*The Diaries
of Jane Somers*

The Diaries
of Jane Somers

by Doris Lessing

Vintage Books
A Division of Random House
New York

Library of Congress Cataloging in Publication Data

Lessing, Doris May, 1919–

The diaries of Jane Somers.

Reprint of two works. Originally published: New York:
Knopf, 1983–1984.

Contents: The diary of a good neighbour—If the old could—.

I. Lessing, Doris May, 1919–   . Diary of a good neighbour. 1984.

II. Lessing, Doris May, 1919–   . If the old could—. 1984.

III. Title.

[PR6069.042A6 1984]   823'.914   84-17245

ISBN 0-394-72955

Contents

Preface

I have been thinking about writing a pseudonymous novel for years. Like, I am sure, most writers. How many do? It is in the nature of things that we don't know. But I intended from the start to come clean, only wanted to make a little experiment.

The Diary of a Good Neighbour got written when it did for several reasons. One: I wanted to be reviewed on merit, as a new writer, without the benefit of a 'name'; to get free of that cage of associations and labels that every established writer has to learn to live inside. It is easy to predict what reviewers will say. Mind you, the labels change. Mine have been—starting with *The Grass is Singing*: she is a writer about the colour bar (obsolete term for racism)—about communism—feminism—mysticism; she writes space fiction, science fiction. Each label has served for a few years.

Two: I wanted to cheer up young writers, who often have such a hard time of it, by illustrating that certain attitudes and processes they have to submit to are mechanical, and have nothing to do with them personally, or with their kind or degree of talent.

Another reason, frankly if faintly malicious: some reviewers complained they hated my Canopus series, why didn't I write realistically, the way I used to do before: preferably *The Golden Notebook* over again? These were sent *The Diary of a Good Neighbour* but not one recognized me. Some people think it is reasonable that an avowed devotee of a writer's work should only be able to recognize it when packaged and signed; others not.

Again, when I began writing my Canopus series I was surprised to find I had been set free to write in ways I had not used before. I wondered if there would be a similar liberation if

I were to write in the first person as a different character. Of course, all writers become different characters all the time, as we write about them: all our characters are inside us somewhere. (This can be a terrifying thought.) But a whole book would be a different matter, mean activating one of the gallery of people who inhabit every one of us, strengthening him or her, setting her (or him) free to develop. And it did turn out that as Jane Somers I wrote in ways that Doris Lessing cannot. It was more than a question of using the odd turn of phrase or an adjective to suggest a woman journalist who is also a successful romantic novelist: Jane Somers knew nothing about a kind of dryness, like a conscience, that monitors Doris Lessing whatever she writes and in whatever style. After all there are many different styles, or tones of voice, in the Canopus series—not to mention *Briefing for a Descent into Hell* and *Memoirs of a Survivor*—and sometimes in the same book. Some may think this is a detached way to write about Doris Lessing, as if I were not she: it is the name I am detached about. After all, it is the third name I've had: the first, Tayler, being my father's; the second, Wisdom (now try that one on for size!), my first husband's; and the third my second husband's. Of course there was McVeigh, my mother's name, but am I Scots or Irish? As for Doris, it was the doctor's suggestion, he who delivered me, my mother being convinced to the last possible moment that I was a boy. Born six hours earlier, I would have been Horatia, for Nelson's Day. What could that have done for me? I sometimes do wonder what my real name is: surely I must have one?

Another influence that went to make Jane Somers was reflections about what my mother would be like if she lived now: that practical, efficient, energetic woman, by temperament conservative, a little sentimental, and only with difficulty (and a lot of practice at it) able to understand weakness and failure, though always kind. No, Jane Somers is not my mother, but thoughts of women like my mother did feed Jane Somers.

I and my agent, Jonathan Clowes, decided in our plan of campaign that it would be fair to submit *The Diary of a Good Neighbour* to my main publishers first. In Britain these are

Jonathan Cape and Granada. Cape (not Tom Maschler personally) turned it down forthwith. Granada kept it some time, were undecided, but said it was too depressing to publish: in these fallen days major and prestigious publishers can see nothing wrong in refusing a novel in which they see merit because it might not sell. Not thus, once, were serious literary publishers. I saw the readers' reports and was reminded how patronized and put-down new writers are.

Michael Joseph, who accepted my first novel all those years ago, has now twice published me as a new writer. On taking *The Diary of a Good Neighbour*, they said it reminded them of Doris Lessing, and were taken into our confidence and entered with relish into the spirit of the thing. The redoubtable Bob Gottlieb of Knopf in New York said at once, Who do you think you are kidding?—or words to that effect. Interesting that these two great publishing firms, crammed with people and the possibilities of a leak, were able to keep the secret as long as they wanted: it was dear friends who, swearing their amazing and tested reliability, could not stand the strain.

Three European publishers bought *Good Neighbour*: in France, in Germany, and in Holland. My French publisher rang up to say he had bought this book, had I perhaps helped Jane Somers, who reminded him of me?

This surely brings us back to the question: what is it that the perspicacious recognize, when they do? After all, Jane Somers's style is different from Lessing's. Each novel or story has this characteristic note, or tone of voice—the style, peculiar to itself and self-consistent. But behind this must sound another note, independent of style. What is this underlying tone, or voice, and where does it originate in the author? It seems to me we are listening to, responding to, the essence of a writer here, a groundnote.

We—that is agent, publishers and I—believed the reviewers would guess at once. But not one did. A few people, not all reviewers, liked *The Diary of a Good Neighbour*. It was mostly women journalists in women's magazines who reviewed it, because Jane Somers was described on the dust jacket as a well-known woman journalist. (It was enough, it seems, to say it for people to believe it.) This neatly highlights the major problem of publishing: how to bring a book to the attention of readers. The trigger here: the phrase *woman journalist*. (Some potential reviewers, male, were put off by it.) It is this situation that has given rise to all these new promotional schemes in Britain: The Best of Young British Novelists, The Best Novels of Our Time, the razzmatazz prizes, and so on. The problem can only exist, it seems to me, because so many good novels are being written. If there were only a few, there would be no difficulty. Ever more loudly shrill the voices, trying to get attention: this is the best novel since *Gone With the Wind*, *War and Peace* and *The Naked and the Dead*! Overkill earns diminishing returns and numbed readers return to former habits, such as relying on intuition and the recommendation of friends. Jane Somers's first novel (first serious novel—of course she had written those romantic novels which were not reviewed at all, but sold very well!) was noticed, and got a few nice little reviews. In short, it was reviewed as new novels are. And that could easily have been that. Novels, even good ones, are being published all the time that have what publishers call 'a shelf life' (like groceries) of a few months. (Once they used the phrase as a joke, sending themselves up, but now they use it straight. 'The shelf life of books is getting shorter,' you'll hear them say. 'It's down to a few weeks now.' As if it all had nothing to do with them. And it hasn't: the mechanisms for selling dominate their practices; the tail wags the dog.) A first novel can be remaindered and out of print and vanish as if it had never been, if unlucky enough not to win a prize or in some way attract a spotlight such as the admiration of a well-known writer who cries (see above), 'This is the greatest novel since *Tom Jones*.' Or, making accommodation to the times, 'More exciting than *Dallas*!'

The American publisher was asked why more had not been done to promote *The Diary of a Good Neighbour*, which in the opinion of the enquirer, a literary critic, was a good novel, but the reply was that there was nothing to promote, no 'personality', no photograph, no story. In other words, in order to sell a book, in order to bring it to attention, you need more than the book, you need the television appearance. Many writers who at the start resisted have thought it over, have understood that this, now, is how the machinery works, and have decided that if—in fact, even if it is not acknowledged—they have become part of the sales departments of their publishers, then they will do the job as well as they can. It is remarkable how certain publishers wince and suffer when writers insist on using the right words to describe what is happening. In very bad taste, they think it is, to talk in this way. This attitude is a relic of the gentleman publisher, a contradiction which has bedevilled the publishing of serious (as distinct from commercial) books. On the one hand, a book has to be promoted: oh, but what a distasteful business it is! One of the problems of the ('serious' as distinct from the 'commercial') author is this attitude on the part of his or her publisher. You are pressured to do interviews, television and so on, but you are conscious that the more you agree, the more you are earning his or her contempt. (But looking back it seems to me that men publishers are more guilty of this hypocrisy than women publishers.) I have sometimes gloomily had to conclude that the only writer some publishers could really respect would be one who wrote a thirty-page masterpiece, reviewed by perhaps three critics, every ten years: this paragon would live on a mountain top somewhere and never, ever, give interviews. Now, there's a *real* artist!

If Jane Somers had only written one serious novel, which sold, as first novels do, 2,800 copies in America and 1,600 copies in Britain, by now it would be remaindered and pulped, and she would be cherishing half a dozen fan letters.

But she wrote a second. Surely this time people must see who the real author was? But no.

Predictably, people who had liked the first book were disappointed by the second. And vice versa. Never mind about the problems of publishers: the main problem of some writers is that most reviewers and readers want you to go on writing the same book.

By now, the results of friends' indiscretions meant that some people in the trade knew who Jane Somers was and—I am touched by this—clearly decided it was my right to be anonymous if I wished. Some, too, seemed inclined retrospectively to find merit.

One of my aims has more than succeeded. It seems I am like Barbara Pym! The books are fastidious, well written, well crafted. Stylish. Unsparing, unsentimental and deeply felt. Funny, too. On the other hand they are sentimental, and mawkish. Mere soap opera. Trendy.

I am going to miss Jane Somers.

Unexpected little sidelights. One review was a nasty little reminder of how many people reach instinctively for their revolvers at the mention of something they don't like. From the hard left (and, perhaps, not so hard left: it is a disease that spreads easily), dislike of Jane Somers's politics was character-istically expressed in the demand that such books should not be published. Just like the hard (and sometimes not so hard) right. 'The publishers should be sued for publishing this book.' (Not Jane Somers's, one of Lessing's.) Alas, poor Liberty, the prognosis is not very good.

Finally, a treasured memory, which I think is not out of place here. Imagine the book editor of a famous magazine (let us call it *Pundit*) standing in his office with books sent him for review stacked all over the table, on the floor, everywhere. He is harassed; he is desperate. He deals me out books to review, and mostly I hand them back again. Then he gives me another: 'Please review this book,' he cries. 'No one wants to review it. What am I going to do? Please, please say yes.'

'But it is a very bad book,' I say, returning it to him. 'Just ignore it.'

'But we can't ignore it. We have to review it.'

'Why do you? It will take up the space that could be used for a good book.'

'The *Viewer* has reviewed it, they gave it all that space, so we must.'

'You must be joking,' I said, thinking that he was, but he wasn't.

Doris Lessing
July 1984

The Diary of a Good Neighbour

The first part is a summing-up of about four years. I was not keeping a diary. I wish I had. All I know is that I see everything differently now from how I did while I was living through it.

My life until Freddie started to die was one thing, afterwards another. Until then I thought of myself as a nice person. Like everyone, just about, that I know. The people I work with, mainly. I know now that I did not ask myself what I was really like, but thought only about how other people judged me.

When Freddie began to be so ill my first idea was: this is unfair. Unfair to me, I thought secretly. I partly knew he was dying, but went on as if he wasn't. That was not kind. He must have been lonely. I was proud of myself because I went on working through it all, "kept the money coming in"—well, I had to do that, with him not working. But I was thankful I was working because I had an excuse not to be with him in that *awfulness*. We did not have the sort of marriage where we talked about real things. I see that now. We were not really married. It was the marriage most people have these days, both sides trying for advantage. I always saw Freddie as one up.

The word cancer was mentioned once. The doctors said to me, cancer, and *now* I see my reaction meant they would not go on to talk about whether to tell him or not. I don't know if they told him. Whether he knew. I think he did. When they took him into hospital I went every day, but I sat there with a smile, how are you feeling? He looked dreadful. Yellow. Sharp bones under yellow skin. Like a boiling fowl. He was protecting me. *Now*, I can see it. Because I could not take it. Child-wife.

When at last he died, and it was over, I saw how badly he

had been treated. His sister was around sometimes. I suppose they talked. Her manner to me was like his. Kindly. Poor Janna, too much must not be expected.

Since he died I have not seen her, nor any of that family. Good riddance. I mean, that is what *they* think of me. I would not have minded talking to his sister about Freddie, for I did not know much about him, not really. But it is a bit late for that.

When he died, and I found I was missing him so much, I wanted to know about times in his life he hardly ever mentioned. Like being a soldier in the war. He said he hated it. Five years. Nineteen to twenty-four. They were wonderful years for me. I was nineteen in 1949, beginning to forget the war, and making my career.

And yet we were close. We had all that good sex. We were perfectly adjusted in that, if nothing else. Yet we could not talk to each other. Correction. Did not talk to each other. Correction. He could not talk to me because when he started to try I shied away. I think the truth is he was a serious inward sort of person. Just the kind of man I would give anything for now.

When he was dead and I was going mad for sex, because for ten years I had always had anything I wanted there for the asking, I was sleeping about, I don't like to think how many. Or who. Once at an office party I looked around and saw I had had sex with half the men there. That gave me a shock. And always I had hated it: being a bit tight and after a good meal I am in a hurry, sex. It was not their fault.

That came to an end when Sister Georgie came to see me and said it was my turn for Mother. I felt very sorry for myself again. *Now* I think she might well have said something before! Husband, four children, small house—and she had had Mother since Daddy died, eight years. I had no children, and with Freddie and I both working there was no shortage of money. Yet there had never been a suggestion Mother should live with us. *Or one that I can remember.* But I was not the kind of person who looked after a widowed mother. Mother used to say what I spent on my face and my clothes would feed a family. True. It is no good pretending I regret that. It sometimes seems to me now it was the best thing in my life that—going into the office in the morning, knowing how I looked. Everyone took notice, what I was wearing, how. I looked forward to the moment when I opened the door and went through the typing pool and the girls smiled enviously. And then the executive offices, the girls admiring and wishing they had my taste. Well, I've that, if nothing else. I used to buy three, four dresses a week. I used to wear them once or twice, then into jumble. My sister took them for her good causes. So they weren't wasted. Of course that was before Joyce took me in hand and taught me really how to dress—style, not just fashion.

It was when Mother came to live with me I knew I was a widow.

It wasn't too bad at first. She wasn't very well but she amused herself. I couldn't bring a man home if I fancied him, but I secretly was quite glad. I can't ask you in, you see I have my aged mother, poor Janna!

It was a year after she came she got sick. I said to myself, Now, this time you aren't going to pretend it isn't happening. I went with her to the hospital. They told her it was cancer. They talked a long time about what would happen. They were kind and sensible. The doctors could not talk to me about what was happening to my husband, but they could talk straight to my mother about what was happening to her. *Because of what she was*. It was the first time in my life I wanted to be like her. Before that I had always found her embarrassing, her clothes, her hair. When I was out with her I used to think, no one would believe I could be her daughter, two worlds, heavy suburban respectable—and me. As I sat there beside her and she talked about her forthcoming death with the doctors, so dignified and nice, I felt awful. But I was scared witless, because Uncle Jim died of cancer, and now her—both sides. I thought: will it be my turn next? What I felt was, *it isn't fair*.

While Mother was dying I was doing my best, not like Freddie where I simply didn't want to know. But I couldn't do it. That is the point. I used to feel sick and panicky all the time. She went to pieces so fast. *Went to pieces*—that was it. I hate physical awfulness. I can't stand it. I used to go in, before leaving for work. She was in the kitchen pottering about in her dressing gown. Her face yellow, with a sick glisten on it. The bones showing. At least I didn't say, Are you feeling a bit better, that's good! I sat down with her and drank coffee. I said, Can I drop into the chemist's—because there were so many pills and medicines. And she said, Yes, pick up this or that. But I could not kiss her. Well, we aren't exactly a physically affectionate family! I can't remember ever giving my sister a good hug. A peck on the cheek, that's about it. I wanted to hold Mother and perhaps rock her a little. When it got towards the end and she was being so brave and she was so awfully ill, I thought I should simply take her into my arms and hold her. I couldn't touch her, not really. Not with kindness. The smell . . . and they can say it isn't infectious, but what do they know? Not much. She used to look at me so straight and open. And I could hardly make myself meet her eyes. It wasn't that her look asked anything. But I was so ashamed of what I was feeling, in a panic for myself. No, I wasn't awful, as I was with Freddie. But it must have seemed to her that there was nothing much there—I mean, as if *I* was nothing much. A few minutes in the morning, as I rushed off to the office. I was always latish back, after supper with someone from work, Joyce usually, and by then Mother was in bed. She was not asleep, I wished she was! I went in and sat with her. She was in pain, often. I used to get her medicines ready for her. She liked that, I could see. Support. Of a kind. We talked. Then Sister Georgie took to coming up two or three afternoons in a week and being with her. Well, I couldn't, I was working; and her children were at school. I used to come in and see them sitting together. I used to feel sick with envy because they were close. Mother and daughter.

Then when Mother went into hospital, Georgie and I took it in turns to visit. Georgie used to have to come up from Oxford. I don't see how I could have gone more often. Every other day, two or three hours in the hospital. I hated every second. I couldn't think of anything to say. But Georgie and Mother used to talk all the time. What about!—I used to listen, absolutely incredulous. They would talk about Georgie's neighbours, Georgie's neighbours' children, their husbands, their friends' friends. They never stopped. It was interesting. Because they were so involved with it all.

When Mother died I was pleased, of course. And so was Georgie. But I knew that it was very different, Georgie saying it, and my saying it. *She had a right to say it.* Because of what she was. Georgie was with Mother every minute of the day and night for a month before Mother went. I had learned by then not to hate the physical side so much, Mother almost a skeleton with yellow skin over it. But her eyes were the same. She was in pain. She did not pretend she wasn't. She held Georgie's hand.

The point was, Georgie's was the right kind of hand.

Then I was alone in our flat. Once or twice one of the men came home. It wasn't anything much. I don't blame them at all, how could I? I had already begun to understand that I had changed. *I couldn't be bothered!* How about that! Not that I didn't need sex. Sometimes I thought I'd go mad. But there was something dreary and repetitive. And the place was full of Freddie. I could see myself becoming a monument to Freddie, *having* to remember him. What was the use of it? I decided to sell the flat and get something of my own. I thought that out for a long time, months. I saw even then it was a new way of thinking for me. Working on the magazine, I think differently, quick decisions, like being kept on the top of a jet of water. I am good at all that. That was why I was offered the job in the first place. Funny thing, I hadn't expected it. Other people knew I was going to be offered assistant editor, not me. Partly, I was so involved with my image, how I projected myself. My image first was light-hearted, funny Janna with her crazy clothes, ever so clever and Girl Friday. Then, after Joyce, very expensive and perfect and smart and dependable, the person who had been there longest, with her smart trendy husband off-stage. Not that Freddie would have recognized himself in that. Then, suddenly (so it seemed) a middle-aged woman. Smart. *Handsome.* It was hard to take. It is still hard.

A handsome, middle-aged widow with a very good job in the magazine world.

Meanwhile I was *thinking* about how I ought to live. In Freddie's and my flat I felt I was being blown about like a bit of fluff or a feather. When I went in after work, it was as if I had expected to find some sort of weight or anchor and it wasn't there. I realized how flimsy I was, how dependent. That was painful, seeing myself as dependent. Not financially, of course, but as a person. Child-daughter, child-wife.

I wasn't in the way of thinking I should get married again. I couldn't see myself. Yet I was saying to myself, you must marry, you must, before it is too late. And it is what even now, sometimes, I want to do. Particularly now that I think I am not quite so awful as I was. But when I *think*, I know I shouldn't get married. Anyway, no one has asked me!

I sold the flat and got this one. A room to sleep in, a room to live in, a study. A large expensive block of flats. But I am hardly ever here. When I am, I think a lot.

This way of thinking . . . it is not so much thinking as holding things in your mind and letting them sort themselves out. If you really do that, slowly, surprising results emerge. For instance, that your ideas are different from what you had believed they were.

There are things I need to *think* out, which I haven't got around to yet.

Joyce, for one. That office of ours, top floor, sunlight and weather all around it. Her long table with her behind it, my long table with me behind it, facing each other. We've sat there for years now, opposite, making the magazine work. Then the long trestle down one side, with all the things we need on it, the machines, the drawing boards, the photographs. And the small table on the other where the secretaries sit when they come in to take notes, or anyone we want to talk to. It gives me pleasure to think of it, because it is so right, so apt, fits so exactly with what goes on. But I must think, must *think* . . . there is a feeling of discomfort, as if there is something *not* quite right.

After I moved into the new flat I soon saw that my life was entirely in the office. I had no life at home. *Home*. What a word! It was the place I prepared myself for the office, or rested after work.

One of the things I am *thinking* is that if I lost my job, there wouldn't be much left of me. I look at the clever girls, fighting their way up. I find myself looking at one, Phyllis, for instance, and reflecting. Yes, she's the right material, she can fit words together, interview anyone, edit, she has a mind like scissors, she never panics.

Does she understand how things *really* work? What do I mean by that? A great deal. Everything. She's pushy and impatient, you've got to know how to let things happen.

What I was thinking most of all was that I had let Freddie down and had let my mother down *and that was what I was like*. If something else should turn up, something I had to cope with, like illness or death, if I had to say to myself, Now, you will behave like a human being and not a little girl—then I couldn't do it. It is not a question of will, but of what you are.

That is why I decided to learn something else.

I saw in the paper the advertisement, Would you like to befriend an old person? The picture of a dear old lady. A dear, sweet old thing. Everybody's favourite granny. Ha! I rang up and went to see them. Miss Snow. Philanthropist. I went with her to visit Mrs York. We all three had tea together in a little flat in Kensington. It seemed to me false and awful. I thought Miss Snow was condescending but didn't know it. Mrs York, a large slow invalid, pale and with a puffy doughy face. Little complaining eyes. I could see she didn't like Miss Snow. I sat there and thought, what the hell am I doing here? What good does this do Mrs York? Am I to visit her once a week on Sundays and bring her cake and ask how her rheumatism is? Miss Snow knew I felt like this, and when we said goodbye on the pavement she was perfunctory. Yes, give me a ring, Mrs Somers, if you feel you want to do this work, and she got into her Mini and was off. A failure. Well, all in the day's work, she was thinking.

Someone else would have to be found for Mrs York. But I did not feel lacking this time. Mrs York was simply not for me. I used to look at the advertisement with the dear sweet old lady and think of awful Mrs York and feel a sort of jeer.

Meanwhile, opposite me, on the landing, Mrs Penny. She is seventy, she is alone, and she is longing for me to befriend her. I know this. I don't want to. She knows it. She would take over my life. I feel smothered and panicky at the idea of being at her beck and call.

But then I was in the chemist's and this happened.

I saw an old witch. I was staring at this old creature and thought, a witch. It was because I had spent all day on a feature, Stereotypes of Women, Then and Now. *Then* not exactly specified, late Victorian, the gracious lady, the mother of many, the invalid maiden aunt, the New Woman, missionary wife, and so on. I had about forty photographs and sketches to choose from. Among them, a witch, but I had discarded her. But here she was, beside me, in the chemist's. A tiny bent-over woman, with a nose nearly meeting her chin, in black heavy dusty clothes, and something not far off a bonnet. She saw me looking at her and thrust at me a prescription and said, "What is this? You get it for me." Fierce blue eyes, under grey craggy brows, but there was something wonderfully sweet in them.

I liked her, for some reason, from that moment. I took the paper and knew I was taking much more than that. "I will," I said. "But why? Isn't he being nice to you?" Joking: and she at once responded, shaking her old head vigorously.

"No, oh *he*'s no good, I never know what *he*'s saying."

He was the young chemist, and he stood, hands on the counter, alert, smiling: he knew her well, I could see.

"The prescription is for a sedative," I said.

She said, "I know *that*," and jabbed her fingers down on to the paper where I had spread it against my handbag. "But it's not aspirin, is it?"

I said, "It's something called Valium."

"That's what I thought. It's not a pain-killer, it's a stupefier," she said.

He laughed. "But it's not as bad as that," he said.

I said, "I've been taking it myself."

She said, "I said to the doctor, aspirin—that's what I asked for. But *they're* no good either, doctors."

All this fierce and trembling, with a sort of gaiety. Standing there, the three of us, we were laughing, and yet she was so very angry.

"Do you want me to sell you some aspirin, Mrs Fowler?"

"Yes, yes. I'm not going to take this stuff that stupefies you."

He handed her the aspirin, and took her money, which she

counted out slowly, coin by coin, from the depths of a great rusty bag. Then he took the money for my things—nail varnish, blusher, eye liner, eye shadow, lipstick, lip gloss, powder, mascara. The lot: I had run low of everything. She stood by watching, with a look I know now is so characteristic, a fierce pondering look that really wants to understand. Trying to grasp it all.

I adjusted my pace to hers and went out of the shop with her. On the pavement she did not look at me, but there was an appeal there. I walked beside her. It was hard to walk so slowly. Usually I fly along, but did not know it till then. She took one step, then paused, examined the pavement, then another step. I thought how I rushed along the pavements every day and had never seen Mrs Fowler, but she lived near me, and suddenly I looked up and down the streets and saw—old women. Old men too, but mostly old women. They walked slowly along. They stood in pairs or groups, talking. Or sat on the bench at the corner under the plane tree. I had not seen them. That was because I was afraid of being like them. I was afraid, walking along there beside her. It was the smell of her, a sweet, sour, dusty sort of smell. I saw the grime on her thin old neck, and on her hands.

The house had a broken parapet, broken and chipped steps. Without looking at me, because she wasn't going to ask, she went carefully down the old steps and stopped outside a door that did not fit and had been mended with a rough slat of wood nailed across it. Although this door wouldn't keep out a determined cat, she fumbled for a key, and at last found it, and peered for the keyhole, and opened the door. And I went in with her, my heart quite sick, and my stomach sick too because of the smell. Which was, that day, of over-boiled fish. It was a long dark passage we were in.

We walked along it to the "kitchen". I have never seen anything like it outside our Distress File, condemned houses and that sort of thing. It was an extension of the passage, with an old gas cooker, greasy and black, an old white china sink, cracked and yellow with grease, a cold-water tap wrapped around with old rags and dripping steadily. A rather nice old wood table that had crockery standing on it, all "washed" but grimy. The walls stained and damp. The whole place smelled, it smelled awful. . . . She did not look at me while she set down bread, biscuits and cat food. The clean lively colours of the grocery packages and the tins in that awful place. She was ashamed, but wasn't going to apologize. She said in an offhand but appealing way, "You go into my room, and find yourself a seat."

The room I went into had in it an old black iron stove that was showing a gleam of flames. Two unbelievably ancient ragged armchairs. Another nice old wood table with newspaper spread over it. A divan heaped with clothes and bundles. And a yellow cat on the floor. It was all so dirty and dingy and grim and awful. I thought of how all of us wrote about decor and furniture and colours—how taste changed, how we all threw things out and got bored with everything. And here was this kitchen, which if we printed a photograph of it would get us donations by return from readers.

Mrs Fowler brought in an old brown teapot, and two rather pretty old china cups and saucers. It was the hardest thing I ever did, to drink out of the dirty cup. We did not speak much because I did not want to ask direct questions, and she was trembling with pride and dignity. She kept stroking the cat— "My lovely, my pretty," in a hard but appealing sort of way—and she said without looking at me, "When I was young my father owned his own shop, and later we had a house in St John's Wood, and I know how things should be."

And when I left she said, in her way of not looking at me, "I suppose I won't be seeing you again?" And I said, "Yes, if you'll ask me." Then she did look at me, and there was a small smile, and I said, "I'll come on Saturday afternoon for tea, if you like."

"Oh I would like, yes I would." And there was a moment between us of intimacy: that is the word. And yet she was so full of pride and did not want to ask, and she turned away from me and began petting the cat: Oh, my little pet, my little pretty.

When I got home that evening I was in a panic. I had committed myself. I was full of revulsion. The sour, dirty smell was in my clothes and hair. I bathed and washed my hair and did myself up and rang Joyce and said, "Let's go out to dinner." We had a good dinner at Alfredo's and talked. I said nothing about Mrs Fowler, of course, yet I was thinking of her all the time: I sat looking around at the people in the restaurant, everyone well dressed and clean, and I thought, if she came into this restaurant . . . well, she couldn't. Not even as a cleaner, or a washer-up.

On the Saturday I took her some roses and carnations, and a cake with real cream. I was pleased with myself, and this carried me over her reaction—she was pleased, but I had overdone it. There was no vase for the flowers. I put them in a white enamel jug. She put the cake on a big old cracked plate. She was being rather distant. We sat on either side of the iron stove, and the brown teapot was on it to warm, and the flames were too hot. She was wearing a silk blouse, black dots on white. Real silk. Everything is like this with her. A beautiful flowered Worcester teapot, but it is cracked. Her skirt is of good heavy wool, but it is stained and frayed. She did not want me to see in her "bedroom", but I took a peep when she was in the "kitchen". The furniture was part very good: bookcases, a chest of drawers, then a shoddy dressing table and a wardrobe like a varnished packing case. The bed had on it an old-fashioned quilt, plump, of chintz. She did not sleep in the bed, I realized, but on the divan next door, where we sat. Everywhere in the room were piles of rubbish, what looked like rags, bundles of newspapers, everything you can think of: this was what she did not want me to see.

When we ate the cake, she said, "Oh, this is real cream," and told me about how, in the summers, she and her sisters were sent to an old woman in Essex.

"Every day of the summer we were out of doors. Lovely hot summers, not like the ones we have now. We got as brown as toffee. The old woman had a little cottage but no kitchen. She built a tripod under a cock of thatch in the yard, and she had a great iron pot on chains and she cooked everything for our dinners in the pot. First she put in the piece of beef, and around it the carrots and potatoes, and she had the pudding rolled in a floured cloth and that went in to boil at the same time. I used to wonder how it was the pudding tasted of jam and fruit and not the meat, but of course it was the flour the cloth had on it. And then she gave us great soup plates, and sat us on the steps, and we ate the meat and the vegetables, and then she peeled the cloth off the pudding, and it came out all crusty and rich, and gave us slices in the same plate we ate the meat off—but we had licked that clean as washed. And then she said, Off with you—and she boiled up water in the iron pot to wash our plates, and to wash herself, after, and we went off into the fields to pick flowers. Oh, I like to sit here and think of all that."

"And how old were you then?"

"Children. We were children. We went every summer—several summers. That was before my poor mother died, you see."

She talked about the old woman, who was so kind, and the little cottage, that had no running water, and only an outside lavatory in a little brick shed, and those hot summers, all afternoon. She talked and I listened. I did not leave till nearly seven. I came home, and switched on the fire, and thought it was time I did some cleaning. I sat by myself and thought of Mrs Fowler, by herself, the flames showing in the open front of her grate. I opened a tin of soup, and I watched television.

Next Saturday I took her a little pot of African violets and another cake.

Everything the same: the fire burning, the yellow cat, and her dirty white silk spotted blouse.

There was a reticence in her, and I thought it was because she had talked last Saturday for three hours, hardly stopping.

But it wasn't that. It came out almost when I was leaving.

"Are you a good neighbour?" she said.

"I hope perhaps I may become one," I said, laughing.

"Why, have they put you on probation, then?"

I did not understand, and she saw I didn't. It turns out that the Council employ women, usually elderly, who run into old people for a cup of tea, or to see if they are all right: they don't do much, but keep an eye on them. They are called Good Neighbours and they are paid so little they can't be doing it for the money. I made it my business to find out all this through the office. On the third Saturday I took her some fruit, and saw it was the wrong thing. She said nothing, again, till later, when she remarked that her teeth made it impossible for her to eat fruit.

"Can't you eat grapes? Bananas?"

She said, with humour, that the pension did not run to grapes.

And she was off, on the subject of the pension, and what coal cost, and what food cost, and "that Council woman who doesn't know what she is talking about". I listened, again. I have not pieced it all together yet. I see that it will be a long time before my ignorance, my lack of experience, and her reticence, and her rages—for now I see how they simmer there, making her eyes light up with what you'd think, at first, must be gaiety or even a sense of comedy—a long time before how she is, her nature, and how I am, my rawness, can make it possible for me to form a whole picture of her.

The "Council woman", a Mrs Rogers, wanted her, Mrs Fowler, to have a Home Help. But the Home Help cheated her and didn't do any work, and wouldn't wash her floors. The Home Help was just the way all these young women are now, lazy, too good for work. She, Mrs Fowler, was not too good to wash floors, she carries her own coal all along the passage, she sweeps her own chimney once a week as far up as she could reach with her brushes, because she is afraid of fire. And so she went on, about the social workers, and Home Helps, and—a Good Neighbour, she was kind enough to come once, and she said it was time I was in a Home, so I said to her, You know your way out.

"But, Mrs Fowler, you and I met in the chemist's, how could I be a Good Neighbour—I mean, an official?"

"They get up to anything," she said, bitter but distressed, for she was afraid I would be offended and not come back.

She went with me to the outside door when I left, and she was doing something I have seen on the stage or written in novels. She wore an old striped apron, because she had put it on to make the tea, and she stood pleating it with both hands, and letting it go smooth, then pleating it again.

"Shall I drop in during the week?" I asked.

"If you have time," she said. And could not resist, "And it

will make a bit extra for you." Yet she almost gasped as she said this: she did not want to say it, because she wanted to believe I was not an official, paid person, but just a human being who likes her.

When I went in after work on Wednesday, I took in a copy of our magazine. I was ashamed of it, so glossy and sleek and slick, so *clever*—that is how it is presented, its image. But she took it from me with a girl's mischievous smile, and a sort of prance of her head—what remained of a girl's tossed hair—and said, "Oh, I love these, I love looking at these things they think up."

Because it was seven, I did not know how to fit myself in to her. When did she eat her supper? Or go to bed? On the newspapers on the table was a bottle of milk stout and a glass.

"I've drunk it or I'd offer you some," said she.

I sat down in the chair opposite hers and saw that the room, with the curtains drawn and the electric light, seemed quite cosy, not so dreadfully dirty and grim. But why do I go on about dirt like this? Why do we judge people like this? *She* was no worse off for the grime and the dust, and even the smells. I decided not to notice, if I could help it, not to keep judging her, which I was doing, by the sordidness. I saw that the electric switches were broken, and made an excuse to go out to the "kitchen": frayed cords trailing over the walls, only one switch for the whole room, up on the light itself, which she could hardly reach.

She was looking at the magazine, with a smile that was all pleasure.

"I work for that magazine," I said, and she let the thing fall shut and sat looking at me in that way of hers, as if she is trying to make things fit, make sense.

"Do you? And what do you . . ." But she did not know what questions to ask. I could not bring myself to say I was the assistant editor. I said, "I do typing and all sorts." Which is true enough.

"That's the main thing," she said, "training. It stands between you and nothing. That, and a place of your own."

That evening she talked about how she had fought to get into this flat, for at first she had been on the top floor back, in one room, but she had her eye on the basement flat, and wanted it, and waited for it, and schemed for it, and at last, got it. *And they aren't going to get me out, and they needn't think it.* She spoke as if all this happened yesterday, but it was about the time of the First World War.

She talked about how she had not had the money for the rent of these rooms, and how she had saved it up, penny by penny, and then it was stolen, two years' scrimping and saving, by the wicked woman on the first floor, and she saved again, and at last she went to the landlord and said, You let me in down there. I've got the money for it. He said to me, And how are you going to keep the rent paid? You are a milliner's girl, aren't you? I said, You leave that to me. When I stop paying, then you can throw me out. "And I have never not paid, not once. Though, I've gone without food. No, I learned that early. With your own place, you've got everything. Without it, you are a dog. You are nothing. Have you got your own place?"—and when I said yes, she said, nodding fiercely, angrily, "That's right, and you hold on to it, then nothing can touch you."

Mrs Fowler's "flat" is rent-controlled, twenty-two shillings a week. About a pound in new money, but of course she doesn't think in terms of the new currency, she can't cope with it. She says the house was bought by "that Greek" after the war—the new war, you know, not the old one—for four hundred pounds. And now it's worth sixty thousand. "And he wants me out, so he can get his blood money for this flat. But I know a trick or two. I always have it here, always. And if he doesn't come I go to the telephone box and I ring his office and I say, Why haven't you come for your rent?"

I knew so little that I said to her, "But, Mrs Fowler, twenty-two shillings is not worth the trouble of his collecting it," and her eyes blazed up, and her face was white and dreadful and she said, "Is that how you see it, is that it? Has he sent you here, then? But it is what the rent is, by law, and I am going to pay it. Worth nothing, is it? It is worth the roof over my head."

The three floors above all have Irish families, children, people coming and going, feet tramping about: Mrs Fowler says that "she" makes the refrigerator door rattle to keep her

awake at night because "she" wants this flat . . . Mrs Fowler
lives in a nightmare of imagined persecutions. She told me of
the ten-years-long campaign, after the first war, not the new
one, when "that bitch from Nottingham" was trying to get her
rooms, and she . . . She, it seems, did everything, there was
nothing she did not do, and it all sounds true. But now upstairs
there is an Irish couple, four children, and I saw the woman on
the steps. "How is the old lady?" she asked, her periwinkle
Irish eyes tired and lonely, for her husband is leaving her,
apparently for another woman. "I keep meaning to go down,
but she doesn't seem all that pleased when I do, and so I don't
go."

I showed Mrs Fowler the issue of *Lilith* that has Female
Images. She took it politely, and let it lie on her lap. It was only
when it was ready to go to press that it occurred to me there
was no old woman among the Images. I said this to Joyce, and I
watched a series of reactions in her: first, surprise. Then shock,
small movements of head and eyes said she was alerting herself
to danger. Then she, as it were, switched herself off, became
vague, and her eyes turned away from me. She sighed: "Oh,
but why? It's not our age group." I said, watching myself in
her, "They all have mothers or grandmothers." How afraid we
are of age: how we avert our eyes! "No," she said, still rather
vague, with an abstracted air, as if she were doing justice to an
immensely difficult subject to which she had given infinite
thought. "No, on the whole not, but perhaps we'll do a feature
on Elderly Relations later. I'll make a note." And then she
flashed me a smile, a most complex smile it was: guilt, relief,
and—it was there still—surprise. Somewhere she was wondering, what has got into Janna? And there was in it a plea: don't
threaten me, don't! And, though she had been meaning to sit
down and join me in a cup of tea while we discussed the issue
after next, she said, Must fly. And flew.

Something interesting has just occurred to me.

Joyce is the innovator, the iconoclast, the one who will
throw an issue we've just got set up into the wastepaper basket,
and start again, working all night, to get it down just *so*; Joyce
presents herself—she *is*—this impulsive, dashing, daring soul,
nothing sacred.

I, Janna, am classical and cautious, conservative and careful—this is my appearance, and how I think of myself.

Yet there are so often these moments between us, there always have been. Joyce says, "We can't do that, our readers won't like it."

Me, I have always believed our readers—and everybody else's readers for that matter—would take much more than they are offered.

I say, "Joyce, can we try it?"

But more often than not, whatever it is lands in the file I have labelled Too Difficult and which I leave out on my desk so that Joyce will see it and—so I hope, but most often in vain—be prompted to have another think.

The Images. (a) A girl of twelve or thirteen, and she gave us the most trouble. We discarded a hundred photographs, and finally got Michael to photograph Joyce's niece, aged fifteen actually but rather childish. We got a frank healthy sensuality, not Lolita at all, we were careful to avoid that. Miss Promise. (b) A girl about seventeen, emphasizing independence and confidence. Still at home but you are ready to leave the nest. (c) Leading your own life. Mid-twenties. Since in our experience women living their own lives, sharing flats, keeping down jobs, feel as if they are walking a tightrope, we chose something pretty and vulnerable. Needing Mr Right but able to do without. (d) Young married woman, with a child. Emphasizing the child. (e) Married woman with part-time job, two children, running home and husband.

And that was that.

Before a few weeks ago, I did not see old people at all. My eyes were pulled towards, and I *saw*, the young, the attractive, the well-dressed and handsome. And now it is as if a transparency has been drawn across that former picture and there, all at once, are the old, the infirm.

I nearly said to Joyce, "But one day we will be old," but it is a cliché so obvious, so boring! I can hear her say, "Oh, Janna, do we have to be so boring, so obvious, they don't buy us for that kind of thing." She always says, They buy *us*, we must make them want to buy *us*. One day I went into a filling station and I was tired after a long drive and I said, "Please fill me up." And the garage man said, "I'll be only too happy to fill your car up, madam."

When Mrs Fowler went into the kitchen to get some biscuits, I went with her and watched her pull up a stool to stand on so she could put on the ceiling light. I examined the frayed flexes, the damp walls.

Later I said to her, "I'm going to ask my electrician to come in here, otherwise you are going to kill yourself."

She sat quite still for a few minutes, then she raised her eyes, looked at me, and sighed. I knew this was a moment of importance. I had said something she had dreamed of someone saying: but now this was a burden on her, and she wished the moment, and me, away.

She said, "I've managed well enough." This was timid, and an appeal, and sullen.

I said, "It's a disgrace that you should have to be in these conditions. Your electricity, it's a death-trap."

She gave a snort of laughter at this. "A death-trap, is it?" And we laughed. But I was full of panic, inside me something struggled to run, to flee, out of the situation.

I felt trapped. I am trapped. Because I have made a promise to her. Silently. But it is a promise.

I went home and, as I opened my door, the door opposite crept open: Mrs Penny, on the watch. "Excuse me," she cried, "but I have been waiting for you to come home. I simply must ask a favour of you."

I said ungraciously, "What is it?"

"I forgot to buy butter when I went out and . . ."

"I'll bring it," I said, and in a surge of energy went into my flat, got half a pound of butter, thrust it into her hands, said, "Don't mention it," and ran back into my own place with a bang of the door. The bang was deliberate. She had butter, I knew that. What I was thinking was, she has a son and daughter, and if they don't look after her, *tant pis*. It's not my responsibility.

I was in a frenzy of irritation, a need to shake something off—Mrs Fowler. I filled the bath. I put every stitch of clothing I had worn that day ready for the launderette. I could feel the smelly air of Mrs Fowler's place on my skin and hair.

My bathroom, I realized that evening, is where I live. Probably even my home. When I moved here I copied the bathroom I had made in the old flat, to the last detail. But I did not do anything particular with the living room and bedroom, the study. Freddie joked that his rival was my bathroom.

I had the paint mixed especially, ivory with a tone of pink. I had Spanish tiles, very delicate and light, coral, turquoise, and ochre, and the blinds were painted to match the tiles. The bath is a grey-blue. Sometimes a room is perfect—nothing can be added and nothing changed. When Joyce saw it she wanted it photographed for the mag. I said no: it would be like being photographed nude. I bath every morning, every night. I lie in the bath and soak for hours. I read in the bath, with my head and knees floating on waterproof pillows. I have two shelves full of salts and bath bubbles. That evening I lay in the bath, adding hot water as it chilled, and I looked at my body. It is a solid firm white body. No fat on it. God forbid! But solid. It doesn't sag or droop yet. Well, no children. There was never time for children, and when I said to Freddie, Yes, I'll fit one in now, I did not get pregnant. He was cheerful and nice about it. I don't know how deeply he felt it. I know he wanted children, but not how much. I was careful not to find out, I suppose.

I came out of the bath and stood in the doorway wrapped in my bath sheet and looked at the bathroom and thought about Mrs Fowler. She has never had hot water. Has lived in that filthy hole, with cold water, since before the First World War.

I wished I had not responded to her, and I was wondering all evening how to escape.

In the morning I woke up and it was as if I was facing some terrible fate. Because I knew I was going to look after Mrs Fowler. To an extent, anyway.

I rang up the electrician. I explained everything to him. I went to work depressed and even frightened.

That night the electrician rang: Mrs Fowler had screamed at him, *What do you want?* And he had gone away.

I said I would meet him there next evening.

He was there at six, and I saw his face as she opened the door and the smell and the squalor hit him. Then he said to her, in a nice cheeky sort of way, "Well, you got at me good and proper last night, didn't you?"

She examined him slowly, then looked at me as if I were a stranger, stood aside, and went into her "living room" while I told him what to do. I should have stayed with her, but I had brought work home and I told her this.

"I didn't ask you to put yourself out," she said.

I struggled with myself, and then gave her a hug. "Oh, go on, don't be a cross-patch," I said, and left. She had tears in her eyes. As for me, I was fighting disgust, the stale smell of her. And the other smell, a sharp sweet smell which I didn't know.

Jim rang me yesterday and said he had done what he could to the place, put in new cable and switches at a height she could reach, and got her a bed lamp.

He told me the cost—as bad as I thought. I said I would send him a cheque. A silence. He wanted cash: thinking I might need him again for Mrs Fowler—and this thought was quite horrifying, as if I was acknowledging some awful burden for ever—I said, "If you come around now I'll give you cash." "Can do," said he. He arrived an hour later. He took the money, and stood waiting, and then, "Why isn't she in a Home? She shouldn't be living like that." I said, "She doesn't want to go into a Home. She likes it where she is."

Jim is a nice boy, not stupid. He was ashamed of what he was thinking, just as I am. He hesitated, and then said, "I didn't know there were people still living like that."

I said, worldly wise, the older experienced one, "Then you don't know much."

Still he lingered, troubled, ashamed, but insistent. "What's the good of people that old?" he said. And then, quickly, to cancel out what he had said, cancel what he was thinking, "Well, we'll be old one of these days, I suppose. Cheers then!"

And went. It was delicacy that made him say, *we'll* be old, not *I'll* be old: because for him I am old, already.

And then I sat down and thought. What he said was what people do say: *Why aren't they in a Home? Get them out of the*

way, out of sight, where young healthy people can't see them,
can't have them on their minds!

They are thinking—I have been thinking—I *did* think, what
is the point of their being alive still?

And I thought, then, how do we value ourselves? By what?
Work? Jim the electrician is all right, electricians are obviously
category one—if you can get them to come at all. What about
assistant editors of women's magazines? *Childless* assistant
editors? How about Joyce, editor, one daughter, who won't
speak to her, she says Joyce is beneath contempt for some
reason or another, I forget; a son, difficult. I get so bored with
these spoiled prima donnas, the teenagers.

How about Sister Georgie? Well, she's all right, children,
husband, good works. But how about Sister Georgie in fifteen
years' time? Statistically she'll be a widow, children gone,
she'll be in a flat, no use to anyone. How will she be judged
then?

How about my Freddie, if he had lived? A saint, no less,
putting up with spoiled child-wife. But in fifteen years? I see the
old men, lean and shadowy and dusty-looking, or fat and
sagging and grey, going about the streets with their shopping,
or standing at street corners, looking lost.

We are to judge people by their beautiful thoughts?

If my thoughts are not beautiful now, what are they likely to
be in fifteen, twenty years' time?

What is the *use* of Maudie Fowler? By the yardsticks and
measurements I've been taught, none.

How about Mrs Penny, a nuisance to her children, to
everyone in this building, and particularly to me—something I
simply cannot face? Silly woman with her plummy I-was-in-
India-in-the-old-days vowels, her secret drinking, her "refinement", her dishonesty.

Well, how about Mrs Penny? There's not a soul in the world
who'd shed a tear if she died.

When I had paid off Jim I had another of my long baths. It is
as if, in such a bath, my old self floats away, is drowned, a new
one emerges from the Pine-Needle Foam, the Satin-Self Gel,
the Sea-Breeze Ions.

I went to bed that night saying I had made a contribution to

Mrs Fowler's welfare that was more than she could possibly expect. And that it was enough. I simply would not go near her again.

In the morning I woke feeling ill, because of being so trapped, and I thought about how I was brought up. Very interesting: you'd say it was a moral household. Religion, of a mild kind. But the atmosphere was certainly one of self-approbation: *we* did the right things, were good. But what, in practice, did it amount to? I wasn't taught anything in the way of self-discipline, self-control. Except for the war, but that was from outside. I wasn't taught how to control my eating, I had to do that for myself. Or how to get up in the morning, and that was the hardest thing I ever had to do, when I started work. I've never known how to say no to myself, when I want something. We were never denied anything, if it was there. The war! Was it because of that, because so little was available, that children were allowed anything they wanted? But there is one thing I can thank Mother for, just one: and I lay in bed saying to her that morning, "Thank you for that. At least you taught me that if I make promises, I must keep them. That if I say I will do a thing, then I must do it. It isn't much to build on, but it's something."

Thank you.

And I went back to Mrs Fowler after work.

I had been thinking all day about my marvellous bathroom, my baths, my dependence on all that. I was thinking that what I spent on hot water in a month would change her life.

But when I went in, taking six milk stouts and some new glasses, and I cried out from the door, "Hello, I'm here, let me in, look what I've got!" and I strode in down that awful passage while she stood to one side, her face was a spiteful little fist. She wanted to punish me for her new electricity and her new comfort, but I wasn't going to let her. I went striding and slamming about, and poured out stout and showed her the glasses, and by the time I sat down, she did too, and she was lively and smiling.

"Have you seen my new boots?" I asked her, thrusting them forward. She bent to peer at them, her mouth trembling with laughter, with mischief.

"Oh," she half whispered, "I do like the things you wear, I do think they are lovely."

So we spent the evening, me showing her every stitch I had. I took off my sweater and stood still so she could walk round me, laughing. I had on my new camisole, *crêpe de Chine*. I pulled up my skirts so she could see the lace in it. I took off my boots so she could handle them.

She laughed and enjoyed herself.

She told me about clothes she had worn when she was young.

There was a dress that was a favourite, of grey poplin with pink flowers on it. She wore it to visit her auntie. It had been the dress of her father's fancy-woman, and it was too big for her, but she took it in.

"Before my poor mother died, nothing was too good for me, but then, I got the cast-offs. But this was so lovely, so lovely, and I did love myself in it."

We talked about the dresses and knickers and petticoats and camisoles and slippers and boas and corsets of fifty, sixty, seventy years ago. Mrs Fowler is over ninety.

And she talked most about her father's woman, who owned her own pub. When Mrs Fowler's mother died . . . "She was poisoned, dear! *She* poisoned her—oh yes, I know what you are thinking, I can see your face, but *she* poisoned her, just as she nearly did for me. She came to live in our house. That was in St John's Wood. I was a skivvy for the whole house, I slaved day and night, and before *they* went to bed I'd take up some thin porridge with some whisky and cream stirred in. She would be on one side of the fire, in her fancy red feathered bed jacket, and my father on the other side, in his silk dressing jacket. She'd say to me, Maudie, you feeling strong tonight? And she'd throw off all that feathered stuff and stand there in her corsets. They don't make corsets like that now. She was a big handsome woman, full of flesh, and my father was sitting there in his armchair smiling and pulling at his whiskers. I had to loosen those corset strings. What a job! But it was better than hauling and tugging her into her corsets when she was dressing to go out. And they never said to me, Maudie, would you fancy a spoonful of porridge yourself? No, they ate and drank like kings, they wanted for nothing. If she felt like a crab or a sole or a lobster, he'd send out for it. But it was never Maudie, would you like a bit? But she got fatter and fatter and then it was: Do you want my old blue silk, Maudie? I wanted it right enough! One of her dresses'd make a dress and a blouse for me, and sometimes a scarf. But I never liked wearing her things, not really. I felt as if they had been stolen from my poor mother."

I did not get home till late, and I lay in the bath wondering if we could do a feature on those old clothes. I mentioned it to Joyce and she seemed quite interested.

She was looking at me curiously. She did not like to ask questions, because something about me at the moment warns her off. But she did say, "Where did you hear about these clothes?" while I was describing the pink silk afternoon dress of a female bar owner before the First World War—who, according to Mrs Fowler, poisoned her lover's wife and tried to poison her lover's daughter. And the plum-coloured satin peignoir with black ostrich feathers.

"Oh, I have a secret life," I said to her, and she said, "So it seems," in a careless, absent way that I am beginning to recognize.

I went back to Maudie last night. I said to her, "Can I call you Maudie?" But she didn't like that. She hates familiarity, disrespect. So I slid away from it. When I left I said, "Then at least call me Janna, please." So now she will call me Janna, but it must be Mrs Fowler, showing respect.

I asked her to describe to me all those old clothes, for the magazine: I said we would pay for her expertise. But this was a mistake, she cried out, really shocked and hurt, "Oh no, how can you . . . I love thinking about those old days."

And so that slid away too. How many mistakes I do make, trying to do the right thing.

Nearly all my first impulses are quite wrong, like being ashamed of my bathroom, and of the mag.

I spent an hour last night describing my bathroom to her in the tiniest detail, while she sat smiling, delighted, asking questions. She is not envious. No. But sometimes there is a dark angry look, and I know I'll hear more, obliquely, later.

She talked more about that house in St John's Wood. I can see it! The heavy dark furniture, the comfort, the good food and the drink.

Her father owned a little house where "they" wanted to put the Paddington railway line. Or something to do with it. And he got a fortune for it. Her father had had a corner shop in Bell Street, and sold hardware and kept free coal and bread for the poor people, and in the cold weather there was a cauldron of soup for the poor. "I used to love standing there, so proud of him, helping those poor people . . ." And then came the good luck, and all at once, the big house and warmth and her father going out nearly every night, for he loved going where the toffs were, he went to supper and the theatre, and the music hall and there he met *her*, and Maudie's mother broke her heart, and was poisoned.

Maudie says that she had a lovely childhood, she couldn't wish a better to anyone, not the Queen herself. She keeps talking of a swing in a garden under apple trees, and long uncut grass. "I used to sit and swing myself, for hours at a time, and swing, and swing, and I sang all the songs I knew, and then poor Mother came out and called to me, and I ran in to her and she gave me fruit cake and milk and kissed me, and I ran back to the swing. Or she would dress me and my sister Polly up and we went out into the street. We had a penny and we bought a leaf of chocolate each. And I used to lick it up crumb by crumb, and I hoped I wouldn't run into anyone so I must share it. But my sister always ate hers all at once, and then nagged at me to get some of mine."

"How old were you, on the swing, Mrs Fowler?"

"Oh, I must have been five, six . . ."

None of it adds up. There couldn't, surely, have been a deep grassy garden behind the hardware in Bell Street? And in St John's Wood she would have been too old for swings and playing by herself in the grasses while the birds sang? And when her father went off to his smart suppers and the theatre, when was that? I ask, but she doesn't like to have a progression made, her mind has bright pictures in it that she has painted for herself and has been dwelling on for all those decades.

In what house was it her father came in and said to her

mother, "You whey-faced slop, don't you ever do anything but snivel?" And hit her. But never did it again, because Maudie ran at him and beat him across the legs until he began to laugh and held her up in the air, and said to his wife, "If you had some of her fire, you'd be something," and went off to his fancy-woman. And then Maudie would be sent up by her mother with a jug to the pub, to stand in the middle of the public asking for draught Guinness. "Yes, I had to stand there for everyone to see, so that *she* would be ashamed. But she wasn't ashamed, not she, she would have me over the bar counter and into her own little back room, which was so hot our faces were beef. That was before she poisoned my mother and began to hate me, out of remorse."

All that I have written up to now was a recapitulation, summing-up. Now I am going to write day by day, if I can. Today was Saturday, I did my shopping, and went home to work for a couple of hours, and then dropped in to Mrs F. No answer when I knocked, and I went back up her old steps to the street and saw her creeping along, pushing her shopping basket. Saw her as I did the first day: an old crooked witch. Quite terrifying, nose and chin nearly meeting, heavy grey brows, straggly bits of white hair under the black splodge of hat. She was breathing heavily as she came up to me. She gave her impatient shake of the head when I said hello, and went down the steps without speaking to me. Opened the door, still without speaking, went in. I nearly walked away. But followed her, and without being asked took myself into the room where the fire was. She came in after a long time, perhaps half an hour, while I heard her potter about. Her old yellow cat came and sat near my feet. She brought in a tray with her brown teapot and biscuits, quite nice and smiling. And she pulled the dirty curtains over, and put on the light and put the coal on the fire. No coal left in the bucket. I took the bucket from her and went along the passage to the coal cellar. A dark that had no light in it. A smell of cat. I scraped coal into the bucket and took it back, and she held out her hand for the bucket without saying thank you.

The trouble with a summing-up afterwards, a recap, is that you leave out the grit and grind of a meeting. I could say, She was cross to begin with, then got her temper back, and we had a nice time drinking tea, and she told me about . . . But what about all the shifts of liking, anger, irritation—oh, so much anger, in both of us?

I was angry while I stood there on the steps and she went down past me without speaking, and she was angry, probably, thinking, this is getting too much! And sitting in that room, with the cat, I was furious, thinking, well if that is all the thanks I get! And then all the annoyances melting into pleasure with the glow of the fire, and the rain outside. And there are always these bad moments for me, when I actually take up the greasy cup and have to put my lips to it; when I take in whiffs of that sweet sharp smell that comes from her, when I see how she looks at me, sometimes, the boiling up of some old rage . . . It is an up-and-down of emotion, each meeting.

She told me about a summer holiday.

"Of course, we could not afford summer holidays, not the way all you girls have them now. Take them for granted, you do! They had put me off work from the millinery. I did not know when they would want me again. I felt tired and run-down, because I wasn't eating right then, they paid us so bad. I answered an advertisement for a maid in a seaside hotel in Brighton. Select, it said. References needed. I had no references. I had never been in service. My mother would have died to think of it. I wrote a letter and I had a letter back asking me to come, my fares paid. I packed my little bag and I went. I knew it was all right, there was something about her letter. It was a big house, set back a bit from the road. I walked up the front path, thinking, well, I'm not in service here yet! And the housekeeper let me in, a real nice woman she was, and said Mrs Privett would see me at once. Well, let me say this now, she was one of the best people I have known in my life. The kindest. I often think of her. You know, when everything is as bad as it can be, and you think there's nowhere you can turn, then there's always that person, that one person . . . She looked me over, and said, Well, Maudie, you say you have no experience, and I value your honesty. But I want a good class of girl because we have a good class of people. When can you start? Now, I said, and we both laughed, and she said later she had had the same feeling about me, that when I arrived it would be all right. The housekeeper took me up to the top of the house. There was a cook, and a scullery maid, and a boy, and the housekeeper, and the two girls for waiting at the tables, and four housemaids. I was one of the housemaids. We were in one of the attics, two big beds up there, two to a bed. I wasn't to start till the morning, and so I ran down to the beach, and took off my shoes. There was the lovely sea. I had not seen the sea since my mother died, and I sat on the beach and watched the dark sea moving up and down and I was so happy, so happy . . . and I ran back through the dark, scared as anything because of the Strangler . . ."

"Because of the *what*?"

And here she told a long story about some newspaper scare of the time, a man who strangled girls when he found them alone . . . It was so out of key with the rest of what she was telling me, and yet this was, is, something in Maudie, a strain of horror-shivering masochism that comes out suddenly and then goes again. At any rate, she ran quaking up through the dark, through the dark garden, with the hot breath of the Strangler on her neck, and the door was opened by the housekeeper, who said, Oh there you are, Maudie, I was worrying about you, but the mistress said, Don't worry, I know where she'll be . . . "You know, I've often and often thought about this, when it is so easy to be nice, why are people nasty? Everything in that big house was nice, all the people in it, and even the guests too, no one unkind or quick or sharp. It was because of her, Mrs Privett. So why are people unkind to each other?

"She had kept my supper for me, and it was a lovely supper too, and she sat with me while I ate. And then up I went to bed. It was dark through the house, with the gas lights burning on the landings, but at the very top the sky was light, there were the three other girls, and oh, we did have such a good time. We lay half the night and told each other stories, ghost stories and all, and we frightened each other with the Strangler, and we ate sweets and laughed . . .

"And next morning, we had to get up at six. And by the time it was breakfast I was so hungry, but she, Mrs Privett, gave us the same food the hotel guests had, and better, and she came into the kitchen while we were all eating to make sure we had it. We ate great plates of porridge and real milk, and then kippers or haddock if we liked, or eggs any way we liked, and then all the toast and marmalade and butter we could eat, and sometimes she sat with us too, and said, I like to see young things eating. You must eat well, or you can't do your work. And that was what all the meals there were like. I've never eaten like that before or since. And then . . ."

"And what work did you do? Was it hard?"

"Yes, I suppose it was hard. But we knew how to work in those days. We got up by six and cleaned the grates through the house and started the fires, and we had the big dining room cleaned and shining before we took the guests their trays of tea and biscuits. And then we did the public rooms, everything just so and polished, and then we had our breakfast. And then we did all the bedrooms, right out, no skimping on the cleaning, Mrs Privett wouldn't have it. And we did the flowers with her, or the silver or the windows. And then we had our dinners, wonderful food, everything the guests had. And then we took the mending up to the attics and while we did that we had a bit of a skylark around. She didn't mind. She said she liked to hear us laughing, provided we got the work all done. And then we came down to do the tea, trays and trays of bread and butter and cakes and stuff, the four of us served all that while the waiting girls went off for the afternoon. And then we had some time off, and we went down to the beach for an hour or so. And then we four maids would sit with the babies and children while the parents went out to the theatre or somewhere. I loved that, I loved little children. We all loved that. And there was a big late supper, about ten at night, with cakes and ham and everything. And we all had either Sunday afternoon or Saturday afternoon off. Oh, it was wonderful. I was there three months and I got so fat and happy I couldn't get into my clothes."

"And then?"

"And then the autumn was coming, and the hotel closed.

Mrs Privett came to me and said, Maudie, I want you to stay with me. In the winters I open a place on the sea, in Nice that was. France. She wanted me to go with her. But I said no, I was a milliner, that was my trade, but it broke my heart not to go with her."

"Why did you *really* not go with her?" I asked.

"You are sharp," she said. "You are right. It was Laurie. I went away from London to Brighton and didn't say where I was, so he would value me, and he did. He was waiting for me when I got off the train, though how he found out I never did know. And he said, So you're back? As you can see, I said. Tomorrow you are coming for a walk, he said. Am I? I said.

"And so I married him. I married him instead of the German. I married the wrong man."

I gave a grimace at this, and she said, "And did you marry the wrong one too?"

"No," I said, "he married the wrong woman."

And this tickled her so much she lay back in her chair, her brown old wrinkled hands squeezing her knees, and she laughed and laughed. She has a young fresh laugh, not an old woman's laugh at all.

"Oh, oh, oh," she cried, "I had never thought of that. Well, Laurie thought he married the wrong woman, but then what woman would have been right? For he never stayed with any one of us."

That was this afternoon. I did not leave her until after six. She came with me to the outside door and said, "Thank you for getting the coal. You mustn't mind me, dear, mustn't mind my ways."

Sunday.

I saw *The White Raven*. I see that I am like Maudie, the housemaids—I like being frightened. After the film I came back here for my usual Sunday evening's occupation, making sure clothes are all prepared for the next week, grooming. I saw that I had spent all day alone and that is how I spend my weekends, usually. Solitary. I did not know I was until Freddie died. He liked us to have proper dinner parties every week or so, and we had his colleagues and their wives, and I asked girls from work, usually Joyce and her husband. My food was perfect, and Freddie did the wine. We were proud of how well we did it. And all that has been blown away, gone. I never saw his associates after the funeral. When I wondered if I would have the perfect little dinner parties, I couldn't be bothered. At work, I am seen by everybody as this self-sufficient competent woman, with a full life. Friends, weekends, entertainment. I go each week to three or four lunches, drinks parties, receptions for the mag. I don't like this, or dislike it, it is part of my job. I know nearly everyone, we all know each other. Then I come home after work, if I am not having supper with Joyce to discuss something, and I buy take-away, and then—my evening begins. I go into the bathroom and stay there two, three hours. Then watch a little television. At weekends I go about by myself. How do you describe such a person? And yet I am not lonely. If anyone had said to me, before Freddie died, that I could live like this, and not want anything different . . . And yet I must want something different? I shall spend a weekend with Georgic. *I shall try again.* I did not go in to Maudie today, thinking it all too much. I am sitting here writing this, in bed, wondering if she expected me. If she was disappointed.

Monday.
   Dropped in after work, with some chocolates. She seemed stand-offish. Cross because I did not go in yesterday? She said she had not gone out because it was cold, and she felt bad. After I got home I wondered if she wanted me to go and shop for her. But after all, she got along before I blew into her life—*crashed* into it.

Tuesday.
   Joyce said she didn't want to go to Munich for the Clothes Fair, trouble with husband, and her children playing up, would I go? I was reluctant, though I enjoy these trips: realized it was because of Maudie Fowler. This struck me as crazy, and I said I'd go.
   Went in to Maudie after work. The flames were bursting out of the grate, and she was hot and angry. No, she didn't feel

well, and no, I wasn't to trouble myself. She was so rude, but I went into the kitchen, which stank of sour food and cat food that had gone off, and saw she had very little there. I said I was going out to shop for her. I now recognize these moments when she is pleased that I will do this or that, but her pride is hurting. She lowers her sharp little chin, her lips tremble a little, and she stares in silence at the fire.

I did not ask what to get, but as I left she shouted after me about fish for the cat. I got a lot of things, put them on her kitchen table, boiled up some milk, took it to her.

"You ought to be in bed," I said.

She said, "And the next thing, you'll be fetching the doctor."

"Well, is that so terrible?"

"He'll send me away," she said.

"Where to?"

"Hospital, where else?"

I said to her, "You talk as if hospital is a sort of prison."

She said, "I have my thoughts, and you keep yours."

Meanwhile, I could see she was really ill. I had to fight with her, to help her to bed. I was looking around for a nightdress, but I understood at last she did not use one. She goes to bed in vest and drawers, with an old cardigan pinned at the throat by a nice garnet brooch.

She was suffering because I saw that her bed was not clean, and that her underclothes were soiled. The sweet stench was very strong: I know now it is urine.

I put her in, made her tea, but she said, "No, no, I'll only be running."

I looked around, found that a chair in the corner of the room was a commode and dragged it close to the bed.

"Who's going to empty it?" she demanded, furious.

I went out of the kitchen to see what the lavatory was like: a little cement box, with a very old unlidded seat, and a metal chain that had broken and had string extending it. It was clean. But very cold. No wonder she has a cough. It is very cold at the moment, February—and I only *feel* how cold it really is when I think of her, Maudie, for everywhere I am is so well heated and protected. If she is going out to that lavatory from the hot fire . . .

I said to her, "I'll drop in on my way to work."

I am sitting here, in bed, having bathed and washed every scrap of me, hair too, writing this and wondering how it is I am in this position with Maudie.

Wednesday.

Booked for Munich. Went in to Maudie after work. The doctor was there. Dr Thring. An old man, fidgety and impatient, standing by the door, I knew because he was farther from the heat and smell of the place, and he was saying, to an angry, obstinate, tiny old woman, who stood in the middle of her floor as if she was in front of the firing squad, "I won't go into hospital, I won't, you can't make me," "Then I won't come in to look after you, you can't make me do that." He was shouting. When he saw me, he said, in a different voice, relieved, desperate, "Tell her, if you're a friend, she should be in hospital."

She was looking at me quite terrified.

"Mrs Fowler," I said, "why don't you want to go into hospital?"

She turned her back on us both, and picked up the poker, and jabbed the flames with it.

The doctor looked at me, scarlet with anger and the heat of the place, and then shrugged. "You ought to be in a Home," he said. "I keep telling you so."

"You can't force me."

He exclaimed angrily and went into the passage, summoning me to follow. "Tell her," he said.

"I think she should be in hospital," I said, "but why should she be in a Home?"

He was quite at the end of his tether with exasperation and—I could see—tiredness. "Look at it all," he said. "Look at it. Well, I'll ring up the Services." And off he went.

When I got back, she said, "I suppose you've been arranging with him."

I told her exactly what I said, and while I was speaking she was coughing, mouth closed, chest heaving, eyes watering, and was thumping her chest with the heel of her fist. I could see that she didn't want to listen to what I said.

*   *   *

Thursday.

Went in on my way to work. She was up, dressed, in front of the fire, face glittering with fever. Her cat was yowling, unfed.

I took out her commode, full of strong stinking urine, and emptied it. I gave the cat food on a clean dish. I made her tea and some toast. She sat with her face averted from me, ashamed and sick.

"You should have a telephone," I said. "It's ridiculous, having no telephone. I could ring you from the office."

She did not answer.

I went off to work. There was no social thing I had to do today, no luncheon, etc., and the photographers' session was cancelled—the trains are on strike. I said to Joyce I'd work at home, and she said she'd stay in the office, it was all right. She let me understand home is difficult for her at the moment: her husband wants a divorce, she does not know what to do, she is seeing lawyers. But she is pleased to be in the office, though in better times she does a lot of work at home too.

I went in to Maudie on my way home, and found there Hermione Whitfield, from what she refers to as "Geriatrics".

We understood each other at first glance: being alike, same style, same clothes, same *image*. She was sitting in the chair opposite Maudie, who was bundled up in all her black. She was leaning forward, smiling, charming, humorous.

" But, Mrs Fowler, there are so many things we could do for you, and you won't co- . . ." But she dropped "co-operate" in favour of " . . . let us."

"And who are you?" she asked me, in the same charming, almost playful style, but heard it herself, and said, in the chummy democratic mode of our kind (but I had not thought at all about these distinctions till today), "Are you a Good Neighbour? No one told *me* anything about *that*."

"No," I said, "I am not a Good Neighbour, I am Mrs Fowler's friend."

This was quite outrageous, from about ten different viewpoints, but most of all because I was not saying it in inverted commas, and it was only then that I thought how one did not have *friends* with the working classes. I could be many things to Mrs Fowler, including a Good Neighbour, but not a friend.

She sat there, blinking up at me, the firelight on her hair. Masses of soft golden hair, all waves and little ringlets. I know what all that careful disorder costs. Her soft pink face, with wide blue eyes, done up with grey and blue paints and powders. Her white fluffy sweater, her grey suede trousers, her dark blue suede boots, her ... I was thinking, either "the welfare" get paid more than I had believed or she has a private income. It occurred to me, standing there, in that long moment of pure discordance, for what I had said did not fit, could not be taken easily, that I was examining her like a fashion editress, and for all I knew she might be quite different from her "image".

Meanwhile, she had been thinking. "Mrs Fowler," said she, getting up, smiling prettily, radiating helpfulness and light, "very well, you won't go into hospital. I don't like hospital myself. But I can get a nurse in to you every morning, and I can send in a Home Help and . . ."

"I don't want any of those," said Maudie, her face averted, poking savagely at the flames.

"Well, remember what there is available for you," she said, and gave me a look which meant I should follow her.

I was then in a position where I had to talk about Maudie behind her back, or say to Hermione, "No, we will talk here." I was weak, and followed Hermione.

"My name is . . ." etc., and so forth, giving me all her credentials, and she waited for mine.

"My name is Janna Somers," I said.

"You are perhaps a neighbour?" she said, annoyed.

"I have become fond of Mrs Fowler," I said; and at last this was right, it enabled her to let out an involuntary sigh of relief, because the categories were back in place.

"Oh yes," she cried, "I do so agree, some of these old things, they are so lovable, so . . ." But her face was saying that Maudie is far from lovable, rather a cantankerous old nuisance.

We were standing in that awful passage, with its greasy yellow walls where coal dust lay in films, the smell of cat from the coal cellar, the cracked and shaky door to the outer world. She already had her hand on the doorknob.

"I drop in sometimes to Mrs Fowler," I said, "and I do what I can." I said it like this so she would understand I would not be relied upon to do her work for her.

She sighed again. "Well, luckily, she has to be rehoused soon."

"What! She doesn't know that!" I recognized my voice had the panic in it Maudie would feel, if she had heard.

"Of course she knows. This place has been scheduled for years."

"But it belongs to some Greek or other."

"Oh no, it can't do!" she began decisively, and then I saw her rethink. Under her arm she had a file stuffed full. She hung her handbag on the doorknob, pulled out the file, opened it. A list of houses for demolition or reconstruction.

I already knew that she had made a mistake, and I wondered if she was going to admit it, or cover up. If she admitted it, I would give her full marks—for this was a contest between two professionals. We were in competition, not for Mrs Fowler—poor Maudie—but for who had authority. Although I had specifically repudiated authority.

A biro between her pretty lips, she frowned over the papers spread on her lifted knee while she stood on one leg.

'Well, I'll have to look into it," she said. And I knew that it would all be allowed to slide away. Oh, how well I know that look of hers, when someone has inwardly decided not to do anything while presenting an appearance of confident competence!

She was about to go out.

I said, "If I could persuade her, what Services is she entitled to?"

"Home Help, of course. But we tried that before, and it didn't work. A Good Neighbour, but she didn't want one . . ." She gave me a quick doubtful look, and went on. "She's not entitled to Meals on Wheels, because she can manage and we are so pressed . . ."

"She's over ninety," I said.

"So are many others!"

"But you'll arrange for the nurse to come in?"

"But she says she doesn't want one. We can't force ourselves on them. They have to co-operate!" This triumphantly, she had scored a point.

She bounded up the steps and into a red Escort, and waved to me as she went off. Pleased to be rid of me. A bright smile, and her body was saying, These amateurs, what a nuisance!

I went remorsefully back to Maudie, because she had been discussed behind her back. She sat with her face averted and was silent.

At last: "What have you decided, then?"

"Mrs Fowler, I do think you ought to have some of the Services, why not?"

Her head was trembling, and her face would have done for The Wicked Witch.

"What I want is Meals on Wheels, but they won't give me that."

"No Home Help?"

"No. They sent me one. She said, Where's your Hoover! Too good for a carpet sweeper. And sat here drinking my tea and eating my biscuits. And when I sent her shopping, she couldn't be bothered to take an extra step to save a penny, she'd pay anything, I could shop cheaper than she, so I told her not to come back."

"Well, anyway . . ." And I heard there was a different note in my voice. For I had been quite ashamed, watching Hermione, seeing myself, all that pretty flattering charm, as if she had—I had!—an eye directed at the performance: how well I am doing it! How attractive and kind I am. . . . I was fighting to keep that note out of my voice, to be direct and simple. "Anyway, I think you should think about taking what is available. And to start with, there's the nurse every morning, while you don't feel well."

"Why should I need a nurse?" she inquired, her face averted.

This meant, Why, when you are coming in to me twice a day? And, too, But why should you come in, it's not your job. And, most strongly, *Please, please*.

If I were with someone like Hermione, my husband, Joyce, Sister Georgie, I would say, "What an emotional blackmailer, you aren't going to get away with *that*." The fine nose of our kind for advantage, taken or given.

By the time I left I had promised I would continue to go in morning and evening. And that I would ring up "them" saying she did not want a nurse. And when we said goodbye she was cold and angry, frantic because of her helplessness, because she knew she should not expect so much of me, and because . . .

And now I am sitting here, feeling quite wild myself, trapped is what I'm feeling. And I have been all evening in the bath, thinking.

About what I really care about. My life, my real life, is in the office, is at work. Because I have been working since I was nineteen, and always for the same magazine, I've taken it for granted, have not seen that this *is* my life. I was with the magazine in its old format, have been part of three changes, and the second of these I could say was partly because of me. Joyce and I made it all happen. I have been there longer than she has: for she came in as Production Manager, mid-sixties, when I had already been there fifteen or twenty years, working my way through all the departments. If there is one person in that magazine who can be said to *be Lilith*, it's me.

And yet I take it all for granted. And I am not going to jeopardize what I really care about for the sake of Maudie Fowler. I shall go to Munich, not for two days, as I said today, but for the usual four, and I shall tell her she must say yes to the nurse.

Friday—in Munich.

Went in to Maudie this morning. She in her chair, staring at a cold grate, inside a carapace of black rags. I fetched her coal, made her tea, fed the cat. She seemed to be cold, yet with the glitter of fever. She was coughing and coughing.

I said to her, "Mrs Fowler, I am going to Munich and I shall be away four days." No response at all. I said, "Mrs Fowler, I have to go. But I am going to ring up Hermione Whitfield and say you must have a nurse. Just till I come back." She went on staring into the cold grate. So I began to lay the fire—but did not know how, and she forced herself up out of her warm nest and slowly, slowly put in bits of paper, bits of wood, a fire-lighter, built up the fire. I looked around—no newspaper, no more fire-lighters, nothing.

I went out to the shop, and on the way back saw that there was a skip in the road outside her door, and there were plenty of little slats of wood, old laths from the demolished walls—she had been collecting these to start her fire. Conscious of how I must look, in all my smart gear, I filled a carrier bag with these bits of wood. While I was doing this, I chanced to glance up and saw that I was being observed from various windows. Old faces, old ladies. But I did not have time to take anything in, but rushed down with the wood and the groceries. She was again in her listless pose in front of the now roaring fire.

I did not know whether a nurse would build a fire.

I asked, "Will a nurse make up a fire for you?"

She did not answer. I was getting angry. And was as distressed as she. The whole situation was absurd. And yet it could not be any other way.

When I stood up to leave I said, "I am going to ring up and ask for a nurse and *please* don't send the nurse away."

"I don't want any nurse."

I stood there, worried because I was late, and it was Conference day and I've never ever been late. And worried about her. And angry. And resentful. And yet she tugged at me, I wanted to take that dirty old bundle into my arms and hug her. I wanted to slap her and shake her.

"What is all this about hospital," I asked, "what? You'd think you were being threatened with . . . what is so terrible about it? Have you ever been there?"

"Yes, two winters ago. Christmas."

"And?"

She was sitting straight up now, her sharp chin lifted in a combative way, her eyes frightened and angry.

"No, they were kind enough. But I don't like it. They fill you with pills and pills and pills, you feel as if your mind has been taken from you, they treat you like a child. I don't want it . . ." And then she added, in the tone of one trying to be fair, and at this attempt leading her into more, more than she had intended. " . . . There was one little nurse. She rubbed my back for me when I coughed . . ." And she looked at me quickly, and away, and I knew she had wanted me to rub her back for her. It had not occurred to me! I do not know how!

"Well," I said, "no one is going to force you to hospital."

She said, "If they'd take me in after last time." And suddenly she was laughing and alert, her enjoying self.

"What did you do?" I said, pleased to be able to laugh with her.

"I walked out!" And she chuckled. "Yes, I had had enough. And I was constipated with all that good eating, because I am not saying they don't feed you, and I was feeling farther and farther from myself every minute with the pills. I said, Where are my clothes? They said, You can't go home in this weather, Mrs Fowler, you'll die of it. For there was snow. I said, You bring me my clothes or I'll walk out in your hospital night-dress. And so they brought them. They would not look at me or speak to me, they were so angry. I walked down into the hall and said to the porter, Call me a taxi. My bits of money had been stolen in the hospital ward. But I was going to tell the driver and ask him to bring me home for the love of God. If God is anyone they know these days. But there was a woman there in reception and she said, I'll take you, love. And brought me home. I think of her. I think of them who do me good, I do." And she gave me the most marvellous merry smile, her girl's smile.

"For all that, I have to go to Munich. I'll be away for four days, and you know very well you can't manage. I want to hear you say, in so many words, you don't want a nurse. I'm treating you seriously, not treating you like a child! If you say no nurse, I'll do no more. But I think you should let me. A nurse isn't going to be the end of the world."

"And how about all the pills then?"

"All right. But say it, you don't want me to ring a nurse." And I added, really desperate, "For God's sake, Maudie, have some sense." I realized I had called her by her Christian name, but she was not put out.

She shrugged. "I have no choice, I suppose."

I went over to her, bent down to kiss her, and she put out her cheek, and I kissed it.

I went off, waving from the door, I hope not a "charming" wave.

* * *

I was late for the Conference.

First time. This Conference is in my view what gives the mag its life. It was my idea. Later I'll write down an analysis, it would help me clear my thoughts, for I see they need clearing, about the office, work, everything. This afternoon I was alone: Joyce at home because she's going to be in the office all the time I'm in Germany. I was trying to get information about the Services. I have all the leaflets as dished out to the consumers, *Your Pension Rights* and that kind of stuff. No, I want to find out how it all really works. After a while I knew what I had to do. I have to find That One Person. If this is a law for our kind of work, then it probably is everywhere. (Maudie talks about there always being *the one person*, though she means it in a different sense.) Joyce and I use it all the time. Long ago, we discovered that if you want to make things work, you have to look for *The One Person* in a department or an office who is in fact running it, or who knows about it, or is—in some way or another—real. Well, Hermione is certainly not that. No. You have to have people like Hermione, if only because there aren't enough of the others: it's not that they don't do any work, or are useless, but they are peripheral. To find out how to get Maudie what she really needs, and what could help her, I can't use Hermione. But I rang her this afternoon—she was out—and left a message that Mrs Fowler will need a nurse for five days. And then something warned me, and I told my secretary to ring Hermione, and then Joyce's secretary too. She can't be left with no one, for four days.

Wednesday.

First, my state of mind *before* I went in to Maudie. I flew back from Munich midday, went straight to the office recharged, all systems go. I adore these trips. What I adore is my efficiency. I like making things work, knowing how to do it. I like them knowing me, giving me *my* room, remembering my tastes. Saw friends through weekend. Rather, "friends", work contacts, then Monday and Tuesday, the Fair. What I like is *being in control*. I am so full of energy, I eat exactly what I should, don't drink a mouthful too much, hardly sleep, rush around all day. I know exactly how to present myself, and how to use it. I saw myself, coming into the Show, Monday morning, sitting down, people smiling and greeting: and at the same time I was back fifteen years, seeing myself through *those* eyes, the way I saw, at thirty, the established women who had been doing it for years. I admired them, wished to be one of them, and while I examined them, minutely, every little detail, I was looking for what *they* overlooked, signs of processes that would lead to their being replaced by others, me among them. Of those women whom I examined then, one remains, though some still are in the field in other ways. I have spent four days wondering what is at work in me which will lead me to be thrown out, or to remain in the office at some less taxing job, while—who?—goes off on these trips. I cannot see what it is. Simply ageing? Nothing to do with it! That I will get bored with it all? I cannot believe that, yet.

When I got into the office Joyce was waiting for me so she could go home: without ever formally arranging it, we make sure one of us is always there. She looked tired. She said she had had a dreadful time since I left, with her husband, she'd tell me, but not now, and off she went. There was a message from Hermione Whitfield that she had not got my message about the nurse till Monday, and that then Mrs Fowler refused to let the nurse in. This brought me back with a bump to my London self. I have worked all afternoon, mostly on the telephone, and then the photographers for tomorrow. But I was thinking at the same time about Joyce. I have understood that this business with her husband means the end of our working together, or at any rate, a change. I am sure of it. This made me depressed and anxious, before I even left the office. Another thing I have understood in a way I didn't before: Joyce is my only real friend. I mean, *friend*. I have a relationship with her I've had with no one, ever. Certainly not Freddie.

I was coming straight home, because I was suddenly tired. But made the taxi put me off at Maudie Fowler's. I stood there knocking and banging on the door. Freezing. Not a sound. I got into a panic—was she dead?—and noted, not without interest, that one of my reactions was relief. At last, an agitation of the curtains at the window of her "front room", which she seems never to use. I waited. Nothing happened. I banged and banged, absolutely furious by then. I was ready to strangle her. Then the door opened inwards, sticking and scraping, and there she was, a tiny little bundle of black, with her white face sticking up out of it. And the *smell*. It is no good my telling myself I shouldn't care about such details. I care terribly. The smell . . . awful, a sour, sweet-sharp reek. But I could see she was only just able to stand there.

There was nothing "charming" about me, I was so angry.

"Why do you keep me out in the cold?" I said, and went in, past her, making her move aside. She then went on ahead of me down the passage, a hand on a wall to steady her.

In the back room, a heap of dead cinders in the grate. There was an electric fire, though; one bar, and it was making noises which meant it was unsafe. The place was cold, dirty, smelly, and the cat came and wound itself around my legs miaowing. Maudie let herself slide into her chair and sat staring at the grate.

"Well, why didn't you let the nurse in?" I shouted at her.

"The nurse," she said bitterly. "What nurse?"

"I know she came."

"Not till Monday. All the weekend I was here by myself, no one."

I was about to scream at her, "Why didn't you let her in when she came on Monday?" but saw there was no point.

I was full of energy again—anger.

"Maudie," I said, "you are the limit, the end, you make things worse for yourself. Well, I'll put the kettle on."

I did. I fetched coal. I found the commode full of urine, but no worse, thank goodness. Thank goodness was what I thought then, but I see one gets used to anything. I then went out into the street with a carrier bag. A grey sleety rain. There I was, in all my smart things from Munich, scrabbling about in the skip for bits of wood. And again, faces at the windows, watching me.

Inside, I scraped out the grate, clouds of dust flying about, and laid the fire. With a fire-lighter. Wood and coal. Soon it was burning.

I made tea for both of us, having scalded the *filthy* cups. I must stop being so petty about it. Does it matter, dirty cups? Yes! Yes, yes, yes, *yes*.

She had not moved, but sat looking at the flames.

"The cat," she said.

"I've given her some food."

"Then let her out for a bit."

"There's sleet and rain."

"She won't mind."

I opened the back door. A wave of cold rain came straight in at me, and the fat yellow cat, who had been pressing to get to the door, miaowed and ran back again, to the coal cellar.

"She's gone to the coal cellar," I said.

"Then I suppose I'll have to put my hand in it," she said.

This made me so angry! I was a seethe of emotions. As usual, I wanted to hit her or shake her and, as usual, to put my arms around her.

But my mind luckily was in control, and I did everything I should, without, thank God, being "humorous" or charming or gracious.

"Have you been eating at all?"

No response.

I went out again to shop. Not a soul in the corner shop. The Indian sitting there at the cash desk looked grey and chilled, as well he might, poor soul.

I said I was buying food for Mrs Fowler, wanting to know if she had been in.

He said, "Oh, the old lady, I hope she is not ill?"

"She is," I said.

"Why doesn't she go into a Home?"

"She doesn't want to."

"Hasn't she a family?"

"I think so, but they don't care."

"It is a terrible thing," he said to me, meaning me to understand that his people would not neglect an old woman like this.

"Yes, it is a terrible thing, and you are right," I said.

When I got back, again I thought of death. She sat there, eyes closed, and so still, I thought not breathing.

But then, her blue eyes were open and she was looking at the fire.

"Drink your tea," I said. "And I'll grill you a bit of fish. Can you eat it?"

"Yes, I will."

In the kitchen I tried to find anything that wasn't greasy, and gave up. I put the fish on the grill, and opened the door briefly to get in some clean air. Sleet notwithstanding.

I took her the fish, and she sat herself up and ate it all, slowly, and her hands trembled, but she finished it and I saw she had been hungry.

I said, "I've been in Munich. To see all the clothes for the autumn. I've been seeing all the new styles."

"I've never been out of England."

"Well, I'll tell you all about it when you are a bit better."

To this she did not respond. But at last, just when I thought I would go, she remarked, "I've a need for some clean clothes."

I did not know how to interpret this. I did see—I have become sensitive enough for that—at least that this was not at all a simple request.

She wanted me to buy her clothes?

I looked at her. She made herself look at me, and said, "Next door, you'll find things."

"What?"

She gave a trembling, discouraged sort of shrug.

"Vest. Knickers. Petticoat. Don't you wear underclothes, that you are asking?"

Again, the automatic anger, as if a button had been pushed. I went next door into the room I knew she didn't like me in.

The bed that has the good eiderdown, the wardrobe, the dressing table with little china trinkets, the good bookcases. But everywhere piles and heaps of—rubbish. I could not believe it. Newspapers dating back fifty years, crumbling away; awful scraps of material, stained and yellow, bits of lace, dirty handkerchiefs, shreds of ribbon—I've never seen anything like it. She had never thrown anything away, I think. In the drawers, disorder, and they were crammed with—but it would take pages to describe. I wished I had the photographer there—reflex thought! Petticoats, camisoles, knickers, stays, vests, old dresses or bits of them, blouses . . . and nothing less than twenty years old, and some of them going back to World War One. The difference between clothes now and then: these were all "real" materials, cottons, silks, woollens. Not a man-made fibre there. But everything torn, or stained, or dirty. I pulled out bundles of things, and every one I examined, first for interest, and then to see if there was anything wearable, or clean. I found at last a wool vest, and long wool drawers, and a rather nice pink silk petticoat, and then a woollen dress, blue, and a cardigan. They were clean, or nearly. I worked away in there, shivering with cold, and thinking of how I had loved myself all these last days, how much I do love myself, for being in control, on top; and thought that the nearest I could get to poor Maudie's helplessness was remembering what it had been like to be a child, hoping that you won't wet your pants before you get to the lavatory.

I took the clothes into the other room, which was very hot now, the flames roaring up. I said to her, "Do you want me to help you change?" The sideways, irritable movement of the head, which I knew now meant I was being stupid.

But I did not know why.

So I sat down opposite her, and said, "I'll finish my tea before it's freezing." I noted that I was drinking it without feeling sick: I have become used to drinking out of grimy cups, I noted that with interest. Once Maudie had been like me, perpetually washing herself, washing cups, plates, dusting, washing her hair.

She was talking, at random I thought, about when she had been in hospital. I half listened, wishing that doctors and nurses could hear how their hospitals are experienced by someone like Maudie. Prisons. Reformatories. But then I realized she was telling me about how, because she had not been well enough to be put in the bath, two nurses had washed her in her bed, and I understood.

"I'll put on the kettles," I said. "And you must tell me what to do."

I put on two kettles, found an enamel basin, which I examined with interest, for I have not seen any but plastic ones for a long time, and searched for soap and a flannel. They were in a hole in the wall above the sink: a brick taken out and the cavity painted.

I took the basin, kettles, soap, flannel, a jug of cold water, next door. Maudie was struggling out of her top layer of clothes. I helped her, and realized I had not co-ordinated this at all. I rushed about, found newspapers, cleared the table, spread thick papers all over it, arranged basin, kettles, jug, washing things. No towel. I rushed into the kitchen, found a damp dirty towel, rushed into the front room and scrabbled about, seeming to myself to be taking all day. But it was really only a few moments. I was bothered about Maudie standing there, half naked, and ill, and coughing. At last I found a cleanish towel. She was standing by the basin, her top half nude. There is nothing of her. A fragile rib cage under creased yellow skin, her shoulder bones like a skeleton's, and at the end of thin stick arms, strong working hands. Long thin breasts hanging down.

She was clumsily rubbing soap on to the flannel, which, needless to say, was slimy. I should have washed it out first. I ran next door again, tore a bit off an old clean towel and took it back. I knew she wanted to tick me off for tearing the towel; she would have done if she had not been saving her breath.

I slowly washed her top half, in plenty of soap and hot water, but the grime on her neck was thick, and to get that off would have meant rubbing at it, and it was too much. She was trembling with weakness. I was comparing this frail old body with my mother's: but I had only caught glimpses of her sick body. She had washed herself—and only now was I wondering at what cost—till she went into hospital. And when Georgie came, she gave her a wash. But not her child-daughter, not me. Now I washed Maudie Fowler, and thought of Freddie, how his bones had seemed to sort of flatten and go thin under flesh that clung to them. Maudie might be only skin and bones but her body doesn't have that beaten-down look, as if the flesh is sinking into the bones. She was chilly, she was sick, she was weak—but I could feel the vitality beating there: life. How strong it is, life. I had never thought that before, never felt life in that way, as I did then, washing Maudie Fowler, a fierce angry old woman. Oh, how angry: it occurred to me that all her vitality is in her anger, I must not, must *not* resent it or want to hit back.

Then there was the problem of her lower half, and I was waiting for guidance.

I slipped the "clean" vest on over her head, and wrapped the "clean" cardigan round her, and then saw she was sliding down the thick bunches of skirt. And then it hit me, the stench. Oh, it is no good, I *can't* not care. Because she had been too weak or too tired to move, she had shat her pants, shat everything.

Knickers, filthy . . . Well, I am not going on, not even to let off steam, it makes me feel sick. But I was looking at the vest and petticoats she had taken off, and they were brown and yellow with shit. Anyway. She stood there, her bottom half naked. I slid newspapers under her, so she was standing on thick wads of them. I washed and washed her, all her lower half. She had her big hands down on the table for support. When it came to her bottom she thrust it out, as a child might, and I washed all of it, creases too. Then I threw away all that water, refilled the basin, quickly put the kettles on again. I washed her private parts, and thought about that phrase for the first time: for she was suffering most terribly because this stranger was invading her privateness. And I did all her legs again, again, since the dirt had run down her legs. And I made her stand in the basin and washed her feet, yellow gnarled old feet. The water was hot again over the flaring gas, and I helped her pull on the "clean" bloomers. By then, having seen what was possible, they were clean to me, being just a bit dusty. And then the nice pink petticoat.

"Your face," I said. For we had not done that. "How about your hair?" The white wisps and strands lay over the yellow dirty scalp.

"It will wait," she said.

So I washed her face, carefully, on a clean bit torn off the old towel.

Then I asked her to sit down, found some scissors, cut the toenails, which was just like cutting through horn, got clean stockings on, her dress, her jersey. And as she was about to put on the outside clothes of black again, I said involuntarily,

"Oh, don't—" and was sorry, for she was hurt, she trembled even more, and sat silent, like a bad child. She was worn out.

I threw out the dirty water and scalded the basin, and filled a kettle to make fresh tea. I took a look out of the back: streams of sleet, with crumbs of greyish snow, the wind blowing hard—water was coming in under the kitchen door; and as for thinking of her going out into that to reach the lavatory, that freezing box—yet she *had* been going out, and presumably would again.

I kept saying to myself, She is over ninety and she has been living like this for years: she has survived it!

I took her more tea, and some biscuits, and left her drinking them by her big fire.

I put all the filthy outer clothes I had taken off in newspaper and folded them up and dumped them in the rubbish bin, without asking her.

And then I made a selection among the clothes from the drawers, and stripped the filthy sheets from her bed, and the pillowcases, and went out into the rain to the launderette, leaving them with the girl there to be done.

I made the place as neat as I could, put down food for the cat, who sat against Maudie's leg, being stroked. I cleared everything up. All this time Maudie sat staring into the flames, not looking at me when I looked at her, but watching me as I moved around, and when she thought I didn't know.

"Don't think I don't appreciate it," she said as I laboured on, and on. I was sweeping the floor by then, with a hand brush and pan. I couldn't find anything else. The way she said this, I couldn't interpret it. It was flat. I thought, even hopeless: she was feeling perhaps, as I had had a glimpse of, remembering myself as a child, helpless in a new way. For, very clearly, no one had ever done this kind of thing for her before.

I went back to the launderette. The Irish girl, a large competent girl with whom I had exchanged the brisk comradeship of equals when leaving the stuff, gave me the great bag of clean things and looked into my face and said, "Filth. I've never seen anything like it. Filth." She hated me.

I said, "Thanks," did not bother to explain, and left. But I was flaming with—embarrassment! Oh, how dependent I am on being admired, liked, appreciated.

I took the things back, through the sleet. I was cold and tired by then. I wanted to get home . . .

But I cleared out the drawers of a large chest, put the clean things in, and told Maudie where I had put them.

Then I said, "I'll drop in tomorrow evening."

I was curious to hear what she'd say.

"I'll see you then" was what she said.

And now I am alone, and have bathed, but it was a brisk businesslike bath, I didn't soak for hours. I should have tidied everything, but I haven't. I am, simply, tired. I cannot believe that this time yesterday I was in the hotel, pampered guest, eating supper with Karl, cherished colleague. Flowers, venison, wine, cream—the lot.

It seems to me impossible that there should be *that*—there; and then Maudie Fowler, *here*. Or is it *I* who am impossible? I certainly am disoriented.

I have to think all this out. What am I to do? Who can I discuss it with? Joyce is my friend, she is my friend. She *is* my friend?

Thursday.

Joyce came in to collect work to take home. She looks awful. I said to her, "How goes it?" She said, "He wants me to go with him to the States." I asked, "For good?" She said, "For good." She looked at me, I looked at her. This is how we converse: in shorthand. She said, "I've got to fly. Tell John I've got the cover finished. I've done the Notes. I'll be in all tomorrow, Janna." And off she went. This means: her husband has been offered a professorship, he wants to take it, he wants her to give up her job here and go with him, she doesn't want to go, they quarrelled to the point of divorce, the children don't want to go to the States—and this afternoon I had the feeling that Joyce would probably go to the States. And that's the end of that.

I went in to Maudie on the way home: her door was on the latch. Fire blazing. Cat on bed asleep. Maudie, asleep. An empty teacup on the arm of her chair. I took the cup to safety, left a note: See you tomorrow, and fled hoping she wouldn't wake before I left.

I am sitting here in my dressing gown by the electric fire. I should clean out this flat. I should really wash my hair.

I am thinking of how Maudie Fowler one day could not trouble herself to clean out her front room, because there was so much junk in it, and then she left it and left it; going in sometimes, thinking, well, it's not so bad. Meanwhile she was keeping the back room and the kitchen spotless. Even now she does her own chimney once a week, and then scrubs the grate, brushes up the dust and cinders—though less and less thoroughly. She wasn't feeling well, and didn't bother, once, twice—and then her room was not really cleaned, only the floor in the middle of the room sometimes, and she learned not to look around the edges or under the bed. Her kitchen was last. She scrubbed it and washed shelves, but then things began to slide. But through it all she washed herself, standing at the kitchen table, heating water in the kettles. And she kept her hair clean. She went sometimes to the public bath-houses, for she had told me she liked going there. Then she left longer and longer between washing her hair . . . and then she did not wash her clothes, only took out the cleanest ones there were, putting them back grubby, till they were the cleanest; and so it went on. And at last, she was upright in her thick shell of black, her knickers not entirely clean, but not so bad, her neck dirty, but she did not think about it, her scalp unwashed. When they took her to hospital, they washed her all over and washed her hair too. She sometimes thought humorously, when they cart me off back to hospital, I'll get another proper wash! But she, Maudie Fowler, was still there, alert, very much all there, on guard inside that old witch's appearance. *She* is still there, and everything has collapsed around her, it's too difficult, too much.

And I, Janna, am sitting here, in my clean, scented dressing gown, just out of my bath. I should do my nails again, though. I should clean my flat, or ask someone in to clean it. I was in my bath for only a few minutes tonight.

By this time next year my whole life will have changed. I know it, though I don't know how.

I shall go down and visit Georgie next weekend. *If I dare leave Maudie*. It is ridiculous. *Where is that one person?*

Friday.

I went in on my way to work. She was better. Had been out to shop for herself. She looked quite nice and fresh—so I see her now, I no longer *see* the old witch. I said I was going to visit my sister Georgie. She laughed at the name. She said, "One of these days I'll visit my sister, I expect." I already knew what that meant, and I said, "I'll take you, Maudie." "Janna and Georgie," she said. "My sister and I, we were Maudie and Polly, and when we went out dressed up in our white coats and little hats, we were a picture." I said, "Georgie and I were a picture too, I expect. I remember pink dresses and berets. I'll see you Sunday night when I come back." "If you have the time," she said. I noted that I could have given her a nice sharp slap, but laughed and said, "I'll see you."

Sunday Night.

The train was very late. Did not go in to Maudie. Now it is midnight. I have done the usual Sunday-night things, seeing my clothes are ready for the week, hair, make-up, nails.

Well, it has been a painful weekend. When I got there Georgie was alone, because Tom and the children had gone off on some visit. Was very pleased, can't stand those brats of hers. Tom is all right, but a married couple is a married couple. I wanted to talk to Georgie. My thought was, specifically: now I am grown up, perhaps she will take me seriously? For years I used to go down, when I *did* go down, rather princessing it. Good old Georgie and good old Tom. She has never bothered about her clothes and things much. I used to wear my most outrageous clothes and take copies of the mag and enjoyed telling her about my life and times. She listened in her way of no-comment. Clever little sister Janna. Correction, Jane. She wasn't going to call me Janna, Jane it was and Jane it will be, to the end. How many times I have said to her, Georgie, no one calls me Jane, no one, I want to be Janna. I can't remember to, says she, making a point, and that's that. She thinks Janna is a smart little name to go with a smart little job. I used to sit through those weekends, when I did go, wondering how she stuck it, but of course she was thinking the same of me. It is not that she despises me, exactly, though she certainly thinks what I do pretty peripheral, it is that she cannot imagine any sane person doing it.

When I went into the house I was very alert to everything, the way I am at the moment—contrasts. Because of Maudie Fowler. Georgie's house is exactly the house my parents lived in always. I call it country-suburban, comfortable, conventional, conservative, all of a piece from the landscapes on the walls to the books on the bed table. My flat is, Freddie's and mine was, both international-contemporary. On the rare occasions Georgie has stayed a night, she has made a point of saying she has *enjoyed* my things. They are such fun, says she.

Georgie had a cold supper for us and seemed at a loss what to do after it. We were in her living room, curtains drawn, some snow outside, not enough for my taste but more than she wanted. She says it makes work. She works hard, Georgie does, the house, the cooking, looks after husband, four children, chairwoman of this, patron of that, secretary of the local reading circle, good works. I sat one side of the fire, she on the other. I tried to talk about Mother. I need to know about her. I never talked to her, a bit more to Father. But Georgie has put me into the category of the irresponsible one who doesn't care about family. And that's that. I kept giving her openings, even asked once, I wonder what Mother would have thought?

At last I talked about my trip to Munich. She liked that. Your glamorous goings-on, she calls all that. She wanted to know how the hotel was, my friends, how the fashion shows are organized, how this is done and that is done. I recognize myself in all this. Not a word about the styles and the fashions, but *how it all works*. So we are like each other after all. Suddenly, when I was in bed, I had a thought that made me sit up again and turn on the light. It was this. Before Granny died, she was ill for about two or three years, can't remember (which is a point in itself), and she was at home with Mother, who was looking after her. I was working like a demon then, it was the first rebirth of the mag, and I simply behaved as if Granny being ill had nothing to do with me. Not my affair! I can remember switching off from the moment I heard the news. But Mother had her at home there, and Father wasn't too well either. Granny had diabetes, heart trouble, bad eyes with operations for cataract, kidney trouble. I used to hear news of all this, relayed in Mother's brisk letters: and I haven't kept the letters, and I remember not wanting to read them. *Now* I know what it costs, looking after the very old, the helpless. I find myself exhausted after an hour or two, and want only to run away somewhere out of it. But where did Mother run to? Who helped her? Not me! Not once, I never went near her.

Sunday morning, Georgie and I had breakfast alone together. Some snow outside. Pretty. Trees and bushes full of snow and birds feeding off stuff Georgie hangs in the branches. She said Tom was coming back with the kids, because the weather was frightful where they were. I said to her, quite desperate because I knew once they had got back, that was that, "Georgie, were you around much when Granny was dying?"

She gave me a surprised look at this. She said, "No, I didn't get home much. I was pregnant twice while that was going on, and Kate was a baby." She was now looking at me in an impatient sort of way.

"I want to know about it," I said. "I have been thinking that I did nothing to help."

She said finally, "No, you didn't," and she wouldn't have said another word. I had to digest that she and Tom had attitudes about me, *my* behaviour, that were established and set, Jane was this and that and the other; and probably these were Mother's attitudes too, and Father's.

I said, "It has only recently occurred to me that I never lifted a finger all the time Granny was dying."

"No, you didn't," she said, in that same shutting-you-out way.

"Well," I said, "recently I've had a little to do with an old person, and I know now what Mother had to cope with."

"I suppose better late than never," said Sister Georgie.

This was much worse than I had expected. I mean, what she thought of me was so much worse that I was burning with—

no, alas, not shame, but it was embarrassment. Not wanting to be so badly thought of. I said to her, "Can you tell me anything about it?"

"Well, what on earth do you want to know?" She was exasperated. Exactly as if some small child had said to her, she having hit her thumb with a hammer, Does it hurt?

"Look, Georgie," I said, "all right, I've seen recently that . . . I could have done more than I did. All right? Do you want me to grovel? It *is* better late than never. I want to know more about Mother."

"She was in *your* flat for two years before she died," said Sister Georgie, making a great amazed incredulous astonishment out of it.

"Yes, I know. But it was since then that I . . ."

Georgie said, "Look, Jane, I'm sorry but . . . you just turn up here after all that, and say, I'd like a nice little chat about Mother. Jane, it simply isn't *on*," she said. She was literally inarticulate with anger. And I, with surprise. I realized that there were years of resentment here, criticism of little sister Jane.

I made a last try. "Georgie," I said, "I am sorry. I am sorry I didn't help Mother with Granny, and I want very much to discuss it all."

"I suppose one of these weekends I'll get a telephone call, when you've got nothing better to do, and you'll turn up, all fine and fancy free, not a hair out of place, and you'll say, Oh, Georgie, I was wondering what was it like having Mother here for ten years, with four kids, no help, and she becoming an invalid . . ."

At which point the telephone rang outside and she went to answer it. I sat there, I was numb. That was the word. Not that I hadn't felt bad about Mother living with Georgie all that time, for after all I was working, and we did only have a small flat, Freddie and I, and . . . and . . . and. But it had never occurred to me that Georgie was not going to talk to me this weekend. If ever. She was too angry. She was, and she is, so angry and bitter about me.

When she came back, she said, "I'm going down to the station to get Tom and the kids." She said to me, "I'm sorry

Jane, but if you are beginning to get some sort of sense of responsibility into you at last, it might perhaps occur to you that it isn't easy to have you just turning up with a light question or two: *How about Granny dying? How was it? Did it hurt?* It was all awful, Jane. *Do you understand?* It was dreadful. I went down there when I could, pregnant as hell or with the baby, and found Mother coping. Granny was bed-ridden at the end. For *months.* Can you imagine? No, I bet you can't. Doctors all the time. In and out of hospital. Mother was doing it all. Father couldn't help much, he was an invalid himself . . . Anyway, I've got to go to the station."

And off she went.

I nearly ran after her, to ask to be put on a train home, but stuck it out. Tom and the kids filled the house with clatter and clang, the record players went on at once of course, a radio, the house vibrating with din. Tom came in and said, How are you?—and went. The kids banged into the kitchen, where I was, Jilly, Bob, Jasper, Kate. Hi, hi, hi, hi, all round. It is established that I think Georgie's kids are awful and spoiled brats, but they might be all right when they grow up. I am the glamorous Aunt from London and the High Life. I send them presents of money at Christmas. When we meet I tell them I think they are awful and good for nothing. They tell me it is because I don't understand them. It is a cheerful game of mutual insult. But I *do* think they are awful. I cannot under-stand how they are allowed to do as they like, have what they like, go where they like. I have never heard either Georgie or Tom say once, No, you can't have that. Never. The whole house is *crammed* with their possessions, clothes, toys, gear, mostly unused or used once or twice. I keep thinking of growing up during the war and having nothing. And recently I have been thinking about the Third World having nothing. Of course, Georgie would say it is *trendy* to have such thoughts, but, as she would say, Better late than never.

Anyway, I sat in the kitchen and listened to the sheer din of those kids all over the house, and Georgie came back and I could see she was ready to talk, if I wanted, but suddenly I found myself saying, "Georgie, you are ready enough with criticism of me, but look at those children of yours."

"Yes, I know what you think," she said, her back turned to me. And I knew at once that this was a sore point.

"Tell me," I said to her, "when have they ever done anything they didn't want to do? Have you and Tom ever tried to teach them that the world isn't a celestial milk bar with milk shakes and cream topping for ever there at the touch of a button?"

"You may well be right. I'm not saying you are not," said she, making it humorous, "and now I have to get the lunch. If you want to help, stay, and if not, go and talk to Tom."

I took her at her word, went to find Tom, but he did not want to talk to me, being busy at something. I found the decibel level in the house intolerable, pulled on my big boots and went for a walk in the snow, came back for lunch. As usual, the parents were like appendages to the scene of the four children, who did not let them finish a conversation if they had the temerity to start one, or talked across them at each other, and behaved exactly as if Georgie and Tom were useful servants they could treat as they liked.

How has it come about that this is what families are like now? In the living room, afternoon, this was the scene. Jilly, seventeen, nagging because she had wanted to visit a friend and couldn't for some reason, so she was sulking and making the whole family pay for it. Bob, sixteen, an over-fat good-looking boy, practising the guitar as if no one else existed. Jasper, fifteen, whining and nagging at his father to go with him to some local football match. Kate, thirteen, cheeks flaming, hair wild, tarting around the room in one of Georgie's dresses, in a sort of locked hysteria, the way teenage girls get. This was for my benefit, because she wants to come to London and "be a model". Poor girl! Tom was sitting in a corner trying to read, and answering questions from his offspring in an abstracted irritable voice, and Georgie was waiting on all of them, in perfect good humour and patience; shouting to make herself heard from time to time, Yes, all right, Kate. Yes, Jilly, I'll do it tomorrow. Yes, Jasper, it's under the spare-room bed. And so on.

I said at last, "Well, this wicked Aunt is about to leave. No, don't bother, I shall go to the station by myself."

With what relief did I turn my back on this scene of happy

contemporary family life and went out to the front door, followed by Georgie.

"Well," I said, "don't say it, I don't understand what children are, and I am not entitled to say a word, because of my selfish childishness, but all I can say is . . ."

"And you are probably right," she said, in exactly the same humorous self-denying voice she uses for the children.

I walked through the already slushy snow to the station, waited a little. I like stations, the anonymity, the freedom of being alone in a crowd. I like being alone. Period.

And here I am alone. I should go to Maudie.

I should, very soon, think all this out.

But what I do know is this. When people die, what we regret is, not having talked to them enough. I didn't talk to Granny, I don't know what she was like. I can hardly remember Grandpa. Ditto Mother. I don't know what she thought about anything, except that I am selfish and silly. (Which is what I think about Georgie's brats.) What did she think about Tom? Georgina? The grandchildren? What did it mean to her, having to nurse Granny, and her own husband, for—I am afraid it was probably four years. What was she like when she was young? I don't know. I shall never know now. And of course, there is Freddie: I lie awake sometimes, and what I want is, not that he should be there to make love to me, though I miss that dreadfully, I want to talk to him. Why didn't I talk to him while he was there?

I didn't want to, that is the answer. *I didn't want to know*.

Monday Night.

I woke this morning in a panic, heart pounding, eyes prickling, mouth dry. I said to myself, a bad dream, that's all; but it stayed. On the way to work, I realized it was because of Joyce probably going to the States. Apart from missing her, everything at work will change. I shall be offered the editorship, but that isn't the point.

As I walked through the secretaries' room, Phyllis looked sharply at me, then came after me and asked, Are you all right? Full marks for noticing. I knew of course that she knew I am anxious about Joyce leaving. But when I sat in a heap at my table, and Phyllis brought me black coffee and said if I liked she would do the photographers' session, I saw that she had thought it all out. She took a heap of files from my table, and I saw her look, long and cool, at Joyce's table, Joyce's place, and she was thinking, that will be mine.

And why not?

Because she isn't Joyce. I mean, specifically, that she is thirty years old, a hard, clever, noticing girl, but that she isn't— cooked. I know perfectly well I don't like her because she makes me think of how I was. But there's more than that. I ask myself, trying to be fair, never mind about what you need, has she got what *Lilith* needs?

I sat there in that office of ours, Joyce's and mine, and decided not to think about Phyllis, I can't cope with that yet. I was thinking about Joyce: what was it I had not seen in her that only a month ago I would have taken it for granted that she wouldn't go to America! But I've been judging her marriage by mine. Of course, she has children; but no, that isn't it. He's a nice enough man. I don't know him. Have never talked to him: we have a joking relationship.

I was wanting Joyce to come in early, but it was nearly lunchtime. She looked dreadful, ill, unkempt. She sat down, got up again to fetch herself coffee, came back with it, sat in a sprawl, lit cigarettes and let them go out, messed with her work, watered the plants on her windowsill, did everything but let herself look at me.

Then she buzzed, in came Phyllis, Joyce said, "I'm not happy about Wine, I've made the notes, please go and see our wine expert, what's-his-name. What *is* his name—and his address, where is it?"

"Don't worry," says Phyllis, "I know where it is."

She takes Joyce's notes, smiles nicely, and out she goes.

And now Joyce allows me a brief smile, a grimace really, and actually looks at me. We laugh.

We look together at Phyllis, through the door into the filing room. We are taking in her clothes, her hair, her make-up, her shoes. Habit. Then Joyce loses interest in her, goes back into her thoughts.

Phyllis hasn't got a style yet. Not as Joyce and I have. I sat there wondering if I could help Phyllis to a style, as Joyce helped me. It is only now as I sit writing this, I think how odd that I was analysing Phyllis and how she could look, when I was wild with misery about Joyce, wanting to say, For God's sake, *talk*. I knew she had made up her mind to leave, and she felt bad about me: I needed for us to *talk*.

Joyce is the only person I have talked to in my life. And yet for the most part we talk in smiles, silences, signals, music without words, 'nuff said.

At last I couldn't stand it, and said, "Joyce, I want to know why, you must see that."

She was half turned from me, her cheek on her hand. She made a leave-me-alone irritable gesture.

I sit here, one in the morning, writing it down. My mind is so clear and sharp, whirling with thoughts. I've just had a new thought, it is this: writing is my trade, I write all the time, notes to myself, memos, articles, and everything is to *present* ideas, etc., if not to myself, then to others. I do not let thoughts fly away, I note them down, I *present them*, I postulate the outside eye. And that is what I am doing now. I see that as I write this diary, I have in mind that observing eye. Does that mean I really intend to publish this? It certainly wasn't in my mind when I began writing it. It's a funny thing, this need to write things down, as if they have no existence until they are recorded. Presented. When I listen to Maudie talk, I have this feeling, quick, catch it, don't let it all vanish, record it. As if it is not valid until in print.

Oh, my thoughts are whirling through me, catch them . . .

I was sitting there with Joyce, both of us cold and sick, miserable, and I was examining us both, out of habit, as I had Phyllis. Two women editors, first-class women's magazine (read by a lot of men), late nineteen-seventies going on to the eighties.

When I read diaries from the past, what fascinates me is what they wore, what they ate, all the details. It isn't difficult to work out what people were likely to be thinking—not so different from us, *I* believe—but how did a woman make up her bed, or lay her table, or wash her underclothes; what did she have for breakfast, in 1780, in a middle-class household, in a provincial English town? What was a day in the life of a farmer's wife, north of England, on the date Waterloo was fought?

When Joyce came to work here she made us all conscious we were tatty! The mid-sixties—tat! And yet her style was, as she said, high-class gipsy, which looks messy easily. She is tall, thin, with a mass of black curls and waves, careful disorder, and a thin pale face. Or that is how her face looks, emerging from all that hair. Black eyes that are really small, but made up huge and dramatic. Her clothes cost the earth. Today she wore a black and rust striped skirt and waistcoat and a black silk sweater and her thick silver chain with amber lumps. Her jewellery is very good, never any oriental semi-rubbish of the kind I can afford to wear, because of *my* style. She is beautiful: but it is a young woman's style. She has kept her hair black. Soon she will have to change her style, to fit being not young.

I was still in mini-dresses, beads and gauds and frips, when Joyce took me in hand. Ever since, my style has been classical-expensive. I wear silk shirts and silk stockings, not nylon, and dresses that look at first glance as if I am not trying. I found a real dressmaker, who cares about every stitch, and I look for special buttons in markets, and handmade lace, and I get jerseys and jackets knitted for me. My style is that at first people don't notice, and then their eyes come back and they examine detail, detail, the stitching on a collar, a row of pearl buttons. I am not thin, but solid. My hair is straight, and always perfect, a silvery gold. Grey eyes, large by nature and made larger.

We couldn't be more different, Joyce and I, except in the trouble we take. But Joyce takes less than me because of her family.

Phyllis is a slight, strong girl, attractive. Fairish. She is always in the new fashion, and therefore there's nothing to remark. I've seen her watching Joyce and, rightly, discarding that style for herself. I've seen her observing me: *how does she do it?* I'll show her if she asks, take her to the dressmaker and the knitting woman, choose her hairdresser . . . that is what I was thinking as I sat there with Joyce, in all that misery: I was mentally abdicating, and expressing it through clothes, through a style!

Yet I have no conscious intention of giving up.

At lunchtime we drank coffee and smoked. Then she said, "I must go home," and I cried out, "*Joyce!*" She said, "Don't you see, I can't do it, I can't!" And I said, "Joyce, you cannot just go off home like that, I have to know."

She sighed, and sat down, made herself come together, and actually looked at me.

"Know?"

"Understand. I don't understand how you can give all this up . . . what for?"

She said, "Have you had the experience, suddenly finding out that you didn't know yourself?"

"Indeed I have!"

"I thought I would agree to a divorce easily "

"Has he got a girl?"

"Yes, the same one, you know. He would take her instead of me."

"All this time he has really been married to the two of you, then?"

"It amounts to that. He said to me at one stage, You have your job, I'm going to have Felicity."

I was sitting there being careful, because I didn't want her to fly off home, and I knew she could easily do that

I was thinking what I call women's lib thoughts. *He* has a job as a matter of course, but when *she* does, he has to bolster himself up with a girl on the side. But I have got so bored with these thoughts, they aren't the point; they never were the point, not for me, not for Joyce. Phyllis is into women's lib, consciousness-raising, and she makes it clear that Joyce and I are unliberated. Joyce and I have discussed this, but not often—because it isn't the point! Once Joyce said to Phyllis, curious rather than combative, Phyllis, I hold down a very good, well-paid job. I have a husband and two children and I run my home and my family. Would you not say I am a liberated woman, then? *Isn't that enough?* And Phyllis smiled the smile of one who knows better and allowed. A step in the right direction. And afterwards Joyce and I laughed. We had one of those sudden fits of laughing, music without words, that are among the best things in this friendship of ours.

"If you don't go to the States, he'll take Felicity?"

"He will marry her."

"Is that what you mind?"

She shook her head. Again she was not looking at me. I was confused, didn't know what it was she feared, in facing me. At last she said, "You are such a self-sufficient one."

This was the last thing I expected—the child-wife, child-daughter—and I said, "I, self-sufficient?"

And she just shook her head, oh, it's all too much for me, and crouched holding on to the desk with both hands, looking in front of her, cigarette hanging from her lips. I saw her as an old crone, Mrs Fowler: fine sharp little face, nose and chin almost meeting. She looked ancient. Then she sighed again, pulled herself out, turned to me.

"I can't face being alone," she said, flat. "And that's all there is to it."

If I say my mind was in a whirl, that is how it was.

I wanted to say, But, *Joyce*—my husband died, it seems now overnight—what is it you are counting on? I could have said, Joyce, if you throw up this work and go with him, you might find yourself with nothing. I could have said . . . and I said nothing, because I was crying with a sort of amazed anger, at the impossibility of it, and worse than that, for I was thinking that I had not known Joyce at all! I would not have believed that she could say that, think it. More: I knew that I could not say to Joyce, Your attitude to death is stupid, wrong, you are like a child! It's not like that, what are you afraid of? Being alone—what's that!

For I had discovered that I had made a long journey away from Joyce, and in a short time. My husband had died, my mother had died: I had believed that I had not taken in these events, had armoured myself. And yet something had changed in me, quite profoundly. And there was Maudie Fowler, too.

It seemed to me, as I sat there, crying and trying to stop, biting on my (best-quality linen monogrammed) handkerchief, that Joyce was a child. Yes, she was a child, after all, and

I could say nothing to her of what I had learned and of what I now was. That was why I was crying.

"Don't," said Joyce. "I didn't mean to—open old wounds."

"You haven't. That's not it." But that was as near as I could come to *talking*. I mean by that, saying what was in my mind. For then we did talk, in a sensible dry sort of way, about all kinds of things, and it is not that I don't value that. For we had not, or not for a long time, talked in this way. The way women communicate—in becks and nods and hints and smiles—it is very good, it is pleasurable and enjoyable and one of the best things I've had. But when the chips are down, I couldn't say to Joyce why I had to cry.

She said, "You are different from me. I've been watching you and I can see that. But if he goes to the States, I'll be alone. I'll not marry again, I know that. And anyway, if you have been married to a man, you can't just throw him aside and take up another—*they* can do that . . ."

"Or think they can."

"Yes, or think they can, without penalties, I mean. And so I don't see myself marrying someone else. The kids, they don't want to go to the States, but if he went and I stayed, they'd commute and I know that pretty soon they'd be there rather than here, more opportunities, probably better for the young. I'd be alone. I don't know how to be alone, Jan."

And I could not say to her, Joyce, your husband is fifty-five, he's a workaholic . . .

"You are prepared to be a faculty wife?"

She grimaced at this. "I shan't get anything like this job, of course not. But I expect there'd be something."

As she left, she said, "No, and I haven't even finally made up my mind. I know how I'm going to miss all this—and you, Jan. But I have no choice." And with that she went out, *not* looking at me.

And that is what I was left with, the *I have no choice*. For I do not know what it is, in that marriage of hers—I would never have suspected—the existence of anything that would make it inevitable she would say, *I have no choice*.

Joyce has been the best editor this magazine has ever had. She has never put her home and family first . . . and yet . . . I see how, when she came in, the flexibility began that everyone welcomed: working at home from the telephone, working late or early when necessary. We all said, It's a woman's way of dealing with things, not office hours, but going along with what was necessary. And now I am thinking that what was *necessary* was Joyce's marriage, her home.

She would easily stay after work to eat supper with me, in the office, in a restaurant: working meals. And yet there were times when she had to be at home. I was what made all this possible: *I* have never said, No, I can't stay in the office late as usual, I have to get home. Or only when Freddie and I did our dinner parties. I've never ever said, This afternoon, I have to go early, Freddie will be in early. But it seems to me that something like that has been going on with Joyce: her marriage, her children, her work. She incorporated all of it, in a marvellous flexible way. "Can you hold the fort this afternoon, Jan?" In a sense, I've been part of her marriage, like that girl Felicity! These wholes we are part of, what *really* happens, how things really work ... it is what has always fascinated me, what interests me most. And yet I have only just had the thought: that I have been, in a sense, part of Joyce's marriage.

Joyce *is* going to America. She will give up a wonderful job. Very few women ever get a job like this one. She will give up family, friends, home. Her children are nearly grown up. She will be in a country that she will have to learn to like, alone with a man who would have been happy to go with another, younger girl. *She has no choice.*

Well, women's lib, well, Phyllis, what do you have to say to that?

What, in your little manifestoes, your slamming of doors in men's faces, your rhetoric, have you *ever* said that touches this? As far as I am concerned, nothing. And, believe me, Phyllis makes sure that all the propaganda is always available to me, spread on my desk.

The reason why girls these days get themselves together in flocks and herds and shoals and shut out men altogether, or as much as they can, is because they are afraid of—whatever the power men have that makes Joyce say, I have no choice.

I can live alone and like it. But then, I was never really married

After I reached home, the telephone: Joyce, her voice breathless and small. Because she had cried herself dry, I knew that. She said, "Jan, we make our choices a long time before we think we do! My God, but it's terrifying! Do you know what I mean?"

"Yes," I said. "I know what you mean."

And I do. And it *is* terrifying. What choices have I already made that I am not yet conscious of?

I have not been in to Maudie Fowler since Friday evening.

Tuesday.

Joyce not at work. Phyllis and I held the fort. After work I went in to Maudie. She took a long time to answer the door, stood looking at me for a long time, not smiling, not pleased; at last stood aside so that I could come in, went ahead of me along the passage, without a word. She sat down on her side of the fire, which was blazing, and waited for me to speak.

I was already angry, thinking, well, and so she doesn't have a telephone, is that my fault?

I said, "I did not get back on Sunday night until very late, and last night I was tired."

"Tired, were you?" And then, "On Sunday evening I waited for you. I had a bit of supper for us both."

I noted in myself the usual succession of emotions: the trapped feeling, then a need to escape, then—of course—guilt.

"I am sorry, Maudie," I said.

She turned her head and stared at the fire, her mouth a little open, and gasping.

"Have you been well?"

"Well enough."

I was thinking, look, I've washed you head to foot, of your stinking shit, and now you . . . but I had to think, too, that I made a promise and hadn't kept it. I must never do that again.

It took nearly an hour before she softened, got up to make us tea. I had to stay another two hours. Before I left she was talking freely again. A long story about her father's fancy-woman, who, her mother "properly and safely" dead, had not only made a skivvy of her, Maudie—"though I've told you all about that, I know"—but then set about poisoning her.

"She poisoned my mother, I know she did, if no one else knew, and my Aunt Mary believed me. She said there was no point going to the police, they'd never take my word against my father, he was in with the police, he was always in with anyone who would do him good, he'd have the inspector in at Christmas for whisky and cake, and he and his fancy-woman'd send a cask of ale up to the boys at the station with a ham and pudding. If I went to them, just a girl, and terrified I was, and ill with it, and said, My father's woman poisoned my mother and now she's doing for me, it's arsenic—well, would they listen? My Aunt Mary said, Look, you leave home and come to me when you can do it without making trouble. I'm not facing that brother of mine in a fight, he's not one to cross, he's one to get his own back. But when it's the right time, you'll find a bed and a bite with me. Well, I got sicker and weaker. Months it went on. I tried not to eat at home, I'd go running to my sister, the one that died—no, I've not mentioned her, she makes me feel too bad. She was always the weakly one, she got on their nerves. She married at fifteen. She married against my father, and he said, Never darken my doors. Her man was no good and couldn't keep her. She had three little children, and my mother would send me with a pie or some bread, anything that wouldn't be missed, and I'd see her, so pale and weak, the children hungry. She'd take a little nibble, to keep her strength up, and then make her children eat the rest. My mother died, and then there was no food in that house at all. I went to my father and said, My sister's dying of lack of food and warmth. Said he, I told her not to marry him, and that was all he ever said. She died, and he didn't go to the funeral. The husband took the one child still alive, and I never heard more. Before she died, I'd be sitting with her, I'd be faint with hunger because I was afraid to eat at home, and she dying of hunger because there was no food, and we were company. It was an awful time, awful—I don't know why people say 'the good old days', they were bad days. Except for people like my father . . ." And Maudie went on and on about her father.

When I asked, "How about your other sister?" she said, "She'd married and gone, we did not hear of her much, she was keeping out of the way of Father, he didn't like her man either. Once I went to her and said, Polly, our sister Muriel is starving, and her children with her, and all she said was, Well, I've got nothing to spare for her. Yet her food safe was stuffed with joints and pies and custards.

"After Muriel died, I did not even have anywhere to go and sit, and I ate as little as I could because I knew there was poison in it. *She* would come up to my room—they'd put me up in the attic, just as if I was a servant—with milk and broth and say, Drink it, drink it, and I'd pour it into the slop pail and then creep down to empty the slop pail so she couldn't know. I could taste the poison in it, I knew there was poison. Sometimes I went to pick up the bread that people threw to the birds, but I was afraid of being seen. We were known, you see, we were well thought of, Father with his goings and comings and his carriage and his free ways, and *she* with her pub. I was the daughter at home, the people envied me for my easy time. Yet I was on a thin bed at the top of the house in an attic, not a whisper of heat, never a new dress, or anything of my own, only her old clothes to cut down, and afraid to eat. Well, one evening it all came to a head, for I was in bed, too weak and sick to get up, and she had a glass full of sugared milk, and she said, I'm going to stay here till you drink it. I don't want it, I said. I don't want it. But she said, I'm going to sit here.

"She had on a pink silk dressing gown with feathers that had grey velvet ruches around the neck, and high-heeled pink slippers. She had put on plenty of weight with all her liking for food and drink, and she was red in the face, and she was sighing and saying, Oh my God, the stairs, and Oh my God, it's cold up here. Yet she never thought that I had to climb up and down the stairs, nor that I had to live in that cold. And yet there were two empty bedrooms on the same floor they had theirs. Later my Aunt Mary said to me, Of course they didn't want you on that floor with them, they didn't want you to hear their goings-on. What goings-on? I said, for I didn't care about all that, I hated all that, I'm like my mother. I shut my mind to it. And besides, they weren't married: she had a husband in a hospital somewhere, so she couldn't marry my father. Now I look back and wonder at it all: people were strict in those days, and yet I don't remember her suffering for her living out of the marriage bond with my father. But I wouldn't have noticed: all I thought of was how not to eat in that house. That night, I had to drink the milk at last, though the taste in it sickened me. Then I pretended to sleep. And she went lumbering downstairs at last. I put my finger down my throat and brought up the milk. Then I put my other dress into my mother's little bag and I crept out of the house.

"I had no money, he never gave me any, ever, though I kept the house for him, cleaned it, did it all. I walked out to the village my auntie was in. It's part of London now, you'd not know it was a village so recently, it was beyond Neasden. I got there as the streets filled with carts and horses and noise. I was nearly falling as I walked. I got to her house and rang and rang and when she came she caught me as I fell. She said I could stay with her, and pay her back when I was well enough to earn. She wrote to my father that Maudie had come to stay with her for a little, that was how she put it. And my father said nothing at all, though I waited and waited for a sign. Not for years did he acknowledge my existence And my aunt fed me up and made me eat. She was poor herself. She couldn't give me what she said I should have, cream and wine and stuff, but she did what she could. I was so thin and small I used to start shaking if I walked a few steps, but I got better, and then Auntie apprenticed me to a milliner in the West End. She got the money from my father. I don't know what she said, but she got it."

It was nearly ten before I got home. I was full of the strong black tea Maudie drinks and feeling a bit sick myself, and so I couldn't eat. Sympathy, no doubt with anorexia, for I suppose that was what poor Maudie was suffering from after her mother died. I have had a brief and efficient bath, and have finished writing this, and now I must go to bed. But I really wanted to write down the thoughts I have been having about the office.

I told Maudie that I would not be in tomorrow night, but that I would definitely come and have tea with her Thursday.

*　　　*　　　*

Wednesday.

Joyce was not in the office and there was no message. That has never happened. The atmosphere in the office restless, a bit giggly, like school when there's uncertainty. Phyllis and I worked together all day, and without a word being said how to behave so as to calm things down. We were brisk and efficient and kept at it. We will work easily together. But oh, she is so *young*, so young, so black and white and either/or and take it or leave it. Her cool crisp little mouth. Her crisp competent little smile. Phyllis has bought her own flat, we—the firm—helped her. She lives for her work, who should know better how than I? She sees herself editing the mag. Why not?

I write that, and wonder at it.

Now I shall write about *my* career, for I am very clear in my mind about it all because of the shocks and strains of the last few days, with Joyce, and then having to be alert and awake all the time with Phyllis.

I came straight into the office from school. No university, there wasn't the money; and I wasn't good enough for university! It just didn't present itself as a possibility.

When I started work for *Little Women*—Joyce and I so christened that phase of the mag, a shorthand—I was so pleased and relieved at getting this glamorous job, in journalism, I wasn't looking for anything higher. 1947, still a war atmosphere. It was a graceless production, bad paper, because of the war: full of how to use cheap cuts of meat and egg powder. How to make anything into something else—Joyce's description of it. I, like everyone else, was sick sick sick of it all. How we all longed to throw off the aftermath of war, the rationing, the dreariness. There was a woman editor then too. I wasn't into criticizing my superiors then, my sights went no higher than being secretary to the production manager. I just didn't think about Nancy Westringham. They were all gods and goddesses up there. Now I see she was just right for that phase of the mag. Old-style, like my mother and my sister, competent, dutiful, nice—but I mean it, nice, kind, and my guess is never an original thought in her life. My *guess* it has to be: if there is one thing I regret, it is that I wasn't awake enough during that phase to see what was going on. But of course then

I hadn't learned *how* to see what was going on: what is developing inside a structure, what to look for, *how things work*.

They were changing the mag all right, better paper, brighter features, but it wasn't enough. There had to be a new editor, and I should have seen it, should have been watching. It wasn't only that I didn't know how to observe: I was too drunk on being young, attractive and successful. At school no one had ever even suggested I might have capacities, and certainly my parents never did. But in the office, I was able to turn my hand to anything. I was soon just the one person who was able to take over from anyone sick or incapable. I cannot remember any pleasure in my life to match that: the relief of it, the buoyancy, tackling a new job and knowing that I did it well. I was in love with cleverness, with myself. And this business of being good at clothes. Of course, the fifties were not exactly an exciting time for clothes, but even so I was able to interest everyone in what I wore. My style then was sexy, but cool and sexy, just a little bit over the edge into parody: in that I anticipated the sixties and the way we all slightly mocked the styles we wore.

I would give a lot now to know *how* it happened that Boris became editor. But it is too late now. When I ask the oldies who are still with us, they don't know what I am asking because they don't think like that.

At any rate, Boris became editor in 1957, and he represented "the new wave". But he didn't have it in him. I was by then in the position Phyllis is now: the bright girl everyone expects great things of. The difference is, I didn't know it. I liked being good at everything, and I didn't mind working all hours. I adored everything I had to do. I was already doing all kinds of work well beyond what I was paid for, beyond what I was described as being. I was a secretary in Production. By then I had begun to watch what was really happening. The immediately obvious fact was that Boris was not very effective. Amiable, affable, trendy—all that, yes. He had been appointed by the Board when Nancy resigned; was asked to leave. He had the large room that is used now by the photographers, a large desk, a secretary who had a secretary, and a PR girl. He was

always in conference, on the telephone, at lunch, giving interviews on the role and function of women's magazines.
"Women's Lib" hadn't been born, though not till I came to
write this did I remember that.

What was really happening was that other people were
doing his work for him, me among them. *The formal structure
of the office did not correspond at all with what was happening.* The mag had brightened up a little, but not much, and Mr
Right was implicit in everything. We did not think clearly
about it, but carried on much as before, with better paper and
some decent photographs.

The moment Joyce arrived, we all became conscious of
exactly what we were doing, and for whom. Market Analysis,
reports from experts; we certainly took notice of all that, but
we had our own ideas. The backbone and foundation of the
mag, what interests us most, is *information*. Birth control, sex,
health, social problems generally. Nearly all the articles we
have on these topics would have been impossible in *Little
Women*, everything had to be wrapped up. This is the part of
the mag I do. As for clothes, food, wine, decor, what has
changed is the level of the photography. Not what is said,
fashion is fashion is fashion, and food is food, but how it is
presented. When I first began working, there were a lot of
articles like "I Am a Widow: How I Brought Up Two Girls", or
"I Am Married to a Paraplegic", or "Alice Is Blind But She
Runs a Business School". All those have gone: too down-
market! *Lilith* deliberately set out to take a step up in the
world, and we made that happen.

I've said that when Joyce came in, mid-sixties, she changed
me: she changed everything else. What interests me now is that
the change took place *against* the apparent structure. She was
Production Manager and I was her assistant. We were together
in the office we have now. It was we two who ran the mag. It
was obvious to us that we ran it, but Boris didn't notice. Joyce
used to say that in her last job she did all the work for her boss,
who had to be allowed to think he was doing it. So nothing had
changed for her. Far from resenting it all, we were worried that
people would notice. And of course they did. Now we wonder
why we thought that they wouldn't. The point was, we loved

the work, we loved transforming the mag. We used to go to the Board Meetings, once a fortnight, sit quietly there, on one side, with Boris at the top of the table, and the Board Reps at the other end, and we hardly opened our mouths. I used to brief Boris before meetings, about what he should say.

The actual structure during that time was Joyce and me running everything, with the photographers coming into prominence, because it was really in the sixties that they did. All the decisions were made in our office, it was always full of people. Suddenly—and Joyce had been there only a couple of years—she was made editor and given complete freedom. New format, new everything. She was clever: several mags that were too Swinging Sixties bit the dust, but the format Joyce created—that we created—survives.

Almost at once the real structure became the same as the formal, the official structure. When Boris left, his great awful *dead* office was turned over to the photographers, and it came to life at once; and the room Joyce and I had been using became the Editors' Room. Then I realized how much effort and nervous strain had gone into everything when what was really happening didn't match with the formal organization. Now, looking around at other offices, other businesses, I see how often there is a discordance.

And what has been growing up inside *this* structure, what is the future? Now I know it is not Joyce and me! But I wonder if it is really me and Phyllis? What is it I am not seeing because I am too involved with what is *now*? It seems to me that things change suddenly, overnight, or seem to: but the change has been growing up inside. I cannot see any change inside: and yet I think about it a good deal.

All I can see is that there is so much less money around for spending, and so our glossy lively even impudent format, or formula, may have to go, and something sterner and more dedicated supplant it.

Dedicated to *what*? Well, if I could foresee that! I do not get any feeling of pleasure or wanting to be part of it when I think that perhaps we will be into "making everything into some-thing else". Clothes to last—well, that has already begun—beef as a luxury instead of a staple, buying jewellery as an investment . . . the last issue but one, we printed recipes from wartime, as a joke, but to those of us who were young during the war and just after it, it wasn't a joke. I heard the girls in the typists' pool laughing, Phyllis making fun of stretching meat with forcemeat balls. I could do a feature on the food Maudie remembers. I expect the typists' pool would fall about if they could hear Maudie on how, when she was a child, the mother of a family made a big batter pudding to "fill them up" before the meat course, so they were satisfied with a little bit of meat, and then after the meat, batter pudding again, with jam. When I think of the war, of that contriving and making-do, the dreary dreary dreary boredom of it, oh I can't face it all again, I can't, I can't . . . but so far no one has said that we must.

I married in 1963. It was shortly before Joyce came. I have written all that history, and only now have thought to mention that I married.

A week since the last—no, ten days.

I went in to Maudie as promised, though I was frantic with work. Did not stay long, in and out. Then, into the office: Joyce not there, no message either again. Phyllis and I coped. Everyone coped. An elegiac mood, for lost lovely times. She made *Lilith*, but if she doesn't come in to work, for days at a time, the waters close over her. She is hardly mentioned. But certainly thought of, by me at least. By me, by me! I have been raging with sorrow. I was uneasy, ashamed, thinking Freddie dies, my mother dies, hardly a tear, just a frozen emptiness, but Joyce slides out of my life and I grieve. At first I thought, look at me, what a wicked woman, but then I knew that since I could allow myself to mourn for Joyce, I have admitted—mourning, have admitted grief. I have been waking in the morning soaked in tears. For Freddie, my mother, for God knows what else.

But I haven't the time for it. I'm working like a demon. Meanwhile I rage with sorrow. I do not think this is necessarily a step forward into maturity. A good deal to be said for a frozen heart.

*   *   *

When I went in to Maudie next I found her angry and cold. With me? No, it came out that "the Irish woman" upstairs had again been turning on the refrigerator to "insult" her. Because I had just come from an atmosphere where things are dealt with, not muttered and nitpicked, I said, "I'm going upstairs to talk to her," and went, with Maudie shouting at me, "Why do you come here to interfere?" I knocked upstairs, ground floor. A lanky freckled boy let me in, I found the large beautiful Irish girl with the tired blue eyes, and three more lean golden freckled children watching TV. The refrigerator is a vast machine, bought probably at the second-hand shop down the street, and it came on while I was there, a trundling grinding that shook the whole flat. I could not say, Please sell the fridge. You could see that this was poverty. I mean poverty nineteen-seventies. I have a different criterion now, knowing Maudie. Everything cheap, but of course the kids properly fed and clean clothes.

I said, Mrs Fowler seemed to me to be ill, had they seen her?

On the girl's face came that look I seem to see everywhere now, a determined indifference, an evasion: "Oh well, but she's never been one for asking, or offering, and so I've given up."

All the time, she was listening—and in fact the husband came in, a thin dark explosive Irishman, and very drunk. The kids exchanged wide looks and faded away into the inner room. They were scared, and so was she. I saw that she had bruises on her forearms.

I thanked them and went off, and heard the angry voices before I had closed the door. Downstairs I sat down opposite that tiny angry old woman, with her white averted little face, and said, "I've seen the fridge. Have you never had one? It is very old and noisy."

"But why does she make it come on at one in the morning, or even three or four, when I'm trying to get my rest?"

Well, I sat there explaining. Reasonable. I had been thinking about Maudie. I like her. I respect her. And so I'm *not* going to insult her by babying her . . . so I had decided. But faced with her that night, as she sat in a sort of locked white tremble, I found myself softening things up.

"Very well then, if it's as you say, why does she have to put it just over where I sleep?"

"But probably it has to go where there's an electric point."

"And so much for my sleep, then, is that it?"

And as we sat there, the thing came on, just above us. The walls shook, the ceiling did, but it wasn't a really unbearable noise. At least, I could have slept through it.

She was sitting there looking at me in a way part triumphant: see, you can hear it now, I'm not exaggerating! and part curious—she's curious about me, can't make me out.

I had determined to tell her exactly what was going on in the office, but it was hard.

"You must be quite a queen bee there then," she remarked.

I said, "I am the assistant editor."

It was not that she didn't take it in, but that she had to repudiate it—me—the situation. She sat with her face averted, and then put her hand up to shield it from me.

"Oh well, so you won't be wanting to come in to me then, will you?" she said at last.

I said, "It's just that this week it's very difficult. But I'll drop in tomorrow if you'll have me."

She made a hard sorrowful sort of shrug. Before I left I took a look at the kitchen; supplies very low. I said, "I'll bring in stuff tomorrow, what you need.'

After a long, long silence which I thought she'd never break, she said, "The weather's bad, or I'd go myself. It's the usual—food for the cat, and I'd like a bit of fish . . ." That she didn't complete the list meant that she did accept me, did trust me, somehow. But as I left I saw the wide blank stare at me, something frantic in it, as if I had betrayed her.

In the office next day not a sign of Joyce, and I rang her at home. Her son answered. Measured. Careful. No, she's in the kitchen, I think she's busy.

Never has Joyce been "busy" before. I was *so* angry. I sat there thinking, I can go in to Maudie Fowler and help her, but not to Joyce, my friend. And meanwhile Phyllis was attending to the letters. Not from Joyce's table, but at a chair at the secretaries' table. Full marks for tact. I said to her, "This is crazy. I'm going to see Joyce now. Hold the fort." And went.

I've been in Joyce's home a hundred times, always, however, invited, expected. The door opened by the son, Philip. When he saw me he began to stammer, "She's—she's—she's . . ." "In the kitchen," I said for him. He had, as it were, gone in behind his eyes: absented himself. This look again! But is it that I didn't notice it before? A prepared surface, of one kind or another; the defences well manned.

I went into the kitchen. The son came behind me, like a jailer, or so I felt it (rightly). In the kitchen, a proper family kitchen, all pine and earthenware, the daughter, sitting at the table, drinking coffee, doing homework. Joyce standing over the sink. She looked far from an expensive gipsy, more a poor one. Her hair hadn't been brushed, was a dowdy tangle, careless make-up, nails chipped. She presented to me empty eyes and a dead face, and I said, "Joyce, it's not good enough," and she was startled back into herself. Tears sprang into her eyes, she gasped, turned quickly away and stood with her back to me, trembling, like Maudie. I sat at the table and said to the two children, "I want to talk to Joyce, please." They exchanged looks. You could say insolent, you could say scared. I saw that it would take very little to make me very sorry for them: for one thing, having to leave their schools and go off to the States, everything new. But I was angry, angry.

"Give me some coffee," I said, and she came with a cup, and sat down opposite me.

We looked at each other, straight and long and serious.

"I can't stand this business of nothing being said, nothing being said."

"Nothing is being *said* here either."

"Are they listening at the door?"

"Don't you see, Mother has been captured. Back from the office."

"Do you mean to say they have resented it, your being so successful and all that?"

"No, they are proud of me."

"But."

"Everything has fallen apart around them, and they haven't known for months if they are going to have Felicity for a mum or me. Now they know it is me, security, but they are terrified. Surely you can see that?" She sounded exactly like my dear sister Georgie, talking to the delinquent—me—and I wasn't going to take it.

"Yes, indeed," I said, "but we are talking of a young man and a young woman, they are not little children."

"Dorothy is seventeen and Philip is fifteen."

She looked hard and fierce at me, I looked angrily at her.

I said, "How did we get like this, so soft, so silly, so babyish? How?"

"Oh God," she said. "Oh God, oh God! Oh God—Janna!"

"Oh God, *Joyce*," I said to her. "But I mean it. And don't patronize me. Is nothing that I say to anyone worth anything?"

"What the hell are you talking about?"

Now we were both furious and liking each other the better for it. Our voices were raised, we both imagined "the children" listening.

"I'm talking about these ghastly *wet* spoiled brats we produce."

"You haven't produced any."

"Oh, thank you—and so that's the end of that then, the end of me! Thank God I haven't then. When I look at—"

"Listen, Janna . . ." Spelling it out, as to an idiot. "Is nothing really due to them, owed to them? They have a father who has had what amounts to a second home for years. Recently they have had to accept their parents are going to divorce. Now the family is going to stay together . . ."

"And what is due to us, your work, to me?"

She sat there, spoon in a coffee mug, and it tinkled against the side with her trembling.

"A crisis in the family, a choice, you wonder if perhaps you might actually have to live alone at some time, along with x billion other women—and all you are in your work counts for nothing, falls to pieces."

By then we were both shaking, and very ashamed. We could see ourselves, two women shouting at each other in a silent house.

"Wait, Janna," she said. "Wait." And she made a business of getting up to put on the kettle again, and took her time about sitting down. And then, "Do you imagine I don't feel bad about you, our friendship? I'm in pain." She was shouting again. "Do you understand? I am in pain. I've never in my life felt like this. I'm being split in half, torn apart. I want to howl and scream and roll about . . . and so I am cooking family meals and helping with the homework. Strangely enough."

"And I, strangely enough, am in pain too."

And suddenly we began to laugh, in the old way; we put our heads down on the kitchen table and laughed. The "kids" came in, hearing us: with scared smiles. I, Janna Somers, "the office", had proved every bit as much of a threat as they had feared. Seeing those scared faces, I knew I was going to give in if I didn't watch it: but my mind was saying, I am right, I am right, I am right . . .

And perhaps I am not right, after all.

I said, "I'd better get back to work."

She said, "I know that you and Phyllis are doing quite well without me."

"Quite well."

"Well then."

And I went back as fast as I could to the office. To my real home. Leaving Joyce in her real home.

Later.

I took the things in to Maudie and sat with her. I was very tired, and she saw it.

She said in a timid old voice, "You mustn't think you have to come in here, if you're tired."

"Why not?" I said. "You need some help, you know that." And I added, "I like you. I like knowing you, Maudie."

She nodded, in a prim measuring way, and there was a small pleased smile. "I'm not saying I'm not the better for it, because I am."

I went out for the second time to the shop opposite because I had forgotten tea.

It was sleeting. I got the bits of kindling from the skip. All along these streets, the houses are being "done up". Four of them in Maudie's very short street. Four skips loaded with "rubbish". Including perfectly good chairs, mattresses, tables, and quantities of wood in good condition. People sneak out for the wood. There must still be quite a few fireplaces in these houses. But not for long, not when they are "done up".

I came out from the shop, and there on the pavement were two old women, wrapped up like parcels. I recognized a face: from the window opposite.

I was frozen. And wanted to get home.

But already I knew that these occasions cannot be rushed. The conversation:

"Excuse me, I wanted to ask, how is Maudie Fowler?"

"She seems all right."

"Are you her daughter, dear? You do take good care of her."

"No. I am not her daughter."

"Are you a Good Neighbour?"

"No, I am not that either." I laughed, and they allowed me small polite smiles.

I say "old women", and that is a criticism of me, no individuality allowed them, just "old women". But they seemed so alike, little plump old women, their faces just visible behind thick scarves, coats, hats.

"Maudie Fowler has always kept herself so much to herself, and we were wondering."

"Well," I said, "she's over ninety, isn't she?"

A reproving silence. "I am ninety-two dear, and Mrs Bates here is ninety-one."

"Well, I'd say Maudie was feeling her age."

This was too direct and I knew it, but had started off like that and couldn't change course. Oh yes, I know very well by now that these conversations should be allowed to develop.

"You know Mrs Rogers, do you, dear?"

"Mrs Rogers?"

"She is one of The Welfare."

"No, I don't."

All this with the sleet blowing across us and our faces turning blue.

"She wants to see you, so she says."

"Well, what about?"

"Seeing as you are a Good Neighbour, then there's another that needs it."

"Well, I'm not one," I said.

"Then goodbye, dear. We mustn't keep you in the cold."
And they went together toddling along the pavement, arm in
arm, very slowly.

Joyce came back next day, and sat at her desk and went
through the motions of working, and did work, but *she* was
not there. She is simply not with us. She looked awful, badly
dressed, even dusty, her hair greying at the roots, and a greyish
edge to her black sweater.

Looking at her, I made an appointment with the hairdresser
at once. And determined to devote an evening to my own care.

This is that evening. I have had a real bath, hours of it. I've
done my fingernails, my toenails, my eyebrows, my ears, my
navel, the hard skin on my feet.

What has made me, for so many years, that perfectly
groomed person, whom everybody looks at and thinks, how
does she do it? has been my Sunday nights. Never did I allow
anything to interfere with that. Freddie used to joke about it
but I said, Make jokes, I don't care, I have to do it. On Sunday
nights, after supper, for years and years I've chosen my outfit
for every day of the week ahead, made sure there has been not a
wrinkle or a crease, attended to buttons and hems, cleaned
shoes, emptied out and polished handbags, brushed hats, and
put anything even slightly soiled for the cleaner's and the
launderette. Hours of it, every Sunday night, and when all those
pairs of skilled and knowledgeable eyes examined me at work,
there has never been, but literally, a hair out of place. Grooming. Well, if I can't keep it up, my style is in the wastepaper
basket, just as Joyce's style is now. A high-class gipsy, turned
slattern, is bizarre; if my style is neglected, there's nothing left
but a dowd.

And now I shall make myself do it: buttons, shoes, collars,
ironing, ironing, ironing, and not so much as a thread of
loosened lace on a petticoat.

*   *   *

Over three months have gone.

It has been a choice between proper baths and the diary. I've had to have something to hold on to.

Joyce came back to work, but she was a ghost, a zombie. Felicity announced she was pregnant, husband Jack asked Joyce to be "generous", Joyce said she wished he would make up his mind, he said, You are vindictive, she said, I must be crazy to want you at all. The poor children are both going crazy and punishing Joyce—she says.

It isn't that she doesn't do the work as usual, but she's not in it. As for what I used to rely on so much, the good atmosphere, the way we used to work together as if we were one person— no, gone. We—Phyllis and I— support her, all the time, tact, tact, tact, oh full marks to all of us, everyone in Editorial, and I watch all this, fascinated, because of *how it works*. The woman who made the mag, because she did, it was her *push*, is fading out. I saw a film on telly, elephants supporting with their trunks a dying friend. It reminded me. Because Joyce *is* fading out. It can't go on like this, is the *unspoken* thought. Unspoken, too, is that I will be the new editor. Meanwhile, Joyce says that she will stay in London, with the children, and she will be divorced. The children for the first time ring up here, making demands. Ridiculous, like, where is the jam, where did you put my sweater? Joyce patient, and *anguished*. For them. Very well, but there are limits to the people one can be sorry for. I'm learning my limits: small ones. Maudie Fowler is all I can manage.

It's been wet, cold, dismal. Nearly every evening after work I've been in to Maudie. I've given up even thinking that she ought to agree to be "rehoused"; I said it just once, and it took her three days to stop seeing me as an enemy, as one of "them". I *am* housed, says she, cough, cough, cough from having to go out at the back all weathers into the freezing lavatory, from standing to wash in the unheated kitchen. But why do I say that? Women of ninety who live in luxury cough and are frail.

It is a routine now. I go in about seven, eight, after work, and bring in what she has said she needs the night before. Usually she's forgotten something, and I go out again to the Indian shop. He, the Indian man, a large pale man, pale grey really, who suffers from this weather, always asks after her, and shakes his head, and gives me some little thing for her: some sweets or some biscuits. When I give these to Maudie, she looks fierce and angry: she's proud, but she's moved.

While I shop she makes us tea. She has had supper at six, when she eats cake and jam and biscuits. She says she can't be bothered to cook properly. She doesn't want me to waste time cooking for her, because "it would take away from our time". When she said this I realized she valued our time of sitting and talking: for some reason I was not able to see that, for I am defensive and guilty with her, as if *I* am responsible for all the awful things that have happened. We sit there, in that fug and smell—but nearly always I can switch off as I go in, so that I don't notice the smell, just as I refuse to notice the smeared cups. And she . . . entertains me. I did not realize it was that. Not until one day when she said, "You do so much for me, and all I can do for you is to tell you my little stories, because you like that, don't you? Yes, I know you do." And of course I do. I tell her about what I have been doing, and I don't have to explain much. When I've been at a reception for some VIP or cocktail party or something, I can make her see it all. Her experience has included the luxurious, and there was her father: "Sometimes, listening to you, it makes me remember how he used to come home and tell us he'd been to Romano's or the Café Royal or the music hall, and he'd tell us what all the nobs ate and drank." But I don't like reminding her of her father, for she sits with her face lowered, her eyes down and hidden, picking in distress at her skirt. I like it when her fierce alive blue eyes are sparkling and laughing; I like looking at her, for I forget the old crone and I can see her so easily as she was, young.

She is wearing these nights a cornflower-blue cotton with big white spots: an apron, made from a dress she had when she was young. I said I liked it so much, so she tore out the sleeves and cut down the back: an apron. The black thick clothes I threw into the dustbin were retrieved by her. I found them rolled into newspaper in the front room. Stinking. She had not worn them, though. There is a photograph of her, a young woman before she was married, a little wedge of a face, combative eyes, a great mass of shiny hair. She has a piece of her hair before it went grey. It was a rich bright yellow.

We sit on either side of the black stove, the flames forking up and around, a teapot on the top, with a filthy grey cosy that was once . . . why do I go on and on about the dirt? Our cups on the arms of our chairs, a plate of biscuits on a chair between us. The cat sits about washing herself, or sleeps on her divan. Cosy, oh yes. Outside, the cold rain, and upstairs, the Irish family, quarrelling, the feet of the kids banging on the uncarpeted floors, the fridge rumbling and shaking.

She tells me about all the times in her life she was happy. She says she is happy now, *because of me* (and that is hard to accept, it makes me feel angry, that so little can change a life), and therefore she likes to think of happy times.

A Happiness.

"My German boy, the one I should have married but I was silly, we used to spend Sundays. We took a penny bus ride up to where we are sitting now, or perhaps a stage further. Green fields and streams and trees. We'd sit on the edge of a little bridge and watch the water, or find a field without cows and eat our food. What did we eat? I'd cut cold meat from the joint, as much as I liked, because Mother wasn't dead then, and clap it between two bits of bread. But I liked his food best, because his parents were bakers. Did you know the bakers were often Germans then? Well, his parents could just read and write, but he was a real clever one, he was a scholar. He did well later, more fool me, I could have had my own house and a garden. But I didn't marry him, I didn't. I don't know why. Of course, my father wouldn't have liked a foreigner, but he didn't like what I did marry, he could never say yes to any choice of ours, so what would have been the difference? No, I don't want to think of that, I spent enough time when I was younger thinking, Oh what a fool—when I'd come to understand what men were. You see, I didn't know then. Hans was so kind, he was a gentleman, he treated me like a queen. He'd lift me down from the stiles so gently and nice, and we spread a little white cloth and put out the lovely white rolls and the cakes from the bakery. I used to say, No, I must eat mine, and you eat yours, and mine always ended up being given to the birds.

"I think of those days, those Sundays. And who would believe it now? Where we sit in these streets, running streams, and birds . . . What happened to the streams? you are thinking. I know, I know how to read your face now. Well, you might well wonder where all that water is. It is underneath the foundations of half the houses along here, that's where. When they built this all up, and covered the fields, I used to come by myself and watch the builders. By myself. My German boy had gone off by then because I wouldn't marry him. The builders scamped everything then, as they do now; some things never change. They were supposed to make the water run in proper conduits, away from the houses, but they didn't trouble themselves. Sometimes, even now, when I walk along, I stop at a house and I think, yes, if your basements are damp, it's because of the water from those old streams. There's a house, number seventy-seven it is, it changes hands, it can't keep an owner, it's because it's where two little streams met, and the builders put the bricks of the foundation straight into the mud and let the water find its way. They did make a real channel for the water lower down, it runs along the main road there, but the little baby streams we used to sit by and put our feet in, they were left to make their own way. And after those Sundays, when the dusk came, oh, how lovely it all was, he'd say, May I put my arm around your waist? And I'd say, No, I don't like it—what a fool. And he'd say, Put your arm in mine then, at least. So we'd walk arm in arm through the fields to the bus, and come home in the dark. He'd never come in, because of Father. He'd kiss my hand, and he'd say, Maudie, you are a flower, a little flower."

A Happiness.

Maudie was apprenticed to a milliner's and worked for them off and on for years. The apprenticeship was very hard. Living with her aunt, who was so poor, and gave her breakfast and supper, but not much more, Maudie had to do without a midday meal or walk most of the way to work. The workshop was near Marylebone High Street. She would calculate whether shoe leather would cost more than her fare. She said she could beg cast-off shoes from her cousin, who never got all the wear out of them, or pick up second-hand boots from a market. But she had to be neatly dressed for her work, and that was her biggest trouble. Her aunt did not have money for Maudie's clothes.

Her employer's wife gave her a skirt and a blouse once. "She valued me, you see. We had to have a decent appearance because the buyers would come into the workrooms. Oh, don't think it was from a good heart, she didn't have one. She didn't want to lose me. It was years before I could buy myself a nice brown cloth dress of my own, and my own shoes. And when I did, oh, I'll not forget that day. I went without so much for that dress. And I wore it on the Sunday first so Laurie could see it. And who gave you that? he said, for that was what he was like, tugging at my arm and hurting it. Who was it, tell me? It wasn't you, I said to him, and as I pulled my arm from him, it tore under the arm. Not much, but the dress was spoiled. Oh yes, a person has his stamp all through him. You know what I'm saying? But *I* didn't know that then. It wasn't long before I knew that in everything he did, it was the same: a new dress I'd saved and gone without for, but he tore it the first time I put it on. But it didn't matter, I mended it, it didn't show, and I went into the workroom and peacocked around, and the girls all clapped and sang 'A Little Bit of What You Fancy Does You Good'.

"That was just before I was promoted, and soon I got another dress, a blue foulard, but I never loved another dress as I loved that first one I paid for myself.

"Oh what times we did have in that workroom. There were fifteen of us, apprentices and milliners. We sat all around a long table, with the boxes of trimmings on trestles behind us, and the hats and bonnets we were working on on their forms in front of us. We used to sing and lark about. Sometimes when I got a bit carried away, *she* used to come up and say, Who's making all that noise? It's Maudie! The rule is, silence when you work. But I had to sing, I was so enjoying myself, and soon we were all singing, but she didn't want to lose me, you see.

"Did I tell you how I learned to know that I was a value to her? If I did, I'll tell you again, because I love to think of it. You see, *he* used to go off to Paris, and see the new season's hats in the shops, and sometimes in the workrooms of the Paris milliners, for he knew people who could snatch him a glimpse. He knew how to remember a hat or a bonnet that would do for us. He used to keep it all in his mind, and nip out quick and draw it. He couldn't draw really, but he'd have the main things, a shape or the set of a ribbon. And then he'd come back and say, You do this, see, it's this shape and that colour, made of velvet or satin, you do what you can. Well, it was as if I could see the real hat behind the scribble on the paper, and I'd work away there, and finish it, and I'd say to him, Is that anywhere near it, Mr Rolovsky? And he'd take it up and stare and say, Well, it's not too bad, Maudie. That pleased me. But then I saw how he'd come and stand behind me and watch while I worked, always me, not the others, and then the way he snatched up the hat when I'd done, for he was so greedy, you see, he couldn't hide it. I saw then I'd come near what he'd seen in Paris. And the girls all knew too, and we'd give each other winks. *She* saw us at it, and she said, That's enough, I don't see what there is to wink at. For she was clever, the missus was, but she wasn't clever at anything but her job, which was making the workroom pay. Have you noticed that at all? A person can be clever as can be, in one direction, and stupid in another. *She* thought we didn't know what she was trying to cover up, and yet it was all plain to us. I had a gift, you see, I had it in my fingers and in my mind's eye, and it was worth everything to them, because when the buyers came in, he always showed them my work first, and it was always my work that he charged the most for.

"I've stood outside the showrooms, just off Bond Street they were, and looked at the hats in the window, only two or three of course, not crammed the way the windows for cheap hats were done, and the hats were always mine. And snapped up as soon as I could do them.

"Yes, I can see from your face what you're wanting to say, and you're right. I never got paid extra for it. I got the top wages for the job, but that was never much, never enough to free my mind of worrying about the future. Yes, you are right again, don't think I haven't thought and thought about why I didn't go somewhere else, or say, Give me what I am worth to you or I'll leave. But for one thing, I loved that work so, I loved it all, the colours and the feel of the materials; and then the other girls, we had worked together so long by then, and we knew each other and all our troubles, and then . . . Well, of course there was more to it. For one thing, it was partly my fault. *He* wanted me to go to Paris. Oh no, if he had anything else in mind, he couldn't let it be that. He said, The wife'll come too, don't you worry, it will all be fair and right. What he wanted was for me to come with him into the workrooms when he could sneak himself in, and look at the hats for myself. He was really getting carried away by it all, he imagined my coming back to London and copying all those hats and bonnets, hundreds of them, I daresay, not just the few he could keep in his mind. And he said he would pay me properly for it. Well, being him, being *that* pair, I knew better than to think it would be much, but it would be a lot for me. And yet I couldn't bring myself, I said no.

"That was twice I was invited to France, when I was a girl, once with Mrs Privett and once with that pair of . . . One a real lady and then two nasty penny-pinchers, the good and the bad.

"Yes, I know what you are thinking. It was Laurie. He'd never have let me hear the end of it if I'd gone to Paris, even if I'd gone with a regiment of guards to look after me, he'd have taken it out of me. And it was bad enough as it was, before we even married, I had bruises on my arms, and it was always: Who was it? Who looked at you? Who gave you that handkerchief?—because I used to pinch and save for proper linen hankies with real lace, I loved them, I loved pretty things. But he never knew I could have gone to Paris then. And if I had, perhaps I might have stayed, I might have married a Frenchie. I could have married a German, couldn't I? Sometimes I look back and I see that my life had these chances, leading to something wonderful, who knows? And yet I never took them, I always said, No, no, to what was offered.

"And yet I had such happy times, I think except for Johnnie they were the best in my life, better even than Hans and our

Sundays. I like to sit here and think back to us girls, sitting around those lovely hats, oh they were so beautiful those hats, singing and larking and telling stories, and *she* always around, Maudie here and Maudie there, it's always you who are the ringleader, she'd say, but I was her best and she knew it, and though she'd like to have seen the last of me, because *he* had his eye on me, and everyone knew it, she had to put up with me, didn't she? And I didn't care. I'd sing away, I'd sing—shall I sing you one of my songs? Yes, I will . . ."

And Maudie sits singing the old music-hall songs, some I've never heard of. Her voice is off pitch now, keeps cracking, but you can hear what it was like in her laugh.

A Happiness.

"I must have got pregnant the night of our wedding. Nine months to the day, it was. And Laurie was so pleased once we knew. Would you believe it, I was so silly, I didn't know what was wrong with me! I crept off to the doctor and said, I am sickening, I'm dying, I feel so ill, and I feel this and that. And I lay down and he felt my stomach, and he sat down behind his table and he laughed. Oh, it was a nice laugh, it didn't make me feel bad, but I did feel silly. He said, Mrs Fowler, didn't it occur to you that you are pregnant? What's that? said I. You are going to have a baby, said he. Oh go on, I said, it can't be—for I hadn't got the expectation of it into my mind at all.

"And then I told Laurie and he cried, he was so pleased. We were in the front room of a house in the next street to this. He painted the room beautifully, for he was a good tradesman, no one could say otherwise, he painted it a lovely shining cream, and the garlands on the ceiling he painted gold and blue, and the skirting boards and the picture rail blue. And he bought a little chest and made that blue, and kept buying little coats and hats—oh, sizes too big, Johnnie didn't get into them for two or three years after Laurie left me. But I was so happy, I thought I was a queen for those few months. He treated me like I was a piece of crystal or a new cup. He kept buying me all sorts of fancies, for I was after pickles and chocolate and ginger and stuff, and they cost him.

"And then the baby was born, my Johnnie. And you'll never guess. From that moment on there was never a kind word for me. How is it a grown man behaves like a little boy? He was jealous, jealous of a baby! But I didn't know then that was how it was going to be. I used to tease him, and then he hit me. All the good times were over. I used to sit there in my nursing chair, which he had made for me, and nurse the baby, and look at the lovely painted ceiling, and think, oh I'm so hungry, so hungry, because Johnnie was such a feeding baby, he sucked and sucked. I'd say, Laurie, get me a bit of lamb for a stew, buy me some bacon, we'll have it with dumplings. And he'd say, What am I going to use for money? And he was in work. Well, I'll not fill your ears with the misery of it when I understood what the future was to be, because what I like is, to look back and think of me sitting like a queen in that lovely room, in my lovely chair, with Johnnie, and thinking how when Laurie got used to it we'd all be so happy."

A month later.

I've never worked as hard as this! If I keep a skeleton of this diary going, then perhaps later . . .

Joyce is just holding herself together, but she is not with us. I am doing all the interviewing, parties, running about, lunches, conferences. We keep her out of sight mostly. Her defences are well inside herself, not where mine are, outside in clothes, hair, etc. She looks awful, a mess. In addition, this series of articles on clothes as an expression of the mood of the seventies, sixties, fifties. They wanted more. I seem never to be able to lose it, undervaluing myself. I would not have thought of myself as able to write for a serious sociological mag, but here I am. So I get up at six to do the work for that.

And I see Maudie every evening, or if not I make sure she knows I'm not coming. I go in, exhausted, but then I shop and do a little bit of cleaning, and then I slump and listen, and listen. Sometimes she tells it well, and laughs, and knows she is pleasing me. Others, she mutters and is fierce and won't look at me, sitting there in my lovely clothes. I have bought a whole new outfit, madly expensive, I feel it as a bulwark against chaos. She leans over and feels the silk of my shirt, none of this cheap Chinese stuff, no. She strokes my skirt, and then looks up into my face, with a sigh, for she knows how good my things are, who better? And then she will turn away her little face and put her hand up to her cheek to shield it, and stare into the fire. Shuts me out. And then she starts again, forgiving me with a little laugh: So what have you been doing today? But she doesn't want to know, my world is too much for her, she wants to talk . . .

"And then one day he left me, he said, You don't care for me now you've got *him*, and he took up his tools and he left. I didn't believe it. I was waiting for him to come back, for years as it turned out. But there I was, with nothing to pay the rent with. I went to the Rolovskys and asked—oh, that was hard, I'd never begged of them before. I had said I was getting married, you see, and *she* had given me a hard time, making me work all hours, to get as much out of me as she could before she lost me. And here I was again, after not even two years. Well, she made a favour of it. And someone else was forewoman now. And it wasn't the same in the workroom. For one thing, I didn't have the heart to sing and dance. I put Johnnie with a baby-minder. She wasn't a bad woman, but it wasn't what I wanted for him. I'd be sick worrying, has she given him his medicine, or his milk? For he was delicate, he always had a cough. But I had enough to keep us. Then the people where I was said they wanted my room. They didn't want a baby, that was what they meant. And they did want all that lovely blue and gold for themselves. And so I came here. The woman who had the house didn't mind a baby, but I had to keep him quiet, she said. I was on the top floor then, the little room at the back. It was cheap, and we looked out at the trees there, lovely it was. But I found it hard to pay for everything. I went to my aunt, but she could only just manage for herself. She said, Go to your father. But he had said if I married Laurie I should never darken his door. And he was right, for once . . . Did I tell you about my wedding?"

And Maudie sat laughing, laughing, and pulled out a drawer and showed me a photograph. A tiny woman, under an enormous flowered hat, in a neat tight dress. "Yes," says she,

"I looked a proper mess. I had been saying yes and no, yes and no, because what would happen was, I'd say, No, and then he'd start his squeezing and wanting, and I'd say, Yes, and he'd say, I suppose Harry (there was another boy who fancied me) won't have you, so I'd say, No. But at last we got to say yes at the same time. I borrowed my cousin Flo's best hat and her church gloves. My dress was my own. I sent a message to Father and said I was getting married on Sunday. He came over to Auntie's and Laurie was there, and he stood in the doorway and said to me, If you marry *him* that is the last time you'll see me. Well, I hadn't seen him for nearly ten years as it was. I said, Will you come and see me married at least?

"On that morning Laurie was worse than I'd ever seen him, fit to burst with black looks and pinches and grumbles. We walked to church with my Auntie, and we were quarrelling all the way. There was Father, all in his best striped clothes and top hat, oh what a dresser he was! And *she* was there too, she had got so fat, and I couldn't help crowing secretly, she could hardly walk, all in purple and black feathers, and by then I'd come to know what was really good and what wasn't, and I could see she was nothing, we wouldn't have her in our workroom. But I was nothing too, that day, I could have got a hat from the workroom for the wedding to marry in, but I didn't want a favour from the Rolovskys. And so we were married, sulking and not looking at each other. After the wedding, there was a photographer who took this, and then when Father went off towards the carriage with *her*, I ran after them and said, Can I come with you? But you've just got married, said she, really astonished she was, and I don't blame her. And Father said, That's right, you come home and don't waste time on *him*. So I got into the carriage and left Laurie at the church . . ." And at this Maudie laughs and laughs, her strong, girl's laugh.

"After I'd enjoyed myself at home for a little, and eaten my fill of everything, I thought, Well, I have a husband, and I said to them, Thanks, but I'd better be off home, and I went, Father saying, Never darken my doors. And I didn't, for he died soon after of a stroke. And they didn't tell me about the funeral.

"But my sister was there, right enough. Suddenly she began

showing herself off and buying herself clothes, and then they moved to a better house. I knew Father had left something to us both, and I went to *her* and said, Where is what Father left me? And she couldn't look me in the face. What makes you think you had anything coming? she said. You never came to see us, did you? But who threw me out? I said. And we quarrelled and quarrelled and she shrieked at me. I went to my sister, willing myself to do it because she always treated me so bad, and I said, Polly, where's my share of the money? *She* has got it, my sister said. You'll have to go to a lawyer. Well, how could I do that? You need money for lawyers. I and Laurie were all lovey-dovey just then, and we both of us found it such a nice change, we didn't want to waste any of it.

"Much later, when I was so down and poor and in need of everything, I went to my sister, and she must have told *her*, for one day when I got back from work the landlady said a big woman in feathers and scarlet had been and left me a parcel. It was some of my mother's clothes, that's all, and her old purse with two gold guineas in it. And that's all I ever had from my father. For I never saw *her* again."

Maudie's very bad time.

"I worked so hard and so hard. I used to get up so early and take Johnnie to the minder's, and then to work, and work all day till six or seven. And then back to pick up Johnnie, and she'd be cross, often, because I was late and she wanted to be rid of him. And I'd get home and find not enough food for him and me. I was earning badly then. Mrs Rolovsky never forgave me for leaving when I married and then coming back. I wasn't the pet any longer, and she was always taking her chance to fine me, or give me a hat that would take twice as long as the others. We were paid by what we'd got done, you see. And I never was able to scamp my work. I had to do it properly even if I was to suffer. And then we were put off. We were put off most summers. Oh, no security then, no pensions, nothing. She'd say, Pick up your cards as you go out, and leave your address, and we'll contact you when there's work.

"That war was coming, it was nearly on us, and times were

bad. I didn't know what to do. I had a little saved, but not much. I had Johnnie home from the minder's, that was something because I hardly ever saw him awake when I was working, but how to feed him? The landlady said, No, no credit on the rent. I kept the rent paid, but often and often I went to bed on cold water so Johnnie could have a cup of milk. It went on and on, and that was such a wonderful summer. I was wild with hunger. I'd go into the gardens and see if there was bread lying there the birds hadn't eaten. But others had the same idea, and I'd be there first, hanging around, pretending I wasn't watching while the people spread out the bread for the birds. Once I said to an old woman, I need that more than the birds. Then earn it, said she. I never forgot that, and I'll never forget it. For there was no work. I tried to get a cleaning job, but they wouldn't have me cleaning with a child hanging around. I didn't know what I would do.

"Then suddenly Laurie turns up, and finds me in bed on a Sunday afternoon, with my arms around Johnnie. I felt so faint and sick, you see. Oh, what a commotion, what a to-do! First, of course, it was all shouts, Why did you move without telling me? And then it was, You know I'd never let you go without! Then prove it, I said, and off he went and came back with groceries. I could have done with biscuits and tea and dried peas and stuff I could have kept, but no, being Laurie, it was all fancy cakes and ham. Well, I ate and Johnnie ate, and after all that he took us out for some food. I'm your Daddy, says he to Johnnie, and of course the little boy is pleased. And then, he went off. Back tomorrow, says Laurie, but I didn't see him for months.

"Meanwhile I'd hit the bottom. I went to Relief. In those days there was a Board stuffed with snobby ladies and gentlemen, and you'd stand there, and they'd say, Why don't you sell your locket, if you're so poor—it was my mother's—have you got any personal belongings, we can't keep people who have their own resources. Their own resources! You say you have a little boy, and they say, Then you must force your husband to contribute. You couldn't explain to the likes of them about the likes of Laurie. Well, they said I could have two shillings a week. That was high summer still, and no end to it in sight.

They sent a man around. I'd pawned everything, except a blanket for Johnnie, for I was sleeping under my coat. He came into our room. Bed with a mattress but no bedclothes, a wooden table—this one here, that you like. Two wooden chairs. A shelf that had on it a bit of sugar and half a loaf of bread. He stood there, in his good clothes, and looked at me and Johnnie, and then he said, Have you sold everything you can? And I had, even my mother's locket. And he leaned forward and pointed to this . . ." Maudie showed me the long dark wood stick with which she pushes back and opens the curtains. "What about this? he said. How am I to open and close my curtains? I said. Are you expecting me to sell my curtains as well? Shall I sell the bed and sleep on the floor, then?

"He was a little ashamed then, not much, it wasn't his job to be ashamed of what he had to do. And that was how I got my two shillings a week."

"And could you live on it?"

"You would be surprised what you can live on. Johnnie and I, we ate bread, and he got some milk, and so we lived until the autumn and there was a note from the Rolovskys: they'd take me on but at less money. Because of the hard times. I would have worked for half what they gave. I slowly got back the blankets from the pawnshop, for the winter, and I got my pillows, and then . . . One day, when I got to the baby-minder's, no Johnnie. Laurie had come and taken him away. I begged and screamed and begged, but she said he was the child's father, she couldn't refuse a child to his father—and I went mad, running about the streets, and going everywhere. No one had heard anything. No one knew. I was very ill then. I lay in bed, I didn't care, I thought I would die and I would have welcomed it. I lost my job at the Rolovskys', and that was the end of them, for me. When I was up, I got myself a job cleaning, to tide me over, because without a child they'd employ me. And when I saved up enough I went to a lawyer. I said, How can I get my child back? But where is your husband? he said. I don't know, I said. Then how can I help you? he said. I don't know, I said. You must advertise for him, he said. But where? I said. Isn't there a way of finding out where people are? Yes, but it costs money, he said. And I haven't got any, I said.

"And then he came over to me and put his hands all over me, and he said, Very well, Maudie, you know what you can do if you want me to help you. And I ran, and I ran, out of that office, and I was scared to go near a lawyer again.

"All this time, Laurie had Johnnie down in the West Country with a woman he had then. Much later, when I met Johnnie again, he told me she was good to him. Not his father, for his father was off soon, to another woman, he could never stay with one woman. No, this woman brought him up. And he did not know he had a mother, he didn't know about me. Not till quite recently, but I'll tell you another time, another time, I'm all roiled up and upset with thinking about it all, and I meant to tell you something nice tonight, one of the times I like to think about, not a bad time . . ."

A nice time.

Maudie was walking down the High Street, and she saw some hats in a window. She was appalled at the way the hats were made. She went in and said to a woman who was making a hat, Don't you know how to put a hat together? And the woman said, No, she had been left a widow with a bit of money and thought she would make hats. Well, said Maudie, you have to learn how to make a hat, as you have to learn to scrub a floor or bake a loaf. I'll show you. She was a bit huffy at first, but she wanted to learn.

"I used to go in there, and she'd show me what she'd done, and I'd make her pick it to pieces again, or I'd make her whole hat, for the skill was in my fingers still, and it is now, I know. And yes, I can see from your face what you are thinking, and you're right. No, she didn't pay me. But I loved it, you see. Of course, it wasn't like the Rolovskys', not the West End, nothing in the way of real good silks and satins, just cheap stuff. But all the same, between us, we made some lovely hats and she got a name for it. And soon she sold the shop for the goodwill—but the goodwill was me, really, and that wasn't in any contract and so I don't know what happened afterwards . . ."

*　　*　　*

A nice time.

Maudie was working for an actress who was at the Lyric Theatre, Hammersmith. She was prepared to take an hour's journey there, and an hour back, because this woman was so gay and laughing and always had a joke. "She lived alone, no man, no children, and she worked. Oh, they work so, these poor actresses, and I used to make her supper ready for the oven, or a good big salad on a plate, and get her fire laid, and go home thinking how she'd be so happy to come in and see everything so nice. And sometimes after a matinée she'd say, Sit down, Maudie, share my supper, I don't know what I'd do without you. And she'd tell me all about the theatre. She wasn't a star, she was what they call a character actress. Well, she was a character all right. And then she died. What of? I was so upset I didn't want to know. It was a sudden death. I got a letter one day, and it was, she had died, sudden. So I didn't go back, though I was owed a fortnight's money."

"When was that?"

For all the time I am trying to get her life mapped, dated.

"When? Oh, it was after the war. No, the other war, the second war."

Maudie doesn't talk about the first war as a war. She was sick with worrying about Johnnie, for she thought that her husband would be in the army, and where was Johnnie? She went "to the Army" and asked, did they know anything about a Laurie Fowler, and they said, But what part of the country does he come from?

"I was so desperate, I went on my knees. I didn't know I was going to, but there I was, with all those officers around me. Please, please, I said. They were embarrassed, and I don't blame them. I was crying like a river. They said, We'll see what we can do. We'll let you know.

"And a long time afterwards, and I was waiting for every visit of the postman, a card: We have been unable to trace Laurence Fowler. And the reason was, he joined up from Scotland, not England, for there was a woman in Scotland he was living with he needed to get away from."

*   *   *

So that is what a month of visiting Maudie looks like, written down! But what of the evening when I said to myself, I am so tired, I am so tired, I *can't*, but I went? It was an hour later than usual. I stood outside that crumbling door, knock knock, then bang bang bang. Faces in the upper windows. Then at last she stood there, a little fury with blazing blue eyes.

"What do you want?"

"I am here to visit you."

She shrieked, "I haven't got time, and dragging down this passage, getting the coal, is bad enough."

I said to her, hearing myself with some surprise, "Then go to hell, Maudie," and went off without looking back. This was without real anger on my part, almost like reading lines in a play. Nor was I worried that evening, but made good use of my spare time having a real bath.

Next day, she opened the door on my second knock, and said, "Come in," standing aside with an averted unhappy face. Later she said, "You don't have to take any notice of my nonsense."

"Yes, I do, Maudie, of course I do. If you say a thing, I have to believe you mean it."

And, a few days later, she was stiff and silent. "What's wrong, Maudie?"

"I'm not going to, I'm not leaving here, they can't make me."

"Who's been this time?"

"*She* has."

"Who is *she*?"

"As if you don't know."

"Oh, so you're back at that, then. I'm plotting against you!"

"Of course you are, you all do."

We were shrieking at each other. I am not at all ashamed of this, yet I've never, or not since I was a child, quarrelled in this way: quarrelled without spite or passion, even with a certain enjoyment. Though I know it is not enjoyable to Maudie. She suffers afterwards.

"But was there someone else to see you, then?"

"Yes."

"What's her name?"

With a blazing blue look, she said, "Rogers, Bodgers, Plodgers, something like that." And, later, "They can't make me move, can they? This house is privately owned?"

I sent for the information. If the flat is condemned, then she'll have to move. By any current housing standard, it should be condemned. By any human standard, she should stay where she is. I want to contact this Mrs Rogers. I know I can ring up the "Welfare" and ask, but this isn't how things happen—oh, no! You have to let things work themselves out, you must catch something at the right time.

I found the two old women again waiting for me the other day. Mrs Boles and Mrs Bates. Bundles of coats and scarves, but their hats had flowers and bright ribbon. Spring.

"Oh, you do run about," says Mrs Bates. "And how is Maudie Fowler?"

"She is the same."

"Mrs Rogers was asking after you," she said.

"Do you know what about?"

"Oh, she's ever so good, Mrs Rogers, running about, just like you."

That is how things happen. Now I am waiting to run into Mrs Rogers somewhere.

Another five weeks have gone. Nothing has changed . . . and yet of course it must have. Same in the office, with Joyce, same with Maudie. But I've met Vera Rogers. On the pavement, she was talking to the old women. They called, she turned, an anxious friendly smile, she was across the street and with me. She is a smallish thin girl. I was actually going to write: *a size twelve.* When am I going to stop thinking of people first in terms of what they wear? Phyllis asked me recently, what was my sister like, and I said, She wears good jersey suits and good shoes and cashmere. Phyllis laughed exactly the sort of laugh I'd have meant her to, only a year ago.

Vera stood in front of me on the windy pavement, smiling an anxious, warm, apologetic smile. Brown friendly eyes. Pink nail varnish, but chipped. Yes, of course this says something about her: she's overworked. Clothes down-market Jaeger, pleasant, not exciting. I knew that here she was, "the one". There was not much need for all the opening moves. I said, "I was hoping to run into you." She said, "Yes, I would so much like to talk to you about Mrs Fowler." I said, "She's terrified she will be forcibly rehoused." She said, "Yes, but we can stave it off a bit." I said, "Meanwhile, what would help her most is Meals on Wheels." She said, "She's active, you see, she can get about, she's not really entitled . . . but if you think . . ." I said, "She can't make herself cook any more, you see, she lives on bits and pieces."

She began to laugh. She said, "I must tell you something really funny, it happened to me last week. I went to see one of my cases, she's ninety-four. Deaf, arthritic, but she does everything for herself, cooks, cleans, shops. There I was, watching her prepare her lunch. A meat pie, cabbage cooked in soda, and then cream cake. I said to her, Do you ever eat any fresh stuff, fruit or salad? What? she shouted at me."

Vera took such pleasure in telling me this, but she was anxious too, in case I wouldn't find it funny, and she touched my arm once or twice, as if to say, Oh, I hope you'll laugh.

"You must eat fruit and vegetables, I shouted at her. You need vitamins. Every time I come to see you, I never see a vestige of green, or an apple or an orange. And she said, What, what, what? though I knew she could hear, and then when I repeated it, she said, And how old did you say *you* were, dear? And then I thought about all my aches and pains, and I've been eating all the right things since I was a child."

And so we laughed, and she looked relieved.

"I've got to get home to the old man," said she. "I'll fix the Meals on Wheels. But if we could get a free moment at the same time we could have a real talk." And she went running along the street to a yellow VW and nipped off, smartly, into the traffic.

Maudie is so pleased about the meals coming in every midday, though they aren't very nice. Stodgy and badly cooked.

I have realized how *heavy* everything is for her. Yes, I knew this before, but not really, until I saw her delight when I said she was on the list for Meals. She thanked me over and over again.

"You see, *you* did it, but *she* wouldn't, oh no, not she!"

"Did you ask her?" I said.

"What's the use, I've asked often enough, but they say I need a Home Help."

"And so you do."

"Oh well, if that's it, then say it! I've looked after myself before and I can do without you."

"Oh, you are so difficult, Maudie. What's the matter with a Home Help?'

"Have you ever had one?"

At which I laughed, and then she laughed.

Now we are nearly into summer.

What has happened since I sat down last to this unfortunate diary of mine? But I don't want to give it up.

I've met Vera Rogers several times, and we talk—on the pavement, once for a snatched half-hour in a café. We talk in shorthand, because we neither of us have time.

Once she asked how I got involved with Maudie, and when she heard, said, with a sigh, "I had hoped you were really a Good Neighbour, because I know someone who I think might accept a Good Neighbour. She's difficult, but she's lonely."

This was a request, put delicately and with embarrassment, but I said that Maudie was enough.

"Yes, of course she is," she said at once.

I told her what work I do, and then she had to be told *why*. As if I understood it myself! Why am I bound to this Maudie Fowler as I am? I said, "I like her, I really do."

"Oh yes, she's wonderful, isn't she?" said Vera warmly. "And some of them, you'd like to strangle. I used to feel wicked when I started this work, I believed I had to like them all. And then, when I'd been with some difficult old cat for an hour, and I couldn't get anywhere, I'd find myself thinking, God, I'll hit her one of these days, I will."

"Well, I've felt that about Maudie often enough."

"Yes, but there's something else."

"Yes, there is."

I told Maudie how much Vera likes her, and she closed up in an angry pinched mask.

"But *why*, Maudie?"

"She didn't lift a finger to help."

"But how can she if you don't tell her what you want?"

"All I want is to be left alone."

"There you are, you see."

"Yes, here I am alone, except for you."

"Vera Rogers doesn't just have one person to visit, she has sometimes ten or more in a day, and she's on the telephone arranging and getting things done. I see you every day, so I know what you want."

"They'll have to carry me out screaming," said she.

"She's on your side, she's trying to prevent you from being moved."

"That's what she tells you They were around here again today."

"Who?"

"Do you know what he said, that Greek? You can stay in one room, and we'll do up the other, he said. And then when we've finished that, you can move in. Me, here in all that dust and mess. And it's months they take to improve a place."

"Then that must have been the landlord, mustn't it?"

"Yes, that's what I said. They are all in it together."

At the Indian shop, I hung around until the owner, Mr Patel, said, "Mrs Fowler was out on the street yesterday, screaming and shouting."

"Oh yes, what did she say?"

"She was screaming, None of you were around trying to get me hot water and a bath when I had a baby, none of you cared when I didn't have food to give him. I've lived all my life without running hot water and a bath, and if you come back I'll get the police."

Mr Patel says all this slowly, his grave concerned eyes on my face, and I didn't dare smile. He keeps his eyes on my face, reproachful and grave, and says, "When I was in Kenya, before we had to leave, I thought everyone in this country was rich."

"You know better now, then."

But he wants to say something else, something different. I waited, picked up some biscuits, put them back, considered a tin of cat food.

At last he says, in a low voice, "Once, with us, we would not let one of our old people come to such a life. But now—things are changing with us."

I feel I personally should apologize. At last I say, "Mr Patel, there can't be very many like Mrs Fowler left."

"I have six, seven, every day in my shop. All like her, with no one to care for them. And I am only one shop."

He sounds as if he is accusing me. He is accusing my clothes, my style. I am out of place in this little corner shop. And then, feeling as if he has wronged me, he takes a cake from the shelves, one that Maudie likes, and says, "Give it to her."

Our eyes meet again, and this time differently: we are appalled, we are frightened, it is all too much for us.

That was eight days ago.

Joyce may go after all to the States. The girlfriend had an abortion. Husband Jack took this badly: he wanted her to have the baby. He has been having a sort of breakdown, and Joyce has been comforting him. This has been going on for weeks.

When she told me:

"It appears he has been longing for us to have another child."

"Did you know?"

"Well, I knew he wouldn't mind, but not that he cared so much."

"If you had known?"

"Yes, I think I would."

"So now you are both blaming the other?"

"Yes."

Joyce with a cigarette dangling, eyes screwed up, holding up photographs, one after another, Yes, to this one, No to that. Her hair dyed again, but with the dusty look. Her hands unkept. She *looks* fifty. There is something weird and witchlike about her. I've said to her, "Joyce, you must change your style, it's too young." And she said, "When I know if I'm going or not, I'll know which to choose, won't I?"

Joyce is always on the verge of tears. A word, a joke, a tone of voice—she'll turn her head sharply, screw up her eyes, peer at me, at Phyllis, at whomever, the tears welling up. But she shakes them away, pretends there's nothing. Phyllis and I have this unspoken thing: we watch every syllable, word, suggestion, so that Joyce will not suddenly betray herself, and start crying.

Later. How long? I forget. Some days.

Joyce said to me today that she said to Jack, Your trouble is, you want to take this situation with you to the States. Home, children, wife the sympathetic comforter—and girlfriend as well, in a separate place. You can't choose. That's why you are so ill.

And he said to her she was heartless and cold.

Four months before he leaves. He should have told them over there if a wife, or no wife, children or not.

"Perhaps he will go by himself in the end," I mused, forgetting about not upsetting her.

She turned her head in that quick startled way she has now, she leans forward frowning, peering at me. My old friend Joyce, she is a thousand miles away, in some sort of black place, and she peers out at me, thinking, who is this quacking idiot?

"Alone!" she said, in a brisk schoolmistress voice.

"Why not?"

"There's something missing in you, I've always said so," she says, coldly, filing me away.

"Or perhaps there is in you."

I told her about Maudie Fowler, who has lived alone now for something like sixty years. Joyce got up as I spoke, picked up her bag, her briefcase, collected things from her desk.

"How did you get to know her?"

I told her. Joyce listened.

"Guilt," she said at last. "Guilt. If you want to let it get to you, that's your affair."

She was on her way to the door. I said, "Joyce, I want to tell you about it, properly, I really do. I want to talk about it."

She said, "Well, not now."

It is summer. Not that I am seeing much of it.

When did Joyce get ill? It must be over a month now. The truth was, we were all relieved, because it made what really was the truth official. I have been running around from morning to night. In the hospital, this scene: Joyce's husband, the two children, husband's *ex*-mistress, her new boyfriend. Joyce lying back, looking at them all from inside this black place she is in, smiling when she remembers to. Now he wants her to go to America, but she says she doesn't have the energy to think about it. But of course she will go.

Because of all this, I don't stay so long at Maudie's, though I have not missed one day. She understands why, I have told her. But the way she *feels* it is, I'm letting her down. I sit there, trying not to look at my watch, and she is remembering only bad things. I say, "Tell me about the day you went to the Heath with Johnnie, and you found blackberries and made a pie with them?" But she sighs, and sits rubbing those old fingers up and down her (filthy) skirts. Then she tells me about . . .

Her sister, Polly, who has had seven children, always summoned Maudie to look after her, each childbed. Maudie was always delighted, even gave up whatever job she might have, and took herself to her sister's, and looked after everything for weeks, more than once months. Then, says Maudie, it was always the same, the sister got jealous, because Maudie loved the children and they loved her. She found an excuse to say, You are turning my children against me, you are after my husband. Is it likely, says Maudie, the nasty scrimping thing, he grudged me the food I ate while I was working as a slavey. He'd say, if I put a bit of meat on my plate, We'll have to buy an extra bit of beef on Sunday, while Maudie honours us with her presence. Meanwhile, I was working eighteen hours a day for them. Between births, Maudie heard nothing of her sister, but she wasn't worried: There'd be another baby, I knew that, because he had to have what he had to have.

Now Maudie talks a lot about sex, and I see that it has been enormous and awful to her, and she has never understood it or ceased to be tormented by it. She says her husband, while he was still treating her like a queen, would leap on her like a tiger, like a wild beast. She says she can't understand it, one moment all lovey-dovey, and the next they have their nails into you. Her husband has been with one woman after another, and she has been brooding about it all her life: *why*? For Maudie has slept with one man, her awful husband. She knows that there are women who like it, and she looks at me while she talks, with a certain modesty and diffidence, because I might be offended if I knew she was wondering if I was "like that".

Yet, she has had other experiences. Upstairs, for some years, there was a woman who became her friend, and this woman "liked it". She used to tell Maudie how she would wait all day until the night, because another life began at night, and it was her real life. Maudie said to me, "She told me that when they had finished all that, she had to sleep lying behind his back, so that she could hold his thing. That *thing* . . ." cries Maudie, almost weeping with disgust, wonder, and disbelief. "Yes, it was out of respect, she said to me." And Maudie sits there, amazed, after thirty or forty years of thinking about it. Suddenly: "I wouldn't give them that much satisfaction, it's the stick they beat you with!"

And then I laughed (and I wasn't comfortable at all, thinking my own thoughts, for that just about summed it up, never mind that we had such a wonderful sex life, Freddie and I), and she said, "I have been watching your face. I can see you think differently. But I can't help it. And now all the time the newspapers, the magazines, the telly, sex, sex, sex, and I think sometimes, am I mad, are *they* mad?"

I laugh and laugh. She laughs too. But it is a wild unhappy laugh, not at all her girl's laugh that I love to hear.

Such is the power of—?—that Maudie refers to that awful husband of hers, even now, as My man. She has seen him half a dozen times in half a century. One day, a knock at the door, and there stood her husband. But this young man said, "Mother? I'm your son Johnnie." "Well, come in then," said she. "I had put it out of mind, you see. I had made myself ill with fretting. Once I had to go to the doctor, and he said, Mrs Fowler, you must either find your child or put him out of your mind. How could I find him? He might be in America or Timbuctoo! And slowly I did forget him. And so when he was there—I am your son Johnnie, he said—we became friends, because we took to each other. And then there was the war. He did well in the war, he was an engineer, and he married an Italian girl, but it came to no good, for she went off with another man, and do you know what I dreamed the other night? Oh, it was a doleful dream, so bad and low. I dreamed there was a wonderful cherry tree, like the cherry tree there was out the back here before it fell down in a big storm. Big black cherries, soft and lovely and shining. And I stood one side of it, and poor Johnnie stood on the other, and we were trying to lean up and reach the cherries, and we tried and tried, but no matter how we pulled the boughs down, they sprang back, and the cherries were out of reach . . . And we stood there, Johnnie and I, and we were crying."

Long after Johnnie was a grown man and had gone to America, where he vanished, and forty years after Laurie had left her, stealing her child, Maudie wrote a letter to her husband, asking him to meet her. They met on a bench in Regent's Park.

"Well, what do you want?" he said.

"I was thinking, perhaps we could make a home for Johnnie," she said to him. She explained that they could find a house—for she knew he always had money, wheeling and dealing—and make it nice, and then an advertisement in the paper in America.

"For Johnnie has never had a nice home," she explained to her husband.

"And what did he say?"

"He bought me a fish supper, and I didn't see him for five years."

A marvellous hot blue day.

I said to Phyllis, "Hold the fort," and I ran out of the office, to hell with it. I went to Maudie, and when she answered the door, slow, slow, and cross, I said, "I'm taking you to the park for a treat." She stared at me, *furious*. "Oh, don't," I said to her. "Oh, darling Maudie, don't, *please*, don't let yourself get angry, just come."

"But how can I?" she says. "Look at me!"

And she peers up at the sky past my head. It is so blue and nice, and she says, "But . . . but . . . but . . ."

Then suddenly she smiles. She puts on her thick black-beetle coat and her summer hat, black straw, and we go off to the Rose Garden Restaurant. I find her a table out of the way of people, with rose bushes beside her, and I pile a tray with cream cakes, and we sit there all afternoon. She ate and ate, in her slow, consuming way, which says, I'm going to get this inside me while it is here!—and then she sat, she simply sat and looked, and looked. She was smiling and delighted. Oh, the darlings, she kept crooning, the darlings . . . at the sparrows, at the roses, at a baby in a pram near her. I could see she was beside herself with a fierce, almost angry delight, this hot brightly coloured sunlit world was like a gorgeous present. For she had forgotten it, down in that ghastly basement, in those dreary streets.

I was worried that it would all be too much for her inside that thick black shell, and it was so hot and noisy. But she did not want to leave. She sat there until it closed.

And when I took her home she was singing dreamily to herself, and I took her to her door, and she said, "No, leave me, leave me, I want to sit here and think about it. Oh, what lovely things I have to think about."

What did strike me, when I saw her out there in the full sunlight: how yellow she is. Bright blue eyes in a face that looks as if it has been painted yellow.

Three days later.

Another gorgeous afternoon. Went to Maudie, said, "Come to the park."

She said irritably, "No, no, you go, I can't."

"Oh come on," I said, "you know you like it once you get there."

She stood holding to the door handle, distressed, angry, dishevelled. Then she said, "No, oh dreadful, dreadful, dreadful," and shut the door in my face.

I was *furious*. I had been thinking, as I drove to her, how she sat in the rose garden, crooning with delight. I went back to the office, furious. Worked till late. Did not go in to Maudie. Felt guilty, as I wallowed about with the hot water making me new again: kept seeing how she stood there, holding herself up, heard the mutter, Dreadful, dreadful . . .

A week has passed, it is dreary and chilly again. End of summer? Maudie seems to me, perhaps, really ill? . . . I know so little about old people! For all I know, all this is normal! I keep setting aside a time to think about her, but I am so busy, busy, busy. I rush in to her, at all hours, I say to her, I'm sorry, Maudie, I've got so much work. Last night I went in late and fell asleep in her chair. This morning I rang up the office and said I was not feeling well. In all my years there I think I've been ill twice, and I never take days off.

Phyllis said, "That's all right, I'll hold the fort!"

Maudie's day.

She wakes inside a black smothering weight, she can't breathe, can't move. They've buried me alive, she thinks, and struggles. The weight shifts. Oh, it's the cat, it's my pretty, she thinks, and heaves. The weight lifts, and she hears a thud as the cat arrives on the floor. Petty? she asks, for she is not sure, it is so dark and her limbs are so stiff. She hears the cat moving about and knows she is alive. And warm . . . and in bed . . . Oh, oh, she says aloud, I must get to the toilet or I'll wet the bed again. Panic! Have I wet the bed already? Her hand explores the bed. She mutters, Dreadful, dreadful, dreadful, dreadful, thinking how, a few days ago, she had wet the bed, and the trouble and difficulty of getting everything dry.

But it is as if her hand has disappeared, she can't feel it. She clenches and unclenches her left hand, to know she *has* hands, and waits for the tingling to begin in her right. It takes a long time, and then she pulls out the half-numb right hand from under the clothes and uses the left to massage it awake. She still does not know if she has wet the bed. Almost she sinks back into the black bed, black sleep, but her bowels are moving and she smells a bad smell. Oh no, no, no, she whimpers, sitting there in the dark, No, dreadful, for she believes she might have shat in the bed. At last, with such effort and trouble, she climbs out of the bed, and stands beside it, feeling in it to see what is there. She can't be sure. She turns, carefully, tries to find the light switch. She has a torch by the bed, but the batteries ran low, she meant to ask Janna to get new ones, and forgot. She thinks, surely Janna would think to look for herself, she knows how I need the torch! She finds the switch, and there is light . . . and anxiously she inspects the bed, which is dry. But she has to get to the toilet. She never uses the commode for more than a pee. She must get herself to the outside toilet. But there is a hot wet thrusting in her bowels and she gets herself to the commode, just in time. She sits there, rocking herself, keening. Dreadful, dreadful, for now she will have to take the pot out, and she feels so low and bad.

She sits there a long time, too tired to get up. She even sleeps a little. Her bottom is numb. She pulls herself up, looks for the paper. No lav paper, because she doesn't use it in here. She cannot find anything to use . . . At last she struggles to the cupboard, her bottom all wet and loathsome, finds an old petticoat, rips off a piece, uses it to clean herself, and shuts down the lid on the smell—and worse, for while she does allow herself a fearful peep, she refuses to let her mind acknowledge that there is something wrong with her stool. Dreadful, she mutters, meaning the stuff her bowels seem to produce these days, and shoves the curtains back off the windows.

It is light outside. But it is summer, it could be the middle of the night still. She cannot bear to think of the difficulties of getting back into bed, and then out of it again. Her little clock has its face turned away from her, she doesn't want to cross the room to it. She pulls around herself an old shawl, and huddles in the chair by the dead fire. No birds yet, she thinks: has the dawn chorus been and gone or am I waiting for it? She thinks of how, a child, she lay with her sisters in the bed in the cottage of the old woman in the summers, and woke to the shrill violence of the dawn chorus and slept again, thinking of the lovely hot day ahead, a day that had no end to it, all play and pleasure and plentiful tasty meals.

And so Maudie drifts off to sleep, but wakes, and sleeps and wakes for some hours, each time remembering to move her hands so that they don't stiffen up too much. At last she wakes to the cat rubbing and purring around her legs. Which are stiff. She tests her hands. The right one gone again. With the left she caresses the cat, Pretty, petty, pretty pet, and with the right she tries to flex and unflex fingers until she is whole again.

Morning . . . oh, the difficulties of morning, of facing the day . . . each task such a weight to it . . . She sits there, thinking, I have to feed the cat, I have to . . . I have to . . . At last, she drags herself up, anxious, because her bowels are threatening again, and, holding on to door handles, chair backs, she gets herself into the kitchen. There is a tin of cat food, half empty. She tries to turn it on to a saucer, it won't come out. It means she has to get a spoon. A long way off, in the sink, are her spoons and forks, she hasn't washed up for days. She winkles out the cat food with her forefinger, her face wrinkled up—is it smelling perhaps? She lets the saucer fall from a small height on to the floor, for bending forward makes her faint. The cat sniffs at it and walks away, with a small miaow. Maudie sees that under the table are saucers, bone dry and empty. The cat needs milk, she needs water. Slowly, slowly, Maudie gets herself to the sink, pulls out of it a dirty saucer which she has not got the energy to wash, runs water into it. Finds a half bottle of milk. Has it gone off? She sniffs. No. She somehow gets the saucer on to the floor, holding on to the table and nearly falling. The cat drinks all the milk, and Maudie knows she is hungry.

Under the table not only the saucers, one, two, three, four, five, but a cat mess. This reminds Maudie she has to let the cat out. She toils to the door, lets out the cat, and stands with her back to the door, thinking. A general planning a campaign could not use more cleverness than Maudie does, as she outwits her weakness and her terrible tiredness. She is already at the back door: the toilet is five steps away; if she goes now it will save a journey later . . . Maudie gets herself to the toilet, uses it, remembers there is the commode full of dirt and smell in her room, somehow gets herself along the passage to her room, somehow gets the pot out from under the round top, somehow gets herself and the pot to the toilet. She splashes a bit as she empties it, and, looking, smelling, her mind has to acknowledge that there is something very wrong. But she thinks, as long as *she* (meaning Janna) does not see what I am making, no one will know. *And they won't put me away* . . .

When all that is done it seems to her that a long time has passed, yet she knows that it is still early, for she cannot hear those noisy Irish brats. She needs a cup of tea very badly, all her energy has gone into the cat.

She stands by her kitchen table, holding on to it, thinking of how she will carry the cup of hot reviving tea next door. But hot tea makes you run, no, better cold milk. She gets the cold milk into the glass. That is the end of the milk. She needs: milk, toilet paper, cat food, matches, tea, and probably a lot else, if she could think of it.

Perhaps Janna will come soon and . . .

She looks sternly at the cat mess, which seems to her a long way down, measuring it in her mind with the need to stoop, and thinks, Janna will . . .

She gets herself and the milk next door. Sits down. But she is cold now, summer or not. She sits in that old chair of hers, by the cold grate, and feels the heat leaking out of her. She has to get the fire made. Should she plug in the heater? But it takes so much electricity, she is only *just* balancing her needs with her pension. She at last struggles up and plugs it in. The room has the warm red glow of the heater, her legs seem to loosen and become themselves. She sits there, sipping her milk, and muttering, Dreadful, dreadful, dreadful.

Then she drifts off into a dream that Janna has taken her into her own home and is looking after her. She is fiercely possessive of this dream, and cuddles and cossets it, taking it out and adding to it whenever she sits there by herself, but she knows it will not happen. *Cannot* happen. But why not? It was impossible that Janna should fly into her life the way she did, who would ever have thought of it? And then how she comes in and

out, with her jokes and her flowers and cakes and stuff, all her
stories about her office, she is probably making it up, after all,
how can she, a poor old woman, know better, if Janna chooses
to embellish it all a little? So why, then, should not another
impossible thing happen, that she should be taken into a lovely
warm flat and there she would be looked after, things done for
her . . .

Or Janna would come and live here. There is that room next
door . . . That is what Maudie really wants. She does not want
to leave here. Get yourself your own place and never let go of
it: Maudie repeats this whenever she is tempted—as now—to
leave here and go and live with Janna. No, no, she mutters, she
will have to come here. And she sits there, sometimes dozing,
thinking of how Janna is living there, looking after her, and of
how, when she wakes in the night, alone and frightened that
she is in the grave, she can call out, and hear Janna's reply.

But soon her bowels force her to get up. Although she
emptied the pot she did not wash it out, and it is disgusting to
her. So she goes outside to the toilet, letting in the cat, who is
waiting and who goes to the saucer with the smelly food in it,
and disdains it, and patiently comes into the room with
Maudie. Who, now she is up, decides to make a fire. It takes
her over an hour, the crawling along the corridor to get the
coal, the crawling back, the raking of the ashes, the lighting of
the fire. She blows at it in small shallow puffs, because she gets
dizzy, so it takes a long time to get going. Then she sits again,
longing for a cup of tea, but refusing herself, because above all
else she dreads the demands of her bladder, her bowels. She
thinks, the Meals on Wheels will be here soon . . . it is only
eleven, though. Perhaps they will be early today? She is
hungry, she is so hungry she cannot now distinguish between
her hunger pangs and the possibility that she must go again to
the toilet. Before the cheerful young Meals on Wheels woman,
who has a key, slams in and out, calling, Hello, Mrs Fowler,
you all right—she has had to go out to the lavatory again.

It is early. Only half past twelve. Maudie at once takes the
two small foil containers to the table and, hardly looking at
what is in them, eats everything. She feels much better. She
thinks, oh, if Janna would come now, and if she said, Come to

the park, I'd not growl and grumble at her, I'd love to go. But she sees out of the window that it is raining. What a summer, she mutters. The cat is on the table sniffing at the empty containers, and Maudie is distressed at her greed, for she knows the cat is hungry and she should have shared.

Out she goes to the cold smelling kitchen and reaches about—yes, oh joy, there is a full unopened tin. So happy is Maudie that she even does a little dance there, clutching the tin to her chest. Oh, petty, petty, she cries, I can feed you. At last the tin is opened, though Maudie cuts her forefinger on the tin opener. The cat eats every bit. Maudie thinks, and now she should go out, to save me letting her out later . . . but the cat won't go out, she takes herself back into the room with the fire, sinks to sleep on Maudie's bed. Which has not been made. Maudie should make up her bed—she thinks, it's not nice for Janna. She does not, but sits in the chair by the fire, and leans forward to stack it up with coal, and then sleeps like the dead for three hours. Though she does not know what time it is, five in the afternoon, when she wakes, for her clock has stopped.

The cat is still asleep, the fire is out . . . she builds it up again. She could do with something. She *has* to have a cup of tea. She makes herself a full pot, brings the biscuits, and has a little feast at her table. She feels so much better for the tea that it is easy to disregard how she has to go out to the toilet once more, twice, three times. Her bowels are like an angry enemy down there, churning and demanding. What's wrong with you then? she cries, rubbing her hand round and round on the little mound of her belly. Why won't you leave me alone?

She ought to have a wash . . . she ought . . . she ought . . . but Janna will come, Janna will . . .

But Maudie sits there, waiting, and Janna does not come, and Maudie gets up to let out the insistent cat, and Maudie fetches the coal, and Maudie attends to the fire, and Maudie searches about to see if there is a little brandy, for suddenly she feels bad, she feels trembly, she could fall to the ground and lie there, she is so empty and tired . . . No brandy. Nothing.

She can go out to the off-licence? No, no, she could not possibly get herself up the steps. Janna has not come and it is getting dark. That means it must be getting on for ten. Janna is not coming . . . and there is no milk, no tea, no food for poor petty, nothing.

And Maudie sits by her roaring furious fire thinking bitterly of Janna, who does not care, wicked unkind cruel Janna . . . In the middle of all this, loud knocks at the door, and Maudie's relief explodes into a raucous shout: Oh, all right, I'm *coming*. And scrambles along the passage, crabwise, to the door, afraid Janna might fly off before she gets there. Terrible, terrible, she mutters, and her face, as she opens the door, is fierce and accusing.

"Oh my God, Maudie," cries Janna, "let me in, I'm dead. What a day."

Oh then, if she's tired I can't ask her . . . thinks Maudie, and stands aside as Janna comes crashing in, all energy and smiles.

In the room, Maudie sees Janna smile as she sees the wonderful fire, and sees, too, a wrinkling of her nose, which is at once suppressed.

Janna says, "I said to the Indian man, Don't close, because he was closing, wait, I must get Mrs Fowler some things."

"Oh, I don't need anything," says Maudie, at once reacting to the news that she has to be beholden to the Indian man, with whom she quarrels nearly every time she goes in . . . he overcharges, he is cheating her over her change . . .

Janna, thank goodness, has taken no notice, but is whirling around in the kitchen, to see what is missing, and out she rushes with a basket, before poor Maudie can remember the batteries. In such a hurry, she always is! And they are all like that, rushing in, rushing out, before I have time to turn myself round.

In no time Janna comes crashing back, slam the outside door, slam-bang this door, with a basket full of stuff which Maudie checks, with such relief and thankfulness. Everything is here, nice fresh fish for the cat and a tin of Ovaltine. Janna has thought of everything.

Has she noticed the cat mess, the unwashed stuff in the sink . . . ?

Maudie goes quietly to sit by the fire, on a smile from Janna which says, It is all right. Janna cleans up the cat mess, does the washing-up, puts away the crockery, and does not think, because she is young and so healthy, to leave out on the kitchen table some saucers and a spoon and the tin opener so that Maudie won't have to bend and peer and rummage about.

Maudie sits listening to Janna working away, *looking after me*—and thinks, oh, if she doesn't remember about the commode . . .

But when Janna comes in, she brings a small bottle of brandy and two glasses, and, having handed Maudie her brandy, she says, "I'll just . . ." and whisks out the dirty pot and takes it away.

I hope there is nothing left in it for her to notice, Maudie worries, but when Janna brings back the scoured pot, smelling nicely of pine forests, she says nothing.

Janna lets herself crash down into the chair near the fire, smiles at Maudie, picks up her glass of brandy, swallows it in a mouthful, says: "Oh, Maudie, what a day, let me tell you . . ." And she sighs, yawns—and is asleep. Maudie sees it, can't believe it, knows it is so, and is in a rage, in a fury. For she has been waiting to talk, to listen, to have a friend and some ordinary decent communication, perhaps a cup of tea in a minute, never mind about her bowels, and her bladder . . . And here is Janna, fast asleep.

It is so dark outside. Maudie pulls the curtains over. Maudie goes out to the back door and sees that all the dirty saucers are gone from under the table, and the cat mess gone, and there is a smell of disinfectant. She lets in the cat, and takes the opportunity for a quick visit to the lavatory. She comes back, and pokes up the fire, and sits down opposite Janna, who is sleeping like . . . the dead.

Maudie has not had this opportunity before, of being able to stare and look and examine openly, to pore over the evidence, and she sits leaning forward, looking as long as she needs into the face of Janna, which is so nicely available there.

It's an agreeable face, thinks Maudie, but there's something . . . Well, of course, she's young, that's the trouble, she doesn't understand yet. But look at her neck there, folded up, you can see the age there, and her hands, for all they are so clean and painted, they aren't young hands.

Her clothes, oh her lovely clothes, look at that silk there, peeping out, that's real silk, oh *I* know what it's worth, what it is. And her pretty shoes . . . No rubbish on her, ever. And she didn't get any change out of what she paid for that hat of hers! Look at it, she flings it down on the bed, that lovely hat, the cat is nearly on top of it.

Look at those little white quills there . . . the Rolovskys used to say that they never had anyone to touch me for making those little quills. I could do them now, it is all here still, the skill of it in my fingers . . . I wonder if . . .

Maudie carefully gets up, goes to the bed, picks up the lovely hat, goes back to her chair with it. She looks at the satin that lines the hat, the way the lining is stitched in—blown in, rather; oh yes, the one who did this hat knew her work all right! And the little white quills . . .

Maudie dozes off, and wakes. It is because the fridge upstairs is rumbling and crashing. But almost at once it stops—that means it has been on for a long time, because it runs for an hour or more. Janna is still asleep. She hasn't moved. She is breathing so lightly that Maudie is afraid, and peers to make sure . . .

Janna is smiling in her sleep? Or is it the way she is lying? Oh, she's going to have a stiff neck all right . . . is she going to stay here all night then? Well, what am *I* expected to do? Sit up here while the night goes? That's just like them, they think of nobody but themselves, they don't think of me . . .

Rage boils in Maudie Fowler, as she sits caressing the lovely hat, looking at sleeping Janna.

Maudie sees Janna's eyes are open. She thinks, oh my *Gawd*, has she died? No, she is blinking. She hasn't moved anything else, but she is lying there in the chair, eyes open, looking past Maudie at the window that has hours ago shut out the wet and blowy night with old greasy yellow curtains.

Maudie thinks, she is taking a long time to come to herself, surely? And then Janna's eyes move to her face, Maudie's: Janna looks, suddenly, terrified, as if she will get up and run—and for a moment all her limbs gather together in a spring, as if she will be off. And then the horrible moment is past, and Janna says, "Oh, Maudie, I have been asleep, why didn't you wake me?"

"I have been looking at this gorgeous hat," says Maudie, stroking it delicately with her thick clumsy fingers.

Janna laughs.

Maudie says, "You could stay the night next door, if you like."

Janna says, "But I have to be home to let in a man to do the electricity."

Maudie knows this is a lie, but does not care.

She thinks, Janna has been asleep here half the night, as if this is her place!

She says, "I have been thinking, this is the best time of my life."

Janna sits straight up in her chair, because, being young, her limbs don't stiffen up, and she leans forward and looks into Maudie's face, serious, even shocked.

"Maudie," she says, "you can't say that!"

"But it's true," says Maudie. "I mean, I'm not talking about the short joyful days, like carrying my Johnnie, or a picnic here and a picnic there, but now, I know you will always come and we can be together."

Janna has tears filling up her eyes, and she blinks them back and says, "For all that, Maudie . . ."

"Will you remember to bring me in some batteries for my torch?" says Maudie, in the humble but aggressive way she makes requests.

Janna says, "I tell you what, I'll bring in my torch from the car, and you can have that."

She goes out, in her usual striding way, but then comes back to say, "Maudie, it's morning, the sky is alight."

The two women stand in Maudie's entrance and see the grey light in the streets.

Maudie does not like to say that now she will probably lie on her bed, with the curtains drawn, and stay there for some hours. She suspects Janna of intending not to sleep again that night. Well, she's young, she can do it. She would so much like to have Janna's torch, because after all Janna might not come in tomorrow—no, today.

But Janna kisses her, laughs, and goes rushing off down the dingy wet pavements. She has forgotten her hat.

*   *   *

Janna's day.

The alarm makes me sit up in bed. Sometimes I switch it off, sink back, today not: I sit in the already bright morning, five o'clock, and look through the day ahead: I cannot believe that by the time I end it I shall have done so much. I make myself jump out of bed, I make myself coffee, I am at my typewriter ten minutes after I am awake. I should have put in: I emptied my bladder, but I am still "young" and do not count that among the things that have to be done! But today I shall write down the visits to the loo, otherwise how can I compare my day with Maudie's? The articles I wrote, so tentatively, and without confidence, last year, have become a book. It is nearly finished. I said it would be done by the end of this month. It will be. *Because I said it would be.* That I do what I say gives me such strength! And then, there is a project no one knows about: a historical novel. It was Maudie gave me the idea. I think of that time as quite recent, my grandmother's; but Vera Rogers speaks of it as I might speak of, I don't know, let's say Waterloo. I plan a historical novel, conceived and written as one, about a milliner in London. I long to begin it.

I work hard until eight. Then I drink coffee and eat an apple, shower, am into my clothes, am off, in half an hour. I like to be there by nine, and I always am. Today, Phyllis was late. No Joyce. I collected mail for the three of us and called the secretary and it was done and out of the way by ten and the Conference. Phyllis most apologetic: she is like me, never late, never away, never ill. The Conference is as usual, lively and *wonderful.* It was Joyce who said it would be like a Think Tank. Everyone, from the PRs and the photographers' assistants to Editorial, encouraged to have ideas, no matter how wild, how crazy, because you never know. As usual, Phyllis writes it all down. It was she who volunteered to do it, and both Joyce and I knew, when she did, that she was thinking, it is a key position. Phyllis does not let these ideas disappear, she lists them, she has them duplicated on all our desks through all the departments. An idea that drops out of sight might emerge again a year later. Today somebody revived one, that the "uniforms for women" series should include the types of clothes worn, for instance, by female television announcers or women going out to dinners with their husbands for career reasons. That is, a certain kind of dinner gown, or style, as uniform . . . that makes my style a uniform! But I knew that! I wear it all the time. Even, said Freddie, in bed. I never wear anything but real silk, fine cotton, lawn, in bed . . . he used to joke that if I were to wear a nylon nightie, it would be the same for me as if I committed a crime.

Thinking about Freddie in the office, I surprised myself in tears, and was glad that I had said I would interview Martina, and got to Brown's Hotel just in time. I am *never* late. She easy to interview, professional, competent, no time wasted, full marks. I got back at twelve thirty, asked Phyllis if she would do the Eminent Women Luncheon. She said firmly no, she could not, I must. I am a stand-in for Joyce, who is the eminent woman, but she is ill, and Phyllis is of course right, was right to look surprised: for it would not be appropriate for Phyllis to do it. Once I would not have made such a slip, but the truth is, my mind is more and more on my two books, the one nearly finished, my lovely historical novel soon to be started.

I look at myself in the washroom. I forgot this morning about the Luncheon, no marks for that, I am slipping! A button hanging on its thread, and my nails were not perfect. I did my nails in the taxi. The Luncheon agreeable, I made a speech on behalf of Joyce.

On the way back from the Luncheon I go into Debenham's and up to the top floor, and there I look for Maudie's kind of vests, real wool, modest high petticoats, and long close-fitting knickers. I buy ten knickers, and three vests, three petticoats—because she wets her knickers now, and sometimes worse. Rush, rush, rush, but I'm back by three thirty. I phone to make an appointment with the hairdresser, another for the car. Phyllis said she felt awful. She looked it. So apologetic, such a criminal! For God's sake, go to bed, I said, and swept all her work from her desk to mine. I did the recipes, summer food, I did Young Fashion, went off with the photographers to Kenwood for a session, came back and worked by myself in the office, no one else there, until nine. I love being by myself, no telephones, nothing, only the watchman. He went out for Indian take-away, I asked him to join me, we had a quick supper on the corner of my desk. He's nice, George, I encouraged him to talk about his problems, won't go into that, but we can help, he needs a loan.

I was tired by then and suddenly longing for bed. I did some more work, rang Joyce in Wales, heard from her voice that she was better, but she was noncommittal. I don't give a damn, she said, when I asked if she were going to the States. She is saying, too, I don't give a damn about you either. This made me think about the condition of not giving a damn. On my desk, in the "Too difficult" basket, an article about stress, how enough stress can cause indifference. It is seen in war, in hard times. Suffer, suffer, emote, emote, and then suddenly, you don't care. I wanted this published. Joyce said, No, not enough people would recognize it. Irony!

I said good night to George at nine thirty, and got a taxi to where I leave my car, and drove up towards home, thinking, no, no, I can't go in to Maudie, I simply cannot. When I banged, I was irritable, I was tired, I was thinking, I hope she is in the lavatory and doesn't hear. But when she opened, I could see by her face . . . I switched on everything I have, and made myself crash in, all gaiety and liveliness, because I am afraid of her black moods, for once she starts I can't shift her out of them. That is why I arrived, female Father Christmas, HM the Queen Mum, all radiant, I have to stop her muttering and raging.

When I reach her back room, it is hot and smelly, the smell hits me, but I make myself smile at the fire. I see from her face what is needful, and I go into the kitchen. I was nearly sick. I whirl around the kitchen, because I know the Indian grocer is about to close, and I run across the road, saying, "Please, just another minute, I need stuff for Mrs Fowler." He is patient and kind, but he is a grey-violet colour from tiredness. Sometimes he is in here from eight until eleven at night. Often by himself. He is educating three sons and two daughters . . . He asks, "How is she?" I say, "I think she isn't well." He says, as always, "It is time her people looked after her."

When I get back, I cut up fish for the cat. It is no good, I cannot make myself appreciate cats, though that makes me an insensitive boor. I clean up the cat's mess, I get the brandy and glasses. I realize I have forgotten the vests and knickers in the office. Well, tomorrow will do. I take out her commode, because she is *not* looking at it, with a trembling pride on her face I know only too well by now. As I wash it, I think, here's something very wrong. I shall have to tell Vera Rogers. I rinse the inside of the commode carefully and use a lot of disinfectant.

When I sit down opposite her, with brandy for her and me, I fully mean to tell her about the Luncheon, with all the famous women, she'd like that, but—that was the last I remember, until I came to myself, out of such a deep sleep I could not find myself when I woke. I was looking at a yellow little witch in a smelly hot cave, by her roaring fire, her yellow shanks showing, for she had no knickers on and her legs were apart, and on her lap she held my hat, and she was using it for some bad purpose . . . I was terrified, and then suddenly I remembered, I am Jane Somers, I am here, in Maudie's back room, and I fell asleep.

She did not want me to go. She made an excuse about batteries for her torch. I went to the door into the street, and it was morning. We stood there, looking up—oh, England, dismal and drear, a grey wet dawn. It was four thirty when I got home. I had a long, long proper bath, and then to my book again.

But I cannot concentrate on it. I am thinking about Maudie's "This is the best time of my life". What I cannot stand is, that I believe she means it. My running in at the end of the day, an hour, two hours, so little, is enough to make her say that. I want to howl when I think of it. And too, I feel so trapped. She might live for years and years, people live to be a hundred these days, and I am a prisoner of her "This is the best time of my life", lovely gracious Janna, running in and out, with smiles and prezzies.

I wrote Maudie's day because I want to understand. I *do* understand a lot more about her, but is it true? I can only write what I have experienced myself, heard her say, observed . . . I sometimes wake with one hand quite numb . . . But what else is there I cannot know about? I think that just as I could never have imagined she would say, "This is the best time of my life", and the deprivation and loneliness behind it, so I cannot know what is behind her muttered "It is dreadful, dreadful", and the rages that make her blue eyes blaze and glitter.

And I see that I did *not* write down, in Janna's day, about going to the loo, a quick pee here, a quick shit, washing one's hands . . . All day this animal has to empty itself, you have to brush your hair, wash your hands, bathe. I dash a cup under a tap and rinse out a pair of panties, it all takes a few minutes . . . But that is because I am "young", only forty-nine.

What makes poor Maudie labour and groan all through her day, the drudge and drag of *maintenance*. I was going to say, For me it is nothing; but the fact is, once I did have my real proper baths every night, once every Sunday night I maintained and polished my beautiful perfect clothes, maintained and polished *me*, and now I don't, I can't. It is too much for me.

Late summer, how I hate it, blowzy and damp, dowdy and dusty, dull green, dull skies; the sunlight, when there is any, a maggot breeder; maggots under my dustbin, because I hadn't touched my own home for days.

Maudie has been ill again. Again I've been in, twice a day, before going to work and after work. Twice a day, she has stood by the table, leaning on it, weight on her palms, naked, while I've poured water over her till all the shit and smelly urine has gone. *The stench.* Her body, a cage of bones, yellow, wrinkled, her crotch like a little girl's, no hair, but long grey hairs in her armpits. I've been worn out with it. I said to her, "Maudie, they'd send you in a nurse to wash you," and she screamed at me, "Get out then, I didn't ask you."

We were both so tired and overwrought, we've been screeching at each other like . . . what? Out of literature, I say "fishwives", but she's no fishwife, a prim, respectable old body, or that's what she's been in disguise for three decades. I've seen a photograph, Maudie at sixty-five, the image of disapproving rectitude . . . I don't think I would have liked her then. She had said to herself, I like children, they like me, my sister won't let me near her now she's not breeding, she doesn't need my services. So Maudie put an advert in the Willesden paper, and a widower answered. He had three children, eight, nine, ten. Maudie was given the sofa in the kitchen, and her meals, in return for: cleaning the house, mending his clothes, the children's clothes, cooking three meals a day and baking, looking after the children. He was a fishmonger. When he came in at lunchtime, if he found Maudie sitting having a rest, he said to her, Haven't you got anything to do? He gave her two pounds a week to feed them all on, and when I said it was impossible, she said she managed. He brought home the fish for nothing, and you could buy bread and potatoes. No, he wasn't poor, but, said Maudie, he didn't know how to behave, that was his trouble. And Maudie stuck it, because of the children. Then he said to her, Will you come to the pictures with me? She went, and she saw the neighbours looking at them. She knew what they were thinking, and she couldn't have that. She cleaned the whole house, top to bottom, made sure everything was mended, baked bread, put out things for tea, and left a note: I am called to my sister's, who is ill, yours truly, Maude Fowler.

But then she took her pension, and sometimes did small jobs on the side.

The Maudie who wore herself "to a stick and a stone" was this judging, critical female, with a tight cold mouth.

Maudie and I shouted at each other, as if we were family, she saying, "Get out then, get out, but I'm not having those Welfare women in here," and I shouting, "Maudie, you're impossible, you're awful, I don't know what I'm going to do with you."

And then, once, I burst out laughing, it seemed so ridiculous, she there, stark naked, spitting anger at me, and I, rinsing off her shit and saying, "And what about your ears?"

She went silent and trembling. "*Why are you laughing at me?*"

"I'm not, I'm laughing at us. Look at us, screaming at each other!"

She stepped back out of the basin she had been standing in, gazing at me, in angry appeal.

I put the big towel around her, that I'd brought from my

bathroom, a pink cloud of a towel, and began gently drying her.

Tears finding their way through her wrinkles . . .

"Come on, Maudie, for God's sake, let's laugh, better than crying."

"It's terrible, terrible, terrible," she muttered, looking in front of her, eyes wide and bright. Trembling, shivering . . . "It's terrible, terrible."

These last three weeks I've thrown away all the new knickers I bought her, filthy and disgusting, bought two dozen more, and I've shown her how to fill them full of cotton wool as she puts them on.

So, she's back in napkins.

Terrible, terrible, terrible . . .

It is the end of August.

I am lying in bed writing this with the diary propped on my chest.

Just after writing the last *terrible*, I woke in the night, and it was as if my lower back had a metal bar driven into it. I could not move at all from my waist down, the pain was so awful.

It was dark, the window showed confused dull light, and when I tried to shift my back I screamed. After that I lay still.

I lay thinking. I knew what it was, lumbago: Freddie had it once, and I knew what to expect. I did not nurse him, of course, we employed someone, and while I shut it out, or tried to, I knew he was in awful pain, for he could not move at all for a week.

I have not been ill since the children's things, like measles. *I have never been really ill.* At the most a cold, a sore throat, and I never took any notice of those.

What I was coming to terms with is that I have no friends. No one I can ring up and say, Please help, I need help.

Once, it was Joyce: but a woman with children, a husband, a job, and a house . . . I am sure I would never have said, "Please come and nurse me." Of course not. I could not ring my sister—children, house, husband, good works, and anyway she doesn't like me. Phyllis: I kept coming back to Phyllis, wondering why I was so reluctant, and thinking there is something wrong with me that I don't want to ask her, she's quite decent and nice really . . . But when I thought of Vera Rogers, then I knew Vera Rogers is the one person I know who I could say to, "Please come and help." But she has a husband, children, and a job, and the last thing she wants is an extra "case".

I managed, after half an hour of agonized reaching and striving, to get the telephone off the bed table and on to my chest. The telephone book was out of reach, was on the floor, I could not get to it. I rang Inquiries, got the number of my doctors, got their night number, left a message. Meanwhile, I was working everything out. The one person who would be delighted—*at last*—to nurse me was Mrs Penny. Over my dead body. I am prepared to admit I am neurotic, anything you like, but I cannot admit her, *will not* . . .

I would have liked a private doctor, but Freddie was always a bit of a socialist, he wanted National Health. I didn't care since I don't get ill. I wasn't looking forward to the doctor's visit, but he wasn't bad. Young, rather anxious, tentative. His first job, probably.

He got the key from the downstairs flat, waking Mrs M., but she was nice about it. He let himself in, came into my room, "Well, and what is wrong?" I told him, lumbago; and what I wanted: he must organize a nurse, twice a day, I needed a bedpan, I needed a thermos—I told him exactly.

He sat on the bottom of my bed, looking at me, smiling a little. I was wondering if he was seeing: an old woman, an elderly woman, a middle-aged woman? I know now it depends entirely on the age of a person, what they see.

"For all that, I think I'd better examine you," he said, and bent over, pulled back the clothes which I was clutching to my chin, and after one or two prods and pushes, to which I could not help responding by groaning, he said, "It's lumbago all right, and as you know there's nothing for it, it will get better in its own good time. And do you want pain-killers?"

"Indeed I do," I said, "and soon, because I can't stand it."

He produced enough to go on with. He wrote out a prescription, and then said that it was unlikely he could get a nurse before evening, and what did I propose to do in the meantime? I said that if I didn't pee soon I would wet the bed. He thought this over, then offered to catheterize me. He did—quickly, painlessly. He had to find a kilner jar in the kitchen, no pot of course, and as there seemed no end to the stream of pee, he ran into the kitchen and searched frantically for anything, came back with a mixing bowl, into which the end of the rubber tube was transferred. Just in time. "Goodness," said he, admiring the quarts of pee.

"How are you going to manage," he asked, "if there's no nurse? Isn't there a neighbour? How about someone on this floor?"

"*No*," I said. I recognized on his face the look I've seen on, for instance, Vera's, and have felt on mine: toleration for unavoidable eccentricity, battiness.

"I could get you into hospital . . ."

"No, no, no," I moaned, sounding like Maudie.

"Oh, very well."

Off he went, cheerful, tired, professional. You'd not know he was a doctor at all, he could be an accountant or a technician. Once I would not have liked this, would have wanted bedside manner and authority—but now I see Freddie's point.

From the door, he said, "You were a nurse, weren't you?"

This made me laugh, and I said, "Oh, don't make me laugh, I shall die."

But if he can say *that*, then it is Maudie I have to thank for it. What would Freddie think of me now?

A nurse came in about ten, and a routine was established—around the animal's needs. The animal has to get rid of x pints of liquid and a half pound of shit; the animal has to ingest so much liquid and so much cellulose and calories. For two weeks, I was exactly like Maudie, exactly like all these old people, anxiously obsessively wondering, am I going to hold out, no, don't have a cup of tea, the nurse might not come, I might wet the bed . . . At the end of the two weeks, when at last I could dispense with bedpans (twice a day) and drag myself to the loo, I knew that for two weeks I had experienced, but absolutely, their helplessness. I was saying to myself, like

Maudie, Well, I never once wet the bed, that's something.

Visitors: Vera Rogers, on the first day, for I rang her saying she had to get someone to Maudie. She came in first before going to Maudie. I looked at her from where I lay absolutely flat, my back in spasm, her gentle, humorous pleasant little face, her rather tired clothes, her hands—a bit grubby, but she had been dealing with some old biddy who won't go into hospital, though she has flu.

I told her that I thought there is more wrong with Maudie than the runs, found myself telling her about her awful slimy smelly stools. And I said that it was no good expecting Maudie to go into hospital, she would die rather.

"Then," said Vera, "that is probably what she will do."

I saw she was anxious, because she had said that: sat watching my face. She made us some tea, though I didn't dare drink more than a mouthful, and we talked. *She* talked. I could see, being tactful. Soon I understood she was warning me about something. Talking about how many of the old people she looks after die of cancer. It is an epidemic of cancer, she said—or that is what it feels like to her.

At last I said to her, "Do you think Maudie has cancer?"

"I can't say that, I'm not a doctor. But she's so thin, she's just bones. And sometimes she looks so yellow. And I've got to call in her doctor. I must, to cover myself, you see. They are always jumping on us, for neglect or something. If I didn't have to consider that, I'd leave her alone. But I don't want to find myself in the newspapers all of a sudden, Social Worker Leaves 90-Year-Old Woman to Die Alone of Cancer."

"Perhaps you could try a nurse again, to give her a wash? You could try her with a Home Help?"

"If she'll let us in at all," says Vera. And laughs. She says, "You have to laugh, or you'd go mad. They are their own worst enemies."

"And you must tell her I am ill, and that is why I can't get in to her."

Vera says, "You do realize she won't believe it, she'll think it is a plot?"

"Oh no," I groan, for I couldn't stop groaning, the pain was so dreadful (*terrible, terrible, terrible!*), "please, Vera, do try and get it into her head . . ."

And there I lie, with my back knotted, my back like iron, and me sweating and groaning, while Vera tells me that "they" are all paranoid, in one way or another, always suspect plots, and always turn against their nearest and dearest. Since I am Maudie's nearest, it seems, I can expect it.

"You are very fond of her," announced Vera. "Well, I can understand it, she's got something. Some of them have, even at their worst you can see it in them. Others of course . . ." And she sighed, a real human, non-professional sigh. I've seen Vera Rogers, flying along the pavements between one "case" and another, her hands full of files and papers, worried, frowning, harassed, and then Vera Rogers *with* a "case", not a care in sight, smiling, listening, all the time in the world . . . and so she was with me, at least that first visit. But she has been in several times, and she stopped needing to cosset and reassure, we have been talking, really talking about her work, sometimes so funny I had to ask her to stop, I could not afford to laugh, laughing was so painful.

Phyllis visited, once. There she was (my successor?), a self-sufficient cool young woman, rather pretty, and I had only to compare her with Vera. I took the opportunity of doing what I know she's been wanting and needing. She has been attempting my "style", and I've told her, no, never never compromise, always the best, and if you have to pay the earth, then that's it. I looked carefully at her dress: a "little dress", flowered crêpe, skimpy, quite nice, and I said to her, "Phyllis, if that's the kind of dress you want, then at least have it made, use decent material, or go to . . ." I spent a couple of hours, gave her my addresses, dressmaker, hairdresser, knitters. She was thoughtful, concentrated, she very much wanted what I was offering. Oh, she'll do it all right, and with intelligence, no blind copying. But all the time she was there, I was in agony, and I could no more have said to her, "Phyllis, I'm in pain, please help, perhaps we could together shift me a centimetre, it might help . . ." than Freddie or my mother could have asked me for help.

And as for asking for a bedpan . . .

Mrs Penny saw my door open, and crept in, furtive with guilt, smiling, frowning, and sighing by turns. "Oh, you're ill, why didn't you tell me, you should ask, I'm always only too ready to . . ."

She sat in the chair Phyllis had just vacated, and began to talk. She talked. She talked. I had heard all of it before, word by word she repeats herself: India, how she and her husband braved it out when the Raj crumbled; her servants, the climate, the clothes, her dogs, her ayah. I could not keep my attention on it, and, watching her, knew that she had no idea whether I was listening or not. Her eyes stared, fixed, in front of her at nothing. She spilled out words, words, words. I understood suddenly that she was hypnotized. She had hypnotized herself. This thought interested me, and I was wondering how often we all hypnotize ourselves without knowing it, when I fell asleep. I woke, it must have been at least half an hour later, and she was still talking compulsively, eyes fixed. She had not noticed I had dropped off.

I was getting irritated, and tired. First Phyllis, now Mrs Penny, both energy-drainers. I tried to interrupt, once, twice, finally raised my voice: "Mrs Penny!" She went on talking, heard my voice retrospectively, stopped, looked scared.

"Oh dear," she murmured.

"Mrs Penny, I must rest now."

"Oh dear, oh dear, oh dear . . ." Her eyes wandered off from me, she looked around the room, from which she feels excluded because of my coldness, she sighed. A silence. Then, like a wind rising in the distance, she murmured, "And then when we came to England . . ."

"Mrs Penny," I said firmly.

She stood up, looking as if she had stolen something. Well, she had.

"Oh dear," she said. "Oh dear. But you must let me know any time you need anything . . ." And she crept out again, leaving the door open.

I made sure after that, that whoever went out, shut it; and I took no notice when the handle turned, timid but insistent, and I heard her call, Mrs Somers, Mrs Somers, can I get you anything?

Supposing I were to write *Mrs Penny's day*? Oh no, no, no, I really can't face that, I can't.

I have been on the telephone for hours with Joyce in Wales. We have not been able to talk at all, not for months. But now she rings me, I ring her, and we talk. Sometimes we are quiet, for minutes, thinking of all the fields, the hedges, the mountains, *the time* between us. We talk about her marriage, her children, my marriage, my mother, our work. We do not talk about Maudie. She makes it absolutely clear, *no*. She has said that she is going to the States. Not, now, because she is afraid of being alone when she is old, because she *knows* she *is* alone and does not care. But it is the children, after all the insecurity, the misery, they want two parents in one house. Even though they are nearly grown up? I cannot help insisting, and Joyce laughs at me.

I said to her, "Joyce, I want to tell you about Maudie, you know, the old woman."

And Joyce said, "Look, I don't want to know, do you understand?"

I said to her, "You don't want to talk about the one real thing that has happened to me?"

"It didn't *happen* to you"—fierce and insistent—"for some reason or other you made it happen."

"But it is important to me, it is."

"It must be to *her*, that's for certain," said she, with that dry resentment you hear in people's voices when sensing imposition.

I said to her, "Don't you think it is odd, Joyce, how all of us, we take it absolutely for granted that old people are something to be *outwitted*, like an enemy, or a trap? Not that we owe them anything?"

"I don't expect my kids to look after me."

And I felt despair, because now I feel it is an old gramophone record. "That's what you say now, not what you will say then."

"I'm going to bow out, when I get helpless, I'm going to take my leave."

"That's what you say now."

"How do you know, why are you sure about me?"

"Because I know now that everyone says the same things, at stages in their lives."

"And so I'm going to end up, some crabby old witch, an incontinent old witch—is that what you are saying?"

"Yes."

"I can tell you this, I am pleased about one thing, I'm putting thousands of miles between myself and my father. He's an old pet, but enough's enough."

"Who's going to look after him?"

"He'll go into a Home, I expect. That is what *I* shall expect."

"Perhaps."

And so we talk, Joyce and I, for hours, I lying flat on my back in London, trying to outwit the next spasm that will knot my back up, she in an old chintz chair in a cottage on a mountainside, "on leave" from *Lilith*. But she has sent in her resignation.

I do not ring up my sister. I do not ring up my sister's children. When I think about them I feel angry. I don't know why. I feel about these infantile teenagers as Joyce does about me and Maudie: Yes, all right, all right, but not now, I'll think about it later, I simply haven't the energy.

Four weeks of doing nothing . . .

But I have been thinking. *Thinking*. Not the snap, snap, intuitions-and-sudden-judgements kind, but long slow thoughts. About Maudie. About *Lilith*. About Joyce. About Freddie. About those brats of Georgie's.

Before I went back into the office, I visited Maudie. Her hostile little face, but it was a white face, not a yellow one, and that made me feel better about her at once. "Hello," I said, and she gave me a startled look because I have lost so much weight.

"So you really have been ill, then, have you?" said she, in a soft troubled voice, as we sat opposite each other beside that marvellous fire. When I think of her, I see the fire: that sordid horrible room, but the fire makes it glow and welcome you.

"Yes, of course I have, Maudie. Otherwise I'd have been in."

Her face turned aside, her hand up to shield it from me.

"That doctor came in," she said at last, in a small lost voice. "*She* called him in."

"I know, she told me."

"Well, if she is a friend of yours!"

"You are looking better than you were, so it might have something to do with the doctor!"

"I put the pills in the toilet!"

"All of them?"

A laugh broke through her anger. "You're sharp!"

"But you *are* looking better."

"So you say."

"Well," I said, taking the risk, "it could be a question of your dying before you have to."

She stiffened all over, sat staring away from me into the fire. It seemed a long time. Then she sighed and looked straight at me. A wonderful look, frightened but brave, sweet, pleading, grateful, and with a shrewd humour there as well.

"You think that might be it?"

"For the sake of a few pills," I said.

"They deaden my mind so."

"Make yourself take what you can of them."

And that was a year ago. If I had had time to keep this diary properly, it would have seemed a builder's yard, bits and odds stacked up, lying about, nothing in place, one thing not more important than another. You wander through (I visited one for an article last week) and see a heap of sand there, a pile of glass here, some random steel girders, sacks of cement, crowbars. That is the point of a diary, the bits and pieces of events, all muddled together. But now I look back through the year and begin to know what was important.

And the most important of all was something I hardly noticed. Niece Kate turned up one night, looking twenty and not fifteen, the way they can these days, but seemed crazy, stammering and posing and rolling her eyes. She had run away from home to live with me, she said; and she was going to be a model. Firm but kind (I thought and think), I said she was going right back home, and if she ever came to spend so much as an afternoon with me, she could be sure I wasn't going to be like her mother, I wouldn't wash a cup up after her. Off she went, sulking. Telephone call from Sister Georgie: How can you be so lacking in ordinary human sympathies? Rubbish, I said. Telephone call from niece Jill. She said, "I'm ringing you to tell you that I'm not at all like Kate."

"I'm glad to hear it," I said.

"If I lived with you, you wouldn't have to baby me. Mother makes me tired, I'm on your side."

"Not as tired as she must permanently be."

"Aunt Jane, I want to come and spend the weekend."

I could easily hear, from her tone, how *she* saw glamorous Aunt Jane, in Trendy London, with her smart goings-on.

She came. I like her, I admit. A tall, slim, rather lovely girl. Willowy is the word, I think. Will droop if she's not careful. Dark straight hair: could look lank and dull. Vast grey eyes: mine.

I watched her eyes at work on everything in my flat: to copy in her own home, I wondered?—teenage rebellion, perhaps; but no, it was to plan how she would fit in here, with me.

"I want to come and live here with you, Aunt Jane."

"You want to work in *Lilith*, become part of my smart and elegant and amazing life?"

"I'm eighteen. I don't want to go to university, you didn't, did you?"

"You mean, with me as your passport to better things, you don't need a degree?"

"Well, yes."

"You've done well in your exams?"

"I will do well, I promise. I'm taking them in the summer."

"Well, let's think about it then."

I didn't think about it. It was all too bizarre: Sister Georgie ensconced in my life, that was how I saw it.

But Jill came again, and I made a point of taking her with me to visit Maudie, saying only that she was an old friend. Maudie has been in better health recently. Her main misery, the incontinence, is checked, she is doing her own shopping, she is eating well. I have been enjoying flying in and out to gossip over a cup of tea. But I am so used to her, have forgotten how she must strike others. Because of this stranger, the beautiful clean girl, Maudie was stiff, reproachful for exposing her. A cold aloof little person, she said yes and no, did not offer us tea, tried to hide the stains down the front of her dress where she has spilled food.

Niece Jill was polite, and secretly appalled. Not at old age; Sister Georgie's good works will have seen to it that her children will not find that a surprise; but because she had to associate old age and good works with glamorous Aunt Jane.

That evening, eating supper together, she studied me with long covert shrewd looks, while she offered prattle about her siblings and their merry ways.

"How often do you go in to see her?" she inquired delicately enough; and I knew how important a moment this was.

"Every day and sometimes twice," I said at once, with firmness.

"Do you have a lot of friends in, do you go out for parties, dinner parties?"

"Hardly ever. I work too hard."

"But not too hard to visit that old   to visit . . ."

"Mrs Fowler. No."

I took her shopping to buy some decent clothes. She wanted to impress me with her taste, and she did.

But at the time Sister Georgie and her offspring were a very long way down on my agenda.

I have worked, oh how I have worked this year, how I have enjoyed it all. They made me editor. I did not say I would only take it for a year or so, was accepting it only for the perks, the better pension, had other plans. Have finally understood that I am not ambitious, would have been happy to work for ever, just as things were, with Joyce.

Joyce left to live in America. Before she went, a dry, indifferent telephone call.

I said to Phyllis, You'd better have Joyce's desk, you have done her work long enough. She was installed in half an hour. Her looks of triumph. I watched her, had my face shielded with my hand. (Like Maudie.) Hiding my thoughts.

Cut your losses, Janna, cut your losses, Jane!

I said, When you are settled, we should discuss possible changes. Her sharp alert lift of the head: danger. She does not want changes. Her dreams have been of inheriting what she was wanting so long and envying.

Envy. Jealousy and envy, I've always used them interchangeably. A funny thing: once a child would have been taught all this, the seven deadly sins, but in our charming times a middle-aged woman has to look up envy in a dictionary. Well, Phyllis is not jealous, and I don't believe she ever was. It was not the closeness and friendship of Joyce and me she wanted, but the position of power. Phyllis is envious. All day, her sharp cold criticisms, cutting everyone, everything, down. She started on Joyce. I found myself blazing up into anger, Shut up, I said, you can be catty about Joyce to other people, not me.

Discussions for months, enjoyable for us all, about whether to change *Lilith* for *Martha*. Is *Lilith* the girl for the difficult, anxious eighties?

Arguments for *Martha*. We need something more workaday, less of an incitement to envy, an image of willing, adaptable, intelligent service.

Arguments for *Lilith*. People are conditioned to need glamour. In hard times we need our fun. People read fashion in fashion magazines as they read romantic novels, for escape. They don't intend to follow fashion, they enjoy the idea of it.

I did not have strong opinions one way or the other. Our circulation is only slightly falling. *Lilith* it will remain.

The contents won't change.

I brought home the last twelve issues of *Lilith* to analyse them.

It is a funny thing, while Joyce and I *were Lilith*, making everything happen, our will behind it, I did not have uneasy moments, asking, Is the life going out of it, is the impetus still there, is it still on a rising current? I know that the impetus is not there now, *Lilith* is like a boat being taken on a wave, but what made the wave is far behind.

Two thirds of *Lilith* is useful, informative, performs a service.

In this month's issue: One. An article about alcoholism.

*　　*　　*

Nearly all our ideas are filched from *New Society* and *New Scientist*. (But then this is true of most of the serious mags and papers.) I once fought a battle with Joyce for us to acknowledge our sources, but failed: Joyce said it would put off our readers. Phyllis rewrote the article, and called it: The Hidden Danger to You and Your Family. Two. An article about abortion laws in various countries. Three. My article about the Seventeeth-Century Kitchen. All garlic and spices! Fruit and meat mixed. Salads with everything in the garden in them. And then the usual features, fashion, food, drink, books, theatre.

I have started my historical novel. Oh, I know only too well why we need our history prettied up. It would be intolerable to have the long heavy *weight* of the truth there, all grim and painful. No, my story about the milliners of London will be romantic. (After all, when Maudie comes to die she won't be thinking of trailing out to that freezing smelly lavatory, but of the joyous green fields of Kilburn, and of her German boy, and of the larks the apprentices got up to as they made their lovely hats, good enough for Paris. She will, too, I suppose, be thinking of "her man". But that is an intolerable idea, I can't stand for that.)

Yesterday, as I drove home, I saw Maudie in the street, an ancient crone, all in black, nose and chin meeting, fierce grey brows, muttering and cursing as she pushed her basket along, and some small boys baiting her.

The thing that at the time I thought was going to be worst turned out not bad at all. Even useful. Even, I believe, pleasurable.

I was standing at the counter of the radio and TV shop down the road, buying a decent radio for Maudie. Beside me, waiting patiently, was an old woman, her bag held open while she muddled inside it, looking for money.

The Indian assistant watched her, and so did I. I was at once matching what I saw with my first meeting with Maudie.

"I don't think I've got it here, I haven't got what it costs," she said in a frightened hopeless way, and she pushed a minute radio towards him. She meant him to take it to pay for repairs he had done on it. She turned, slowly and clumsily, to leave the shop.

I thought it all out fast, as I stood there. This time I was not helpless in front of an enormous demand because of inexperience, I had known at first look about the old thing. The dusty grey grimy look. The sour reek. The slow carefulness.

I paid for her radio, hastened after her, and caught her up as she was standing waiting to be helped across the street. I went home with her.

For the pleasure of the thing, I rang Puss-in-Boots when I got home.

"You are the person I saw with Mrs Fowler?"

"Yes, I am," I said.

A silence.

"Do you mind if I say something?" said she, efficient, but not without human sympathy. "So often we find well-meaning people making things so much worse without intending to."

"Worse for whom?"

I was hoping she might laugh, but she is not Vera Rogers.

"What I mean is, specifically, that often well-meaning people take an interest in some geria— . . . some old person, but really it is a hang-up of their own, you see they are working out their own problems, really."

"I would say that that is almost bound to be true, in one way or another," said I, enjoying every minute of this. "But while it might or might not be bad for me, the poor old geriatric in question is likely to be pleased, since she is obviously friendless and alone."

Another silence. Evidently she felt obliged to think out my remarks to their conclusions, in the light of her training. At length she said, "I wonder if you'd find an Encounter Group helpful?"

"Miss Whitfield," I said, "there's this old woman, don't you think you should drop in and visit her?"

"If she's so bad, why hasn't her doctor referred her?"

"As you know, most of these doctors never go near the old people on their lists, and the old people don't go near the doctors, because they are afraid of them. Rightly or wrongly. Afraid of being *sent away*."

"That is really a very old-fashioned concept."

"The fact is, at some point they do get sent away."

"Only when there is no other alternative."

"Well, in the meantime, there's poor Annie Reeves."

"I'll look into it," said she. "Thank you so much for involving yourself when you must be so busy."

I then rang Vera.

Vera said, What was her name, her address, her age, her condition. Yes, she knew about Mrs Bates, who lived downstairs, but Annie Reeves had always refused any of the Services.

"She won't refuse them now," I said.

Vera and I met at the house. I took a morning off work. The door was opened by Mrs Bates, in her fluffy blue dressing gown, and her hair in a blue net.

She looked severely at me, and at Vera. "They took Mrs Reeves to hospital last night," she said. "She fell down. Upstairs. It's not for the first time. But she hurt her knees. So it would seem."

Between Vera and me and Mrs Bates vibrated all kinds of comprehension, and Mrs Bates's disapproving looks were meant to be seen by us.

"Well, perhaps it's a good thing, we can get her rooms cleaned."

"If you think you can do thirty years' cleaning in a morning," she stated, standing aside to let us in.

The house was built about 1870. Nothing cramped or stinted. A good staircase, with decent landings. Annie Reeves's place at the top full of light and air. Nice rooms, well proportioned, large windows.

The front room, overlooking the street, larger than the other. Fireplace, blocked up. A brownish wallpaper, which, examined, showed a nice pattern of brown and pink leaves and flowers, very faded and stained. Above the picture rail the paper was ripping off and flapping loose because water had run in from the roof. There was an old hard chair, with torn blue cushions where the stuffing showed, near the fire. Some dressing tables and a chest of drawers. Linoleum, cracked and discoloured. And the bed—but I feel I cannot really do justice to that bed. Double bed, with brown wood headboard and footboard—how *can* I describe it? The mattress had been worn by a body lying on it always in one place so that the ticking had gone, and the coarse hair inside was a mass of rough lumps and hollows. The pillows had no covers, and were like the mattress, lumps of feathers protruding. There was a tangle of filthy dirty blankets. It was *dirty*, it was disgusting. And yet we could see no lice in it. It was like a very old bird's nest, that had been in use for many years. It was like—I cannot imagine how anyone could sleep in it, or on it.

We opened the drawers. Well, that I had seen before, with Maudie, though these were worse. And I wondered, and I wonder now, how are these hoards of rubbish seen by those who let them accumulate?

One of Annie Reeves's drawers contained—and I make this list for the record: half an old green satinet curtain, with cigarette holes in it; two broken brass curtain rings; a skirt, stained, ripped across the front, of white cotton; two pairs of men's socks, full of holes; a bra, size 32, of a style I should judge was about 1937, in pink cotton; an unopened packet of sanitary towels, in towelling—never having seen these, I was fascinated, of course; three white cotton handkerchiefs spotted with blood, the memory of a decades-old nosebleed; two pairs of pink celanese knickers that had been put away unwashed, medium size; three cubes of Oxo; a tortoise-shell shoehorn; a tin of dried and cracked whiting for ladies' summer shoes; three chiffon scarves, pink, blue, and green; a packet of letters postmarked 1910; a cutting from the *Daily Mirror* announcing World War Two; some bead necklaces, all broken; a blue satin petticoat which had been slit up both sides to the waist to accommodate increasing girth; some cigarette ends.

This had been stirred around and around, it seemed, so that the mess would have to be picked apart, strand by strand. Well, we didn't have time to deal with that: first things first.

Vera and I went into action. I drove to the first furniture shop and bought a good single bed and a mattress. I had luck, they were delivering that morning. I came back behind the van with two young men to make sure they did deliver, and they carried it upstairs. When they saw what was there, they looked incredulous. As well they might. I bribed them to take the old bed down, with the mattress, to the dustbins. Meanwhile, Vera had bought blankets, sheets, pillows, towels. There was exactly half of one old towel in the place, and it was black. Looking out of the filthy windows, we could see neighbours in their gardens speculating over the mattress, with shakes of the head and tight lips. Vera and I wrestled the mattress to the top of my car, and we took it to the municipal rubbish heap.

When we got back the Special Cleaning Team were on the doorstep. Since the place was far beyond the scope of ordinary Home Helps, this flying squad of intrepid experts had been called in by Vera. They were two weedy young men, amiable and lackadaisical, probably from too much take-away junk. They stood about upstairs in the front room, smiling and grimacing at the filth, and saying, "But what can we do?"

"You can start with buckets of hot water and soda," I said. Vera was already looking humorous.

I have not yet mentioned the kitchen. When you went into it, it seemed normal. A good square wooden table in the middle, an adequate gas stove, two very good wooden chairs, each worth at present prices what I would pay for a month's food, ripped and faded curtains, now black, once green. But the floor, the floor! As you walked over it, it gave tackily, and on examination there was a thick layer of hardened grease and dirt.

The two heroes winced about on the sticky lino, and said, How could they use hot water when there wasn't any?

"You heat it on the stove," said Vera, mildly.

"Look," I said, "aren't you for the rough work the Home Helps can't do?"

"Yes, but there are limits, aren't there?" said one of them reproachfully.

"Someone has got to do it," I said.

They did sweep the front room, and pushed a mop hastily over the floor. But over the kitchen floor, they went on strike. "Sorry," said they, and went off, good-natured to the end.

Vera and I pushed the big table out, with the dresser and the chairs, though they were stuck to the lino with decades of grease. We prized up the lino: it would not come up easily. Under this layer was another, and between them was a half-inch layer of grease and dirt. In all we prized up three layers of lino.

Then Vera had to go home to her family problems.

That weekend I scrubbed the floors, washed down walls and ceilings, emptied drawers, scrubbed them, cleaned a stove encrusted with thirty years of dirt. Finally, I filled plastic bags with this silent story, the detritus of half a lifetime, and took them to the municipal dump.

Mrs Bates marked my comings and goings up and down the stairs, sitting in her little parlour, drinking tea, and from time to time offering me a cup.

"No, I haven't been up there, not for ten years," she said. "If you give her an inch, it's make me a cup of tea, fetch me this and that. I'm nearly ten years older than she is. Are you going to be her Good Neighbour, may I ask? No?"

Her rosy old face was distressed, reproachful. "You had her old mattress out there for everyone to see. Outside *my* place—they'll think . . . And your hands, all in that dirt and muck . . ."

What was upsetting her as much as anything was that it was not for me, such a lady and all, to do this filthy work.

She gave me a key. I took it knowing she was offering me more than I was ready to take. Oh, I'm under no illusions now! Every street has in it several, perhaps a dozen, old women, old men, who can only just cope, or suddenly can't cope; who dream of absent daughters and sons and granddaughters, and anyone coming near them must beware, beware! For into that terrible vacuum you can be sucked before you know it. No, I shall not put myself, again, into the situation I am with Maudie, who has only one friend in the world.

I drop in, for a few minutes, in the character they assigned me, because I am not in any of their categories, am unexplainable, of wayward impulsive benevolence. My main problem is that Maudie should never know I am visiting anyone else, for it would be a betrayal. Eliza Bates, Annie Reeves, live around the corner from Maudie.

If I take Annie a present, I have to take Eliza one, for Eliza watches me as I go up past her to the top floor. Eliza was in service, and knows what is good, and gets it, thus exemplifying, I suppose, To those who have will be given. I take her bread from the good bakery, a new romantic novel, a certain brand of Swiss chocolate, chaste white roses with green fern. Annie knows what she likes and that British is best, and I take her chocolate like sweet mud, a sickening wine that is made specially for old ladies, and small pretty flowers tied with satin ribbon.

Annie Reeves was in hospital for six weeks. She bruised a leg, but although they tell her she could walk again properly, she is on a walking frame and refuses. She is now a prisoner at the top of that house, with a commode that must be emptied, and Meals on Wheels, Home Help, a nurse.

Eliza Bates disapproves utterly of Annie Reeves, who let herself go, who was drinking up there by herself—oh yes, Eliza Bates knew what went on!—who let the dirt accumulate until Eliza sat imagining she could hear the bugs crawling in the walls and the mice scuttling. "I'm not like *her*," says Eliza, firmly, to me, with a little churchy sniff.

"I'm not like *her*," says Annie, meaning that Eliza is a hypocrite, she never was interested in church until her husband died, and now look at her.

Annie yearns for the friendship of Eliza. Eliza has spent years isolating herself from the woman upstairs who has so rapidly gone to pieces, and who is not ashamed now of stumping about on a frame when there's no need, and of getting an army of social workers in to her every day. They call each other Mrs Bates, Mrs Reeves. They have lived in this house forty years.

The Welfare are trying to "rehabilitate" Annie. I would have reacted, only a few weeks ago, to the invitation to this campaign, with derision, even with cries of But it is cruelty! Since then, I've seen Eliza's life, and understand why these experts with the old will fight the lethargy of age even in a man or woman of ninety or more.

I have become fond of Eliza; this quite apart from admiring

her. If I am like that at ninety! we all exclaim; and feel the threats of the enemy ahead weakened.

Eliza Bates's day.

She wakes at about eight, in the large front that was where she slept in the big double bed with her husband. But she has a nice single bed now, with a bedside table, and a little electric fire. She likes to read in bed, romantic novels mostly. The room has old-fashioned furniture: again this mixture of "antiques" and stuff that wouldn't fetch fifty pence. It is very cold, but she is used to it, and goes to bed with a shawl around her and hot bottles.

She makes herself a real breakfast, for she learned long ago, she says, never to let yourself get sloppy with meals. Then she does out one of her three rooms, but not as thoroughly as she once did. About eleven she makes herself coffee. Perhaps one of her many friends comes in. She has a special friend, a much younger woman, of about seventy, from opposite, who is "very young for her age", wears fancy hats and clothes, and is a tonic for Eliza, always running over with something she has cooked, or making Eliza go out to the pictures. Every day Eliza goes to a lunch club, run by the Welfare for old people, and may afterwards detail everything, such as that the meat was boiled to rags, the sprouts too hard, or the rice pudding had just the right amount of nutmeg. For she was once a cook in a family. Until recently she stayed for a couple of hours to "work": old people make calendars, paint Christmas cards, do all kinds of small jobs, some very well, for they may use skills of a lifetime. But now, says Eliza, she feels she must begin to cut down a little, she is not as strong as she was. After the lunch, and a cup of tea and a chat, she and one, or two, or three friends will go shopping. These are the old ladies I once did not see at all but, since Maudie, have watched creeping about the streets with their bags and their baskets—and I could never have guessed the companionableness, the interest of their lives, the gaiety. They love shopping, it is clear; and what shop they will patronize and what not on a given day is the result of the most intricate and ever-shifting tides of feeling. That Indian doesn't keep a clean shop, but he was observed sweeping out yesterday, so they'll give him a second chance. They'll go to the supermarket this week, because there's a new girl with a lovely smile who puts things into their baskets for them. The man at the hardware spoke roughly to one of them last week, and so he will lose the custom of five or six people for weeks, if not for ever. All this is much more to their point than cheap lines of biscuits or a reduction in the price of butter for old-age pensioners. After shopping, Eliza brings one of them home with her to tea, or goes to them. When she gets home she sits down for a little at the kitchen window, where she can see all the washing lines that dance about the sky when there's a wind, and she looks down into the jungle of the garden, and remembers how the lilac there was planted on that afternoon thirty-five years ago, and that corner now so overgrown that used to be such a picture.

She is rather afraid of early evening, so I have discovered. Once, going past to Annie, I saw her, her cheek on her hand. She turned her face away as I said, Oh, Eliza, good evening!— and then, when I went in, concerned, she gestured at the other wooden chair and I sat down.

"You see," said she, "you should keep busy, because if you don't, the grumps lie in wait for you . . ." And she wiped her eyes and made herself laugh.

And then, amazingly, she put on her hat again.

"Eliza, you aren't going out? Shouldn't you rest?"

"No. I should not. I must keep moving if I feel low . . ." And she went off again, creeping around the block, a dumpy brave little figure in the dusk.

She does not bother with supper, perhaps a piece of cake, or a salad. She is often visited by her friend from opposite after supper, or she listens to the radio. She doesn't like the telly. And so she spends her evening, until she goes off to bed, very late, often after midnight.

And, two or three times a week, from spring to late autumn, she is off on coach trips to famous places, or beauty spots, organized by the Welfare or one of the two churches she uses. For Eliza is very religious. She is a Baptist, and she also goes to the Church of England church. She goes to church on Sundays twice, mornings and evenings, and to church teas and bazaars and jumble sales, to lectures on Missionary Endeavour in India and in Africa. She is continually attending weddings and christenings.

When she asked me what I did and I told her, toning it down a little, she understood everything, for she has worked for people in positions of responsibility, and asked me all kinds of questions that had never occurred to me, such as: Did I think it right, having no children, taking the job of a man who might have a family to keep? And loves to talk about—not the clothes she wore half a century ago—but the fashions she sees on the streets on the young girls, which make her laugh, she says, they seem so crazy, they seem as if the girls are having such a good time. She likes to see them, but she wonders if they know what it is like not ever to have a new dress, only what could be got in their sizes at the pawnshop.

For her poor mother had been left by her husband one day. He went off and was never heard of again. She had three small children, two girls and a boy. The boy, says Eliza, was not up to anything, he was born lazy, and would never work to help out, and he too went off when he was fourteen, and never sent back so much as a card at Christmas. Eliza's mother had worked for the two of them. The pawnshop at the corner had their sheets, and often their clothes, from the Mondays to the Fridays, when they were redeemed again. And the woman who kept it used to put aside a good coat for the girls, or a pair of shoes she knew would fit. And she would say, "Well, if that poor soul can't get in in time to redeem it, you'll have first chance."

Eliza brought out one evening an old postcard, *circa* World War One, of a ragged orphan girl with bare feet. When I had examined it, thinking how romantic, for that was how the poor girl was presented, all the harshness taken away from the truth, Eliza said, "That girl was me—no, I mean, I was like that. When I was twelve I was out scrubbing steps for the gentry for a penny. And I had no shoes, and my feet were sick with the cold and blue, too . . . They were wicked times," says Eliza, "wicked. And yet I seem to remember we were happy. I can remember laughing and singing with my sister, though we were often enough hungry. And my poor little mother crying because she could not keep up with herself . . ."

Eliza, disliking televison, will go across the road to watch *Upstairs, Downstairs*. This makes me cross; but then I ask myself, Why then am I into writing romantic novels? The truth is intolerable, and that is all there is to it!

Gracious Lady!

It occurred to me that Hermione Whitfield and the rest of them (male and female) and Vera and myself are in fact the legitimate descendants of the Victorian philanthropist lady, and have taken her place.

Here is my new romantic novel:

My heroine is no titled lady, but the wife of a well-off man in the City. She lives in Bayswater, one of the big houses near Queensway. She has five children, to whom she is a devoted mother. Her husband is not a cruel man, but insensitive. I described him using language frankly stolen from a letter in one of the virulent Women's Movement newspapers Phyllis used to leave on my desk. He is incapable of understanding her finer points. He has a mistress, whom he keeps in Maida Vale, much to our heroine's relief. As for her, she occupies herself in visiting the poor, of whom there are very many. Her husband does not resent these activities, because it takes her mind off his. Every day she is out and about, dressed in her simple but beautiful clothes, accompanied by a sweet little maid who helps her carry containers of soup and nourishing puddings.

Of course, I do not allow that these invalids and old people she sustains are in any way difficult (though one, an ancient who carries wounds from the Crimean War, she describes with a small deprecating smile as *difficile*). None of them screams and rages, like Maudie, or repeats the same ten or twelve sentences for an hour or two hours of a visit, as if you haven't heard them before hundreds of times, or gets sulky and sullen. No, they may be living in dreadful poverty, never knowing where their next crust is coming from, living on tea and marge and bread and potatoes (except for the offerings of the

Gracious Lady), they may have not enough coal, and have vile or brutal husbands or wives dying of tuberculosis or childbed fever, but they are always fine and gallant human beings, and they and Margaret Anstruther enjoy friendships based on real appreciation of each other's qualities. Margaret A. certainly does *not* have the vapours, the languors, the faints; I do not permit a suggestion of the dreadful psychosomatic illnesses those poor women actually suffered from. For she does not allow herself to be bored, which was the real cause of lying for years on a sofa with a bad back or the migraine. (I have been brooding about writing a critical book called *The Contribution of Boredom to Art*. Using Hedda Gabler, whose peculiar behaviour was because she was crazy with boredom, as exemplar.) No, Margaret suffers nothing but unspoken love for the young doctor whom she meets often in those poor homes, and who loves her. But he has a *difficile* invalid wife, and of course these fine souls would never dream of transgressing. They meet over deathbeds, and sickbeds, and alleviate the human condition together, their eyes occasionally meeting, songs without words, and even glistening, very rarely, with the unshed tear.

What a load of old rubbish! Rather like *Upstairs, Downstairs*, and I adored that and so did everyone else.

But the research I've done (extensive) has led me to a real respect for those unsung heroines, the Victorian philanthropist ladies, who were patronized then, probably (how do we know, really?) by their husbands, and despised now. A pity they were so often silent about what they did, are so often written about rather than speaking for themselves. For they must have been a really tough breed, knowing by every-day, year-in-year-out slog and effort what Jack London and Dickens and Mayhew got by brief excursions into poverty and then retreating again, enough facts garnered. When I think of what it must have been like for them, going into those homes, late nineteenth century, early twentieth, the sheer, threadbare, cold, grim, grimy *dreadfulness* of it, worn-out women, rickety children, brutalized men—no, no, I won't go on. But I know one thing very well, and that is that Maudie and Annie and Eliza are rich and happy compared with those people.

Annie will say, as the helpers go flying in and out, "I think of my poor old mum, she had none of this."

"What happened to her, then, who looked after her?"

"She looked after herself."

"Did she have her health?"

"She had shaky hands, she dropped cups and plates a lot. She used to push a chair around as a support when she fell and broke her hip. And we took her in some food and a bit of stout sometimes."

"Was she alone then?"

"She was alone—years. She lived to seventy. I've done better than her, haven't I? By ten years and more!"

I know very well that what I hear from Eliza about her life is not all the truth, probably nothing like it; and I commend her, as I would the writer of a tale well-told. Those long hot summers, with never a cloud! Those outings with her husband! Those picnics in the park! Those Christmases! That group of loving chums, always meeting, never a cross word!

Occasionally there are moments when the veil is lifted, oh only for a moment. She is very condemning, poor Eliza, full of morality, cannot understand how this woman can do that, or that this. She was angry for days over a newspaper story about an elderly woman who left her husband for a young man. It's filthy, she said, filthy. And, a few moments later, in another voice, a hurrying light dream-voice: If it'd been now I could have left, I could have left him, and been rid of . . .

I am very much afraid that, yet again, what it was she wanted to be rid of was sex . . .

Eliza has not had children. She wanted them.

Did she ever go to the doctor and ask?

"Oh yes, I did, and he said there was nothing wrong with me, I should ask my husband to come."

"I suppose he wouldn't?"

"Oh, you couldn't ask him a thing like that, he wouldn't have heard of it," she cried. "Oh no, Mr Bates knew his rights, you see . . ."

Downstairs, Eliza, an example to us all . . .

Upstairs, the deplorable Annie Reeves.

Vera Rogers and I have lunch, half an hour as we fly past each other.

I say to Vera, "What interests me is this: *when* did Annie make that decision to become as she is now? For we make decisions before we know it."

"Oh no, it's not like that at all. Eliza has always been like that, Annie has always been like that!"

"What a pessimist. We don't change, then?"

"No! Look at Maudie Fowler! She was always like that, I expect. Recently I met a cousin after twenty years—nothing changed, not a syllable or a habit."

"Good God, Vera, you're enough to make one want to jump off a cliff!"

"I don't see that at all. No, people are what they are all through them."

"Then why are you trying so hard with Annie?"

"You've got me there. I don't think she'll change. I've seen it before, she's decided to give up. But let's try a bit longer, if you don't mind, and then we'll know we've done our best."

Our campaign for Annie is everything that is humane and intelligent. There she is, a derelict old woman, without friends, some family somewhere but they find her condition a burden and a scandal and won't answer her pleas; her memory going, though not for the distant past, only for what she said five minutes ago; all the habits and supports of a lifetime fraying away around her, shifting as she sets a foot down where she expected firm ground to be . . . and she, sitting in her chair, suddenly surrounded by well-wishing smiling faces who know exactly how to set everything to rights.

Look at Eliza Bates—everyone cries. See how she has so many friends, goes on so many trips, is always out and about . . . But Annie will not try to walk properly, go out, start a real life again. "Perhaps when summer comes," she says.

Because of Eliza Bates I have understood how many trips, jaunts, bazaars, parties, meetings Maudie could be enjoying, but does not. I thought it all over. I rang Vera, whose voice at once, when she knew what I was asking, became profession-ally tactful.

"What are you saying?" I asked at last. "You mean, there's no point in Maudie Fowler starting anything new because she's not likely to stay as well as she is for long?"

"Well, it is a bit of a miracle, isn't it? It must be getting on for a year now, she's holding her own, but . . ."

I went off to Maudie one Saturday, with some cherry liqueur I brought back from Amsterdam, where I was for the spring show. Like Eliza, Maudie knows, and enjoys, the best. We sat opposite each other drinking, and the room smelled of cherry. Outside drawn curtains a thin spring rain trickled noisily from a broken gutter. She had refused to let the Greek's workmen in to mend it.

"Maudie, I want to ask you something without your getting cross with me."

"Then I suppose it's something bad?"

"I want to know why you didn't ever go on these trips to country places the Council organizes? Did you ever go on one of their holidays? What about the Lunch Centre? There are all these things . . ."

She sat shading her little face with a hand grimed with coal dust. She had swept out her chimney that morning. Fire: she tells me she has nightmares about it. "I could die in my bed here," says she, "from smoke, not knowing."

She said, "I've kept myself to myself and I see no reason to change."

"I can't help wondering about all the good times you could have had."

"Did I tell you about the Christmas party, it was before I met you? The Police have a party. I got up on the stage and did a knees-up. I suppose they didn't like me showing my petticoats."

I imagined Maudie, lifting her thick black skirts to show her stained knickers, a bit tipsy, enjoying herself.

"I don't think it would be that," I said.

"Then why haven't they asked me again? Oh, don't bother, I wouldn't go now, anyway."

"And all these church things. You used to go to church, didn't you?"

"I've been. I went once to a tea, and then I went again

because that Vicar said I wasn't fair to them. I sat there, drinking my tea in a corner, and all of them, not so much as saying welcome, chatter chatter among themselves, I might as well have not been there."

"Do you know Eliza Bates?"

"Mrs Bates? Yes, I know her."

"Well then?"

"If I know her why do I have to like her? You mean, we are of an age, and that's a reason for sitting gossiping together. I wouldn't have liked her young, I'm sure of that, I didn't like her married, she gave her poor man a hard time of it she did, couldn't call his home his own, I don't like what I've seen of her since, she's never her own woman, she's always with ten or more of them, chitter-chatter, gibble-gabble, so why should I like her now enough to spend my dinners and teatimes with her? I've always liked to be with one friend, not a mess of people got together because they've got nowhere else to go."

"I was only thinking you might have had an easier time of it."

"I'm not good enough for Eliza Bates. And I haven't been these last twenty years. Oh, I'm not saying I wouldn't have enjoyed a bit of an outing here or there, I sometimes go up to the church when they've got a bazaar on, I look out for a scarf or a good pair of boots, but I might not be there at all for all the notice those church women take of me."

"Why don't you come out again to the park? Or I could take you for a trip on the river. Why not, it's going to be summer soon?"

"I'm happy as I am, with you coming in to sit with me. I think of that afternoon in the Rose Garden, and that's enough."

"You're stubborn, Maudie."

"I'll think my own thoughts, thank you!"

Some weeks after she had left, a telephone call from Joyce, at five in the morning.

"Are you ill?" was what came out of me; as if I'd written her off somewhere inside me.

"No, should I be?"

"Ringing so early."

"I'm just off to bed. Oh, of course, the time difference."

"It's all right, I'm just getting up to start work."

"Good old Janna," says Joyce, in a new vague way, and it is derisive.

"Oh, Joyce, are you drunk?"

"You certainly are not!"

"Did you ring me up actually to tell me how it is all going? Flat? Husband? Children? Job?"

"Certainly not. I thought to myself, how is Janna, how is my old mate, Janna? So how are you? And how is that old woman?"

I said, "As far as I can make out, she is suspected of having cancer."

"Congratulations," says Joyce.

"What is that supposed to mean?"

"Cancer. It's all over the place. Well, I don't see that it's worse than anything else. Do you? I mean, TB, meningitis, multiple sclerosis . . ." And Joyce went on, a long list of diseases, and I sat there thinking, she can't be all that drunk. No, she's pretending to be for some reason. Soon she was talking about how diseases fall out of *use*. Her very odd phrase. "If you read Victorian novels, they died like flies of diseases we don't have now at all. Like diphtheria. Like scarlet fever. Like, for that matter, TB."

And so we went on, for half an hour or more. At last I said, "Joyce, this is costing you a fortune."

"So it is. Good old Janna. Everything has to be paid for?"

"Well, yes, it has been my experience."

"Because you have *made* it your experience." And she rang off.

Soon she rang again. Five in the morning.

"I like to think of you working away there, me old pal, while I fiddle at parties . . ."

"I've done a romantic novel," I told her. "You're the first I've told. And they like it."

"Romance . . . quite right. I, for one, have never had enough of it. I look back and what I see is, me always working too hard for any fun. And that's what *you* see when you look back, Janna. Obviously."

"I'm having fun now."

A long, long silence.

"Don't tell me, because I won't believe it."

"I enjoy writing these romantic novels. I've started another. *Gracious Lady*, do you like it?"

"Gracious. That's a word I've understood. I've come on an important clue to the American female character. Graciousness. It comes from *Snow White*. Generations of American girls see *Snow White*, model themselves on her . . . bestow themselves graciously on this one and on that one thereafter . . ."

"And I enjoy writing serious articles."

"You must be working too hard to enjoy yourself."

"Nonsense. It's because I am working so hard. And I enjoy the old ladies. I enjoy that world, what goes on, I never suspected it even existed before."

"Good for you."

Joyce again: "Another party?" I asked.

And she said, "That's what one *does*, here."

I always ask her what she is wearing, so as to get a picture of her, and she always says, Exactly what everyone else is.

For she says the Americans are the most conforming people on earth, and even when they rebel they do it in droves, and always wear the same as the other non-conformers. She was taken to task several times for her style. She thought it was because she was really too old for it, but no, she was asked severely why the British "always look like gipsies". It is our wild romantic nature, said she, but abandoned her style, cut her hair, and now has a wardrobe full of well-cut trousers, shirts, sweaters, and variations on the little dress. When you enter a room, she says, the eyes of everyone present give you the once-over to make sure you are inside the prescribed limits.

She is enjoying herself, because that is what one *does*. Her husband is enjoying himself: he has a new girlfriend, who happens to be Joyce's colleague. Good God! cries Joyce, at one, two, three in the morning (there) before she goes to bed, to me surrounded by early-morning cups of coffee (here), when I think of all that ridiculous anguish before I left! Here no one dreams of staying married for one second after one of them has stopped enjoying it.

The children too are enjoying themselves, and look on their native land as backward and barbarous, because we are poor and do not have such well-stocked refrigerators.

There has been a new development in the office: politics.

I don't know whether to count it as serious, or not. I think, probably, serious. There is something in the air, something new, I don't like it, but then, I am getting on, and I don't like change . . . because of this was tolerant, to start with. Patronizing? But I saw *them* as patronizing. Revolutions are hardly my line, but they have after all not been absent in my lifetime, and it seems to me that I do not deserve to be tolerated as I am being. As I *was* being. For I have put my foot down. Suddenly, as I moved about the office, it seemed that I was met by groups or couples who fell silent, as if their exchanges were too deep for understanding by this outsider. Yet what they say we have all heard a thousand times; the political clichés scattered about, I could not take them seriously. Most of all I could not take it seriously when these young ones, all middle-class, go on about middle-class values, the destruction of, the replacement by, the rottenness of, the necessity to expose of. There is, actually, one really working-class young man in the place, a photographer, and his father is a printer: which remark could lead me into a long analysis of what is and isn't working class in this our so middle-class land. But I am not going to follow these schoolmen into hair-splitting. What is real about them is not the infinite variety of their religious stances, their dogmatism, but the passions they bring to their arguments. There is a spirit in the office that was never there before, a snarling, envious nasty atmosphere, which makes it inevitable that everyone has to criticize, to diminish anyone not aligned in precisely the same way as themselves; and, as well, to criticize and condemn most of the time everyone in the same group who temporarily or otherwise disagrees with them. What gets me about all this is that we have learned about all this from a thousand sources, books, TV, radio, and yet these youngsters go on as if they are doing something for the first time, as if they have invented all these stale phrases.

It was about the time I was becoming really perturbed by all this that I understood what Vera had been telling me.

Vera and I enjoy our lunches, baked beans or an omelette and a cup of coffee, as we fly around. We enjoy what we do, or rather, to be accurate, we enjoy being able to do it, and do it well.

"Gawd," says Vera, sitting down with a flop, letting a pile of files two feet thick drop to the floor as she reaches for a cigarette, "Gawd, Janna, I tell you, if I had only known when I applied, no you sit there and let me blow off steam, you'll never believe it . . ."

"I wouldn't have," I say, "if I hadn't been watching it in my own office."

What I would never believe is that it is now Thursday, and there have been seven meetings already that week which she ought to have attended.

"These meetings are about nothing, *nothing*, Janna, please believe me, any sensible person could fix whatever it is up in five minutes with a few words. There are so many meetings because they adore meetings, meetings are their social life, honestly, Janna, it is the truth. It took me a long time to cotton on, but once I saw it . . . What is the matter with them? To begin with, when I started, I asked myself if there was something wrong with me. You know how it is when you are new? They'd say, Aren't you going to come to this meeting, that meeting? I'd go. Do you know, they actually set up meetings where they act out each other's roles, can you beat it? They say, Now you be an old woman, you be her husband. Or they discuss this and that. Do you know, there are some part-time workers who are never out of the office at all actually working with the clients? My assistant, so-called, she's part-time, and she hasn't been out of the office since Monday morning, she's been at meetings. I believe she thinks that is what her job is. And it's every evening after work, every blasted night. And then they go off to the pub together, exactly the same lot of people. They can't bear to separate. And if you think that's the end of it, no, the birthdays, the anniversaries, I tell you, if they could hire a bed of Ware large enough, they'd spend all their lives together in it, having a meeting. Well, I did go to some, I did my best, and then I said, Count me out. So they think I'm very odd now. They are always saying to me, as if I were peculiar, and perhaps I am, though I doubt it, There's this meeting tonight, aren't you going to come? I say, Tell me all about it in the morning. You can explain it all to me, I'm stupid, you see, I don't seem to be able to understand politics."

I went back to the office armed by this new insight. It was all true. They call meetings every day, to discuss work hours, lunch hours, work loads, management, the policy of the mag, me, the political bias of the mag, the state of the nation. Many of them in working time. I called Ted Williams, the Trade Union representative, and said as far as I was concerned he was the only sensible person among the lot and I was going to forbid all meetings except for those which he called. He laughed. He thinks these middle-class revolutionaries a joke. (Let's hope they don't have the last laugh.)

I called a meeting of the entire staff, nearly a hundred present, and I said this was the last meeting permitted in working hours except for those convened by the Trade Union representative. And from now on, they could conduct their social lives outside the office. Shock. Horror. But of course they were thoroughly enjoying this confrontation with the Enemy, namely me, namely the Force of Reaction.

I had lunch with Vera, and I said to her, as she moaned about that week's ten meetings, "Hold your horses. You seem to think this is a disease peculiar to your Welfare Workers. No, it's a national disease. It's everywhere, like a plague. Meetings, talking, it's a way of *not* getting anything done. It's their social life. They are lonely people, most of them, without adequate social outlets. Therefore, meetings. Anyway, I've forbidden them in *Lilith*."

"You haven't!"

"I've instituted one meeting a week. Everyone has to come. No one can speak at all for more than a minute unless it is extremely urgent. I mean urgent. And so they go to the pub to have meetings about me."

"The thing is, poor creatures, they don't know it's their social lives, they really believe it's politics."

I sit here, conscientiously looking back over my year . . . I look at that word, conscientiously. I am not going to repudiate it! As I look I think of Joyce's lazy, affectionate: *Good old Janna*.

Well, all right. As I sit here, conscientiously looking over the year, I note again how hard I have worked, how hard. And yet, as I said to my dear niece Jill when she rang to inquire, "I hope you aren't working too hard, Aunt Jane?" meaning, Oh, don't work too hard, don't be boring, don't do difficult and dutiful things, what will happen to my dream of glamour and easy fun?—"I've never in my life worked as hard as your mother, and that would be true if I worked twenty hours a day."

"Can I come and stay the weekend?"

"Please do. You can help me with something."

She came. That was only a month ago.

I told her to write an article about the influence of two world wars on fashion. I watched her face. I had already tried the idea out in the think session. I said that, in the First World War, everyone in the world became used to pictures of masses of people in uniform. For the first time on that scale. Conditioned to the idea of uniforms, you are more amenable to following fashion; following fashion, you are more amenable to uniforms. In the Second World War, everyone in the world *saw* millions of people in uniform. The boss nation wore tight sexually provocative trousers, buttocks emphasized. Since the Second World War, everyone over the world wears tight sexually emphatic uniforms. A *world* fashion. Because of a world war.

I made this dry and factual, no excitement in it. I wanted to see how she would react. She listened. I watched her. Strained she was, but trying.

"I don't think I can write an article like that."

"Yet, or not at all?"

"Yet."

"When are you sitting your exams?"

"In a few weeks. Are you still seeing Mrs . . . ?"

"Mrs Fowler? Yes, I am."

Suddenly her passionately rejecting face, her real distress, which told me how threatened she felt.

Just as I would have done—alas, so recently—she cried out: "Why doesn't her family look after her? Why doesn't the Welfare put her into a Home? Why does she have to impose on you?"

I've just taken three weeks' leave. I have a lot owed to me. I've never taken all that I could, even when Freddie was alive. Nor did Freddie. It has occurred to me: was Freddie's office *his* home? If so, it was only because of what he had to put up with from me. We went for short motoring holidays, usually in France, and ate and slept well. We were pleased to get home.

Phyllis was, of course, delighted to be left in charge. She has a look of satisfaction, which she has to keep hidden. Why? Everything has always been given to her so freely and easily. Take her clothes. Her style, mine adapted, couldn't be better for her. Soft silky clothes, everything sleek and subtle, golden brown hair. Sometimes little frills at wrists and throat—I could never wear those, alas, I'm too solid. Slim good gold jewellery showing in the opening of a plain coffee shirt that has the gentlest shine to it, a fine chain visible under a cuff whose thin stripes echo it. She goes to my dressmaker, my hairdresser, my knitter, she uses the shops I told her about. And yet it is as if she has had to steal all this expertise from me: because I unfairly kept it from her. Thus, when she sees me observing her new outfit, thinking, oh well done, Phyllis!, she has the need to hide the small superior smile that goes with: That's right, I've got one over on you! Amazing girl.

It is not only I who am wondering if Phyllis's new lusciousness mirrors something inward. I watch her in the photographers' rooms. They, their working areas, have always been the pole, the balance, to our office, Joyce's and mine—Phyllis's and mine. Two power centres. Michael, who never took any notice of the girl, is now interested. And she in him. Quite different from me and Freddie: slapdash, casual, *equal*. At any rate, neither of them ever concedes an inch. I watch them in a characteristic scene. He is slanted back against a trestle table, legs crossed at the ankle, thus exposing the full length of his front in soft corduroy, the promising bulge on show. His head is slightly averted, so that he smiles at her across the curve of his cheek. He is good-looking, this Michael, but until just recently I haven't been faced with it. And Phyllis has one buttock on a desk, the other leg a long angled curve. In something pretty and soft, like black suede, or an unexpected bright colour, she presents the length of herself to him, and her hair slips about her face as they discuss—and oh how competently—their work. He lets his eyes travel up her body in a sober appreciation that mocks itself, and she opens her eyes in sardonic appraisal of the soft bulge presented to her. Then they go off to lunch, where, more often than not, they discuss layout or advertising.

I enjoy watching this game, but could not let my enjoyment be evident, for Phyllis would feel something was being stolen from her. Oh, *Joyce*, I have no one with whom to share these moments.

How I have enjoyed my three weeks. I did not go away, because I could not bear to leave Maudie for so long: if that is crazy, then let it be.

Joyce rang up. She is drinking far too much.

"Why do you never ring me, Janna?"

"It is your place to ring me. It was you who went away."

"God, you're relentless."

"Very well, I am."

"I see you sitting there, writing—what is it? *Gracious Lady*?"

"I've nearly finished another serious sociological-type book called *Real and Apparent Structures*."

"I suppose you have all this energy because you have no emotional life?"

"Emotional life being defined as husband, children, or even a lover?"

"Even a lover. Don't you want one, Janna?"

"I'm afraid of one."

"Well, that's frank at least."

"More than you are, these days, Joyce."

"Frank? I reek of emotional sincerity. I'm in an Encounter Group, did I tell you? Ten of us. We scream abuse at each other and relive our ghastly childhoods."

"I didn't know you had a ghastly childhood."

"Neither did I. But it seems I must have had."

"The truth at last, is that it? Emotional truth?"

"You wouldn't know about that, Janna."

"Love is what I know nothing about. Yes, I know that."

"*Well?*"

"Well, do you know something? Those years we sat working together, never a cross word, understanding each other, that was love, as far as I am concerned. *You* think now that love is all this screaming and shouting and *relating.*"

"Of course, I'm now an American. As good as."

"I'll think my own thoughts then, thank you."

And again:

"What are you doing, Janna?"

"I finished *Real and Apparent Structures* ten minutes ago."

"That's going very fast, isn't it?"

"I've had three weeks' leave."

"No temptation for a little trip to Paris, Amsterdam, Helsinki?"

"I've been very much enjoying my own city, believe it or not."

"Talking to dreary old women?"

How I do adore the feast of possibilities this city always is. But I didn't know how much until I had three long lovely weeks, all by myself, long spring days, to please myself in. Suddenly I was surrounded by oceans of time. I understood I was experiencing time as the old do, or the very young. I would sit on a wall along a garden and watch birds busy in a shrub. I don't know a blackbird from a starling. I'd sit in a café and, with all the afternoon in front of me, listen and look while two girls giggled about their boyfriends. Their intense enjoyment. Enjoyment, it's what I've missed in my life, what I've scarcely known the name of, I've been so busy, oh I've always worked so hard.

I could learn real slow full enjoyment from the very old, who sit on a bench and watch people passing, watch a leaf balancing on the kerb's edge. A small wind lifts it: will it fall over, be blown under wheels, be crushed? No, it rests, a thick juicy green leaf, shining and full of sap, probably plucked off some branch by a pigeon. The wheels of a shopping basket spin past, just missing the leaf. The shopping basket belongs to a girl who has a child in it. She is in love with the child, smiling and bending to it, as it looks confidingly up at her, the two isolated by love together on the pavement, watched by old people who smile with them.

I love sitting on a bench by some old person, for now I no longer fear the old, but wait for when they trust me enough to tell me their tales, so full of history. I ask, Tell me, what did you wear on your wedding day? And for some reason there's always a laugh, a smile. "You want to know that then, do you, well, it was white, you see, with . . ." Or I ask, Did you fight in the old war, you know, the 1914–18 war. "You could say I did . . ." And I sit and listen, listen.

I love—all of it, all of it. And the more because I know how very precarious it is. My back has only to say, No, stop! I have only to break a bone the size of a chicken's rib, I have only to slip once on my bathroom floor, whose tiles are dense with oils and essences—at any moment, fate may strike me with one of a hundred illnesses, or accidents, all of them unforeseen, but implicit in my physical make-up or my character, and there you are, I shall be grounded. Like Maudie, like all these old things whom I smile at now as I go about among them, because I know them now, can tell from how they bend so carefully to jerk the wheels of a shopping basket on to a pavement, from how they pause to steady themselves against a lamp-post, how precarious their being upright at all is to them—for they have already been felled several times, and picked themselves up, put themselves back together, each time with more and more difficulty, and their being on the pavement with their hands full of handbag, carrier bag, walking stick, is a miracle . . . Solitude, that great gift, is dependent on health, or an approximation to health. When I wake in the morning, I know that I can shop, cook, clean my flat, brush my hair, fill my bath and soak in it . . . and now I greet each day with—*what a privilege, what a marvellous, precious thing, that I don't need anyone to assist me through this day, I can do it all myself.*

I blow in to Maudie, who these days, because she is feeling better, is pleased to see me, does not shout and slam doors.

She can't get enough of anecdotes about my glamorous life. I search my memory for things to tell her.

"Can I have some tea, Maudie? Listen, I want to tell you something that happened . . ."

"Sit down, darling. Have a rest."

"It was in Munich."

"Munich, was it? Is that a nice place, then?"

"Lovely. Perhaps one day you'll see it."

"Yes, perhaps I will. Well, what happened?"

"You know how quickly these models have to change their clothes at the shows? Well, there was this girl, she came on in a green evening dress, and her black hair fell down . . ." I watch Maudie's face to see if she has seen what I am seeing, but not yet. "A gorgeous green glittering evening dress, and her hair piled up, black and gorgeous, then suddenly, down it slides . . ." Maudie has seen it, she tosses up her hands, she sits laughing. "And all of us, the buyers, the presenters, everybody, we laughed and laughed. And the girl, the model, she stood there, sheets of black hair all down her back and shoulders, tossing her head and making a theatre out of it."

"And you all sat there laughing . . ."

"Yes, we laughed and laughed . . . you see, it never happens. It's impossible. That's why we all laughed."

"Oh, Janna, I do love hearing about what you do."

I have had time to listen to Annie Reeves, to Eliza Bates.

Annie sits in a hard little chair by a blocked-in fire, wearing an old flowered wrap. Down the front of it rivers of food, cigarette droppings.

"Don't think I don't appreciate what you did for me, Mrs Bates said you did all this cleaning."

"I and Vera Rogers."

"You are a Good Neighbour, I suppose."

"No, I'm not."

A long, thoughtful inspection.

"Vera Rogers is not so much a Good Neighbour as she's a social worker?"

"That's right."

"Well, it's all too much for me." She says this giving due allowance to every word. Annie Reeves talks almost entirely in clichés, but for her they aren't clichés, they are words shining with evident truth. Listening to her is like hearing an earlier stage of our language. She says, "You are not old if you are young in heart. And I am young in heart." She has heard these words, thought about them, knows they apply to her, uses them with respect. She says, "I don't like being with old people, I like the company of young people like you." She says, "If they had told me when I was young I could end up like this, then I wouldn't have believed them." She says, "Time doesn't wait for any of us, whether we like it or not."

Annie has been a waitress all her life. From fourteen till seventy, when she was retired against her will, Annie has tripped from a serving hatch to a table with eggs, chips, spam, baked beans, fried steak, and fried fish. She has worked in cafés and dining rooms and in canteens for the staff in big stores, and in two world wars fed soldiers and airmen from Canada and Australia and America, some of whom wanted to marry her. But she is a Londoner, says she, she knows where she belongs. Annie achieved the summit of her ambitions when she was sixty. She got a job in a real posh coffee shop. She cut sandwiches and filled rolls with amazing foreign cheeses (which she would not taste herself) and served espressos and cappuccinos and rich cakes. She worked ten years under a man who was clearly a nasty piece of work and exploited her, but she loved the work so much she didn't care. When she was seventy, she was told to leave. As she had only worked ten years there, she did not get a pension, but a clock which she had to pawn when bad times began, which they did at once, for she went to pieces. Her life had always been in her work, since her husband died, as a result of getting a shell splinter in his lung in the First War. She went to pieces very fast, drinking, and thinking about the good times and how in the last place, the coffee bar, she knew all the customers and they knew her, and sometimes they took her to pubs and bought her a nice port, and the barrow boys in the streets used to call out, There's our Annie, and gave her peaches and grapes. She was, for fifty-five years, one of those smiling, maternal waitresses who make a restaurant, a café, bringing people back to it.

In her bad time she sat drinking in the Private Bars till they closed. Then she wandered about the streets by herself, having no friends in her own area, since she had hardly ever been in it, except at night or on Sundays, when she washed her hair and prepared her uniforms for the week ahead. Meeting impeccable Eliza Bates in the streets, herself a dirty half-drunk old woman, she would turn aside and look into a shop window and pretend she hadn't seen her.

Annie talks of food a lot. Again I listen to details of meals eaten sixty, seventy years ago. The family lived in Holborn, in a now demolished tenement that had stone stairs and two lavatories, one for one side of the building, one for the other. Everyone was supposed to clean the lavatories and the stairs, but only two or three women actually did this work, the others shirked. The father was a labourer. He drank. He was continually losing his job. Three children, Annie the oldest. In hard times, which were frequent, the children would run down to the shops for six eggs, sixpence; for yesterday's stale bread, kept for the poor by the German bakers. For the liquid from boiling sheep's heads, given away free to the poor; they brought back a jug of this, the mother made dumplings, and that is what they ate for supper. They got sixpennyworth of scraps from the butcher and made stew. Enormous boiled puddings full of fruit, with sugar sprinkled on, were used to stay appetites—just as Maudie remembered. When they were flush, the family had the best of everything in the food line, for the father went up to the butchers' auctions on a Saturday night, when the meat was sold that would spoil, and came back with a large sirloin for half a crown, or a leg of mutton. They ate eels and potatoes and parsley sauce, brought from the eel shop in a basin, or thick pea soup with potatoes in it. They got their milk from an old woman who had a cow. The cow had its head sticking out over the door in a shed in the back yard, and went moo when the children came in. The old woman sold buttermilk and butter and cream.

The family bought "specks" from the greengrocer: apples that had a brown spot on them; or yesterday's greens. Just as good as new, they were, and sometimes no money asked at all, just given away.

At the baker's, if they bought that day's bread, the German woman would always give the children a makeweight, cakes from yesterday. And in the market a man made sweets standing at a stall under a canopy, boiling toffee over a flame, and then spread it with coconut or walnuts or hazelnuts, and he always gave the children the little crushed splinters from when he broke up the toffee with his little hammer.

And then, the clothes. Annie, as she says herself, was a good-time girl and did not marry until she was over thirty. Her money went on clothes. She was slim, she had her hair marcelled for half a crown every week, she would buy clothes on the never-never from the shops in Soho. She had a black lace dance dress with a red rose on it, and wore it at the policemen's ball. She had a navy-blue costume with white piping that fitted her like a glove. She wore little hats with veils, because the boys liked them. A brown skirt wrapover, buttoned all down one side with buttons the size of spoons. A coat-dress, in blue velour with revers. Each time she summons the ghost of yet another garment from sixty, fifty, forty years ago, she says, They don't make the clothes like that now, just as she says about the yellow fat on the beef, There's no food like that now, and she is right.

I asked her what she did with all her old clothes: this always interests me, for very few garments actually wear out. "I wore them until I got fed up with them," she says, not knowing what it is I want to know.

"And then what?"

"What do you do with yours, then?"—examining my clothes, but not as Maudie did, with such skilled knowledge. "You've nice clothes, do you wear them out, then?"

"No, I give them to Oxfam."

"What's that?"

I explain. She simply cannot take it in. But this is not all she can't take in: Annie's mind froze, or stopped, or reached saturation at some point probably about ten years ago. Sometimes, as I sit up there, listening to the same stories, I try something new.

I've told her that I work for a women's magazine. She knows the name, though she has never read it. She is incurious. No, that's wrong: the machine that is her mind cannot admit anything outside an existing pattern. Thus, I will say, Today I went to see a new young dress designer, she's making clothes for . . . But almost at once I must retreat from the general to the specific, for I see from her eyes that she has *not taken it in*. "I saw a lovely dress," I say, "it was blue with . . ."

Annie often sits at her window two floors up, watching the street, waiting for something interesting to happen. She is alone except for when the Home Help, the nurse, the Meals on Wheels are rushing in and out. All her life, until ten years ago, was spent in company, and she was never alone, she says. But people are indoors these days, with their tellies, not milling about the streets having adventures, as she and her sister did, two bright pretty young things, the West End their oyster, using it, knowing how to evade dangers. They would allow themselves to be picked up by a pair of calculating salesmen, were taken to Romano's, had a real slap-up dinner, and then, when some kind of reward was due from them, said, We'll slip into the Ladies, if you don't mind, just for a moment—but they knew ways out and about and around, and remained in debt to their salesmen. Or they got themselves taken to the music hall or the theatre, and faded away into a crowd, or into a police station with a false story, or the Underground. For they were good girls, they were, as Annie tells me every other day. That part of her life, the five years before her sister married (more fool her) and the two young girls were not yet twenty, Annie in her first job, these years were the best of her life, she sits thinking of them—those and the coffee bar. That is what she would like to see now, looking down out of her window, a lively quick-witted noisy crowd, and if there were barrows and street trading, so much the better. But no, nothing like that these days. And as for those young people she sees down there, she doesn't have a good word for them. The young people, the descendants, in fact, of her young self and her sister, ten or twelve boys and girls from the flats at the corner, lively, black, brown, and white, unscrupulous and thieving, sometimes go strolling through this street, part of their territory. But what they see is old faces looking from windows, these houses are all full of the old and elderly, and the area is too dull for them, as it is for Annie.

How Annie grumbles and complains, she is so dull, it is so dreary . . .

Poor Eliza Bates's tales are all of the very far past, when her husband was alive, her sister.

Now she has no one. There is a niece somewhere, she believes, but she's lost her address. A brother-in-law has just died. She sighs and looks distressed when she mentions him. "He was the last, the last, you see," she murmurs. Then makes herself smile.

And her "young" friend, the woman of seventy, married a man she met at the Lunch Centre and has gone off to live in Scotland. This has shocked Eliza Bates. She is often scandalized. I never appreciated that word until I knew Eliza Bates. Hearing something that shocks her, which is often, she lifts both hands, fingers spread, to the level of her shoulders, her eyes widen, she gasps, she cries, Oh, oh, oh! I never would have thought it!

About her lost "young" friend, she expostulated, I wouldn't ever have believed *she* was like that!

Meaning, believe it or not, she suspects the poor woman of marrying her raddled stick-like old swain for the pleasures of the bed.

Not so Annie upstairs, who at moments may look like that worldly-wise, world-loving female who turned the handle of the barrel-organ while Irene was being raped in *The Forsyte Saga*, her ravaged face a grinning triumph. Our Annie has created—to suit what she thinks we expect from her—a timorous, refined, refraining persona, one from whom all unpleasant facts must be kept. For instance, she delights in telling us how often her father, her mother, her husband, kept from her the sight of a dog run over in the street, news of a dead relative, even a passing funeral. For she was such a sensitive, delicate soul. (Child-daughter! Child-wife!) Oh yes, Annie, the pretty raider of the West End streets, fashioned for herself at the same time a pouting, coy, simpering style which, I think, was all her swains saw of her. Probably the Canadian airman, the Australian soldier, the American sailor, fighting men of two world wars, all of whom "took her out" and bought her presents, the salesmen and the Burlington Berties, never ever saw this exulting unscrupulous, exploiting female who now, when forgetting about her simper and her refinement, may wink and say, Oh, *I* knew how to take care of myself, *I* knew my way about, *I* never gave anything I didn't mean to!

But almost at once this female will vanish, as Annie remembers the needs of respectability, and she will again become a coy little girl; even sitting—this eighty-five-year-old woman—in the simpering pose of a three-year-old, which says silently, Oh I'm such a delicate little thing, so sweet . . .

I have a feeling that Annie has done a lot of thinking about what she may and may not tell us, and that her tales will always be heavily edited.

But sometimes there are flashes: a phrase from an advertisement, or from a popular song, and she'll light up—Little night nurse, he called me, she crooned the other day; and then, remembering I was there, she shot me a half-scared, half-triumphant smile. Yes, night nurse—well, I like to sit here and remember I've had a good life.

Driving home, I saw a company of old ladies on the pavement, all hatted and scarved in the chill spring evening. They had all been to Hatfield, by coach, on a church outing. Among them, Eliza Bates. Little old ladies, chirping and chirruping away. The company that is too good for Maudie. The Vicar was there with his lady aides. Eliza was being supported by her friends. I realized that she is seen by them as frail, getting frailer. I rang up Vera; she said, "She's lost her last relative, her best friend's married and gone, you've got to expect . . ."

I also saw Maudie again, out in the harsh spring light, toiling along, gasping. The bright yellow of her face, that painted look. I don't have to ring Vera to ask.

At the end of the three weeks, I decided, simply, to work less. They like my *Milliners*. They like my *Fashion Changes*.

I shall work part-time, and they must get a new editor. I want to enjoy myself, to slow down . . .

My sister Georgie rang, in the way she does now, in a cautious noncommittal way, checking up on her irresponsible sister. I, without thinking, said that I will work part-time and inside two minutes Jill was on the telephone.

"Aunt *Jane*," she was gasping. "It can't be true. It can't."

I was silent, for far too long.

She was weeping. "Aunt Jane, you *promised*."

I did? I made a promise?

After thought, I wrote to her, encouraged her to do well in her imminent exams, and told her to come and see me when she knew how she had done. I can almost hear the cold and censorious breaths from the Arctic of my Sister Georgie: Really, Janna, do you never think of anyone but yourself?

Joyce again:

She says, "I've been working away at fixing up our new apartment, and I've just finished scrubbing the kitchen, and I thought of *you*."

"And how is the new apartment, how is America, how is university life, how is the campus wife?"

"I think I am about to get a job as counsellor."

"What council?"

"No, counselling, I am going to counsel."

"Whom?"

"Those who need counselling."

"On behalf of whom?"

"Those who know the answers."

"And you are of course going to be properly paid for it?"

"Adequately. Money for jam. But it really ought to be you, Janna. Advice has been less my forte than yours."

"I have never given advice."

"What are long erudite articles of a sociological bent if not advice?"

"And how is your husband liking America?"

"He is adjusting."

"And how are your sprightly children?"

"They are adjusting and relating to peer groups."

"And how are *you*, Joyce?"

"It is possible that I am too old or too stiff-necked to adjust."

"Oh, does that mean you are coming home?"

"I didn't say that, Janna."

"I see."

"I thought you would."

"Well, I miss you."

"I miss you."

"Goodbye."

"Goodbye."

Well, so that was the year. As Virginia Woolf said, It is the present moment. It is Now.

I have told them they must get an editor, I want to come in perhaps two, three days a week, or mornings. Phyllis's reproach. She is good as assistant editor, working with me. Am I to stay full-time because of Phyllis, because of Jill? That is what their demands amount to. Silent demands—Phyllis. Most voluble and exclamatory—Jill.

But the waters will close over me as easily and thoroughly as they have over Joyce.

The young ones in the office treat me with charming casualness, the new house style—certainly not mine, and where did it come from? Everything is much more inefficient, slapdash. They have started meetings again, lunch hours, coffee breaks. "Oh, excuse me, Janna, we are having a meeting."

"Enjoy yourselves," I say, having given this battle up. Revolutionaries to a man they are, these well-educated, well-paid, well-fed young people who, like me, spend as much on their clothes as would feed families. Well, the house of revolution has many mansions, I say to them, and they agree to find it amusing.

Michael and his mates are "into" a serious study of brain-washing techniques, propaganda, the use of slogans, conversion—all that kind of thing. From the point of view, of course, of combating them when used on them and their comrades.

I say, "But it doesn't seem to have occurred to you that *you* and your employees will be using them on your opponents—probably me?"

"Oh, Janna, don't be like that."

"No, I'd find it all rather endearing than not," I say, "if there's not a quite serious prospect of you and your lot getting into power. Not, of course, that any of you would survive ten minutes. You'd be eliminated in the first wave!"

"We're realists, we are."

"Romantics every one. Romanticism is not the best quality in a new ruling class."

"Well, you should know about romance," says Michael, brandishing the proof copy of *The Milliners of Marylebone*, which is being avidly read in the office by everyone. "But why not a *serious* novel about them? They were shamefully exploited," he cries.

"I shall leave that to you," I say. "In my opinion the truth is intolerable, it is more than we can stand, it has to be prettied up."

"Escapist."

But when I gave him the proofs of my serious book, *Fashion Changes*, he didn't read it. This is because, I know, he wants me in a certain category: elderly reactionary who cannot face reality.

Maudie is ill. She looks dreadful. She sits opposite me, and draws the curtains in full daylight so that I can't see her face, but I hear her breathing come short as she shifts position in her chair, see her hands go protectively over her stomach. She drinks little sips of tea, as if they might be poison, then drinks, suddenly, cup after cup as if it might wash something away.

All this last year I've been going to the doctor to get her prescriptions, and getting them made up, because she won't see the doctor. She won't.

I said to her today, "Maudie, you ought to let the doctor see you."

"If you've all decided it, then I shall have to do as I'm told." Sullen.

"No, it's up to you."

"That's what you say."

I realized in fact she wants me to call the doctor, but won't say so. Is he going to prescribe new pills? If a dictator wished to subjugate a population, all he would have to do would be to come on the telly screen and say, And now, all of you, it is time to take your little white pill. Just take your little white pill for me, dear . . .

For if you ask Annie, you ask Eliza, What is that pill you are taking? they never think of replying, I am taking Mogadon, Valium, Dioxin, Frusemide, they say, It is a big yellow pill, it is a little white pill, it is a pink pill with a blue band . . .

The doctor came today. I wasn't there. Maudie: "He says I've got to go for another examination."

"I'll go with you."

"Please yourself."

Today I took Maudie to hospital. I filled in the form for her and said she was not prepared to be examined in front of students. When our turn came, I was called in first. Large many-windowed room, the table of Authority, the big doctor, and many students. Their *young* unknowing faces . . .

"How am I going to teach my students if I can't show them any patients?" he asked me.

I said, "It's too much for her."

He said, "Why is it? It's not too much for me, and I am sure it is not too much for you when you're sick."

This was so *stupid* I decided not to bother. "She's very old and very frightened," I said, and left it at that.

"Hmmmmmmmm!" And then, to the students, "So I suppose I'll have to order you to take yourselves off."

This was my cue to give in, but I wasn't going to.

Off went the students. There remained the consultant, myself, a young Indian man.

"You'll have to put up with my assistant."

Maudie comes slowly in, not looking at us, supported by the nurse. She is put in the chair next to me.

"And what is your name?" asks the big doctor.

Maudie does not look up, but she is muttering. I know she is saying that she watched me fill in the form with her name.

"How do you feel?" asks the big doctor in a loud clear voice.

Now Maudie lifts her head and stares at him, incredulously. "Have you got a pain?" asks the doctor.

"My doctor said I had to come up here," says Maudie, trembling with fear and with rage.

"I see. Well, Dr Raoul will examine you for me, and then you'll come back here."

Maudie and I are taken to a cubicle.

"I'm not going to, I won't," says she to me, fiercely.

I simply begin taking off her coat, a bully just like the doctor, and then the smell hits me. Oh, if only I could get used to it.

"Why should I?" she complains. "It's not what I want, it's what you all want."

"Why don't you let them examine you while you are here?"

I take off her dress, and see that her underclothes are all dirtied, though I know she put out clean ones for today. She is shaking. I take off everything but her knickers and hide her in the enormous hospital dressing gown.

We have to wait a long time. Maudie is sitting upright on the examination table, staring at the wall.

At last in comes the Indian doctor. Charming. I like him and so does Maudie, who patiently lies down for him and allows him to examine her very thoroughly. (Please lie down for me, Mrs Fowler, please turn over for me, please cough for me, please hold your breath for me; it's the formula, insulting, used in all hospitals and Homes, by everyone working with the old, who have to be treated like small children.) He listens to her heart, he listens for a long time to her lungs, and he then, very gently, uses his brown hands to feel her stomach. A tiny little belly, you wonder what happens to all the food she eats.

"What's there? What's in there?" she demands, fierce.

"So far, nothing, as far as I can see," smiling, delightful.

And suddenly, in strides the big doctor. He shouts, "What do you mean by sending the X-rays for the oesophagus to the Records? I need them now."

The Indian doctor straightens, stands looking at his boss over the body of Maudie, his brown hands on her yellow stomach.

"I must have misunderstood you," he said.

"That's no excuse for incompetence."

Suddenly, Maudie: "Why are you cross with him? He's very nice."

"He may be nice, but he's a very bad doctor," says the tyrant, and withdraws.

We three do not look at each other.

The Indian doctor is pulling up Maudie's knickers and helping her sit up. He is angry, we can see.

"Well, I suppose he feels better after that," says Maudie, bitterly.

Back in the big doctor's room, Maudie, the Indian, and I, in three chairs facing him.

I know that things are bad, because of the bland competence of the man and because of something about the Indian doctor's attitude towards Maudie. But Maudie is leaning forward, her bright blue eyes on the big man's face: she is waiting for the word from Olympus. It comes: oh, very nicely done, I admired that, full marks.

"Well now, Mrs Fowler, we've examined you thoroughly, and there's nothing that we can't get under control. You must be sure to eat . . ." And so he goes on, looking from his notes, to her, smiling, looking back as if to check up his facts, a beautiful performance. And I was thinking, I won't know till the report has gone to Maudie's doctor, and Vera has rung him up, and I have rung Vera, and then I can know: meanwhile, because I'm not real next of kin, but only the person who's nearest to Maudie, I'll have to lump it.

In the taxi, Maudie is an upright tense suffering trembling bundle of thick black, and she says, "What about the pains in my stomach, what about those?"

She has not said anything to me about pains before, and I did not know what to say, except that her doctor would come.

"Why? You take me up there, all that performance, that consultant, whatever he calls himself, Lord Muck, but after all that, back home I go, and I can't even be told."

It has taken ten days, while Maudie has been ill with worry. She knows she has something badly wrong. The big doctor wrote to the little doctor. Vera rang him. Vera rang me: Maudie has cancer of the stomach.

Vera says to me, "It's bad, it's awful—but you know, they can control pain now, they know exactly how to do it. So when she has to go into hospital . . ."

Vera is worried that I am worried—and I am. Very. Meanwhile, Maudie is told she has a stomach ulcer and is given mild pain-killers. But unfortunately they muddle her mind and so into the lavatory pan they go, more often than not.

Vera and I have telephone calls in which more is understood than can be said: Maudie must be kept out of hospital as long as possible. She must not be worried with Home Helps if she doesn't want, or with nurses coming in to wash her. We must make sure her landlord takes no notice of threats from the Council that he will be taken to court for the condition of her flat, and meantime Vera will have a word with the relevant official.

And how long can all this last? I find myself suddenly desperately wanting it all to be over. In short, I want Maudie dead.

But Maudie does not want to be dead. On the contrary. She is raging with a fierce need to live. It is Vera who has forced her up to the hospital, who made her doctor come, who has caused this diagnosis of stomach ulcer to be forced on her. It is Vera who is the enemy: but, as Vera says, this is a good thing, because the old have to have an enemy (only the old?), so she can have me as a friend and Vera as an enemy. Vera is used to it.

Maudie says to me, "Stomach ulcer?" She sits with her two large knotted hands on her stomach, gently feeling. There is sweat on her forehead.

Vera says that the cells of the old reproduce themselves slowly, and therefore the cancer may take a long time to become fatal, and Maudie may live three years, four—who could know?

Vera and I have tea in the café on the corner and eat baked beans on toast. We are both fitting a meal in, somewhere, before we fly apart to our different spheres of labour.

Vera says to me that yes, probably Maudie knows, but she also does not know: and we have to take our cue from her.

Vera tells me about an old man she is watching over who has

cancer of the bowel and has been keeping himself upright and viable (her word!) for two years. He knows. She knows. He knows she knows. His anguish, his contrivings, his slow deterioration—the squalor—they both of them ignore it. But yesterday he said to her, Well, it won't be long now, and I'll not be sorry to die. I've had enough.

Maudie won't have a Home Help, she won't. As she talks, I see that for years this or that social worker has been trying to get Maudie to see reason. The stories Maudie tells about them, you'd think they were a race of sluts and thieves. But now I know a bit more, because I see Annie's Home Help. And Eliza Bates is ill, quite suddenly very ill, almost helpless, and Annie's Home Help is now hers too, though one of the things she had been so proud of all these years is that she has never, ever, asked anyone for anything, ever let her place go, ever been a burden.

A Day in the Life of a Home Help.

She may be Irish, West Indian, English—any nationality, but she is unqualified and has a dependant of some kind or children, so that she needs a job she can fit in around her family. She is young, or at least not elderly, for you need strength for this work. She has bad legs/a bad back/chronic indigestion/womb trouble. But nearly every woman has womb trouble these days. (Why?)

She almost certainly lives in a Council flat and is a Council employee, as a Home Help.

She wakes at half past six or seven, when her husband does. He is in the building trade and has to get off early. One or other of them puts the kettle on and sets out the cornflakes for the kids, and both parents jolly them out of bed and through the business of washing and dressing. While she keeps an eye on everybody's breakfast, state of health, the cat's meal, the weather, her voice competes with the elder child's cassette player, kept low because she nags at him. But she is simultaneously planning her day. It is raining . . . the kids must take their macs . . . Bennie needs his football gear . . . she must pick up her husband's prescription for the skin infection that announced itself last week and shows no signs of going. While she telephones for a dentist's appointment for her "baby", now five, she urges on the middle one, the girl, to be quick and get the five-year-old's coat and scarf on, for it is getting late. Her husband has shovelled down cornflakes and toast and jam, while he reads the *Mirror* and absently scratches his neck, which is flaming red. She doesn't like the look of that at all. He says to the boy, the twelve-year-old, Come along, then, and as he goes past his wife takes from her hand (the one not holding the telephone receiver) the packet of sandwiches she made for him while he was in the bathroom. See you later, he mumbles, for he is thinking about whether he should drop into the doctor for his rash. She yells after them, Bennie, your football things, and the two males are gone.

There are left the two girls. The sound of music is stilled. Silence. The "baby" croons as she picks up her toast, and the girl sits efficiently ingesting toast and jam.

The Home Help lets herself flop into a chair, bringing the telephone with her, and she hooks the receiver under her chin while she pours herself tea and reaches for her son's unfinished toast and jam because she can't bear waste.

She makes half a dozen calls, all to do with husband and children, and then rings the Home Help Office to find out if there is anything new. They want her to do old Mr Hodges today, for his Help has just rung to say she has to take her mother to hospital and won't be working. The Office sounds apologetic, as well they might, for Bridget is already doing four a day, and they are all difficult. She gets the difficult ones because she is so good with them.

As she sits there, watching how the "baby"—oh, look at that, over goes the milk, what a mess—she plans how to fit in Mr Hodges. Then she gets up, says, Come on now, school time. She acquires from all over the kitchen, handbag, shopping bags and baskets, money out of a drawer, a plastic scarf for her head, the packets of sandwiches for the children, a dozen small items they need for school: books, exercise books, crayons. Objects seem to dance about her, in and out of bags and drawers and off hooks, and then the three of them are ready, all done up inside plastic for the bad weather outside.

When they are out, though, it is not so bad, damp but not cold. The school is only five minutes' walk away, that's something; Bridget never ceases to give thanks that this part of her life, at least, is so convenient. Having seen the two little girls run off across the playground, she turns away, thinking, Oh, she's not a baby any more, little Mary isn't—is it too late for me to fit in another? She yearns for a fourth, part of the time; her husband tells her she is mad when she mentions it, and she agrees with him . . . As she whisks past another mother coming to leave a child at the school gates, Bridget smiles at a small baby in a pram, and thinks, now stop that, girl, stop that! You know where *that* will lead you.

She goes back home for the few minutes in every day when she enjoys perfect peace. Sits at the kitchen table, sees if there is any tea in the pot—there is, but it looks too black and she can't be bothered. Sits in a heap, breathing steadily, in and out, a young woman still, on the right side of forty, and you can see in her the wildly pretty Irish girl she was when she came to this country with her husband twelve years ago. Cornflower-blue eyes, pink skin, a mass of dark waves and curls. Nevertheless, she is tired, and looks it. What she is—is tired.

In her mind she is listing all the things she has to buy, for her four regular customers and her own family and—of course, she was nearly forgetting—for old Mr Hodges. Is he on the phone? Oh *no*, Mother Mary, help me! Does that mean she will have to go out again to buy in food and stuff for him? No, she'll drop in and do him first before the shopping. A nuisance.

She does not look forward to Mr Hodges, whom she knows of old.

Bridget takes another look at the sky, decides it is safe to leave off her plastic wrap, and again gathers together her bags and baskets. Mr Hodges is ten minutes' walk away. She does not have the key, so she stands banging and banging, till at last the head of a cross old man appears in the window above and he says, "What do you want? Go away."

"Oh, Mr Hodges," cries Bridget gaily, "you know me, I'm Bridget. Do you remember? Maureen can't come today, she's taking her mother to the hospital."

"Who?"

"Oh, do be a dear now and let me in. I haven't all day."

This threat makes him open the door, and she casts the rapid skilled glance of a doctor, nurse, psychiatrist—or Home Help—over him, and decides that—thank God!—he's not too bad today. Mr Hodges is eighty-five. His wife got past it and she's in a Home, much to the relief of Mr Hodges. For they were near to killing each other from exasperation. Mr Hodges is a little stick of a man, his clothes hanging on him. He has got very skinny recently. Bridget thinks, cancer? Diabetes? I must mention it at the Office.

As he clambers up the stairs in front of her, he is grumbling, And she didn't get me the sugar, and I've no cheese, nothing to eat, no one does anything . . .

"Mr Hodges," cries Bridget as she reaches the two rooms he lives in—if that is the word for it—and examines everything at a glance, "I can see you are in a bad mood today. Now, what can I do for you?"

"Do for me? You're doing for me, the lot of you," he snaps, and he trembles all over, with age and with rage.

He has no one to talk to but the Home Help, and for hours of every day he engages in angry fantasies because of his helplessness. He was (only the other day, it seems) an energetic and independent man, the careful and tender support of his wife, who cracked up before he did. And now . . .

Bridget sees that she need not clean today, the place is not too bad. It is no part of her job, but what he *needs* is to talk and to scold, and so she sits herself down on a kitchen chair, and listens to the old man's complaints and accusations while she examines the kitchen for what he might be short of.

"And what shall I get you?" she asks, interrupting the tirade when she feels he has had his allowance.

"I need tea, can't you use your eyes?"

He says nothing about the cheese and the sugar, and Bridget thinks, I'll get him those and anything else I think best, and if he doesn't want them, then Mrs Coles might . . .

Soon she has left him, urging him to remember that she will be back later with his things and she needs to be let in. Now she knows everything she has to buy, and she takes a bus down to Sainsbury's.

She has no lists, not even a scribble on the back of an envelope, but she keeps in her mind the requirements of ten people, and after half an hour or so emerges on to the pavement with basket-on-wheels and four heavy baskets. She is thinking as she proceeds soberly up the street, and for God's sake now, Bridget Murphy, mind your back ... you don't want *that* again. And so she walks, does not take the bus, which means so much lifting and managing. It takes her half an hour to walk back up to where her work is. She feels guilty about this, but tells herself, It's sensible, isn't it? What use would you be flat in bed? She passes Maudie Fowler's place, from which she has been ejected more than once; thinks, thank God I've not been given her again, that'd be the last straw, really it would.

First stop, Mrs Coles. She is an old Russian woman who was once a beauty, with photographs stuck everywhere around her rooms to prove it. Furs, saucy little hats, naked shoulders, gauze—this great mass of a woman sits torpid in a big chair most of the day, gazing at her past. She is a complainer, and drives Bridget mad with it.

Bridget switches off as she goes in, always; and lets the heavy greasy voice sag on and on about this and that, while she puts away bread, butter, tins of soup, detergent—but then she realizes she ought to be listening, for Mrs Coles is saying, "And it was bright red . . ."

Bridget asks sharply, "What was bright red? What have you been eating, then?"

"What could I have been eating? What can you eat that makes your water red?"

"Did you keep it for me?"

"How? What in?"

Bridget whirls about and goes into the bathroom.

Mrs Coles has been rehoused, and this is the middle floor of a house, done up. Done up very nicely, but Mrs Coles doesn't like it because she never wanted to move at all. And she brought everything she owned with her. The two rooms are crammed with old heavy furniture, two wardrobes, three chests of drawers, a table the weight of a rock. You can hardly move. But there is a proper bathroom and a good toilet. Bridget peers in. It has been flushed. But there is a smell to the place. What? Something chemical?

She goes back to the other room, and Mrs Coles is sitting where she was left, still talking as if Bridget has not been out of the room at all.

"I think I might have strained myself, that's what it might be. I lifted that chair yesterday, when I shouldn't."

But Bridget is on the track of something.

"Have you been taking those tonic pills again?" she suddenly inquires, and darts off to the bedroom, and there she finds a bottle of enormous pills, good enough for a cart-horse, and they are virulent scarlet.

"Oh, my God," she says, "oh, Holy Mother, give me patience." She marches back and says, "I told you to throw that rubbish away. It's nothing that will do you good. I'm going to throw them right away, it's them that are giving you the red water."

"Ohhhhh," wails Mrs Coles, "you are throwing them away, you have no right . . ."

"Oh, keep them and take them, but don't complain to me about your water. I told you when I saw them, remember? I told you, they bring on red water. Because another of my cases did the very same thing."

Mrs Coles is holding out a fat dirty hand for the bottle of pills. Bridget puts them into it. Then Mrs Coles herself throws the pills into a pail and murmurs, "Good riddance, then."

Bridget has been here for fifteen minutes. She is supposed to be here an hour and a half. But included in that time is the time for shopping. Yet she shops for everyone together. She includes that shopping time as half an hour, separately, in the mental account she makes for each of her charges. And then she walked up the street for half an hour. That means she has fifteen minutes to go. Bridget's conscience troubles her daily over these calculations of hers. But she always makes it come out like this: and in the end she spends half an hour with Mrs Coles, if that. But then, what about those times when she has run around and about getting medicine, fetching the doctor, coming specially to let in electricity men, gas men, the man who mended the leak in the ceiling—and for these times she does not seem to charge. No, it probably all balances out. Yet she knows that, like Mr Hodges, Mrs Coles relies on her for company, and so she sits down again, fidgeting with impatience to be gone, and listens while Mrs Coles grumbles.

At twelve o'clock she hears the Meals on Wheels in the street, throws up the window, checks that she is right, and says, "Well, your dinner is here, and I'll see you tomorrow."

And she runs down the stairs, her mind already on Annie Reeves, who is next.

Oh, dear God, let her be in a good mood, she prays. For sometimes, after Mrs Coles's incessant grumbling, to walk in to Annie and yet another dose of the same is more than she can stand. She is thinking, if she's in one of her moods, I swear I might kill her.

She finds Annie sitting in a heap by the radiator and notices how the old woman looks up blinking, vague, a miserable, strained old face.

Annie starts at once, "I feel so bad, my legs, my stomach, my head . . ."

"Wait a minute, love," says Bridget, and goes into the kitchen, where she fumbles for the kettle and puts it on. It is all too much, too much . . . Perhaps I could do some other kind of work, thinks Bridget, her eyes shut . . . what, cleaning? No, wait a minute . . . "*coming*," she shrieks as Annie shouts, "Where are you? Are you here or aren't you?"

She goes into the other room and tidies this and that. While Annie complains. Bridget empties the commode. She sees the cat has made a mess and it has to be cleaned up. She sees that Annie's cardigan is grey with dirt and really ought to be changed.

But first . . .

She puts the Meals on Wheels food on to plates, helps Annie to the table, sits her down, puts the food in front of her, fetches cups of tea for both of them. And sits down, with a cigarette and her own sandwiches.

Annie eats heartily, and when she has finished, pushes away her plates saying she has no appetite. She complains the tea is cold, but Bridget does not budge and she drinks it, grumbling. Whining, she allows herself to be taken back to her chair. She says she doesn't see anyone, she doesn't get out, she never . . .

At this, Bridget, as she does every day, lists all the things Annie could be doing: she could go down and sit outside on a fine day and watch the people passing, she could walk up and down on her frame, like old Mrs This and That and the Other One, she could go on a Council holiday, she could go on coach trips, like Eliza used to do, she could say yes when Janna asks her to go for a drive instead of, always, no.

"Perhaps, when the weather is fine," says Annie, looking triumphantly at the rain, which has started to fall. "And I suppose you haven't brought me in the things I asked for?"

Bridget heaves herself up and brings in the things she has brought so that Annie may see them.

"I asked you for a bit of haddock," says Annie at the end.

"No, you didn't, love, but I'll get you some tomorrow."

"And where are my oranges?"

"Here, three lovely oranges. Would you like one?"

"No, my stomach isn't too good. I don't feel like eating."

Bridget fetches the work sheet, and sees to it that Annie signs in the right places.

As she goes down to Eliza Bates, she hears, "An hour and a half, I *don't* think. The Irish. Scum. They send all the scum to us."

Bridget finds herself muttering, "Scum yourself!" Annie's parents were both of them Irish, and in better moods she may say, "I'm Irish, like yourself, although I was born in the hearing of Bow Bells." And she will tell stories of her mother, who picked cockles and mussels off the rocks in Dublin Bay, who went to the races dressed in sprigged muslin—Annie has a photograph of her—in a jaunting car; of her father, who was six foot four inches tall and fought in the British Army in India, in China, and in Egypt, before he became a labourer, but always said to his family, I'm an Irishman, and I don't forget it; of how on St Patrick's Day he and her mother always drank to Ireland together, though they never had the money to visit it after they left it.

Bridget knocks on Eliza Bates's door, and there is no reply.

Her heart begins pounding. She lives in dread of walking in and finding one of them dead. It hasn't happened to her, but it has to other Home Helps. One of these days, it will. Bridget rang Vera yesterday to say that Eliza was not well, she was going downhill fast, they ought to be thinking of getting her into a Home. This was Bridget's tactful way of saying that she was not going to put up with it for long: Eliza's staying out of a Home was because of what she, Bridget, did for Eliza, beyond the demands of her job.

Eliza is sitting upright in her chair by her electric fire, asleep. It is very hot in the little room. Eliza is flushed with the heat, has sweat on her face. She is wrapped in shawls and blankets. Her legs are up on a pouffe, because she has suddenly developed a bad ulcer on one, and both of them are swollen.

Again Bridget sets out the food from Meals on Wheels, left outside the door in little flat foil containers, on plates. For Eliza she takes trouble finding pretty plates, for Eliza still cares and notices, not like that Annie, who wouldn't notice if she ate off a dog's plate. Bridget makes tea, remembering just how Eliza likes it, and then arouses Eliza, who comes awake staring and wild.

"Oh, Bridget," she says, in a trembling old voice, out of a bad dream, and then, hearing her own voice, changes it to her usual sprightly cheerfulness, "Oh, Bridget, Bridget dear . . ." But because of her dream, she puts up her arms to Bridget like a child.

Bridget, her heart at once melted, takes the old woman into her arms and kisses her and rocks her.

She could weep for Eliza, as she tells her husband, who has so suddenly found herself in a chair with her legs propped up, an invalid. It's not as if it was that Annie, who does everything to get herself waited on. No, Eliza is not like that, is independent, suffers. Bridget knows that twice recently Eliza has woken soaked in urine: Bridget has rinsed out the sheets for her. She knows that Eliza is afraid to go too far from the lavatory, for fear of worse. Eliza, who has spent the last fifteen years of her life in the company of the old, knows exactly what can happen at the end, the miserable humiliation that might be in store for her.

Bridget sits by Eliza, coaxing her to eat, chats about her children, her husband, says that the weather is not so good today as it was yesterday.

She establishes that Eliza has not been to bed all night but has sat up in the chair, sleeping. She has not had anything to eat yet, though the Good Neighbour made her a cup of tea. "Who is this Good Neighbour?" she asks Bridget, peevishly. "She comes in and out, I am sure she means well, but I don't know her."

"She lives next door," says Bridget. "Do let her in, she just drops in and out to make sure you are all right. We are worried about you, you see."

"Janna hasn't been in for days," says Eliza, but questioningly, for she knows she sometimes doesn't remember who comes in.

Bridget does not want to say that Janna has probably been busy, in what time she has, with Maudie Fowler, who is on her last legs—these old things are all so jealous, you've got to be careful what you say.

"Janna has got a lot to do," she says vaguely. She decides to leave a note addressed to Janna on the stairs, asking, if she does drop in, to make sure Eliza is all right.

Then she starts on the business of getting Eliza to take her pills. She herself is horrified at the number of pills Eliza is supposed to take, is sure that they must all quarrel together in the poor old thing's stomach, but the doctor says so, the nurse does what the doctor orders, and she, the Home Help, at the bottom of the heap, cannot disobey.

"Come on, love," she murmurs, beseeches, implores, handing Eliza pills and pills.

The nurse comes in to give her pills in the morning. The Good Neighbour gives her pills at night. But the midday pills (or some time in the day, for Bridget can never be sure of exactly when) are her job, for she has agreed to do it.

Eliza sits there, with tight lips, looking at the heap of pills, her face knotted up with resentment. But the habits of a lifetime's obedience keep her silent and she swallows them down, slowly, one, two, three, four, five.

Bridget has sworn that she would not be here more than an

hour at the most, but by the time she leaves it is nearly three hours, and she has the comfort of knowing that Eliza is almost her old self, alert and awake because of all that affectionate attention, a little tart perhaps in her comments, but smiling, even joking about her weakness, saying to Bridget that one of these days Bridget will come in here and find her gone.

Well, she's not so bad then, thinks Bridget to herself, if she can joke about it, but then, who can tell . . . ?

It is getting on for the time she should pick up her two girls. She never lets them go to school or come back by themselves, because of a big main road they have to cross.

She runs into a telephone booth, is lucky to find a friend at home, asks her to collect the two girls and take them to her place.

For it is nearly four, and she still has Mrs Brent and Mr Hodges.

The old man is easy, she has only to take in his food, having again banged and shouted and banged to be let in, and to say that either she or his own Help will be in tomorrow.

And now for Mrs Brent. Bridget does not have to pray that she will be in a good mood, for she always is, although she is part-paralysed. Not yet thirty, a beautiful young woman, she has a child of three, and it is Bridget's job to bring the child back from the nursery, where the young husband takes her every morning. At moments when Bridget thinks that she cannot endure this job one day more—though on the whole she does not mind it, it is only on a day like this, when there are the straws that *nearly* break her back, that she thinks she will give up—then she remembers Hilda Brent, who is always good for a laugh, even in such a sad situation.

Bridget runs as fast as she can along several streets to the nursery, finds the child ready, the teacher reproachful, for Bridget is late, and then goes to the little flat the Brents live in. She loves the little girl. She looks forward every day to this hour when she takes the child home to her mother, and gives her tea, for Hilda cannot do it, is dependent on her husband and Home Helps. But today she finds Hilda lying back in her chair, eyes closed, her pretty face all grey hollows.

Oh, Holy Mother, says Bridget to herself, oh no, *stop*, it's too much, *no*.

She knows what has happened, Hilda has these turns.

"Have you rung the hospital?" she shouts.

Hilda, without opening her eyes, shakes her head.

Bridget rings for an ambulance, and then rings the office where the young husband works. But, as she suspects, he will not be back until seven, he has to work late.

She gets the young woman's things ready for the ambulance, helps the ambulance men with her, sees her off, promises her she need not worry about the child, and then locks the flat, and puts little Rosie into her push-chair.

She wheels it to her friend's flat, collects her two children, and goes home with the three of them.

She is thinking that the last time there was an emergency, there had been a strike of the social workers for more money, and the Home Helps were supposed to be working to rule in sympathy. This struck her then and it strikes her now as the ultimate in stupidity. How can one work to rule in this job? How, tell me that! But she had been officially ticked off by some bright spark, who was organizing the pickets at the Office, for strike-breaking. But what was I supposed to do, then, let the baby fend for herself alone in that flat? What?

But the young hero had said to her, "If you ever do it again, you will be penalized."

Well, she was doing it again, but with a bit of luck there wasn't a strike on. She hoped.

At home she rushes about, getting her husband's tea. He needs it when he comes in, for he is working out on site this week and he is not well anyway, what with that nasty rash of his.

The boy comes in. "What shall I do with my football clothes?" he asks, and she says, "Throw them into the bath."

She has the table laid, tea made, the three children eating, and little Rosie on her lap drinking milk, when her husband comes in.

Again that rapid skilled expert glance. She knows at once he is ill and is not surprised when he says, "I'm going up to get into my bed, that's how I'm feeling."

"I'll bring you some tea, then."

"Don't trouble, love, I'm going to sleep it off."

And he goes upstairs.

Perhaps I can get Vera in her office now, sometimes she works late . . .

Bridget rings, and is lucky.

"Oh, thank God, Vera," she says, "thank God it's you."

"I'm just off," says Vera warningly.

"It's Eliza Bates. She can't go on. She can't."

And suddenly Bridget is weeping.

"Oh, it's like that, is it?" asks Vera. "Well, don't tell me, I know, I could howl my eyes out, what a day, and now they want me to go to a meeting on top of it."

"I'm going to ring off," says Bridget, doing so.

But by the time she turns to face the four children, she is smiling.

She cleans vegetables, puts them with a chicken into a pot, puts the pot into the oven, clears the tea things away, and says to the two older children, "And now get your homework done and you can watch television."

She sits down, cuddling the little girl, who, because of her father always being so desperate to catch up with himself, having a paralysed wife, and her mother not being able to hold her properly, is starved of proper comforting and cuddling.

The two needs are fed, together, for a blissful half an hour, the child crooning and snuggling, and Bridget sniffing at the deliciously smelling curls, which she washed herself yesterday (though it is not her job to do it), and stroking the soft plump little limbs.

Then she says to the older boy, "Keep an eye on them for me," and to the girl, "If you smell burning, then turn the oven down to three."

She ties a scarf over her head, pulls the plastic hood down over that and ties it fast, encloses little Rosie in plastic, and sets off along the dark streets to the Brents' flat, half a mile away. The young husband is back, grateful for her taking his child, wanting to know about tomorrow. For again he will have to work late, though he said his wife was ill, and he won't be home till later than today.

"Don't you worry about it," says Bridget, and she kisses little Rosie with all her heart, and goes home.

It is nearly eight. She will give her children supper, she will make herself take a bite, though she isn't hungry. She thinks that her husband had said something about their going to the Club for a drink tomorrow. Well, if he's up to it . . . And there's that wedding next week, of her husband's young sister, that's something to look forward to. She sits by herself, half watching television, listening that the children are not making too much noise and disturbing their father. There is a lot of cleaning she should be doing, but she seldom has time for her own place in the week. Bridget does not work at weekends. That is, she does not work as a Home Help.

Today, this happened. A telephone call from Jill, screaming, exultant. "Auntie, Auntie Jane, I've just done them, and I know I've done well."

"Done what?"

"Auntie! Oh *no*. It is too much." Tears. I thought, it must be that ghastly Kate, but no, it was Jill. What, then? I realized I'd been really stupid. "I'm sorry, it's your examinations, isn't it? They've gone well?"

Sniff. Sniff. "Yes, I am sure they have. I've worked so hard, Auntie, I've *worked*."

"Come up and tell me about it." I didn't mean that moment, but that is what I was inviting, and she shouted, "Oh, thank you, I'll be there this afternoon, but not till late, it's my turn to feed the neighbour's cats, she's away, and Mother is visiting Jasper in hospital, he's broken his ankle playing football."

I made myself sit down and think. Jill has never been renowned for her schoolwork, I remembered. She hated examinations, tended to fail. Now she's done well. She's been working: for Auntie Jane. She's been determined to pass well: for Auntie Jane. The whole family have been involved. Cheers and jeers, happy families. But Auntie Jane says, "Done what?"

She arrived, exuberant, shining all over.

She kissed me, spontaneously. Then seemed embarrassed.

"Tell me all about it."

"I know I've done well. The results won't be in for *weeks* but I know it."

She chatted on, giving me such a picture of what it must have been, Jill getting up at five to work, working all evening, and at the end of it the prize, a job in *Lilith* with Auntie Jane.

"When do you think I'll be able to start?" she inquired, and I realized she expected me to say, perhaps, "Next Monday." I was startled into silence. A long one. I was realizing a very great deal. She was waiting to move in here, with me, and to start work in *Lilith*—waiting for her adult life to begin. And I sat there looking at—myself, at her age. All pleasure, confidence, relish. She's not ambitious, Jill. She's being eaten up with excitement at the idea of being part of it all, *being able to do things well.* Emerging from loving family life, which grinds people down so, "Poor Jill, she's bad at examinations, poor Jill, she's not an academic". She is full of confidence at her abilities, which are bubbling in her; she doesn't know herself yet that she can do things; she knows only that she can't wait to start.

And suddenly as I realized that I had not *really* taken in that Jill, Sister Georgie's child, was going to come into my life, and take it over—I knew suddenly, beautifully, absolutely, how right it was, how apt, how fit, and I burst into laughter and sat laughing, unable to stop, while poor Jill sat there, all her joy ebbing away, tears coming into her eyes.

"Why do you hate us all so much?" she gasped. "Why, what have we done? You think we are all awful, that I'm no good, oh I know!"

"No, you don't know," I said. "I'm laughing at me. It is you lot down there who think *I* am no good, that I'm awful, and do you know what, Jill, at this moment I agree with them."

I watched her face, that had shrunk and gone white and pinched, absorb colour and confidence; and soon she smiled.

She said coaxingly, "You know, Aunt Jane, you've got me wrong. I never make scenes, slam doors, pout, leave things about, expect to be waited on . . ."

Teasing her: "A likely story, from your mother's daughter."

"I am *not* Kate. And I've been telling Mother, Why have you always let us do as we liked? Why are you a doormat?"

"And did she have a sensible reply?"

She laughed. I laughed.

"You could begin ingratiating yourself with me by not insisting on calling me Aunt Jane, or Auntie."

"Right, Janna, you're on."

"If my sister's daughter will allow herself to call me Janna, then . . ."

"Oh, Auntie, oh, Janna, what you don't realize is, you see, we were discussing it . . ."

"You *were*? A nice family discussion?"

"Of course. You can't believe, surely, you wouldn't be discussed? Why, you've been a sort of *focus* for—well, everything. There are splits and schisms in the family over you."

"There are?"

"Yes, and the way I see it is, it must go back to when you and Mother were children. Because it is quite clear to *us* that in let's say ten years we'll all have conflicts because of how we are *now*. Particularly Kate and me. If we ever want to see each other at all. She's such a *drag*."

"And it would help your mother and I to remember what we quarrelled about in our teens?"

"What did you quarrel about? Mother says you never quarrelled."

"What rubbish. She made my life a misery. It was the war, you see. Everything in short supply. She filched my rations. I had to wear her cast-offs."

"Ah," said the young psychologist.

I told Jill that of course she could not start at once. She will have to wait until there's a vacancy, and she won't get the job if there's an applicant who's better equipped than she.

"I don't believe in nepotism," I said.

"I hope you do, to a certain extent," said she, in the humorous voice that I know will be used to "handle" me.

When she went, I collapsed. I had taken it in, as a fact, as something that will happen. When Jill moves in here, my life will become shared. It is the end of lovely solitude. Oh, oh, oh, I can't bear it, I can't. Oh, how I do love being alone, the pleasures of solitariness . . .

*　　*　　*

I told them in the office I was going to take another two weeks' leave. Phyllis's look. She murmured, "Aren't you going to be here when the new editor comes in?"

"I shall take two weeks now. I'll be back by the time he comes."

Her look was meant to say, I don't understand you. My look at her, I understand myself, and that's enough.

Pleasure.

I woke early, the sun wasn't up, gold and pink cloudlets in a grey sky waiting to fill with sunlight. Early summer, a real summer's day. I lay in bed, looking, listening, the birds, the milk bottles clinking. I was inside my strong body, jam-packed with health and energy, and it stretched and yawned itself into being awake, and I jumped out of bed, with my mind on *Gracious Lady*. I wrote and wrote, Joyce rang, just off to bed. Amiable insults. I said, Niece Jill was going to take over my life, and she said, "Wonderful, now you'll really have a burden. A blossoming young soul and if she goes wrong it will be your fault."

"Your thoughts, not mine."

"Oh, yours, too, but they are unconscious, you can't win at this game. No, no, your portion is guilt, Janna."

"Not yours?"

"I'm liberated from it. By the way, how do you feel about taking on my two guilt-makers? The sooner the better as far as I am concerned."

"No, I don't know anything about *love*, you see. I'll leave your love-reared offspring to you, Joyce."

"I must say it's the neatest alibi you could imagine."

"What are you talking about?"

"If you have Niece Jill with you, you can't have your own life, you'll have no personal life, and as for a lover, out of the question."

"You assume I want one."

"Of course you want one. At least unconsciously. It is your right to have one. It is our right to have *good* sex. Surely you know that?"

"But I had good sex."

"No, it's your *right* to have good sex all the time. Until you are ninety."

"If you say so, Joyce. How's your good sex?"

"I'm working at it."

Then I had a bath, a quick one. What has happened to my long lovely baths, my scents and my oils and essences? I haven't time, that's what.

By nine I was down in the streets, sauntering along, enjoying myself in the way I do. Oh, the good humour of this city, the pleasantness, the friendliness! The sun was shining fitfully, in and out of rapid white clouds. Mild. I went into the boutique cum coffee room cum health food shop, and since there was no one in it, Mary Parkin left her counter and sat with me and told me the latest instalment in that long serial, her war with her neighbour over that wicked woman's insensitive treatment of her cat. I ate healthy, rich, delicious whole-grain cake. Then I walked on down the High Street, and in the newspaper shop stood on one side while a tall, rakish, handsome young labourer teased the two middle-aged and respectable women behind the counter because of a magazine they sell, which advised a young wife trying to reattract her husband to cut her pubic hair into a heart shape.

He had bought this mag yesterday for his wife, they had had a good laugh over it, and now he couldn't resist, he said, dropping in to share the joke with Madge and Joan.

"Well, you never know," says he, "we thought we should point it out, after all, you might not have noticed it, and you wouldn't want to let your pubic hair go ungroomed, would you?"

"I don't think I've had much occasion to notice mine recently," says Madge, and asks Joan, "How about you, dear?"

"My pubic hair is not what it was," says Joan, handing the *Sun* and the *Mirror* to an old woman (as it might be Maudie, or Eliza Bates) who is listening to this unable to believe her ears.

"If I wasn't married," says the young man, "I'd see what I could do, but as it is ... well, ta, then, keep *Homes and Gardens* for us then, Lily says if she can't afford a new decor, then she likes to read about it at least."

And off he goes. The two women look at each other and share that laugh which means, Those were the days, and turn their attention to the old woman, who is scrabbling about in her handbag for change. They wait patiently, realizing she is upset by what she has heard, and then ask after her husband.

She and I arrive on the pavement together. She looks straight at me with shocked eyes and whispers, "Did you hear?"

I switch roles and say, "Disgraceful," thinking of the real pain of Eliza when she reports of the radio, the telly, the papers, But what is happening to everyone, why are young people like this now?

But Joan and Madge are not young, that is why she is miserable. We walk along the pavement, while she gently grumbles herself back into balance.

And now the bus. By now the office workers have ebbed from this area, and the bus is full of women. The freemasonry of women, who sit at their ease, shopping baskets and bags all over them, enjoying a nice sit-down and the pleasant day. A bus at half past ten in the morning is a different world: nothing in common with the rush-hour buses.

These women who keep things together, who underpin our important engagements with big events by multifarious activities so humble that, asked at the end of the day what they did, they might, and often do, reply, Oh, nothing much.

They are off to a shop three stages away to buy knitting wool for a jersey for a grandchild, buttons for a dress or a shirt, or a reel of white cotton, for one should always have some about. They are going to the supermarket, or to pay the electricity bill, or to get their pensions. The Home Helps are on their way to get prescriptions made up for Eliza Bates, Annie Reeves, Mrs Coles, Mrs Brent, Mr Hodges. Someone is off to the stationer's to buy birthday cards for all the family separately to send to Uncle Bertie, aged sixty-four. A parcel is being sent to Cape Town to an emigrated niece and her family, for she has asked for a certain make of vests you cannot, it seems, get in South Africa. Or a parcel containing homemade biscuits to Wales, for a cousin. Some are off down to Oxford Street, on a weekly or monthly jaunt, regarded as a holiday, a rest, and will spend hours trying on dresses and keeping a sharp eye open for clothes that might be suitable for mothers, daughters, husbands, sons. They come home from several hours' hard labour around the shops with a petticoat, two pairs of nylons, and a little purse. All of which they could have bought in the High Street, but it's not so much fun. They will later go to visit housebound relatives, taking with them all kinds of specially needed commodities, like tooth powder, or a certain brand of throat lozenges; they will go to the hospital and sit for hours with a granny; they drop in to have a cup of tea with a daughter or take a grandchild to the park. They are at it all day, these women, and the good nature that is the result of their competence at what they do overflows and splashes about the inside of the bus, so that smiles get exchanged, people remark on the weather—in other words, offer each other consolation or encouragement—and comment humorously on life through events glimpsed on the pavement.

The Victoria and Albert, all the time in the world, I looked at a little chair, early eighteenth century, of wood like silk, and its life and times seemed so enormous, all-encompassing, like listening to Maudie talk, or Eliza, such a statement it was, sitting demurely there, *Look at me!*—it was enough and I went off to the restaurant, and there was a gentleman, that's the word, courtly and humorous, ready like me for a few amiable words over a meal, and we sat together and did not say more than we had to about our lives and times. Enjoyable. On the steps he went his way, and I mine to the top of a bus this time, for it was afternoon, and it was no longer women's time, and I listened to the conductor's back-chat with a passenger, the London style, sardonic, dry, with its flavour of the surreal.

In the High Street, the café where I sometimes manage to find time for half an hour's lunch with Vera, but now I sit for an hour or so, listening to a couple of out-of-work youngsters at the next table. One black, one white. Youths. Passing the time away, like me. I said to myself, This is a tragedy, you should be feeling bad, but their faces were not tragic, but good-natured; yes, I would say sad, but far from hopeless about it all. They were making jokes and planning to go to the cinema. I was determined not to be sad, not today, not this perfect day. I talked to them a little, but I was this thing outside their experience, at their age probably the "old woman"; they were nice but not going to open up and share anything. They went off saying to me, "Ta, then, see you. Take care."

I went off to Maudie, and no, that was the bad part of the day. Maudie is so ill—but enough, I left her to walk up past the deer and the peacocks and the goats in Golders Park, to drink good coffee on the little terrace with all the shrewd comfortable elderly Jews who sit through the summer there, getting brown and shining, and with the mothers and the little children. On the long acres of green grass, the deck chairs were like sails, like coloured sails, miles of blue sky, with not a cloud anywhere, and people scattered about soaking in the sunlight.

I came back home in the dusk, late, after nine, and here I sit, at my desk, Diary Time, and I am trying to capture this day, this lovely day, so that it doesn't vanish away for ever. Because it is precious, it is rare. Oh, I know how to value it, such a day, time for the spending, all the time in the world—but only for one day, nothing I *have* to do, no one I *have* to see, except Maudie, oh, poor Maudie, but I'll not think about her until tomorrow. A day in London, the great theatre, lovely London whose quality is sardonic good humour, and kindness, a day to myself, in solitude. Perfect enjoyment.

The two weeks are over. That was the best day, because of the sun, but I enjoyed all the days, fifteen of them, long and lazy. Except for Maudie. I am doing all kinds of things for her again.

It is late summer. I have been working, working, how I do work, how I do like being able to—and how much I will enjoy not working so hard, when I go on part-time. Soon.

Jill is in my flat, my home, she is in my "study", a decent room, not too large, but she's hardly ever here. She's taken to the office—as I did, all those years ago. She's taken to Phyllis, and Phyllis to her. They work together, Jill soaking it all up. She does not see Phyllis as I do—as I *did*; Phyllis has changed, she's lost her cutting edge. She is kind to Jill, sensitive, generous.

The new editor. He was not the one I voted for, he's the

Board's choice. At first glance it was evident to me and to Phyllis, in fact to everyone, that he'd be a passenger. Phyllis was wild with the injustice of it: she's too young to be editor, the question did not arise of course, but she was fit for it. Now she has to work *through* him. I cannot say, My dear girl, take no notice, don't waste time being upset, nothing much will change.

Indirect instruction. What I did was to talk a great deal about when Joyce and I worked together in the old days, ran everything, while the so-called editor danced to our tune. Phyllis, with a small nice smile, listens, her eyes full of ironical enjoyment. Jill doesn't yet understand what I am saying, but she watches Phyllis with such concentration that she soon will. I have never once denigrated poor Charlie.

I'm engaged in "working in" Charlie, who will take my place at the end of that time. He's a nice man, I'm fond of him. Product of the sixties. What a sloppy lot, no discipline, they had everything too easy. Agreeable, greying, bit too fat, you almost expect to see food stains on his roll-neck. *He doesn't pay attention.*

I've been wondering for years what makes the difference between the ten per cent who really work and the rest who float along appearing to work, perhaps even believing they do. Poor Charlie arrived in the office, and waited to be told. I had given thought, of course, to *where* he should be. I wasn't going to turn the photographers out, they need the space. I didn't see why our room should be given up, and it has never been one of the best. No, the room used for board meetings, officious and rather upholstered and apart. I moved into this, with Charlie, and left the two girls where Joyce and I had been. Now I sit opposite Charlie, as I did with Joyce. We get on like anything.

Charlie has been running a trade mag, a clean, bright, good-looking production. (But who *really* ran it?) He sits there, sliding papers about all over the large desk, while I tell him the history of our mag, the changes, how it should be now "in my opinion"—God forbid that I think my opinion should matter now, I'm on my way out. Oh but Janna, of course we must take your ideas into account . . .

He never ever initiates anything . . . Well, does that matter?

Passivity is a great virtue, sometimes. To be able to let things happen: oh yes, one must know how to do that. But then to take control, at the right moment, make the machinery start, use inertia, *make* things happen.

Joyce was good at waiting, listening, then moving in and controlling. Perhaps, I thought, Charlie is such a one. But no, I am pretty sure not. *He does no work*—well, very few ever do. It is interesting, watching people not working. The mail comes in, he hands it over to me, I go through it with him. He says, How about this or that? I say, Don't you think if we . . .? He says, Well, perhaps . . . I find myself making the telephone calls, and then I have my secretary in, and Charlie is busy with papers as I dictate. He has a business lunch every day, with someone. He is back late in the office, and by then everything is under way. He sits around, we talk, he dictates a letter or two, and the day is over. *He has done no work at all.* He has even said to me, smiling, but the smile did have the faintest tinge of anxiety, A good organizer knows how to delegate.

Well, fair enough: all our departments would go along quite well under their own momentum for a long time, without intervention.

Meanwhile, there is Phyllis, there is Jill, and they have already got the idea. It is to them that he is—Charlie thinks—delegating responsibility. I watch Phyllis as she comes in to take instructions, to make suggestions. She does *not* allow her eyes to engage with mine, never is there the faintest suggestion of complicity. Oh, full marks, Phyllis! She sits there, competent, quiet, of course dressed in her soft silky reassuring clothes, and says, "Charlie, I was wondering what you'd think if we . . ."

"Well, I was rather thinking along those lines myself," he will say, half an hour later. And when I go into their office, to have a chat, we talk as if in fact it is Charlie who has initiated this and that, Charlie who is in control.

The wonderful autumn continues, day after day, and this afternoon I had cleaned out my flat (Jill's room is kept very nice indeed), and actually got my clothes, hands, nails, etc., up to the mark, and I was looking at the sky, and suddenly I was running down the stairs, into my car and to Maudie.

"Maudie," I said, "come to the park."

It could have gone either way, I saw that, and I said, "Come on, Maudie, do . . . Just for once, say yes."

And she smiled her sprightly amenable smile, the one I see with such relief, and she says, "But there's my sandwiches cut and the cups out . . ." I fly in, fetch her coat, her hat, her bag, and she lets me take over. In ten minutes, Regent's Park. I drive around and around the Inner Circle, looking at the gold and bronze and green under the blue blue sky, and Maudie has her face averted and her hand shading it. I think, she's crying, yes, but no, I *won't* notice it. So I keep my eyes well away.

"Can you walk a little?" I ask.

Luckily, a free space only twenty yards from the entrance to the café. It is a long twenty yards, and I see how she has deteriorated since we were here last summer. I hated that word when I first heard that snide little pretty-boots Hermione use it, and now I hate it when Vera uses it, and yet I use it myself. Maudie is deteriorating fast . . . like groceries.

At last we got into the place where the tables are. There are roses still, blobs of colour and scent, in their proper places, and the well-fed sparrows hopping everywhere. I settle Maudie and fetch cakes and coffee. Maudie eats, eats, in her slow methodical enjoying way, and in between cakes she sits smiling at the sparrows. *The darlings, the darlings* . . .

I cannot believe how much she can eat, when I think of that little yellow belly. And Maudie says, You must feed an ulcer, they say . . . not apologetic, but wondering, for she too is amazed at how she has to eat and eat, sometimes cutting bread and butter after she has polished off the Meals on Wheels or eating a whole packet of biscuits.

And then I drive her around and around and around the Inner Circle while she shields her face and gazes at the yellow trees and the shadows coming under them.

Maudie. She seems to be better: if you can say that of a woman with cancer. Her dreadful rages infrequent, her mood often friendly, even gay. This, paradoxically, because she feels that I have let her down. Just after I took her to the park, I again woke with my back in a knot. Nothing like as bad as last time, and it was gone by next day. But I knew what I had to do.

I rang Vera Rogers, we had a long talk, and I went in to Maudie, sat myself down, and said, "Look, Maudie, I have got to explain something and please listen, without getting cross with me."

This "getting cross" was already a note I had decided not to use: for I had spent hours the night before telling myself, she is an intelligent woman, she is sensible, I only have to explain . . . Oh, what nonsense; for almost at once she had turned her face away, and was staring with her hard trembling forlorn look at the fire.

I was telling her she had to have a Home Help, even if only twice a week, to do shopping; she had to have a nurse in to wash her. Or I would be permanently on my back in bed and she wouldn't see me at all.

She did not say one word. When I had finished, she said, "I have no alternative, have I?" Later she made it clear she blamed Vera Rogers, that villain.

I realized then that I must no longer expect sense from her.

The Home Help is a nice Irish girl, who was told Mrs Fowler was difficult and who stood patiently knocking until Maudie let her in, grinding her teeth and glaring and muttering.

Molly said politely, "And what can I fetch you in?"

Maudie said, "I've got everything."

"Oh dear," said Molly, trying something that works with another difficult old woman, "I am so tired, can I sit down and have a cigarette?" She looked at the dreadful armchair, and sat on the hard chair by the table.

Maudie did not miss that repugnance, although it showed itself for no more than a moment, and she decided she hated this girl. "I can't stop you sitting," she said.

And Molly knew that in this place she must not sit and be chatty. Soon she put out her cigarette and said, "If you've got nothing for me to fetch in, I'll be off."

At which Maudie was silent, and then said in a hurried offhand angry way: "There's biscuits . . . and you could get in something for the cat . . . don't want you to put yourself out."

On this basis poor Molly manages to get some of the things Maudie needs: but when she tried to see into the kitchen, where she might be able to use her intelligence to find out what was missing, Maudie said, "I don't remember asking you in." And so when Maudie forgets, which she so often does, she goes without. And when I get in, I go out again for her. I feel ridiculous; after all, it only takes a few minutes. She thinks it is ridiculous, that she has to put up with that Home Help, and all because I have gone cold and unforgiving.

But the worst, of course, was her being washed by a nurse who is black, too young, too old, white, and with hard hands or cold hands—who is not Janna. She would not let the nurses in; then found I was being unkind and would not respond to her silent appeals. Then she did let them in, but they could not find washing things, could not find clean clothes, and their at first gentle and patient, then increasingly irritated and peremptory queries received only muttered replies. The first nurse was black, reported that she thought Mrs Fowler would not stand for a black nurse; the second, white, tried twice and gave up; the third actually managed to wash Maudie, who found it so shameful and painful a business that next time a nurse came, she was screamed at: "Go away, I don't want any of you, I can manage by myself."

Then there was a ridiculous time when, as I arrived in the evening, I was confronted by Maudie, smelling horrible, looking desperate and ashamed. We sat there as usual, on either side of the fire, and she entertained me with the same stories, for she has run out of memories, and between us was this knowledge that I would not wash her, that I her friend was no longer her friend.

"When you were still my friend," she began once, not meaning it as pressure, but because it is what she is thinking.

And soon I was thinking, this is an old woman dying of cancer, and I won't even give up half an hour of my time to wash her.

I rang up Vera, told her to cancel the nurses, but keep on the Home Help, and I have been washing Maudie since. But not every day, I simply cannot. I am afraid of that silent enemy, my back.

When I arrive, Maudie is wondering, sometimes in real misery and horror at her condition of dirtiness and smell, is she going to be in a good mood today? And I sense this, and say,

"Do you feel like a wash, Maudie?" And her face! The relief on her poor old face . . . How she does hate being dirty, being repulsive to herself. And in a way my coming into her life was a bad thing for her, because before she had been able to forget it a little, had not been noticing her filthy clothes, her grimy wrists, the dirt in her fingernails.

And so, every third day or so, I wash her all over. And she has not been dirtying herself at all, though she is sometimes wet.

I partly understand the vigilance and effort that goes into keeping herself unsoiled: how often she drags herself out to the cold lavatory; how she studies to outwit her bowels. And besides, there is something else: she does not want Janna—the spy for Vera Rogers—to know what she is making; so she will do anything, even sit up all night, so as not to use the commode. But once she had to use it, she could not get out in time, and I came in before she could empty it. She did not stop me from taking out the pot, but she stood looking into my face in a way that told me this was a moment she had dreaded, and now it was here. I thought she had been drinking real coffee: then I remembered something about coffee-ground stools. And I did ring up Vera next day; and she said, Oh, I should call the doctor in, I *should*. Don't, I said, please don't. Leave her for as long as you can.

And so, now, instead of Janna the real friend, the *one person* (who is your other self) who can be relied upon, who will always say yes and do what is needed, she has this other Janna, who sets limits and sometimes she will and sometimes she won't.

I took Maudie to visit her sister. She chose a Sunday when she believed she would be well enough not to disgrace herself. She rang her sister, dragging up the steps to the telephone box at the corner, and told me afterwards it was arranged, and she would take herself by bus, she had done it often enough, I needn't put myself out.

It was a warm November day. Maudie had on a best dress of dark blue silk with grey and pink roses on it. It was given to her by her actress friend from Hammersmith soon after the Second World War. She wore a black coat with it, and a black straw hat with black satin ribbon and a little bunch of roses: she bought it forty years ago, for a wedding. When I went in to pick her up, I thought she could be Liza's mother in *My Fair Lady*: a shabby poverty, but gallant. But there was, too, something sprightly, even rakish about her, and thus it was that Maudie, visiting her relatives, whom she had not seen for years, presented herself to them as they think of her, an eccentric, gone-to-nothing poor relation whom they wish they could forget.

It was a nice little house, old, with a garden, one of several dotted about among the great new tower blocks, the massive shops, the garages, the roaring roads. We drove around for a while, looking for the place, and there it was: almost a village, or the fragment of one. A painted garden gate, a path up between autumn-dimmed roses, and there was the clan, waiting to receive Aunt Maude and her new friend. Curiosity. They are an awful lot, hard, bright, *common*—a word that should never have been allowed to go out of use.

The sister, older than Maudie, is a matriarch, still active and in command. She cooked the dinner, ordered daughters and granddaughters how to lay the table, instructed sons and grandsons that she needed the rubbish taken out, a jammed window opened, the lavatory chain lengthened.

Twelve of them, all in smart nasty clothes, talking about their cars, their lawn mowers, their holidays. They are all a good step up from Maudie and her sister Polly, but then, how would you assess them in relation to their wicked grandfather, Goodtime Charlie? I sat there brooding about our class system, not always easy to sort out; while I answered questions about what I did—I certainly did not tell them, for they would think I was lying, said I was a secretary; questions about Maudie. But I knew what was coming, and it came: "So you are Maudie's Good Neighbour?"

I was determined not to let Maudie be cheated out of a real friend of her own; and I said, "No, I am not. I am Maudie's friend. We have known each other for some time now."

They did not accept this, exchanged knowing glances. They

addressed loud patronizing questions and remarks to Maudie, as if she were a half-wit; and she sat there among them in her best clothes, her head trembling a little, defiant and guilty, and obviously unwell, and tried to stand up against this truly awful pressure that made her ridiculous and stupid. A timid question to her formidable old sister: "Polly, do you remember how I used to make fruit roll for Paul?" "Did you, Maudie? You were always busy with ideas of your own, weren't you?" And: "Polly, do I see that old sauce boat still? I remember it from home." Polly, then, with a large, angry sniff: "Well don't think you're going to get it now, because you aren't. You've had what you are entitled to!"

"Oh Mother!" "Oh Mum!" "Oh dear!" From the "children", elderly themselves now; and from the grandchildren, in their twenties and thirties, exchanging merry glances because here is a family tradition bought to life: how Auntie Maudie was always trying to make off with Granny's things, she was always scrounging and begging, and now she's at it again.

Maudie, realizing what is happening, goes silent, and stays silent, except for Yes and No, through the meal.

The fourteen of us around the long table that has a leaf put into it cram the dining room, which is the room everyone uses; there is a front room, like the old-fashioned "parlour", which is unnaturally clean and shiny. We pass around old-fashioned vegetable dishes full of greasy roast potatoes, watery cabbage, soggy parsnips. There is rather good roast beef. We pass around bottled horseradish sauce and ketchup and a silver cruet large enough for a hotel—or for this family gathering. We eat stewed plums, bottled from the garden, and marvellous suet pudding, light and crusty, with jam sauce. We drink cups of strong milky tea. The middle-aged ones talk of their vegetable gardens and bottling and freezing what they grow; the young ones talk of pizzas and foreign foods they eat on their travels. Apparently there are plenty of young children; but they have not been brought to this gathering, it would be too much for Auntie Maudie, they say; and the thrust goes home, for there are tears in her eyes; but I did not find out what it referred to. These people do not see each other except at Christmas, when they gather together here, all of them. They joke *at* each other all the time, a hard, cruel game, keeping alive moments of weakness, failure, treachery. Their faces are glistening with strength and confidence and this careless cruelty. And the matriarch sits calmly there, smiling. I easily see her father in her: I have never been able to catch a whisker of him in Maudie. She has a broad red face, under fluffy white curls that show the red shiny scalp. She has a massive body, in a crimplene brown and white figured dress, very tight and awful. She has heavy reddish hands, with shiny swollen knuckles. She walks with a stick. Ninety-six, she is: and good for another ten years. They eat, they eat, they eat; we all eat. And Maudie eats most of all, sitting silent there, her eyes kept down, thorough and methodical, she keeps us all waiting while she demolishes every last crumb.

And they all sit nicely around the loaded table, with their superior smiles, their false good humour, and they tease her with Auntie Maudie did this, Auntie Maudie did that.

And she answers not a word.

When the meal was over she said to me, "And now it is time for us to go." She looked straight at her sister, raised her voice, and said, "Now that I've eaten you out of house and home."

Uneasy titters from the children; amusement from the grandchildren. The absent great-grandchildren may never have heard of Auntie Maudie.

The matriarch merely smiled, queenly and hard. Said she, "I've made you a nice little Christmas pudding as usual, to take away home with you."

"I don't remember seeing one last year, or the year before."

"Oh, Auntie," said a niece.

The matriarch gave a directing nod at a young man, who took a little white bowl to Maudie. At first she was going to leave it, and then gave it to me: "Take it."

I took up the little pudding that might perhaps have fed a few sparrows, and we all went together slowly to my car, Maudie setting the pace. Oh, how yellow and awful she did look in the late-autumn sunlight. And the family saw it, and understood. Suddenly a chill on them, these large well-off fresh-faced people, as they stared at the family's little black scapegoat. They exchanged frightened looks and raised their voices and cried, "Goodbye, Auntie, come and see us again soon!"

"That's right," ordered her sister, "you must get your Good Neighbour to bring you another Sunday. But give me enough warning next time." For she had decided not to understand that Maudie would not come again. She said to me, "It is so nice for Maudie to have a Good Neighbour. If I've told her once I've told her a hundred times, you need a Home Help, I've said."

And in this way was Maudie finally robbed by her family of this achievement of hers, a real friend of her own, someone who loves her.

For I do love Maudie, and I couldn't bear it when she sat there beside me, trembling, whimpering.

I said to her, "Maudie, you're worth a hundred of that lot, and I am sure you always were."

And so we drove home, in silence. I stayed with her all afternoon, making her tea, making her supper, cosseting her. But she was listless and distressed. And next day there was a real change in her. That was three weeks ago. And it's been downhill ever since.

A week ago she began talking of how once, when she was a child, she was taken to Christmas Eve service, and she had never forgotten the Child in the manger, and the angels. I asked my secretary to find out where there would be an easily accessible service, but at last settled for the church down the street from Maudie, so she would not have to manage a long journey.

She has talked for the whole week, and for the first time, about the church services she was taken to as a small girl, but clearly Burlington Bertie and his fancy-woman and the poor wife didn't go in much for religion. What she talks about is the singing, the prettiness of the church, the coloured-glass windows, "the nice smell of the wood", the flowers.

I drove her last night very slowly the hundred yards or so to the church: and could see how much—again—she had deteriorated, for only five weeks ago I took her to her sister's; but now the gentle movement of the car was distressing her. I helped her out of the car and walked with her into the church. Outside it was the usual quite pleasant little building, nothing remarkable, but as soon as we reached the entrance, I saw through Maudie's eyes. She stood quite still gazing, lifting her eyes up to the dark spaces of the roof, and then to the blaze of candles on the altar. On one side, a pretty baby in the crib, and the angels, in blue and scarlet robes and gold crowns, knelt behind Mary, who was a shining young girl with pink cheeks and a lovely smile. The three kings stood near, their hands full of gifts wrapped in gold and silver, tied with scarlet. And all around, on soft glinting straw, were lambs. And a real dog, the vicar's, a white woolly terrier, lay among the lambs.

Oh the pretties, cried Maudie, so that people turned to see the old, bent, black-clothed crone smiling and trembling there. And they smiled too, for there was only the blurring gentle light of the candles, and no one could see how ill and yellow she was.

We went very slowly up the aisle, because she was not looking how she walked but at the beautiful scene there by the altar, and we sat right at the front, where we could see the obedient dog panting a little, and yawning because of the heat from the candles. Oh the lovelies, oh the pretties, oh my petty, my little petties, wept Maudie, stretching out her hands; and the dog, responding to her, came halfway towards her, and then, at a low command from someone out of sight behind a pillar, went back to lie among the lambs. The service was ordinary enough; and I am sure the scene was tawdry.

Afterwards she was worn out with it all, and I put her to bed, with some hot milk, and her cat beside her.

Lovely, lovely, my lovely petties, she was murmuring, and smiling at me, the cat, her memories, as I left.

But . . . she has to go into hospital. The doctor came last week, and not because the wicked Vera asked him to. He was expecting, he told her, that Maudie was "about ripe" for hospital, and what he found made him say that if it wasn't for Christmas she would have to go in at once. But she has a week's grace. We know she will not come out again.

Does *she*?

Oh no, that's another two weeks gone . . .

A nightmare. Maudie boiling and raging. Vera Rogers is away on a training course, and since there has to be an enemy, I'm it. "Maudie," I said, when she'd slammed the door in my face one night, and admitted me next day, white-faced, eyes blazing, "why are you treating me so badly?"

We were sitting opposite each other, the fire out, the room cold, her unfed cat restless and yowling. I was expecting her capitulation, the sharp turn of her head, the prideful lift of her chin—then the sigh, the hand up to shield her face, and, soon, the small reasonable voice in an explanation. But no, she sat sullenly there, her lower lip thrust out, eyes staring. I coaxed and cajoled, but no; and I am wondering if perhaps I shall not see *my* Maudie again. For there is no doubt of it, she is a little mad. I have been thinking about this, what we tolerate in people without ever calling them mad. What is madness, then? Surely, losing contact with reality? For Maudie to scream and rage at her only friend, to treat me as an enemy, is not rational.

Nothing that is happening touches reality, it is all a horrible farce, because I cannot say to her, Maudie, you have cancer. I think of my mother, I think of Freddie. I lie awake at night and wonder, what has made that difference, that those two people could say, I have cancer, but Maudie cannot? Education? Nonsense! But at no point before my mother, my husband, died were they out of touch with what was going on. It was I who was out of touch!

And Vera is not here, and so I cannot ask her . . . what? All kinds of things I need to know. I cannot handle Maudie. In hospital or not.

Vera has come back, we have taken Maudie to hospital.

*   *   *

I had to arrange for Maudie's cat to be fed by the woman next door, who said I mustn't expect that she would give it a home, so why not take it to the RSPCA? I went through the place, to make sure there was nothing that would smell—the commode, the kitchen. I found horrible caches of soiled knickers and underclothes and was able at last to dispose of them into the dustbins. And, as I did so, said to myself that it was as if I was disposing of Maudie.

It is true that I am thinking, why does she have to go through with this, the long sordid process of dying? If she could only just die in her sleep. But what right have I to feel like that, if she doesn't?

She is in our newest large hospital, in a ward that takes four, getting the best of modern medicine, modern nursing. She is surrounded by solicitude, tact, charm. And there she is, that poor Maudie, a little yellow angry old woman, propped up in bed, held up on cushions in a chair, brought food, brought medicines, and she does nothing but rage and rebel and mutter and curse . . . and yet they all of them love her. It is true. At first I thought it was just their marvellous training, but no. There's something about her, each one of the nurses has said to me; and the junior doctor said, "How did you get to be a friend of hers?" Really wanting to know, and it was because he, too, feels it in her. "She's very lovable," says the male nurse, who has just spent twenty minutes persuading her to take her medicine. It is a pain-killer. Not the ferocious potion she will be getting when the pain gets bad enough to make it essential: this is an intermediate brew. But Maudie says, It takes away my mind, my mind feels full of cotton wool, and she puts off taking it until, with an angry whimper, she jerks her head at the glass that is standing on her table, indicating to me that she will take it.

I go up every day after work, for a couple of hours.

"Oh, there you are at last," says Maudie.

And, when I leave: "Going, are you?" And she turns her face away from me.

The relief of it, not having to wash her and keep her clothes more or less clean; not having to sit opposite her, keeping down anger, depression, spite while she spits venom at me.

The family have already been, the tribe, admitted to her presence in twos and threes.

"Are you coming to see if there's anything for you when I'm dead?" she inquires. "You should know better than that, you've had everything off me years ago."

"Oh, Auntie!" say nieces, nephews, and, "What sort of talk 's that, Maudie?" inquires the matriarch.

"You know what kind of talk," says Maudie, and turns her face to stare away from them; and she does not reply to their Goodbye, Auntie, Goodbye, Maudie.

I asked to start part-time earlier; I now go in two full days, flexibly according to need; one half-day on the Think Session morning; and I've agreed to another full day and a half in the few days before the mag goes to the printers.

Phyllis asked me to have lunch with her. A formal invitation. This is because she and Jill are inseparable now, Jill has attached herself to Phyllis, and it is not easy to find even a few minutes for private talk.

I thought she wanted some advice about the office, Jill perhaps, but she took my self-possession away by saying that Charles wants to marry her.

The possibility had not crossed my mind, and as I sat there, dabbing my mouth with a napkin, and taking some wine, to gain time, I was thinking it had not come into my mind because it was preposterous. That was my first reaction, and as I sit here writing (midnight) I think it was the right one.

Almost at once I recovered myself and sat there all sympathetic attention, and trying to make myself feel less critical of it all, by repeating silently that, as is well known, I am not equipped to make judgements in this area, due to my never having been really married, there is "something missing".

But how can she marry Charles, or rather, how can she stay married? He is getting a divorce, has three children, so there is so much to pay out for their education. Phyllis will have to support their life-style. What about children? All this was running through my head; while she sat there, leaning forward in her anxiety, such a pretty thing in her soft clothes. I would never before have thought to call her pretty, but she is these days. Hair shining, eyes shining, she seemed to gleam and glow against the dark wood walls of the restaurant.

She wanted advice. Well, I know better by now than to give people advice.

I wanted to find out how clear she is in her mind about what she is taking on; for that is the essence of it, surely? What she was talking about was how she and Charles worked together so well on the mag, how easy everything is: she talked on and on restlessly about work, and her eyes were expectantly on mine, for I had not said, Oh, Phyllis, you are crazy, or, What marvellous news. And I let her talk, and talk, saying not very much, but supplying the occasional worldly-wise remarks that one needs such a large supply of to cope with the moments when people expect you to tell them what to do.

And by the time our meal was finished, she was mentioning for the first time that they would not be able to afford to have a child, for she would have to work, and that she did not know what she felt about children. She kept giving me small hopeful looks, as if even now at this late stage, I might say, But of course, you must marry him!

But what I did ask was, in the hurried embarrassed way one uses when a topic you want to introduce is foreign to the texture of a conversation, "But what about your Women's Meetings, that sort of thing?"

She averted her eyes, smiling, and said, carelessly, "Oh, he doesn't mind what I do, he's quite interested, really."

That struck me as so off the point that I heard myself laughing nervously, as if at a joke that had fallen flat.

Charlie invited me to lunch too. He wanted to tell me about his problem. He feels it is unfair to marry Phyllis and burden her with his past. He is having second thoughts about marrying her? I had polished up an extra supply of remarks like, You must think it over seriously and do what you think best! And, I do see that you must feel like that! I used them while listening to what amounted to a two-hour monologue. When we parted outside the restaurant, he thanked me for good advice. Phyllis is too clever: when we parted (outside the same restaurant) a few days earlier, she gave me a cheeky grin and said, "Why won't you tell me what to do, and then I can put all the blame on you!"

It seems at least possible that these two might get married out of inertia; if then, after all, the marriage turns out well . . . ?

I had looked forward, now I have more time, to getting my clothes up to the mark. What hard work it is, my style. I stood in front of the glass in my best suit. Honey-beige wild silk. My bag. My gloves. My shoes. There is a roughness over the seat, and no way of curing it. The edges of the revers have a slightly dulled look. Two buttons are working loose. A thread showing from the dove-grey satin lining. My shoes have creases along the fronts. My gloves are less than ideal. All my silk stockings have ladders. What is to be done? Throw the whole lot out and start again! But no, the problem is, if I have the time now for my style, I do not have the inclination. I have been remembering how Colette's, or Chéri's, Leah greeted her old lover with the information of how she put on a suit and a good lace jabot and there she was, ready for anything and in full fig. And what hurt him (hurt Colette?) was that she no longer cared about these careful time-consuming luxuries. But I am not going to be slovenly, I will not. The trap of old age—after all, I am in my fifties, hardly time to abdicate—is a tired slovenliness. If I no longer can care about my style, which depends on time, trouble, detail, then I shall think out something intelligent, a compromise. Meanwhile, I have taken a load of stuff to the charity shop, and have asked my dressmaker to repeat certain items. I have never done that before; we have spent hours in consultation over materials, buttons, linings. She was surprised, rang me up on getting my letter, and what she was really asking was, Have you lost interest that you simply tell me please make the pale grey woollen suit again, and the material is in Bond Street?—Yes, my dear, it is so, I have lost interest; but after all, I did introduce Phyllis to you. And I shall ask you to make again for me the brown trouser suit, the black *crêpe de Chine* shirt, the cream silk dress.

* * *

How long has it been? Two weeks, I think.

Every day, in to Maudie. Hello, I say, how are you, in the same smiling friendly way that everyone uses, and which—putting myself in her position—I know seems to her a nightmare of dissimulation, of deceit. Here she is, trapped, our prisoner; and she is surrounded by our lying smiles. *Which she herself imposes.* I long for her to come out from her yellow sullen hostility, I long to communicate, if even for a few moments, with Maudie herself. But she is shut inside her rage, her suspicion; and from that prison, looks out at that *awful* charming smile which I can feel my face organizing itself into as I go in.

What an ordeal, what a horror! I am talking about my ordeal, not Maudie's now. Selfish still, obviously, though I believe that this Janna who goes in every day to sit with Maudie one hour, two hours, three (though never long enough, she always feels rejected when I leave), is not at all that Janna who refused to participate when her husband, her mother, were dying. I sit for hours near Maudie, ready to give what my mother, my husband, needed from me: my consciousness of what was happening, my participation in it. But what Maudie wants is—not to be dying!

She mutters at me, in a new hurried breathless way, "*I* know who to thank for this, *I* know who ordered me here!" And does not look at me, for she so much hates what she sees.

She means me, and she means Vera Rogers, whom she told not to come near her again, when she visited. "Don't want you," she said to poor Vera, "don't show your face to me again." And turned hers away.

I sit quietly there, in a chair that is rather too high, for she is propped in the low one. The big chair, the expertly set pillows, the blanket over her knees, seem to be trying to swallow little Maudie, who, whatever position she is put in, stares ahead of her. "How are you, Mrs Fowler, would you like some tea—some hot milk—some chocolate, some soup?" No queen, or rich Arab's wife, would get better nursing than she does. But what she wants is—not to be dying!

I sit by her thinking, ninety-two years old, and Maudie seems to believe that an injustice is being done to her! One of

the night nurses, witnessing Maudie's dismissal of me—
"Going, are you?"—ran after me down the corridor and said,
Mrs Somers, Mrs Somers . . . and took me by the arm, looking
into my face with the same gentle friendly smiling persuasive-
ness that Maudie experiences as a prison, a lie . . .

"You mustn't let yourself mind," said she, "it is a stage they
go through. You'll see, there are stages. First, patients, when
they begin to understand, think it is unfair. They are sorry for
themselves."

"Unfair? Unfair that one has to die?"

"Sick people aren't always the most rational folk in the
world. And then, next, they get angry."

"Yes, you could say she is angry!"

"Well," she said whimsically, while her expert eyes searched
my face for signs of over-stress, "it isn't nice to die, for anyone,
I expect."

"Is it possible that these stages get a bit mixed up?"

She laughed, but really, enjoying being able to laugh at "the
book". She said, "The books says, three stages. I would agree
that in life things are not so clear-cut!"

"And the third stage?"

"That is when they accept it, come to terms . . ."

A nurse came running up, Nurse Connolly, Nurse Connolly,
and with a quick, Excuse me, off she ran, back to some minor,
or major, crisis. And I went home.

It isn't fair . . . anger . . . acceptance.

An over-ninety-year-old woman finds it *unjust* that she is
dying?

And next day Maudie, allowing her sombre yellow gaze
actually to reach my face instead of—mostly deliberately, or so
it seems—avoiding it, said in a clear contemptuous voice, "It's
a tragedy, a tragedy!"

"What is, Maudie?"

She looked at me—contempt! "A tragedy," she said loudly
and clearly, and then averted her eyes, before saying in a soft
distressed mumble, a tone I do not hear from her these days,
"Now that we were so happy, you coming in every evening and
me telling you my stories. A tragedy this has happened . . ."

I hold Maudie's hand while I sit there, though she always lets hers fall, inert, from mine, once, twice, sometimes three or four times, before clutching at me. Turned from me, her eyes never looking at me, her mouth falling open, because the drugs make her lose control of herself, a sullen sulking furious old woman, her hand nevertheless speaks the language of our friendship.

Maudie feels it is unfair that she is dying.

Yesterday, she said again, a soft hurrying mutter, "A tragedy, a tragedy, a tragedy," and I hear myself saying, not in the "charming" winning concerned way that is, so to speak, the house style of the hospital, "Maudie, you are ninety-two years old."

Her head moved slowly around, and then the blaze of her blue eyes. *Furious.*

What I am thinking about is, who, or what, in Maudie believes herself to be immortal, unjustly sentenced? It seems to me there are several Maudies inside that tiny yellow cage of bones, dying at different rates, and one of them has no intention of dying!

Another of the nurses asked me, "Are you religious, perhaps?" I know why she did. It is because my general air, manner, behaviour belongs to those who are not upset by dying, death, instead of to those—whom I can easily pick out, as I look at other visitors, relatives and friends—who are.

She meant, I suppose *you* think there is an afterlife! The little sniff, due to the backward, was implicit.

I said, "No, I'm not religious," not answering her real question.

Again I brood about what I do, or might, think about a possible afterlife—for my mother, my husband, Maudie. I think one thing one day, and another the next. Have "believed" one thing one decade, its opposite the next.

Another week gone.

As I leave her, about nine or ten, Maudie's hand tightens around mine and she leans forward, with amazing energy, and says, Take me home with you, take me out of here! Her eyes, which have been avoiding mine for two, three hours, are suddenly all there, a furious demand.

How can I take you home with me, Maudie? You know I can't, I say, every evening, sounding distressed, and *guilty*.

To involve oneself with the infinitely deprived means you take on a weight of guilt. They need so much: you can give so little.

I have been going home every evening, thinking, Perhaps I could take Maudie home? She could have a bed in my living room. I could get in day and night nurses . . . Jill would help. This is stupid, but her need forces me into it. And it isn't even what she wants, which is that I, her friend, Janna, should nurse her, day and night, always be there, and there would be no smiling skilled nurses.

It is impossible; yet, every evening, I wonder how it could be managed.

Why not, why not, why not? she wants to know.

I would not be able to look after you, I say.

Why would it be any more absurd than my becoming Maudie's friend to the extent that I did, or visiting Eliza and Annie as I have done for months now? All that is judged, by Joyce for instance, as worse than eccentric. Looking at my behaviour from outside, as I would have judged it before my husband and my mother died, it has something about it obsessive and even unhealthy. (Of course, this view does not take into account that my lunacy might add something to the lives of these unfortunate old women.) And yet why? What has happened that, for someone like me, well off, middle class, and in possession of my faculties, to undertake such tasks without any necessity for it means that I am wrong-headed? Sometimes I look at the thing one way, and sometimes another: first, that I am mad, and then, that the society we live in is. But I do take on this responsibility, and I am a friend of Eliza's and of Annie's, and I am a friend (more than that, I think) of Maudie's only because it was something I decided to do. I did it. Therefore it works. If you undertake to do something, then it is not absurd, at least to you.

To Joyce I say, "What is the difference between your 'counselling', whatever that may mean, and my being a friend to people who need it?" I say this because I want her to say, "The difference is, I am paid for it!"

But once said, it is exposed as ridiculous.

"Are you saying, Joyce, that none of us should ever do anything we aren't paid for?"

"Well, all right, Janna, if you want to be *logical*, but all I know is, there's something neurotic about your doing it."

"I wouldn't argue about that."

So we wrangle, across all that water, but nearly always it sounds as if we are in houses half a mile away, so clear are our voices to each other.

For me to take Maudie into my flat for the weeks or months or even years before she dies, would be absurd, because I couldn't do it.

And yesterday she leaned forward and announced, as if regretfully, "You are a fair-weather friend."

I had to accept this.

And this afternoon she said, "Why can't I go home, why can't I?"

"You know you can't, Maudie! You can't look after yourself any longer."

"But I look after myself perfectly well, I always have," she says, amazed.

Maudie ought to be, she knows, in her sister's house, where she has given so much time, amounting to years, of her love and service to the family; she should be in bed there, and her relatives should be around her, with hot broth and hot milk, handing her medicines.

Something from *War and Peace* teases my memory, it is about the old Countess, who is in her second childhood. She needed to be allowed to cry a little, laugh a little, sleep a little, quarrel a little ... In that household, many servants and hangers-on and dependants and family; and an old woman, sitting in a corner in a chair, or propped in bed, would be assimilated.

I cannot think of any household I know where Maudie could be accommodated now, we all work too hard, have too much responsibility as it is; our lives are all pared down to what we can fit in, we can all just cope and no more.

What I think when I sit there, holding Maudie's hand, that she ought to be in a large loving family like a rubber net that could stretch a little here and there to fit her in, is of course nonsense. I am saying, as well, that she should have been an intelligently loved child of sensible parents, and that her mother should not have died when she was fifteen, and that she ought, *by right*, to have been happy healthy wealthy and wise her whole long life through. When I say what she, what an old woman, *ought* to have by *right* as she dies, forbids hardship, suffering, injustice, pain—denies, in short, the human condition.

Take me home with you, Janna, take me home with you.

I can't, Maudie, you can see that for yourself! And I have to run off home now, it's getting late and the night staff have just come on. I'll see you tomorrow, Maudie.

Today I went to the wedding. As always, relatives one had never heard of: one sees people known (in Phyllis's case), for years, in their matrix of work. Phyllis's family like mine. But—surprise! Charles turns out to be an exotic with wildly elegant mother from Paris and two fathers, real and step, both worldly, witty and charming. Phyllis looking marvellous, a credit to us and the mag. I enjoyed it.

Two weeks.

Maudie's pain is getting bad now. She has carefully adjusted doses of pain-killer, three times a day, but they watch her, with those skilled, careful, smiling eyes, question her gently, and according to what they see, what she says, gradually increase the dose.

At six in the evening, when I come in, the medicine glass is sitting on the table by her. They know that for her to take the stuff is a defeat, the worst—*the end.* So therefore they do not force her, or jolly her into taking it. "In your own good time," they say. "Take it when you need it."

Maudie sits there, and I feel her bony grasp tightening. She swings her head to look at her enemy, the glass with its contents. Then she makes her eyes turn away again. In a moment, her gaze returns to it. I can hear her gasping, as the pain burns in her stomach.

I have learned not to say, too soon, "Would you like the medicine, Maudie?" When I do, she nods, in a quick abstracted way, as if thinking of something else much more important; and I hold the glass to her lips, which reach forward in her eagerness, as if they were creatures independent of her, and curl around the glass's lip so as to suck the deadening stuff into her.

"They are taking my mind away from me, they are deadening my thoughts," she has whispered to me, reproachful, sorrowful, angry. At least she did not say, "*You* are . . ."

The last two nights, a night nurse has sauntered in, smiling around the room, checking her kingdom, one, two, three, four; has gone to one bed after another, eyes casually, but so efficiently, at work on each sick old face—they are all old women in this room—and then, having stood for a while by Maudie, "And how are you tonight, Mrs Fowler? Good evening, Mrs Somers"—has said to Maudie, "If you feel you'd like a little something to make you sleep, you have only to ring."

This means, "If the pain gets too bad . . ."

And both nights, before I have left, Maudie has grabbed at my skirt as I stood up, and whispered, "Tell them, tell them, don't forget—I'll take a bit of hot milk or something."

I go to the duty desk and translate this, "I think Mrs Fowler will be needing a bit more pain-killer."

"Don't worry about her, we'll be along to her in a moment."

And indeed they are.

And I can positively hear Maudie's thought, as I hurry away to get home, to reach my bath, which is *my* medicine and my oblivion: if I had had some of this offered me when I needed it, when I had nothing to give my Johnnie, and so he was stolen from me . . .

A month.

Oh, it goes on, and on, and on, and on . . . I am so *tired*. I am so absolutely *done*. I say to myself, What are you feeling tired for? This is nothing to how it was when you were in to Maudie sometimes twice a day, shopping and cleaning and doing her washing, and washing her. This is a picnic, going in to that lovely new clean ward, gentle smiling nurses, and Maudie looked after, and all you have to do is to sit there and hold her hand. And, of course, trying not to react when she blazes her eyes at you and says, "Why, why, *why*?" or "It is a tragedy, that's what it is!", for she is likely to say these things still. The truth is, it wears me out and there seems no end to it. I know the nurses expected her to be worse than she is by now: you can pick up what they are thinking, usually because they want you to! There has never been any place like a hospital for the unsaid, the unspoken, people understanding everything on a look. I was called to the duty desk and told that Maudie would probably be transferred to the old hospital, for old people, up the road. This appalled me. Because it will appal Maudie. Because, quite simply, I want her to die. It is all *awful*. And yet I cannot allow myself to think like this. She does not want to die, and that's all there is to it! It seems to me legitimate to want someone dead if they want to be dead, but certainly not when they are not ready.

I have been looking for signs of the beginning of "the third stage". Maudie seems as angry as she ever was. Perhaps there are only two stages, It's not fair!, which is anger surely; and acceptance. Oh please, let Maudie accept, and let her accept soon! There is something terrible about seeing this ancient woman die in this way, as if something were being stolen from her. If she feels her life has been stolen from her—by her own mother's early death, by bully-boy Papa, by the feathered fancy-woman, by her nasty sister—fair enough, I suppose, but where does that end? The point is, what does she *still* feel was owed to her that was taken from her? What does she feel is owed to her *now* that is being taken away?

If only I could get her to talk to me. But we sit in that large clean light room, at the top of the big hospital, with sky and air all around us, the birds going past, the pigeons cooing outside, and there are three other people in that room, and the nurses in and out, and the visitors and the doctors . . .

The doctor who is on duty most of the time is nice, and she

likes him—I can see she does, though he could be pardoned for believing she hated him. But the big doctor comes around with his chorus once or twice a week, and Maudie is still angry, more than angry, incandescent with fury, when I arrive at night.

"*He* was here again today," says she, her little yellow face working, lips trembling.

"And how was it?" I ask, though of course I know.

"They stand in the doorway, *he* and all those boys and girls. Doctors, are they? They look like children to me. And they have black ones too." Maudie, who is scrupulous, when herself, always remembers to say, if she has criticized a black person, "They are human just like us," has lost this now, and knows only that they are different and alien. In a churn and a tumult of contradictions, she is; for two of the nurses are black, and she likes them very much. But still, they are black, and a focus for her angers. She likes, particularly, the way one of them lifts her up and settles her in a chair, without hurting; I can see the softness on her face, just for a moment, before it is swept away—but she *is* black, and reminds Maudie that she has not chosen to be here, in this hospital, with no decisions she can make on her own account.

"Well," I say, "there have to be black nurses and black doctors trained, and this is a teaching hospital."

"Why should I have to be the guinea pig? They never asked me. And they are so young, how can children like that know anything? And he came over, Lord Muck, and stood over me, and he was talking to them the whole time about me. Oh, they think I am stupid! And then when they were all standing around me . . ." she went on; and I could see the scene, tiny yellow Maudie against her white pillows, and the forest of tall young men and women, and—not among them, but opposite them—the big doctor . . . "After he had finished talking, he said, And how are we today, Mrs Fowler? And then he started talking to those children again, about me. Does he think I am an idiot?" (This is a gasping shriek, she is so furious and so distressed.) "He said to me, Please pull up your gown, Mrs Fowler. I wasn't going to, why should I? And the nurse stepped forward, all ready to oblige, and up came my nightie, in front of them all, everything on view. And then *he* began his prodding and his pushing, I could have been a bit of pastry on a board, and he said to *them*, See that swelling there? Feel it. And not a word to me. They felt my stomach, one after the other. Thank you, Mrs Fowler, he said, but he hadn't ever asked me my permission, had he? See that swelling, he said, feel it—as if I can't see it and feel it! I'm not a fool, I'm not stupid, I'm not an idiot—" And Maudie is beside herself with anger, with helplessness. "*He didn't look at me, not once.* I might just as well have been a stick or stone. He looked at *them*, they are what is important to him. I was just here for their convenience."

They are going to tell Maudie that she is being moved to the other hospital. And indeed she is not stupid, and—I dread it.

They have told her. When I went in tonight, she was sitting turned away from me, from everything. After I had been there half an hour, not a word said, she began muttering, "I am not going, I'm not going into the workhouse."

"What workhouse? What are you talking about, Maudie?" She persisted, "I'm not ending up in the workhouse!"

I found out the hospital she is going to was once, a long time ago, the workhouse. I rang up Vera Rogers. She sounds tired, distrait. "And what did you ring me for?"

"I want to know what Maudie means when she goes on and on about being put away into the workhouse."

A sigh. "Oh God," says Vera, "not again. All these old dears say it, We won't be put away into the workhouse, they say. There haven't been workhouses—for, well, I don't know. But you see, when they were young, a workhouse was what they dreaded. The idea was, if you were sent there, no matter how old you were, you had to work. They scrubbed floors and washed linen and cooked. And don't quote me, but let me tell you, I don't see what was so terrible about it. Because what happens now? We shovel them off into Homes where they aren't allowed to lift a finger, and they die or go mad of boredom. If I had any say, I'd have them all working from dawn to dusk, keep their minds off themselves. Oh, don't take any notice of me, Janna, I'm letting off steam."

I ought to be visiting Annie Reeves and Eliza Bates, just

occasionally, but I have no energy over from Maudie.

Today I went with Maudie to "the workhouse". A pleasant indifferent girl called Rosemary came with us. Her function was, she said, so that Maudie could see a familiar face and not feel abandoned. But Maudie asked her, "Who are you?" And Rosemary said, "Oh, Mrs Fowler, you know me. I've been in to see you." "I don't know you," said Maudie. "But I've been in nearly every day, Mrs Fowler."

"Janna?" asked Maudie, in a small weeping voice, "Janna, are you there?"

"Yes, I'm here."

In the ambulance, the three of us, Rosemary holding Maudie's possessions, a carrier bag with a comb, a washcloth, soap and her handbag. In her handbag are her marriage lines, and a photograph of "her man", a sulking handsome hero of about forty, in jaunty clothes, and another of a small boy, tidily dressed, smiling unhappily at the cameraman.

At the entrance to the hospital, the wheelchair was lifted up the steps by the matey reassuring ambulance men, and Maudie was holding on tight, and did not realize, until she was inside, that here it was, the dreaded workhouse.

"Is this it? Is this it?" she whispered to me, as we went along the passages, that had on them an exhibition of art done by the inmates, staff and patients. And, on the landing, a poster of Beardsley's *Salome with the Head of St John the Baptist*, put there by some joker (I suppose). But Maudie's astonishment at this took us up to the first floor. "Is this it?" she was asking, clutching on tight to the chair, sliding this way and that, despite all the care of the men, for she is so light she could blow away.

"This is the Old Hospital," said Rosemary cheerfully.

"They've changed it, then," said Maudie.

"Have they?" said Rosemary. "I know it's been painted recently."

But Maudie was here round about the time of the First World War, to visit an aunt, and she could not make these memories match with what she saw.

The wards we got glimpses of are the traditional hospital wards, with twenty or so beds, and the great windows all along. But when we reached Maudie's room, she had a room with one bed in it.

There sat Maudie, upright in bed, full in the bright light from the window, which showed her yellow against the massed white pillows. Through the window, a church spire, a grey sky, the tops of trees. Maudie was silent, looking bitterly round the room—as far as I was concerned, a hospital room, that's all—and then out of the window.

"Then this is the Old Hospital," she confirmed, staring at me, at the nurse who had settled her in, at Rosemary, who was on the point of leaving, her arms cradling a heap of files.

"Yes, love, this is the Old Hospital."

And Maudie bared her teeth at us, in a hissing gasp, and said, "Then that's it, then, isn't it? I'm here, then? And that's the end, then?"

"Oh, Mrs Fowler," said Rosemary, benevolently, "don't be like that. Well, I'm off, see you when I drop in next time."

And off went Rosemary, back to the new hospital.

I stayed with Maudie all afternoon. I wanted to find out who among the staff was the one I needed to talk to, establish relations with. This hospital is different in atmosphere from the other, something relaxed, amiable, slack about it. Of course, the other is one of the world's great hospitals, and the nurses there are the cream, and the doctors too. Nearly all the old men and women in this place will not leave it till they die. It is not exactly a hospital; it is not a Home—it is a compromise. The big doctor from the other hospital comes over with his retinue to teach Geriatric Medicine. Some of the nurses are the ambitious ones from the other hospital, here for a few weeks to learn what they can learn only in a place like this, full of old men and women who will never leave here, and who have the kinds of lengthy lingering diseases appropriate to their condition.

I was thinking, how lucky for Maudie to be in a room by herself; but Maudie, I knew (and I know now rightly), was interpreting it as her death warrant. And the place was abominably noisy. As so often with us all, beaten into submission as we all are by the noise and clatter and din, it was not until I saw that Maudie was suffering from noise that I opened my ears, which I had shut, to the swing and the bang of the doors, the crash and clang of food containers from the little kitchen just opposite Maudie's room, the grinding of the food trolleys.

Noise! I said to Maudie, "Let's shut the door," but she said, "No, no, no," breathlessly shaking her head. She is afraid of being shut in.

They had given her no medicaments when she arrived; and she was in pain. I went to find the sister, and asked if Maudie could have something.

She is an elderly woman, with the look of an old inhabitant, for this place is probably her home as much as her own home is. She looked at me in the shrewd skilled way they use to assess you, Sensible, Silly, to be Relied On, to be Told the Truth, to be Shielded . . .

She said, "You do know that we try to give as little as we possibly can, so that when we have to use strong doses they will have some effect?"

"Yes, I know," I said. "But she's had that move, and she's frightened, because this is the Old Hospital—and she's in pain."

"Oh dear," said the sister, sighing. "You know she might live for weeks, even months. And it's a question of the pain at the end, you see?"

"Yes, I do see."

But Maudie got something "to tide her along", and it wasn't enough to send her under, though it was to stun the pain, for when I left she was awake, alert, listening to everything, and grimly silent. Is this, then, the "stage" of acceptance? Oh God, I do hope it is.

Do not go gentle into that good night! Indeed. What wet, slobbery, self-pitying rubbish! What self-indulgence! And how like *us*, spoiled brats, with our demands, and our "it isn't fair", and our *I haven't been given enough*.

Jill and I were both early this evening. I came in from the hospital so tired I didn't know where to put myself.

Jill saw how I felt, made me tea, a sandwich.

She sat down opposite me, waiting for me to recover.
Underneath her good nature, her need to please, her new
confidence—for, as I did, she is learning with every day how
much she can do, that she is clever and flexible—was something sullen and critical. I knew what was coming.

"Why do you do it, Janna?" And this had behind it all the
explosive protest of the young: No, no, I won't, I can't, keep it
all far away from me. Above all: *If you, who are so close to me,
are prepared to accept this frightful, appalling ugliness as part
of your life, then what is to prevent it all coming into my life
too?*

"I suppose it is all discussed in the office, on its merits," I
said.

She looked embarrassed, because the niece of Janna, living
in Janna's flat, cannot resist: Janna says, Janna does, Janna
is—this and that.

"Well, I suppose so."

"Typical upper-class behaviour," I said, "the tradition of
visiting the poor, useless benevolence, but the revolution will
do away with all that nonsense."

She was red and angry. Jill has become a revolutionary.
When I teased her about it, she said angrily, "Well, what do
you expect? You never have anyone here, there's no social life,
what do you expect?"

"I expect," I said, "that, just like all the other revolutionaries, you make a social life for yourself—and call it something
else." She did laugh, after a bit. But today she was too
threatened to laugh.

"Never mind," I said. "She'll die soon. It will soon be over."

"I think it is ridiculous, ridiculous," she said, furious
aggressive. "Hours and hours, every day. Who *is* she, who
Maudie?—I mean, of course, she's just a substitute f
Granny, you weren't nice to her, so you are making it up wi
Maudie Fowler."

"What subtlety, what insight, what penetration!"

"Well, Janna, it's obvious, isn't it?"

"And if so, what of it?"

"Well, it's so peculiar of you, you must see it."

"Listen to me, my dear, when you came to live here, I

no promises about adjusting my life according to the prescriptions of my sister, you—or anyone else."

Silence. A proper full-blown sulky silence, adolescent pouting lips, imminent tears, lowering looks.

But it has been the first, and I give her full marks, seeing that in her mother's house this kind of thing is *de rigueur*. And this was our first quarrel, too.

"If you like," I said, "when Maudie's dead, we can have nice little dinner parties. I'm very good at them. You can ask your comrades, and we can talk about class warfare."

She *almost* laughed.

Maudie has been in the Old Hospital a week now. She is no less angry than she was, but she is more silent. Grim. She is holding on. She has so little energy, because of the pain, which is much worse. The sister, without words, showed me the glass she took in to her last night, with a gesture that said, You see? I did. It's the potion they use when the pain is really bad, though it is a killer, a mixture of morphine and alcohol.

Maudie sits straight up, staring, her lower lip pendulous, a drop of saliva gathering there and falling, gathering and falling, her eyes sullen. As soon as I arrive, it starts: "Lift me up, lift me up." I stand by her, lifting her so she is sitting straight up. But no sooner have I done it and I have sat down, ͜e whispers, "Lift me up, lift me."

͜ lift her, sit down. Lift her, sit down. Then I stand by ͜ lifting her so that she is leaning forward, unable to stop ͜lf.

͜audie, you are already sitting straight up!" I protest.

͜ *"Lift me up, lift me up!"*

͜ ͜t because at least she feels she is able to exert some ͜ on this world she is now in, where things are done to ͜he cannot combat them; and because I can hold her ͜ her. Though she never says, Hold me, I want to be ͜ys, Lift me up, lift me up.

͜vo days I've stood by her, lifting and settling her, ͜lding her, an hour at a time. I've said, "Maudie, ͜ I've got to rest." She acknowledges this with a little jerk of her head, but in a moment it begins, "Lift me up, lift me up."

I think perhaps this is a way of keeping herself awake, because the potions are now so very strong.

She is drowsy for a good part of the time. They say she is asleep most of the night. But she is conscious, knows what goes on, suffers, badly, from the clang, the clash, the loud feet on the uncarpeted corridor, the grinding wheels of the food carts. Crash, go the doors, every few minutes. I find myself sitting there, nerves alert, waiting for it.

Yet still the door must be open, for Maudie fears the silence and indifference of the grave, where she will be shut in.

Maudie is not ready to die.

I do not now have long periods of sitting by her *thinking*, for I am too busy lifting her up, settling her pillows, cosseting her, but here at home, in the bath, I think. What about these euthanasia societies? I do not believe my mother, or Freddie, wanted to go before they had to; they were resigned, they were *grown up*, but I am sure I would have known if they had been longing for one of us to slip them a deadly draught. (Would I, though? I must ask Sister Georgie, when I see her next. If I ever do.) *Why* is it so hard to die? Is it legitimate to wonder that? Useful? Oh, it is hard, hard, hard to die, the body doesn't want to let go. There's a struggle going on, it's a battlefield.

But suppose Maudie's will and mind wanted her to go, would that mean her body would fight less? If it *is* her body that is fighting.

Maudie is sitting there, willing not to die. I simply do not understand it; and that's all there is to it!

Contrasting myself with Maudie, I know that sometimes not possible to put oneself into the place of another. Though know that what I am doing is to contrast my present state mind, that of the woman of fifty who is physically not death, with that of a woman of over ninety who is near One's frame of mind changes as death comes near? course there is some absolute barrier, or wall, between mind and knowing I shall die. I mean, I know I shall not as a vivid violent fact. Perhaps we are programm animals, not to know it; because knowing it would pr from living. For whatever else Nature is interested in, she wants us to live, breed, populate the earth, perpetuate—anything beyond that, Nature can't care about. And therefore do I, Janna, or Jane Somers, sit by a dying woman, fighting to make my mind change gear, lose a layer or become more raw and exposed, so as *really* to know that I shall die. But Nature won't let me.

I imagine, deliberately, all kinds of panic, of dread: I make myself visualize me, Janna, sitting up on high pillows, very old, being destroyed from within. I reduce my outer boundaries back, back, first from my carapace of clothes, how I present myself; and then to my healthy body, which does not—yet—suddenly let loose dirt and urine against my will, but is still comely and fresh; and back inside, to me, the knowledge of I, and imagine how it is a carcass I am sitting in, that's all, a slovenly mess of meat and bones. But it is no good. I do not fear death. I do not.

And, paradoxically, watching Maudie die, I fear it even less. For those who are concerned with dying, these professionals, have a brisk intelligence about it all that is exactly what I would like for myself. And even an honesty, for I know now hat if Maudie is not told "the truth"—as if she didn't know it ready—she would be told it, for the asking, by the nurses. d if they didn't say in so many words, Maudie Fowler, you , dying, they would allow her to know it. Which now, use of her attitude, they are not doing: no, they under- that she is "not ready to know"—the sister's phrase, to d so the atmosphere in her room continues friendly, lmost indifferent, as if she had no more than a cold or leg.

for living afterwards: the fact is, I cannot make ieve that this furious bundle of energy which is oing to disappear altogether. It is more than I can believe. Good God, Maudie makes such a claim or sick; such a statement does she make about life, the nature of what she has experienced; so Maudie come over that I cannot believe she e vapour when the air warms up. No. d with the *now* of Maudie that what might survive of her impresses itself on me not as a question at all, such as, what will she look like, will she be young or old, would "her man" recognize her, or her son as a baby or as a middle-aged man, all this is irrelevant.

"Lift me up, lift me up," says Maudie, and I pick up this little bag of bones and set it upright, and smooth back her wispy hair, and say, "Enough for a minute, Maudie, I must sit down."

For, a little bag of weightlessness she might be, but with enough repetitions, my back starts complaining. My back is very vocal, in short, and I find myself apostrophizing it, Just hold on there, wait a little, you've got to hold out, you can't give in yet.

For the first time, I find being in the office a strain, I am too tired to do more than go through the motions, and Phyllis covers up for me, and Jill too as much as she knows how.

When I come home with Jill from work, I let her drive, climb the stairs like a zombie, fall into my big chair and sit there, absolutely done, hardly moving, getting up energy to drive to the hospital. Jill says, "Don't go, Janna, don't, you'll be ill."

"Of course I have to go."

Coming back at ten, or later, I fall into a bath for an hour or so, or lie on the floor in the living room with a cushion under my head. Jill brings me tea, soup. Like Eliza Bates, I have more than once not bothered to go to bed, but have sat through the night contemplating Maudie's drama as if it is being played out somewhere inside me, on my stage, while life goes on, noises off, elsewhere. Jill has come in, two, three in the morning, and I've said, "Never mind, leave me." But if she had not been here, I would not have seen anything untoward in all this. Of course I'm likely to be "upset", as Jill puts it, and it's only a question of living it out. It is Jill who is upset, she is frightened when I don't go to bed, or fall asleep on the floor. But she is being sweet, considerate; her mother's daughter.

This has not stopped her, more than once, from saying, "Living with you, Janna, I'm going to become a real chip off the old block." Meaning me. This with hard, amused looks, and an expression of well, if so, it's because I have to look after myself!

"You mean, I'm such a hard taskmaster?"

"Not that, exactly, but I have to give as good as I get, don't I?"

"I didn't realize I was as bad as that."

"I don't mind really. I told Mother it's good for me. Bracing."

"Like cold baths."

There's also the problem of Mrs Penny.

"Why do you hate her so much?" asks Jill, quite amazed, so I have to ask myself why I do. "She's quite nice really, she's quite interesting, she has all those stories about India, and she's so lonely, she's such a poor old thing."

"I've been doing great damage to my character by being unkind to Mrs Penny, for she's one that if you give an inch to, she'll take a mile."

"You go and visit those other old women, you put up with them. When Mrs Fowler's dead, are you going to visit the other two?"

"I can't drop them just like that, can I?"

"You really are very stubborn, Janna, you must see that."

What I must see, have seen in fact, is that having admitted Jill into my life, so that my gates are down, the defences breached, my territory invaded, no place I can call my own, Mrs Penny is irrelevant. I find Jill and Mrs Penny enjoying a nice cup of tea in the kitchen, and I nod with a calculatedly stern absent-mindedness, a busy woman with important things on my mind, and retreat to my bedroom, the door firmly shut.

From where, very soon, I go up to sit with poor Maudie. I am thinking of her, at home, when "resting" as Jill recommends, so I might just as well be with her, which I am all the time in thought. And the nurses and the doctors are used to me, I go in at all times, without their minding.

I have been seeing something of the life of the big ward. Maudie has been going off to sleep after her midday potion, and I was sitting there for an hour or more, waiting for her to wake up.

The ward sister came to stand at the bottom of Maudie's bed and began chatting in that apparently vague way in which so much information is given in hospitals. And directives, too. She said that some of her patients never got a visitor at all. "They might just as well not be in the land of the living as far as their relatives are concerned."

So, keeping an eye on Maudie to make sure I am there when she comes fully awake, I go into the ward and talk to whoever seems to welcome it.

Once I was so afraid of old age, of death, that I refused to let myself see old people in the streets—they did not exist for me. Now, I sit for hours in that ward and watch and marvel and wonder and admire.

The nurses . . . what patience, what good sense, what good humour! How do they do it? For there are eighteen or so old people here who are difficult in one way or another, incontinent, or lame, or witless, or ill, or—like Maudie—dying. Here they are, these aged creatures, together in this intimacy, in a ward with beds all along both sides, and what they have in common is their need, their weakness. And that is all. For they were not friends before they came in. At the other end from Maudie's room is a ninety-six-year-old woman, a grinning clown who is totally deaf and quite mad, who does not know where she is. She is put to sit in her chair, and remains there, perhaps for an hour, two hours, and then up she jumps, and takes herself for a walk between the rows of beds. But at once she is lost, and everyone is watching her, perhaps smiling, perhaps irritable, for now she cannot find her way back. She will stop arbitrarily at this bed or that, and try to get into it, regardless that there is someone in it already. "Maggie," shouts the occupant, "can't you see I'm here?" "What are you doing in my bed?" shrieks old Maggie, and at once the call goes up, "Nurse, Nurse, it's Maggie!" And the nurses come running, laughing usually, and say, "Maggie, what are you doing?" and take the opportunity to lead her off to the lavatory, since once she's up they might as well . . .

In the bed next to Maggie is the "difficult" one.

Oh, you are so difficult, sigh the nurses, as she asserts herself yet again. She is a massive woman, with a strong face always on the watch for threats to her sense of what is due to her. She has bad legs, which are propped in front of her. She sits with her arms folded, watching. Or she reads. Romantic novels, usually, or sometimes sea stories, of which she is fond—*The Cruel Sea, Hornblower*.

She has been in for three months. Some of these people have been in for years. When she came in, she said, My name is Mrs Medway. I am not going to be called Flora. And I'm not going to be treated like a baby.

When a new nurse comes into the ward and calls her love, dear, darling, or Flora, she is told, "Don't baby me, I'm old enough to be your great-grandmother." "Oh," says the poor nurse, who has been trained, by watching the other nurses, to coax a difficult eater to "take another spoon for me", as one does for a child, or "eat up your pudding for me, lovie", "Oh, Mrs Medway, just as you like, but you call me Dorothy, I don't mind."

"*I* mind," says this formidable one, and while she listens to the nurses discussing their tasks, Maggie needs this or that, and Flora needs . . . "Mrs Medway," she corrects them, calmly and loudly.

"Oh, Mrs Medway love, why are you so difficult, darling?"

"I am not a darling."

"No, sometimes you aren't . . . Can we take you down to Physio now, please?"

"No."

"Why not?"

"I don't like it."

"But it's good for you."

"I don't want to be done good to."

"Oh, Mrs Medway, don't you want to get your legs right?"

"Don't be silly, Nurse, you know they won't get right for a few kicks and bends."

"No, but it will stop them getting any worse."

"Well, I keep them moving all the time up here."

And she does. Every half-hour or so she removes the light plastic boots she has on, I suppose to stop sores from pressure, and moves her legs and feet about, and rubs them with her hands. Then the loud flat voice: "Nurse, I want you to put my boots back on. And I want to be walked to the door and back."

In the bed opposite her is a woman of over ninety who was,

so the sister told me, "a lady". The sister is that person in this cast of people, all of whom seem to be admirable, who represents "the one" that Joyce and I used to talk about. It is she who sets the tone of the ward. She is middle-aged, rather tired, has thick legs that seem to ache, and a broad sensible pleasant face that gives confidence. She is always on the watch for the slightest sign of unkindness or impatience by her nurses. She does not mind that they are slapdash, casual, and—apparently—sometimes inefficient, forgetting to do this or that, recovering the situation with a laugh and an apology. On the contrary, I have understood she encourages this atmosphere. But when I saw one of the more brisk quick nurses using a sharp edge on her voice to old Maggie, Sister White called her over and said to her, "This place is her home. It's all the home she's got. She's entitled to be silly if she wants. Don't hurry her and harry her. I won't have it, Nurse!"

Sister White said to me that the woman who is a lady was a countrywoman in Essex. She used to breed dogs. She rode to hounds. And she had a large garden. How did she come to be here, in a London hospital? But Sister does not know, for Ellen has been here seven years now and does not like to talk about her past.

Ellen is completely deaf, and she has bad legs, so that when she goes to the lavatory it might take her ten or more minutes to get there, and as long back again. She has to be helped to sit. She has a thin sweet keen face, and her eyes are full of life. For she sits watching everything that goes on, misses nothing, smiles to herself when something charming or funny happens, sighs at the bad things . . . She will smile at me as I come in, and indicate with a gesture that she has been reading the magazines I take in for her: *Country Life*, *The Lady*, *Horse and Hound*. She cannot hold a conversation, because she is so deaf.

Sometimes I talk to Mrs Medway, who was not so long ago the proprietor of a newspaper and sweet shop in Willesden, and whose husband died last year. She has one daughter, in the West Country, who comes up sometimes to visit her. Mrs Medway does not have visitors much. Ellen never has visitors, she has been forgotten. Except, of course, for the ministers of various churches and for the young people who volunteer to visit the old and whose visits charm them. Mrs Medway, the terror of Tennyson Ward, entertains her visitors with reminiscences of her young self, at their age—back in World War One. When they go off, shaking their heads and laughing, exchanging glances because of the nearness—to her—of that impossibly distant world, she looks at me, and we, too, laugh because of time, and the tricks it plays. "Well," she might say, as she imperiously waves a hand towards the nurse, for she wants her glasses brought to her (they are to be reached by leaning over four inches, but she doesn't see why she should), "well, I tell you something. I could have danced any one of that lot into the ground, any night! A poor lot, compared to us, I'd say." And she picks up her novel, probably called *Passion at Twilight*.

What I am thinking about, as I sit in that ward, watching; as I sit with Maudie, watching; is a possible new novel; but this time not a romantic one.

I want to write about these ward maids, the Spanish or the Portuguese or Jamaican or Vietnamese girls who work for such long hours, and who earn so very little, and who keep families, bring up children, and send money home to relatives in Southeast Asia or some little village in the Algarve or the heart of Spain. These women are taken for granted. The porters are paid well in comparison; they go about the hospital with the confidence that goes with, I would say, not being tired. I know one thing, these women are tired. They are tired. They are so tired they dream of being allowed to get into bed and to stay there sleeping for weeks. They all have the same look, of a generalized anxiety, that I recognize; it comes from just keeping on top of things, from a fear of something happening, an illness, a broken bone, that may make them fall behind. How do I recognize this look? For I cannot remember seeing it before. I have read about it? No, I think it comes from Maudie: probably, when Maudie talked, dredging up from her past some tale that now I have forgotten, there was on her face, because it was in her mind, this look. These women are frightened. Because their poverty allows them no margin, and because they support others. In the wards it is they who slip purses out from handbags, help themselves to a pound here, a few pence there; nick a bit of jewellery, transfer an orange to a pocket. Nothing is safe from these needy fingers, and it is because of them that the great hospitals of London, the exemplars for hospitals all over the world, hospitals with names that inspire doctors and nurses in poor countries from North India to Southern Africa, are unable to protect their charges from the theft of everything that is thievable. I watch these women work, putting a hand briefly to the small of their back and letting out a sigh that is a half-groan; slipping off their shoes, while they stand for a stolen few moments behind a half-shut door to ease their feet; drawing in a couple of breaths of smoke from a half-smoked cigarette squeezed out and replaced in a pocket. They are kind, too, bringing cups of tea to such as me, or putting into the hands of some crazed old one a bright red flower which she may sit and stare at, seeing it perhaps as she has never done in her life, or popping into the mouth of another who never has visitors a chocolate which has been filched from the box of one who does have visitors. They observe everything, know everything that happens, are everywhere—and, as far as I can see, no one notices them. They are taken for granted. And why aren't the bully boys and girls of the barricades, or our busybody unions, doing anything about them?

Well, that is what I would like to write, but a novel of this kind is hardly the same task as one about those gallant milliners or the sentimental lady.

Today, the big doctor and his neophytes.

I was sitting with Maudie, with a sound as of a herd of goats, clatter, click click, on the bare cement stairs. Voices, and above them, the firm loud voice of *him*.

Maudie's door is open. Outside the flock comes to a standstill.

The big doctor, the expert on the aged, a world expert at that, so I am told, is holding forth.

This is the stomach cancer, they have their notes. They have seen the slides. It is typical in that . . . I do not understand the next few sentences. It is atypical in that . . . again, I lose the

thread. And now if you ladies and gentlemen will kindly . . .
The flock appears, all at once, crowding into the doorway.
Maudie is sitting straight up, bent forward a little, her head
hanging, awake, staring at the bedcover.

She looks uncomfortable. The nurse who is with the doctors
sees Maudie through their eyes and comes forward to say,
"Mrs Fowler, lie back dear, yes, lie back . . ." Yet she knows
how Maudie says, Sit me up, sit me up, and how I do this, over
and over again, and how Maudie sits exactly like she is now for
minutes, for hours at a time.

We play the charade through: Maudie is laid back on her
pillows, silent, and the mass of doctors watch.

Maudie has her eyes shut.

The big doctor is in two minds about whether to examine
her, for the benefit of the student doctors, but decides not: let
us hope humanity is making up his mind for him.

They all retreat a few steps, to outside the door.

The big doctor explains that Maudie is now in a coma and
will slip away in her sleep.

This astounds me. It shocks the nurse, who lets out, involuntarily, an irritated sigh.

For Maudie is awake most of the time, fighting pain. She
sleeps heavily for an hour or two after she has had the potion,
and then fights herself awake again.

The big doctor is saying, to a respectful silence, that Mrs
Fowler is a woman of great independence, self-respect, who
has never wanted to be drugged at all, and in such cases, of
course, it will be necessary for them to monitor very carefully—and etc., and so on—but luckily she is in a coma now,
and she will die without coming to herself.

The nurse is angry. Her discipline makes it impossible for
her to exchange a glance with me, but we vibrate with understanding. Because, of course, it is the nurses who monitor, the
changes of need, of mood, of the patients, and the doctors
appear from time to time, issuing commands. For that is the
most striking thing that is to be seen while I sit there, observing, listening, the utter and absolute gap between doctors and
nurses. It is the nurses who know what is happening, the nurses
who adjust, temper, and very often simply ignore the doctor's

instructions. How did this extraordinary system grow up, where those who issue the orders don't know what is really going on?

The noise of the doctors diminishes as they all disappear into the main wards.

The nurse gives me an apologetic smile, as Maudie whispers, "Lift me up, lift me up," and I get up to put her back as she was, where, for some reason, she is more comfortable.

"I'll just shut the door a minute," mutters the nurse, meaning, The doctors won't know you've sat her up.

She does so. Maudie: "Open the door, open it, open it."

"Wait a minute, Maudie, till they have gone."

In a few moments, they all come clattering and chattering back and off down the stairs.

I open the door again. The food trolleys are approaching, crash, bang.

"Mrs Fowler, soup? A sandwich? Jelly? Ice cream?"

I say for her, "Some soup, please, and jelly," though she doesn't eat anything at all these days.

I hold the soup to her lips, she shakes her head, I offer a spoon of jelly, "No, no," she whispers, "lift me up, lift me up."

I do so, on and on, through the evening.

And then, it is nine, the night staff are on. I wait to establish contact with the night nurses and tell them myself what sort of a day she has had—the same as yesterday and the day before—and the night nurses smile and bend over Maudie and say, "Hello, love, hello, dear, how are you?"

There are three brown night nurses and one white one, and Maudie feels herself surrounded by the alien.

"I'm off, Maudie, and I'll be in tomorrow."

"You're off already, are you? Good night then."

Milliners came out today. They reprinted twice before publication. I've been too busy with Maudie to enjoy it all as I would otherwise have done. It is going to be a wild success. My secret moments of terror that I was mad to jettison my lovely well-paid job were for nothing.

I read it very early this morning, a dark winter's morning,

dreary and cold, but the jacket of *The Milliners of Marylebone* bright and pretty. How I did enjoy making Maudie's relentless life something gallantly light-hearted, full of pleasant surprises. In my version Maudie has her child stolen from her, but knows where he is, visits him secretly, they support each other against her wicked lover, whom she loves, heigh-ho! But then a long mutually respectful relationship with an older man, a rich publican, who cherishes her, and helps her get back her son. She is the valued head assistant in the milliner's workrooms, and with the aid of this disinterested gentleman buys her own business, which flourishes, enjoying the patronage of the nobility, even minor royalty. Maudie would love her life, as reconstructed by me.

Maudie has been in the Old Hospital three weeks now. I see no difference in her except that she is steadily more restless. She asks to be put flat, and then, when down, asks to be put up. She begs incessantly, Lift me up, and when she is lolling forward, for she can't help but do that, hisses, Lay me back.

The nurses come in and out, watching, "monitoring". Maudie gets these terribly strong doses, Maudie is not really sane at all, but the one thing she is not is in a coma. Maudie is not resigned, not accepting, not anywhere near resignation or acceptance.

Maudie is still saying to me, or muttering rather, "Take me home with you—yes, take me with you when you go home."

Maudie knows and does not know that she has cancer of the stomach and is dying.

Rather, there is a Maudie who knows this, and another who does not.

I suspect that it is the Maudie who does not who will still be there when Maudie actually dies.

Oh God, if only Maudie would die, if only she would. But of course I *know* that is quite wrong. What I think now is, it is possible that what sets the pace of dying is not the body, not that great lump inside her stomach, getting bigger with every breath, but the need of the Maudie who is not dying to adjust—to what? Who can know what enormous processes are going on there, behind Maudie's hanging head, her sullen eyes? I think she will die when *those* processes are accomplished. And that is why I would never advocate euthanasia, or not at least without a thousand safeguards. The need of the watchers, the next of kin, the nearest and dearest, is that the poor sufferer should die as soon as possible, because the strain of it all is so awful. But is it possible that it is not nearly so bad for the dying as for those who watch? Maudie is in pain—intermittently, in between those ferocious doses she is getting—but is pain the worst thing in the world? It certainly never has been for me. It wasn't for Maudie when she was herself. Why is it, as soon as the dying move away beyond a certain point, that the decent, human criteria are no longer used, or are not so easily used, for them? Maudie would never in her life have judged what happened to her by the physical pain she felt. So why should we assume she is different now? She is still afraid of dying, I know, because of her need to keep open the door, that terrible door which admits so much noise (admits *life*)—the banging feet, the voices, the wheels, the clatter of crockery. But what she is really thinking is probably nothing to do with pain at all. The pain is something she has to cope with; it is there, she feels it come and go, lessen and become sharp, she has to shift her position—Lift me up, lift me up!—but we don't know the first thing about what is really happening.

Maudie died last night.

The last few days there has been a pretty little dark nurse, I mean a white girl with dark hair, dark eyes, not a black nurse. She is vague and good-natured and careless. She drifted in and out of Maudie's room, helped me lift Maudie, helped me lay her down, brought me cups of tea. I knew that Maudie was deemed worse, because I was offered tea several times yesterday. But I couldn't see much difference, except for her truly incredible restlessness. In that high smooth tailored hospital bed, that jet of energy, Maudie, wearing me out, tiring the little dark nurse too, who said, "Goodness, Mrs Somers, but you must be a strong one." Last night this happened. The nurse brought in Maudie's potion, which nearly filled the glass, there was so much of it. As it was not quite time for it, she put it down on the table, went out. She came back in a hurry about something, said, "Oh, I forgot Mrs Fowler's medicine," and, in picking it up, knocked it over. All the wicked liquid lying splashed about.

The old dramatic gestures are quite true, accurately observed: she gasped, her eyes widened in terror, her two hands flew to her mouth, and she stood biting her nails, staring at the spilt concoction. Then those eyes were on me, in the most abject appeal: Was I going to give her away? she was demanding.

I was astounded, not being able to see that nice, rather vague ward sister in the light of a tyrant, but I assured the poor girl silently that I would not.

She fetched cloths and pads and mopped it all up, and meanwhile Maudie was sitting silently there, head hanging, needing her potion.

It happened that last night I had to go off half an hour before I usually do, at nine or after. I had said I would take at home a telephone call from Rome about next week's shows.

So I said to the nurse, "You'll see that Mrs Fowler does get her medicine?" Though now I see quite well that she was likely not to report her crime, seeing the state she was in. But anyway, if Maudie has been bad in the night, I know she has been given extra pain-killers, the sister told me so.

But I wonder now if the nurse did not get the spilt dose replaced, and if perhaps Maudie was wanting something in the night and did not get it—whether, in short, she died of an excess of pain? I don't know, and I won't know.

I took the telephone call, worked for a while on files I had brought home from the office, had a bath, got very late to bed, and was woken about four by the telephone: Mrs Fowler has just died, would I like to come?

I was at the hospital in ten minutes.

At that hour, the place had a dimmed humming quality, a soft vitality to it, that was pleasing. I raced up the cold stone stairs and into the ward. Caught a glimpse of two minute brown girls, they are Vietnamese I think, wrestling an enormous mass of aged woman out of bed. They saw me. I saw their harassed faces: Oh God, one more thing to cope with. But their faces had all the harassment wiped off by the time they reached me and they were smiling nicely, and they said that Maudie had died about an hour before, they thought; but they had had a difficult night, with a sick old woman, and when they went in to check, Maudie was gone.

The last thing she had said was, "Wait a minute, wait a minute," as they left her, because they had to leave her, with so many others to deal with.

"Wait a minute," she had muttered, or cursed, or cried, as life went surging on, leaving her behind, but life had taken no notice and had gone on past her.

I would not be at all surprised if Maudie hadn't died of —well, yes, rage. Janna not there, but then she never was!— and the black nurses, look at them, in and out, no time for me . . . In this way, probably, Maudie had died. But I don't believe that that was what really went on behind her scenes.

One of the girls brought me a cup of tea. The ritual. There I sat beside dead Maudie, who looked exactly as if she were asleep, and who was warm and pleasant to the touch, and I held her dead hand, and in my other hand a cup of tea. The decencies must be preserved.

When a patient dies, the nearest and dearest should be offered a cup of tea. And quite right too.

In came the sister, another one, the night sister; or perhaps she was the matron. At any rate, she stood there, chatting away, restoring normality. It was necessary for me to say certain things, and I said them: such as that Maudie was a wonderful woman, and that she had a hard life, and she had faced all her troubles with such resource and courage.

And the matron stood there smiling and sympathetic, listening.

And then there was nothing more for me to do.

The trouble was, I could not feel that Maudie was dead at all, although this was the first time I'd seen her still for months; I was even worrying that she was not dead, not really. But her hand was stiffening and cold when I put it down. The moment I stood up and was collecting my things, in ran one of the little brown nurses, laid Maudie's hands together on her breast, and whisked the covers up over her face. She had the look of a housewife: That's done! And what's next? Yes, now I must...

As I drove along the front of the hospital, homewards, I saw the pretty nurse of yesterday evening. She looked like a soft ripe raspberry, in a reddish jumpsuit, with a vast pink scarf wound around her neck and shoulders. She was smiling, flushed, indolent, assuaged: every atom, every movement shouted that she had been making love all night, and that she was still in imagination back in the warm bed she had left with such reluctance a few minutes before. She had her uniform in the carrier bag in her hand, and she was swinging the bag around and back and forth, and she smiled... She was early for her shift, and planned to creep into the hospital, find a bathroom, and use it, hoping that the matron or sister would not see her. Though it was easy to imagine how this older woman, ready to reprimand, would find herself saying, "Well, never mind, but don't do it again"; and then, feeling the total, reckless, unfair claim, find herself examining the sleepy happy face, and understand her own capitulation. And she would think, well, she won't be with us for long...

The bath over, this lucky one would go from ward to ward, where everyone was frantically busy getting things done before the day shift began, but find a friend who'd say, "Of course, use our kettle, what's it like outside? Warm, is it?"

Coming on duty, the girl would yawn, think, well, the day will soon pass, and then... Oh, Mrs Fowler's dead, is she? Has she been prepared? She has, oh super! For she of course loathes the task of laying out the dead, and always tries to get out of it.

Going into Maudie's room, and seeing the white tidy bed hardly disturbed by the slim mound that is Maudie, she remembers, and again her hands fly towards her mouth in that ancient gesture, *Oh, what have I done?*—but thinks, well, if she did die a day or two earlier than she needed, what of it? Thinks that she will go and look at the chart and see if Maudie was given extra potion in the night, she would like to have the reassurance that it was not pain that killed the old woman, but she forgets.

I rang Vera as soon as the office was open. She burst into tears, surprising me and herself. "Oh God," said she, "I'm sorry, it's the last straw, it's too much—how silly, she was due to go, but . . . Are you all right? I hope so. Oh, I don't know why, there was something about her, what was it?" Vera chattered on; it was a nervous reaction. She wept again. She said again, "How silly . . . take no notice. You say you met the relatives? Will they pay for the funeral, do you think?"

"They can certainly afford it."

"I'll ring them . . . Oh dear, I do feel low. No, it's not just Maudie, I've such problems. No, I don't want you to ask. When I got this job, I said to myself, my job is going to be one thing and my home life another, and I'm not going to mix them. So far, I've done it. I got the job because if I hadn't I'd have gone mad. Though you could say, frying pan out of the fire, I do the same kind of thing at home as I do at work—and let's leave it like that, if you don't mind."

She rang up later to say that Maudie's sister had said that Maudie had paid for years to get herself buried decently, and she couldn't afford to put anything to it.

"God," said Vera, "doesn't it make you sick? Funny thing, I had a feeling she'd say just that. Right, it will have to be the Council, then. And now I have a favour to ask—will you do something about the cat? It's the one thing I can't bring myself to do, when these poor old things die, taking their cats to be put down."

Frightful rushings about and commotions in the office because of Phyllis getting to the spring shows in Rome—said I wouldn't go. Said I had "problems"; the problem being Maudie's death. Crazy, and I know it. Except that it makes sense, to me. Late snow, airports tricky—well, we got that over and she's off, and I went to Maudie's. Oh, the smell of the place, the dark nastiness! Without that blazing fire there, there was no life. I spent half an hour sweeping all the old food into carriers and dumping them into the bins. Including perfectly good tins and jars, unopened. But I was in the grip of a need to be done with it. And that is why, Vera says, when old people die, the second-hand dealers get windfalls: everyone feels the same, including the Council people who come in to sort and assess: Oh, let's be done with it, let's get it over. Maudie's bookcases, I think, would fetch a bit in an antique shop; she has some engravings that aren't too bad; there's a fine chest of drawers. But who will get the benefit of it, if I say to Vera, Make sure whoever it is who goes in gets the value of those good things? That sister of Maudie's that's who . . .

The cat. I went out the back and found the poor beast sitting outside the door, waiting, I suppose, for Maudie to come back. About fifteen years ago, this cat arrived on Maudie's back step, crying for help. She was pregnant. Maudie took her in, found homes for the kittens, had the cat operated on. Love and kisses ever since and now, suddenly, again, a homeless beast crouched on a back doorstep. I went to the woman who had been feeding her, hoping for a bit of luck. But she was angry and said, "If I'd known it was going to be so long! I didn't bargain for weeks of it . . . I've got a cat of my own . . ." Then, she softened and said, "I'd have her if I could, but . . ."

I got the cat into Maudie's cat basket and put the animal, crying, into my car and drove down to the RSPCA. Just in time before it closed.

Maudie's funeral today.

Maudie paid weekly for many years into a Funeral Benefit. In hard times she went without food to keep up the payments. When she had finished, there was fifteen pounds. Enough, then, to bury her properly. She wanted to lie near her mother, in Paddington, but those graves had been emptied and built over long ago. She did not know that cemetery has gone, nor that her fifteen pounds would hardly pay for the hire of a spade.

The funeral the Council lays on for those who die without means is adequate: I wouldn't mind it for myself, but then I don't care about all that.

I realized today that I switched off for my mother's funeral and for Freddie's: I was there, I suppose, but that's all. I was certainly *there* for Maudie's . . .

A nice spring day, pale blue sky, busy white clouds, some snowdrops and crocuses in the grass around the graves. An old cemetery full of birds.

The clan turned out, but not the great-grandchildren whom Maudie longed to know. And besides, these days *of course* children are not supposed to put up with anything as basic as death and funerals.

There were thirty-three people, all well off, well dressed and complacent.

I was *furious*, through the whole thing. And there was the matriarch, predictably blubbering away, being supported on either side by her elderly sons.

Afterwards, up came the son of a nephew and began to talk about Maudie. I could see us standing there, near the great mound of fresh-smelling yellow earth, me impeccably dressed for a funeral, dark grey suit, black gloves, my black hat (that Maudie adored so much, she said it was a wonder!), black shoes with heels about a foot high, black silk stockings. I had taken all the trouble I could, to signal to that lot that I valued Maudie. And there he was, a grey, paltry, diminished man, and I began to wonder *who* I was being so angry with. He was smiling, doing his best.

He offered, "Auntie Maudie had her sense of humour all right, oh she liked her little joke . . ."

And he told me a story I had heard often from Maudie. People she cleaned house for had a fruit and vegetable shop, and the woman said to her, "Would you like to taste this season's new strawberries?" And set in front of the expectant Maudie a single strawberry on a good plate, with the sugar bowl and the cream. Maudie ate the strawberry, and then said to the woman, "Perhaps you'd like to sample the cherries on the tree in my back garden?" Brought the woman a single luscious cherry in a large brown-paper bag, and gave her notice there and then.

By then several of them had crowded up. Some I had seen at the famous lunch, and others were new. They were curious about Maudie's fine friend.

I said, "There was another story she used to tell, it was this. She was out of work, because she had flu and had lost her cleaning job. She was walking home with no money at all in her purse and she was praying, God help me, God please help me ... And she looked down and saw a half-crown on the pavement. And she said, Thank you, God. She went into the first shop and bought a currant bun, and ate it standing there, she was so hungry. Then she bought bread, butter, jam, and some milk. There was sixpence over. On her way home she went into the church and put the sixpence in the box, and said to God, You've helped me, and now I'll help You."

Around me faces that said they did not know whether to laugh or not? A joke? For Maudie was always such a joker! Very doubtful they looked, they glanced at each other, they wondered whether to offer more reminiscences. And I was thinking, what is the point? They had simply written Maudie off years ago. The sister (still weeping noisily as the earth thudded down), unable to come to terms with how she used Maudie, and then dismissed her, used her and dismissed her, had said she was *impossible*—for one reason or another; and therefore had the family been able to forget her. I stood there looking at the uneasy *stupid* faces, and decided not to bother.

And they had the last word, after all, for, as I reached my car, one of the elderly sons came after me and said in a kindly patronizing way, "And now I suppose you'll get yourself another little job, will you?"

And so that's that.

I got home raging, went around the flat slamming and banging and muttering to myself. Like Maudie.

When Jill came in from the office she stood looking at me for a while, then she deliberately came over, took me by the hand, and led me to my big chair.

As I stood by it, she reached to take my hat, and I pulled it off, and gave it to her.

"Lovely hat, Janna," she said.

She looked at my gloves and I peeled them off and handed them to her.

"Lovely gloves."

She gently sat me down in the chair, fetched a stool and lifted my legs on to it.

"Lovely shoes," said she.

"I'm so angry," I said, "I'm so angry I could die of it."

"So I can see."

"If I let myself stop being angry, I'm going to howl and scream."

"Jolly good idea, that."

"Meanwhile, I am angry."

"Provided you know *who* you are being angry with," said Niece Jill, and she went off to make me a nice cup of tea.

If the Old Could...

If the young knew...
If the old could...

French proverb

My heel caught as I stepped off the train. My right foot went into the gap. I fell. I was on all fours on the platform, among the people waiting to push on to the train. As I scrambled up, they were jostling all around me. I stood teetering, and saw a man stepping fast towards me, and was struck at once, even in that confused moment, by his command, his competence, his quickness. He caught me as I was going down again, and as a result of our joint attempts I found myself lying in his arms, one of my hands, the one clutching my handbag which I had held on to through it all, at the back of his neck. I began to laugh. A sad enough wail, but a laugh. His face, so close to mine, was attractive, intelligent. All that energetic incisiveness would have led me to expect a face much less—I am afraid there is only one word for it—sensitive than his. His smile was inquiring. I explained, 'I am a romantic novelist.' After the briefest pause he laughed, appreciatively, and then I was standing up beside him smoothing down my clothes, returning to myself.

We took each other in, liking what we saw, and showing it. And then I noticed, past his shoulder, that a girl stood watching us with a fierce closeness that dissolved the moment, for as my face changed he turned fast and, saying to me, 'Are you all right?', he went to her, took her arm and led her away. I was struck again, and painfully—though I need to understand and to study that pain—how his vigorous, almost careless, yes you *could* say debonair insouciance vanished, and even the set of his shoulders changed, as he took charge of the girl and was all responsibility.

I stood watching them go. Would he turn around? No. But the girl did. A suspicious and hostile face: his mistress?

Young girls fancy handsome elderly gents. In his fifties, I should say. Like me... I went slowly up and out, shaken more than I had thought, and by more than my fall. I was thinking, That was an unusual man, one that would stand out anywhere, in any crowd. You forget how mediocre most people are. Then, suddenly, one of the other kind. What did he think of me? Well, I knew, there was no mistaking that.

On the street, April showing itself in wild fast-fleeting cuds of white on bright blue, and a fitful sunlight. Oh, to be anywhere in northern Europe now that April is here. That was what I was thinking in Madrid only two days ago. I answer yes to more and more travelling for the mag. They say elderly women get itchy feet, travel all the time if they can. But I insist still that I am middle-aged. Oh, I do feel low. It is as well I didn't maintain a stiff upper lip and go to the office, but went home, rang them up, and said not today, tomorrow.

None of this would have happened were it not for Niece Jill's announcement yesterday. How many thousands of times have I got off the train at Tottenham Court Road? No, *don't* work it out. Have I ever fallen there—or anywhere else—before?

When I got back from Madrid yesterday the flat was not as usual as neat as a filing cabinet, but there were clothes everywhere, and Jill was in a state, all sighs and concerned looks. I knew. I was ready to weep and howl, and this it was that bouleversed me, for until it happened I would not have thought that hearing Jill was leaving would hurt me so.

'When and where to?' I asked.

'Oh, Jane, I might have known you'd get it at once.'

'I haven't asked *why*,' I said.

She said, 'I'm moving in with someone.'

'Male or female?'

'You know, Mark. The photographer.'

'Oh, Mark!'

At once, anxious: 'Don't you like him?'

'But, Jill, I've not done much more than approve his pictures. It hadn't occurred to me to think of him as a possible nephew.'

'I didn't say I was going to marry him.'

'What would your mother say?'

'It is what *you* say that I mind about,' said Jill softly, and I sat down with a bump and tried to be normal. She was near the window, watching me. The curtains were not drawn, and beyond her was a fast-moving sky full of white clouds lit by, presumably, the moon. There was a full moon in Madrid, so why not here? I thought again how very fond of her I had become. There she stood, slim, erect, for she holds herself very well these days, and very pretty. I might have guessed she was in love, so animated and alive is she. A credit to everyone concerned, Jill is.

I was thinking fast; and there was nothing to disturb, or to warn. Why should I be upset? What had happened? Everything was as it should be. Three years ago Jill had come to London town to seek her fortune, aided by her wicked worldly aunt who, with shameless nepotism, had got her a job in *Lilith*. There Jill had flourished, turning her hand to anything, mistress of all trades. She had been an amenable, sensible, kindly flatmate, handling her tricky aunt with tact. She had made friends, got a prophylactic dose of revolution-ary socialism, now over. She had found herself a young man and wanted to live with him. What could be more of a success story than that?

'Jill,' I said, 'I shall miss you most horribly.'

And began to cry. Jill, too. First, sniffs and deprecating little self-conscious smiles. Then slow painful tears. Then hot sobs, and we flung ourselves into each other's arms.

'Oh, Aunt Jane!' cried Jill.

'Oh, Jill!'

'And you didn't even want me here, to start with,' she accused.

'More fool me.'

We separated, with many a little pat and stroke, and stopped crying. She made us tea, and we drank it.

I saw there was more.

'Well?'

'Jane, you do realize that Kate will be on the doorstep as I move out?'

I thought about it, while she watched me, her great grey

eyes in lakes of glaucous paint over the edge of her cup. Kate
has gone from bad to worse in the last three years. She did
badly in her A-levels, refused to take them again as her
parents wanted. She had asked me to get her a job in *Lilith*,
and I had said she must see that there were limits to my
introducing young female relatives into the mag. Sister
Georgie, predictably, had rung up to say, Surely I could see
my way to doing something? I said, 'As you know, I have
your daughter Jill living with me. I would say that was
something.' She said, 'Kate thinks it is very unfair, and I must
say we do too.'

That had been last year. Since then Kate had been mooning
around the house, deciding whether she would or would not
study Spanish.

At last I said to Jill, 'I know I didn't want you here to start
with, and as it turned out I enjoyed every minute. But Kate
surely is a very different thing?'

There is nothing skimpy or dishonest in Jill. She did not
say, 'Oh, it will be all right,' or, 'She's not so bad.' She said,
'Yes, she is a different thing. Altogether. I wonder if you
really know how different?'

'Probably not. Though I have seen quite a few spoiled brats
making the lives of my peer group miserable. You, my dear
Jill, are the only young thing I have actually lived with.'

'Well, I would say that Kate is in a bit of a mess.'

'Do you know why? I mean, *really*?'

She thought. She sat there holding her cup on the arm of
the big red linen chair, she in a white negligé, her—at the
moment—red hair loose, eyes blank with memory. She was
looking back into scenes of family life.

'Well, I don't know. Would you agree that people are
born?'

'Yes, I would.'

'I would say that of us four Kate is going to turn out the
mess.'

'Is that a life sentence?'

'I wouldn't be surprised.'

'Hard words.'

'Oh, you are thinking, *Sisters! They never got on. . .* It's true, we never have. My idea of a bad time is one spent with Kate. It always was. But, the point is. . .'

'All right, I get the point.'

'As long as you really have, Jane. Because I wonder if you realize. . . it takes a strong person to stand up to you!'

I was sloppy enough to allow my sigh to be a bit theatrical: the start of a familiar joking game we have, Jill and I, where she says how I can't tolerate weakness and I'm tough as old boots, and I say that it is I who have to stand up to her. 'No, no, listen,' she was going on. 'Believe me, I am grateful—oh, no, not just for your letting me live here, though that is the best thing that ever happened, or for *Lilith*—I hope you won't think I'm ungrateful if I say that *now* I know I would have done well anywhere. But I learned *that* in *Lilith*. But it is *you* I'm grateful for. Because you never let anyone get away with anything. You have never let me . . . well, not everyone could take it.' A small 'humorous' smile, but only because the situation prescribed it, and her great sea eyes anxious on my face.

'Very well,' I said.

'Good.'

And soon she gave me a hug and went to bed.

I stayed on for a while, alone in this room, thinking that soon being alone would again be my condition. Oh, it was not that I minded. Aloneness has never frightened me, on the contrary. But I was going to miss, more than I want to admit to myself, the *youngness,* the freshness of Jill.

Who really is my younger self.

In the office I heard them calling her Chipov. So I thought, Why a Russian nickname, what is Russian about this brisk English girl? But no, it was 'Chip off'. A chip off this block. When Jill came to live here she was a tentative, watchful creature, all great eyes and apprehension, held together by her resolve that she would live here and benefit from her Aunt Jane. She tended to droop, to become listless. But she was herself, was Jill . . . Very soon, she became me, put on my characteristics, my mannerisms, my walk. Her voice is mine.

No, I did not see this at once; needed to hear the nickname first. Then I thought, Of course! And I started to observe

myself in her, this mirror, on the whole flattered, thinking;
Well, I am, rather *was* not so bad! But then, seeing something
else, began trains of very different thoughts. . . . A competent
girl she is, every movement so right, her mind behind it. But
controlled . . . over-controlled? Her quick grace, her flair—
well, I never had that, or I don't think I had, or have. She
seems to take command of a place as she walks into it, or
expects to. Bossy, in short. Her voice is measured, usually
humorous, or with an edge on it, signpointing absurdity or
incongruity. It is the voice of one who has decided to give the
impression that she sees the world as a comedy, on the whole
an agreeable one. But this posture is an effort, a strain; she is
by no means sure of the comedy. Every note and change and
pitch of that voice is mine.

There is also, in Jill, a little hard streak of something—
perhaps even an obtuseness?—that gives the impression of
self-satisfaction. But is it? Does it not come from the effort it
takes her to prove herself, self-absorption because of the
difficulties of what she confronts, and which she is not going
to admit to, even to herself.

Very interesting questions, this raises. First, and one that I
have brooded about not a little: why did Jill not choose to
model herself on those admirable citizens, her mother and
father? If there were ever exemplars bound to be approved by
every authority I can think of, then Sister Georgie and her
husband Tom fit the bill best. If the textbooks are right,
surely Jill would have 'internalized' one or the other or both
long before she came to me? But no, it was Aunt Jane, of
whose selfishness and shallowness she has been hearing all
her childhood, on whom she chose to model herself.

Secondly, and I brood about this too: if that tentative
uncertain girl *was* Jill, and what people see now a skilled
adaptation, then with whom is Mark, her boyfriend, in love?
For the rest of her life Jill will be a version of her Aunt Jane;
and that is what people will mean when they think of her,
speak of her.

Thirdly. On whom did I model myself? For I resemble
neither of my parents, those worthy souls of whom I have to
say, They had no style, no dash, no flair, no kind of

distinction. No, probably when I was about Jill's age I admired someone in the old office, the pre-*Lilith* days, and admiring, became. And for thirty-odd years Janna James, then Janna Somers, has presented herself polished, finished, arranged, and this is what people see and know. But it is an artefact! I am even asking myself, When Sister Georgie complains of my superficiality and all the rest, perhaps she means that in my late adolescence I quite simply acquired a personality that seems to her false? Is there any point in asking her? As for her, *she* 'internalized' our mother, and that was that. Every gesture, tone of voice, habit. And very early.

And so Jill is off, having done everything right. I am sure she will continue to do things right; will not make a bad marriage, have a breakdown, become a whine in middle-age. I feel sure about her.

Yes, of course she will come and see me, I will see her in the office, we will be friends. It won't be the same.

Well, cut your losses, Janna. Cut your losses, Jane.

That's *that*.

What is the point of dreaming of wild April from the solid bourgeois pleasures of Madrid, and then seeing nothing of it? This morning I was up and out by seven, had breakfast in the little workmen's café, where they exchange pleasantries with me now, and walked slow, savouring, through the budding lanes of Hampstead down through Swiss Cottage and to the park. There I sauntered about, listening to the birds and wishing I knew cherry from apple blossom. Around me a pristine spring was dismissed by half an hour of hot summer, a big black summer cloud, a growl of thunder and a clap of warm rain, and spring came back, with innocent fickleness, for its blue and white was at once absorbed into a uniform grey, from which floated down a dozen large loose damp snowflakes to disappear on the unnaturally green grass. Autumn did not appear, and I walked out into the Marylebone Road and approved some rather good outfits in the windows of Monica, where I bought my white linen last summer. I was window-shopping, not for myself, but for Jill; and told myself to stop it. It was then nine. I had not wanted to be late, so I got on to the underground at Baker Street and got out as usual at Tottenham Court Road, not catching my heel this time but with a pang for this man I would never see again. Walking slowly down to Soho Square, where I proposed to linger, not wanting to relinquish the joys of this delicious morning—for it was a spring morning again, and the spring flowers were massed in tiers at the street corner—I saw in front of me a man's back, and then, as he felt my eyes on him, his face, for he turned with his characteristic swift way and, seeing me, smiled as if this was nothing more than what he had expected, and said, 'Ah! So there you are! I hoped you might be somewhere about. Have you time for a coffee?' And we sat opposite each other at a table on the pavement, while people raced past to work.

He had his first breakfast, and I had my second, sticky nut cake and marvellous coffee.

We were both of us filled with a wicked, wild, racing delight, we could not stop smiling while we looked at each other with a frankness which, because it was so natural, was the best of it. He is weathered-handsome, tawny, with grey-blue eyes, not sea eyes like Jill's, but direct and shrewd. His hair is yellow, not silvered like mine, for I propose to keep my metallic locks, gold and silver. He is not tall, but taller than I am. A handsome man: what must he have been like when he was younger? And I was thinking how well we were matched, physically, and how well we would have been, younger. And he knew I was, and matched these thoughts with his own. Everything we said on no matter what subject seemed to be about us, and this amazing meeting of ours. It seemed impossible not to talk about ourselves, and yet by the time we parted I knew nothing about him except his name, Richard, and that he had just come back from abroad.

'What a marvellous time to come home,' he said. 'Not that it was an accident. I said to myself, No, I am not going to miss one more spring. And look how right I was!'

'Where have you been?'

'In America.'

'I was recently in New York. And I still wanted to come home.'

'Well, if I had been in New York—but no. There is only one country in the world to live in, and only one city. And here I am.'

The sky flung a handful of rain at us, with a *soupçon* of ice in it, then the sun came out hot, and we went on down to Soho Square hand in hand. We made, I know, a handsome couple: or at least, I knew, trained as I am to keep an exterior eye focused on how I look. As for him, he could scarcely have been unaware that people looked at us as we stood together in the middle of the square, spring on the trees and the white clouds racing.

We stood facing each other, quite ablaze with love.

He stammered a little as he asked, 'Will you have breakfast with me again? It can't be tomorrow—on Friday?' And as I smiled, 'I am taking the most appalling risk, not even knowing your name . . . where you live . . . no, don't tell me, just be here, same place, but an hour earlier?'

And so we parted.

I arrived in the office knowing that every gland in my body was shooting out magical substances and that my blood must be pure ichor. I had to go into my own room and shut the door and calm myself down with steady hard work.

I am working as hard as I have ever done. I still talk about retiring to live on my royalties, which I could do, and live very well; but when I did go on part-time, thinking to slide out that way, I came back again. The board asked me, and they were right. To lose both editors, Joyce and me, more or less at once: too much.

But when I do think about it, I have to be a bit uneasy. If *Lilith* would find it hard to do without me—fair enough, I've worked with, for, by, and from *Lilith* for—when I write down how long, it's a shock. Since the end of the last war. Decades. But suppose I can't do without *Lilith*? That's not so funny. Jill remarked, casually, not to be provocative, 'You're married to *Lilith*.' I didn't like that. Who really runs *Lilith*? Phyllis does, in tandem with Jill. These two clever young women are *Lilith*, and nothing happens anywhere in any department without their knowledge. They come to me for advice, but less often now. I travel to dress shows all over Europe, and do the public lunches: I am the public face of *Lilith*. These two girls, both of whom learned about clothes from me, will watch me as I prepare myself for a luncheon at the Savoy, or as I leave for Munich, and say, 'Janna, I loved that dress you had on last week!' Or, 'Jane, do you think that suit would be better with a cream. shirt?' For I have been unable to recover my total dedication to how I look: I feel that keeping myself groomed and my clothes up to the mark amounts to a holding operation against an invisible enemy who is every day becoming stronger.

The formal structure is that poor Charlie is editor, with Phyllis as assistant and me as consultant, Jill as my helper. Oh, the amiable social Charlie, how fond we all are of him! Phyllis, who is after all married to him, and who manages him at home as pleasantly as she does in the office, genuinely seems to love him. But then, as Jill remarks, 'And so she'd better, if she's seven months pregnant.'

But so much time gets wasted while Phyllis makes sure that Charlie does this or that, or Charlie consults with Phyllis or Jill; people approach the editor, needing quick decisions, but cannot have them because first everything has to be discussed with Jill or Phyllis. A snap and a sparkle have gone out of *Lilith*. Never mind. It does well enough, making less money, but then so does everything now, and it is still a household word, bought by 'upmarket' women, mostly working. But we do wonder—perhaps it is bought as much by housebound women who want to be working? For, after all, cookbooks and fashion magazines are not bought to be used, but read, for pleasure: doors into fantasy worlds. . .

Lilith's formula is as it always has been—three quarters solid common sense, information, medical advice, the problems of being a consumer in a consumer economy; one quarter outrageous clothes and glamorous food which practically no one ever actually wears or eats.

I enjoy being in the office, and my travelling and my business lunches, but the thing is, it's all more of an effort.

The effort is in always having to be on show, presented, observed. At home I have been careful to be *there* for Jill; responsible, not a source of that dread infection (despised by me, and of course by worthy Sister Georgie whose life might be defined as a war against it) sloppiness, whether of behaviour or of anything else. *My* place, my refuge, the only spot on this wide earth where I can be myself, do not feel the presence of possibly critical eyes, is—my bed. Not even my room, for Jill has needed to be able to come in and out, so that she may be reassured her rights in me are not restricted. Oh, not too often, not annoyingly: but the fact is, it is not when I have shut my bedroom door that I have felt responsibility take its weight off me, but when I turn off the light. I lie in the dark and look at changing skies over rooftops and trees.

Jill moved out today. She stood with her cases and her bundles in the middle of the living room, waiting for the taxi, and looked at me appalled at the cruel choices that life imposes on us. Her young man is very nice. I approve of him.

I went to the little café at exactly the time of the tryst. He was not there. I sat at a corner table, pretending to be amused at myself, but my heart was a clench of apprehension. No one there but Gino, the handsome Italian behind the expresso machine, in a gorgeous black and white sweater which made him look, with his polished black head, like harlequin. The café is a cosy box lined with wood and trailing plants. Only the two of us. I refused to watch the door, then could not stop myself. I was wondering when in my life have I been in such a state over anyone? Never. My poor Freddie? Certainly not, and as a matter of principle! And, thinking of Freddie, which as a rule I try never to do, I realized I had been dreaming of him all last night; as if it were Freddie and not Richard with whom I was in love.

And I tried to exorcise him thus: I have been dreaming of my husband, badly treated by me when I was married to him, not that I knew it until after he had died, nastily, of cancer. And so what is the point of dreaming now that I loved him, when I certainly did not then? It's sentimental rubbish!

And then, I realized I had used the words of Richard, 'in love', and this touched off a typhoon of contradictory emotions. First of all, I am afraid, pride: I, Janna Somers, in love, and in this sudden inappropriate way, at first sight, with someone whose name I still did not know. I, Janna, always in command of my decisions... But all this was being put at nothing, quite simply, by an outrageous delight, an energy that made it hard even to sit still, and which was drawing the young Italian's eyes to me though he did not know why. A smart elderly? middle-aged? lady, ever so well groomed, that was what he was seeing: and approving: the wearer of that sweater would have to give me full marks for what I was wearing. When Richard came in, or rather blundered in because of panic, for he had imagined I would be outside at the table on the pavement, his face cleared into a wonderful smile, and he came fast to the corner where I was, and sat down not looking what he was doing, but exactly as I was at him: is it possible that this miraculous person actually exists, I haven't imagined it all?

'It's raining,' I said.

'Is it?'

And we began to laugh, peal after peal, relief after tension.

'Gino,' said this man, Richard, 'coffee, cakes, cream—everything!' And laughed.

'Certainly,' says Gino, all smiles and style and connivance with our holiday mood, and in no time our little table was set for a feast. Which, however, we were unable to touch.

This man, Richard, whoever he was, like a tarnished lion, seemed all out of place in this domestic interior, too large. And I felt, excessive, even dangerous to it. And yet I didn't want to move, or to do anything, but sit there for ever, and look at him. It wasn't only that he is handsome, and so forth; no, it was that he seemed so familiar to me, this stranger, kin—flesh of my flesh? Oh no, that's dangerous, that is! Sitting here in my—for the first time in three years—empty flat, writing, I think, Would I like to go to bed with him, and I feel quite shocked. There is a *no* there, but why? I hold out my hands and look at them, so well kept and nice, with the rosy soft nails, and the rings. The hands of a matron, however.

We didn't say anything very much, sitting on either side of that table, leaning towards each other. We could not stop smiling, waves of energy flowed back and forth between us.

Then he said, 'Look, why don't we simply go for a long walk? In the rain?'

'I adore walking in the rain,' I said, and he: 'Of course you do! Well then!'

And, as he turned to signal to Gino, whose eyes had not left us for a second, I saw beyond him, on the pavement through the door, a girl standing, apparently lost, indecisive—the sombre dark girl he had been with when we first met. And some instinct made him turn too to see her, and with an exclamation he got up and was out of the café at once. I saw him take her by her two arms and bend over her, anger contained by tender expostulation. And then he moved her on out of sight. I felt as if the plug had been pulled out; dismay was now in the air of the café; and Gino was *not* looking at me, but polishing glasses, holding them up to the light one after another, and squinting at them as if into a kaleidoscope.

I was there alone for perhaps fifteen minutes. I knew that he must be walking her well away from where I was. What I was examining in my mind's eye was the way, from the moment he had seen her, he had damped himself down; that cautious set of his shoulders, the responsibility.

When he came back, I saw a different man. This sober and responsible person sat down opposite me and looked at me, and was choosing words.

I said, 'It's your daughter, is it?'

'Yes, that's Kathleen.' Then he took both my hands, leaned forward and looked at me. 'Why don't we decide not to talk about any of it?' he said. Now what characterized him was a patience, a carefulness; there was irony but no criticism. I knew I was seeing the man as he was in his ordinary life, and wondered if I too dimmed down and diminished as soon as my claims and my boundaries imposed themselves?

'It is at this stage,' said he, smiling, but with a grimness in it, 'that I tell you, and then you tell me, all about ourselves. But why don't we decide not to?'

I said, 'Well, I know something pretty important about you already.'

'Yes, I know, I know. But let's try.'

'Very well.'

We went out, and I saw him look swiftly up the street and then down into Soho Square. A soft glistening rain. A tender veiled sky.

'I ought to be at work anyway,' I said.

'Tomorrow?' he said. 'Rain or shine?'

After work I went to bed at once. I have woken from a dream of Freddie. *Why?* A dream of loss and emptiness. Freddie was on the other side of a deep and dangerous river, full of black twisting water, and he stood there looking at me. I can't make out what it means, that look of his. If I'm not careful I am going to cry—and once I start, what sort of a flood will that be? Dare I go back to bed?

Well, I didn't. I sat by my window and looked up into the sky where a deep black had floating on it small white islets; I longed for the light to come. And here it is.

It is night again: and what a day it has been.

Just as I was leaving for the café, the bell rang. Before answering it I stood in the middle of the living room, now my own again, as orderly as if Jill had never been here. I was looking for something, anything of hers—a book, a scarf—but no. I had tears in my eyes when I answered the entryphone and heard Kate's voice. At once, anger! I said, 'Kate, it is eight in the morning, and I didn't know you were coming.' Sniff, snuffle, gulp. 'Oh, Aunt *Jane,* and I've been sitting on a bench in the street all night and it is so *cold.*'

I pressed the button. I waited, astounded, even alarmed at myself. I was a rage of emotion. Which I must not inflict on Kate. What I let in was a snuffling waif, an infant clown. Her hair is neglected punk, she wore baggy pink dungarees, soiled of course, and a T-shirt, orange. She was shivering violently, and gazing at me with hopeless eyes, china blue. Her grubby fingers plucked at her lips.

'I know it is no good my asking why you didn't even telephone first?'

'Oh Jane, but I was afraid you'd say no.' But she was stammering with cold.

She had let down a small (soiled) bundle near the door.

'Now you've made your effect, you could put a sweater on?'

She shook her head: helplessness.

'You haven't got a sweater? You have no clothes at all with you because you mean me to buy you a new outfit?'

She nodded, biting her nails, her face awash.

I got her one of my sweaters, and her listlessness vanished as she scrambled into it: I saw how she had been dreaming of getting warm.

'What time did you get into Paddington?'

'Eleven last night.'

'You were engaged perhaps in exciting metropolitan adventures?'

'I sat on a bench there, till the fuzz moved me on. They were horrid. And then I walked and walked till I got here. . .'

'My sister Georgie doesn't know you are here? She didn't give you money for the journey?'

'All my money was stolen. I was mugged.'

'The first thing you've got to do is ring your mother and tell her where you are.'

She drooped away to an armchair. Seeing her where so often Jill had been, contrasting the two of them, sent away my anger. Besides, I was realizing just what I had to contend with. Everything Jill does is characterized by competence: Kate bungles the setting down of a coffee cup.

I said, 'I have precisely fifteen minutes.' I rang Sister Georgie. Her voice, Home Counties homogenized.

'As I am sure you know,' I said, 'your daughter Kate is here. She arrived in London in the middle of the night, has already been robbed, has been wandering about by herself without so much as a cardigan. She simply arrived on my doorstep.'

'I suppose she was afraid to telephone,' said Georgie. 'She's afraid of you.'

'Then why did she come?' I said, and put down the telephone.

Seeing how much I wanted—but really!—to assault that girl physically, not from anger now but from sheer exasperation, I took my time in turning around to face her. She was not looking at me, but gazing dolefully out of the window.

Her hair, in yellow, pink and green tufts, stuck up, and she was gnawing her grubby little fingers.

'What does my sister Georgie make of your punkhood?' I inquired, but she did not answer or turn around.

'How about making yourself a cup of tea, getting yourself warm, having some breakfast?'

The blue doll's saucers of her eyes at once became visible, all hope.

'Tell me, can you really not get yourself some tea, at least?'

'I . . . I . . . I . . . was afraid to suggest it.'

'Well, I have suggested it.'

She did not move. I saw that her whole body was clenched in a steady deep shiver.

I went to the kitchen, switched on the kettle, cut some bread and butter, took it to her with some tea on a tray.

I was about to say, 'Never, not once, in the time your sister was here, did I have to wait on her.' But something stopped me. The something was, I am afraid, pity. I do not propose to be sorry for this Kate! I do not believe that it helps people to be sorry for them! The best you can do for anyone is to help them to independence. But *Kate*—the sight of this poor little tyke, wolfing down bread and butter, slopping down tea . . . shivering . . .

How was it possible she could turn herself out like that?—not care? Punk is *style*. I admire it, properly done. There's a girl at the corner, she's a pleasure, we exchange

smiles as she even peacocks about a little for my benefit,
miming a fashion model there on the pavement, often not
only for me, but for her mates who are also punks, but not so
elegant. She can look like a cat, little black ears carved out of
her golden hair, black arms (gloves from a stall?), a
suggestion of gallant tiger around the shoulders. Or a
highwayman, black swinging cloak and a mask done in black
paint from which gleam painted eyes, all enjoyment. It must
take her hours: as long as I used to need when I still cared
enough. Her style is intransigence, contained and formalized;
poor Kate has taken some bottles of hair dye to the
bathroom, stood on tiptoes before the mirror, probably
sniffling, daubed paint on tufts of hair cut as she works, and
then stood in the doorway waiting for her parents to say, 'Oh
Kate, what have you done to yourself?'

'I've got to go,' I said.

'When will you come home?'

'I don't know.'

At this she looked at me differently. I am not saying that all
that had happened had been a pose, an invention: she was
too cold and miserable for that: but she had been for weeks,
months, rehearsing claims and just demands: she had known
what she was going to say to me and was determined to say
it.

Her look was not at all that of one alarmed at being told
she was to fend for herself: it was a thoughtful assessment.

I was interested that I was pleased to see she was capable of
any kind of rational thought: simultaneously I noted panic in
myself. I am not going to have my relationship (whatever it
is) with Richard spoiled by this girl.

'How old are you, Kate?'

'Don't you know!' she sniffed.

'No. Eighteen?'

'Nineteen.'

'I'm not babying you, Kate! I'm off now. We'll talk when
I've time. Here's some money. We need bread. I don't aspire
to that healthy wholemeal your mother doubtless insists on,
you can get in some decent French. Butter: I like Normandy.
You'd better get some paté, eggs. If there's anything you want

for yourself. . .' I added this last, forcing myself.

Before I left I stood at the door, examining her again, conscious that I had been in too much of a rush about everything.

I saw her hands trembling, around the cup.

'Kate,' I said, 'I'm not going to clear up after you, tidy up, be your nursemaid.'

She nodded, eyes down.

As I left the building I forgot Kate.

Everything in movement. Above raced, from west to east, plump white clouds on shallow healthy blue like Kate's eyes. As I passed the cherry at the corner, the wind lifted off a pink froth of blossom and dumped it with a flourish on the pavement. My hair was frisking around my face.

I was late, *late*: and as I ran into the little street and saw Soho Square a shrill spring green, Richard hastened towards me, took my arm, and said, 'Let's go.' I could not help glancing around for his daughter Kathleen, but he said, 'No, it's all right.' All the same he too looked around as we got into the taxi. He took my hands and held them to his face, and we sat dissolving in smiles.

'At this point, when people fall in love,' said he, 'it is customary to tell each other the story of their lives. Let's not make a present to each other of our pasts.'

'So you have already asked,' I said, or queried.

And he said, or stated, 'It signals the entrance into responsibility.'

'I have already seen that you have too much.'

'Then that's more than I want you to see.'

We went to St James's Park. It was just right for our mood. The grey waters, where we caught glimpses of the frivolous blue spring sky reflected, were crammed with fanciful ducks, in style rather like punks (when they get it right!) if you come to think of it. We stood hand in hand among the crocuses and daffodils and marvelled at the inventiveness of the world, while the spring exploded all around us.

How fresh and dazzling everything was; each flower or bird an amazement, a gift of love. And we realized our senses were at peak and a day like this might not come again, not ever, so rare it was; and how rare and hardly achieved our meeting. We walked about for hours, and felt life tingling in each other's hands, and if we looked at one another we could not stop smiling.

But somewhere else in me the thought kept popping up, to be suppressed: this has never happened to me. Not ever!

There was a point when we separated, he going off along one edge of the little lake, I on the other, and this parting was done with style, as if as a symbol or a foreshadowing, and because of the way this struck to the heart I was perhaps too ready to linger there watching him, only a few paces away but divided from me by water. It was my dream, Freddie standing on the other side of impassable water, and his long grave look. For a moment the intoxication of the day went, and I saw a man bereft of splendour, a middle-aged man, slightly stooped because of some invisible burden he carried, his tarnished locks adrift, a patient, quizzical face. I could see it all there, saw life, the way it drags down, pulls low, weighs, tugs, erodes; and I was trying to make myself see, there, where he was, himself as the young man; for there are times I don't know if it is this one I am seeing, my sudden companion who is battered and beaten like I am, or the young man I can see all the time more and more clearly: a light-stepping charmer, with a grave smile and blue eyes between fringes of sandy lashes.

And he too was staring at me.

I wanted to cry out; say, 'No, no—don't.' For if he was seeing the girl I was once, then that was even worse; for it was bad enough that Freddie should return to remember me, that cold girl, negotiating allowances of emotion, of sex—did I ever use the word love?—and who never, ever, had looked at him as if he might be the door to some wonder or astonishment.

That was a bad cold moment, as we stood separated by the muddy waters of the pond where the coloured ducks bobbed and dived, their orange feet scrabbling in the air as they forced themselves down, down, to puddle for weed at the bottom.

I felt so emptied and nothing, and he too; and we turned, but with an effort, dragging ourselves out of it, and met again at the corner of the lake, linking hands tentatively, as if what had brought us together to link them at the beginning might have gone for ever.

'You see,' he said, 'you see what lies in wait, if we are not careful.'

I, then—and my voice sounded to myself a stubborn, forlorn little statement: 'But perhaps we can't shut it all out.'

'Ah, I don't want to hear that from you. I mean, common sense.'

And I, dryly: 'I am famed for my common sense.'

And he: 'Yes, I daresay, but that's not what . . .'

And he quickly pulled me to him, and we stood, lightly enlaced. It is a strange thing, standing body to body with one's love, if the bodies are not young ones. The clothes we wore and which divided us seemed like statements, or reminders, of our real lives—not, as they were once, hardly to be distinguished from hot flesh. And, as I stood with Richard, there flashed into my mind a memory of me with Freddie, in some foreign place, Spain perhaps, one of our holidays, and me pulling off skirt, panties, to stand naked; while he stripped on the other side of a bed. I remembered and wondered, How was it that he did not take off my clothes, I his?—I was remembering the efficiency of the operation.

If I were with Richard, and *young*—I would wait for him to unbutton, slide sensuous stuffs off flesh, *take possession*. But Freddie was never allowed to possess me, perish the thought.

I felt Richard's rough cheek slide against mine, and he said, 'Do you have a photograph of yourself when you were a girl? Yes, I know that is crass, I should be able to imagine. Before you were married, or *serious*. Were you married? No, I don't want to know.'

'I was. I've been alone for—let's see. Yes, it must be five years, six. *Can* it be—really.' And dismayed, I stepped back out of the embrace.

'Let's go and have breakfast, lunch, something, a drink, we need it.'

We walked out of the park and found a little restaurant off St James's Street. The vividness of our senses had come back, and every mouthful seemed a miracle of tastes and savours. We ate—it didn't matter. A corner of bread with a bit of butter would have seemed a feast. We drank quite a bit of wine though, holding our hands around the glasses as if they warmed what we looked at, always each other for we could not take our eyes away.

And then we went through a showery glittery afternoon and walked and walked with no intention of ever stopping, until straight in front of me I saw a couple, a girl and boy. He had his back to a tree trunk, and held her in his arms, and her black Mediterranean hair sprawled all down her back and over his arms, and they were kissing.

Suddenly I was in a flood of tears, I who find myself in tears once a year with surprise and annoyance; but how many times have I wept in the last few days?

'Good God,' I heard myself say, as I stared at this young pair, lost to the world. 'What a fool I've been, what a fool I was.' When I came to myself I felt his comprehension of me, the moment, and was not able to return his look. For it was Freddie I was thinking of. If I could now separate them at all, Freddie, Richard. Richard put his arm around my shoulders and we walked past the lovers and towards a shop window where we saw ourselves. Some trick of the fading and changing lights in the glass made it easy to see myself, the pretty fresh girl with the crisp light hair and smiling eyes; I saw him beside me, the young man.

I don't know what he saw, or wanted to see.

We wandered on through the afternoon, stopping twice for coffee, and then it was early evening.

There was a withdrawal in him, and I was not surprised when he said, 'At six, I must leave you.'

Then: 'Tell me—on some other occasion, could I come to your place? You can't to mine.'

I said, 'This morning my niece Kate, my sister Georgina's second daughter—she has another daughter and two sons—arrived on my doorstep. It is her intention to live with me.'

'You have no children,' he stated.

'No.' Then I made myself say, 'It was not that I—that *we* decided not to but. . .'

'*I don't want to know* . . .' Then: 'I suppose we can't avoid plunging into each other's lives like dirty swimming pools, but let's put it off please for as long as we can.'

'My life,' I said, 'has been on the whole well ordered, often rechlorinated, the water changed.'

'That is what I am afraid of,' said he, and there was a pain behind the dryness that I, in my turn, was fighting not to have to know about.

But before we separated we walked along the Bayswater Road, and suddenly we saw a building being done up, with scaffolding up its side for four storeys, and on a platform on the fourth-floor scaffolding a little house, in scarlet, set there for the workmen to have tea in or to rest, and in the doorway sat a workman with a bucket in front of him in which must be a wisp of fire, for he held a sausage on a fork over the heat and waited with his knees apart for his meal to cook. And there was something so comical and pleasant in it that we laughed, holding on to each other, for the absurdity of the little red house so high up there and the sausage on the fork.

The strong exultation came back into us, and the burden fell off his back and he stood free and laughing, like me. Then we separated, with an assignation, but not for tomorrow. I do have to work some time, after all, even though I am a privileged elder stateswoman.

I went to the office anyway, to see if there was mail. Phyllis had gone, but Jill was there.

'I know about it,' said she. I thought she meant Richard, because of the vitality I could feel booming in me, but no, it was Kate of course.

She saw that I had had to tell myself she must mean Kate. She said, 'Has she been alone all day?'

'Presumably.'

'*Well!*'

'You are saying she can't be alone?'

'With all of us, the family, she hasn't had much practice at it.'

I seemed a long way from Kate, her problems, and I was not thinking of her as I sorted out my letters and looked at the diary for tomorrow.

Jill, who was at her desk which was piled with work, went on with it all for a few minutes, and then said, 'You should decide what to do about her. She's waiting for that. To call her bluff, if that's what you are going to do.' And then as I didn't answer, Jill cried out, 'Jane, you are sorry for her, aren't you?'

I said, 'I suppose so—if that's the point.'

'It is the point if it lets you in for more than you want.'

I said, vaguely, for I was thinking of Richard and if he had got home, what 'home' was, and what was the problem with Kathleen, 'I suppose after all it is just a question of having a sensible talk with her.'

Silence. When I looked up, Jill was smiling, as if to herself, but I was meant to notice it. 'It occurs to me, Aunt Jane, that in many ways you have had a very sheltered life.'

'You mean that Kate will be too much for me?'

'All right, don't say I didn't warn you.'

When I left she was still working. Enjoying it. I could see that pleasure of it in her: being able to do it, to do it well.

Pleasure: when I looked back at my life since I started working—before I was twenty—the strongest thing in it, in the way of pleasure, is how I felt when I proved to be so good at things. A consistent, years-long theme: me, working, *doing it,* doing it well. That has been my life's theme. And poor Freddie? The background to it.

And as I came home I was thinking of Freddie, though I try often enough not to. If he was the background to my life, was I to his? Probably. When he died and made a reckoning or account of his life, as I suppose one does, did he say to himself, My enjoyment was in my work? For he couldn't have said, Pleasure, that was Janna, that's what fun, pleasure, accomplishment has meant to me.

When I opened the door into the living room, I saw Kate asleep on the sofa, where she was when I left. The tray I had brought her was still by her, swept clean of every crumb. The sight brought home to me what Jill had said, and to collect myself I got through the usual small chores of homecoming, drawing curtains, switching on lights, getting myself a drink. In the middle of my cool and elegant room, lights so tastefully and efficiently disposed here and there, a vase, candy-striped cushions on the pale yellow chairs—amid all this, like a curtain going up on a play, the pathetic waif, her great clumping dirty shoes making marks on the grey linen sofa, the bundle still lying where she had dropped it near the door.

'Kate, wake up.'

She woke, stretching and yawning, but I still don't know if she had been awake all the time, listening to me move about.

'And now,' I said, 'we are going to talk. First of all, you will tell me what plans you have.'

Those pathetic, blinking baby-blue eyes! The slightly open, wet, pinkish mouth! The stubby childish hands plucking at her clothes.

'Kate, you are not going to work in *Lilith*.'

At this she flung herself about, heaved some desperate sighs, and ended by fixing me with a dramatic betrayed stare. I did not know, do not know, how much of all this was a prepared 'scene', for she must of course have known, for I have said so, that she will not work in *Lilith*. What I was convinced by was not the histrionics, but the limp defeated-ness of her.

I was thinking, Suppose she was as clever and well presented and as 'together' as Jill was, would I introduce her into *Lilith*, nepotism or not? Actually, not; but I might ask one of the other magazines, in which of course I know so many people, to take her on.

I realized that the speech I had in my mind to make, was simply not on:

'Kate! You have not passed your A-levels. You have no intention of passing your A-levels. You are not fitted for anything at all—not even, as far as I can see, to do a little shopping when asked. First of all, your appearance. You will decide on what style is going to be yours, and I will go shopping with you. But whatever it is, it will be a lot of trouble. Life is a lot of trouble! Punk is a lot of trouble: so if that is what you want, then you must get up earlier in the morning, or set aside so many hours in the week. Think carefully about all this. Decide what you are going to study so as to. . .'

This speech, which could have been addressed to Jill with effect, even if she teased me for it, calling me pompous, headmistressy, disappeared into the limbo of unsaid things, and what I said was, 'Do you think a bath would help? Are you hungry?'

I ran the child's bath, lent her my best nightgown, in which she looks like a nine-year old aspiring to grownuphood, cooked her an egg and some toast. All the while, I have to report—with distaste—attacked by tenderness for the poor little grub. What is the point of tenderness? I can't do anything for her. I made up the bed where Jill had slept, and put her into it.

I then telephoned Jill. Her young man Mark answered. His voice reminded me that Jill was the past: it set bounds and limits. But I had to say to Jill:

'This is the wicked and worldly but sheltered aunt. No—listen. I have a question, specific. Right? Very well. I find that, sitting in front of your sister Kate, any sensible remark or suggestion dies on my tongue. It is because, clearly, she is in some sort of breakdown or collapse or something of that kind. Right?'

'Jane, she has always been like that.'

'Very well, infantile. But. I was sitting there realizing that I literally could not say anything like that about Kate to Sister Georgie, your mother, either.'

'Ah,' said Jill, having got the point at once. 'Well no, you can't, can you?'

'I expect you to tell me why not?'

'Things are not easy at home.'

'It goes without saying that your adolescent siblings, the two boys, are making life hell for everybody, because it is expected of them—is that it?'

'Oh, not worse than anyone else's family. . . No, it is Kate, Kate herself. You see, my mother and father succeed at everything. That is their thing. What they turn their hands to, then in their hands it blossoms. Kate does not blossom.'

'Does your mother know this child is such a mess?'

'I think Daddy does, but I don't think my mother can face it. Because there is no cause for it, you see.'

'Yes, I do see. Very well, Jill. And thank you.'

'Any time. But if I were you, I'd send her home. She'll take you over, Jane.'

'Not if I don't let her.'

A week has gone. We are into May. The sun has been shining on trees covered with pink and white blossom, on tulips, and on acres of green grass where I have been walking with Richard. I took a week off from work; as always, I have quite a bit of leave owing to me. Instead of saying to him, But I have to work tomorrow, I say, Yes, where shall we meet? We have met in Regent's Park and in Green Park; in Hyde Park and on Hampstead Heath. When we meet at once springs up that reckless gaiety that characterizes *us*: we hurry towards each other, looking to see if *it* is still there, if, as we approach, we can feel the energy of delight that carries us through our long days together, our long and energetic days. Never have I walked so much! Richard laughs at me because I walk in my lovely smart shoes, over heath and heather, vale and hill. 'Why don't you get some walking shoes?' 'These *are* my walking shoes,' I say, holding out to him, as I stand on one leg, an elegant shoe that looks as if it is fit for no more than simpering around a drawing room. But I keep up with him, striding about and up and down. 'You are ridiculous,' he says, laughing, and his eyes take me all in and eat me up, for I know he likes my lovely clothes, though they aren't what they were in my dedicated days, and he notices, saying, 'That's a wonderful blouse,' and his hands on my arms are aware of the texture of the cloth there as well as of the warmth of the flesh under them.

I looked out old photographs. A discovery! I have very few of me. Or of Freddie. There are group photographs, *Lilith,* or of me in all my best clothes at some fashion do in Paris or somewhere. But photographs of *me*? A thought: I have spent thirty-odd years working in the fashion trade. For years of my life I cared so much about what I looked like that I was conscious if there was a strand or two less of thread on one button than on its neighbour; I am aware of the impression I make entering a room, or on colleagues, can assess what they think of what I wear by an inflection of the voice or a glance. My poor husband used to joke that he came second to what I wore. Yet not only have I seldom been photographed, but when I came on a photo of me at probably twenty-three or four, I was amazed. A really quite extraordinarily pretty girl. It was the freshness and vitality I had. This lovely thing is standing by a flowering bush, though I can't remember where, smiling quizzically at the camera. She wears a charming little flowered dress (I remember the dress!). Yet I never say to myself, as I know women of my age and old women do, 'How beautiful I was,' as I put out pictures of a younger self (the real one) on a shelf or table.

Finding this little picture gave me a bad moment or two. For I really had not made that effort, done that balancing act where you say, That's what I was, and this is what I am now. I assumed, vaguely enough, that I had not much changed.

I stood in front of my mirror, with the little photograph in my hand, and looked from one image to the other. If that girl had been asked to glance into the future, to see that woman there, what would she have said? I don't know. I can remember only that she was full of confidence and enjoyment. I saw in the looking-glass this rather good-looking woman, not badly made, solid rather than slim, with a face redeemed from ordinariness by the great grey eyes, and the pretty silvery chunks of hair that make people look: Is she grey, or is it a dye? That's compliment enough, I suppose, that they have to look. Taken feature by feature, putting one part of the body with another, shoulder, knee, neck, my smooth white forehead, you could say, Where's the difference? But the whole ensemble . . . oh, that's a very different thing, and I have to face it; for the girl in the little photograph is so strong an assault on the senses, all dew and juices, that I can hardly believe I was unaware of it. And now, here is this solid woman with no light in her, no grace. It is all achieved, done for.

I saw something else as I stood there, looking from the photograph to *me*—it was me as I must seem to Kate. The unreachable accomplishment of it, this woman standing there so firm on the pile of her energetic and successful years. What a challenge, what a burden, the middle-aged, the elderly, are to the young. I never saw that before, or suspected it. I didn't want to think of Kate, at that moment, there; but I *was* thinking of her. Also of Kathleen, Richard's daughter.

As we were striding across the Heath on Saturday, hand in hand, laughing—for we laugh all the time, it seems—he stopped dead, pulled me up to him. Wandering away in front of us, there she was. I had a good look at her. A sleepwalker, that is the impression she makes first. The way she walks, or trails, her slow indecisions, for she stops, hesitates, goes on, might turn aside one way but then goes another. She's all stops and starts: a rather large dark girl, in her uniform of jeans and sweater.

But I was struck most of all by her watchfulness, her suspicion.

'Does she trail you all the time?'

'When she can.' The helplessness was back in him, and the burden was on his shoulders. He even seemed to stoop.

'What is she so afraid of?' I could not stop myself asking. Yet I most passionately approved his warning look at me: *I don't want this to end;* and yet I did ask.

'She is afraid I might vanish.'

'Because you have already?'

'*I* haven't. I have been careful not to.'

'Well, I see. Or I think I do.'

He said, 'Jane, Jane, let's *not*. Let's stave it off, do.' And he caught my hand and we began running across the rough grass. This was, I knew, to bring back the energetic wildness of being together, and he teased me as we ran: '*Ridiculous*—shoes; *absurd*—Jane,' and we ran into the little road where the good coffee shop is that has the wonderful cakes, and we found a table in the corner and stayed there all afternoon, because the rain came down outside too hard for walking in.

Would I have believed I could spend three, four hours, simply sitting by a man, sometimes not talking, in content-ment? We watched the people coming and going at the tables near us, and might exchange a smile or a look that summed up what we thought about them. We watched the little dramas and eavesdropped. Or we talked—what do we talk about, when so much cannot be said, or even approached? We make up stories about what we see; we tell each other about people we know. What this is, is a shared solitude. I spend so much of my time doing things by myself: walking, going to the cinema, sitting in cafés, talking to strangers, visiting galleries and museums, always by myself. And now there is someone else with me: and it is as easy and natural to be with him as to be with myself.

I asked him, though I knew, 'You spend a lot of time by yourself?'

'Oh, I don't mind, I like it,' he said quickly. And then: 'It's not that, I mind . . .' And the look at me: I have said more than I meant to. Don't take advantage of it.

I have also, this week, spent some time with Kate.

First of all, I bought her some clothes. The helpless passivity of the poor thing, always looking towards me to suggest, prompt and even decide. Jill on a similar jaunt only needed my chequebook.

Kate did not 'really' want to be a punk; 'did not mind' if she wore this or that. I took trouble, finding things that are well made, with some style, but as she puts them on, they dwindle into ineffectiveness. The pink and the green have gone from her hair, and she has an uneven crop, midbrown. I showed her how to use make-up, and said that with such eyes she could hardly go wrong. But she can and does.

I said to her that she must study something. I've sent out for pamphlets from schools, colleges, polytechnics.

I rang Sister Georgie and said, 'About this daughter of yours. Tell me, is there anything you have in mind for her to do?'

'Well, I don't know, you could have a talk with her, couldn't you?' This was so feeble, compared with ordinarily, that I was deflated. Where was my crisp and disapproving sister? Do I get good marks, perhaps, for having assisted her Jill towards this satisfactory condition of hers: job, London flat, young man? Half a good mark? At some point will I be judged as having atoned for my delinquencies? I have a feeling that this profit and loss account will never be balanced...

Kate rings her mother quite often. When I am there. I suspect not so often when I am not. Her voice is small, obedient; and on her face is the smile that goes with it, it is a biddable good-child's face, and she listens with little nods of agreement and consent.

I do not think Georgie has rung Kate. Certainly not while I have been there.

This afternoon, the last of my week in Elysium, we parted at a bus stop outside the Victoria and Albert. But as I stood in the queue and saw him walking away under the trees, up towards the park, I found myself in a panic that made me start shaking. I ran up after him, calling, Richard, Richard, and heard my voice weak and inadequate. He turned, smiling, but puzzled, because he could see my state. 'Do you realize,' I said, 'that if either of us failed to turn up at a rendezvous—well, we might never see each other again? I don't know your name, and I can't bear it,' I heard myself plead.

He put his arms around me and we stood resting side by side under a plane tree in full leaf. Late afternoon, a rich yellow light, and a bird was cheeping away about something or other overhead.

'My name is Richard Curtis. And yours is Jane Somers.'

'I never told you.'

'No, but you did mention your magazine and I rang up, got your name. I wasn't going to have you vanish.'

'I'm ridiculous,' I said, and left his embrace. 'The thing is...' I don't know why it was, but the future was casting long shadows, and I was thinking, This will soon have to end.

But why should it? I went back to the bus stop, and turned to wave: he was waiting for me to do it.

I can't bear that this will end, so I won't think about it.

I don't know when I have worked as hard as I have this last

fortnight. Three distinct and separate lives. First, the office. Because Phyllis has left to have her baby, Jill and I are doing her work. We sit opposite each other in the room where Joyce and I sat. Some of the old hands among the staff come in and say, 'It's like old times.' We make everything happen, and make sure that Charlie has plenty of business lunches. He's not bad at those, provided he is well briefed. He comes late and goes early, without apology. Phyllis's baby is an enterprise shared by the whole office. As he comes in, affable, smiling, he will say, 'The doctor says it might be earlier than we thought.' Or, 'Poor Phyllis slept very badly.' His secretary brings him tea with a little solicitous air and a connivatory smile. At this Jill and I exchange glances, as Joyce and I used to. Nothing disturbs our speed, efficiency, harmony, but Kate, who rings up several times a day. 'Jane, I can't find the sugar.' 'Can I borrow your silk petticoat, the one with the lace?' I swallow down distaste, for everything she wears is left with a sickly smell of sweat, no matter if she does bath every day, as I insist, and say, 'Yes, of course.' While Jill raises her pretty eyebrows and regards me, sighing at my folly.

I say, 'She tries on every stitch I have while I'm out anyway. I believe that is the only thing she ever does.'

Jill puts her chin in her hand, one, two, three, four pink nails emphatic against a pearly cheek, coral lips, that would be better set off by a pout, decisively set to match her mind, and she examines me with the frankest curiosity. 'What's got into you, Jane?'—and she really wants to know.

I don't want her to know, and I offer her symptoms rather than root, saying, 'What I can't stand is writing her off.'

'Who's writing her off? It's a question of her finding her level.' She says this with a little air of finality, like a housewife who says, Yes, now I've arranged everything: satisfaction in proper order. 'Don't you see?' she goes on. 'She's simply not *up* to what's been expected of her.' And, as my look indicates that I am willing, indeed need, to hear more, she says, 'She will get married, won't she? Someone of her own kind. Or become a nun, or something.'

'I've seldom heard anyone being disposed of so finally.'

'Well, Jane . . .'

Twice the telephone has rung, not Kate but Richard, and Jill has not watched me with frank curiosity, but busied herself, and even made a point of going out of the room.

I cannot prevent my voice changing—I am sure, my whole body—when Richard rings. I hear my voice lift into the gaiety of intimacy, and everything outside this magical unity, Me and Richard, goes away into a stupid darkness.

It takes time for me to come back to the ordinary world after these calls.

After the last, Jill left a good hour before asking, 'Jane, do you ever think of marrying again?'

She looked a little furtive, for she had not really wanted to ask, and for a moment I didn't like her, my lovely Jill. The word *marry* was like a whip, some deliberate hurt. I said, after a while, 'I have no plans at all to get married again.' And sat scarcely breathing; for to be married to Richard—well, I could not begin to conceive of such a happiness. And yet it was all nonsense, for everything that marriage has to be has been left out of our being together, even thinking about it. I was full of distress, and I had not expected it, and I went out of the room. When I came back, Jill was sitting, stricken, and her great sea eyes were swimming.

'I am *sorry*,' said she.

I sat down, I took the things to do up my smudged eyes from my bag, I began work on them, before saying, 'As you will have seen—I am well out of my depth.' I finished my eyes, put everything away, set my bag down tidily, and after all that said, 'Your frivolous Aunt Janna has had a depth charge set off in her, and she does not understand what is happening. And *no*, Jill, I do not want you to explain it to me.'

On the evenings I was not with Richard, coming back into my flat was an effort of my whole self: not because I don't know what I will find, but because I do. Kate flumps in the corner of the grey sofa, which is already her territory. It is a grubby island in my lovely room, covered with bits of clothing, odd bits of crockery such as an empty cup rolling there amid the detritus of assorted make-up, magazines. Kate does not read, but like a child looks at pictures. Usually she has plugged herself into a radio, and from between the wires that trail on either side of her head her face responds to the unheard (by me) din, and her eyes have the characteristic hypnotized look of these poor zombies. Her body might be moving rhythmically too.

I say, 'Kate, it makes people deaf, do you want that?'

She says, with the bright prattling eagerness which characterizes her manner with me, 'Oh, no, Jane, I'd hate it.'

'Then why don't you stop it? When I'm not here you could listen in the ordinary way.'

But she likes being plugged into her secret world, safe from outside impacts. And she is already a bit deaf. When she has unplugged herself, I have to shout for some minutes.

In Kate I am meeting an entirely new experience: someone who literally cannot hear what you say, quite apart from this intermittent real deafness. I have never before known anyone, I think, who, informed that to do something will make her deaf, would not decide to stop.

I go to the kitchen to see if she has in fact done the shopping I asked, not that I can't do it myself, but as a way of getting her active. She does go out, and she gets an approximation of what I've asked for, but it is never exactly what I've said, and I am even quite interested when I go into the kitchen: what will be there this time? A certain brand of coffee because the tin has an attractive pattern of gold and black; a red cabbage, because she was drawn to the colour; some tangerines, which she hasn't eaten, but she liked the sunny display on the pavement; five giant packets of potato crisps and some sticky buns.

I make supper for us out of what is in my cupboards and what she has brought, not wanting to discourage the child. But probably she doesn't connect the red mush on her plate which sets off the slim brown frankfurters with the silken magenta marvel she brought in from that wonderhouse, London.

What an effort it is to dim myself down, defuse myself, during the long evenings with Kate! I watch every word as it forms in my mind, I stumble about among words and phrases that won't 'upset' her; though it is not that, more choosing words that can arrange themselves into patterns that connect with her. I ask her what she's been doing during the day, as if it cannot possibly matter that she slept until twelve, tried on my clothes, trailed around a shop or two, and then sat jerking in the corner of my sofa to that violent music. I try to find out anything in the world that really interests her, but apart from Jill, about whose doings she is fanatically curious, there is nothing. She wants to be with Jill, to *be* her. She asks about Jill's flat, but I only glimpsed it briefly and cannot answer what she wants to know: is there room in it for her? If she knows Jill's escape from home three years ago was as much an escape from her as anything, she does not admit it. She asks what clothes I bought Jill, and I see her looking hopelessly at her own, already a collection of sad jumble. She wants to know about Jill's flatmate—which is what Jill calls him: 'Meet my flatmate,' says she, introducing her love, and I look on and want to say, Jill, Jill, *don't*—warning her against I know not what; and I really don't, sitting there examining her as I do the photograph of my youthful self, incredulous that she doesn't know what treasures she is—I think—locking up: hands off.

Then I talk to Kate about what she is going to study. She could, if she had the will, go to all kinds of classes and courses now, though it is drawing near to the end of the student year—a new arrangement of the calendar for me. But in the autumn she will go to the polytechnic and learn Spanish. I cannot think of anything easier. I talk of it, and she does because I do, as the entrance to some fabled existence (like Jill's) where everything will become possible: friends, accomplishments, independence.

In the meantime she proposes to droop around here. It seems as if the vitality that surges and jigs and flies about everywhere in the world is something she knows nothing about: she is not connected to it. There's a short circuit. An evening with Kate: I am exhausted. I even go to bed an hour earlier than usual, as early as eleven, to try and recover. I am appalled that this girl is here. I don't see how I can, as Jill says, tell her to leave. 'Well, tell her to go home, Jane!' I really would feel as if I were condemning her. But if she were not here, then Richard and I could . . . what? Come here for a meal? Lovemaking presents itself from time to time as an imperative, and then takes itself off again. How is it that two people who cannot meet without sending the temperature up all around them, nevertheless do not make love, nor, much, think of it?

It is that little picture of the young girl, what that means, that stops me? Stops *us*?

I have stood in front of my glass, naked. Oh, I certainly have been deluding myself. Not much changed, I've been thinking vaguely, adjusting over my ageing body the clever clothes I wear, with their textures and substances like skin, or flesh . . . When I do think—which I prevent myself doing— about making love with Richard, woe invades me, an emptiness, as if I were proposing to bring a ghost to a feast.

I dream about Freddie every night.

We make love all right. Strange, I have never had sexual dreams about Freddie. Sex we had; good sex, as the phrase goes, so what was there to dream about? I remember asking myself, when other people said they dreamed of sex. When he died I did not dream of sex, not as a feature of my dreamlife that I needed to take notice of: I had orgasms, I remember, in my sleep, but that was functional. Masturbation for me has always been practical rather than sensuous: I need it, I must relax, I get it over with, has been my attitude. It is because I have known what sex can be. But now when I go off to sleep I make wild and passionate love with Freddie, full of regret and longing. Crazy. We are crazy creatures, there's no gainsaying that.

Kate has asked, because of the evenings I have spent with Richard, 'Are you going to friends?' 'Have you been with friends?' I say, firmly, 'Yes, I am.' 'Yes, I was.'

'Are they nice?' she asks pathetically. Meaning, Would they like me? She even said sullenly once, 'Why can't I go? Are they famous?'

'Look, Kate, I have my friends, and you will have yours.'

As I said this, I experienced it, through her, as a rejection, a cruelty: like being told she was not going to be working in *Lilith*. Door after door closes in her face, and the glamorous world of real achievement is continually being withdrawn from her as she approaches it.

The poor bundle dwindled into the corner of my great sofa, and the tragic eyes of a mistreated child mourned at me.

When I see her to bed at nights—for if I did not she would sleep where she was, in a mess of crumbs, fragments of chocolate and potato crisps—I seem to see the ghosts of teddy bears and dolls. Should I buy one for her? Would that be another cruelty?

And then, my life with Richard. It really is another life, and I fly into it, my heels winged. Sometimes I arrive at our rendezvous with my hands full of flowers, somewhere to put my joy. Richard laughs when he sees them, straight into my eyes, so that my eyes dazzle with it, like too strong sunlight. He takes flower after flower, putting them in my hair, my belt, a buttonhole. I stand bedecked and people look, at first ready to be critical, but then getting the benefit of the spin-off from our enjoyment. Wherever we go, we pull others into our pleasure. Yesterday, we stood by a fountain in Trafalgar Square and one by one, like coins for luck, threw in freesias and late daffodils. We bought these off the pavement together, and the man said, 'The last of the daffs for this year,' and we bought bunch after bunch. When one of us stopped buying, the other bought another, until our arms were full. The flowers lay floating on the fountain, a drowned greeny-yellow on the light blue, and a couple of small girls pulled off their shoes and socks and paddled in to get them, shrieking and slipping while they threw the flowers to the edge of the fountain. 'Why do you want to throw them *away*, mister?' they yelled, paddling about to collect them; so we gave the small girls bunches of fresh ones from our mountain of flowers, and went on up St Martin's Lane, distributing daffodils to startled people who looked into our faces and then laughed. They probably thought we were actors from one of the theatres, creating a 'happening'.

We go into many pubs. We started by going into one to have a drink before the theatre, and Richard said he had forgotten about pubs, how marvellous they are. He said he misses them more than anything, abroad. He says there is nothing like them, anywhere else.

I have never been much of a pub-goer, and now I am wondering why? Well, for one thing, you need a companion, for a pub.

And how pleasant they are, London pubs. Every public place is like a theatre, but pubs most of all, because people coming in are so often regulars. Richard and I sit where we can, until we can get into our favourite place, which is a corner, so we can be out of the way and no one need notice us.

We drink Scotch, he with ice, and I without, and the two glasses stand close together and the light makes oily golden patterns in the liquid that repeat themselves on the table tops. What companionable and good-natured places they are, these pubs; how people do come and go, apparently without reason, but each caught tight into his or her little pattern, their trip into the pub a fragment of the pattern which is invisible to us. How various we all are, never a face repeated, the amazing mix and match: the doors swing in, a new face appears, you could never have foreseen its uniqueness.

And then we have our conversation. Well, if it is only one of our conversations, it certainly repeats most often:

Richard says, 'How is it they don't see what they've got, why do they all run it down so?' Changes it to, 'How is it *you* don't see . . .' Says, another time, 'I, we . . .' 'If we could only . . .'—see this or that, do that or this. It's nothing but woe, he says, on the television, in the newspapers, never a good word to say for—themselves, yourselves, ourselves.

I say, 'But things are bad.' I list unemployment and industries running down; and say how awful is the inefficiency, the muddle, so that you feel as if it is all running through your fingers, you can't grasp anything . . .

And he says that that is true of everywhere, it is because of everything being too big and unwieldy, that has nothing to do with Britain—us, you, them.

I tell him stories about *Lilith,* the grind and grit of making things work against what seems to me an amiable indifference to everything, a tacit agreement that it all doesn't matter.

He says that we—you—they, don't know what we have got. And what we have got is—people. He says there is a sanity and a sense, and a balance and a rightness; and we don't value it.

I say, 'I do value it.' And I tell him how I walk and walk around this city, and feed—which is how I feel it—on the people: the little scenes that stage themselves, the comedies, a spirit of surreal enjoyment that is always there, coming out in what a man says in the greengrocer's, or two girls on a bus.

He says, 'All the same, you are spoiled, all of you. You live here in this little oasis, surrounded by chaos and terror and by people who have to be afraid to say what they think.'

I say, 'It's time you came home to live.'

He says, 'I couldn't stand the way you are letting it all slide. Sometimes, when I'm away too long, I come back and it hits me, that there's something here, something special, but this time what is new is that you never stop running yourself down, and you let things go to pieces.'

He pulls a newspaper out and lays it on the table between us, and he has marked with heavy double lines: unemployment, the pound, strikes, Ireland, the state of our sewers, the crisis in the railways ... And then, as I glance around the pub, at *them, you, us,* wondering if that man is without a job, or if that young couple over there have ever had one, if this apparent good humour, ease, confidence, is all a mask, he will say, 'How is it possible you don't see what you are doing?'

Today he said, 'Well, perhaps you deserve to lose it all. If you don't value a thing, you lose it.' Anger: a passionate and indeed violent regret. In Richard violence lies coiled, restrained.

But he was talking about us, him and me, just as much as about *them,* or *you*—he was skirting the edge of the personal that is forbidden us. And I was careful not to look at him, for I want him to believe that I am keeping the rules. *His* rules; for it is his rules that I am obeying. But is that true? Why have I been so reluctant to take out of my handbag, where it lies in an envelope that is getting soiled, the little photograph of me? Oh, I am as afraid as he is! Of the big issues—yes; but they are too much for me, as they are for us all; and very much afraid for Richard and me. So vulnerable are we, so easy would it be to blow what we have apart. A word could do it; a word or a look does often rip aside our enjoyment in each other, leaving us fumbling, so that we both scramble with words or a movement to cover it all over, talking about something else, making up nonsense as we do, for the pleasure of words, words, the game of them; or we get up from where we sit in a pub or on a pavement and we walk rapidly away from where the danger was.

It has been very hot. The spring trees, all pink and cream and white, are gone, and there is a full green instead. Summer. Yesterday I wore my yellow linen dress and sat with Richard on the pavement in the yellow sunlight, and he said, in the way he has of paying compliments, warm but with a regret in it that pays tribute to some ineluctability or other, the worm in the apple, 'Pretty Janna!'

I told him that to nearly everyone I am Janna, but not the family, and he said at once, 'Janna, of course you must be Janna, Jane is so solemn,' and he said the word heavy and dragging, Ja—a—a—ne, so that we both laughed at it. But I wasn't laughing altogether, because I could hear in that *Jane* the weight and the strictures of the family.

And that was the moment I was inspired, God help me, to take quickly from my bag the photograph, and give it to him. He did not know what it was as he took it, was uncomprehending, and then as he looked, his body tensed and he even sat up to put the picture down flat between the white china ashtray and the tall glasses of orange juice, and he stared down at that girl in her flowered dress for a long time. His breathing was shortened. I saw he was flushed. How I regretted giving it to him! How I suffered sitting there, my heart beating, knowing that something quite terrible had been done: by me, by me! I kept my eyes away, but could not prevent little anxious glances, and still he sat there, looking at me, thirty years lost and gone. Now he looked tired, even drained. And pale. Our gorgeous day, sunlight and hot blue skies and people in summer clothes, all relaxed and smiling—where was it? Or where were we? Not part of it any longer. All kinds of thoughts presented themselves to me, to be dismissed. Like: It's unfair. Like: He *asked* for a photograph of me as a girl. Like: Is he blaming me for not looking, at fifty, as I did at twenty? Like: *You're punishing me!*

He was in fact suffering, and badly.

He did not look at me: he would not. There was a wildness, a bitterness there, and I felt that this was not to do with me. Which made things worse; and I sat there scarcely breathing, for breathing hurt, and what I wanted was to move, fast, away from this scene, to almost anywhere at all.

And then he said, judiciously, giving me, or the situation, its exact due, 'Congratulations!'

A little wind blew up the paper corners, red white and blue, of the table cloth, and the photograph tilted up and would have blown away. But he put his hand quickly over it, as if over a butterfly, something he wanted to capture, and then he looked at it again, with real pain on his face, and put it into his breast pocket.

'Let's go,' he said, and hastily emptied money on to the table for the drinks, much too much, and he walked off, with me following him. We walked along the Old Brompton Road, found ourselves in Cromwell Road, and did not notice how the buildings were lowering themselves and becoming shabbier until we found ourselves between Shepherd's Bush and Hammersmith, in a maze of streets, the dense crammed London people live in, not work in, and stroll and push prams and shop for everything from Rice Crispies to yams and flying fish and Mars Bars, and stand talking on pavements saying, And then she said, and then he did … And we still had not looked at each other. The hot sun came down, the hot pavements hurt our feet, and we were breathing fast because of how fast we had walked. We came to a stop under a plane tree growing, it seemed, straight out of the warm pavement, with under it two Pepsi-Cola cans, a litter of ice-cream sticks, a bit of dirty newspaper, and a child's blue ball with a jolly face painted on it in yellow. We were looking into a minute front garden where a girl in an orange bikini was directing a black snake at seven bright pink tulips growing out of a square foot of black earth. Glittering water encompassed the tulips; dark hair, iridescent in the sun, tossed about her shoulders, and on one hip she held a small, almost naked baby, browned by this week's heat. She saw us, playfully waved the hose so that the rays of water splashed about us, said, 'Hi!' and then, 'Have a good day,' in a strong Midwest accent, flung down the hose to lie in a coil, dribbling water, and lolled very white thighs indolently up her steps into her house: the door was standing open, to get a bit of air in.

And now he sighed, and still without looking at me, put his arm around my shoulders and we stood there gazing at the pink tulips, sparkling in the sun.

The heat continues. We all know that this week-old summer may at any minute vanish away for another year, and it is as if England breathes in sunlight as if each breath may be the last before blizzards strike. Everywhere bodies sprawl around on the grass of London's parks, acres of naked flesh; along the city streets go girls dressed for Hawaii or the Riviera, with naked shoulders that are flushed dangerously, white legs that seem to blush, and hair spread about to catch every luxurious ray. Jealous hoarders of every golden moment, we—Richard and I, together with the rest of the inhabitants of this chancy island—spend every second out of doors. Every second, that is, that we can; he with his still untold—to me—responsibilities, I with so much work in the office because of Phyllis's pregnancy. Nevertheless, I escape all the time and we sit in Soho Square among the pigeons and office workers and eat Jumbo Sweet and Sour Chinese Special Take Away Snacks, or pizza smelling of olive oil and real tomatoes, and then one or other of us says, 'But I have to go. . .' I cannot remember ever in my whole life feeling my heart go grey as it does when Richard says, 'My love, I have to leave you,' as it does when I have to say, 'Goodbye,' leaving him there alone on the bench.

*　　*　　*

Our summer has vanished. Fitful rain, and everything soaked and green and lush. Richard said today, 'What was the reason you said you couldn't ask me to your place, I forget?' This was said hard and rough. And reluctant. Because of our nomadic, peripatetic life on pavements and in parks, in cafés, restaurants, theatres and pubs, always in public: our real life.

'I could ask my niece to go away for the weekend,' I said, after thought. At this he laughed; and so did I. It sounded so forlorn and ridiculous. But his eyes, resting on me, were critical. *Of me?* I am not sure.

Today, this scene. I had come in late, after supper with Richard. But I brought in take-away Chinese for Kate, because she never eats a proper meal unless I arrange it. She was, as usual, sitting in the corner of the sofa, plugged in and jigging her limbs about. She did not unplug herself as I put the food on plates and brought it in to her. She smelt sour, her face had that grimy look that some old people have when it has become too difficult to keep up maintenance.

She was going to eat, still plugged in, but I as it were waved to her from a farther shore and she hastily, but reluctantly, took the wires away from her ears. Then she fell on the food.

'Kate,' I said, 'I want you away from this flat this weekend.'

It was as if I had slapped her, and very hard. Her mouth, with food in it, fell open, and tears sprang from her eyes. Genuine tears. She was stammering with shock.

'But . . . but . . .'

'Kate . . .' I said, 'you must see that . . .' But she was incapable of seeing anything of the kind; it was as if I had said to a child of three: You must be out of your home this weekend. Incomprehension. Then frantic rejection.

'Why? Why?' she wailed. 'What have I done?'

'You haven't done anything, Kate! Surely it isn't odd that I should sometimes want my own home for the weekend?'

'Who are you having here?' she demanded. Now she was sullen and scarlet with anger. I was amazed. I was sitting there opposite her, trying to make sense of it all. Surely she didn't think . . . hadn't imagined . . . didn't believe . . .

'Well, I wouldn't be in the way,' she expostulated, indignant now; and the idiocy of it all made me lay down the law:

'Look, Kate. For this weekend. Saturday and Sunday. Surely you can go home for two days?'

She stared at me. I stared at her. What defeated me was the sheer lunatic impossibility of it all!

'How can I go home?' she wailed, turning it on, or so I sounded, so that I was even, for a moment, encouraged: I find that when she is play-acting in a rehearsed scene, is genuinely sullen, I am pleased. Anything that has an origin in energy, drive, self-assertion.

'I really cannot see why not,' I said. Then I saw her face change: excitement was there, a soft pleasure.

'I'll stay with Jill,' she announced. And far from having been insulted and injured, she was all expectation, and she sat there chatting away about Jill's flat and her boyfriend and how Jill and she had done this and that together at home.

I said to Jill today in the office, 'Would you mind having Kate for two days, this weekend?'

And now I saw that this was what she had really been afraid of all the time, for she was stricken, afraid—trapped. I saw her scrabble for a cigarette, saw her fingers shake. Where was my self-possessed and efficient Jill? An injured, threatened young thing, all pleading eyes and anxiety, sat there staring at me.

'There is something out of proportion, *ridiculous* about this whole thing,' I said. 'What am I asking? That you take your sister for two days—one night! She won't go home!'

'Jane! If you can't see—'

'She's bound to come to your flat some time. You can't forbid her to!'

'Once she's in, she'll never leave.'

'Jill, don't be so feeble. Where is Mark going to be then?'

'He certainly won't be there when Kate is.'

'Has he met her?'

'No, but I'll make sure he doesn't.'

'That's silly.'

A long silence. She sat hunched, puffing out smoke, rubbing her cigarette into the tray, then picking it up, looking at it abstractedly, throwing it down, lighting another, puffing away, until she was in a haze of blue smoke.

'You are not saying, I hope, that you are afraid you'll lose Mark because of Kate!'

She thought. 'No. Well, perhaps I am. Why should he put up with her?'

'Families,' I said, 'families.'

'Look at you and your sister. Jane and Georgina! You've always hated each other.'

'Nonsense,' I said briskly. But was struck: did I hate Sister Georgie? 'She may hate me,' I said.

'Obviously, you've hated each other's guts all your lives. You've both been reacting against each other, *off* each other, in everything.'

'Well, Jill, I don't want to spoil family mythology, but if Georgie has been obsessed with me, then I have not been with her. She may have spent her life talking about her awful sister, but I can assure you there have been years when I have scarcely thought of her at all.'

'Happy years,' said Jill.

'She hasn't been all that important to me.'

'Then why don't you simply send Kate *home*?' she demanded fiercely.

'I didn't send you home.'

She did take thought a little at that, looked conscious, made a little negative movement of her head, as if to say, I'm sorry. But she was too possessed by her fear.

'All my life I've been scared of one thing, that I would be landed with Kate for some reason. You say, *your sister*—but I didn't choose her.'

'Jill,' I said, 'for two days. That's all. I'll come and pick her up from your place on Sunday evening.'

'All this is because of that man. A weekend's love-in. Why don't you go to a sex hotel?'

I don't know how to write down what I felt at that. To say

I felt attacked . . . She might have hit me, thrown a sack of garbage at me . . . filth could have spewed from her mouth. I sat there, sick and dizzy.

'Oh God, Janna, Jane, I am sorry, I didn't mean it. Oh, how could I have? Oh, oh, what shall I do?' She was up, striding about the office, her hands clenched at her cheeks, staring at me, beating her clenched fists up and down in front of her as if hitting something in the air with them, invisible to me. Tears were shaking off her face and splattering about, she was ill with remorse and pain. And so was I.

'Oh, Jane,' she cried. 'Of course I'll have her. Of course. I'm sorry.'

And so, the weekend that caused so much emotion before it even started, is gone. Kate is in bed, after a bath and a good feed.

I am sitting in my bedroom which has until now seemed so comfortable and right for me, my setting, my home even; at odds with it. I look up out of my large window at the theatrical London sky, purple and mauve, hazy with reflected light, a sky that is never dark because of London lying there beneath it, throwing up its image to dazzle off cloud or dark. I have my diary here in front of me and I am writing in it, and it is as if there is no substance in me, I am empty, something has been taken away. But it is not sensible for me to feel like this . . .

I shall put off writing this until tomorrow.

Perhaps I'll have a bath. I hate bathing after Kate, it is as if her grime has got into the pores of the enamel, as if her stale odours are mingled with bath salts and the smells of warm dry towels. I shall get into bed and think of my love Richard with whom, it seems, I will never share a bed. A thousand swords lie between us.

On Saturday morning I wrestled Kate out of bed. Literally: she was curled up head to knees, her muscles clenched against me. By then I was feeling so awful about it all I nearly left her there, meaning to intercept Richard and say it was off. But if to go forward was clumsy, riding rough-shod over not only Kate and Jill, but me, too; then to retreat was absurd. I made her get up, did everything but actually put her clothes on her, put into her hands a cup of hot chocolate and a croissant, and then gave her money and a map of how to get to Jill's. Full of sullen and revengeful anger, she left, slowly. I saw her on the street staring up at my windows. My heart hurt me. And what of it? I am now expert in this world of the heart, that recalcitrant, obstinate, self-determining organ. For Kate my heart reacts with a dull grief, like hopelessness. Jill: a warm glow, probably a variety of selfishness, because of my part in helping her on. Richard? It is not a question of an organ situated in the middle of my chest: I think of him and I feel a smile on my face, and my feet begin to tap as if I want to dance.

I begin to see that dull pain which is what that sad bundle Kate demands of me as a symptom of inadequacy: mine.

I rang Jill to say that Kate was on her way. Mark answered. He sounded pleasant, but abstracted. They were laying the carpet in the bathroom, he said.

I then started on the business of tidying this flat. Mrs Brown comes as usual twice a week, but there is an unspoken agreement that she will not clear up after Kate. I did as well as I could, and shopped for a meal. A good one. What a long time since I used this—after all—not inconsiderable talent of mine. When I think of those little dinner parties Freddie and I used to give: well, perhaps I won't think about them. The fact is, for both of us, what was enjoyable was the doing of it, the perfection of it all, and probably the guests were only the setting for this presentation of ourselves. Do I want to think on these lines? No, I definitely do not; but it seems as if every day what I had with Freddie is being rubbed out, made to seem nothing at all. That it wasn't what it ought to have been—yes, I know that. But—so little? This business of dreaming of Freddie: night after night, he is the landscape I walk into, and yet between me and him are always barriers. Or *I* am the barrier, as if my substance, what I am, is inimical to him, to what I see but cannot touch. Mists come down between us, or he walks away as I approach, or I stand close to him, looking in hope and longing at his dear face, but he is not smiling, and I cannot move from where I am, and even my hands, which I would like to stretch out to him, are too heavy to lift. When we make love it is full of regret, pain: he is going away, or I am.

When the rooms were all tidy, I had a bath, not one of 'my' baths lasting hours which are so rare now, but a bath for effect. I stood in front of a mirror in my Janet Reger knickers and let the silk of the petticoat slide over my head, ivory with coffee lace, and I felt soiled and vulgar, and wished very much that I was to look forward only to a weekend with Richard at large in London.

We met at the Indian restaurant down the road. For the first time. They greeted me as I came in, and we chatted: Richard has not before come into my territory, and I saw him watching something new to him: me in my setting. Mr Lal asked for Jill, who has eaten here with me often, then after Kate—in a different tone of voice, which did not make judgement.

Saturday lunchtime: the place agreeably full. You can eat well enough, reasonably. Richard was subdued. So was I. Our chemistries were working against us, and even the food seemed dull. Richard sat opposite me, his back to the room, but he turned his head to see who came in, or to watch a couple at the next table: two young men, who had come back from a trip down through Africa in a Land Rover. Many adventures, including being arrested by some army some-where as spies. They were brown, very fit, full of energy, already planning another trip: probably through India. This was discussed with the waiter, who was interested. Also, behind his courtesy, amused I think. Envious? Angry? Here were these two young princes, able to take off across continents: how about the desert in Australia?—No? You don't fancy the Aussies? Then why not South America?—Too many wars and revolutions? Then why not India!

Richard was sitting with his arm hooked over the back of his chair, listening: he had not finished his food. Everything about his pose said he was not comfortable in this, my restaurant, and was waiting to be able to go. And yet we have been, it seems, in a hundred restaurants and never have we wanted the hours to pass.

Outside, the cinema was showing *Les Enfants du Paradis*, and I said, 'I've seen it six times at least.' 'Like everybody,' he said, and we stood thinking, Is this what we want? Very privately thinking, If this weekend had been going right, then *Les Enfants du Paradis* would have been a miraculous juxtaposition, a bonus from the Gods, but as things were . . . yet it was raining, more like the cold rains of winter than a summer rain, and it seemed that not to go in was churlish.

We sat well apart, and it was not future partings I was mourning for, in the film, but now, in this little cinema, my favourite, where I've sat so often nearly always alone, in an intense secret pleasure, like eating chocolates by yourself knowing you shouldn't. But not this afternoon. I could not feel Richard as I do usually, like an electric extension of myself, for there was a heaviness there. And when the lovers were caught in the crowds, at the end, and he tried to reach his lost love, the people jigged and swirled all around him so that he could not move, then could not even see her, and she went away, for ever—then what I felt was, *So what? That's how it always is.*

It was then eight o'clock, and a wet, chilly, gusty evening approached. We went into the pub, my local, but it is not a very nice pub, or was not that evening, and Richard was fidgeting with his glass, and sitting as he had in the restaurant, arm hooked over his chair back, half turned away, as if he had already left the place.

We stayed there a couple of hours though because neither of us in fact wanted to come here. But then we did. The evening was fine, but windy. The trees along the pavement were being tugged and pushed every way by a gusty wind that seemed to have blown off some icefield. The wind was from the north-west, and I imagined a black ocean like a field of icebergs over which our wind was blowing, for beyond them up in the Arctic of course it is their summer, or will be shortly, the tundra is putting out bright brief flowers and clouds of mosquitoes, and the little lakes and streams have ice-cold water under a hot blue sky. It will be June very soon.

We came slowly here, and up the stairs to this third floor, and as I opened the door he took a step in and stood there, as if he had come to do just that—have a swift, thorough look around, and then leave. I saw the room through his eyes: large, low-ceilinged, with beige walls, vast expanse of floor, parquet, with the good rugs—Freddie knew all about buying rugs from Persia and from India and from Bokhara and from far Cathay—among which floated my pale grey sofa, and a couple of lemon-yellow chairs and a red one: I utterly loathed this room, from the plants all along the far wall, captured from the jungles of South America, to the enormous crystal ball hanging in a window which sends little rainbows spinning about over everything if you touch it.

Saying not a word, but with a tight, enduring look to his shoulders, my handsome beau went to the sofa, stood looking down at the grubby depression that was Kate's natural home, and sat down beside it.

I went into the kitchen, wishing I was dead, and arranged a tray with drinks. Which I brought in and put on the long glass table between us. For I could not sit near him.

And still he had not said a word, nor looked at me.

I imagined him taking out the little photograph and laying it gravely on the glass of the table, and then raising his eyes to say: What? But he said nothing, only shook his head, discouraged, and leaned back, legs crossed, head lowered rather, looking past me at a rug or something.

I said, 'This is the most dreadful mistake.'

He shrugged. 'Yes, but why should it be?'

'That's the point.'

We drank a little, Scotch, and more Scotch, and the ice made little oily patterns in his glass.

'I've bought food,' I said at last.

He said, grim, 'It's as well to be sure you can cook.'

And then we were able to laugh, at last. He patted the sofa beside him, realized it was where Kate had left her ineradicable deposits, patted the other side. I sat by him, and we held hands.

'What an accomplished lady you are,' he judged me. 'I suppose I should have expected no less. Your clothes—never have I seen a hair out of place.'

'It's my job.'

'Of course.'

Our two hands, tightly clasped, were like allies against everything else around them, including us, who sat feeling our distance.

'Have we imagined all this, Janna?' he asked, grave, anxious. 'Have we made it all up?'

'It seems so at the moment,' I said, and our two hands tightened in protest, and said no, nonsense.

'Do you think so?' he inquired.

'No, I don't.'

'We have not been alone before,' he said.

'Haven't we?'

A silence.

'Why don't I get the food?'

'You have of course prepared a meal that will give the maximum of pleasure with the minimum of trouble.'

I had to laugh, though I knew well enough this was some ultimate complaint he was making. Against me?

'Well, I shall enjoy it. I like food. As you may have noticed.'

In the kitchen I did this and that, wondering what he was doing, but did not want to look. I heard him, though, and went out, leaving my pots and pans a-bubble, and saw him in the door to my bedroom, leaning there, taking his time. I went to stand by him; again I saw through his eyes: a square, not very large room, all softly gleaming ivory, with sunny yellow Casa Pupo rug and soft yellow curtains. My bed is quite large, with an ornamental brass head to it, and with a Portuguese cover in white. On it a couple of bright cushions. My bedroom, all white and yellow. Little furniture: a chest of drawers, a bookcase. And of course this desk where lies this diary, and against the wall, reference books. Also, copies of my novels.

'But where are *you* in all this?' he demanded at last, in protest at it all, and left the door to go to the desk. He took my *The Milliners of Marylebone* first, and then *Gracious Lady*, and leafed through them.

'The first thing you said to me was—do you remember?'

'I write romantic novels, yes. Or I *did*.'

'Have you stopped?'

'I wanted to write a serious novel. But I couldn't.'

'What about?'

'The ward maids in a big London hospital. You know—or perhaps you don't, why should you? They come from everywhere, Jamaica perhaps, or refugees from Vietnam, or Portugal. They send home everything they earn, and work—they are very poor. They bring up children, maintain husbands, and ... well, I tried to write about them but couldn't. Reality is clearly too much for me.'

'So you are a romantic novelist.'

'So it would seem.'

'Are you going to write another?'

'Perhaps I will.'

'Perhaps you will write a romantic novel about us?'

At this I felt as I had when Jill said what she did, and I could not answer. But he was not cut to the heart by remorse, as she had been. He stood by my desk, this one, he stood there, just behind where I sit now writing this, and he had his hand on the desk and was looking around the room, again and again, as if he simply could not come to terms with any of it. He picked up *The Milliners of Marylebone* and stood reading it for a while. Then he put it down, without saying anything. He went to the window at last, and with his back to me stared up at the sky. The light was concentrated in the white clouds that were being ripped and hustled and rolled across a mauve silk sky by the same chilly north-west wind of earlier. I went to stand by him, and heard him say, 'Well, I can't see you in this home of yours, but I can in that sky.'

I felt grateful and put my arm in his and we stood side by side, our backs to the room—and the bed—and watched how the light flared up on the clouds and began to dim. The smells from the kitchen summoned me and I ran to move a saucepan off the flame, just in time.

We ate in the kitchen, for which he said he was grateful, making a joke of it. I asked him, 'What is your home like?'

'Very nice. Being American middle-class. Suburban. And before you ask, our home here, in London, is currently rented to someone else.'

'You aren't living in it?'

A long silence.

'Janna, look how wrong things go when we do this! Do we have to?'

'No, we don't.'

'And *of course* you are a perfect cook.'

When we went back to the living room we were restless, did not sit down for a time, then did; but got up, and went strolling about, he to examine my—I nearly said *our*, since Freddie bought it—Picasso lithograph, and set of flower prints. Very nice, they are; but then, so is my living room, this whole flat. I offered him a drink. We both had another Scotch, and then it was eleven o'clock and both of us knew it was all impossible.

We were stricken, shocked, shaken, but it would not have been possible for us to go into our bedroom, take our clothes off and make love. I was thinking wildly, If all the lights were switched off, what then? A thought which utterly amazed me, so foreign was it to me.

And he said, just as I thought it, 'If all the lights were off, Janna—but then, who would we be making love with, I wonder?' And he was looking at me from an unfriendly distance, and even laughing, a most masculine laugh I judged it, full of irony—and finality. Yet I felt my spirits lift as I heard it, for there was a sanity there which had been missing.

Then he said, 'I'm going. I shouldn't have come.'

'Yes, you must,' and I couldn't wait for him to leave.

'I've taken your telephone number, and so we are one step nearer to—' He left it unfinished. I went to the door with him. He went out quickly, with a small, baffled, impatient shake of his head, and a smile that said, It's not you, it's both of us. What he said was, 'Shall I ring you here or at your office? No, better the office—' And he went.

I stood at the window to see him go, and thought that Kate

was lurking there, on the pavement, gazing up. But it was dark outside the pool of lamplight, and then I believed I was imagining it.

As for me, his going was a load off me; literally, I felt myself expand and breathe again and want to move about and do things. So I did—tidied, cleared up, put on the radio and danced a little by myself, which I do very often, coming back from Richard. But last evening, it was sheer relief. Yet of course I could have wept, too. Not so much for 'the night of love' which had been presenting itself to us so unpleasantly, like something on an agenda, provided for by circumstances and by careful planning—was *that* the rub?—but because we had both been in such disarray that we were forgoing the treat of a whole day together, today, which we were to have spent free of all other ties.

It goes without saying that I dreamed of Freddie, my lost love. Who was never my love. Or I don't think he was. It is strange what a bad memory I have for the things that matter. I can remember exactly what I wore and what he wore, where we were: we were married in Kensington Registry Office and Freddie's parents and my parents gave a reception at the Savoy. My parents could not have afforded it by themselves. Joyce was my matron of honour. We never saw Freddie's best man, or I don't think we did, after the wedding. We were all jolly. I looked, I had no doubt, very pretty: after all, I was very pretty. But what was I feeling? I have no idea at all. The honeymoon, motoring in the Dordogne, is a mystery to me. I remember lovely scenery, wonderful food. I am sure we had wonderful sex, because we did. What did I feel? As for what he felt, I am sure I didn't give that a thought. Did I ever ask myself what Freddie felt about anything, until after he was dead? And yet, what a credit I was all round! I do remember strolling back into the office, after the honeymoon, and the satisfaction of it, as after a job properly done! I've done that, done it well, everything is as it should be!

This morning I woke very early, grieving, I shouldn't wonder, and lay in bed and examined my pretty room, this simple, pretty room. What is wrong with it? Nothing! I love it. I feel myself in it. But Richard says he can't see me in it and has to look out of the window at the elements, at nature! What a joke! Surely that says everything about him; nothing about me.

This morning was fine. I walked down to the supermarket and bought food for the next few days, thinking of Kate's needs. I put everything away, and the telephone rang. No, it was not Richard, but a neighbour of Annie Reeve's saying that her Home Help was ill, and the woman upstairs was away, and would I go and see her.

It is not that I haven't been visiting Annie. I continue to drop in, rain or shine, two or three times a week, I take her flowers, a cake, I sit with her an hour. But this is something I do, like—I was going to say—cleaning my teeth. With Richard here, three or four times recently I've said I would go and then didn't. This afternoon I bought dwarf tulips at the corner, pink, with some gypsophila, because she likes the small and the pretty. And then, instead of walking on up the street till I reached this one, 'my' street, I turned a corner, and then another, and was in Annie's street, and as I went in at her door entered the world I once hardly knew existed, that of the poor, the old, the sick; and those people who minister to them, social workers, Home Helps, Good Neighbours, Church Visitors; a world so different from mine, which is populated with those who keep themselves successfully balanced on life, people who do not expect (for it is something which happens to others) to trip, fall over, and find themselves incapacitated in a bedsitting room some-where, being kept going by visits, food brought in, moral support; a world which few of us, ever, want to think about until we have to. If I decided to abandon Annie, and stopped turning that corner, and then the next, into her street, I would walk past that submerged struggling place in which millions live and soon forget it exists.

And in fact during the last fortnight, when I haven't been in to Annie at all because of Richard, I've thought, Oh, well, there's that Irishwoman upstairs, and, Never mind, the Home Help will ... And I've caught myself thinking, But really I need never go back, no one would blame me, probably not even Annie, who has seen so many people flit into her life, all smiles, and then vanish for ever, as Home Helps and Good Neighbours and social workers come and go, and she'll probably only mutter fiercely, She's got better things to do with herself, oh, you can't tell *me*.

'Where is Janet?' she might complain, of some Home Help who has been in every day for months, and then not come. 'Oh, Janet Collins, you mean? She's been moved to Geriatrics in Paddington, didn't she tell you?'

I have even managed to forget that it is those who visit the old and the cantankerous often and regularly who get shouted at and abused: when I see Annie nearly every day I am treated as if I am her enemy. But, dropping in after a week, I am greeted with smiles, even formality, for she has been afraid I may never come again. In fact I can judge the degree of intimacy I have achieved with Annie by how much she grumbles, accuses, rages.

Today, appearing in her door, which I always open with the key that is beside mine on my key-ring, as noisily as possible so that she will not be startled by me, I was ready for reproaches and bitterness. She leaned forward out of her chair, for her sight is failing, and examined me with screwed-up eyes. 'Who's it this time?' she demanded; and then seeing my contrite posy, my placatory smiles, she said, 'Oh, it's you,' and sighed with relief of it—and the bad temper which would have unleashed on me had I been in during the last two or three days was set aside. 'Oh, what a stranger,' she remarked graciously, and became a sweet old thing. Not the real Annie, someone we glimpse rarely enough if we have ever seen her at all, but someone who has excised all sorts of memories, behaviour, experiences, so as to present to all these respectable mentors of hers a bland and jolly personage who can be blamed for nothing, a dear old lady.

I made us both tea. I set out cakes. I put the flowers in a jam jar. I sat on the little stool near the blocked-in fireplace. I waited, tensed, for her to say, 'Been busy, have you?' in a hard, sour voice.

But I could see from her face how afraid she had been I would not come again. 'How long is it since you were here?' she inquires cautiously, for really she cannot remember.

'Two weeks,' I said. 'No, two weeks and a day.' For I always give her exact information, hoping to arrest the slow muddling of her mind.

'And I've been sitting here,' she began, and stopped herself, checking, with a physical effort I could see in her restless movements and a swerve of her distressed eyes away from me, the impulse to let herself go into anger.

'It has seemed a long time,' she said meekly, but her voice was cold.

It is crazy, but now I am the person whom Annie has known longest. I've been her friend now for five years, more. For five years she has sat in a chair, in one room, moving less and less, while I've rushed around London, travelled to and from the office every day, been to a thousand Lunches and Dinners for *Lilith*, been to dress shows in Kyoto, and Madrid, Barcelona and Amsterdam, most of the cities in Europe in fact; jaunted off to Somerset and Dorset with Jill, taken myself to Iceland because the place, let alone its fashion, interests me. I have spent hundreds of enjoyable hours by myself in and around London, my great bazaar, my lucky dip, my private theatre. Recently I have been in love—I do not see what other word I can use—unsuitably and ridiculously; and have walked back and forth and around and across London with my blood fizzing in my veins like champagne. Meanwhile, old Annie has been sitting in this chair.

I saw today that she was troubled, wanted to find out something, was trying to come around to a subject sideways.

It is her memory: she can remember less and less. She does not like to confess how the map of her past is blurring and shifting. Her recent past, that is. Her memory is in fact the opposite of mine. What she was at ten years old, eighteen, thirty, forty—it is all there. What she felt, wanted, got, or didn't get; her clothes, her food, her boyfriends, her dead husband; every detail of it all, it's there. But she doesn't know if the Home Help came in yesterday or not. She talked on and on about the Home Help while I sat there, drinking tea, and thinking how my memory is like a busy broad and populated road just behind me, but then, quite soon, it begins to narrow and dwindle, and by the time I get to my twenties it is patchy, and then it becomes a little patch and often vanishes for months or even years at a stretch, except for strongly illuminated childhood scenes, mostly to do with my sister Georgie.

The Home Help ... on and on about the Home Help, Maureen. The trouble is, Annie grumbles; she is a grumbler; when she starts, one has to switch off. And so I listened with half an ear, and yet I encountered Maureen before, with old Eliza, and I know she is a crook. Annie says that Maureen has not been in, not for three days now: true or false? There is no way of finding out. Maureen only stays fifteen minutes instead of the hour and a half she is paid to stay. True? Very likely. Maureen said she would bring in this or that but hasn't, and now Annie has nothing to eat.

I cannot abandon Annie, no matter how much I would like to.

Do I love Annie? I am fond of her. Is that all, after five years or so? Well, I would very much like to know the real Annie, who I believe to be there somewhere, but I never will.

I sat on, and I made some more tea, and sat on again, and then listened to what I call Gramophone Record Number 3, which is how she went to the policemen's ball wearing the black lace dress with the red rose on it, and she drew all eyes (and probably really did, for she was lovely when she was young, a photograph avers that she was), and danced every dance. She was paying for the dress on the never-never in a dress shop in Wardour Street. She knows I have heard this often, but her need to talk is so great she has to pretend that I haven't: as she talks, she stops herself to say, I think I told you?—and as I shake my head, No, she smiles a little sour smile that refuses to be grateful but insists on its rights. She wore this afternoon a rather nice viyella skirt I ran up for her, in dark red, on elastic because of her ever-expanding girth, and over it a dirty cotton housecoat, because she can't find anything to wear 'because of the Home Help'.

I looked, saw that indeed all her clothes are dirty; that there was almost nothing to eat. I went out to buy her the necessities. When I do this she always says, over and over again, 'Oh, you shouldn't, don't bother, there's no need for it . . . don't forget the cigarettes.'

By the time I had done everything, emptied the commode, rinsed out a pair of knickers, made her some jelly, she had talked herself out and sat quietly, watching me.

'Don't forget poor Annie,' she said as I left.

When I was on the stairs here I heard the telephone and wondered if I had missed Richard. I had not been in five minutes before Kate rang at the door. It seems she has lost the key. She went to the sofa and slumped on it, repossessing her own.

'How are Jill and Mark?' I asked.

'I don't know.' This was smug, even vindictive, and I said, 'Very well, you didn't go there. Did you go home?'

'No.'

I decided I was not going to ask, but would wait for her to tell me, and she decided to match me: she plugged herself into her machine and was engulfed by sound.

The telephone rang: it was Jill, who had been ringing me all day, she said. Kate had just arrived last night, been admitted by Mark, who had asked her to make herself at home, 'Quite nicely,' Jill thought. But he went back to laying the carpet, and when he returned to the living room, Kate had gone.

Jill was beside herself with anger. Many years of it hissed there, concentrated in her shrill breathless voice. '*Get* her on the phone,' she commanded.

'It's for you,' I said to Kate, and Kate went to the instrument, and held the receiver up, not detaching herself from the wires. Through God knows what din came Jill's vituperations, and Kate listened, saying once in a low voice, because she did not want to disturb the glories of what she was listening to, 'I was in a squat, that's all.' Quite soon she put down the telephone and went back to her place.

I made her supper, demanded that she should unplug herself.

I said to her, 'Was that you on the pavement down there last night?'

She nodded, eyes down.

'I saw him leave,' she remarked. It was not a question, I think. Just another manifestation of the adult world which she will never—I am sure she is sure—understand.

'This squat, what is it?'

'Oh, just a squat.'

'There are squats and squats. I've done a whole series of articles on them. I might even know it.'

'I've only been in one,' she triumphed with an ugly little jeer. As if I were a competitor for squats.

As usual, I had to remind myself that the child is crazy, or not far off it.

'They are decent people,' she cried, sounding like my sister, my brother-in-law, who will diagnose people as decent or not, in which first category they will benefit from Georgina's and Tom's sincere regard. 'I know you wouldn't think so,' said Kate, stuffing in all that was left of the stew from last night, and mopping it up with chunks of French bread.

'You mean, they treat you well, unlike me, your sister, and your parents?'

'They judge people for what they *are*,' she insisted piously, eyeing me in a putting-down way that she had learned over the weekend.

'I'm glad to hear it, but who are *they* who have such perfect and instant judgement?'

'He recognized me from when I came, you know, to Paddington, when I came up to stay with you. I went to Paddington to go home, but he saw me and said Hi. I said Hi. He said, What are you doing here? . . .'

'You said, My aunt has thrown me out, my sister Jill showed me the door, and now I have to go home to my horrible cruel parents.'

That this was exactly what she had said was acknowledged by a shrill, frightened little laugh, which was nevertheless exultant.

'So I went with him to his squat. They are ever so kind.'

'Well, now you are home again with your wicked aunt and you have eaten up everything'—for of course she had not noticed that she had put all the stew on to her plate, and all the vegetables, so that there was literally none for me— 'how about a bath?'

At which she stood up, a tragedy queen, and laughed theatrically. 'I said to them, I said, the first thing she'll say is, Go and have a bath. That's what they are *like,* I said.'

'It is very simple, Kate. You smell horrible and I'm not going to put up with it.'

This hurt her. I had not expected it to reach her at all: if she did not even notice that she ate all the food on a table which had two people at it, why hear what I said about a bath? I gave up. I handed her a vast fluffy towel, put bath salts into the water, and she got into it gratefully. I picked up all the clothes on the bathroom floor for the launderette. I put her pyjamas on the warming rail. I made her a cup of chocolate before she slept, which she did at once, like an infant. Then I rang Jill.

'What happened?' we asked together.

'I think we will never know,' I said. 'I do know she was standing outside this building at eleven last night.'

'Perhaps she was not in a squat at all,' said Jill.

'You mean, a squat is some beautiful and unachievable dream?'

'You sound stricken by the thought, are you?'

'Yes, I think I am. She probably spent all night wandering about.'

'She could have been here. Mark made up the sofa for her.'

'But in her mind had been a dream of some amazing welcome, Sister Jill all smiles and kisses.'

'I don't know and I don't care. At least I hope you had a nice weekend?'

'Well,' I said, 'you could put it like that.'

And then Jill said, not at all putting the knife in, but in her parents' manner, diagnosis and judgement, 'The thing about you, Jane, reality isn't your strong point.'

'It isn't? Are you sure?' I heard my voice come anxious, as if she had said, You must realize that the prognosis is not very good.

'Oh, Jane, dear Jane,' breathed Jill, all remorse again, though I didn't need that this time.

And so here I sit, and it is midnight, and my heart is full of woe. I know one thing, that things won't be the same with Richard after this weekend, and after the little photograph.

I have been watching Jill. If Phyllis had not been off having her baby, I would be with Charlie in Editorial, not sitting opposite Jill, looking—or so I believe—at my past.

She works quickly and well, with concentration, at a desk spread about with a hundred tasks, while the telephone rings, people come in and out from the other departments with queries. They go to her, not to me. She has been working here three, nearly four years, knows as much as I do, or as Phyllis does. She defers to me, asks advice, takes it: but I know, if she does not, that if I were not here, if Charlie were not, she would manage.

Responsibilities, tasks, decisions, pile up all around her, and the surface of her desk begins to look like battlements behind which she operates, always alert and moving, like a brigand or guerrilla fighter expecting ambush. Her appearance relates not at all to the detailed complexities of her working life. She, like me all those years ago, is not ready for a personal style, but presents herself differently every day, even sometimes like a competent office worker with clothes subdued to her calling.

Today there was a crisis over an article that got itself mislaid and people came running in and out, telephone calls, exclamations of despair, exasperation, petulance. Through all this a handsome young bandit sat swashbuckling, swivelling about on her high stool, legs set apart in black highwayman's boots, striped cotton full trousers tucked into them, a black cotton jacket tied at the throat and held by a wide shiny black belt, dark hair a mass of little curls, kept off her brow by a yellow bandanna. She looked extremely pretty. Mark has been making excuses to come in and see her, to look at this girl of his, a nut-brown maid equipped for a life of piracy, his superior in the office while Phyllis is away. He brings in batches of his photographs, and stands very close while she bends over them. He is large, amiable, comfortable, whose style with girls is to be elder-brotherly; he has a hand on the back of her chair, and as she pores over his work so that he is forgotten, he runs a tender forefinger down where one might suppose her backbone is under the black envelope. She slightly tenses, then frowns, then looks up smiling, but it is a protest. She had decided to smile. It is because they have had a spat, I know: he complains that in the office she 'puts him down'. 'But we met in the office,' she said, threatened and breathless, reminding him with a quick smile of their long courtship, which was shared in (like Charlie's and Phyllis's baby) by everyone. What he is saying is that now he is her 'flatmate' her manner to him should not be so offhand. She does not like this; but thinks it over; wonders why, if he fell in love with her 'offhand' he now wants her different. But feeling the tender finger, she remembers their arguments, decides to smile, and does so, but there is an edge to it, and he moves away, to stand against the wall, and light a cigarette, while she gives him a smile which is not so much remorseful as an allowance of what is due.

And I look at two people who are like characters out of different plays: the elegant young bandit, concentrating over her decisions, sliding photographs behind each other, having given each its exact amount of attention, the large and amiable young man, standing against the wall. Then suddenly the June sun floods in, dimming Jill's colours, and illuminating the clouds of cigarette smoke he stands in; swirls of hazy blue lie around him and cling to his shaggy dark hair and loose dark shirt, which is like a moujik's tunic.

What I am waiting for, I realize, is the moment when, as she leaves, she relents, acknowledges this flatmate of hers with a glance or, as he takes the photographs, a touch. But she says, 'I think these two, here . . .' And it is only when he has gone out that she casts over her shoulder a single, remorseful look that says, 'If you were still in the room I'd give you—' but what? A kiss?

While they were manoeuvring towards love—a word which I suppose they do use—you might come on them as they separated from an embrace, or hear a laugh from behind a door, but now all that is relegated to their other life. I can hear, and so can he of course, her thought: One should keep things in their proper place!

I have not heard from Richard. It is almost a week. Well, I have been working hard. I have been spending evenings with Kate, trying to—what? What *do* I expect? I realize that I expect to have a beneficial effect on her! Suddenly this deplorable waif will sit up, unplug herself, shake off the crumbs and the dust, the grubby rags she wears will put on shape and decision, and she will actually hear what I say. 'Of course, Jane,' she will reply. 'I'll enrol tomorrow, I'll get some qualification, I'll take myself in hand, you will find me a job when I'm viable, and then . . .'

Last night when I was ready for bed she had dropped off to sleep on the sofa, the cup of chocolate I had made for her knocked over in the saucer, spilling everywhere, table, carpet, her knees. I had practically to lift her to bed, and this morning she was so dead asleep I left her, curled into a foetus, her back to me and the world, in a small dark room.

Today Richard rang. He said at once, 'Janna, you must not think that I haven't rung because of our—fall from grace.' That was so apt that I was grateful for it, and reconnected in this way with *us,* what we are, I said at once that I didn't . . . though I had.

'I have problems, Janna. No, really. But they are sorted out . . . Will you still be there next week? Early, probably Monday?'

There was such anxiety in this I was grateful for that too, and I laughed and said, 'But where else could I be?'

'Oh, I don't know. You do get around a lot, don't you?'

'I'll be here,' I said.

It is hot, hot, hot; June flames and smoulders. I look up from my bedroom window into lakes of pure blue where perhaps may amble a single white cloud; I stand at the office windows and look over the little hedge of greenery, maintained by Jill and Phyllis, down into the hot streets full of genial sun-worshippers, then up into the dazzle of blue. I ache for Richard. What I want is to be with him. That is all. How can we be wasting our blissful summer like this?

Jill said to me today, since I am not always running out for an hour, or two, or leaving early, 'What's happened to your handsome boyfriend?' And, at my look: 'I saw you two together on a bench in the square. Like two pigeons in spring.' And, as I did not say anything—I was waiting, I know, for her knife-thrust: 'Personable, I would say he was. And you, of course, but you always are.' She sat back on her swivelling chair, and examined me, from across the gulf of thirty years, with as strong a curiosity as I watch her.

Today Jill said to me, 'Do you like Mark?'

This ridiculous question was answered by the quizzical smile I put on my lips, while I went on with my work.

'Well?'

'What actually are you asking?'

'What's so silly about it?'

'Very well, I like him, very much indeed.'

She staged an exasperated sigh. Then: '*Jane!*'

'You're not asking my advice, surely?'

'Well, if I am? Do you think we are well suited, all that kind of thing?'

I said, after some time, for the words that presented themselves all seemed wrong, 'He's a very warm and affectionate man . . .'

Before I could finish she flashed, 'And I am not, is that it? Well, I can tell you, I feel suffocated sometimes. Did you, ever? Sometimes it is as if I want to explode with irritation— just run away.' I said nothing, because my memory tugged, and I was trying to lure that fish back into consciousness, when she said angrily, 'Well, did you feel like that ever?'

'I can't remember . . .'

'It's never being alone. I ask him, I say, tell me truthfully, don't you mind never being alone? He says, I can't say that I do.' She copied his manner, humorous, indulgent, to perfection, and her whole body showed how she had wriggled in irritation out of his embrace.

'Well, perhaps you are too young for it all?'

'*What does that mean?*'

And, suddenly, I was in tears. From out of my depths somewhere welled great surges of woe and loss.

'Jane,' expostulated Jill, shocked at me.

'I know one thing,' I said, between sobs and sighs, 'I look back and think I was the greatest bloody fool . . .'

She was scared: frightened, not at anything I had said, but at my weeping. She went on working, subdued.

Monday. Richard did not ring.

The lovely weather continues. Today I watched this scene.

Jill wore a thin white dress that has a wide scooped-out neck and arm-holes, and a dropped waist from which flounces white broderie anglaise. She sat with her legs apart on her stool-like chair. She is brown with the summer, and really lovely, her hair, still dark and curly, today tied with a white bandanna. She is all delicate thin brown arms and legs, and angles and hollows. And this vision sat there, concentrating on her work while occasionally dabbing at her damp forehead with tissues. Mark came in with two girls from the agency, dressed for the autumn, to illustrate the article Jill was writing: 'You will be wearing the colours of a forest in October . . .' All over her desk photographs of autumn forests, from Vermont as it happened, golden grass, red berries, yellow trees, and so on. The girls, intrepid as is expected of them, were sweating inside tweeds and jerseys, and making jokes about Jill and me wearing cotton. Mark wanted to know if Charlie was expected in because the light was just right in the big room. Charlie is with Phyllis, who has gone into hospital to have her baby. Mark also wanted his Jill to go with him and the girls into the big editorial room, on the pretext that his usual assistant is on holiday, the other one off sick, and—in short, he wanted Jill.

Jill said, 'But Mark, I've got my work to do.'

She was, of course, quite right. But in her tones rang other expostulations, such as: why should *I* be your assistant!

Both the girls had worked with us before, and knew Mark. One, Edna, said, 'Oh, we'll manage, Mark.' She is a striking, dramatic, olive-skinned dark-eyed beauty, whose scarlet sweater succeeded in dimming our wilting pastels, the kind of girl whom you have to look at, like an actress projecting herself. Mark put his arm around her, as he stood gazing, baffled rather than hurt, at his love Jill. This was not designed to gain advantages. Mark is too generous in his instincts to bargain or manoeuvre; just as he had not said, though I know Jill had been expecting him to, I've been taking orders from you, this last week.

Edna, who cannot help playing up to any situation she is in, was acting the part of a flattered preening beauty inside Mark's arm, and the other girl, Sally, was laughing with me. The three of them, Mark, Edna, Sally, seemed self-contained there, the indulgent, easy man, and the two girls whom he was about to photograph, they being obedient to his spoken and unspoken wishes; they were laughing, expansive, enjoying it—and suddenly Jill, with a little exclamation 'Oh very well . . .' got up, and as she did so the group broke up, and four people, Mark and the three girls, one for summer and two for the months still a good way ahead, went into the editor's room, where they worked all day, Jill frequently emerging to collect cold drinks, tea, beer, for the others. Meanwhile I was working like a donkey: I am doing Charlie's job, and part of Phyllis's. Today I was doing Jill's as well, and I called June from the pool to help me.

She is a very nice girl: good-natured, ready to please and to do what is needed. She has to be given an exact and precise task, with explanations, when she will finish it, bringing it to me with the air of a willing servant. She has been with us seven years, and yet has never seemed to want any more than what she has: a decent little job that does not ask much of her. She is a great favourite with the others, something of a clown or a comic, and with me was entertaining about minor events in the pool, and at the end of a story would wait hopefully for my laugh, her bold jolly blue eyes fixed on my face. She knows everything about her own department, and has no capacity or desire to think of *Lilith* as a whole. Having spent a day with June, I realize what a treasure Jill is, who had grasped everything of importance in *Lilith* within a month and never has had to have anything explained to her. Yet June is not stupid! It is a mystery to me, this business of capacity, people's innateness. It is more of a mystery now that I spend so much time with poor Kate. How is it possible that these two girls emerged from the same family, the same influences, the same everything! Kate lives in a dazzle of confusion. She has a great gaping pit or hole somewhere in the region of her solar plexus, all need and craving, and nothing, or so I begin to fear, will ever fill it.

Today Richard rang, said could I meet him at twelve in Soho Square. I was sitting there in a riot of joy, pulses hammering, my whole body ready to take off, but I said, 'I can't, we are so short-staffed . . .' But Jill was leaning forward hissing, 'Go on, Jane, don't be so silly.' I covered the mouthpiece and said, 'Jill, but how can I?' And heard in my voice a plea that she would say it was all right. 'Of course you must go,' she said. And I said to Richard, 'Yes, it's all right. . .'

As I walked into Soho Square, he was standing over some begonias, turned away from me, and his look up as I approached was wary, then he was delighted, straightened, put his hands on my arms, looked smiling down at me, and at once the miracle started, the reckless, delicious delight, but he said, 'Janna, we must move out quickly . . .' And we ran out of the square, hands linked, while he hissed at me, stage villain, 'I have reason to think we are being followed.'

We ran past 'our' little café, where we have had so many encounters, and in Oxford Street leaped into a taxi. 'Just drive along,' said Richard to the taximan. We fell into each other's arms, and I felt the warm roughness of his cheek, and the heat of his arm coming through the linen of his jacket radiating into my back.

'Janna,' said he, 'I've missed you every minute.'

'And I you.'

And so we sat, close. And the strange thing was that this closeness was warm, intimate, with the friendliness of sensuality. But it was not sexual. This was because we cannot let it be. And I am wondering as I write if, in times when sex was not the first thing people had to think of, some woman (or man for that matter) writing in a diary would have bothered to say, 'But it was not sexual.' Why is it we have made an imperative of sex?

Soon Richard said, 'What would you feel about going up to Richmond on the river boat?' It seemed to me perfect, but of course I had to niggle and object inwardly, because I would not be back in the office at all. But I thought, To hell with it, Jill will cope.

At the pier we were lucky. You'd think all of London would have thought of going up to Richmond that day, but only half had. The queues were long, but we got on a waiting boat, and went forward to sit by a rail on deck. The river seemed full of pleasure, little boats, other river boats, even the river patrol boat seemed to be frivolously darting about, and the heat was weighing the green trees along the banks with a look of summer repletion, and the buildings were on holiday. The sky was faultless, the blue so seldom seen in England, with a couple of negligible clouds to set it off. Balmy breezes and seagulls and the voices of children rushing about below eating potato crisps, completed the scene, and we held hands and were happy.

My head rested against Richard's shoulder, and just above my ear he was humming, 'London, London, London, I love you, how I love you, London, my love.'

About being happy, what is there to be said!

At Richmond we found a pub, and ate quantities of pie and potato salad, and he said, 'There's one thing about you, you never fuss about a diet.'

'But I don't get fat,' said I, and then had to add, 'But on the other hand, I must do, since I'm fatter than . . .' I was going to say, when that photograph was taken, but even a reminder of it seemed dangerous. Yet he took it out of his top pocket, where he must have put it that morning, and that girl lay on the dark green paint of the pub table with shadows from a chestnut tree in full flower sifted over us and her. I knew he had taken it out so promptly, and laid it there so as—so to speak—to defuse it, make her harmless, but I was looking at that slight lovely girl, all angles and hollows, just like Jill, and I said, 'I've got solid.' And he put the photograph back in his pocket, and put his brown hand over the pocket with a protective gesture, and smiled. And at that moment his smile faded; and his face, then his body, were wrenched with anxiety. I looked around and saw, walking past the pub, slowly, not looking at us, his daughter, Kathleen. We watched her together, as she went away down into a road full of chestnut trees.

'Why?' I had to ask.

'I have been out of London for over a week, and while I told her—truthfully—what I was doing, she suspects I have been with you.'

'I wish you had.'

Again I could not stop myself having to know and he knew it, and hesitated, then said, 'My mother is very old, nearly ninety. She has been living by herself, and managing. Now she can't. I've found a Home for her. It's not bad, as these places go. She's being allowed some dignity. She'll have her own room. She hates having to go in, but she knows she must.' There was a long silence after this. He answered it with: 'If she lived with us, things wouldn't be any better, there'd be no one to look after her properly, we both work all day.'

This was more information than I'd had, or wanted; and I felt a resistance in all of me, No, no, don't tell me, *I don't want to know.* He saw it and held out his hand to me, and pulled me up in the same movement as he got to his feet, and we went out of the pub garden into a street and saw, right at the far end of it, Kathleen turning to come back. We went fast in the opposite direction, through the leafy summer gardens of Richmond, full of people in bikinis, summer dresses, shorts; full of dogs and cats and children; and everywhere the trees and flowers of full summer, English summer the vagrant, the delinquent, which when it is with us says, Why do you worry so, this is what summer *is,* aren't I here?—but then vanishes, with a smile. And does not return, perhaps for years. No wonder we talk about the weather, think about it, are obsessed by it. What a theatre it is, what a pageant, what a free show, in lovely England, where one hour is so seldom the same as the one before. But today it was summer all through, hour after hour, and we went slowly, hand in hot hand up into the park, and sauntered about over the thick grass with the deer that once fed commoners and kings, and now are like harem beauties, sheltered in special places and loved for their rarity. We walked and we walked, I as usual in my madly unsuitable Kurt Geiger shoes, but feeling secure in them, my sturdy feet going down strongly over the thick tussocks of grass, my hand held tight by Richard, who was a tawny lion indeed in all that hot yellow light, and we walked clear across the park, and around it, and I don't think we spoke, only smiled, and felt life moving in our linked hands.

By seven in the evening we had walked in a great circle and came back to houses and gardens where people still lolled and played, enjoying our summer, and groups idled about under the trees of the streets. We found another pub and there was a little garden at the back. We were hungry by then, and we ate steaks and salad and apple pie and cream and drank a great deal of red wine. It seemed as if we could not stop smiling, or looking at each other. My eyes were like hands, for I could sense, as I looked at his cheek, how the cool skin was very slightly damp, and his sandy lashes brushed my fingers; and how, under his blue shirt, for he had taken off his jacket, his body was strong and full of vitality. And I could feel his gaze, like a touch, on my face and on my arms. They were bared, though I had wondered if I should, and they satisfied me, because his eyes seemed to be finding pleasure there.

The garden of the pub was crammed full of people, and this made a setting for our solitudes. It was bounded by a tall rose hedge: several kinds of rose grew there, white and red and pink, and the scent was strong. As the dusk came down, the roses became mild blobs against the dark; and then the lights were on, and we went down to the river again and waited for a boat. We sat together on the bench up at the front, and headed downstream between the lights on the banks. It was so warm that we sat with bare arms and his hand was close on the flesh of my shoulder.

As we came off the boat at Westminster, we saw ahead of us in the crowd Kathleen, who must have been on the boat without us knowing, and perhaps even sitting close to us. She might have been following us all day, at a distance, as we wandered through Richmond Park. She did not turn to look at us. We did not walk faster, to catch her; nor slow, to avoid her.

I have by now seen her quite often; yet I feel I do not have a clear picture of her: for surely when she is normally occupied she does not seem powerful or even threatening? Richard felt I was thinking this, for he said softly, 'There is no reason to believe this, but Kathleen is actually a very sensible, very nice person.'

What did that mean? When people say someone is 'sensible' and 'nice' usually there is an implication of reassurance. And this girl still trails us, as far as I can see, whenever she suspects we might be together, and often when we are not. What can she want?

As we walked towards Charing Cross station, I was thinking, Perhaps we ought simply to go after her; say, Kathleen, let us meet!—to put an end to this. But what would not be put an end to is our meeting. Which presumably is what she wants, this sensible and nice spy.

We saw her go down into the underground, and we went on to the Strand and up into Soho where, suddenly, we were engulfed by the sex shops and sex shows, and this was so painful to us in the mood we were in that we almost ran out of it again. 'You keep saying England, England,' I heard myself saying in a hot distressed angry voice, 'but that is England now too.'

'All right, all right,' he said. 'But let's not . . .'

How often, and about how many things, do we now say in words or by implication, *All right, but let's not . . .*

He said as we parted, 'I suppose I can't tempt you away from your office tomorrow as well?'

I knew it was impossible but I could not bear to be final

about it, and I said, 'Ring me—early. I'll do what I can.'

We laid our hot cheeks together, and smiled and parted.

And here I am, sitting in my bedroom, which I like so much and which he says is not me, writing this. Have I caught anything at all of this day we have had, so perfect, even if threatened by that thundercloud Kathleen?

Kate was not here when I got home. I was so relieved: what a burden she is, even when she does nothing, sits silent on my sofa in her world of sound. She seems to weigh down the air, weigh me down. Then, of course, anxiety. Then, a cautious beginning of the thought: Perhaps this means she is getting more self-reliant, grown-up. She came in furtive and pleased with herself. I was not going to ask what she had been doing. She was not going to tell me, though many a triumphant little glance came winging my way.

I keep saying to myself, She is nineteen, an adult. Though what dishonesty, since she is nothing of the kind.

She made herself a sandwich, made herself coffee, she got herself into a bath without being asked. Perhaps she is getting over—whatever is wrong with her.

But I don't care, not tonight. I am sitting here in my white cotton nightgown, and I am looking into the sky, which has light in it even though there are no clouds and nothing to reflect back London's brilliances. Is London ever dark? Is our sky ever without light? I don't think it is.

Wednesday is Editorial conference day, but there were only Jill and me from Editorial to confer. Phyllis is in labour, induced. Jill has been furious all day because of this: it appears my sister does not hold with induced labour and has fought four successful battles to be permitted to have her babies her own way. The doctors told Charlie that Phyllis was 'too old' and nature could not be trusted. Charlie went along with all this. 'As he *would*,' cried Jill, distressed out of all proportion: how often in Jill do I hear these violent echoes of family battles.

What is evident is that Editorial needs to be rapidly enlarged. I keep going on part-time, and then pressures and my own interest in it all brings me back. Phyllis is going off for three months to enjoy motherhood. Jill, while a jewel and a boon, is still so young, and I know that there are mutters about nepotism. Today, while working like a madwoman, I also reviewed everyone in *Lilith* who has a spark, a flair; who has, as well, ambition. It is extraordinary how few people are ambitious, how many are content with their lot.

Two interesting points emerged from all this: one was brought to my attention by Jill, who inquired why, when talking about possible candidates for rapid advancement, I talked only about the women? This was a real shock to me. It is true, I do see *Lilith* as run by women, Charlie notwithstanding. In my mind I then went carefully through all the men. There is a very bright, quick, ambitious young man in Production, Henry. I had to fight against reluctance, though: which surfaced as, When there are so few jobs for clever women, why waste even one on a man? Jill was watching me, not ceasing her work of course, as I wrestled with this one.

'Well?' she inquired at the end, and when I said, 'I'll put it to him, it wouldn't be fair not to,' she laughed in triumph, 'You said that exactly as mother would.'

Richard rang about ten, and I had to say that it was impossible to leave the office, even for lunch. Outside the windows the sun dazzled.

In the middle of a frantic afternoon, telephones ringing everywhere, there was a call from Joyce. I thought at first from New York, but no, she is in London. Her voice unchanged, slow and deep. A gipsy voice, we used to joke; full of fate. But now it has a slur of America in it, and the depth and pitch and range is considered, as voices get when one is out of one's own country and is having to contrast one's voice and the use of it with everything one hears. I could tell at once that Joyce was determined *not* to acquire an American accent, as a matter of principle, and listened to herself, a severe monitor of every inflection of her voice.

'Well?' came this voice that was once part of my life, teasing me with memories that on the whole I resist, 'and how fares the old bitch *Lilith*?'

Once Joyce would not have said anything so brutal, but I

understood it was only her new style. Perhaps even a bulwark against unwanted memories: she was feeling like me, as we sat in different parts of London, she in Hammersmith as it happened, in a room overlooking the river with swans on it, she said.

'This old bitch,' I said, 'is very pleased to hear your voice. Joyce, I've just had a brilliant idea. Why don't you come back and work here? We need you.'

A silence. I was even hopeful, thinking she might have been wanting me to say it.

'You don't change, Janna,' said she. 'My husband? My merry moppets?'

'Who *must* be adults by now, surely?'

'Sometimes I believe one thing, but then another.'

I thought of Kate, and was silent.

'Well, am I going to see you?' I asked.

'I wondered about tomorrow evening?'

Richard had said he might be free tomorrow and I was just about to say no, then thought, Joyce was my friend, the person closest to me for years, and now ... I said, 'Very well. But I am not going to ask you home, there are reasons ...'

'Then we'll spend a cosy evening in a restaurant. I'm out of touch, which?'

I was going to suggest my local Indian restaurant, then thought, No, too near home, meaning Kate, again, and said, 'Bertorelli's.'

Richard rang up just before I left to say he would have tomorrow evening free—and how bitterly I regretted then, giving it to Joyce.

'I can't,' I said.

'Ah ...'

'I'm spending it with a woman who was once my best friend. We worked together for years and years.'

'Old friendships should never be sacrificed for new loves.'

'Is there no chance at all,' I asked, breaking all our—unwritten—rules, 'of meeting this evening?'

'I wish there were.'

Waves of regret washed to and fro between us, charging

the ether I am sure with all the colours of the rainbow.

'I'll ring you on Friday.'

Today Charlie rang to say Phyllis was sleeping off childbirth; she had had a bad time of it; they had a baby daughter. As for him, he was at home proposing to sleep it off too. And I said, 'No, Charlie, you can't. You must come in. We are going frantic.'

'It's no good,' he said, in the cheerful, expansive way that is his style in storm or in calm, 'I'm washed up, Janna.'

I said, 'But Charlie, it's simply not on,' for I was afraid he might decide to give up coming in altogether while Phyllis was in hospital.

'I'll see if I can come in later this afternoon,' said he, and did, briefly, accepting the congratulations of the entire office in a careless, regal way which everyone knew was a front: he is, there is no other word for it, radiant. We all saw this afternoon that we were looking at one of the world's natural fathers: he misses the three from his other marriage, sees them all the time, Phyllis accommodates the offspring of her rival with efficiency and tact, and this fourth baby is seen by him, we understood, as only an item in a continuing production line.

'I have been at all the births,' he said, smiling, smiling, helping himself to cigarettes, bits of chocolate or sweets off people's desks. 'It is the most exciting thing in the world, there's nothing like it—the moment when the babe pops forth all *there*, don't you know, ready for it all, I always weep, I cry my eyes out, I can't help it!'

And having shed beneficence and blessings from his heights, he wandered off again, back to the hospital, to see if Phyllis was awake.

Jill was thoughtful. Of course. I am sure children are not on her agenda. Why should they be at her age? The right age, according to those moguls, the doctors, for childbearing. Mark however was attentive to the radiant Charlie, listening to the siren song. And Jill knew it.

'I wonder if Phyllis realizes Charlie's plans for her future?'

'It's all right, they can't afford it,' I said.

'Want to bet?' And to Mark, who had come in to be with her, propelled by borrowed emotional fuel from Charlie: 'Are you looking forward to seeing our babies born?' She sounded so threatened, almost tearful, and Mark felt her panic, and laughed and teased her out of it. He really is a most extraordinarily decent young man.

Three evenings with Kate. She weighs on me, oh how she does. I find myself thinking of her when I'm at work, wondering, Has she got up out of bed yet, it is nearly midday? Has she eaten anything? Perhaps she has actually gone for the shopping I asked her to do? Perhaps when I am not there she actually reads something, or at least is not as hopeless as when I am?

Today I was thinking so hard about Kate that I had stopped working, in spite of all the pressures, and I looked up to find Jill watching me with the small shrewd smile I am familiar with from Phyllis. Jill has acquired that characteristic from Phyllis, along with those she has taken from me. (Where, *who*, is Jill?)

'Do you realize how worried you look?'

I did not reply, was thinking that if all of me is an artefact, put together from those earlier influences I have forgotten, then it might explain why Richard could stand there looking at my bedroom, and say, You are not in this room.

'Why don't you just send her home?' Jill was going on, and I recognized the extra determination that comes with having planned a conversation, and making oneself do it. 'You do really think you are going to change her, don't you?'

'Yes, Jill, I have caught myself in just that silly and unworthy thought.'

'Yes, I know. There's going to come a point when Kate suddenly changes from an unremitting, hopeless, useless *slob*'—I really do not know how to convey anything of the helpless anger that went into those words— 'and sits up all bright and washed, her mother's daughter and her aunt Jane's niece.'

This hard driving insistence of hers, the *need* of Jill that I should see it.

'Aren't you at all fond of Kate?'

'Oh no!' she exploded, and even got up from her desk, to move about, pulling out and sliding in filing-cabinet drawers. Her emotions were pushing her around the office; twitching her into abrupt, uncoordinated movement. 'I've had it all my life! "Don't you love your sister?" No, I *don't*. Don't you see?' She was shouting at me—or her mother, 'I don't. Why should I?'

'I did not use the word love,' said I, sitting heavily there while this wild creature—today as it happens the picture of a girl dressed suitably for the office, in a nice little pleated dark blue skirt and dark blue shirt—went banging and crashing about. 'But I am certainly thinking about it a lot.'

'I bet,' said she vulgarly, but at my look desisted.

'I mean, about Kate.'

'I'll save you the trouble. I am an expert on love, being one of four siblings. All the degrees and kinds of it. I have had to be. "Don't you love your sister?" "No, I don't love my sister." "Heartless wicked girl." Not that they said that except in *joke.* Oh, you don't know anything about the jokes of large families, Auntie Jane, and aren't you lucky.'

'Pity the poor filing cabinets,' I said, as a drawer slid in with a dull crash and the cabinet banged back against the wall.

'*But.* Having been forced into this minute and I maintain untimely examination of my soul, at about six I could say that I didn't love Kate, but I did love Jasper. I have always loved Jasper. More than anyone in the world? If Jasper was in the *mess* Kate is, then yes, I would do anything, *everything*— When Mark and I got together ...' I smiled at this euphemism, she saw it and was impatient, 'I said to him, you had better know that there's Jasper, I love him, and I want to see as much of him as I can.'

Now she retreated to her desk, shook back her dark curls, and lit a cigarette. She seldom smokes. Calm after the storm.

'As for me,' said I, 'it is not so simple.'

'Perfectly simple. You keep saying to yourself, But what

will become of her! Why can't you face it, Jane? Are you going to be house-mother to Kate for the rest of your life?'

After some thought I said carefully, 'In three years, getting on for four I suppose, I've watched you change. You came into my flat—very different from what you are now!' I could hardly say, I've watched you become Aunt Jane, model II.

'Well, of course I've changed. I've learned so much, from you mostly.'

I saw then, finally, that Jill does not know of her transmogrification. Perhaps she never will.

'If I tell Kate I won't have her, she's not going home, I am sure of that.'

'No, she would pester me, day and night, to live with me. And I *won't*,' she shrieked. 'You have no idea what it is like. All my life, she's been there, just a great gaping *void*, sucking up everything, *me*. I've never had anything, ever, in my whole life that she didn't try and get from me. It used to be toys. Then my clothes. Suddenly, they were Kate's. "Poor Kate," Mummy would say, and there went my new dress . . .'

'She probably thought that since you had so much else, a dress was neither here nor there.'

'I might at some point attain such heights of sainthood, but then, aged five or ten or whatever, a dress *was* important. Shoes. Gramophone records. I never could have anything— they were hers. Her room was stacked with everything of mine. Then it started—friends. I deliberately started to make friends out of our circle. It was marvellous. Quite apart from discovering that the world did not consist of the British middle class, a useful discovery at that, for I would never have suspected it, from dear Mummy and Daddy. But suddenly, guess what? My little Kate was there too. She has a way with her, or she used to have when she was of the right age to go with her babyings. I used to be absolutely amazed that people couldn't see what she was doing—coming after me. "Your sister Kate," they'd say, "Kate is coming with us, to the pictures." "I thought how nice for you if Kate came too." In no time, Kate would be *there* more than I was. It happened again and again. I couldn't have a friend of my own. Not ever. Once I asked mother if I could go for two months to visit a school friend, I really liked her, she lives in Galway. The whole of the summer holidays. Guess what, but I hadn't been there a week before Kate turned up. She'd hitch-hiked. She made herself at home, ingratiated herself with the parents, was ever so useful about the house . . .'

'You mean to say she can be useful about the house?'

'Oh, Jane, of course she can be, when she wants.'

'I am infinitely reassured. There is a difference between can't and won't.'

'The point is that at the end of two weeks I left Ireland and came home, thinking that all right, let her have my lovely friends, I'd enjoy a peaceful month at home, but then she came back after me.'

'I begin to see how very galling it must be for you that she is in my flat now.'

'Yes.'

'But she wasn't, not once, when you were there. And that was for three years.'

'It was because this worm finally turned. I told my mother that, if Kate came after me, I'd kill her. And I told Kate that, if I found her in your flat when I was there, I'd—'

'What?' I am really interested what the final threat could have been; but Jill simply shook her head, breathless, speechless, played-out. She was white and pinched about the nostrils, she looked a poor little thing, vulnerable; not unlike, for those few moments until she had recovered, Kate.

'If I told Kate to go now, I think she'd be in the hands of the police within a week.'

'Yes, she probably would. On purpose.'

'And that doesn't seem to you to matter?'

She shook her head irritably, made a gesture that said, *Enough*.

Today I met Richard for a quick sandwich. Our summer has departed, trailing black clouds and cold rain. We went to a McDonald's, delicious, and held hands. Outside the rain plunged down.

'Janna,' said Richard, 'what would you say if we went

away for a week? I'd like to say, of course, for ever. But a week it would have to be.'

'When?' I said; and I half understood when he laughed.

'Things are very difficult at the moment,' I said, and told him for the first time about Phyllis, about Charlie, about Jill About *Lilith*. It took all our lunch hour. I was absorbed in telling it, for particularly at the moment, now, it is interesting. *And, after all, it is my life. . .* I noticed him sitting back, arms folded, watching me, as I sat there, all animation no doubt, Phyllis's baby, Charlie the father, the lot, and there was something final there, on his face. Affectionate, yes. Love—yes, I think so. A warm, close look, but detached too. I am not saying that anything was missing of what we feel. But an assessment had been made, and then a judgement. I heard myself say, faltering, apologetic, 'It is my life, after all.'

And he put out this strong quick hand of his, laid it on top of mine—all rings and prettily varnished nails—and left it there while he said, 'All the same, can you spare me a week?'

'Why does it have to be at once? Couldn't it be in a month's time?'

These words struck painfully into both of us, because his answer would take us right into what we both most of the time avoided. For I was also asking, Are you going away again? I have been most carefully preventing myself having any such thoughts; and I am not having them now, I will not live through this thinking all the time: But it will end, he is going away.

'Janna, it can't be. It will have to be in the next fortnight or not at all. Oh no, I'm not saying that,' for I knew that I must have gone pale. I could feel my whole body cold, as if a shadow had passed over me after hot sunlight. My hand under his was trembling, and his closed hard over it. 'I'm not saying that I am leaving now, Janna. But if it's a question of my getting a week away . . .'

'I'll see. Well, I'll have to see what I can arrange.' But I was thinking that it was impossible. Even without Kate it is impossible. I can't take a week's leave now. It wouldn't be fair to *Lilith*.

Today I had dinner with Joyce, my old mate, my cobber, my pal, my *friend*.

I made a fuss on the telephone when booking, asked for a table in a quiet corner, and we got it. We sat opposite each other, as we have done so often talking about work, and examined each other with a frankness we acknowledged with a smile.

My wild romantic Joyce, high-class gipsy, has vanished. The truth is, I would not have known her. All her thickets of black hair gone, and she has a neat little head. Bronze. Her beautiful crazy clothes—gone. She wore a 'little' black dress, and even a diamanté brooch on one shoulder. The thirties. She is extremely well groomed. Smart. She is bony and pale. Her shoes: she used to sit, anywhere she was, with one shoe off perhaps, or held by its toes, her feet hooked around each other or a chair leg; tonight she wore little black pumps like chisels, placed correctly side by side.

'Well, you haven't changed,' says Joyce, as she makes sure that she is not eating anything that could put on an ounce. Or a gramme. 'You wear well, as they say. Good for you. I *don't* wear well.'

I didn't say anything, and she said, 'If that is tact, then you have changed.'

'You look lean. And handsome.'

'You look plump, and pretty.'

'Good God.'

'But those frail, fair wisps of hair, around a winsome face. Yes, I'll stick to pretty.'

'I don't know why you think it's an insult. Besides, I am in love. It is an infallible recipe.'

'Really in love?'

'Really implies permanence.'

But she let it slide away. She was sipping a cocktail. Examining me. Little black eyes. Now they are not made-up, immense and exaggerated, an old woman's eyes? Yes; and my heart ached for her. I don't know why: but I swear it was not because of our lost closeness. I was sitting there thinking, We worked all those years, she was closer to me than anyone, even Freddie. And now . . . this was to make sense of it all.

After she left for New York, she used to ring me; those crazy drunken conversations in the middle of the night. I could see she drinks a lot. Needs to. She had two cocktails and a lot of wine and then brandy. She ate very little; she used to love food. We had many a good tuck-in. We had a lot of good things together: but that is all ghosts and the past. I do not know Joyce now.

She talked about her job. She counsels the students about their problems. Life problems and work problems, she explained; and I imagined her asking some anxious young thing, Is it a life problem or a work problem you are bringing to me?

Her qualifications for this job? That she has never had anything but problems of every kind with her own two.

They are at university and she sees little of them. They are both 'into' the new technology. She says she does not understand what they say, most of the time.

Her husband: he is in his element in America, and hopes he may never have to leave: teaching Dickens, Trollope and Hardy. I picture these three men, sitting side by side behind a table, smiling benevolently on the labours of their proselyte, a decorated scroll saying, 'Well done!' above each august and whiskered head.

His affair with her best friend (still her best friend) is over; and he is having an affair with a girl who was his student last year: discretion made them 'wait' until she was no longer his student.

She is having an affair with a student. But not from her husband's department. She says she has reached the age for this type of affair; all her women friends have one, or have had one, or plan one. She finds it rejuvenating. For her ideas, she means—catching my involuntary glance at her arid self. It's not that she shares their ideas—the young; but that's not the point.

By now we had reached the pudding, which I insisted on having while she watched, her thin freckled hand protective around the brandy.

At any moment we would be brought the bill.

'Joyce, are you enjoying yourself here?'

'I've come to get my father into a Home.'

'Ah. It seems to be the thing one does, at our age.'

'If they haven't already died.'

'Don't you ever miss—' I had been going to say *us*, but said, 'England?'

There was then a rather long silence. She cuddled the brandy glass and did not look at me. I realized that what I was looking at was anxiety. Joyce has achieved this equilibrium of hers at the cost of being locked inside anxiety.

I was waiting for her interest in me to manifest itself. *How are you, Janna, but I mean, really?*

I was sitting there, wondering, Was she ever interested in me? *Really?* Was I ever anything but a background to her amazing competence, her juggling acts of work, family, success at everything?

'It does seem all rather quaint,' she pronounced at last. 'A dear little country, preoccupied with important problems, such as, are you going to have television at breakfast time.'

'Unemployment, the recession, the rage of the young . . .'

'We have all those too . . .'

We, she had said.

'You don't think you will come home?'

'My husband,' said she, using the word deliberately, 'sometimes prattles away about *home*, but I notice that when he's got leave, he chooses Canada or Mexico.'

'Yes, but what about *you*?'

Another silence. 'It's like this, Janna. I made a mistake when I went there. Now I know it. You were right. You must be pleased at that. Being in the right is so important to you.'

First what I felt was anguish, on her account. I realized, sitting there, painfully looking, and looking again for some sign of the wild, successful energy that once characterized her, how much Joyce had meant to me because of that energy, the generous carelessness of it that invigorated everything about her. Oh, how measured and careful she has become. . . And then, I was feeling pain on my account. Yes, of course we always said what we thought, did not wrap things up; our criticisms of each other, heard from outside, must have sounded like—well, like the vigorous home truths that fuel family life. But this was different, it was the spite of weakness.

After some time, I said, 'But there's *Lilith*, we would love to have you back.'

'You don't see that if something is done wrong, then there are consequences, and—that's that!'

'No, I don't. You could make an effort, heave yourself out of there, and come home.'

An angry smile, even vindictive. 'It's the making an effort,' she said. 'I couldn't do it. I'm burnt out.' And as I hesitated: 'Oh, shut up, Janna. You don't understand. Look at you sitting there, all fat and happy, like a cat full of cream.'

She scrambled for her bag, a nice little packet of tissues appeared, she dabbed and patted, and then did a quick, adequate repair job.

'Well,' said she, pushing everything away out of sight into the mad jumble of her handbag, sitting up severe, tailored and contained. 'And you are still living there in lonely satisfaction in your impeccable flat, and I hear that every time you leave *Lilith* for good you are back again inside a month.'

I signalled for the bill, and paid it. She did not offer to share: it was because she was not aware of anything but her misery.

We left the little nook I had asked for, the table behind a bank of flowers around which waiters and trolleys laden with food appeared out of the busy crowded spaces beyond, and we went into the street.

'That wasn't much of a success, was it?' she announced, with a smile that was meant to be friendly.

'No.'

'If I have time before I go back, I'll ring you. But getting my father settled in is not leaving much time for anything else. When I get to that age I'm going to jump out of a window. Oh yes, I remember, you have progressive thoughts on the subject, don't you? Well, good for you.'

And she went off along the pavement, while I stood there simply not believing it. Not possible for us to separate like that, enemies, or at least seeming to hate each other.

I watched how her walk slowed. I nearly ran after her, to

say—but what? I could not move. She stopped. In the street lights she was a small, solitary figure. Only we two were out, but the restaurants presented well-lit, discreet and satisfied façades to Charlotte Street.

I watched Joyce turn, hesitate, and then come wandering back. I had not moved an inch. She came to a stop in front of me. We looked at each other. Her face was small, and pinched with—anger? No, it was grief.

In that *other* voice, the one we use, or hear, so seldom, she said as if she was listening to herself, and even with surprise, 'Clever Janna, not to have children.'

I hadn't expected it and it hurt. I cried out, 'But you can't mean that, Joyce!'

'Why not? Yes, I'll stand by that. Sensible Janna, you didn't have any children.' And she smiled. A real smile at last, bleak enough, but friendly, and said, 'I'll write,' and this time when she turned, she walked directly off, brisk and in command of herself.

And so, that's that.

Upheavals and turmoil in the office! It's Charlie. If he were not such a passenger ... but he's always been one, and it's only because there is a crisis that it matters. There is an empty space where Charlie ought to be. Phyllis at home, and Charlie does not come into work. Jill and I do everything. We get it done, borrowing people from all the other departments, but it's mad.

I rang up Charlie today and said, 'I know you are editor, Charlie, but I swear I'll give you the sack if you don't come and *work*.'

'Oh, everybody knows who runs *Lilith*,' said he, comfortably. In the background I could hear a baby cry. 'Can you hear Caroline?' he inquired. 'What a pair of lungs!'

'Charlie, it's not *on*.'

A silence. 'Jane, very well. I'll take leave.'

'You can't abandon us like this.'

'Are you coping or aren't you?'

'That isn't the point.'

'It is my point. As far as I am concerned, this is what is important.'

'When one of your wives has a baby?'

'Now, now, now,' says Charlie. Avuncular.

'Supposing I said to you, The most important thing has happened to me I can ever remember. I need to be free to meet this man . . . *Lilith* can go hang.'

'Are you saying that Janna? Good for you.' And he rings off.

Jill listening to all this, smiles. 'I don't think that at my tender age I can be expected to run *Lilith* single-handed.'

'Have I said you should? Not that you couldn't.'

'Because what you have forgotten is that there is this meeting of the Fashion Syndicates in Amsterdam next week.'

'Oh *no*, yes I had forgotten. Well, I can't go.'

'Has *Lilith* ever not been represented?'

'No.'

Jill and I sat, stymied. We were also laughing, it was a kind of elation.

'Oh,' I said, 'you can go!'

'No, I can't go. Charlie could go. Phyllis could go. But I can't. I haven't the experience. You know that.'

'Yes.'

'But it is all utterly impossible.' I waited. And what I meant was that I should have to go to Amsterdam for the meeting but not with Richard.

'The person we must talk to is Phyllis,' said Jill. 'She'll get Charlie back to work.'

And so Jill talked to Phyllis, and Phyllis talked to Charlie, and I am going to Amsterdam. For four days.

I went into the Jackdaw at lunchtime, coming in out of warm splashy summer rain, and saw Richard sitting at a table against the wall. He was listening to a young man who was leaning forward, talking earnestly. Something about Richard, the way he sat, considering and considerate, his thoughtfulness, the way he was examining this youth, taking everything in, made it come into my mind: Richard is a doctor.

I saw I should not interrupt this consultation, any more than I could in a doctor's rooms, and sat down at a near table to wait. Richard smiled at me, with a small grimace. The youth did not see this: he was too absorbed in his ills. There was a discouraged look to him, and he was tearing off chunks of bread from a pub sandwich, and cramming them into his mouth, chewing as he talked. He was hungry, I thought, and wondered, Unemployed? A junkie? Perhaps he is trying to touch Richard for a pound or two.

He went off in an effusion of thanks, and I joined Richard.

'Unemployed,' he said. 'He can't pay his electricity bill. His wife has just had a baby. Their second. She's been ill. He has bronchitis and a rash that looks to me like the beginnings of erysipelas. His baby has a cough.'

'You are a doctor,' I announced.

'Yes. And reality is breaking in everywhere, no matter how hard I try to exclude it. My mother does not like the Home I found, and I must try to find another.'

The Jackdaw is old-fashioned, and has dark brown panelled walls in which the lights gleam, and a dark red carpet. It is like a chocolate womb, full of warmth and comfort. It was full. It is always full. On hot days it is a cool cave. It may be the middle of June, but coolness was the last thing anyone was in search of today.

I had on my white cardigan. This morning when I dressed I thought of Joyce's 'plump and pretty'. Size 16.

Richard said, 'You look like a meringue, always my favourite food,' and I decided to hell with Joyce.

'As a doctor you should be against them.'

'A little of what you fancy does you good. Solomon himself must have said it. I have it done like a Victorian sampler, very pretty it is, and it hangs behind me on the wall in the consulting room. When I hand out diet sheets it is written at the top: A *little* of what you fancy does you good.' He sounded offhand, almost brusque, as he does sometimes when he is very serious and does not, perhaps, want to be. 'Advice which you and I are perhaps following too strictly, Janna?'

Knowing what I had to tell him, I put it all off, wanting to enjoy this hour, lunchtime at the Jackdaw, and he and I, sitting together at a small table, with all around us people standing, the lively noisy crowd. Good-natured. A lot of laughter. Somewhere among them presumably, though we could not see him, was that one among three million casualties of the Depression.

'Quite soon we'll know everything about each other.'

I said, 'Reality does keep breaking in.'

'I picked up a paperback of *Milliners of Marylebone,* and I read it last night. How do you come to know so much about all that?'

'There was an old woman I used to know. Her name was Maudie Fowler. She died aged over ninety. Furious.'

'Ah. I recognize that.'

'I knew another about the same time. Very old. And she was furious. Is your mother angry? If so, I wish you'd explain it to me. Because when my time comes, I propose to avoid that one. To watch aged crones angry because they are dying is not the most heartening experience.'

'My mother is not angry at being old. But she does not like being patronized. I said to the staff, "To be old does not mean to be half-witted." At least, not in my mother's case. But I am not *their* doctor. I am in the role of customer. I called the doctor in charge of the Home as a colleague and said, "Is it possible to do something about the staff's manner to the patients?" He said, "Dr Curtis, you said? We have not had any complaints about our treatment of the residents."'

'They can't afford to complain,' I said. 'They are too dependent on others' goodwill. And of course they have to be patronized. The very old are too frightening, too much of a threat, we can't stand it, *mementoes mori,* one and all, so they have to be dear little children. For our sakes. And I'll have another whisky.'

He reached up past someone, put our two glasses on the bar counter and signalled to the barman.

'Am I to take it you are or have been a doctor among your many specialities? No? A nurse? No. A social worker? No.'

I had been shaking my head, at more than being expected to answer. 'Yes, you are right. But, Janna, at the moment you are like one of those pictures children get: they look quite blank, like empty paper, then you start shading them with a pencil and a picture starts forming. My picture of you is half shaded in. Well, if we spend a week together, who knows what we'll find out.'

Again I slide away from it. He reached down the whiskies.

'I've been thinking,' I said. 'When a young person gets married, there's not much to them, is there? No wonder they find it all so easy. I, John, take Mary. I, Mary, take John. And they are both all there to be taken. Well, more or less. But people of our age, it's like two continents in collision.'

He said, very dry, with the rough edge of his voice that both thrills me and makes me fear him, 'And were *you* all there to be taken?'

I faced him steadily, though I knew I was blushing, 'I know why you say that, and you are right. But I was over thirty when I married. And Fred was forty. We weren't a couple of children.'

'I was nineteen when I married. I was all there to be taken.'

'And you weren't?'

'No.'

'You've been married to the same woman all that time?'

'Thirty-five years, more or less.'

I felt this literally as a blow to the heart. It hurt. I could feel how I must be pale, where I had been hot and uncomfortable a moment before. Suddenly the whole thing—I there with him, this man who had lived with one woman thirty-five years, *thirty-five years*—seemed paltry and ridiculous. And for some reason these dreams I have every night, of Freddie, seemed very close, the atmosphere of them, lost, sad, bleak. Last night I dreamed of us two, Freddie and I, on some chalky, low, pale shore, with sea birds crying overhead. The cries of the swooping birds sounded in my heart and woke me.

'I told you,' he said, in a low, quick, unhappy voice, 'I told you we should leave it all alone. Why *do* we . . . We simply should not talk about anything of the kind.'

I was crying.

'I do cry a lot these days,' I said. 'Take no notice. You'd not believe that normally I never cry. If I find myself crying, my first impulse is to check my digestion.'

'Drink up.' He swallowed his Scotch, put mine into my hand, I drank it, and he pulled me up and we went out of that pub into the Marylebone Road. High up above the city a periwinkle-blue sky accommodated some lively clouds in grey and mauve, and everything about us glistened and sparkled. At a flower stall he bought an armful of yellow roses, and we went on together to the corner.

'Well,' he said, stopping me there, and facing me so that we stood with the flowers pressed between us. 'Are we to go to Paris? Edinburgh? Munich? You say where.'

I said, 'Next week I have to go for four days to Amsterdam. For a meeting of the International Fashion Syndicate.' I could not look at him, and then I did. He was incredulous . . . angry . . . even violent. He stepped back, suddenly, letting go my arms, and the yellow roses fell on to the pavement.

'I have to. I have to.'

'It's your work,' he said, and now he sounded quite wild, and even uncoordinated, as if he had been knocked hard, mid-centre. I had known he would be disappointed. I felt miserable myself. But this reaction was past anything I expected.

'Richard,' I pleaded.

I saw him as sharply as I did the first time, this quick, vigorous man, who seemed to have more energy in him than fifty normal people: but all this was directed against me now, and I knew he could have killed me.

Then he held himself in, his shoulders took on his characteristic hunched look, and I thought, Have *I* become a burden that he has to assume and bear?

'And now you have to go back to the office,' he said steadily.

'Yes, I do.'

He nodded, very distant from me now. He said, almost abstracted, 'I'll ring you, Janna. I'll ring you tomorrow.' And he strode off as a summer shower came splashing down through sunlight, and people looked up and around and laughed at it and at each other.

I went back to the office, and Jill said: 'The path of true love.'

Today, as the telephone rang and rang, each time I hoped to hear his voice, but it wasn't him; and it was not until nearly six that he rang, when I was leaving. He sounded distant, but it was because, I knew, of some kind of restraint or discipline.

'Janna,' he said, 'when did you say you were coming back from Amsterdam?'

I told him, Thursday.

He was quiet for a moment, thinking, then said, 'Very well. I have to go up to Hull again to move my mother, and settle her in, but if I'm going to be free when you get back, I must go now. So—I won't see you till next Friday.'

With anyone else this would be some kind of tit-for-tat: you are going away, so I'm exacting due measure; but not Richard. I realized, standing there holding the receiver with one hand, my other holding my handbag and work to take home as if I were already off to Amsterdam, that I knew how this man's mind had been working, could follow his thoughts stage by stage. Leaving me on the wet pavement with the roses scattered all about, he had said to himself, 'That's it, it's not worth it. I'm going to walk away from the situation for good.' Then he had felt the chill of loss, and thought, Be fair, it *is* her work. Then, this thought bringing with it the weight of associations with something very heavy in his life that I can only surmise—his wife does not love him? They stay together because of their child (or children? Kathleen is not the only one?)—he thought again, No, it is all too much, I *shall* tell her I can't go on with it. But remembered that when we are together it is truly as if we are the separated halves of some whole that has been unjustly severed, remembered all the good; and so thought carefully how he would arrange his comings and goings to fit in with my going and coming back; and yet the thinking, the arranging, had an all too familiar feeling of duty to it. Yet again—he thought, as he said to himself, Yes, if I do this and that I can be back to be with Janna on Friday—yet again I am fitting myself in, and adjusting, and taming myself and *scaling myself down*. If he did not think this last, sensing himself as something splendid, caged and held in restraint, then I did. How we are when we are together must surely have added, as it has to me, to his knowing how much potential we have we do not use. I would never, before Richard, have believed that merely to be with one other person could bring into being areas of oneself; like the pictures he talked about that children bring into being by rubbing a pencil over them. Surely, for him as for me, what we are together makes palpable a fact: that we live at half pressure, while all around the small lit stage that we move about on in strict determined patterns surges and beats, but is held back from us, the energy of delight, of joy. I know that when he has said, No, it is not worth it, he has only to remember what happens when we meet; I know this because I am the same. Sometimes I have thought, No, enough, the strain is too much. But what I want to put an end to is Freddie! I have been waking in the mornings from these dreams of him, thinking, When Richard comes to an end (it is extraordinary, I suppose, that I have never questioned it must come to an end), then perhaps Freddie will go away. What do I mean by that? That Richard is an aspect of Freddie, or Freddie of him? Richard gone, Freddie will sink accommodatingly back into oblivion?

Is this remorse? If so, I don't see the point of it! Given what I was when I married, and what I was all the time I was married, then that was what I had to be, with Freddie. To say I should have been this or that is feeble. And I am not at all convinced I should have been something else. I don't even now know what Freddie was, in himself, not really. This Freddie I dream about: did he exist? Who is this courteous ghost who stands there, slightly bowed, looking at me, not to remind me of something but to state a fact: that he *is* there. He is there, and I should be with him, or going towards him, but then he is not there, or is wandering away, or I nearly reach him but cannot. When I think of Freddie, it is true that it is restraint, a holding-back, that I see, or sense in him. And I know I was not what he wanted.

But how much of all this am I making up? Richard has

said, Janna, are we inventing this? Am I to sit down and bring back into my mind the years of my being married to Freddie? Make myself remember? What for? To say, finally, I should have been this or that? To what purpose?

When Richard goes . . . but why should I keep saying that? I don't know what he is doing here, assume it is some sort of long leave. For all I know his marriage has broken up; no, I don't think it has. Why should Richard and I not marry? Or live together? The thing is impossible, that's why. *Why is it*? He has been married for thirty-five years to one woman. Who wasn't me. And because Freddie with whom I was married for twelve years haunts my sleep, is on the wings of my stage, unsatisfied. It is not Richard I ever dream of . . . no, all this is too much. I don't understand it, and I shall go to sleep. It is long after midnight, and I have too much work to get through tomorrow. Kate is asleep in the sofa, still plugged into her private concert. What can it possibly be doing to her brain, let alone her ears? I can see her facial muscles move and twitch, tugged by the music.

Today Charlie returned to us, with carefully measured petulance, just a little cat's claw of spite, that reminds us all—as if we needed it—that affability is not all there is to Charlie. He said no, he would not interview Hannah from Production, I could do it.

Hannah will join Editorial. I have been thinking of her as a pleasant and obliging girl, with a taste for bizarre clothes that made one often look at her more than twice. When I had her sitting opposite me this morning I wondered at my laziness: I have simply not been paying attention. The reason why one was aware of her, had to look at her, was because her personality was too large for her job. It demands more scope. She is formidable. Like one of Picasso's monumental seaside women, you imagine her bounding along a shore, hair afloat in a balmy breeze, dark brown limbs agape, hands star-fished up towards a striped beach-ball that is somewhere at the level of the sun. She has dark doe eyes, black glittering hair. She comes from many-fathered Liverpool. De Loch. I wonder where that name originated?

Hannah de Loch seemed not surprised that I offered her this very good job, with such prospects, seemed, even, unimpressed. She said yes, she wouldn't mind having a try, but she likes working in Production too. As if the really remarkable difference in salary was not an issue. I asked myself my private question for such occasions: *Has she got the cutting edge*? Then Hannah makes me put another: *Very well then, what do I mean by that*? She is one of the people who make you define yourself.

Hannah has a desk in with Jill and me, and will be working with Jill from now on. I shall move back with Charlie, to keep him up to scratch, as Jill remarks, without acidity, stating the case.

Charlie says Phyllis will not be coming back to *Lilith* after three months, leaving the baby with a nanny. Charlie is blossoming, is in the state not far off that which Richard and I are in when together. He cannot stop smiling; he is half the time on the telephone with chums and cronies, telling them about the baby, Phyllis's ups and downs of health, the milk supply, and their disturbed nights of which he is clearly very proud and in which he takes his share of responsibility. He buzzes from his room to summon Jill, Hannah, Mark, June, me, or a typist or a photographer—anyone who will share his pleasure. And we all do. We do not know if it is Charlie who cannot bear for Phyllis to lose the full benefits of mother-hood, or Phyllis, for we have not seen her alone. A brief telephone call to her unfortunately coincided with baby's feed, and she said, 'It's a drag, Janna, I know, but I think I'll stay home for at least six months. After all, I do want to breast-feed.' This was news to me, but if Charlie can't breast-feed, then Phyllis must; we do all see that.

I sat opposite Charlie this afternoon, with a lot of things prepared to discuss with him, decisions that if he doesn't actually take he should know about, and listened to him talking about fatherhood.

Large and expansive, affable and generous, this good soul, our Charlie, editor. of a first-class women's magazine devoted, to judge by its appearance at least, solely to glamour, says to me, 'Janna, this is my fourth, and God forgive me the best! I know you shouldn't like one more than another, and in a sense I don't, they are *miracles*, I simply can't believe it, how utterly amazing and marvellous each baby is, each in its own way. But this one, there's something about her . . . perhaps it is because of Phyllis, and the way I feel about her . . . it is not that I didn't love my first wife, I did, she is a good person and all that kind of thing, and I hope we'll never be less than the best of friends—but Phyllis is something else. Do you know what I mean, Janna? Yes, I am sure you do, a little bird has told me, I hope you won't mind my saying this, that something lovely has happened to you too—don't mind, *please*, I am so happy for you. But there is such a thing as something that is *meant*, and that is what Phyllis is for me. And so I know you understand. When little Caroline was born—although I had seen it all three times before and every time it was just the most *perfect* thing— when this little being appeared, and they put a towel round her and put her *straight* into my arms, because I am afraid poor Phyllis was not with us just at that moment, she opened her eyes and looked at me. She wasn't crying or shocked or anything like that—I know now because after all Caroline is my fourth. And my heart gave way. Do you know what I mean? There she was, this little scrap, still a bit bloody from her ordeal, and she looked straight up at me. She has wonderful dark blue eyes. Deep deep blue eyes. Like dear Phyllis. It was a moment of *recognition*. I swear it. I was so *moved*, I couldn't speak. I had been crying like a baby girl anyway while she was making her appearance, because of Phyllis—she had a bad time, you know, and I'm not at all persuaded about this damned induction business, they *will* use it—and because I get so excited waiting for the moment of truth, the actual moment the baby pops forth, all new-minted, into this wicked world. And I sat there, crying my eyes out, holding the little thing, and I swear I fell in love with her at that moment.'

Tea appeared, in the Wedgwood Charlie insisted on buying for the office. A chocolate cake. Ever since Caroline was born

Lilith has been awash with champagne, sweets, and cake from the Swiss *pâtisserie* at the corner. June ran out to get the cake, and on an impulse got flowers for Charlie at the same time. When she brought them in she was shy, elated, blushing, delighted. Charlie was delighted. Everyone is delighted. If I know nothing else it is that there are going to be weddings or at least pairings through all the departments of *Lilith*. The whole place is broody. There is an atmosphere of secret, wicked delight; and people smile for no particular reason. All this is the doing of not Caroline, but Charlie, *Lilith*'s editor.

Charlie sat in his great chair, in the sombre elegance of the editor's office, all dark red leather and teak panelling, and poured tea and cut cake and smiled and said, 'I cannot understand how any man would not insist on being in on it all. It is absolutely the most exciting thing that ever happens. Oh, I'm not saying sex isn't wonderful, but after all, compared to a new human being just appearing "out of the everywhere into the here"—isn't that how it goes?—well, I am afraid I know what takes second place. And how girls can want to get back to work as fast as possible, leaving all that fun to a nurse. I don't understand that either.'

I listened to all this, feeling horribly excluded from it, refrained from chocolate cake, and drank Charlie's (for he brings it in) Orange Pekoe tea. What I wanted to know, boringly practical as I am, is about finance. If Phyllis is not going to work, who is going to pay for everything? They need the two salaries because of his alimony, which takes every penny of his salary for educating his other children.

But how to introduce these sordid thoughts? And quite apart from money, how about Phyllis herself? When I think of Phyllis, what she was when she started in Editorial, this sharp, needy, ambitious girl, clever as a cat, always on the lookout for advantage, and think of her only four years, is it? five? years later, someone who will willingly stay at home with a baby, with an uxorious husband. Is there such a word as uxor? There ought to be. There is no word in the dictionary for an excessively fond father. Charlie is a fondly paternal uxor married to one of the most coldly ambitious and clever and competent girls I have ever known. And I have been watching clever and competent girls flowing through *Lilith,* often of course on their way to being married, for thirty-five years. Since I started work in these offices. (While I have worked in *Lilith,* my Richard has been married to—his wife.)

But Phyllis may have changed. People change. I have changed.

Listening to Charlie prattling away about how he feels in the middle of the night when he hears Caroline wake, I feel rather as I do in these dreams (these *dreams*) I have. 'We never let her cry, Janna, we simply cannot bear it. Why should she have to cry for something she needs, like a clean nappy?' And he goes to her, because he wants Phyllis to have her share of rest, and there is the infant in her little nest. 'I see her smiling up at me. Yes, I know *they* say babies are not supposed to smile for weeks, but they do talk the most amazing rubbish. She knows me at once, and she lies there gazing up, quite still, with those wonderful deep eyes, not like baby eyes at all, really Janna, but a human being's eyes. I stand looking down, and I do feel such an immense height and size, I can't tell you how crude and awful I feel, trying to see me from her point of view, the tiny thing, looking up. And then when I pick her up, very gently, because she's such a little princess, and I hate to think of her feeling *whisked* up—you know how you see mothers grab up quite tiny infants sometimes, the poor mites can hardly keep their breaths, they gasp and struggle for balance—well, I just gently scoop her up, in her little blanket, and put her on her table where she is put to be changed, and we have this little lovely intimacy going on, in the middle of the night. And I look forward to it. I don't know why people complain at being disturbed by their babies. Not that she cries. It is a privilege, that's what I feel. I adore it. And Phyllis does too, I am sure of it. Sometimes there is even a little competition at four in the morning, about who is going to change Caroline.'

I was sitting there, with the tears running. I had my back to the tall windows, and it took some time for him to notice, he was so absorbed. I had been planning to make an excuse and go out, but my voice was too unsteady to use. Then he was up in a bound and he had his arms about me. 'Oh, Janna, don't, don't, I am so sorry. Of course, I had forgotten, you haven't had children, oh poor poor Janna, I am so sorry, how awful of me.'

And he was off to his store of goodies, and in a moment I had a cognac sitting there in front of me, and a little packet of tissues, and he had his arm around me coaxing me back to normality. 'We are all so used to you, dear Janna, always so cheerful and sensible and *perfect*—and that's why we exploit you. Yes, I see it now. We take it all for granted.'

I swear he could have said, 'And now, *blow*. . .' holding a tissue to my delinquent nose. But how could he have been more kind?

And how can Phyllis stand it? I went back into our office, where sat Jill and Hannah working away—Jill, aged twenty-two, directing Hannah, who is ten years her senior and makes no claims on that account—and I had red eyes and did not care.

'It's got to you, has it?' said Jill carelessly. 'Well, he had me crying like a baby yesterday.'

'And me,' said Hannah.

'This is an *office*,' announced Jill, like a scandalized schoolgirl, trying out how it sounds. 'An *office*.'

'Offices are very peculiar places,' agreed Hannah, in her amiable indifferent way, working at her pace, which is that nothing seems to happen but everything gets done. While Jill works in a whirl and everything gets done.

'I suppose Phyllis will come back some time?' said Jill jealously.

Hannah said, 'Perhaps she won't.'

'Of course she'll come back,' I heard myself protesting—threatened.

'Not if he has his way,' said Hannah.

Jill and I found ourselves looking at this new colleague of ours with respect. She is a large young woman, dark, even swarthy, her straight black hair worn to the shoulders with a fringe. She is handsome, like a tamed young Indian from a jungle. She is full of eighteen-carat femininity, which enables her to judge matters of the emotions with authority.

'If Phyllis is going to come back to work, then she'll have to fight every inch of the way,' said she.

'But,' I said, 'luckily, there is a financial problem.'

Jill said to me today, 'Are you going to leave Kate in your flat for four days? Without a baby-sitter?'

'What else can I do?'

Leaving Kate is bad, but what *can* I do? Mrs Penny, my dreaded neighbour, has succumbed to senility and has gone into a Home. Irony! I would be pleased to have her here now, so as to say, 'Would you keep an eye on my niece? You know what these young things are.' I cannot say to my new neighbours, a successful, busy, energetic young couple, the Jefferies, 'Please keep an eye on my poor niece. She's a bit of a derelict, you know.' I can ask them to get in a plumber, or keep an extra key. 'What is wrong with your niece?' I imagine. 'Oh, nothing much, apart from being an infant in adult guise. I'm afraid she may leave the bath taps running all night or start a fire.' This set off an interesting train of thought: who you can ask to do what. The number of people is limited to whom you can say, 'I know it's a drag, but she's not crazy really, she simply hasn't jelled! You need to treat her like a child but talk to her as an adult, so as she can develop some self-respect, don't you know!' It's a question of what one has experienced.

What I am really afraid of is that Kate will ask in some of her friends from the squat she admires. 'Oh, my aunt won't mind, just help yourself.' I believe she wanders down there sometimes in the afternoons, and I am even pleased. I have told her I am going, given her a calendar with the dates marked in bright red, said that she is not to have people in here, I would not stand for it. 'Oh, Aunt Jane, you are so horrible,' she wailed, predictably. But she seemed to brighten really, as if she was pleased this ukase has been issued. This made me wonder if her squat friends had put pressure on her to let them into her rich and reactionary aunt's flat, and she had found it hard to refuse. There are squats and squats. I made inquiries about the one she has made her second home, and it is a haunt of drug pushers and petty criminals. I came in unexpectedly once from the office, and found Kate dressed up in an evening dress I have for glad-rag occasions. Kate was standing in front of the glass, her orphan much-dyed locks, pale green at the moment, were brushed straight up, like rough green flames, her face made up like Dracula's. I saw that she probably visualizes herself as a gangster's girl.

A career, of sorts, I suppose.

A worse problem than Kate is poor old Annie. I have been in as usual, two or three times a week, and sat with her. It is always late, about seven, before going home. But last weekend I was there on both Saturday and Sunday. Since the Cuts, old people who are not actually crippled do not have Home Helps on the weekend. Her wonderful Home Help, Bridget, is for some reason allocated elsewhere. Her new one, Maureen, is a nasty piece of work, but who would know it from meeting her? For at first you are reassured by her: as she means you to be. She has been working as a Home Help for some years. A large, jolly woman, in her mid-thirties, she has her hair cut short all over her head in black curls, she has a pudgy baby-face and pudgy little white hands (with bright pink nails) that dart about like little white rats. She comes in for a few minutes, instead of the time she is paid for, might not come in at all, forgets what Annie needs, but presents herself always as very busy (true), kind-hearted, overworked (true), devoted to her charges. She has taken the trouble to make friends with Vera, her superior, who thinks she is wonderful. And in times of crisis she is there, working like a horse, thinking of everything.

She is also a thief, helping herself to Annie's pension. I know what ought to be in Annie's purse, for I keep an eye on it. This Maureen, from Belfast, is in sole control of what gets given to Annie and what gets spent. It is she who collects the pension and who buys everything, and pays electricity and gas bills and the rent. She who explains to the Services that Annie needs extra for this or that. I reckon that about ten pounds a week goes into Maureen's budget from Annie's, and since she deals with four or five other people apart from Annie, this would add up to quite a bit.

Maureen, all amiability and flurries of competence in between nice sit-downs when we—she and I and Annie—sit around drinking tea, greets me as if I were her best friend as well as Annie's; but a few months ago, when I was sitting there, having emptied Annie's commode and made her bed and brought her some groceries because Maureen had not come and Annie was afraid of being left unhelped, Maureen did come in. She was very pleased I had done her work; for she was tired. She has four children, a husband who is not in the best of health, and she does indeed work very hard. But I had been asking Annie about the money in her handbag, and Annie had told Maureen, and now Maureen, standing with her back to me as she fussed about cutting Annie a sandwich, said in a low voice, 'I am afraid of you.' Here it was again, the other voice, the voice we seldom use. This was an interesting moment for a variety of reasons. There was nothing in it of our usual relationship, that of the two busy women meeting over an unfortunate old thing, to help her, taking each other's competence and expertise for granted. Nothing that we had ever said to each other before—Hello, Mrs Somers—Oh, how are you, Maureen?—Oh, fine and dandy, Mrs Somers, and I hope you are feeling yourself?—all that nonsense, could have accommodated even a hint of what lay behind Maureen's low 'I'm afraid of you.' Coming in after three or four days of *not* coming at all, realizing she had forgotten Annie's tea, or butter, or cigarettes; seeing that I had taken down and washed Annie's curtains or stood on a chair to clean her windows, she checks over Annie's money, for two reasons. One, to see if enough has accumulated for her to slip out a few more pounds for herself. Two, so that Annie might notice it and say, 'Janna was saying I should have more money than I do,' and then she can contradict it. Going home she broods, probably vindictively, or fearfully about this irritating visitant from the glamorous world of the rich and successful. When Maureen was allotted Annie as her new charge, she encountered me, who on Annie's cards is marked as next-of-kin. She has heard how I have visited Annie, am Annie's friend, how I 'always' come in and 'never' miss. Alas, I, like Maureen, do miss. But Annie uses this as a spell, like magic: 'Janna never misses, she always comes in,' says Annie severely to the airily dishonest Maureen.

The story of how I met Annie in the radio shop and came home with her, and then bought her things and looked after her ever since, has become one of Annie's 'gramophone records' which I never hear, but which Maureen or Vera or someone else has to hear for the umpteenth time.

'*I am afraid of you,*' that low, just-breathed visitor from her real thoughts about me was left unremarked by me. I sat on, drinking tea. What was I to say: There is no need to be afraid of me, I won't tell?

If there really are impossible situations—and my nature refuses to accept such a thing!—then I am in one.

For one thing, I am not at all with Annie as I was with poor old Maudie, totally committed, an affair of the heart.

I know what it is to become committed to an old woman whose needs are so great that your own needs become secondary, your whole life gets swallowed up. I've done that, once; I am not sorry I did it—far from it, for I loved Maudie, and I suppose when you've used the word love, then that's it. But said to myself I wouldn't let it happen again; for after all, I like Annie but I don't love her, and I said to myself, So far and no farther. This private bargain I have made with myself means that I do not throw a nasty and even sneaky spanner in the works, such as ringing up Vera suggesting we meet, and tactfully conveying to her that her favourite Home Help is making free with the pathetic little pensions of her helpless charges. I can't, and that is all there is to it. Besides, as I sit there with Annie, knowing that yet again Maureen has not done this or that, I myself have all kinds of thoughts which can be classed as 'black market' or 'second economy' thoughts; those which all over the world in fact motivate most citizens. Who have long ago abandoned honesty as my parents would have recognized it, an absolute: 'You do *not* steal, lie, milk the rich, even if you are dying of hunger in a hovel. It is wrong.' It is because everything seems to be seizing up, going wrong; because our money, the citizens', is spent so wastefully in ways we feel we have no control over.

Maureen thinks like this. The old people's pensions are too low, are they! I know better than that! When her rent is paid and the electricity and the gas, and I've bought her little bits of food, there's five pounds left over, ten in a good week. That Somers woman will run her up a bit of a skirt if she needs it, and she gets her her vests and knickers, and there's Welfare if she's in want of a jersey. The woman upstairs from Annie said she had a pair of slippers she's not in want of. Besides, Annie's entitled to that clothing grant. I'll see she gets it, and that will make a bit extra for my Lorna when she goes to Boulogne with her school at half-term. And there's that ten pounds slipped down the side pocket of Annie's bag. She won't even notice if I slip it out. I can put down the deposit on our holiday. It's a shameful thing the way they waste the country's money on these old people. Not that I grudge them what they have to have. If Annie was in need for anything, I'd see she got it. And now there's old Mrs Baker, I'll have a word at the office about her supplementary. She's entitled to a good bit more, the way I look at it. There's no point in wasting a good opportunity of getting a little bit extra for them. All the government does is waste it anyway on their crazy ideas. If they had an ordinary working woman running things—oh, I'm not saying myself, that's not it—but someone who has had to balance the budget a bit, then we'd not have all this waste. They said in the office they were going to give me that poor old man, he's not long for this world, what's his name? Yes, Dick White. Well, I'll just make sure he's getting everything he's entitled to. If I don't put that deposit into the office before next week we won't have a holiday this year.

I was thinking this evening, as I sat drinking tea with Annie, that I was doing more or less the same as my love Richard with his mother. But I am afraid that from the perspective of Annie's little room, which is neat and nice *when* it is cleaned, but smells of old age, Richard and I, what we are, seem another world. I think of how we range around London, from Greenwich to Richmond, from Highgate to the docks, of how on a whim we go to the theatre or decide to walk ten miles; the glitter and colour of our being together—all this fades, becomes paltry and nothing. There is a cheap pinchbeck look to us, as I sit there, seeing the food stains down the front of Annie's blouse, and hear her sighing and complaining; that couple there, Janna and Richard, walking away hand in hand, that handsome pair of adventurers, for so we seem seen from that close confined room, are even an invention, only the play of two indulged people; and yet we are neither of us that, for we both work so hard; and putting myself back, in my mind, into that woman there, Jane Somers, walking across a field on Hampstead Heath, beside Richard, the sun on their backs: for I was choosing to remember that wonderful week of summer which seems such a long time past—I feel in a sudden amazing surge of love and happiness the truth of being with Richard. Which can best be expressed, quite simply, thus: There is nothing we could not say to each other, as if our two lives, running for so long invisibly to the other and coming together so improbably in that comic little accident on Tottenham Court Road underground, carried along with them a rich cargo that had been invisible, too, to ourselves, like rivers whose depths know nothing about the baulks of good timber, green boughs from some far-off flood in the mountains, packing cases that have who knows what things in them—silks? books? special scented teas from North India? a consignment of rare plants from some jungle destined for a garden in northern Europe?—seventeen disconsolate chickens sitting on a bucking and rearing log, a drowned horse, and the light worn bones of an ancient dinosaur that has been washed off some eroding hillside. All these things, carried along so far by the flood, swirl into a side-reach of the river, toss a little, and subside in brown froth on a beach of white sand whose river waves run past in a normal season smooth and orderly, each modestly crested with white.

*   *   *

I wanted so much today to be able to ring Richard, that's all, only to hear his voice and say, Next Friday, we will meet. Next Friday, it's only five days away, well, you could call it six. . . He has my two telephone numbers, but I do not have his.

If I did have his home number—if it is not a hotel he is at, for he did say that his own home was let—who would I get, with Richard, presumably already departed up to Hull? Kathleen, that sombre presence? Should I say, oh, this is Jane Somers, you know, we have *almost* met so often.

Usually I love getting ready for these jaunts abroad to dress shows, conferences, or with a team of Photography to get pictures of some special shop or place or person. I adore it all, everything, from the packing of my clothes which give me so much pleasure, to the business of actually getting processed on to the plane, and then the plane, and the pleasant hotels I go to, for I know now where all the real hotels are everywhere in Europe. What fun I do get from all this. And as I write I remember I cried out to Richard once that what I had excluded from my life was pleasure, I had worked too hard. And it is not true. My days are full of pleasure, delights, little treats, listening to the amazing exchanges between people on London's pavements, so surreal and suggestive of hidden continents of experience, looking at people in restaurants, buses, shops . . . but today I feel no pleasure at all. Leaving England is leaving Richard.

A Day in the Life of a Derelict Girl.

She wakes in the dark, her stomach sour, her heart painful, and it is as if she is being pounded and wrenched by powerful waves. The waves are sound, a thud of rhythm. She feels caged by them, assaulted, and scrambles up away, feels pain in her ears and remembers: she tugs out the plugs and sits stunned, bereft, in the silence of deafness: her ears are ringing. Where is she? It takes some time for her to realize that she is sitting on the edge of the sofa where she has fallen asleep. A vast resentment possesses her as she thinks that Janna did not wake her, detach her from the machine, take her to bed. She does not think, Janna is this or that, but the resentment she feels *is* Janna, just as, until she came to live here, the resentment she lived with *was* her family, her parents. Now, with bitter and vindictive thoughts raging, she totters up to the light switch and makes the room spring into being. She is looking around for signs of Janna and thinks, seeing its emptiness, that Janna has gone off to her room. She has got chilly and stiff. She thinks, Shall I have a bath to warm up? She runs a bath, as she sits vacant on its edge, her eyes held by the spume of bubbles under the taps. She even smiles a little, like a small child, because of the pretty bubbles. Then she loses interest, because sitting in the warm steam has livened her, and she wanders off to her bed. As she collapses she remembers the water is running; thinks, Well, let it run, but does get up, and turns it off, or nearly: the hot tap is trickling as she staggers back to the bed, and flings herself dressed under the duvet. She lies for a long time, quite straight, stiff with a kind of apprehension, the lights beating on her face. She thinks, Janna will come and turn them off; then remembers Janna is in bed; then, that Janna is not here, but in Amsterdam.

She sits up straight, in a surge of anger. She is all alone in this flat, abandoned. With this thought comes some relief from the tension, the apprehension, which is in fact connected with Janna, who, she knows, seldom approves of her or anything she does. For four days, she thinks, she will be free of that critical presence. She sighs and relaxes, feels the light dazzle on her lashes, just manages to get up and turn it off, and collapses back into bed. She sleeps very soundly while the morning comes, and she wakes in full day, with the birds noisy in the tree outside. She wakes with an apprehension of pleasure; wonders what it is she is expecting, remembers it is that she will be alone. Her frank sigh of relief sounds like contentment. She thinks, And I'll get up and make myself some breakfast, and I won't have to be worrying all the time what *she* is thinking. She lounges around under the covers, savouring her freedom, then gets up, and sees from the clock by her bed that it is not yet five. But it is much too early to get up, she says indignantly, as if she has been cheated or hoodwinked by the early summer light, and she goes back to sleep. She does not wake until ten or so, and this time she is heavy and flaccid. She sleeps again, wakes at midday, and again lies for some time, thinking that it won't be long until Janna comes in at six and makes her some supper.

Again she remembers Janna is away, and this time there is no pleasure in it. Four days she thinks, dismally. At last she drags herself up, thinking that she will have a hot bath, but the trickle of water from the hot tap running for hours has drained the tank. The cold water makes her shudder, so she does not wash, but goes in the dress she has worn now for four days to the kitchen, where she looks into the fridge, where she expects to see butter, eggs, bacon, and an assortment of cheeses. They are all there, for when have they not been there? All her life she has opened refrigerators knowing that the shelves will be full. She checks jealously, Is there enough here till Janna comes back?—for she plans not to leave the flat at all, but to stay here timeless, unpressured, free. She starts off by being hungry, but cannot be bothered to cook anything, and eats bread and strawberry jam and drinks very strong tea.

Then she wanders around a little, looking in the bedroom which looks as if no one has ever been in it, so neat and tidy is it, with the square brass-framed bed in its thick folded white, the cushions just so. Kate stands there looking in for some time, for nearly every morning when Janna has gone she does this, and what she thinks first, in a sort of panic, is: How can anyone keep a room as neat as this, there's *nothing* out of place. From this grows a fantasy of her own room, the one she will have, which is far from being like Janna's, all white and yellow, clear bright colours, but is like a dark luxurious cave seen in some magazine, of a hundred different textures and stuffs, all in sombre rich colours, an essence of a thousand paisley shawls, every inch of the room clothed, ceilings, walls, floor; and the bed is loaded with dark intricate cushions among which Kate, unvisualized but strongly felt, lolls. She is far from alone in this room; she never imagines a man in it, or a girl alone, but a group of loving friends, whom she allows in, but on her terms: they resemble her friends from the squat, but these, to use the jargon of Janna's trade, while remaining themselves, free and freewheeling spirits, owing allegiance to no petty Caesar or censor or censure, have taken several giant steps upmarket, are rich jetsetting youth with the world their oyster, Hong Kong one day, Buenos Aires the next. In this room like a Victorian pasha's den, Kate spends a lot of her time, while she is in actual fact trying on Janna's clothes, so that as she stands looking in the long mirror, an unformed girl who might be eleven wearing one of Janna's outfits, she certainly does not see what is there, but something resembling a photograph from *Lilith,* and her unkempt spikes of hair, green, pink or blue, are those of some preposterous beauty pouting in self-mockery at the public.

Today she decides not to try on anything, though she checks to see what Janna has taken. Very little seems to be missing: Janna's cream linen suit, which Kate adores as she might some fabulous being like a film star, for ever beyond her: how *can* anyone wear that all day and take it off in the evening without a crease or a stain? (When Kate tried out her fantasies in it, and took it off after an hour, there were stains from her chocolate bar all down the skirt, and she had to run out to the one-hour cleaner's at the corner with it, hoping that Janna would not ever know.) What else? A pale blue *crêpe de Chine* suit. Kate does not care for this, even more because Janna looks so well in it. It makes her feel diminished, that suit, which apart from anything else has rows of minute tucks in the lining that no one would ever see except for Janna herself—a revelation of secret perverse enjoyments, these tucks seem to Kate; and she had entertained the members of the squat with them: 'Where no one would ever *see* them!' she had exclaimed, virtuously, but felt as if she had missed a trick or two when Brian, the squat's leader, said vulgarly, 'No one but her lover.' When Brian said this, emotions rioted all over her, even while she felt stupid. She imagined Janna taking off that slinky little jacket and laying it over the arm of a chair, deliberately exposing on one side only the little field of tucks that ran from below the breast to the bottom of the jacket.

Janna had taken too a creamy silk shirt that has very fine brown stripes, so that if you turn it this way and that it glistens like pale toffee. And a cotton T-shirt, sleeveless, in cherry pink. And a jersey dress in pale grey. Kate is affronted when she realizes that was all Janna had taken: herself, she could not imagine going off for four days, and on such a posh trip too, with fashion experts and models (Kate supposes), unless she took suitcases crammed with everything she had, just in case. Kate checks on the underclothes that are not there: remembers that she secretly removed a pair of knickers in pink and coffee last week, which she wore herself all one day, meaning to put them back. Where were they? Kate stands chewing her fingernails in a panic. Where can she have put those knickers? Janna would *kill* her. Shame engulfs her: she still has them on. Of course, for she hasn't got around to changing.

It is the dead middle of the day, one o'clock, and the sunlight is filling the sky, for the rain has gone away as if it has never rained in London and never will.

Kate pulls a chair to the window in Janna's bedroom, and gazes down into the street. She sees herself down there, dressed in Janna's cream suit. She walks with negligent charm to the corner, swings on to a bus acknowledging the admiring glances of a group of young people sitting just inside. They long to be like her, so cool and elegant; but do not dare to address her. She gets off the bus at Baker Street and walks at her leisure down to Upper Regent Street, where, being late, she takes a taxi to *Lilith*, and she walks through offices smiling, being greeted by everyone; and when she reaches the office she shares with Jill, her sister cries, 'Oh, Kate, I've been waiting for you, what shall I do about. . .' Kate advises Jill what to do, and then goes out to lunch at a restaurant with three famous models. One of them says to her, 'Kate, you are wasting yourself! You should be a model. Only the other day I heard someone say, What a pity, Kate would be perfect for this type of clothes.' 'Who was that?' asks Kate, and hears, as she expects, 'Mark. Mark was talking about you.' Kate has known, of course, that Mark admires her, and that she has only to say the word... But now she says, 'Well, I don't mind trying it out for a week or so.' 'Oh, super,' says Olivia, the red-haired model, 'I'll arrange an appointment for you with the agency...'

This fantasy occupies Kate for some hours. She has dreamed it all so often that it is like a book that one may open anywhere and read on. It is detailed and intricate, so that she knows what the young people on the bus are like, what they are wearing, can smell the sharp stuffy air of the bus, knowing that as she is walking down Wigmore Street there is a quick flurry of raindrops so that she must step in off the street to a florist's, where the girl who has watched her so often walk down that street, presses on her a single pink rose, her eyes shining with secret admiration. She knows how, after the office, she will say to Jill, 'No, it is sweet of you to ask, but I have another engagement,' and she is off to meet the woman who runs the modelling agency, who says, 'Kate, I don't often say this, unfortunately, but you are—simply—a natural. Born for it!'

Kate finds she is hungry. Her stomach rages. Again she pokes her head down to inspect even the deepest corners of the fridge, but does not see what she yearns for, something like a whole basin of sweet custard, or a cake full of jam and cream. Though earlier she had been comforted to think she need not go out, now she runs down into the street and to the corner shop, where she buys a dozen Mars Bars, six giant packs of potato crisps and some samosas. As she gets back into the flat she hears the telephone, goes as fast as she can but it is too late. It stops as she puts out her hand. There she stands, for about five minutes, her heart beating, hoping it will ring again. She fears it is Janna, ringing to 'check'. Even more, she fears it is someone from the squat, because she knows if she says Janna is away they will insist on coming up, and even sleeping here, taking over. 'It is your duty to take everything you can get from your bourgeois relatives' is the slogan. At the same time she hopes they will ring, and then she can say, 'Can I come and visit?' When she is with these squat-mates, she is swung every minute between moods and choices. She admires them for being so independent, living their own lives on the dole, moving from one desolate house to another; admires them for their brave scorn of the police; at the same time she is afraid, for she certainly does not want to go to prison, and some of them have been in prison, and two are on parole, and there was even talk of her going with them to 'do' a sub post office in Hendon. It sounded as if they were joking, but perhaps they weren't. And then, again, she loves being with them, just to sit quietly in a corner while they talk, or play music, or smoke a bit of pot. She is quite happy there, for hours; there are no pressures on her, that is it; none of them are up to much (as she knows quite well), and there is nothing to measure up to. With them she feels nothing of that burning nagging pain somewhere near her midriff, or even in her throat, like a need to vomit, which she has felt with Jill ever since she can remember.

Perhaps it was Jill who had rung. She puts out her hand, thinking she will ring Jill: dare she? Will she? Knowing that several times before she has nearly got to the point of ringing Jill, and then failing, she now stands there wondering, *Will I?* She does: before knowing it she has dialled *Lilith* and asked for Jill. 'Hallo,' she heard her voice trailing off.

'Oh, Kate,' said Jill. 'I'm just off actually.'

'Oh.'

'It's getting on for six, did you know?' Jill sounded censorious, as she always did; like a tutor. Kate ought to know it was six; she should have some bearings in her timeless days, and Jill was doing her a favour by telling her.

'Oh, is it?' wailed Kate.

'Well, are you all right?' sighs Jill. Then she adds, and Kate can hear that she is forcing herself, 'Do you want me to drop in on the way home?'

'No, it's all right.'

'Very well. Be careful about everything, Kate.' And rings off.

She might have asked her to come to supper, at least, thought Kate; and then she runs to the heap of stuff she has bought, and she gets into her place in the corner of the sofa, spreads crisps, chocolate and samosas all over the coffee table, puts the leads to the machine in her ears, and is welcomed into the world of sound. Yet, not without a moment's reluctance, even fear: she knows she is often deaf for minutes after she unplugs herself; she cannot bear to give up this addiction of hers, where she is cut off from everything painful and difficult.

And so sits Kate, eating and listening, while the sunlight hangs in the sky outside, then dims, and it is night, and soon it is time for bed. About midnight Kate feels sleepy. She is grateful that she does. Also, she is rather sick, for she has eaten every crumb of what she bought.

She now takes a long very hot bath, syrupy from a concentration of Janna's bath salts, several varieties of them. She is ashamed and distressed that the water seems to be brown. Had she really been as dirty as that? But never mind, she is clean now. She even washes her spiky Strewelpeter head. Her parents had said to her, You look like Strewelpeter, and she had sought out the book from the nursery cupboard, looked at the illustrations, and was pleased: she felt like Strewelpeter.

She got into bed very late, in a nightgown of Jane's, and lay awake for some time, in a dream of how she was with Jane in Amsterdam, the most famed fashion model in five continents: 'This is my aunt, Jane Somers. Yes, she works at *Lilith*. . . oh, you have heard of her?'

We are into July, my least favourite months of the year are here. All the spring blossom gone long ago; the trees are full and heavy, of a dowdy green; I think of it as the year's middle age, when nothing much happens for what seems like for ever, only insidious intimations of the changes to come. It rains or it doesn't, but it is summer rain, with nothing of the shocks and delights of spring rain which can be snow, ice, hail and warm showers all at once. I was thinking all this as I drove back from the airport in the taxi, and looked at London, London, with the eyes of a lover, not seeing the dreariness of the approaches from the airport, welcoming scarlet buses and telephone boxes; and seeing how, just like

Amsterdam, the streets seethe with tourists staking a claim in the famed city. How extraordinary a thing is this exchange of populations, and yet we have got so used to it, we don't think it strange. A hundred years ago, a few people went on jaunts to the seaside, and the well-off visited suitable bits of 'the continent'. This whole business of *having to see* has evolved in a handful of years. In Amsterdam I was sitting in the hotel coffee room waiting to be fetched for the conference, and at the next table were young people, establishing themselves with each other. One said, 'I saw the Grand Canyon. It was cool.' The other: 'Yes, I have to see that; maybe next year.' With a little anxiety, as if something essential had been for overlong neglected. If it is there, then it must be seen—*had*; as I have been *having* Amsterdam, for in the evenings I made a point of walking around the canals and having dinner in the proper places, for it would not have done simply to eat in the hotel and neglect the canals.

I have been working extremely hard at the conference, which was a success, and at *having* everything I could. And, all the time, Richard, Richard, was beating at the back of my mind; an anxiety, which has been growing to a fever. As much as the longing to be back, and to be with him, I have been asking myself, But suppose the whole thing *is* nonsense?—and at such moments I seem to be breathing something stale and rancid; I seem to myself pathetic. And he, the image of him, acquires a tinge of the ludicrous.

These were my thoughts as I came into London. I went first to the office. Hannah and Jill were working away together in perfect harmony; and Jill said, even a little irritated, 'But, Jane, there's no need for you to be here. You said tomorrow!' The splendid young savage was amused at *family* in the office; and poured oil—which is her nature—saying soothingly that she for one wanted to see me, because a slight problem had arisen. It seems that Hannah is a member of the Women's Action Group Phyllis was once so busy with. They have been keeping tabs on Phyllis, who, from their point of view, sold out by marrying at all, and particularly Charlie who can be nothing else but a male chauvinist pig. It is truly very odd to hear these words being used as if they are a

political label, like: a social democrat, a left-wing deviation-
ist, a right-wing extremist. When Hannah said, 'He is a male
chauvinist pig,' it was without the edge of humour or satire
the words once had; she has long since ceased to think of
what the words mean, they are no more than sounds.

From time to time members of the group have visited
Phyllis, full of passionate sisterhood, to rescue her from her
victimization.

'How?' I asked Hannah, not meaning to be provocative.

We were all sitting in our office: Hannah at 'my' table,
which I am giving up to her anyway since I must go back to
Charlie's room. Jill was as usual just visible behind piles of
work. I sat tactfully to one side, with my hat still on, my
suitcase by my side—a visitor.

Hannah was wearing a striped tunic, belted with black,
over full Turkish-style trousers. Her magnificent black hair
swung as she turned her head to inspect me: in her women's
group I am of course a reactionary, a woman who has
succeeded in the man's world and does not care about her
ground-down sisters. It has long seemed to me that this is not
what anyone actually feels, but what they feel they have to
say: like 'male chauvinist pig'. Hannah considered me, and
said, 'It was all discussed. We decided that if Phyllis had had
enough, she could come and live with the sisters in the
commune.'

Jill gave me a glance which meant: *Don't.* I had no
intention of being abrasive. And while I was in the grip of a
familiar need to laugh, so inappropriate and off the point did
this seem to me, I said mildly, 'Well, surely that isn't very
likely?'

Hannah said seriously, 'Earlier on, before she was
pregnant, Phyllis was thinking of it—leaving Charlie.'

We all sat silent for a while, but we did exchange looks
which admitted what it must be like being married to Charlie,
that perfect husband.

'*Well,*' I said, 'you could knock me down.'

'Why?' Hannah really wanted to know.

I had been trying to get rid of the subject because of its
dangers to office tranquillity, but Hannah is not one to be set

aside if she wants a subject dealt with. I now faced her squarely, and said, 'Because: Phyllis is a very intelligent young woman, one of the cleverest I have known.' Hannah nodded, waited for the point. 'She worked with Charlie for a long time, knew exactly what he was, before she said she would marry him.'

'That's got nothing to do with it, I think,' said Hannah. 'If you haven't been married, then how do you know?'

'You have been?'

'Yes. For long enough. . .'

I said, 'I have only got to look at you, Hannah, to know that you were the stronger, you took on someone problematical, and that he found you too much.'

I had taken a chance, but she gave me an agreeable smile and nodded: 'Right. I probably shouldn't marry at all, or take on a man. I do better with women.'

This was the shock it always is: a shock of the nerves, but not of the mind. Once it had been said, it was obvious, if for no other reason than that Hannah has that comfortable maternal kindness that some lesbians have.

I said, 'But Phyllis is a man's woman.'

'Yes, I agree,' said Hannah. 'If not Charlie then someone.' There was no contempt here, though I was on edge for it, only assessment. 'That's why I was the odd man out in my group—the odd woman out,' she corrected herself with a smile. 'I said you are making a mistake, sisters. Phyllis would not settle for one of us. She's very attractive, you see,' she explained. 'More than one of the girls has been in love with her. Not me, not my type. But I like her, if I think she's a fool.'

Jill said, quick and fierce, 'If it's what she wants, why is she a fool?' From this I saw that Jill has been under attack from Hannah because of Mark. And I wondered for a little what they had against him: for Mark is the modern young man, equal, takes it for granted that housework must be shared, responsibilities be equal. But, to be a man is the crime.

And then Jill, to me, with a scandalized laugh—but a real one, not the try-out, shocked air of the very young girl she often still is: 'They went to Charlie and said that he was exploiting Phyllis, using her salary to pay off his other wife.'

I said, 'But she chose that situation.'

'All the same,' said Jill, '*I* think it's awful. They rang up Charlie, asked to meet him, he said he had nothing to say to them, they trailed him in the street, jumped into a taxi with him that he got into to escape them, and shouted at him that he was a wicked exploiter.'

'And what did Charlie do?'

'*They* say that he threatened them with the police.'

'Is that true?' I asked Hannah, for it didn't sound at all likely.

She looked thoughtfully at me; she knew I didn't believe it. 'I don't know.' Then she swung that glistening black hair back, reached for a cigarette, signalled she had had enough of it, and remarked, 'It sounds all a bit much, I agree, but they were concerned for Phyllis.'

'She chose it,' I said again; and again she dismissed it, this time with a shake of her head, as she took in great draughts of smoke. It is only when she smokes that one sees Hannah as under stress, needing it.

'I knew nothing about all this,' I said. 'But the person to tell me would be Phyllis, for Charlie certainly wouldn't.' And at this I had a sudden picture of the affable Charlie shut into a moving taxi with two shrieking sisters, and I had to laugh, though laughter was not appropriate, not with Jill so anxious and on the defensive. I laughed, and I laughed, while Jill typed very fast, annoyed with me; and Hannah stood four-square on two brown and sturdy legs, smoking, looking out of the window.

When I'd stopped, she said, making judgement, 'It is not funny to Phyllis. Not funny to Charlie. Not funny to the girls who tackled Charlie.'

'So much the worse for all of them,' I said. 'And now I have to go home. Did you hear from Kate?' I asked Jill.

'She rang up every day; I *did* offer to go round, Janna.' And then, apologetic: 'I think there were other people there: she rang up to ask when you were coming home, and someone was telling her what to ask.'

'I see.'

'I hope you do,' said Jill, virtuously.

Hannah said, 'I spoke to her once. I invited her to visit us at the commune.'

The suddenness of this new perspective was too much, and I was not able to say anything but 'Goodbye, see you tomorrow.'

I came home with of course apprehension, expecting I knew not what. Kate was in the corner of her sofa, plugged in. Her face lit up pathetically as I came in, and she voluntarily removed the leads. She stood up, and uncertainly came towards me. I embraced her, for the first time; and what was in my arms was a plump child.

'Oh, Aunt Jane,' sniffed Kate, 'it seemed so long.'

Over her shoulder I looked around: I knew at once that people had slept here. The yellow chairs were grubby, had cigarette burns on them. There was a smell of marijuana. I could see a crust of bread in a saucer full of cigarette ends under a chair. I could feel her tense up, knowing that I was looking around, seeing . . . 'Never mind, Kate,' I said, and she burst into floods of relieved tears. Smiling through them, she backed away, and fell into her corner, her legs set apart, looking like two little fat black dogs in the thick black of her trousers. She was wearing a fluffy white sweater—mine. She put the leads into her ears and sent grateful smiles to me as she sank into her noisy world.

And so here I sit, at one in the morning. Kate has gone to bed. I have rung Mrs Brown and offered her a large bonus to clean up tomorrow. My clothes are ready for the cleaner's, including those worn by poor Kate. I am about to get into my square white bed; I have finished today and tomorrow is Friday, and Richard will ring . . .

Richard did not ring. All day I worked like a black. I said to Jill, 'I have been working like a black,' and she said, 'Janna, you must not say that.' I said, 'Why not? The blacks' case all over the world is that they have to do everyone's dirty work, and I agree they do. So why not say, work like a black? It is descriptive, not insulting.'

'If you can't see why not!' said Jill.

'Oh, I can see why not, all right, but there's no one here but you.'

Charlie had gone out to lunch with our main advertiser. Before he left I saw him slip the pack of new photographs of Phyllis and Caroline into his pocket. He saw that I had seen and he laughed, comfortably.

Hannah had gone to the Professional Women's Lunch. I've announced that she will have to learn to tackle these 'at least for a few months'—meaning Richard; but really I mean to slide out of all I can. But so I have said before.

I am sitting here, looking up at an absolutely clear dark sky, not a cloud anywhere; a small slice of yellow moon, and a couple of emphatic stars. There is a cat yowling for love down there in the dark. Me. All I want is to be with him, with him. That's all.

The weekend I expected to spend with Richard has been spent alone. Yesterday, Saturday, I woke Kate, said I was going to do the shopping, probably buy myself a dress, have lunch out. Would she like to come with me? It was hot, London's streets full of the indolent good-nature that comes with the sun. I stood by Kate's bed, looking down; and as she stared up, befuddled, I thought of how Charlie, looming over his daughter's cot, feels himself oppressively large. How often with Kate do I see myself through her eyes: confident, careless, large, daunting. To make myself less so, I sat down on the edge of her bed. She was lying on top of the bedclothes; fully dressed. She smelled sour. I was asking her to share this day with me because of the spontaneous embrace when I got back from Amsterdam, which I felt marked an entrance into a new stage. Of affection? Of sisterhood! But that pasty formless little face of hers was hard and suspicious. After a while she said, 'Where is *he,* then?' This surprised me, for she had not challenged me before. A savage protectiveness for me and Richard came to the fore, and I said, 'Kate, that's not your affair.' I got up from the bed, dismayed at my own anger. I stood at the window and looked down, not seeing what I looked at, for I was conscious of Kate, who turned her head to look at me with a hard, triumphant little smile. What I was upset about more than anything was that I could see—much too late—that Kate's question meant she had all this time been thinking, or rather feeling, that on her arrival in my life I should have given up all else, for her; or, that I should have taken her when I went to meet Richard. Of course she had felt that, for she was really a small girl. Probably it was her strongest feeling about being here, about me.

At last I said, 'Kate, we could have quite a pleasant day, if you like. Well, it's up to you. I'm going to have a bath and go out in about half an hour . . .'

I did this and that, but she did not emerge from her room. Glancing in, I saw she was still lying in that twisted position, to look up at the square of sky in her window: it was as if she was examining something seen by her for the first time: foreign to her, and hostile.

She had not moved, and I was ready to go. I was telephoning to make an appointment for my hair, when I saw her standing in the doorway, her face hard with suspicion. Listening, through her, I was making a date for some delight with an unknown called Anton. I said, 'That is the hairdresser.' Coldly, angry that I had to explain myself to this—interloper, which was how I was feeling her at that moment. She did not believe me. Her thumb went into her mouth, she stood indecisively, than I saw her whole person set into some purpose or idea. With a glance at me that announced: You needn't think you are fooling me! she went off fast to the kitchen to get some breakfast.

'Are you coming or not?' I called.

No reply.

I went out to do some shopping, and came back an hour later with groceries. Kate was not there. When I had put everything away I went out again and sauntered down the pavement for the pleasure of Saturday morning busyness. I know most people's faces; they know mine; we smile, we nod, we comment on the weather, our voices contented, acknowledging the hot sun, summer beneficence. At the fruit and vegetable stall I bought an apple to eat as I walked. The man always has to deal with a queue because his good humour, his jokiness, attracts people. I stood behind a pretty black girl, with her hair in a thousand tiny pigtails, each tipped with a blue bead. She wore a short, red, cheeky skirt, with comic faces all over it in yellow, like suns, and a white singlet. Thin black arms were loaded with brass, copper, bead bracelets, and in her ears hung loops of red beads, like cherries, to her shoulders. The stall man, confronted by this charmer who stood grinning at him, folded his arms, raised his brows, and said, 'Marylyn, you've been robbing my stall.'

'I've done no such thing,' said she, mock indignant, and swung her cherry earrings.

'Every day I say to myself, What's that Marylyn going to come up with today? But you've outdone yourself. Well, what can I do you for?'

'You're not going to do me today as you did me yesterday. Those strawberries were all squashy at the bottom of the punnet.'

'But that's why they were half price. I was doing you a favour.'

'You can do me again with another one, for free.'

These two people speak the same, quick, cocky cockney, watching each other's lips so as to come in fast with the next riposte. The people behind me were involved, and amused. A woman said, 'You have to watch Benny's strawberries, you do. They are not always what they seem.'

'I'll thank you, Marylyn,' said he, closing his eyes with the pain of it, and wagging his head slowly, 'not to put down my strawberries. Listen to them!' Addressing the queue: 'I was selling strawberries for ten pence a punnet, less than half the cost, for jam. And they complain.'

'The ones you gave me were lovely,' said a crone, all wrapped in thick scarves and jacket against the dangers of the day. 'I had mine for tea.' She was not in the queue, but humbly, at one side, looking at some bananas that were set aside as being past it.

He said, 'Try banana and cream today,' and he slipped a couple of bananas into a bag, and handed them to her with a wink. She opened her hand to show she had some change in it, but he shook his head. She went off, stuffing the bananas into her bag, looking pleased with herself.

'And now, Marylyn, you haven't vouchsafed your needs.'

'Vouchsafe,' said the urchin, daintily, 'I am vouchsafing all the time.' And she stuck out her hand towards a pile of toffee apples. But did not take one, for she knew what he would do now. His face screwed up with the agony of indecision, he peered down at the heap, then chose one, holding it up on its stick towards the sky, dodging his head about so as to get a good look from every possible angle. Then he sighed, dramatic, put back that apple, and took up another. She was giggling, her hand clapped over her mouth. This he held down, towards the pavement, and pulling back his head as far as he could, he examined it first with one eye, the other closed, then with the second eye. Again, he sighed: 'Not good enough.' He dropped it back disdainfully and picked up a third, which he brought close up to his face, and squinted at it, moving it quickly about, his face an intent frown. Then he slowly moved it back from his face to the length of his arm, still frowning, permitted himself to nod and, taking the stick daintily between forefinger and thumb, presented the toffee apple to the black girl, who bobbed him a curtsey and at once started to lick the brown crust with an astonishingly long soft red tongue.

'And, madam, now for your ears.' And he took from the pile of cherries a linked pair, which he held out towards the girl. She inclined her head, still licking the apple. He solemnly removed the vast hoops of miniature cherries on that side and hung the two bright red cherries there. Then she stuck out her other ear. 'You want your pound of flesh, sorry, cherries, I mean,' and he hung the looped red cherries on the other side. With the two removed red bead earrings dangling from his forefinger, he contemplated them. Then he looped them over the end of the pole that held up the awning over his display of fruit.

'I'll keep them for you till you come again,' he said, and the girl went off, laughing.

He sold me my apple, remarking only that if he was to do

business that day in units of one he would soon be broke.

This was rather more lenient than I expected, though his eyes with me had been hard, not, as with Marylyn, indulgent. I could easily have been presented to the rest of the queue as an enemy, served up to them with a remark that stripped the clothes and skin off me, or with a tone of voice, or even in the way he handed me the apple, deferential. This has happened before, if he has felt the need for a victim. I have stopped there in my good clothes, the very picture of expensive well-being, and all that quick joky good humour has suddenly, savagely, been switched off, and I have stood there, exposed, the enemy: his hard, cold eyes flicking over me, once: his palm like a salver—probably copied from *Upstairs, Downstairs*—offering the paper bag with the tomatoes: 'Veenay great?' And the faces of the people in the queue as suddenly as his changed to their reverse: full of a secret, gloating malice. The enemy: the rich. England. There is a vein, or a streak, or a mine, of sadism, cold and expectant. A stall-holder playing at being a stall-holder, with all the tricks: entertainment, people queueing for that as much as for a lettuce or a toffee apple. I have been the entertainment. Also, going to his stall alone, we have exchanged amiabilities, fellow good citizens of this agreeable city. But: let there be a queue, and I stand in it waiting to see if it will be I, today, who will be served up.

I walked on towards the underground, melting, like the pavements, but with pleasure. And I wanted this mood to last, for woe lay in wait for me . . . where was Richard? I was trying to remember when in my life I have waited, helpless, for a telephone to ring.

I dawdled down into the underground. The carriage had in it some French students, several middle-aged Americans, a group of young Germans, some middle-class Russians presumably from the Trade Delegation in Highgate—all spies, I recall, with an agreeable shiver—three Indians, and two very large black ladies, Nigerian, looking like sailing ships. I think I was the only native there. My spirits rising every moment, with the inventiveness, variety and interest of the journey, I travelled on towards Baker Street station, where I went out into the street in a rush of schoolchildren going to the Planetarium, crossed it and made my way to Marylebone High Street, where I went to Monica's and tried on half a dozen sun-dresses, none of which I intended to buy. This is a game I play, accompliced by Monica herself, who is well used to the middle-aged—I will *not* say elderly—taking time off into the past. Monica left some other customers, elegant French women, to an assistant, and came with me into the trying-on which just had room for her to lean, arms folded, back against the wall, watching. Monica looks French and elegant, wears severe dark hair and neat little outfits, but when the shop is empty she will throw all this off, with me, and join in an orgy of retrospection, she lilting up and down in *Jeune Fille* skimpy frills, while I return to my early twenties in fantasy outfits, rather like Jill's and Hannah's now, emerging from the changing rooms like a buccaneer, or a beefeater. The two middle-aged ladies, in fancy dress, parade before Monica's wall of mirrors, and collapse on to her grey velvet sofa in fits of laughter, which are cured by the assistant bringing us cups of coffee and indulgent smiles from which she banishes the slight hint of impatience or criticism.

Monica today knew at once when I stood in the white *piqué* dress with a halter neck and a bare back, that I could easily have bought it; for what I was seeing in the looking-glass was a not *so* solid, tentative, attractive woman who had a look of youth about her as she fingered, in an uncertain, appealing way, the white *piqué* line that cut across her chest, and smoothed down the blonde wisps of disarray around her ears. Monica said quietly, 'My dear Janna, *no*,' and I took off the dress, and handed it to her. She went out with her armload of sun-frocks, while I stood emptily, waiting for the depression I was so afraid of to strike home. But she came back with a beautiful blouse, silky and gentle, in dove grey, and slid it over my head, and made soothing, almost cooing noises, as I saw how it became me.

As I paid for it, and they wrapped it, the coffee: and Monica and I drank it, watching the two French women walking up and down in the suits they might buy. Their complete, close, silent concentration, hardly speaking; you'd think they were not breathing, as they turned and walked one way, stopped, presented their backs to the glass, then their sides, then their fronts, then walked back, slowly, like models. First one, while the other watched, making little exclamations, or a breath of comment; then the first became critic. A beige linen suit, and a white one; each expensive, and you'd think perfect, but they were both rejected, for neither was quite right, not absolutely and utterly, and Monica stood for a few minutes with these two experts, smiling and agreeing that they were quite correct to go on with their quest, for everything in this world depends on detail.

The beige suit, the white one, were in the hands of the assistant, about to be hung up, when in came some American girls who were in search of sun-dresses. They went into the changing room with the ones I had just rejected. Monica and I exchanged small ironies with our smiles, and I went out into the street. It was dazzling, full midday, and I did not believe my eyes when they told me that on the opposite pavement Kate was standing, staring at me. She looked both furious and guilty; and I went across to her, fast, knowing that cars would hoot, and they did as they stopped for this crazy woman.

'Kate, is anything the matter?'

'No.'

'Well, if you've come to join me—good. Have some lunch?'

'Oh . . . no . . . not really. I'm going to the squat.'

I exclaimed, 'The *squat!*' For it is in Chalk Farm.

'You don't own the pavement,' she burst out, and hearing the ridiculousness of it, went red, and said, 'Anyway, I'm late, Aunt Jane!' And went off towards Oxford Street.

This brought down my spirits, already dented in Monica's, and I went on draggingly, feeling hot, knowing that this business with Kate meant ill, to her, or to me; knowing that I had consistently refused to face how dislocated and lost she was; knowing that I ought to be doing something about her, but not what . . . In this state I walked past a little restaurant I was in once with Richard. I went in, was recognized by the German who runs it, given a little table at the window and served a large plate of very likeable *hors d'oeuvres* ordered as a main course; but could not finish them, for everything on my tongue tasted flabby and heat-limp, but this was my fault, not the restaurant's. I was thinking, of course, of Richard. I left quickly, went into the hairdresser's to cancel my appointment, and came home, having used up all my vitality.

The flat without Kate in it offered an opportunity for tidying up; a task that I as usual do not shirk; and it needed it, although Mrs Brown had done a little before giving up.

I took the yellow linen covers with the cigarette burns off the armchairs, and thought then that I would need to get new ones made. The chairs without the yellow are a soft rust, almost cherry; and I used to love them, only covered them up when I had to. I sat on the sofa, but not in the grubby depression that is Kate's, and looked at the chairs and thought that Freddie and I had sat in them opposite each other, and this brought such a flood of misery that I simply went to bed. It was three in the afternoon. I don't remember ever doing anything like it before. I wept and slept, and woke looking at a square that was full of evening: a late, soft, beguiling sunlight, trailing fleecy clouds.

I made supper for me and for Kate, waited for a while, but she did not come. Anxiety. I kept repeating that lying litany: But she's nineteen, she's an adult . . . while I wondered if I should ring the police.

In the end I did not; I bathed, attended to my clothes, and went to bed to read myself to sleep. Which was not until after four in the morning when the sky was again filling with another hot summer day. I don't know what I dreamed, but it was a very sad dream; and I got myself out of bed early and went off to Regent's Park, and there I spent the day, by myself, walking through roses, roses, and sitting near the fountains by the tall poplars.

Kate came in an hour ago, looking awful. She had been smoking pot, and was fuzzy and vague and did not answer when I asked her what sort of weekend she had had. When I came in here, to go to bed, she took the things out of her ears and asked, 'Are you going to work tomorrow?'

'But of course I'm going to work tomorrow!'

It was all beyond me; Kate is beyond me. She is sitting

there now, jiggling away to her music, and I am going to sleep.

Today I was in Archives all morning with June looking up back numbers of *Lilith* for an article on fashion in the sixties. It goes without saying that for her it was an historical epoch, like the Edwardians for me; but it certainly puts a perspective on things when of your yesterday a young adult remarks indifferently, 'I think they were rather silly.' At my look, she expounded, 'I mean, they had no social conscience in those days. Waste not, want not.' This agglomeration of improbables in two sentences addled my tongue, and I did not go on with it. I like Archives—a grand name for what might once have been the butler's pantry, twelve by twelve of a concentration of social history crammed to the roof on shelves. We had to have the doors open into the typists' room. Ten of them; and with half my mind I enjoyed the lively goings-on, and with the other judged the work we did fifteen, twenty years ago. Things change, and you don't know how much. We have made successive decisions not to change *Lilith;* precisely, not to accommodate ourselves to harder times, on the grounds that people need glamour. Well, *Lilith*'s covers have become wilder, more surreal, with girls that resemble tropical birds or insects.

I asked June, for curiosity, if she'd like to be moved up into another department, into Editorial, and she said no, she liked it where she was. And anyway she was engaged to be married, and next May she'd be leaving us. 'It'll be sad, leaving the old place,' said she, meaning the typists' room.

When I went back up, Jill said that Richard had rung. Yes, she had said, of course, that I could be fetched, but he said he would ring again. I knew that I had gone white; I could feel my flesh chilly on my face. Hannah is not one to be inhibited by false tact; and I was grateful that she put a chair under me, then stood behind me, massaging my neck and shoulders. 'There, there,' said she, 'poor Janna.' I could feel the heat of her large breasts, and her hands were strong and calm. It was a shock to me, the pulsing warmth of that young Aztec. I hardly ever touch anyone, after all. Sometimes poor old Annie, when she's sick or needs helping up from her chair. I allowed my head to rest back, and was accepted into her maternal plenitudes.

The telephone rang; it was Richard, and I took the receiver from Jill. I was feeling more than foolish: behaving like a teenager with a boyfriend. I noticed the composure with which Hannah laid her hands on my shoulders, pressed them, and went back to her desk.

'Richard!'

'Janna, you are there.'

Linked with his voice, and our certainties—which exist, though about what I could not say—my anxieties left me, and I was myself.

'I said I would ring, but I thought I would wait till I got back, and then that was delayed . . .'

'Where are you?'

'Boston.'

At this, that moment when I will hear, Boston—or Tasmania, or Greenland—and know it is for ever, came towards me from the future, and I could not say anything.

'Janna!'

I found I could not speak.

'Janna, are you there?'

I croaked out, 'Yes.'

'I'm booked on a flight back tomorrow. Janna, it was an emergency.'

I croaked, 'When will I see you?'

'Lunchtime on Wednesday. The square.'

'Yes.'

'Without fail.'

'Janna, I couldn't honestly say I wish you were here, but I wish I was there.'

'Me too.'

I sat on in the chair, recovering, while Hannah took the telephone receiver, replaced it, and set a cup of coffee in front of me.

Jill was typing as if she were running a race with her own sense of the outrageous: she was embarrassed because of me;

flushed, and tight-lipped. I noticed I needed, very badly, to put my arms around her and warn her—but say what? No words! To communicate as Hannah did, waves of communication from, was it?—her solar plexus?

Hannah was standing with her back to the filing cabinet, her coffee cup in her hand, contemplating me and my condition and what it demanded from her. Today she was wearing a dress of strong blue cotton, loose because it was so hot this afternoon, the sun streaming in. Her arms were bare and brown, her strong legs brown and bare. Everything about her is so healthy, sound and right. I swear she would only have to stand in a room anywhere, and life would obediently have to order its waves to flow around her and the faces of everyone would turn towards her. 'There, there,' she would say, to life.

Suddenly I found myself thinking, What would it be like to be in bed with Hannah?

If there are generation gaps, this is one. The only lesbians I ever met before the Women's Movement were evident as being full of suppressed intensities, seemed to want to insist on perversity, paraded miseries before you, and—in my case at least—attempted (twice) seductions that had about them an air of the theatrical, as if they were play-acting seductions that had a script and which did not come from their real natures.

It came into my head that if I said now, at this moment, to Hannah, 'I was wondering what it would be like to be in bed with you,' she would remark, 'Well, you should give it a try one of these days,' and I could hear the unspoken addendum: Do you good.

This made me want to laugh; I choked, Hannah neatly fielded my coffee cup and saucer, and I sat laughing helplessly.

These day, girls discuss it as if they are or are not going to try on a dress. Jill remarked once, when she was quarrelling with Mark, 'I said to him, Mark, you are all too much. I'm going to live with a woman. They are not so demanding.'

'And what did Mark say?' I asked.

'He said, How you do know, you've never tried one? I said,

Well, perhaps it was time I did. He said, Well, if you do, let me know when you need a change. I said, You're so damned cocky. He said, You've put your finger on it.' At which she had said he was vulgar, crude and conceited beyond bearing. A few minutes later she remarked that she enjoyed quarrelling with Mark: this with the little air of satisfaction that is so characteristic of her.

I said to Hannah, 'Thank you,' meaning it from the heart, and then, that I had to go to see how Charlie was getting on.

In the great cool room Charlie was sitting at one end of the long table, smoking a Gauloise. Three tall windows admitted summer, and on a windowsill two pigeons sat basking. Charlie was looking rather flushed, as if he had drunk too much at lunch. I said to him that we had problems to discuss, decisions to make, policies to decide. He said comfortably that he had every confidence in my judgement.

I said to him, as I do it seems every other day, 'Charlie, the world is full of people who never dream of doing any work, but most at least put on a show of working.'

'Why should I, Janna? I've always found things went along very well for me. There are always people who adore working, and are good at it.'

'Well, let's pretend, at least.' I handed him the pile of *Lilith*s from the sixties, and he sat turning them over, appreciative, even proud, as if he had been responsible for them all.

I got on with my work. Time passed. Then he yawned, stood up, collected the pile of magazines and brought them to me. 'If I don't leave now I'll miss Caroline's six o'clock feed,' he said.

From the door he gave me a smile that combined the determination to do exactly as he wants; a slight, rather pleasurable guilt; a twinkling complicity that made me laugh, though I was annoyed. Then he escaped. I hear his voice in exchanges with Jill's and Hannah's. Laughter. Then two typewriters started off together.

When I got home, I knew that someone else had been there; and understood Kate's inquiry, Would I be going to work? The two cherry-coloured chairs were covered with ash and crumbs. In the kitchen I found that the fridge had been cleared out of everything, even milk and butter. They had made sandwiches of the cheeses I had brought from Holland, eaten the steak I had put to thaw out for tonight, drunk all the Bols, demolished a large cake. The sink was full of plates and glasses. Three of them had been here.

I did not know what to do. Kate could say to me, as she was probably planning to do, 'But are you saying I can't have my *friends* here?' And what was the use of saying to her, 'You know perfectly well their coming here and making themselves at home is a deliberate act of defiance, or aggression, like raiding foreign territory.'

I was very angry. Then I was cold and discouraged. I stayed for a long time in the kitchen and washed everything up. Then I took a bag and went fast down to the shops and bought everything again that we needed. I brought these home, put everything away, tidied everything; I had been walking in and out, to and fro past Kate, because I did not know what to say. She sat on in the sofa corner, sullenly staring ahead of her, her ears harnessed.

Then, having done it all, I went up to her, took the things out of her ears, and shouted because I knew she would be deaf, 'Kate, if that ever happens again you are going to have to leave.' Then I put the two leads back in her ears, without waiting to hear what she had to say. But I saw on her face pleasure, as well as a sullen triumph. I don't know why; because I had put my foot down, and now she could say to them all that her unkind aunt had said she could not have her friends in: she needs me to lay down the law?

I have no idea. When I think that she might indeed leave, then panic surges up. Because I shall have to ring Sister Georgie and say, Your daughter has joined the flotsam and jetsam, the derelicts of London? I have not heard one word from my sister. This is so unlike her, and outside the codes and mores spoken and unspoken of our family life (such as it is), that when I think of it I feel as if solid ground has given way. Whatever else one has to say about my sister and her kind, they are not people who renege on their responsibilities.

I said to Jill, 'Do you realize I have not heard from your mother?'

'I hear from her,' she said composedly.

'What does she say about Kate?'

'She hopes Kate is all right.'

'But that is preposterous!'

'What can she say?'

'But she knows Kate is a disaster area and can't be "all right".'

'Jane,' said Jill, laying aside her work, and giving me her full attention. 'Why is it you can't see it? Don't you *see*? My parents don't know how to cope with unsuccessful people.'

'But they are full of good works, dishing out aid and comfort.'

'Yes, but that's for people who are like that—old people, junkies, delinquents.'

'If Kate is not a delinquent, what is she?'

'Yes, but she is one of *us*, don't you see? She's not out *there*. My parents can't hand out goodies or tender loving care and then say bye-bye and go back home. *She doesn't measure up.* To them. She makes them feel a failure and they can't have that.'

'Tell me, then, what do you suppose they have in mind for Kate long-term? That she will be slumping around my home for ever? Yes, yes, don't bother to say it, I chose it. But what do they think will happen?'

'They *don't* think. They say to themselves that Kate is just a late starter, or something like that.'

'Well, perhaps she is.'

Silence, from me.

Then: 'Hannah thinks Kate should go to their commune.'

I looked at Hannah.

She said, 'It's the worst possible thing for her, to be with you.'

'Are you sure?'

'She can't measure up to you, any more than to her parents.'

'You, Hannah, are hardly inadequate, in any area!'

'No,' said Hannah, 'I am not. But there are ten women in

our commune, and some of them are like Kate. People who need time.'

'I'm not going to throw her out.'

'Of course you mustn't throw her out,' directed Hannah, 'but she'll leave, won't she?'

'Will she?'

'You don't love her,' announced Hannah, without criticism.

'I think I'm fond of her, in a dreary sort of way, hopeless. She makes me feel inadequate. It's like sliding into a fog.'

'Well, there you are,' said Jill. 'But who wouldn't feel that?' This was a sniffing little challenge to Hannah, who merely smiled, knowing better.

But now I have told Kate I will throw her out—if.

Love! Love! Love!

I love Jill, but I don't love Kate. I love Richard. I am rapidly getting very fond of Hannah. I feel fondly affectionate towards Charlie. I feel affection for Mark. I like Phyllis very much, whereas at first I disliked her. I loved Joyce—oh, yes, I did, no doubt of it. But now, where is all that? And Freddie? No, I did not love Freddie. My heart aches tonight, it aches. Tomorrow I shall be seeing Richard, so my heart ought to be skipping like a sparrow.

This morning I was glad to be working in the big room, away from those two sharp-eyed women, Hannah and Jill. Charlie and I discussed the article about that remote epoch, the sixties, while he amused me with a hundred agreeable little reminiscences. Meanwhile, I was in a turmoil, like an adolescent, thinking about Richard. But waiting to see him, today, was not as it has been, a rapid rise of temperature knowing there would be calm and pleasure when we met: no, I was anxious and restless; a condition that no one could describe as pleasurable. Love! An anguish. This morning I was in a sharply opposite mood to the one I was in when I wrote my acid piece last night: thinking that, if I did not love

Freddie, so much the better. If love is suffering, and a lot of useless emotions, then why bother ... And did Freddie suffer? Oh, that is what I can't stand, it is coming closer, crowding in: it is what I really can't face.

I went to Soho Square early. It was humid and airless. The sky had a hazy occluded look. I wanted to sit quietly by myself and let the anxiety go away. But as I came into the square I saw Richard, sitting by himself at the end of a bench. He was not expecting me yet. What I saw was a middle-aged man, evidently tired, staring at some pigeons feeding in a flowerbed. When I sat down by him, he looked up as at an unwanted stranger, then he smiled and his whole body seemed to fill with energy as he turned and put his arms around me. We sat like that for a few moments, then I heard him sigh, and we moved apart.

'Two weeks,' he said, as if in accusation.

'Two weeks,' I accused.

'How was Amsterdam?'

'As it always is.' I didn't want to talk about what to me is only something that I have to do; I wanted to know about America, Boston. I said, 'And how was America?'

He shifted his legs, lost some of his confidence, and said, 'I had to go. All right, I see I shall have to tell you. But first, let us go to a pub and get ourselves cushioned against fate.'

We got up together and went out of the square, and I heard myself asking anxiously, 'What fate? Are you going away again?'

'Not yet.'

This did not assuage me: I was actually thinking, as we walked towards *our* pub, If it's going to end anyway, then what's the point: but that was because today it was as if two weeks of not being with Richard had accumulated need that had been, during the time we were meeting so often, fed little by little, but now nothing he said or did could stop that tormenting ache. It seemed to me then, in that heavy hazy sunlight, that damp heat, as if the ache, the want, had swelled up, too large to be contained by Richard. All I wanted was to be rid of this burden, this ache.

Our table was free, and we squeezed ourselves in, sitting

low among the tall noisy lunchtime crowd.

'What fate?' I asked, as soon as I sat down.

He gave that snort of laughter that means someone has behaved as expected; endearingly perhaps, but too predictably, and I said, 'Suddenly I can't bear it. But bear *what*? If I knew...'

'I understand perfectly.' He reached down from the counter two double Scotches, which the man had supplied on a nod and: 'The usual,' and he handed me mine. 'Drink up.'

'I want to know.'

'Yes. First, Amsterdam. I want to know. Yes, I've been saying no, no, no, let's *not,* but I find myself more and more thinking about your life. I know nothing at all about you. And I'm jealous.'

'I'm so jealous that... and I've never ever been jealous...' My voice trailed off; for what I was saying, and I knew it, was that I had not loved before. I said, very low, not looking at him, feeling my face hot: 'I don't think I've loved like this...' I could feel his eyes close and keen on my face, wanting me to look up, but I couldn't. I was afraid to see what there might be there on his face. Some kind of pain, I knew that, and not on my account. Oh, our thoughts fly back and forth between us, so fast; we think the same thoughts.

'Amsterdam. What do you do on these—jaunts?'

'It's not a jaunt. I work, very hard. Very well. There's a hotel I always go to. It's one of the tall old houses, on a canal. They try to give me a room right at the top, which I like. You look at trees, and the water and the boats going past. Once, in winter, there were people skating, like a Breughel. They bring me coffee and bread and jam, early, at seven. I hate being rushed and fussed. I take my time. Then I walk to wherever it is. This time another hotel, used a lot for conferences. And then, when it's over, I have dinner with someone—I know a lot of people in the trade, of course.'

'Of course.'

'And then I usually walk back, because I like walking in Amsterdam, and I go to bed and read.'

He was regarding me with irony. We held our glasses, and were drinking with the intention of finishing and ordering more. The glow of the drink and the noisy cheerful crowd made me feel better; and he said, 'Well, that's better.' And he took our two empty glasses and set them on the counter to be refilled.

'I know I am an oaf and a bumpkin, but what do you do all day?'

'This time, I listened to reports and speeches. From all over the world. Fashion—the state of—the crisis in—there's always a crisis in fashion . . .'

'There's always a crisis in everything, hadn't you noticed?'

We laughed. It was easy to laugh: we looked at each other, our eyes not wanting to look at anything else; he reached down our two glasses, and I suddenly said, 'I'm going to phone and say I won't be in this afternoon, if you're free?'

'I'm free.'

I told Hannah to tell Charlie, who had not yet left, that I was taking the afternoon off and this and this and this was to be done. By him.

Back at our table, I slid into my chair as if into a happiness that would never end, for the afternoon stretched away in front of us, and he said, 'You had breakfast, walked to the other hotel, and there you listened to speeches. All day?'

'Yes. And I made one. People from South America and Canada and the States. From every country in Europe. From the Soviet Union. Everywhere. You know—fashion. Big business.'

'What was your speech about?'

'A report. I was speaking on behalf of the upmarket women's magazines in Britain.'

'You listened to speeches for four days?'

'We also split off into smaller groups—committees and subcommittees. Discussing aspects of. Aspects of, mostly the Depression.'

'Ah yes, the Depression.'

'This *is* the real subject of conferences everywhere at the moment.'

He said, 'Are we going to admit the Depression?'

I said, 'It is not just the Depression. Last time, there was Depression, and then War.'

'Yes.'

'Yes.'

I lifted my glass to him and knew that my smile was strained. His was bleak.

'Let's *not*,' I said.

'No. But I suppose this is where I tell you what I was doing in the States?—Yes? Right. We had an urgent call. We have a son, Down's syndrome. A mongol. John. We've not put him in a home or an institution. We've not wanted that. But when we both came away this time, in April, we did not bring him. It would have been impossible. He needs to have someone there with him all the time. In Washington we have a woman who lives in our house. Cuban. She's like one of us now. But she had a family crisis of her own, her mother, and at first we thought there was no one to leave him with. It's not everyone who can cope with—the inadequate.'

'How old is he?'

'By age, sixteen. Two years younger than Kathleen. But he is really about four or five. He's very lovable—they are, you know. We never wanted to put him in an institution. We'd have missed a lot. Sometimes I think he's the only person of the five of us in our house who is happy.'

Listening to this, what I was doing was putting the flesh of detail, detail, on to the plot. The house, and in it Richard; Kathleen, the elder daughter; the idiot boy around whom everything—it would have to—adapted itself; his wife, that unknown quantity; the large, sensible southern woman ... he had said five.

'Five?' I asked. 'The Cuban lady?'

'No. With Maria, six. Our son Matthew is an extremely ambitious and hard-working young man. Like my wife,' he put in quickly, with a glance at me: you have to take it, at some time. 'Yes. But no one could describe Matthew as one of the world's sunbeams. He works and plays with equal dedication. Kathleen has always been shadowed—by John. She was two when he was born, and for some reason he afflicted her. Matthew has never been involved, he accepted it, went his own way, cutting himself off emotionally from us early. But Kathleen loved John, she loves him, she suffers over him, she is embarrassed by him, when people come and there's this happy idiot, a sort of deformed dwarf, always laughing and there, like a happy puppy, you know—but people coming for the first time always have to be put in the picture and then adjust. It is always Kathleen who mediates. She can't stand it, I believe, somewhere deep inside. I believe it is a sort of permanent anguish for her. Sylvia and I . . .' Again the little glance, assessing, even diagnostic: she must take it, is she taking it? And he put his hand down over mine and squeezed it and sighed, and his face was the same as a mother or nurse who has to make a child take medicine, and is so involved with the act that the physical relief of having swallowed shows on her face. 'Oh, Janna . . .' he breathed, but went on: 'I and Sylvia had discussed this often enough, as you can imagine. We were always arranging for Kathleen to be away, staying with friends, at holiday camps—you know, they have them in the States for young people in the summer, marvellous things, you should do more of it here . . .' I was noting, of course, the *you*: but he didn't notice. 'But it did no good, you see. We could send Kathleen off to camp for a summer, but she'd be on the telephone every other day: How is John? No, the person who has taken the real burden of John is Kathleen.'

'Not Maria?'

'No. Not emotionally. Quite rightly. She's not had children of her own. Unmarried. She is by nature a cheerful and busy person.' I was smiling to myself, because this sounded like a doctor's notes. 'So-and-so is a cheerful and busy person with many interests, and the prognosis is good.' 'Kathleen loves John. No, but really. He loves her. It's not I or Sylvia who have suffered over John. We both work very hard, you know. We both say—though it is not very easy to understand—that coming home to John is like a tonic. There's a kind of joy they have.'

'I've read about it.'

'Well, it's true. Extraordinary. It's a kind of irrepressible exuberance welling up.'

I sat silent, weighted with all this, feeling those years, Richard and Sylvia, three children, the house, the cheerful and busy woman from Cuba ... doubtless cats, dogs and hamsters. It was all too much for me. Over thirty years, he had said.

'How old is Matthew?'

'Twenty-two. I was waiting for you to ask. No, we did not have children, not till we were both over thirty. We were both nineteen when we married. Children. There should be a law against it.'

'Why? You are still together?'

'Yes—no, that's not it. I don't regret ...' Again he put his hand over mine, tossed the whisky into the back of his throat, indicated I should finish mine. I did, and he set the two empty glasses back on the counter.

'I am getting drunk.'

'Good. How can we get through this otherwise?'

'Why did you wait for so long without children?'

'We were both too busy. We waited ten years. Working. Working. Isn't that enough for today?'

'Yes, it is, more than enough. I don't think I can ...' I shook my head. I was full to the throat with that 'over thirty years' of crammed, packed, family life, the intensity of it, the *organization*—two working parents (what did Sylvia do?), an ambitious and clever elder son, Kathleen whose spirit was darkened by the irrepressibly jolly and happy mongol boy who would never grow up.

'Just one thing, and that's enough for today. What was the crisis you had to go back to?'

'John has never been without one of the family around, at least one of us, and Maria has been with us since he was five. Suddenly, we all went away, except Matthew, but he's at university, he's there in the mornings and evenings, and he's never been anything more than pleasantly distant with John. And we had Maria's sister in the house. John is not used to her. And so he got ill. That's the real reason he was ill, though it's pneumonia. Was. He's over it.'

I was digesting all this: questions emerged. I decided not to ask any of them.

'I think we ought to have some lunch,' I said.

'Good idea.'

We walked down to Wheeler's. But our two lives, the real lives, the texture and pattern and weight—the weight, the *weight*—was there now, between us. Is there. Then we went to the pictures like children and saw—but what does that matter? We held hands. He said he had to go home at about seven. Outside the pub where we had a drink before parting, Kathleen was standing, her back to us, staring across the street. She's a handsome girl; but heavy, slow, because of her hypnotized look.

It seemed to me that we ought to go up to her in an ordinary way, so that we could meet, she and I: and I think that was what Richard meant to do. But as he hesitated slightly, she walked straight across the road and away. A heavy, blind walk.

'Was she upset about John's being ill? Didn't she want to go with you.'

'We didn't tell her. Yes, that sounds strange. But it was hard enough to get her to accept coming to university here. She didn't want to be parted from him. We'd been fighting it all out—for months. It seems like years now. We wanted her to be severed from him, do you see?'

He had his arm in mine, and I could feel from the pressure of it how much he wanted me to understand.

'Yes, I do see.'

'Good.'

'If she found out he was so ill and she didn't know, would she forgive you?'

'Ah. Yes!' He stopped, turned, took my two upper arms in his hands and smiled straight into my face. 'Yes. Yes. That was my position. But Sylvia . . . We discussed it, it seems to me we have been discussing nothing else since we came here, Sylvia said, we've *got* her away from him, she's made the break.'

That we, we, we, we! Each time it said to me, You interloper, you *nothing*. And 'we have been discussing nothing else'—I could see myself, way off on the periphery, someone met when there was time, a pleasant entertainment outside the real business of life.

He was saying, 'It's not like that, Janna,' squeezing my

arms, gently rocking me back and forth. His face was close, urgent, concerned.

I shook my head, I could not speak. He put his arm about me and we walked soberly along Old Compton Street. His arm, the strong warmth of it, said to me, Nothing has changed.

At the corner he said, 'I had hoped we could spend tomorrow evening together?'

I quavered, 'I wouldn't have the strength of mind to say no!'

'The pub?'

I nodded again, and went on up Charing Cross Road, half blind and choked.

By the time I got to *Lilith* I had recovered. I stood as I sometimes do, looking at the old houses, externally unchanged, and wondering what the people who lived in them—let's say, up to the First World War—would make of us, of *Lilith,* who spreads herself over two houses, who has knocked down walls and removed barriers and boundaries where once separate families might have heard the odd sound through thick brick and plaster. I was thinking of how these houses were layered once, the family on the ground floor, first floor, second floor; the servants in the basement and at the very top; and, as I thought of those servants, going in and out down the steps where now the typists and secretaries go, it was as if there was a time-blur, for there was a skivvy, a kitchen maid, someone like that, standing on the pavement, wearing a dragging long skirt and a flowered blouse, and what from this distance looked like a bonnet. I walked fast towards this visitant from the past and saw it was Kate, who stood humbly on the pavement gazing up to where her lucky sister worked. It was her streaky hair, pink and green, that looked like a bonnet. 'Kate,' I said, and she turned with a start, and said, 'Oh, you did go out then . . .' but her voice trailed away, and she went an ugly red. This was so much not what I expected, I did not at first hear what she had said. Besides, I was in the grip of such pity for the wretch. All bouleversed, soggy, and sagging with emotions as I was, only just in command of myself, there was something about Kate that went, smash, to my heart, and I could have hugged her,

like a small, disconsolate child, or perhaps the sentimental-
ized version of a put-upon put-down pre-First World War
scullery maid. Then I did hear, retrospectively, what she had
said; and I stared at her and she at me. Suddenly, things
clicked into place. *Kate has been following me.* Following
Richard and me. Just like Kathleen. How often? For how
long? Where to? I don't know, and I don't propose to think
about it.

But that girl had gone to *Lilith* in order to trail me while I
went off to my assignation with my demon lover—but I had
left early—for she had known he was back; because of my
manner? She had overheard me on the telephone? I could not
remember whether she had been there or not.

She knew I had understood, and her stare was hard, bold,
triumphant. Far from wanting to embrace her, I wanted to hit
her, hard. And I went on up the steps into the hall where once
ladies and gentlemen handed cards to parlour maids or took
off their coats and hats, and then to the third floor, hoping
that Charlie would not be there. I needed to recover. I was
suffering from as bad a fit of panic as I can remember. I was
feeling caged. I felt like that when Maudie made me her
prisoner, not by what she said but by her need. I have felt like
that sometimes with poor Annie. But this child is in my home,
my life; and there is no way I know I can use to get rid of her.
The idea that she follows Richard and me . . . But how is it
we have not seen her? We have not been looking for her,
that's why! Richard has known once or twice that Kathleen
has been with us when I thought she was not: told me
afterwards, not at the time.

I sat alone at the long table where the heavy damp trees of
midsummer stood around beyond the windows, and thought,
No, it is all too much. I cannot see Richard again. Being with
him is simple and easy; as if we had both been born for it. But
we both drag trails of muddy circumstances with us, and we
cannot even meet without spies and observers. And yet I
knew quite well that I will be in the pub tomorrow. And who
else will be there?

Kate was not in when I returned this evening. She did not
come until about eleven, and said she had been at the squat.

She was quite terrified, putting on all kinds of little airs of bravado, expecting me to say, And now you must go. When I said goodnight, her eyes were brimming with tears, and she came to embrace me. It was a sad little embrace. I feel so lacking, holding that poor child in my arms, this nineteen-year-old who is like a dumpy apprehensive child, I don't know what to say or do. She needs—everything!

Richard rang before lunch. Charlie had already gone. I was alone. As I worked I was listening to Jill and Hannah in the cheerful outer office. Wishing I could be there and not in the big dreary editor's room. I don't know why, but it has always been a lifeless room for some reason. Whereas the outer office where I worked so long with Joyce, then with Phyllis, then too briefly with Jill, has always zinged with life. I was thinking that this move in away from that room to work finally with Charlie meant the real severance with Jill, who, naturally enough, has more attention to pay her flatmate and to Hannah, than to her aunt. I was altogether in a low mood, and thoughts of Richard were not helping at all. It was at this point that he rang, sounding harassed, asked if I had a car; I said I used to have, but sold it, I used it so little. The trouble was, said Richard, that he thought we should not meet in our pub, but somehow if we could get away, perhaps to the country, he couldn't explain now, but ... I said he didn't need to explain.

We eventually arranged that he would pick me up exactly at five thirty in a taxi and we would drive to Baker Street, and from there go by underground to Wimbledon, where there was a restaurant he had discovered. All this came to pass. On my way past Jill and Hannah, I sneaked a look down on to the pavement to make sure Kate wasn't there, or Kathleen. I couldn't see either. I knew I was looking furtive, and that Hannah and Jill would start commenting on me the moment I had left. How primitive we all are: by leaving that room, leaving *them* their closeness, I had become *other*, and I would be discussed in a way that I would not have been while actually working with them, in that room.

Richard's taxi drew up as I got to the door and I sneaked into it.

'All clear?' I gasped.

'As far as I can see.'

We embraced. A strange flavour, our embraces have. Friendship, yes, that above all, instant intimacy, always, as if we have never been apart. The warm understanding of the flesh, his hand on my summer-bared forearm, mine behind his neck. Passion, oh yes, it is all there, imminent, incipient, like a country stretching all around us that some mysterious law forbids us to enter. Thus far and no farther is written on our invisible tablets, so that we may repose inside each other's arms, feeling them burn and promise; but we may not turn our heads to kiss. If our lips did meet, good God, what an announcement that would be but—and this is the point—something would at that moment die. What? Do we know? I don't. My God, what a world I have locked away from me! I feel his breath on my cheek, and at once a warning sounds: Be careful, even as I long to turn my face so that my mouth would, for the first time, arrive in the same place as his. Oh no. No, no, no.

Disengaging, and *not* looking at each other, for it is amazing how, when we move out of these dangerous and sorrowful embraces, we are careful not to let our eyes meet, he said, 'I am sorry about the cloak and dagger stuff. But something happened.'

He said this with a long, contemplative inward stare: as at ranges of possibilities of things that could happen. All, I feel, for the worst.

And I felt with him that my life, as well as his, could present us with something not explosively but insidiously bad. *Is* presenting us with: as we crawled up Tottenham Court Road, I was examining the pavements in case Kate should appear there, standing with her face to the traffic, her eyes at work on the interior of every taxi, to catch me out.

'You'd better tell me,' I said.

'Matthew, you know, our oldest, let Kathleen know that John had been ill. No, no, it wasn't malice, or mischief-making, or anything like that. It was—indifference. You see, he has turned a key on caring about John, he did that long ago. So when we, in fact it was Sylvia, wrote to ask him not to tell Kathleen, he didn't take it in. He sent a postcard to Kathleen, added as a postscript: And John is out of danger. He didn't think.'

'So Kathleen doesn't forgive you.'

'Ah! But what is she not forgiving us for? Of course, for making John a mongol in the first place.'

'Not very rational.'

'But what, dear Janna, is rational?'

This struck me as being well over the line of tolerance, into—what? I was thinking that in Richard and in Sylvia, these two by definition rational and sensible people, was something altogether out of proportion when it came to talking of Kathleen. For a healthy eighteen-year-old to trail her handsome father and his wicked mistress week in week out, not even making much secret of it, but standing around on pavements and on river banks quite openly, if with that heavy, brooding, almost hypnotized look—well, it is surely beyond what is to be expected of adolescence; though of course I know that that has to be bad enough. In short, I was sitting there thinking that Kathleen was more than somewhat crazy. And that Richard and Sylvia refused to recognize it; just as my ever-loving Sister Georgie and her mate refuse to see that Kate is fit for a loony-bin. Well, not far off.

'She hasn't announced that she is going back to John? To be with him?'

'We asked her not to. But I don't think she can. You see, she has to stay here to make sure that her father isn't going to . . .'

'Richard,' I said. 'Look! It is an utterly marvellous evening. Let us not talk about these ghastly children . . .' I saw his half-annoyed, half-appreciative glance, heard his snort of laughter, noted his querying look. 'Yes, we do not have only one of them on our trail. Now there's one of mine. No, I am *not* going to tell you about her now. For God's sake, let us enjoy this evening . . .' And I stopped myself from adding, It might be the last chance we get. But he heard this, though I didn't say it, and his fingers tightened on my hand.

We slid out of the taxi at Baker Street, both with furtive glances over our shoulders, we ran inside, and in the carriage knew that we were checking up on the faces of everyone in it, and those who came in. But we were alone, and our spirits rose, and by the time we got to Wimbledon we were able to forget poor Kathleen, poor Kate.

We wandered for a while among Wimbledon's leafy streets that were hot, heavy and spicy, noted the admirable roses, and then went into our restaurant, which has tables in a garden at the back, and a little pool with irises, and birds swooping in to splash and drink.

And so: it was a lovely evening. It *was* a lovely evening. It was. But there was a heaviness and an anxiety there, just behind our pleasure in each other. More than once, our eyes meeting, we acknowledged it in a small grimace, a smile. And there we parted, in the bowels of Baker Street underground, he said, 'I've got to rush. Matthew said he would ring us. Midnight. That's seven there. He gets in from college about seven. He's very regular in his ways, Matthew is. To be counted on in all things.' We shared a smile at this, and a sigh: censored, by both of us.

'If you are free, Janna, do you suppose we'd be safe in our pub tomorrow?'

'We could try. What alternative do we have?'

'We can't go off to Wimbledon or up to Hampton Court every lunch hour . . .'

When I got home, I stood in the doorway seeing my beautiful room now and *then*. Two shabby little cherry-coloured chairs, off some junk heap. A handsome red linen chair. A grey sofa, filthy and creased. A pile of dingy garments lay on the floor. My carpet looked soiled. There were smears on the walls. On the sofa Kate sat, her terrified eyes on my face. She was not plugged in. I knew that her friends from the squat had come, and she had not wanted to let them in; had had to let them in; they had deliberately made as much mess as they could, while she wailed and beseeched. Now she was literally trembling with fear that I would throw her out. That threat I made was the most stupid thing I ever did. I went to the kitchen. They had cleared the place out, and left the remains of their meal on the kitchen table. I knew that they had made a point of being as messy and clumsy as they could. A bottle of milk had been overturned and there was a pallid lake on the brown wood of the table, with a crust or two afloat and many crumbs.

I went back to the living room, and did not know what to say to Kate. The point was, she did not have the strength to say no to these people; it did not make any difference what I said, or threatened.

The enormity of Kate came into me. The inexorability of her. How one could not go around her, avoid her, refuse her: or for that matter, cope with her.

On an impulse I went to the telephone: I wanted to talk to my sister. As I reached it, Kate was there, already, cowering and shivering, her fingers in her mouth.

'Who are you going to ring up?' she begged.

'I am going to talk to your mother.'

'Oh please, please, please,' she squeaked, and squirmed, 'oh please . . .'

'Go and sit down,' I said, snapping, suddenly furious. 'Go and sit down. *She's my sister*. Now shut up and sit down.'

Of course she did not move, but stood staring as I dialled. My sister was not in: she was, no doubt, administering to the poor or the distressed in some way or other.

And what had I wanted to say to her? Something like: But how did Kate happen?

How did Kathleen come about?

When I left this morning, I woke Kate up where she was lying asleep in the sofa, surrounded by the usual mess of crisps and chocolate: 'Kate, I don't want to be followed today. Do you understand?'

She gazed up at me, blank. Then she nodded, remembering, an anxious nod. As if I had said something like, Please remember to open the windows, or do the washing-up.

But as soon as I had said it I felt silly. It was like saying to her that she mustn't have her friends in. Like saying: Since they've eaten everything up, if we are going to eat tonight, then you'd better buy some food.

Kathleen was outside the pub. I went straight up to her and said, 'Kathleen . . .' She lifted those sleepwalker's eyes to me. She is really a very handsome girl, this Kathleen, with her large rather protuberant hazel eyes, full of light, and a glowing healthy skin, full, naturally red lips. She seems made for activity, for accomplishment; yet there's something in her that contradicts all that. She didn't recognize me at first. It took her some time to put together this appearance of me, the hated one—for I suppose I must be that—immediately before her, saying, 'Kathleen . . . Come in and have a drink,' with her doubtless horrible fantasies. She gave an unwilling half-smile, as if this was an invitation on an ordinary occasion; then looked annoyed, and walked away, in that slow, ponderous way as if she has invisible chains on her.

I went into the pub, and there was Richard at our table. The barman, an Irishman, gave me two completely different looks: one, due to this good customer who is in so often at lunchtime, the obviously well-heeled woman from the world of fashion. For of course he has found out everything about us both. And the other a quick hard stare from the surface of his blue Connemara eyes, which is for this middle-aged woman who is in some kind of relationship unsuitable for her age with this doctor man, who, like an Irishman, travels to do his work in another country. He made the comparison himself. My whisky was already waiting at my place, and I slid into it saying, 'I asked Kathleen to come in and join us.'

'So did I.'

'I don't think she liked it.'

'No.'

I looked around that pub, our pub, our cosy brown-wood-walled, red-curtained, brass-railed lair; and I saw it all as a bit tawdry and faded, and the customers, that splendid lunchtime mob of enjoyers and good fellows, as people putting a face on things, with anxiety not far behind. The doors were open on to the hot dusty street, the noise of the cars was too loud. In short, reality was too much with us; and I said, 'Perhaps we should try another pub.'

And Richard said, 'No, we should stick it out.'

'Do you think Kathleen will go on trailing us? Now that her two worlds have been brought together. Now that we have invited her?'

'Not at once. She is off today to see her grandmother. My mother is unhappy in this new Home I found. No—she's not going to move again. She said on the telephone that she had understood it was herself she can't stand, not the Home.'

I suddenly said, 'Ah, Kathleen wants you to have her grandmother in America with you? And blames you because you won't?'

'How can we? Maria can just about cope with John. She couldn't manage an old woman who has to have everything done for her.' Again that unknown, Sylvia, presented herself, and after a while Richard said, 'My wife is very eminent in her field. Much more than I am. If anyone was to give up working to look after my mother, then it should logically be me.'

'How long is Kathleen going for?'

He said in a low, tired, distressed voice, 'I hope for a long time. She is giving us hell. Isn't it extraordinary how they blame us for everything? Take it out on us? Punish us? Did we do that? I don't think I did. I don't remember anything of the sort. I left home before I was twenty. What about you?'

'I found myself a flat, and I went home when I had to out of a sense of duty.' After a silence I found that I had to add, 'But that was not the end of it of course. To put it mildly!'

'Well, I suppose I shall in duty be bound to listen to all of it, Janna. And so will you—to my perplexities. But I feel very cheerful as I have had a reprieve. I really did think that I was going to have to go up north again and settle poor Mother into yet another Home. And that would have taken away another two weeks from our time together.'

I sat silent, thinking of how we had been in what I found myself thinking of as 'the early days', when we first met, in April; being with each other was a dazzle and a freedom, inside a magic circle where ordinary life was not . . .

He said, 'All right. I know that look on a woman's face. I know it only too bloody well. You are thinking very practical thoughts. And the words *ought* and *should* and *have* to are about to make an appearance.'

'In my experience they do.'

'Something to do with this expertise of yours, about the aged?'

I said I wanted another drink. Patrick, the barman, slid to the edge of the bar with a practised air the two glasses, one with ice and one without; and he stood for a moment looking out past the heads of his customers into the glare of the street. He is a proper Irishman, jaunty and fluent, and uses the charm of his voice for all he is worth, and of course people like him for it and incite him to use all his wild inventiveness, smiling as the English do at our lack of what they have so much of; but today he was rather bony and gaunt, and there was sweat on his forehead: I was looking at some kind of anxiety. Until that morning I had flatly refused to think of this charming witness of our meetings as a man with the weight of an ordinary life on him, but now I had to. Oh, a great pity the pub doors were open, heat or no heat.

I told Richard about Maudie. It was difficult, because I had this strong sense of her, that awkward old woman, and how we were so involved, she and I, how—and here is this word again—I loved her; and yet the words I had to use seemed so inappropriate, did not convey anything. I said that I had met this old woman, she was in need of help, I offered it, got in deeper than I had meant, and had ended by being something not far off a daughter to her, for a long time—years. She died. And how that had led to my befriending Eliza Bates and Annie, and how I still see old Annie at least two or three times a week; and how it has become so much a part of my life that dropping in for an hour or two is like shopping, or seeing my clothes are in order. I go in, finding *her* despondent and bloody-minded; and slowly absorb like a sponge all her miseries, till she is quite sprightly and nice, and I go out, and give myself a great shake outside her door, and feel all that weight of depression go flying off and away.

I had my eyes on his face, of course, needing to know how he would take this eccentricity, as Jill insists it is; or worse, a sign of some horrible elderly perversion, like approaching senility. He did not comment until I had stopped and his face was kept noncommittal, with the look I describe to myself as the doctor's look.

'Yes, but why?' he asked quietly.

'It was like this. When my mother died, I was useless. Good for nothing.'

Unexpectedly he laughed, and said, 'You couldn't stand being inadequate in that? You had to feel you could cope with that—as well?'

I said, and with difficulty, 'First of all it was my husband. He died first. Of cancer. I didn't want to know. I simply cut myself off from it all. Now I cannot bear to think . . .' But I couldn't go on with that thought, then: I steadied my voice, and said, 'Not long after, there was my mother. Cancer. I can say I was a bit better than with my husband. At least I was ashamed at how awful I had been with Freddie, so I tried with my mother. Well, a little bit. But I couldn't. I didn't know how.'

'Ah,' he remarked, as I sat silent, hoping he would fill it all in for himself.

'And so that's it,' I said.

'Are you afraid of cancer?' he asked, unexpectedly.

'No. I simply cannot see why it should be worse than other things. I know that is quite an eccentric thought.'

'I agree with you.'

'And I'm not afraid of dying. And that is so eccentric that I don't dare to say it. People don't believe it, for a start.'

'It is one thing sitting here on a warm July day, saying, One day I will die—and actually dying.'

'I know that,' I said. I was disappointed. In him. But then he remarked, redeeming himself, 'Again, I agree with you. But then I've seen so much of it. Death, I mean.'

I said, 'I have learned to keep quiet now. If you say, I am not afraid of death, of dying, people react as if you are lacking in proper feelings. And it is not only in that area either. It seems to me that nearly all the things I really think, really believe—I can't say. For one thing, that I like living alone. That's another . . .' But as I said this I heard my voice shake, and it was because it came over me that if I could live with Richard I might not prefer solitude. But then I thought

that for all I knew this ease of being with someone was
because it was not tested by the grind of bed, board and
conversation about grubby chair covers.

'I can't even imagine what it might be like to live alone,' he
said. 'I went from home to share a room with Sylvia, and
that's been it. I think I admire you. I don't even know
whether I could do it.'

This word *admire* was cold, or it seemed so to me.

I wanted most desperately to weep, to put my head under
the covers, to shut out glare, light, noise—reality.

He saw this, and said, 'Perhaps we should try another
place. Let's make a move.'

Outside Kathleen was standing. Richard and I went up to
her. He said nicely, 'Kathleen, aren't you going to miss your
train?'

'I'm not going till eight.'

'Ah.'

There we stood, the three of us. Were we all three to go to
another pub? But Kathleen again solved it by turning away,
as if she had to; as if she were being forced to by some power
outside or in her. There was something blind and mechanical
in it; and she walked away across the road not seeing a car
which had to grind to a halt, hooting.

I said, 'But Richard, surely this isn't *normal,* it isn't sane
behaviour?'

Richard said, 'My dear Janna, it's no more crazy than
anything else!'

I said, 'Do you mean us, you and I?'

'No, I didn't mean that. But I suppose I could have!'

I said, 'I think it is crazy—I mean, Kathleen. And you and
Sylvia are like my sister and her husband. There's this *mess*
Kate, and they simply pretend nothing very much is wrong.'

Richard took this seriously: though if he had matched my
seethe of distress and anger he would have shouted at me or
been unkind. He said, 'Is that what you really think? Is that
what you've been thinking? But what can we do, Janna?' This
we I first took as he and me—*we:* then realized the *we* was he
and Sylvia. I shook my head, too full of the need to cry. He
turned me to him, took me by the arms, and stood holding

me, his hands on my elbows, looking into my face.

'Janna,' he said, 'but what can we do?' Meaning, this time, he and me, Richard and Janna.

I shook my head: 'I don't know.'

'Would you like to go and have some lunch? Shall we walk for a bit?'

I shook my head. A taxi came creeping down the narrow street, hooting. I said, muffled and shocked. 'Ring me, Richard, you must ring me, I don't have your number remember.' This sounded like the wildest accusation, a lover's complaint, and I got into the taxi and burst into tears at last. His concerned, weary face: it is in front of me now.

I was very hungry. I forgot to bring in food: Kate of course is never hungry because of her eternal crisps and Mars Bars. There is literally nothing in the place but some dried milk. I shall make myself hot chocolate: a comfort drink; and go to bed thinking, like a young girl, But *will* he ring me tomorrow?

He did ring me, but I was out at the Eminent Women Luncheon. He left a message that he would ring again. But not when.

Tonight I rang my sister, and she said, 'How's Kate?'

I said, 'Kate is as she always is.' (She was out at her squat, or trailing me for all I know, so I could talk freely.)

I was waiting for Georgie to say something to the point. But she said, 'It is very kind of you, Jane, to have Kate.'

I didn't know what to say. 'Georgie,' I said at last, feeling the uselessness of it, 'surely there is something very wrong with Kate?'

'No!' This was quick, defensive, offended. 'She'll be all right. Her trouble has always been Jill. Jill always over-shadowed Kate, but now, you'll see, she'll find herself.'

'Ah,' I said, sounding like Richard, noncommittal. 'In that case, all right.'

But I didn't put down the receiver. I could not. I was waiting for Georgina to say something, almost anything, that wasn't inane. I was feeling that she couldn't possibly be meaning it, be serious. And then, in fact, came *the other voice*, and I wondered if I have ever heard anything like it from Sister Georgie before? She said, 'Well, why shouldn't you take Kate on? Why not? Why should it be any problem to you? Everything comes so easily to you, you are such a success at everything, the world's your oyster, isn't it, it always has been.' Her light, hurrying voice, almost indifferent, as if in this way she need own no responsibility for them, for Georgie's thoughts thus blown or breathed at me, but then probably at once forgotten, for she remarked quite casually, 'I've got to rush, Jane, Tom's chocolate is on the hotplate. It is our bedtime, you know.'

I was out all this afternoon, interviewing Randy Sykes, the Singing Footballer, very attractive, so I'm told, but not to me; a dish, the would-be upmarket career woman's secret dreamboat, her bit of rough. And when I got back to the office they said Richard had rung to say he would be outside here, my place not the office, at six. It was already half past five. Hannah and Jill watched me, no comment, as I scrabbled for my things and fled down the stairs to the underground. I made it—just. A dark blue Volvo waited under the plane tree at the corner. I could see Kate's face at the window above, an anxious blur. I escaped into the car, and there he was.

We drove up past St Albans, and found a pub and spent the evening there. We did not discuss his problems or my problems, or the state of the world or of Britain. Taboo! I have just got in: after twelve, and Kate is not here. I am too happy to worry.

Richard has got the loan of a colleague's car for a fortnight. We intend to make the most of it.

This morning I found Kate asleep on the sofa, bedraggled, sullen.

I said to her that I was not going to be in in the evenings, and suggested she should arrange to spend them with her pals in the squat. This enraged her: for I was supposed to be hating her and her squat-mates, and was probably meant too to have thrown her out, or to have called the police to threaten them, I don't know, and I don't care.

I have also rung up old Annie's neighbour to say I will be on holiday for a fortnight. When we—I, or her Home Help, or the woman upstairs—go on holiday or away even for a weekend, Annie shows all the anxieties of a child who has good reason to think a parent might disappear for ever. I feel more disquiet about abandoning Annie for two weeks than I do over Kate. Annie has nothing, no one, no hope. Kate has a future. I'd rather not think *what*; but there is now a curious little toughness between us, which we both recognize. I have not performed that act, like a turning of a key, which divorces one from somebody, when you have had enough: I am not inwardly pushing her away, meaning this to be felt by her as an edict: Now, go! On the contrary, this inner strengthening is more like an acceptance. I cannot change her, nor do much for her; but I am not going to throw her out. There is no point in doing anything about my poor living room, which looks like a slum. It can stay as it is—until *she chooses* to leave.

'My mother wouldn't like it if she knew I was spending time at the squat,' said Kate virtuously and pathetically, with a small child's sniff, tears welling.

'I don't like it either,' I said cheerfully, 'but I didn't notice that that stopped you. And as for trailing me about, it is a waste of time because we won't be in London.'

'Where will you be?'—as if she expected me to give her exact information.

What a lovely time we have had. Three weeks of it, not two. Warm, indulgent weather, everyone and everything slowed by heat, and good-natured, the way we all get in England when it is really hot. Every afternoon Richard has waited for me, at six, and we drove up into the little villages of Essex and Hertfordshire, a different one every day, not getting back until twelve or one. During this time everything but our being together has been 'noises off'; the office—well, I've been in it, I've done what I've had to do, and Charlie, Hannah, Jill, have accepted my condition. A wonderful thing, people working together when they are working well, making allowances, giving a little here, staking a little claim there, like a sort of amoeba, flexible and encompassing. All that Charlie said, and he has had to work harder than usual: 'Well, Janna, it's nice to see you being so relentlessly bent on pleasure.' All Jill said was: 'Mark says you look more relaxed with your boyfriend than I do with mine.' Hannah hasn't said anything, but her smile offers well-considered encouragement.

But now that's over; and it is because, I know, Sylvia has come back from somewhere or other, for when I said I could easily hire a car, Richard shook his head. She hasn't been mentioned; nor Kathleen, who has been in Hull with her grandmother; nor Kate; nor John, nor Matthew. All that has been far away, on the other side of the hill, beyond a screen of leaves and flowering shrubs and roses. Summer. Nearly every evening we have sat out in gardens at the backs of pubs. It is amazing how many pubs have a garden, even a little one, a couple of wooden tables at the edge of a patch of drying lawn; the scent of roses. It has been very dry. We have sat on and on in long slow twilight, watching the light leave the garden and go up into banks of white cloud, or become absorbed into the dazzle of streets. Driving back, on different little roads every night, we have stopped the car on a hill, and watched a yellow field flash out as the car lights swept across it, like a knife cutting, slice, slice, slice, in regular illuminations with soft blank dark between; or we have got out of the car in a wood and crept a little way into it, afraid of disturbing the life that goes on just out of the scope of the passing traffic. We have sat on a log under silent trees for an hour, two, holding hands, hardly breathing, listening. I have never done anything like it in my life, my urban, street-loving life. And in three weeks I've seen more little pubs, cafés, restaurants, curiously inventive and original places, run by people with a talent and a gift, than I have in years. Nothing to stop me, any time, doing the same: looking from this high point, a Sunday evening after this marvellous time, at my ordinary life, it seems so flat, and I think that *one day*—meaning, when Richard goes away—I shall hire a car, or borrow one, invite Jill or Hannah or someone, and jaunt off, without a destination, as I have been doing with Richard. And of course I shan't. For it is Richard who has made it possible; Richard and me: fit us together, like hands joining, and it seems we have only to drive into a village in the late sunlight of this summer, and at once walk into some bar or restaurant or garden so full of character and charm that we are amazed the whole world does not know about it.

Richard said tonight that he will be out of London for a week on a visit to relatives. I take it that means, with Sylvia.

It is already August.

Every night, instead of coming back to the blue Volvo, into which I escaped, I've been going first of all in to Annie. Oh, what a load of misery! Annie has come to anchor in her large chair, which I got her off the pavement outside a shop. It was once a grand chair, of crimson brocade, with tall back and wings, deep and comfortable, draught-excluding. Sometimes I brood that I should never have brought it in, to swallow Annie's life up.

Her day goes like this. She wakes early, at six or seven, and at once gets up, for she is not one to lie in bed. She struggles to the commode, using her frame. She returns to sit on the bed, where her clothes are, at its foot. She has not taken off her vest, so she puts on over it, fumbling and angry with the intransigence of *things*, a man's white cotton singlet, extra outsize, since she can get nothing else on comfortably. Then a skirt made for her by me, on an elastic, then a cotton cardigan which though outsize hardly covers her. She balances to the big chair, where there is a thermos of tea. She switches on a bar of the electric fire, summer or winter, for its companionship. 'It's not as nice as a cat though,' says Annie. Her cat was run over a year ago and she will sit and weep for him, alone.

She switches on the radio, and twiddles from station to station in search of her need, which is for the popular songs of any time up to about twenty years ago. Failing that, she listens to news, or the disc jockeys joking away between records that don't interest her: 'Funny music,' she says, 'like mad people howling.' She drinks all the tea in her thermos. Everyone who comes in, me, the Home Help, the nurses who come to wash her, the nurse who comes to check her pulse and breathing and give her pills, tells her she is capable of going to the kitchen to make her own tea. She did it for a long time, filling the thermos and carrying it back looped over her frame. But she won't. She won't use the lavatory in the bathroom, but insists on the commode: says it takes too long to get to the bathroom. 'It's such a long walk down the passage,' says she, to the bathroom, to the kitchen, 'not like my own home.'

For Annie is not really living in this nice little two-roomed flat, which 'they' insisted on moving her into. Annie lived at the top of the house down the street, in two large airy rooms where she had been for forty years and never wanted to move. 'But there's no bathroom,' expostulated successive social workers, scandalized at her indifference to this. 'I have never lived anywhere with a bathroom,' said she. 'You can keep yourself clean without that.' 'But it's so draughty.' 'I don't mind the cold.' 'But it's so *old*.' And these young people one and all have looked around the two beautiful shabby rooms, efficiently visualizing how they will look when done up. As her rooms look now, in fact; for I went up to see. They have sliced off the end of the big room, reducing it to a pokey one, and put in a bathroom. The place has lost its symmetry and rightness. It is as well Annie will never see it.

Annie's second room at the back of this new flat of hers is never entered—by her. She lives totally in the front room, the commode at the foot of the bed. And when the nurse who washes her once a week comes and begs her to go to the bathroom and have a lovely shower, she says she will, one day. The nurse brings in a basin and washes her in it as Annie stands naked in front of the fire.

Her clothes accumulate on the back of her regal chair, and she picks out what she needs from them. Her meals are eaten at the window. But in her imagination she lives in her own home, which is in fact now occupied by a single parent with two small children, going mad because of all the stairs.

When Annie has drunk all the tea in the flask she waits until the woman upstairs drops in on her way to work with another cup of tea. A few moments of lively chat, while the woman cries, 'I must go, I'm late, Annie,' and Annie cries, 'Oh, how are you, have you heard from your nephew?', trying to keep her. But Mrs Mount flies off, and Annie sits, angry, discarded, drinking the tea in small sips to make it last.

'And now I'm alone for the rest of the day,' she sniffs, and goes to the table to have breakfast, eating and eating to pass the time. The Home Helps bring to that room with the fat old lady in it enough to feed a family. And Annie eats it all, from boredom. She sits there, the curtains drawn back, throwing a few crumbs out for the sparrows, who entertain her well, cranes to see if the cat from next door is out on the little wall, and can she entice her in? She sits behind her yellow curtains, half hidden, watching and watching and watching, while the people go past on their way to work. But then one turns in at the gate and comes running in: Annie hears the outer door go crashing back, and then the flat door bangs inwards. It is the little lively nurse who gives her the pills. Which are hidden somewhere in the back room. Annie has even dragged herself in there once to look for them. Meaning to throw them all away. She hates the pills. She grumbles incessantly that they make her feel funny and fuddled, that she never feels herself, that she doesn't want them. But 'they' make her take them. The little nurse, all bright black eyes, red cheeks and jolly black curls, stands over her. 'Now Annie, take these two.' 'I don't want to.' 'But the doctor says you must.' 'What are they for?' 'They are for your heart.' 'But what's wrong with my heart?' 'Oh, it's what the doctor says that goes dear, you know that. If he says it's your heart, your heart it is.' For the nurses don't always like these handfuls of pills they have to force their poor old crones to take. Annie swallows six pills in all, two for her heart, two for her water, and two to counteract the side effects of the other four. And just as Annie is crying, 'Then sit down and have a cup of tea, take the weight off your feet,' the nice nurse is on her way out: 'Not today, Annie, I can't, I'm doing someone else's work as well as my own.' And bang, bang, the two doors are shut, and Annie watches the girl fly off, waving as she goes behind the hedge. Annie sits burping, raging but dully, for she knows it is no use. Before they sent the nurse in every day to make sure she took the pills, she used to throw them into the toilet, or into the bottom of her handbag, or into a drawer, but they always found out, sniffing and snooping about among her own personal things. The only one who doesn't say, why have you thrown away your pills? is Janna, and she, Annie, knows what Janna thinks of all these pills, oh, I'm not a fool, I can read her face, and I can read all their faces, they think I'm stupid and dead and gone, and I'm not.

There is a clock by Annie's chair which she tries not to watch. It is only nine o'clock in the morning: she seems to have been up and about for hours. She finds some chocolate, and nibbles: the pills give her a nasty taste in her mouth. And now she is drowsy, but is afraid to sleep, because if there is one thing she dreads it is lying awake at night thinking. Of her life; of what it has become. She pulls herself over to the commode, relieves herself. Shuts down the lid at once, goes back to her big chair, and is about to drowse off when she sees that another nurse, one she doesn't know, is standing over her. Come to wash her, she says. 'I don't want a wash,' mutters Annie. 'Well, that's what you've got to have,' says the nurse. 'You've got a bathroom here, it says on my sheet.' 'I am washed in this room here,' announces Annie, energy coming into her with the battle. 'If you want to wash me, then you can bring a basin in.' The nurse, well used to ancient cantankerousness, stands with her fingers pinching her hips on either side, as if they had a throat between them. Annie and she exchange long combative stares. The nurse recognizes that this stubborn old woman is not going to give in. With an angry mutter not unlike Annie's, she marches off to the kitchen, puts on a kettle. There could be hot water, but that is only switched on for special purposes. As Annie keeps saying, I've never had hot water laid on, why should I have it now? When the kettle is hot, the basin full of warm water is carried in, put on newspapers on the table where Annie eats;

and Annie strips herself naked, winter or summer. For she really doesn't feel the cold. Years of living in inadequately and unevenly heated rooms have given her immunity, and when we, her mentors—and jailers—stand about shivering in coats and sweaters, Annie may well be sitting in a cotton cardigan, saying she wants to switch a bar of the fire off, she's too hot. The nurse washes Annie, efficiently, but not with tenderness for this white plump delicate flesh. Annie, standing nude, because she is fat is comely, does not sag, is all comfortable rolls and curves. 'And where are your clean clothes?' demands this nurse, who hasn't said a word, since she is cross, starving poor Annie of the chat she craves for. Annie says, 'I can dress myself,' though on her card it states she cannot. She swings herself naked on her frame to the big chair, and puts on a vest that is in fact stale and an uncertainly clean pair of knickers. The nurse shrugs, picks up the clothes Annie has discarded, whisks off the basin and the towel, and disposes of the lot next door for the Home Help to deal with. She has said, 'Goodbye, I'm off,' before Annie can cry out, Have a cup of tea, and a sit-down.

Incredulously, Annie sees that it is only ten o'clock. She is no longer sleepy. She yearns, longs for tea. But she feels tired after all that effort, and does not move. She listens to the radio. She is waiting for the the Home Help: she knows Janna never comes in the mornings, or only when Annie is sick. So it shows she could come in the mornings, if she wanted. But the Home Help does not come. Annie is now limp with self-pity and loneliness. How would they like it sitting here all day, alone, with nothing to look forward to?

She moves back to the window, but there's nothing to see. Mid-morning, everyone at work now, only a few old people crawling along the pavement. The woman next door who has four small children gives Annie some interest, but today is not to be seen. Nor is her cat. A shaggy brown dog who sometimes begs Annie for something noses after the sparrows' crumbs, and Annie shouts at him, enraged, 'You filthy thing!' The dog trots off. 'Leaving nothing for the poor sparrows,' sniffs Annie, and she has a bit of a cry. She is also frightened, for her heart is feeling funny. It often does these days. 'Once I didn't even have a heart,' mutters Annie, and it is as if 'they' have caused this to happen too.

Now she is waiting for the Meals on Wheels. It makes a change. She is praying that the dinner and the Home Help don't come together, for she doesn't get the fun of either of them then. She likes her pleasures one by one. Tea! She scrambles along to the kitchen, makes herself some tea, and drinks it sitting with her face to the wall at a little table that 'they' have put there, saying that she can use it as a place to eat if she can't be troubled to eat at the big table next door. How would they like to sit with their faces six inches from a nasty white wall? She drinks two cups of tea, and drags herself back to her big chair. It is twelve o'clock. *Half the day gone, that's something*. She rests there, gets her breath back, empties herself into the commode, and goes to the table. The young lady from the Meals on Wheels knocks on the window. Annie slides it up, knowing better than to hope for her to come in for a bit of a chat. Annie longs for this to happen. These girls seem to her so lively and so friendly. 'Hello, Annie, hello, how are you? But we have to rush.' And they do. Of course it is a charity, they say they do it for nothing; all the same, it would be nice. The two little oblong containers are sitting one above another, on the sill. Annie carefully opens the first, and she is sick with disappointment. It is Wednesday, she had forgotten; Wednesday they bring this great sog of a pie, all damp crust with some dubious mince in it, a spoonful if that. She loathes cabbage. She hates carrot. She picks at the mince, her face squeezed up with distaste. No, she cannot. She investigates the pudding. It is a sponge, in custard. 'On a hot day like this, you'd think they'd give us a bit of salad,' she moans. And eats slices of white bread and jam and biscuits, one after another, till she's full.

She goes to her big chair and sleeps like death. She awakes to find Maureen standing over her; 'Annie . . . Annie . . . are you asleep?' She comes up out of deep dark miles of sleep, muttering, 'My mouth, my mouth, I'm so dry . . .' 'I've got the kettle on,' says Maureen, and bustles about. Annie knows by the haste of Maureen, and because she has put on the kettle at once, that she need not expect the pleasure of her company for even a quarter of the time she is supposed to stay. 'And they pay her for it too,' as Annie mutters every day as Maureen trips off, saying that she has to rush, because— whatever she says the reason is on that day. Annie is so pleased to see Maureen, but she cannot help herself. Out pours the long day's and the long night's deprivations, in a savage, dirty stream. Annie says that she's sick of this life. Sick of it all and sick of all of you. She sometimes wishes she could go right away somewhere. To a little cottage some- where, that would be best. Or she could go and stay with her sister ... While Annie shouts and moans, Maureen is whisking up the bed covers and emptying the commode. In a moment there is a cup of tea for Annie, and the thermos flask is full again. Maureen has sat down, on the little seat by the fire, with her own cup in her hand. She has a sandwich in a piece of clingwrap on her knee. Annie likes it better than anything when the Home Help, or anyone else, has time to sit and have a cup with her, but she cannot stop her shouting and complaining, and she can see from Maureen's face that she—Annie—is going to get it back in full measure. And she does. Maureen drinks all her tea at once, brushes off the crumbs from her lap into the grate, and stands up. She tells Annie she has no one to blame for her solitude but herself. She could go to the Lunch Centre, and she won't. She could have a Visitor to come and talk to her, and she won't. She could go on a council-paid holiday, and she won't. 'Why should I go off with all those old people?' shouts Annie. 'And they'd send me with all those cripples, oh yes, I know, you can't tell *me*.' And she stares triumphantly at Maureen. Who sighs, and decides she won't bother. Silence. Maureen unpacks her shopping bag, putting out bars of chocolate and a pound of sweets, cigarettes, loaves of sliced white bread, some ham, some tomatoes. 'And you're eating yourself silly,' she announces, 'where do you put all this food?' 'I couldn't eat the dinner,' whines Annie. Maureen inspects the Meals on Wheels dinner and knows it is not appetizing. All the same, as she tips it into the bin, she is thinking, And all those starving people, etc. She has not been there half an hour, when she announces her departure. She has not swept, or cleaned, or done anything very much. Annie does not care about all that; she cares that Maureen is going. And she goes. Saying, 'See you tomorrow, about three.' She has taken some notes from Annie's handbag for the things Annie has requested: sweets, cigarettes, chocolates, a decent bit of fruit, a bit of chicken, something I can *eat*.

Annie thinks, Surely there should be more money than this! I had all those notes. But what is the use, they'll say it's my fault.

It is half past one. Annie stares, appalled at the long afternoon ahead. She can't face it. Every day, at this time, she thinks of killing herself. But how? Killing herself has an abstract, vague quality for Annie: she does not think of actually doing anything, like swallowing all her pills at once, but it is dramatic, like something on the telly. She sees Vera and Janna and Mrs Mount and Maureen standing around her corpse and asking, How could she do that to us? The long, long afternoon wears on. She sits at the window. She watches some television: but it is getting more and more incomprehensible to her. She eats bread and jam and cake and biscuits and chocolate. She drinks up all her tea. She listens to her radio. All this in short, fidgety snatches, unable to settle. At five o'clock she is at the window, waiting for the people to come home from work. Soon Mrs Mount comes in, says hello. Says she is in a hurry, collects her empty mug and goes up. Now Annie can listen to her moving about upstairs.

Suddenly the lights click on in the passage, the door opens: it is Janna. How smart she looks, thinks Annie, in a respectful way: not for the person of Janna, but for her clothes. She looks like something out of a magazine, Annie knows. She knows too, from a hundred little signs, that Janna will not be staying long. She is determined not to drive her away with her tongue. Janna is examining Annie as Annie examines Janna: how is she, what is her mood, what can I expect? But everything is all right today. Janna has brought in a small bottle of Scotch, and pours them both out generous drinks. She has brought Annie some freesias and a single pink rose with some maidenhair fern. Although it is still light outside, Annie asks Janna to pull the curtains. Inside there is an air of companionship, festivity. Drinking their Scotch, Annie smoking, Annie listening to how Janna has been driving around Essex or somewhere. With some friend. Janna does not say with whom. Annie has never been to Essex, does not know where it is, so she cuts in to what Janna is saying with an account of how she went with her husband to the dog racing. She knows she has often told Janna the story, but she feels it doesn't matter, Janna is listening so nicely.

'And he always bought me some eels, because he knew I loved them. He didn't like them. Lovely stewed eels with green sauce and mashed potato. He bought me white port to drink with it, and he drank stout. Oh, he spoiled me, my husband did. We used to go every weekend, the two of us, and he always gave me the money for a bit of a bet.'

Janna says, 'But weren't you working then?'

Annie hates these practical questions, pinning her down, suspects Janna of not believing her. 'Yes, but I never had any money, did I? I used to spend it on my clothes. I used to look nice, I did. What money did I have to put on a bit of a bet? And I won once. I won five pounds. That was a lot! He said to me, And aren't you going to give me the bet money back? Not I, I said. I bought myself a coatdress I had my eye on, in Oxford Street. It was of black cloth with a big fur collar. I looked a treat, he said. Oh, he was good to me, he was.' And Annie sits snuffling, but there is also something else on her face: she is remembering—what? Sometimes Annie says in that other voice, the one that intrudes, breaking in through the crust of ordinary life, 'When I married, I didn't know what I was doing. I was used to the West End, wasn't I? I knew my way about I did . . . and he never wanted to go out.'

Minutes before Janna actually rises to leave, Annie knows she is going to. Then Janna says, 'I've got to go home, Annie.' She gets up, puts down by Annie some cigarettes she bought for her. She smiles, lingers by the door, says, 'I'll be in tomorrow if I can.' Annie knows she feels guilty. She wasn't in at all for three weeks.

And now Annie feels better. The day is gone; the night is here. She's got through another of these dreadful dragging days. She makes herself some supper, ham between bread, thick with delicious salty butter, tomatoes. She has some more of the Scotch Janna has brought.

When the Good Neighbour arrives at nine thirty, Annie is watching television, and does not want to be interrupted. It is a film of Vivien Leigh, made in the days when they knew how to make films. The Good Neighbour, Lucie from three doors down, makes sure the thermos is filled, the windows are locked, and that Annie seems adequately cheerful. She sits for a while, watching the film. Which ends. And now Annie turns to her, all animation, wanting her to stay. But Lucie has to get back to her own husband and her three children. She says good night cheerfully, and goes. It is ten o'clock. Annie watches some television, listens to some radio. The one thing she will not do is to go to bed one minute before midnight. Even so when she does, lying there in vest and knickers, she lies awake for some time. The light from a car swirls across the ceiling, and she thinks, That's funny, that light reaching all the way up here—for she is back in her mind in the old place, her home, at the top of the house opposite where all that can be seen from the windows is the sky. 'No, I must be here then, not there,' she mutters, and drops off into black sleep.

It seems to me that Annie is going downhill fast. 'Deteriorating', as the geriatric specialists put it. There's the external evidence: the nurses coming in every day to make her take the pills; this is a new thing, in the last month or so. But there's an angry restlessness in her, a distress. Her fantasies are those of a desperate person. She has a sister, as old as she, crippled with arthritis, chair-bound, the scourge of three children who take turns to come in to her. Years ago this sister shed Annie, who, when she was retired against her will at seventy from the waitress job she had off Oxford Street, went to pieces. Her husband long dead, her life and interests were in her work. Her work gone, there was nothing. Annie drank, became a disreputable and dirty old hen snuffling about the streets waiting for the pubs to open. Her sister told her not to come again. Not in a thousand years would her sister allow Annie to live with her; the nieces and nephew would not dream of taking on two burdens where now there was one. All this Annie must know, in some part of her mind. Or knew. Now she has chosen not to know; for 'they' have started talking about a Home, even Janna. 'They' say she would have more company there, not be alone all day. 'They' say that they will take her into a Home for a week to see if she likes it, and then if not she can come home to her flat again. They are like a cloud of flies buzzing in and out, with bad news, and she can't escape from them. But over in Seven Sisters Road there's her sister, and she will go and live with her and ... Where's that address, I'll get Janna to write.

I have written to this sister probably twenty letters of every kind, politely giving information: 'Your sister Annie is well, and sends her regards to all the family,' letters that are dictated by Annie and beg for help. 'How are you, Lil? I sit here and think of all the good times we had. I do not seem to have had a letter from you. Did you get my Christmas card?' I send Christmas cards, Easter cards, postcards that I bring back from my journeys abroad for *Lilith* with views of canals in Amsterdam and the blue Danube and cafés in Paris, and these pathetic pleas are never acknowledged.

'Yes,' I say, 'I wrote two weeks ago, don't you remember?'

'Two weeks, no, it wasn't two weeks,' she says, sullen. 'How could it be two weeks?'

I am silent; for she is really protesting about time itself, the deceiver, who has whisked her life away from under her feet.

'Well, you just find my writing paper and I'll tell you what to say.'

Dear Lil, How are you? I am not what I used to be ...

She painfully signs it, and her *Annie* looks like the first attempt of a very small child.

I sit there, as I did with Maudie, and with Eliza, looking at an old woman who I know, if she could be with a family, or even one other person, would live another ten years, or twenty years. As it is, she is being eaten up with unused vitality that beats through her on the rhythm of her bitter lonely thoughts: 'High blood pressure, they say I've got,' mutters Annie, her face flaming scarlet, feeling the blood thud and pound. 'High blood pressure, is it?'

Annie, I know, is going to die of rage, like Maudie, and like Eliza. And the rage is fed every day by us, by 'them', who drop in and out, with our smiling, lying faces; the faces of good friends, who will leave two containers of food, wash her, sweep her floor, make her a cup of tea, but who—now it has come to the point—fade out, start talking of a Home. 'A home! But I have a home,' mutters Annie, and sighs; meaning the beautiful rooms from which she was taken, surrounded by friendly smiling faces, though she had said a thousand times she did not want to go, did not need a bathroom, hot water.

'Liars,' I can hear Annie mutter, after I'd remarked that she could perhaps try the Lunch Centre.

'But you have never even tried it, Annie.'

'I don't know them. Who are they?'

'You would know them, once you've been.'

Annie sits solid, this fat little woman who comes up to lower than my shoulders, her flowered skirts spread about her, her broad red face lowered as she stares angrily at the dirty rug, thick with cigarette ash, food scraps, dust. The Home Help said this morning that she had done it yesterday, and she wasn't going to do it again!

When she lifts her small blue eyes to me they are full of resentment. And my look at her, I know, is exasperated.

I contemplate the closed circle that is Annie's mind, her life. She will *not* take one step out of her lethargy, will not break this circle. If she did—so we, her tormentors, like to fantasize—she would find someone, perhaps more than one, at the Lunch Centre, or on the coach trip, or the church bazaar, who would like her, who would come and visit her. For she's likeable enough, old Annie, when she's lively. And from this one friend would come others. Annie would become part of the community of old ladies in the area, who live sprightly brave lives, gossiping and visiting, making little trips and dropping in and out of each other's houses.

Think of Eliza Bates, we all cry, think of how she got out and about!

'But she's dead,' says Annie triumphantly, with that knowing wag of the head that means: I've got you there.

'But when she was alive. She was doing all sorts of things almost until she died.'

'How can I, with my frame?'

'But lots of people have frames, and get about.'

Cornered, Annie mutters that she will, when the weather is fine. Every day this last week she has said that she will, when it is fine; and the sun has been blazing down in its heavy insistent late-summer way. One little step out of this revolving circle of hers, and Annie would . . .

But this decision was made years ago, when she decided she would have a walking frame, though all of 'them' said she could walk perfectly well without a frame.

'One day, when it's fine . . .' Annie muttered then.

Oh, what a horrid warning Annie is to me; as I sit opposite, listening for the hundredth time to how she wore a pink dress with blue spots, when she and her sister went out together that night; how she used to cook apple sauce for her husband to eat with his pork chops, but she wondered how he could like it; how when he died of cancer—because his lung had got that shrapnel in it in the First World War—she got compensation and she spent it on a black rabbit-fur coat with silk buttons, and a fox-fur stole which is lying, a ragged brown smelly lump, in a drawer. It has bright button eyes that appear suddenly, as one of our hands dislodges a scarf or a stocking. 'What have you done with my pink chiffon scarf?' 'I don't know, Annie, I'll have a look.'

All this I listen to, and think about and say to myself, as I keep my face smiling and friendly, I will not be like her, I will not. I will not die of rage, nor blunder about a dirty room like a bedraggled old bird, knocking against a hundred things that stand up against me like enemies. Annie's life is being banged, beaten, eaten out of her by things. Walls of them close her in. The passage to the kitchen is so long and slippery. She puts down a glass and cannot find it, for it has maliciously concealed itself. She has broken the lenses of her glasses and has hidden them, because she can't bear Janna or Maureen to nag at her to get new ones. Her hands slip on the grips of her walking frame, because for some reason butter has got there. Her fingers have become thick and difficult, and let things slide through. On the table where she sits to eat, she will look for a bottle of ketchup for half an hour and find it right by her plate, where it must have walked. Sometimes it seems to her as if she sits crouching like an animal in some dirty corner, afraid to creep out because *things* will trap her; or as if she has some mysterious illness, about which she even speculates—Have I got a bit of flu then?—whose main symptom is that *things* have become her enemy. Perhaps I've got a bit of that paralysis, is that it? Isn't that what they call it when you can't move as you fancy?

I find myself, as I sit there, surreptitiously rubbing one hand with another, moving my fingers about, twining them in my lap; as I watch Annie fumbling among objects that slip and slide away.

On the first evening I came in after work, after visiting Annie, there was Kate, hugging her little machine in her arms, gazing at me from between the wires, sitting in the corner of the sofa.

I leaned down and shouted, 'Do you want some supper?'

She stared, then slowly removed the earphones.

'Aren't you going out?' she pathetically asked.

'No. Will you help me put things away?'

She slowly got up, and trailed after me to the kitchen. I had brought in a great deal; meant to re-stock the cupboards and the refrigerator. As I put a packet of sliced ham down, Kate avidly reached for it and started cramming it in. She seemed unaware she was doing this.

A half-pound of ham disappeared in a moment; she wiped her pudgy grubby hand across her mouth and burped. 'I was hungry, I think,' she volunteered, realizing what she had done.

Then she went scarlet with anger. At me, I suppose. I indicated a heap of packets, and said, 'How about putting them into that cupboard?' She stood fingering them for a while, interested in the packaging, the presentation, then started pushing them anyhow on a shelf. Soon, she stopped and watched me doing it.

'Are we going to have supper together?'

'What would you like?'

'Oh, I don't know . . . anything.'

'Well, sit down, then.'

She dumped herself in a chair, and soon started to look restlessly about: she wanted her music machine.

'No, let's have supper, Kate.'

I put out various cheeses and patés, made a salad, arranged fruit, sat down. Kate was no longer with me. Her eyes were dull and absent.

'Have you been to the squat?'

No reply.

'Kate, have you been here all these three weeks? At the squat? Have they been here?'

'Yes, I think so. Sometimes.'

They have been here, more than once, I think, but while the grubbiness and dinginess increases, no actual damage has been done.

But I wasn't going to ask, because then she would lie. Immediately I had finished this meal, that with Richard would have been so pleasant, and with her was a graceless filling of the stomach, she got up and went back to the living room, reaching for her machine as she flumped into the sofa. I stopped her. 'Kate!'

'What—?'

'Kate, I don't want you to plug yourself into that damned machine yet. I want to talk.'

Suddenly she screeched in a tantrum like a baby, 'Why do you get at me, why do you stop things all the time?'

I shrugged, and let it go.

That was the first evening.

The next night, she was sitting alert and ready for me: she had thought it over, decided she had behaved wrongly, was not going to do it again. It is this in her that encourages me: she does in fact quite often live in the same world as normal people.

I had brought home a lot of work: for of course it has piled up during my three weeks in Arcady. But I put it aside, took trouble over the supper, and made the table look pretty. Smiling hopefully, she trailed about after me, waiting for the chance to be what I wished.

I sat fumbling among words that would do, or would not; offered remarks which were eagerly awaited but then died between us in silences, not embarrassed so much as hopeless; smiled, pressed food on her. But she wasn't hungry: several packets of biscuits had gone from the cupboard.

After supper, baffled, I thought I might as well work, but as we went into the living room she said shyly, with anxiety, 'Aren't you going to put the chair covers on again?'

'But they are full of cigarette holes.'

Restless evasive movements of her whole person: a denial that she was responsible. 'But aren't you going to have new covers?'

'Sit down, Kate.'

She sat opposite me in that filthy sofa, in her mess of crumbs and wrappers and dirty tissues.

I sat, reluctantly, in a chair that had had jam on it, scraped off.

She was so woebegone and pathetic; but I didn't know what to say. I could see it was important to her that I should say, Yes, I am going to do the room up. She had been thinking about it.

What I should perhaps have said was: But, Kate, what is the point of doing the room up, when you are going to ruin it again, you and your friends! But I couldn't say it. Say: *When you've left,* then . . . But that was what she was hearing, as she gazed at me, her eyes frantic.

I said, 'I will get things put right, Kate. Don't worry.' Meaning, Don't worry, I'm not going to throw you out.

Meanwhile, Mrs Brown has finally given me up. She will not clean up after Kate: and that's that.

Every night, leaving Kate there, when I go to have my bath and retreat to my bedroom (the room in which Richard says I am not!), I find myself slumping into discouragement because of Kate; then I rally into energetic decision-making. I marshal sensible remarks to make to her; I imagine conversations.

'Kate, are you planning to go on like this?'

'Well, Jane, I can see that . . .'

'It won't do, Kate. It isn't doing any good, slumping around here, week after week! No, we have to make a real plan for you. What about that Spanish you said you would study? What have you done with the books.'

'I'll find them, Janna. I'll do at least a couple of hours every day.'

But when, with these conversations blue-printed in my mind, I sit down with Kate at the supper table, or in the chair opposite her, they simply evaporate. They had not been addressed to Kate at all: the words for her are some I cannot even imagine, cannot find in my mind. Somewhere inside me I must be convinced that the words exist which will reach Kate. I have only to find them!

Tonight Kate again asked about the covers for the chairs. They have become a symbol to her. I took the wretched yellow covers down to the shop at the bottom of the road and asked them to repeat them. 'In yellow linen?'

'In yellow linen.'

Crazy. I can't put them on the chairs! I can't not put them on, because it will be some kind of blow for Kate.

Today, Jill said to me, as I went through past her and Hannah, 'Did Kate tell you I was in your flat last week?'

'No. Did she ask you to go?'

'When you were off pursuing your love life—*sorry*, Jane, she was ringing me two or three times every evening.'

'Well, I'm not going to apologize for that,' I said, knowing that Jill and Hannah both watched me closely for symptoms of all kinds.

'Who said you should? But one night she sounded quite peculiar, as I went over. I saw the flat.'

'Ah.'

'*Well,* Jane!'

'So what have you decided?'

'Don't be like that. No, it's like this, we—I mean, Mark and me—thought you'd like to come to supper with us.'

'To discuss Kate?'

'And you haven't really seen our flat, have you?'

'Flats,' I said, 'can be quite easily put to rights if they've gone downhill.'

'But people can't.'

'Well, I'm going to trust that means Kate and not me, because I don't propose to apologize for anything.'

I was really quite angry: as I went off into the amiabilities of my office and Charlie's, I heard Jill cry, 'Oh, Jane, of course I didn't mean you, I meant Kate.'

Richard rang. It's been a week. He sounded far away, and he was. Near Dundee somewhere.

He said, 'Jane, it seems we have an inordinate number of relatives, all of whom have to be seen.'

I said, 'Richard, when you're not here it is as if you've dropped off the edge of the world.'

He said, 'It's funny about relatives. I don't think I've given any of mine a thought in five years. Suddenly it's a family necessity. I'm with my cousin William and his family.'

'And then?'

'Oh, Janna. I'm sorry.'

'What's it like, where you are?' For I was remembering that time with Joyce, when she had left *Lilith* and we talked on the telephone, she in places in Wales, and then it was New York: friendship at the end of a long, fading wavelength.

'As I look out of the window I see a small rather cosy lake, with three tourists in a rowing boat; a hillside covered with gorse, and a garden where my cousin's wife Betty is picking asters.'

'Well, I shall be here,' I said.

Supper with Jill and Mark, in Kentish Town.

It is the first floor of a Victorian house, a very large room, off which is a tiny room that has a shower and a lavatory. The place was converted to Mark's prescription. When I shared my first flat with a girl all those years ago, the pattern was the conventional one, scaled down: we had a minute bedroom, small living room, and both of us deciding to eat in the kitchen were defensive with our parents, for it was not then common. But Jill and Mark live in this big room, putting down futons at night, that are rolled up during the day in cupboards, eating at a large low table which is the focus of the sitting area, near the kitchen, which is an assemblage of the most advanced gadgetry: I did not at once recognize these scarlet cabinets and steel surfaces as ovens, grills, refrigerators, etc. Jill and Mark and Hannah and I sat around in low canvas chairs looking out of french windows, uncurtained, but with the old-fashioned wooden shutters painted scarlet, folded back, and a frivolous scalloped scarlet blind half lowered to display a church spire, rising from a sober little garden that allowed itself an exclamation mark: a sheet of purple clematis over the fence. In the street outside, a black youth dressed in a brilliant yellow tracksuit was caressing a dark blue Mercedes with a vast sponge that showered rich white lather everywhere over it and over three children— white, male, adoring—who wished to take part in this ritual of love, but who had to be repelled by continuous assaults of foam. They kept rushing in to touch the car, shouting triumphantly at the black guardian, who shouted at them, but stylishly, in the pace of the game, and then they rushed off again, giggling. The black youth's ears were occluded by the plugs that fed music into his brain and set the rhythm of his smiles and circling, sweeping, smoothing arm. One hand held the transistor. The late sunlight left this scene as we drank various anticipatory mixtures of alcohol, and withdrew itself to the church steeple which glowed a mellow golden brown.

Mark spread plates of bread and olives and tomato salad about on the table while Jill worked on with the next course. Strict equality. 'But I cooked the stew, so you do the vegetables, Mark.' 'But I made the pudding.' 'But I made the pudding on Sunday.' 'All right.'

Jill is wearing jeans and a fantastic harlequin sweater, and her hair, done that day, is dyed purple, the same colour as the clematis, now a sombre inky splodge in the twilight; it is brushed straight up, in short vibrant flames. She looks like a parakeet. Mark is wearing jeans and a cerulean sweatshirt that says on it: Funky III, Montezuma! To ask what it meant would seem to expose a lack of imagination. Hannah, the earth mother, is wearing a full dark green long skirt, and a tight yellow top that leaves her large brown arms bare and exposes the tops of bulging brown breasts where slides a turquoise Navaho necklace. She looks massive. She is sitting slightly back from the three of us, reposing in her chair with her two arms hooked back behind her exposing the salubrious black tufts in her armpits. It goes without saying that she does not wear a bra. Her Aztec face, all proud fine curves, surveys all, and reserves judgement.

The focus of this scene, the sun to whom we turn, is Jill. Why? I wonder often enough what it is that makes this or that person the loadstone in a group for an occasion. Our eyes follow her as we talk: she is all quick, fine, accurate little movements; and her face is concentrated on what her hands do. Mark goes to her, to stare into the stew she is stirring, but really to be close to her. I see how her body gathers itself together at this closeness, not repudiating him, but saying, Later! And, as he slides a kiss on to her neck, she looks up, quick and annoyed, and makes herself smile. He lays a large arm on her shoulders. He looks like a suppliant; but not a humble one. Oh no: Jill need not think . . . Her shoulders did not refuse that lover's arm, but she moves away to reach for the salt, as if she had not noticed the arm. Mark stands there, quietly, looking at his love deliberately moving about out of his reach, and then she flicks up her cockatoo head, gives him a brisk little smile that has imminent in it a promise of better things, but at the right time: and comes past him to sit down. He remains standing for a moment, behind her. He holds his arms in: they long to put themselves around her. But she makes no sign, merely piles tomato salad on to her plate, and he sits down, roughly, knocking something over: an explosion of frustration which makes me look quickly at Hannah. For some reason I don't want this skilled observer to see what I am seeing, but of course she does; and I don't want to share a look with her, which is what will happen if I allow our eyes to meet.

On the wall opposite me there is a large mirror salvaged

from some pub that has—mistakenly—been modernized. Art-deco lilies engraved in silver and gold and black loll in the arms of a girl not unlike Jill when she first came to my flat, all long floating hair and tender uncertainties. Reflected there I see myself reclining in the canvas chair, a woman who, with the room's distance away, and the scarlet-framed window full of evening light behind her, seems, in her misty lilac-blue dress, with her soft wisps of silvery hair, to belong more with the lilies and the floating girl.

My heart is aching.

We eat our admirable salad, praise the olive oil, comment on the Greek bread; Kentish Town is fantastic for Cypriot food, Mediterranean food. We comment on this and that. And I know that Jill is containing a head of steam fuelled by a lifetime: she wants me to see Kate as she does, at last; but this item on our agenda, Kate, is in fact the least of it; I am watching Jill and Mark, close to each other in low chairs, and see how he looks at her. A hunger. And deeper than that, anger burning there in eyes which reflect exactly what is happening to him. Later that night, Jill will allow some switch or other to be turned, and will—what? I find it hard to imagine this girl amorous. One has only to look at Mark to know that he is not one who will settle for a cold girl; but when that switch is turned, how does this efficiently airy one become a lover? Or loved?

What I am saying to myself, as Jill—it is her turn—serves lamb stew and mange-touts, is some kind of prayer or a plea: Jill, don't; don't Jill. Oh, *don't* . . .

She raises the subject, as we reach the end of the stew. She stammers slightly, showing for how long and with what intensity she has prepared fantasy exchanges of intelligent words, just as I do for Kate. 'Jane, about Kate, I really do think—'

'Let the poor woman have her food in peace,' says Mark, swilling red wine about his glass and squinting at it, in a way that says he is embarrassed by Jill, or feels himself out of his depth. And indeed we all have to be embarrassed and controlled, for her voice trembles and we know we are seeing Jill's past, embodied there now in the dusk of the big room, as she says, 'Jane, look, surely you must see that something has got to done about Kate? Your *flat*. Your lovely *flat*—it's like a dustbin. When I went in and saw it, I wanted to weep. I simply do *not* understand you, Jane.' And tears threaten her voice. Mark gets up, switches on the lights in some contraption, like the fairy lights in a summer garden, that dangles from a bracket. The dusk springs back outside. Mark pulls down the scarlet blind. Mark—it is his turn—clears away the plates; and Jill sits staring woefully at me, and she looks at this moment not so different from the poor waif Kate, the hopeless one.

Now I do look at Hannah, straight, wanting to know what she thinks; and she gives me a smile and a companionable nod, as if to say, Never mind!

'Are you going to go on like this, Jane?'

'Of course not,' I say at last. 'Something will happen.'

'Like what? Did you know those squatters are making themselves at home in your place?'

'It had occurred to me.'

'But what are you going to *do*?' Here Mark wants to know what I am going to *do*; making it plain from his tone that he knows jolly well what he would do. And I can see that no squatter would get anything but short shrift if they managed to enter this shrine of modern living.

Mark is revolutionary. Of course. I cannot make out what brand. We have occasionally discussed his 'line'; but it seems to me like a piece of abstract patterning, one premise flowing from another, very agreeable to do, as a relaxation, but nothing much to do with life.

I say, 'Are you worried about my chair covers, Comrade Mark? Tell me, would you call the police?'

Committed to not calling the police, until they are on his side—which my private thoughts convince me they may very well soon be—he looks put out; but then says that he would get rid of them himself. He wouldn't need the police.

It has ever been my observation that revolutionaries are sticklers for the law; and I say, to try him, that I was much too wary of the processes of the law to attract them: if squatters were to be thrown out forcibly from one's home, surely that would be aggression?

'They are *trespassing*,' says Jill fiercely 'They are causing damage to property.'

I look at Mark; and see him reluctant to criticize assaults on property; but he says briefly, 'You shouldn't let them get away with it, Jane. If you like, I'll go down to the squat myself and have a talk with them.'

I say, 'Are you going to complain about my chair covers?'

At which Mark looks offended; and Jill springs up, to get the pudding. A summer pudding oozing delicious red and black juices appears before us, and our annoyance dissolves in exclamations, and doses of heavy cream.

And that amazingly was the end of the subject of Kate, which Jill had been privately suffering over, I am sure, for days.

We sat on over the wreckage of the pudding. We drank more red wine. We drank brandy. We drank coffee. Jill, whose turn it was to do the washing-up, allowed herself to be assisted by Mark. Hannah and I sat together, and currents of good feeling washed back and forth.

In a low voice, she said, 'Jane, when you can't cope with Kate, let me have a try, will you?'

I said, 'I think she's rather worse than you allow for.'

She said, 'All the same . . . I've seen her, you know. She's hung about sometimes on the pavement outside *Lilith*. She's no more of a mess than many.'

'If there *are* many, then I think I am discouraged. I mean, for us all.'

Hannah smiled, acknowledging this; and then laughed a little. She said, in a very low voice, 'The thing is, people like you and Jill, you don't find it easy to be efficient, it's all a great effort for you, that's why you have to overdo it. And you don't see how much it intimidates the rest of us.' She was looking at Mark, very close to Jill; he was doing the washing-up while she dried. Her whole person said, Not *now*.

I laughed. She laughed.

'What are you laughing about?' inquired Jill, quick and on guard.

'I am not really laughing,' I said, speaking truly.

And I am sitting here tonight, having insisted that Kate should run a bath and then actually get into it, thinking that Hannah has looked at me, the efficient, competent, always on top of everything Jane, and said casually, as if there could not possibly be any argument, that I was not efficient by nature. I am staring back into my past tonight—back, back, before— but *who* was it, who was strong enough a personality to make me model myself on her? I'd give anything to have my mother here now, to put this question: What was I really like as a girl, before I came to London and became the success of the family? Was I like Kate, perhaps? And, as I write this, I know that my mother would look puzzled, even annoyed, and say, 'What do you mean? You and Georgina quarrelled all the time, that's all I know.'

We are halfway through August. My least favourite month sags past. It rains quite a bit, heavy and slow. London explodes with people from everywhere, and on the underground and buses I look to see a homegrown face. I enjoy this, every year, the feast of people, Babel, even if I shut my senses to the month, waiting for the crisp pleasures of September. But this year I hold on to every day, willing it to slow, and stay. Richard has still not said when he will leave, and I don't want to know—but autumn is coming. He has not rung, and a week has gone since he did.

I spend my evenings with Kate, wrestling for her soul: if Hannah can do it, why not I? is my thought. But the gods would laugh, the gods probably are laughing, at the sight of me and Kate, at my table in the kitchen, opposite each other; or on either side of my low glass table in the living room, Kate reluctantly unplugged, while I fight to bring her into ordinary life. Every remark I gather out of the assortment in my brain to present to her dies in the space between us. Sometimes she does not hear at all, I am convinced, though an abstract smile is set on her face, to appease me. She is probably listening still to the seas of sound, though not plugged into them. Or, I can see words reach her, and she seems to consider them, one by one. She smiles, politely, but puzzled. Why is Jane saying that? she is wondering, while I am asking myself, What is the use?

Why does she want to know what I did when I was at school? She is sullen, and I censor the subject for the future. Why is Jane talking about the flamingoes in some park or other? Why is Jane describing what Amsterdam is like?

Well, why am I?

I think then that after all, with ordinary people, nearly everything is said without words; I can work with Jill, the amiable Charlie, all day with hardly a need to say more than: I'll do Wine, but you must do Food; and I'm going out to interview X, but you have to do the Luncheon. All the rest is a flow between you, both know what is necessary.

Very well then, let's establish between Kate and me the companionable silences where things are understood: but if I stop talking, she reaches for her earphones.

But I've kept at it, wearing her out, and me too.

I go to bed exhausted. And dream, I dream, oh I dream.

I also go in to old Annie every day for an hour after work. That I have finally become her nearest and dearest is marked by the fact that she starts raging and abusing me as I go in. Because I am going in, Maureen, hearing from Annie that I go every evening, hasn't been bothering, except to fetch in supplies of food, a quick dart in, then out with the cry: 'Oh, but I've got to fetch my youngest from school, and I'm late.'

'She's ready enough when she hands the book to me to sign,' shouts Annie at me.

I say, 'Then don't sign.'

'I won't, one of these days,' she screeches.

'The book is there for you to say no, I won't sign, if they haven't done their work.'

'Their work? She was in here five minutes this morning, but she takes the money for it.'

'Then don't sign.'

This futile circular conversation may easily go on for half an hour. For Annie needs to talk and to shout, to dispel some of the energy that rages in her. It exhausts me. I reach home and Kate, exhausted.

❖   ❖   ❖

Richard rang. He is in Somerset. With his wife's brother's family. He said, 'I will be back next week. Will you be there, Janna?'

The anxiety in that appeased me; but I cried, 'You will have been gone three weeks.'

'I know.'

Richard rang. I was already in bed. His voice, in my ear, as I lay in my white thick cool bed, alone. His voice goes right through me, makes my heart beat, delights me: I suppose a romantic novelist (*manqué*) is entitled to say something of the sort.

He said, 'Are you in bed?'

'Yes, are you?'

'Yes, in an ancient four-poster, in a little attic room at the top of an old manor house. England is very extraordinary, Janna. You've got used to it all and don't notice. It is a treasure house. You go into some dump of a village—sorry, but I'm more American than I know. You turn in at some gates and there's a house like an illustration. It is packed, crammed full of goodies which the owners take for granted. What's in this room up here would fetch thousands in the States.'

'But they don't take it for granted. You are meant to think they take it for granted.'

'Is that it? I've been away too long. Janna, up here tonight I feel as if I am in a fairy tale. The door will open and you will walk in . . . Janna?'

'I'm here. Listening.'

'Why can't you and I go to bed together? When it is obviously the one thing we were born to do? Are you there?'

'Yes.'

'Is it vanity, Janna?'

'My vanity, you mean?'

'Do you suppose I don't have any, Janna?'

'Do you still have that little photograph?'

'What do you think!'

'Is it there, now?'

'Yes. Propped against the lamp.'

'Ghosts,' I said. 'Ghosts are why we can't make love.'

'Janna, I've been thinking these last weeks. I've never, ever had with anyone else in my life the sort of thing I do with you. Have I told you that?'

'No.'

'I feel there is no need to tell you things.'

'I know.'

'Good night.'

'Good night.'

Ghosts were in my room, all right. Of course I didn't sleep. I've wept. Snuffled and groaned and mopped up floods. I've caught myself thinking that when Richard goes this dreadful pain will go away.

Richard rang.

He said, 'Are you alone?'

I was amazed. I said, 'But Richard, how could I be anything else?'

He said, 'Well, I don't know anything about you, not really.'

'You do,' I said, the bottom dropping out of something; my idea of him, my idea of his idea of me . . .

'Do you have affairs, Janna?'

'No, I don't.'

'I thought you didn't. But I was thinking tonight, lying up here, why should I take that for granted?'

'Are you lying up there alone?'

'Yes.'

'Do you have affairs?'

'I have had one or two. The *willed* affair. Do you know what I mean?'

'You mean, you felt an affair was due to you?'

'Exactly. Not to be recommended.'

I said, 'I've only slept with one man. Freddie.'

A silence. Then I said, shocked at myself, 'What an extraordinary thing to say. In fact, after he died, I slept around quite a bit.'

'Why not!'

'But that didn't count.'

'Of course it didn't,' he agreed at once. 'I'll allow that you are a one-man woman.'

'Mockery?'

'No, I assure you.'

'Perhaps we are both monogamous, and that's our trouble?'

'Oh, how I wish I could be monogamous with you.' And he started humming it as a blues-style Billie Holliday. 'Ohhh—ho-o-w I wi-i-sh I could be mono-o-ogamous with you-u-u.'

They delivered the new chair covers today. I suppose I had planned to put them away—until! But Kate had the package open, and was waiting for me to make the decision to put them on. Together we fitted them, she taking one chair, I another. Two elegant little armchairs, yellow and bright, with candy-striped cushions. Tears in her eyes—of gratitude. She rushed into my arms. I held her tight: the thought in my mind being, I have so much energy, can't I press some into her? She held me frantically, and snuffled. Then we separated, beaming with pleasure at the pretty chairs. We sat on them, opposite each other. Then, the impulse of this little ceremony exhausted, Kate, still smiling, went back to her sofa and blissfully plugged herself in.

Something awful, *awful*—I cannot get to grips with it. Earlier this evening, about eight, the telephone. Richard. Richard's *voice*.

At once my heart melted, senses swooned, etc., and so forth.

'Richard,' I said.

'It's not Richard. It's Matthew. Matthew Curtis.'

I really could not speak. It was such a shock . . . and my mind began racing in all directions, frantically trying to take it all in. A thousand things at once.

'Is that Mrs Somers? Janna Somers?'

'Yes.'

'Is my father there?'

'No, he is not.'

Silence. Which I could not break.

'He's not there?' *Richard*'s voice, but brisk and trying to sound offhand. Now, of course, I heard the American accent, quite strong; which I had not at once, because all I could hear before was Richard.

Waves of light and dark were breaking through me, and I thought I was going to faint.

'Well, thanks. I'm sorry I bothered you.'

I sat on the edge of my bed for some time, trying to get back to myself. Then I told Kate I was not well, and I came to bed.

The telephone. Richard's voice. My mind went reeling about and I held fast to the thought: Matthew's voice has an American sound.

'Janna?'

'I'm here,' I said, rather faint.

'What's wrong? Is there something wrong?'

'Your Matthew rang me this evening. To ask, were you here?'

'What . . .' It occurred to me, I had not ever seen my love angry. The air was sizzling with anger. 'He rang *you*? Jane, I'm sorry. What can I say?'

'Did you know he was in London?'

'Sylvia told me today he was coming. For a month. *Jane?*'

'I'm all right.'

We went on like that for a little and rang off in a misery of apologies, and, of course, anxiety.

Kathleen must have telephoned Matthew, saying that their father was being enticed from his responsibilities.

Today this happened. I rang the office to say I was not well. This never happens. Charlie said, Oh all right, but Caroline was not well and he was going home early to accompany

Phyllis and the baby to the doctor. Jill rang to say she hoped
Kate was looking after me. Hannah rang to be instructed on
how to do my work. She remarked that I should be thinking
of getting someone else into Editorial, because Phyllis has
said she won't be back for at least another year. 'It will be
more than that, to my mind,' commented Hannah. I said I felt
too awful to care about *Lilith,* and they must all get on with
it.

I made myself bath and dress. Like old Annie, I was never
one to loll in bed. (Or was I once, I don't remember!)

The doorbell. I thought, The milkman. No, four young
people, instantly recognizable as from the squat. A young
man, three girls. It was ten a.m. and I knew they had decided
to spend the day at my expense.

I said, 'Kate is still asleep.'

The young man, Brian, a pack leader, with an air of
responsibility, even solemnity. He improvised: 'I would like
to have a word with you, about Kate. If that is all right,
Janna.'

(*Janna!*)

I said, seizing, I was sure—and as it turned out rightly—an
opportunity, 'Please come in,' and stood aside, smiling like a
hostess as they crowded in. And shut the door, and invited
them politely to sit down. Never have I been so grateful for
the support of civilized intercourse. Held together by that, I
asked them if they would care for tea or coffee, and stood by
while they settled themselves. They all looked hard and with
antagonism at the new yellow chairs, and they exchanged
glances. They sat, two on the dirty grey sofa in Kate's mess,
and two opposite. I went to the kitchen to put on the kettle,
and so on.

I was just holding myself together. Not because of them.
This business of Matthew—it has gone right *home*—
wherever home is, in me. I feel quite sick with it, I am not
myself. I did not care about these four outriders from the
armies of the future, which is how I felt them, as they came
into the flat with the sort of assurance that comes from
knowing, absolutely, that they are in the right. I knew that
each one of them, taken by herself—and Brian too—is a

perfectly pleasant and decent and ordinary young thing (in their early twenties, Brian is perhaps getting on for thirty), and that if I were alone with any one of them we would 'get on' and like each other. I knew that the four of them together were a closed group, a pack, and that everything I could say would be judged by their group faculties, and that Brian would be the arbiter. I knew that every one talked the language of revolution, of women's lib, and all that jargon, and that Brian held their destinies, boss male, even while he—I have no doubt at all—nicely assesses the rights of women. I knew. I felt, standing there, arranging my pretty cups and plates, nothing but an immense weariness.

I carried in the tray, loaded with delicious coffee and a large fruit cake from the health-food shop which I buy for Kate, hoping in this way she will get into her, at least sometimes, a little real food.

I sat down, and invited one of the girls to pour the coffee, remarking that I was not feeling very well. This I did because I wanted to observe them. A bit of a fuss over the coffee, jokes about the cake—'Very healthy'—vast chunks cut for them all. They all wore jeans and varieties of singlet. The girls looked unspeakably scruffy. Since the mode—alas—at the moment demands that a model should spend three hours to get turned out with her hair looking as if she has just been in bed for three weeks with pneumonia and she hasn't got around to tidying it—a state of disorder that is almost impossible to preserve for five minutes without constant recombings by the beauticians—these girls, emulating, had rats' tails and spikes and tufts of rubbishy hair all around attractive little faces, and Brian, a well-set-up and brisk young man, seemed like the owner of a harem of freaks.

But all this—the scene, Brian, that commissar, the girls— seemed a long way off from me.

Tidily consuming cake, his coffee cup lodged on the edge of the chair, Brian said, 'Janna, I wonder if you have ever seriously considered Kate's problems?'

Four pairs of eyes were fastened, with identical expressions of withheld condemnation, on me.

I said, 'Obviously, not.' And waited.

They looked at each other, frowning.

'Janna, she *needs* help.'

'But isn't she getting it—from you?'

Brian, who isn't stupid, whatever else, said, 'No, Janna, this must be a serious discussion.'

I said, 'Don't you think you ought to wake her? I for one don't want to discuss her behind her back.'

At this, minor consternation. Clearly I had invoked some code of theirs. 'I do agree that that would be best,' conceded Brian, with a glance at the three girls to keep them in order, 'but I—we—feel that it is a serious situation.'

'What do you suggest?'

'She shouldn't be alone all day,' said one of the girls, fierce and accusing.

'Sometimes she is alone from early morning until late at night,' said another.

'Very true, she is.'

My reactions were not what they had expected; this confrontation might have been planned in four separate minds, but had been directed by Brian. What I was to say had been imagined quite differently.

'But if she came to live with us, she would have company,' said another girl.

'Oh, I know what people like you think of squats,' said the fierce girl, who, now she had started to hate me, was sending me forceful, accusing glances between gulps of coffee.

'As it happens I once wrote a long article for *Lilith* about squats, and I said that some of them are rather good and useful. You may need to think of yourselves as a persecuted minority, but I can't help that.'

'No, wait, just a minute,' commanded Brian, obviously well used to this situation of directing discussion. If discussion this could be called. 'This is not helpful to any of us, and particularly not Kate.' Here he looked inquiringly at me, then gave a little nod which told me it was my turn to speak.

I said, 'Well, why doesn't Kate move in with you? I have never, not once, said she shouldn't. Or for that matter criticized you. Though perhaps you might agree that I have had good reason to . . .' And here I indicated the state of my living room. They frowned, looked away, glanced at the two little yellow chairs which more and more assumed the character of symbols, though innocent ones, of some shockingly sybaritic state, the mere contemplation of which—even a glance—was strong enough to feed the strength of moral disapproval in them.

'Yes, well, let's keep things in proportion,' said Brian to me coldly; and again quelled his girls with a glance. 'You say you haven't stopped Kate coming to us?'

'No, never.'

'That is *not*,' said he, 'what she has told us.'

I said nothing at all. I was suddenly fed up with them all. I got up—noting that I had to put my hand out to steady myself on the chairback. I put the coffee cups, half full or empty, not caring, on to the tray. I swept together plates full of crumbs. I lifted the whole load out and into the kitchen. When I got back they were all on their feet, conferring.

'Perhaps we have made a mistake,' said the fierce girl, but not as if she felt it.

Brian said, 'If there's been a misunderstanding, then . . .'

'Look,' I said. 'Kate is nearly twenty. She came here because she wanted to. She invited herself. If she wants to leave, she may. I think I had better say I would prefer her to move into a place where people have better manners, but I am sure you think that is a very reactionary thought.' And at this my energy ran out, and I heard myself say in a quite different tone, the voice of what I really did feel, 'Oh, do go away, I am so fed up with it all. I'll tell Kate you were here and that you want her to live with you. And now—get out.'

They went out, silently, each alone. I mean, not cementing their togetherness with a dozen little glances, the almost imperceptible movements of their solidarity, the way the gestures of one will echo another, or they will turn to share a look at the same moment, or stretch out their hands together as if in a rehearsed gesture for a piece of cake.

At the door Brian said, finishing the interview in command, 'Janna, we all feel that it was a good thing we have had the chance to speak to you. Our minds are much clearer.'

'I am glad,' I said. 'Mine, on the other hand, remains at sea.' And I shut the door.

When Kate woke, I said they had been here, and she was at once in a panic. 'What did they say, what did they say?' For she knew that I knew she had been saying her wicked aunt had forbidden her to see them, let alone go to live there.

'Oh, don't worry, Kate,' I said. 'And anyway, I rather liked them.'

'You did?' she exclaimed, pleased, cheering up. 'Oh, I am glad. I knew you would if you met them.'

But I am sure they will not come again here.

My little yellow chairs are safe.

Today I saw Richard. He rang at the office, saying could I be downstairs in half an hour. I was. A taxi. We collapsed into each other's arms and held on tight. We told the taxi to go to Knightsbridge. 'To meet you has involved lying to Sylvia, so as to find an excuse to take the train after hers, because Matthew met that one and I have no doubt was preparing to follow me.' He sounded despairing, angry, incredulous. 'Janna, how do we come to be in this situation?'

We sat on there, close, not saying a word, imbibing each other, with our eyes closed, cheek against hungry cheek.

When the driver put us down in Knightsbridge, we walked till we found a pub, and dived into it.

It was full, crammed, jumping with London's visitors. Enormously enjoyable, colourful, and we found our spirits soaring with the alcohol and lack of food, for we couldn't be troubled to eat. When the pub closed we left. We have worked out a series of rendezvous and exact dates, the hour, the minute, where we may with luck encounter each other without having to use the telephone.

Conversation with Kate.

'I went to the squat today.' A pause. She looked miserable.

'They are cross with me, Janna.'

'Well, never mind . . .'

Sniff, gulp, snuffle.

'Kate, have you met Hannah? You know, the girl who works with Jill in the office?'

Her face froze; her eyes darted suspicion.

'Well, have you, Kate? Do you like her?'

Kate became virtuous and scandalized, just as Jill does, copying their mother.

'Well, but she's a lesbian.'

'I think she's very nice.'

'Jill says she lives in a commune.'

'It's rather like a squat.'

Suddenly, a swirl towards me, like a caught fish, the wild accusing eyes: 'Why do you want me to go there? Why do you want to get rid of me?'

'I don't, but I thought you might like Hannah.'

And then: 'Are you going to leave?'

'Where to?'

'Are you going to get married? Go away?'

'No, Kate, I am not.'

She is not reassured; her face is pinched and full of dread.

I am beginning to regret the squat: at least she did have some resources apart from me.

It occurred to me today: the three weeks Richard and I had together, that time: when we were in it we thought there was plenty to come. But perhaps that was the high point, that was it.

I met Richard in Holborn, looking over my shoulder for Kate, for Kathleen—even Matthew? I felt silly, cheapened. So did he. We went into a pub, to a corner well out of sight of the doors, and smiled at each other, grim.

'What price love?' said he, using the word with precision.

'It can certainly be high enough,' I said, and with the intention of entertaining him told him about Phyllis, the sharp ambitious multi-talented girl who, feeling she *ought* to marry—for what else could have made her?—married one of the world's natural marriers, natural fathers; and who, wed, found her work was not for her, her own advancement, but for maintaining her husband's first wife and three sons. Pregnant, she thought of abortion, so much of a threat did a baby seem to her; her husband was appalled, scandalized. The baby born, the world revolved around it. She, we believe, but it is hard to get past that protective barrier, Charlie, would like to get back to work, if for no other reason than to do something about the debts that are mounting rapidly. At this point, Charlie summons his rich mother and two rich fathers, real and step. A family conference, centred on the baby. They will fork out, very handsomely, to allow Phyllis to stay at home and be a good mother to her baby, and for the period of a full three years.

This tale, which has been entertaining me, Jill and Hannah, started off lamely, for the rich hilarity of the office had not survived the sneaky journey here, and Richard's and my discomfort. I talked on, watching Richard's face for signs that he did find it at least a comment on something or other, life or sex. Or even love. He did smile at the end, a little, but sighed. He looked forlorn.

In the stridently lit pub, for this was a modern one, nothing like 'our' Soho pub, he seemed tired and drained, though he was brown and glistening with his country days (and, presumably, nights). He had on a cream linen suit. Summer. But suddenly it did not seem summer at all, the cream suit looked skimpy and washed out, and the rain on the window panes was not a summer rain.

I felt impelled to go on. 'And there's another,' I said. 'Hannah, you remember her, I've told you about her?'

'The warrior on the frontier of women's rights,' he said.

'You could put it like that.'

'I thought that was how she put it.'

'It's just that . . . she's not a fanatic. Today she told us this story. One of the girls who had been living in their commune and had got married has a baby. Before she had the baby she kept coming to visit the commune, her sisters, to say how she missed them, missed communal life, and how she was dreading having to give up her job—'

'I take it her husband doesn't contribute anything one way or another,' he remarked, distant.

Richard is far from monotone, can be sarcastic, sardonic, witty, angry, ironical. But hostile he has not been.

I was silent. Now it seemed a foolish tale to tell, though with the three of us it had seemed funny enough.

'Well, go on.'

'When the baby was born all the sisters went to visit her, and found her radiant.'

'Glandular,' he remarked.

'Quite so. But when they went visiting, to commiserate with her on her incarceration, for so she had been expecting it to be, they found her pleasurably immersed in maternity. Invited to come and visit them at the commune, she did not come. She did not ring. There were consultations, and a rescue operation was planned. They visualized her beaten down by maternity, wifehood, domesticity. Several times they arrived outside her door and, though convinced she was within, there was no answer when they knocked. This went on for some weeks. They waylaid the husband, who naturally they saw as an enemy, and he treated them accordingly, with a Yes, and a No.

'But they weren't going to give up on their distressed sister. Finally they found her in the park, with her baby, drinking Coca-Cola while she lolled on a deckchair in the sun reading. Guilt personified, she sat up, and behaved as if she had committed some crime. But what she was concealing was happiness, as Hannah slowly became convinced.'

'Ha, Hannah again.'

'Yes. Hannah saw that all this girl wanted was to be rid of her. Finally she said that she had never been more happy in her life. She had been working since she was sixteen, and as far as she was concerned, to be allowed, with the full permission of everybody, to do nothing all day but look after a baby and sit around in parks and gossip with strangers and chat with other mums was, simply, heaven. Her life had become pure pleasure. But she did see that the sisters weren't likely to go along with that, so Hannah would have to forgive her, but please, would she just go away. She could tell the girls in the commune anything she bloody well liked, as far as she was concerned. She thought they were all looneys.'

Richard, sitting in his hunched position, shoulders loaded, cosseted his drink. He has very fine hands. When I look at them my heart turns over. And so forth. But my love's hands were very tense around that glass.

'Hannah was telling the story against herself, against the commune,' I pointed out.

'Well, I don't know,' he said at last. 'Look, let's get out of here and walk. If you think we can do it without finding some obsessed waif in our path.'

We walked around the streets of Holborn in the rain.

I went to our second rendezvous, in Shepherd Market, but he did not come. I waited an hour and left.

Back in the office, Jill said he had rung, would ring again. But he did not ring until just as I was leaving.

Kathleen had tried to commit suicide. Not really, more a 'cry for help'.

He will try and make our next rendezvous the day after tomorrow.

When I put down the telephone, Jill and Hannah were both silently regarding me. So I must have looked shaken.

I said, 'Can you explain why a girl who has always had the best of everything, and two perfectly satisfactory parents, should stage a cry for help?'

Hannah remarked, in the studied way that says something has been mentally prepared, 'Janna, have you ever thought that Kate might try it?'

This was such a shock, I had to sit down. 'No, it hadn't crossed my mind.'

They were both *not* looking at me, nor at each other: pennies must drop: mine.

I said, 'But Kate is such a long way from any sort of reality.'

'You mean,' said Jill, 'that to commit suicide you need to have a sense of reality?'

I thought. 'Yes. Clearly that is what I must mean. The one thing about Kate is that she seems such a long way from understanding her situation.'

A short snort of laughter: Jill. And Hannah's full, queenly contemplation of other people's inadequacies.

'Poor Janna,' said Jill.

'I would say,' I persisted, 'that that is the definition of Kate.'

'No,' pronounced Hannah, 'that's not it.'

Jill: 'You didn't know that Kate tried to commit suicide? Or rather, staged some stupid bit of melodrama?'

'How should I know, if no one told me?'

'No one told you because as far as my clever parents are concerned it never happened.'

'But you knew and you didn't tell me, Jill.'

'I've been telling you and telling you, you're crazy to have Kate.'

'What did she do?'

'She took twelve of Mother's sleepers, when she knew she would be found half an hour later.'

'All the same,' said Hannah.

'I take it that is judged as being within the scope of a cry for help, if not a suicide attempt?' I was very angry.

'And one of these days,' said Jill, 'you are going to get back at one in the morning and find Kate moribund.'

Hannah said, 'I think she's particularly at risk now she's not going to the squat.'

I said, 'How does it come about that I am some sort of a criminal? Kate isn't my daughter. Thank God.'

'Well, you've taken on the responsibility for her, haven't you?' said Jill, fussed and cross and accusing.

'And you, her sister, won't even have her around for a meal,' I said.

Hannah, pacemaker, peacemaker, pronounced, 'I don't see that either of you is to blame.'

'Thank you,' I said.

'Thank you,' said Jill.

Richard telephoned to say he couldn't make our next, tomorrow: Holborn again.

Tonight I am so sick with it all, with wanting to be with

him, with not wanting to be with him because it is getting so painful. I even catch myself thinking that if this is love, Love, that I've missed out on, then I am glad that I have.

But now I am going to sleep and I suppose I shall be dreaming of Freddie.

Kate wasn't in when I came in. Frenzies of worry! I nearly rang the police. At twelve, just as I was going to bed, she drifted in, smelling strongly of drink. This is a new and nasty development.

'Where have you been?' I demanded, breaking my own rules with her.

'Oh, just around . . .' she smiled vaguely, and reached for her transistor.

I was with Annie. She in a misery of helplessness. 'Where did you put my blue shoes?' she screamed as I entered. 'The blue shoes with the silver buckles?' It turned out that they were shoes she had twenty years ago. She never wears anything but slippers.

She raved on and on, until I was so identified with her feelings that when I stood in the doorway and saw my own living room, dirty, smeared everywhere, Kate asleep in a lump on the sofa, it was as if everything was being taken away from me; above all, my control of my life. And for the first time I have to wonder what it represents, this necessity to have perfectly tidy rooms, the chairs set opposite each other just so, cushions poised at such an angle, so that when I have walked into my home it has always been into order. My bedroom still remains exact—but I am 'not in it'!

I feel as Annie does: that things slide away between my fingers, that I cannot grasp hold of them.

I sat for a long time tonight thinking that I ought to ring up my sister and say, Enough! She's your responsibility. But I can't. *What would happen to her*?

This morning I woke drowned in sorrow. When I opened my eyes on the fresh white and yellow of my room, the sunlight outside, I seemed to be looking at it all from some dark sad place. Of course, I had been dreaming. An embrace, full of sweetness and longing. '*I love you*'—the words were in my mind. But who had said, 'I love you'?

I lay thinking about Freddie, not wanting to. All too much, this obsession with a dead marriage. Dead. It's the right word. Only something dead and gone can haunt, and taunt. I was wondering if Freddie had said, 'I love you.' Presumably these surely essential words did make their appearance, when we decided to marry? 'I love you, Janna,' he had said; and I replied, 'I love you, Freddie.' Is it likely! I simply don't believe it. But I can't remember. I can remember easily, though, our efficient and prompt sensuality, the understanding of the flesh. 'I love you!' Freddie whispered to me as we went off to sleep afterwards? No. And I have to ask myself if I ever did say, 'I love you,' to Freddie. It would probably have seemed some sort of capitulation, or weakness.

But, suddenly, as I lay propped on my (of course) snowy pillows, watching how the yellow curtains moved a little, so that the oblong of sun on the carpet wavered at the edges in a dreamy, hypnotic way, it came into my mind that Richard never said, 'I love you.' Of course, that was what I had been dreaming. And the sadness of the dream dragged me down, so that I could have wept, and wept . . . and meanwhile, my mind was sitting there quite cool and intelligent, thinking that Richard and I had no need of saying I love you, when we had only to meet to feel part of each other, thinking the same thoughts. In fact, there would have been something false about it, prescribed.

Well, the words are prescribed. Like weddings. At this very moment a million girls tapping away at their typewriters or doing little sums on their calculators are dreaming while they do it—not of women's lib and emancipation—but of *I love you* and a wedding dress: and we know, for *Lilith*'s researchers tell us so, that the wedding day is still the golden moment of these infant dreams. Why? For one thing, because of the efforts of *Lilith* and her sisters.

I was lying there in bed, my arms behind my head, in the posture—as I now see—of a captive's surrender, making myself truthfully imagine a real embrace, inside Richard's arms, and his *I love you*. With part of myself I was—*I am*—quite simply discomforted. Because of the unnaturalness of it. At the same time my senses were dissolving with the wanting just that and nothing else, I love you, I love you. I love you—what nonsense, like a spell or a drug, the words feeding fevers, the tongue fattening on the pleasure of saying them, but the mind is brooding: Love? *What* love? Love *whom*?

What circumstances could possibly make 'I love you' natural between us, as natural as that we exchange looks acknowledging a shared thought or an impulse. In bed? Well, I suppose so. But no, absolutely *not*. I will *not* have with Richard the horizontal handshake. One of the men I had sex with after Freddie died remarked over the parting cup of coffee as he returned to his wife, 'It is the horizontal handshake, that's what it amounts to.' Expressing what we both felt about this performance of ours. Nothing. Good-humoured enough—but nothing. Nil. The point was: it wasn't dangerous. I was going to say *Like real sex*. But of course, this thought is not on for post-Freud and post-Johnson and Masters women.

This scene: Joyce had had lunch with her elder sister, living in the country and up for the day to shop at Harrods. Joyce came in, thoughtful; remarking that her sister was happily married. Joyce, at that time, was just beginning to know how unhappily married she was.

Joyce told me, deliberately, watching my face for reactions, that during the war this sister, then unhappily married, met a man whose girl had been killed early in the Blitz. For four years these two worked in the same office. War work. They loved each other, told each other so, but did not sleep together, for words like betrayal and loyalty, fidelity and deception, were used and respected. Sometimes he drove her home, and they held hands in the dark. They hardly dared to kiss: kisses were dangerous. After the war, there was a divorce, and the two married and at last they slept together. Joyce said that *she* said, It was worth waiting for.

'Now there was a couple who gave sex its proper due,' I

said to Joyce, choosing my words, and as her face said yes, that was it, exactly, Phyllis came into the office with some papers. She looked so young and competent and just-so; and Joyce's eyes and mine met on the same thought, and Joyce said, 'Do sit down a minute, Phyllis. I've been having lunch with my sister and—well, I want to tell you something. If you like, it's a little experiment. The generation gap thing . . .'

Down sat Phyllis, composing herself, her face prepared with an alertly discriminatory smile. And Joyce told Phyllis the story. We both watched, Joyce and I, Phyllis's inner processes reflected on that neat and pretty face. First of all, unmistakably, a flash of envy, at once succeeded by a small—at first incredulous and then patronizing—smile. As if at an account of behaviour in some backward tribe. She said at last, 'But what for? It was silly not to.'

She looked at Joyce for enlightenment, and then to me. This was before Joyce's introduction to the pleasures of the horizontal handshake, for she had never slept with anyone but her husband. Joyce was speaking out of an absolute identification with the chaste pair. As for me, I was able to partake of both states, for until Freddie died I had never slept with anyone else. Then the horizontal handshake had been my lot briefly, until I sickened.

Joyce said gently, from her still intact certainties, 'Phyllis, you have to believe that there are people like that.'

Phyllis seemed threatened. She protested, 'But why do you believe your sister? They probably had it off every time they could, but lied about it.'

'No,' said Joyce. Phyllis smiled, knowing better.

She looked at me. I said, flippantly enough, I thought,'Now there was a couple who gave sex its proper due.'

'*What due?*' flashed Phyllis, getting up to leave.

'Dangerous,' I said. Important. Threatening. Full of fate. Fraught with risks of pregnancies, diseases, commitments. The great gamble with the unknown. Ecstasy, and all that.

'Rubbish,' said Phyllis. 'All that sort of thing is simply not *on* for post-Freud and post-Johnson and Masters people.'

Joyce and I, left alone, looked at each other and laughed. And laughed.

When I at last dragged myself out of bed, I took myself out of the flat, leaving Kate still asleep. I was consciously in search of solace, a lift, nutriment, like the tonics they gave us when we were children. 'You need building up, perhaps a tonic?' But I saw nothing in the streets except dinginess, and the heavy late August skies fitted over the city like the pewter lid of an old-fashioned meat dish. On the underground at Baker Street, standing all by herself on the platform, an inordinately pretty girl dressed like a milkmaid out of Laura Ashley, all prim ruffles and flowered muslin, was holding open in front of her a vast illustrated book called *The Frogs and Toads of Great Britain*, which book she continued to hold at a precise angle, as if to catch a light coming from behind her shoulder, until the train came in, whereupon she clapped the book shut, slid it into a lacy reticule, and strode into the carriage.

This would normally have cheered me up, but I remained dismal and down. I was dawdling my way to a meeting with Richard. Or so I hoped; for he might have been prevented, as I was so often prevented, or he was. I was thinking, When we used to meet *then*—as if that was years ago, instead of four months—it had been always with that uprush of zestful, almost savage, unscrupulous enjoyment that carried us on and up over all difficulties. And now ... my feet dragged, and my mind was full of the sad longings of the dream.

The café was in Wigmore Street. After I had suggested it I remembered that sometimes Freddie and I used to meet here, but thought, Well, what of it? I was in a corner inside, not on the pavement, and ordered myself some coffee, in case Richard wasn't going to come. I was thinking of Richard, of Freddie, when against the light I saw what for a moment I thought was Freddie. There was a moment of panic, an absolute NO, as he came stooping towards me; then I thought, It's Richard, of course, well they are similar, and I said, 'Richard ...' as I saw him transfigured, young, smiling, debonair, but with something about him deceiving, even malicious, as when, in a dream, someone well known and friendly appears as an enemy. All this took a few seconds, my moment out of ordinary sense; and as my heart thumped and my pulses bumped, I saw this was not Richard, but a young man who looked like him. He stood with his hand on the chair painted a bright sailor's blue, and smiled down at me, politely but winningly.

My mind was a long way behind my apprehensions, and when he said, 'I am Matthew, may I sit down?' it took some moments for me to take it all in; for I was staring, helplessly, at my Richard, miraculously delivered to me as a young man. But the voice, Richard's, was American; his clothes, self-consciously neat and proper, American, and his politeness not homegrown.

He sat down, since I did not speak but went on staring, caught from the start in his net.

'Janna,' he said, in Richard's voice that was not, 'I thought I would come and get to know you.'

The effrontery of this, the bullying, vulgarized that discreet American politeness; and I went on saying nothing now for another reason. I had understood it all. Knew that he had found his father's little pencilled list of our meeting places; Richard could not come, probably because his son had seen to it that he could not; and that this insolent attack was not only his, but also Kathleen's. I even looked past him out through the glass of the window into the street to see if that familiar heavy sentinel was standing there, monitoring her brother as she had to do her father. I was determined, now, to sit it out, remaining passive, if for no other reason than that I could not trust my senses—my mind being another matter. I was being absolutely pulled to pieces, from within, for I was fascinated by this, my young love Richard, and could not take my eyes off his face.

But there was this triumphant glisten there, in his eyes, and his voice, and he leaned towards me as if taking possession, and said, 'I am sure you will understand me. Of course I wanted to get to know my father's new friend.'

To sit opposite your love, as you have done for months of times, exactly the same eyes, hands, brown forearms bare, the fair Viking hair, all, all the same, but magicked: an imposter sitting behind the eyes, so I felt. So it was! And still with me was that flash of a moment, no more, when this man appeared dark against the heavy light of the street, and I thought, Freddie.

'And so here I am, Janna,' he was saying, for I had missed quite a lot of what he had said. 'And I hope to be forgiven.'

I still had not said anything. Now he was silent, not put out at all—I mustn't think that!—but using the moment to give me a good looking-over. He sat quite still, those brown healthy shining forearms crossed, like a tidy buccaneer in his blue buttoned bush shirt: he wore a suit that made him look like a young doctor in one of those American war films, where callously wisecracking heroes are always about to take off in a helicopter into impossible dangers. But this one was no hero. If I had not been told by his father that this was the one who had shut off the pains and impositions of the happy idiot, his brother John, I would have known that this young man was as self-contained as a walnut, tidily sorted out in compartments. He was looking at me with an open assessment of me as a woman; making sure that this would be evident as appreciation. He meant me to imagine him licking his lips. What he really was thinking of course I was not to guess: but he was making an exact inventory of every asset or liability. He had given me good marks for my hair, so cleverly tinted it would have appeared, on a girl's head, as natural. He had noted my hands, which owned frankly every one of my years; he had taken in the fine wrinkles around my eyes.

After all this, he sat back, raised a hand with an appropriate gesture at the waitress, and said, 'May I have some coffee here, please?' And, to me, he leaned forward slightly, all winning smiles, and said, 'And you, Janna?'

'Thank you, no,' I said. And gathered my handbag, for I was about to leave.

He changed his voice, put on the look of a man who was being made to deal with someone unreasonable, and said, 'Janna, I had really hoped that we could get to know each other. No? What do you say?'

This really fatal vulgarity of his, which came from a complacency that seemed to be part of his texture, overflowing from his eyes and his voice, was what undid me. Richard was being diminished for me by his son! I was consciously forcing the image of the real Richard, that carelessly confident, faded lion of a man, who seemed to be made of a different stuff altogether, back into my mind, to stand there as a protection, warding off this assault.

'Matthew,' I said, 'there is just one thing I have to say. Not that I can easily imagine, having met you, that you are capable of taking it in. It is this. My friendship with your father has nothing whatsoever to do with you. Nor with your sister. And that is all I have to say.' I was about to get up, but he shot out his hand and laid it on my wrist to keep me. I wasn't going physically to tussle with him, so I remained on the edge of my chair. I was conscious that now people around were looking at us. A couple, probably French, were watching with discreet malice, their vivacious salacious faces saying that everything was understood: and I saw us, Matthew and I, reflected in those faces: son and father's still-attractive mistress, poised on the edge of—The waitress slid a cup of black coffee in front of Matthew, and then with a glance at us swiftly withdrew. Camera! Action!

'But just you wait a little,' said Matthew, still grasping my wrist while he fumbled in his breast pocket and brought out, with a smile towards me that both entreated my appreciation of his efforts, and expected them, the little photograph I had given Richard. There it lay on the jolly red tablecloth, the ghost of myself. But I saw that it was not the actual photograph. This young man had somehow stolen my photograph from his father long enough to take it off and have it copied, then—presumably—had replaced it.

'I haven't been parted from it,' announced Matthew, playing out this role as he had planned it in his mind: for I knew there was nothing he said that had not been rehearsed.

He was looking at me, leaning forward, his hot palm an intimate pressure on my wrist, the blue eyes at work on my face; I was looking at him, disliking him as much as I ever disliked anybody in my life.

Then he said, and for him it was the culmination of this willed scene, 'I love you, Janna. I feel as if I have loved you all my life.'

These words went through me in shockwaves. I then got

up, shaking off his hand. I collected my bag, my scarf. I went out, past the pair of Latins whose eyes were misted over with the satisfactory perverseness of it all.

I don't remember how I got onto the street, how I walked to the underground up along Baker Street. I was in a welter and a fever and wished only to be in some cool dark place, alone. I found Kate still asleep in bed. I thought for a moment of Jill's 'One day you'll find her moribund', and bent over to make sure she was all right. She breathed regularly. Beside her a tumbler was rusted with last night's vino.

I went into my room, drew the curtains, put on a wrap, and went to bed and wept.

The thing is, I had fallen in love.

That was . . . days ago. What a horror and a humiliation. That rather unpleasant young man pushed a button, set off a tripwire; at any rate, put his finger on some unknown part of me that had been programmed to hear just those words and no other: and Wow! Blam! I fell in love. I am poisoned. I am possessed by a sickly sweet fever. I am obsessed.

Richard rang, and said, Why had I not been at the pub in Shepherd Market today? I had both forgotten and not forgotten it. I was in that state of mind where one hopes that if one doesn't take any notice a problem will take itself off.

At the time I was supposed to be meeting him I was working like a maniac in the office with Charlie so as not to think of anything.

I said to Richard, 'I am very sorry. I just couldn't.' I heard my voice, cold but distressed.

Richard asked, 'Janna, is there something wrong? I mean, worse than usual?'

I said, 'No.' It occurred to me that until now I have said everything to Richard, there was no need for me to censor my thoughts.

I heard him say, 'Don't you want to meet me, is that it?'

I hear myself crying out, 'Oh, Richard, don't say that, don't, don't.'

He was silent. For that was not a note we had permitted ourselves.

'Janna . . . then when can we meet?'

I can't meet him when I am in this state. How can I? It's disgusting, all of it.

It comes to me that if I were twenty-five and not fifty-five I would marry that nasty little piece of work on the basis of what I *feel*, and live for ever after . . .

Phyllis came into the office with the baby Caroline today, looking cool, a little amused, very pretty, very pleased with herself. Also, wistful. We don't have to be told that she misses *Lilith*. Charlie: proud, fatherly, both with little Caroline and with Phyllis.

Everyone in the building, it seemed, dozens of people, milled about, admiring Caroline, bringing little offerings, a flower, a trinket. Charlie sent out for champagne, which went foaming around Editorial and we all got a little drunk.

Phyllis was in the big room with me for a moment alone, Charlie having borne off Caroline for a fresh orgy of admiration.

She looked at me, and said in a low voice, in case Charlie should hear from next door, 'Janna, I often wonder what you are thinking of me, about what has happened.'

I looked at her, this Phyllis, who had been so sharp and hard, now rather plump with maternity and all the milk she has to carry about for little Caroline, and I said, 'I am thinking of absolutely no one but myself at the moment.'

My voice shook a little. I had the stupid impulse to tell her everything. I needed to let it all out. But I thought, No one under the age of forty could understand this one! If not older . . . She looked at me. I looked at her. She said in a falsely jaunty voice, 'Love makes the world go round.'

* * *

Richard rang today, said he had managed to 'get a week off from family duties'.

'I think I could actually get away with you somewhere unfollowed. How about it, Janna?' He sounded confident I would say yes. And rightly; for I would have overturned everything, thrown Kate to the Fates, given up my job, anything, to be with him. For what I know is the last chance we will have.

But I said, 'Richard, you will have to believe me, I simply cannot. It isn't that I don't want you . . .' I had meant to say, don't want to . . . but it came out like that.

'You really can't?' he said, and his voice was thin with disappointment.

'I *can't*.'

It is ten days since I met Matthew. We are into September. There is a crispness where there was a heaviness. The sunlight slaps you pleasantly across the face, and tingles on your arms.

I think I am getting over this. It's like an attack of something. Shingles. Measles. Chickenpox. Some indisposition that has an exact term. For being in love with some man you dislike intensely, so and so many days. In the meantime I rage and burn, and wake in the night, pulled up into the sitting position, my arms out, my breasts burning, for *him*. Who? Him. *Who*?

Richard rang to say that if we couldn't get away for a week, why can't we at least have lunch? I cannot bear to meet him in this state. I said I couldn't meet him until next week. Suddenly he said, 'Janna, you know that I am going away soon? I mean, for good? Back to the States?'

'Yes, I thought you were.'

I am watching these splendid September days race past, while my fever abates, and I long to be with Richard, but cannot be. It is not that I feel ashamed, but rather as if I have been convicted of bad taste. But worst, worse than anything, is that I cannot tell him about any of this.

At two in the morning, the telephone. Even half asleep,

though those tones beguile me, I know it is Matthew. Fury slaps me awake, adrenalin races, I sit up.

Every syllable has been measured, calculated. 'Janna, I was thinking of you. I felt I should ring you. Do you mind?'

The *do you mind* stopped my tongue: it had been meant to.

I sat looking at the dark wall, with its oblong of illuminated cloud. I could hear Kate moving about in the kitchen.

'I am thinking of you all the time, Janna. Please don't think I blame my father. I understand him absolutely! I—'

I dropped the receiver back and then, at once, took it off again.

I went into the kitchen. Kate sat eating shortbread biscuits with a total avid concentration, both hands at work, one lining up the next biscuit to be consumed, while the other actually fed her mouth.

Knowing the folly of saying anything like: Kate, why don't you eat a proper meal? I hung about for a little, watching how my fury over Matthew transmuted itself into anxiety over Kate.

'Are you all right, Kate?' I asked her suddenly, as one says it to a friend, meaning, really, that one recognizes a need, a situation, saying, really, *I am here*.

A good little girl, with a weakness for nibbling sweet biscuits, she smiled blandly, her eyes empty.

I went back to bed with a cup of tea, and stayed awake till now, morning, making an inventory thus:

I hate Matthew with a pure, cold, even dispassionate hatred. I am in love with him, but am almost getting over it. I am sick with concern over Kate, and helpless. When I think of Jill, it is as if I want to put my arms around her, shielding her from—herself. I admire and rely on Hannah. When I think of Charlie, I surprise an affectionate smile on my face. Phyllis: she makes me want to cry. I don't allow myself to think of Sister Georgie too much, for at once I fill with incredulous rage. I like thinking about Mark: there is a pleasantness and strength there. I love Richard. Period. I dream about Freddie.

*　　　*　　　*

Richard rang today, his voice cold and furious. 'Janna, tell me, did you meet Matthew?'

'Yes, he was at the café where I thought you and I were going to meet. It was he, and not you.'

'Why didn't you tell me?'

'It seems I was right, there is no need to tell you.'

'It is utterly unforgivable, awful ... I am sorry, Janna. What can I say?'

Today I said to Richard, when he rang, just as if nothing had happened, because that was how I felt it, 'Yes, let's meet, where?'

A silence from him. 'Very well Janna, I'm not going to ask for explanations! I've no right! Still, you are rubbing it in—or that's how I feel it. Where then?'

'Could we meet in Soho Square without our attendants, do you think?'

'We could try.'

I met Richard in Soho Square.

I did not look to see if I was being followed: I did not care. Anyway, Kathleen seems to have relegated this duty to Matthew.

Blue September sky: nostalgia in its warmth. A sparkling air. As I walked to the bench where my love sat, a yellow leaf spun down.

With a distance between us we sat and smiled, wryly. It had been nearly three weeks. He looked tired, drained.

'I am sorry about Matthew,' he said; but I saw that he didn't know the half of it.

'It was not your fault.'

He said deliberately, 'I have never liked Matthew.'

'But you always did everything you should.'

'Yes. I suppose I projected on to him what I could not allow myself to feel about Sylvia.'

At this invitation to talk I seized up and stalled. 'I don't want you to think I haven't wanted to be with you,

Richard . . .' This came out false, for it was not the kind of thing we have said.

'But you had more important things to do,' he stated.

I could not say anything.

'In some ways, Janna, you are very much what I know only too well . . .'

A couple of pigeons bobbed around hopefully. We had nothing for them; they flew off to another bench, where two office girls fed them bits of sandwich.

'Yes, I know. A career woman. Well, you had better tell me; I know when you have gone I'm going to be anguishing over the things we haven't said and didn't get around to discussing.'

'I'm not flying off to the moon!'

'It might as well be the moon. Intimate conversations on the telephone? "I wish you were here." I think you ought to tell me.'

'Well, I wonder if you'll even see any of it. Why should you? Your whole life shows . . . Well, where do I start?'

'She didn't care for you?'

'Oh yes, all the proper feelings. In appropriate measure. Oh, I forgot.' Here he rapidly produced two limp packets of sandwiches in cellophane, and, as he unwrapped his, another pigeon materialized and waited by our feet.

'We were both nineteen. Cambridge. She had had to fight to get there. Her parents—they didn't care. A girl, you see. There were three clever brothers. She was clever, but a girl. They didn't really want her at Cambridge, said she would get married, that kind of thing. She did not have a scholarship. But the thing was I knew she was brilliant, but really. It was that quality she had—has. A total commitment. A straight line through to—she did not know her goal, then. She was having a difficult time. Not really enough money, with the parents having to finance four of them at university. We became very close, helping each other with our work, and I helped her with money. I am not one of the world's spenders by nature. And then we moved in together; it seemed the sensible thing to do.'

'Too sensible?' I asked, for there was something not

coming through.

'No. That's not it.'

A pigeon, little rainbows on its pearly feathers, flew between us on the bench, and pecked at Richard's sandwich. We watched it.

'I loved her,' he said. 'I loved her from the very first moment I saw her. At a lecture. She sat there, seeing absolutely nothing and nobody, only the teacher. I saw only her. I sought her out. I made it all happen. I found our room, I paid the rent, I saw to it that we ate—I did all that. She—fitted herself in. Took it all. It wasn't a question of her grabbing, Janna, do you see? It was there. I was there. It was what she needed. She took it all, expected it. *Do* you see?'

What I saw first was that he didn't want me to condemn Sylvia. I could say, truthfully, that I did see.

'We both worked very hard. I because I had to. I was never brilliant. She because she was. Halfway through university, her father died. Only just enough money for the three boys to finish. Her mother expected her to go home, and she would have done, except for me. I knew that it would be a crime to let her throw herself away. I could not get money from my parents, they had only just enough. I earned the money to pay for her. Of course now, looking back from the dizzy heights of the American way of life, it was peanuts, nothing. But then—'

'What did you do?'

'What didn't I do? I can't believe it now, when I think of how I worked, for those two years. I did dog's-bodying for my tutor. He was well known. I proof-read, I researched, I even wrote some of his papers. He knew I needed money, and got me that kind of work with other people. I used to be working until four in the morning. At weekends I cooked in a café, underpaid of course, it was moonlighting. And there we were, the two of us, working. That is all we did, work.'

'You didn't make love?' I asked, deliberately laying ghosts.

'I suppose we did. Yes, of course we did. But it wasn't an issue. Not even for me, not then. I was too bloody tired all the time. We had that damned narrow little bed, crammed into the corner of the room. The room was almost filled by the table we worked at. We used to roll into bed at four in the morning, in each other's arms, and fade out.'

'And you did well, both of you?'

'She, brilliantly, of course. I, passably. But her success was mine. I felt it like that. She didn't, of course. Then we came here to London, and we were in different hospitals. She knew by then she wanted to be a surgeon. I merely wanted to be a doctor. Unfashionable, then. We had a room at the top of a house in Bloomsbury. She was at the Middlesex. I rated a humbler hospital. We had just enough money to get by. We worked. We worked. Janna, if you knew how we worked. Well, I suppose you do, you do.' And he smiled at me, direct, wry and hard and savage, but the savagery contained. I could see there in his face old bitterness, transmuted. For a moment I saw him as old, an old man, smiling dryly at his life.

'She had outstripped me of course, long before we got to the end of it, the training. I was the second-best, and it had to be like that. That's how it was. Do you see? Well . . . and so we went on. She went from achievement to achievement, getting better all the time. I was always—there. And now of course it wasn't only me who knew she was special, really quite extraordinary. It has always been that deadly single-mindedness of hers that she isn't even conscious of . . . she was expected to do brilliantly.'

'And you? You never say . . .' For I was waiting for something. All the time it seemed as if the real subject of all this had not appeared.

'Me? Well, I loved her, of course.'

'And she loved you?'

'She has never, I believe, loved anyone else.'

'Richard, all this doesn't explain why you are like a damped-down volcano.'

'It doesn't?' he said, in real surprise. 'Do you mean to say . . . ' He studied me, leaning forward to do it in a movement so sudden that two pigeons took to their wings and swerved off up into the trees.

'I just don't see you as a man eaten up with unfulfilled ambition.'

'Ambition? Have I said anything about ambition? No,

you're right. I've enjoyed what I've done. I'm even glad I didn't go in for years of specialization. I'm coming back into fashion, the ordinary family doctor. I, with a group of others in Boston, run a new and very influential type of clinic: medicine for the consumer, the patient treated as a grown-up human being with choices, medicine as prevention—all that. Do you know about it? No, how should you? It is taking on. So I can't say I have anything to regret. *That isn't the point.*' And, leaning forward, he put his warm hand on my forearm resting on the back of the bench. I felt the lively pain of it, skin to skin, pulses beating, everything that had not been, and my eyes filled with tears. 'Ah yes,' he said, in a low voice, smiling straight into my face. 'Well, that's it, you see. All my life. And with you, again.'

He removed his hand, sat back, facing out from the bench, folded his arms.

'Tell me, romantic novelist, have you thought about the situation of a man hopelessly in love with his wife, who has long decided that his place in her life is just so much and no more? Would you say that was a romantic subject?' And he laughed.

I sat there, feeling as if all the dreams I have been dreaming over the last months about Freddie had ended here, on this bench, at prosaic lunchtime, in the square.

I could have told him my story, I suppose, spoken of Freddie, exposed myself, but I did not. Not cowardice. It was more like: he'll never say it to Sylvia, let him say it to me.

'Of course for the first years we were working so hard. But then, there seemed a bit of room to turn around, to feel . . . What I saw was still Sylvia, I was just as much in love with her as when we were nineteen, but when we had stopped working like slaves or dogs—or rather, when I could stop working as if there was nothing else in life but that, she just went on working. If we took a holiday, it was because she knew one should sometimes relax, but she took work with her. If we went out for the evening, she was thinking of what she would be doing next day. If we went to bed, she was thinking that if we overdid it, she would be tired in the morning. I had an exact place in her life, just so much, at certain times. And—I could have killed her for it.' The last came out dispassionately, between lips that smiled, but I knew that he had meant it. And often.

'I loved her,' he said, sounding quite surprised as he said it, as he looked back and saw yet again how much. 'I adored her. I used to court her. We had been living together for years cheek by jowl, in rooms like matchboxes, but all that didn't matter, that we knew each other as brothers and sisters do, for intimacy. For me she was always the most beautiful, glorious, *unreachable*—do you suppose that was the point, Janna?' he asked, with his characteristic quick turn to me. 'I remember sitting and watching her sleep, and aching with wanting her. But I knew if I woke her she would smile, after a minute, conscientiously banish her tiredness, and then say, Oh, Richard, do you want . . . ? And move over in the bed, to give me my due space. And she would smile at me, oh quite sweetly, and we would then make love, oh very nicely, I have no complaints. But never, *not once,* Janna, has she ever . . . I used to find myself dreaming about her when we were there in the same room, she working of course. I'd be dreaming about her as if she had an *alter ego* she knew nothing about, and which was my possession, not hers. Mine.'

A long silence. Lunch hour over, the office workers were going off, dropping sandwich wrappers and bits of plastic into the rubbish container. A pigeon cooed. The sun was hot and delicious, and there was a smell of newly cut grass.

'For years I was unconsciously thinking that one day she would suddenly realize and turn to me and *then*—I remember the day I understood, finally, that it would never happen, that this *alter ego* of hers I had invented, this loving *glorious* girl, just did not exist. Never would.'

'And then?'

'She was moving, from hospital to hospital, perfecting her training. She understood one morning she was in her thirties. She decided it was time we had children—doesn't do to leave it too late, said she, doctor to doctor. So Matthew was born in London. It was very difficult. We were both working like dogs. I think I can say I took my fair share—much more. I was closer to Matthew than she was. Yet Matthew is her child, I think of him like that. Sylvia's son. I think Sylvia had thoughts about leaving it like that, one child. She knows that it cost me a lot, her children, but not how much. She's not good at putting herself in other people's places. Just before we went to the States, because she got this job, you see, she wanted it desperately—very prestigious, first-class hospital—she had to have it—'

'Did you want to go to the States?'

'No. Not particularly. I like it here. You might have noticed.' And he turned to give me that direct marvellous look, full of the reckless pleasure that characterized our first meetings. 'But how could I say no, when it was everything she wanted? Just before we went off, it was crazy, she decided to get pregnant again. The argument being that we could get the pregnancy over here; once there, arrangements could be made—and she was right, practically. Her salary has always been enormous, by European standards. So has mine, but much less than hers. We got a house and arrangements were made, we had a living-in maid. And from that time Matthew and I have been strangers. I don't know him. I only know that he's a chip off her block, all right! And then, there was Kathleen, and I loved her from the first moment; and I understood then that I hadn't ever loved Matthew. Funny, that: if there had never been the second child, I would not have known that that wasn't love for a child, not really, I would have thought that was what it was, a sort of dutifulness. But Kathleen: when she was born—I was there of course—and I looked at the little thing sprawling there between Sylvia's legs, she was like a crushed strawberry. Poor mite. I picked her up, and I felt ... but you never had children,' he ended, and my breath stopped from the pain of it. Which he couldn't know, nor should know, so I made myself go on breathing, made life go on, and sat looking at how the sun made minute dazzles on the hairs of his cheeks and on the lion-coloured locks of his hair. A tawny, warm, fine man, he is, my love Richard.

'And then,' he said, after a long time, 'there was John. And you know all about that. And Maria came into our lives, and lived with us, and the real heart of our house is John. The idiot child. And I've wondered often enough, though of course that is probably some sort of superstition, something of that kind, if John was *necessary*. Do you understand? Something joyful and crazy and plain bloody irrational. For *why* should these creatures be so full of love and joyfulness? It doesn't make sense. What have they got to be so bloody happy about? But our household had to have it, that quality. Poor Kathleen, she has a dark sorrowful little spirit, I don't know why. Probably that's why she adores John as she does, he has something she will never have.'

Suddenly anger seemed to explode out of him, even propel him forward in a violent movement, and he struck his fist down on the back of the bench. 'I wonder what your woman-liberating Hannah would say to all that? It seems to me everything gets referred to her, in your life.'

I said, amazed, 'But Hannah's only been in Editorial a few months.'

'It sounds as if . . . Oh, don't take any notice, Janna. I suppose I'm not rational on some subjects. But in the States this women's movement thing—is *cruel*—do you know that? They have institutionalized cruelty. And I come back here and fall in love with you and there it is again, in your office. Hannah says this and that.'

'I think you are being a little unfair,' I said.

'I am? Well, do you know something? I don't care! I've been too conscientious and *fair* all my life. I've had the best of tutors! *Ought. Should.* I *ought* to be fair about Hannah and the rest of the army, but I am not going to be! My life gives the lie to the whole lot of them, anyway.'

I was sitting there thinking of Freddie, Freddie; wondering perhaps if he had sat watching me sleep, hoping that this time, when I woke, I would . . .

'Why *do* you love her so much?' I asked. 'You haven't ever said.'

'Why? What a bloody silly question—no, I suppose it isn't. It's a good question. She was so beautiful, you have no idea! She never has known it herself, she's no time for that kind of thing, but she's the most beautiful . . .' He turned slowly, with that unscrupulous freebooter's smile spreading all over his face; he leaned forward to look at me, laughing. And I was laughing helplessly, at the sheer lunacy of it all.

He kissed me, then, on the lips. For the first time.

We then briskly separated, and stood up.

We walked up to Oxford Street.

'Will you have time to meet tomorrow?' he asked.

'When?'

'Evening. I'm free from six on.'

'Yes. The square?'

'Yes.'

At five thirty, as I was leaving to meet Richard, the telephone. Annie's Good Neighbour. Annie had fallen down in the morning. It had taken hours to get the doctor, and then there was a delay with the ambulance. She, Lucie Fox, had gone up with her, Annie was in such a state, you'd think she was being killed, you know how she goes on. But she, Lucie Fox, had had to get back to her children. The Home Help wasn't in today. 'Goodness knows where she had got to, but I thought you'd like to know, Mrs Somers, you being such a friend of Annie's.'

This means, You are supposed to be such a friend, now over to you.

I said I would go up and see Annie. I rang the hospital. The nurse said Annie was in a state, crying and carrying on, were there any relatives? Who is next of kin? I suppose I am, I said. A silence. I said what I *ought,* which was that I would go up now.

No one left in *Lilith* but Hannah, sitting, sturdy brown legs wide apart, on her chair as if it were a horse, contemplating the plants on the windowsill. She wore a striped purple and red dress, and a purple bandanna, all of which made her look even more like Pocahontas. She fanned herself equably with the last issue of *Lilith,* which has on it the picture taken earlier in the year of girls striding through autumn woods, and regarded me, no comment, as I said I had to go up to the hospital.

'Kate?'

'No. An old woman. And so I would like you to do

something for me . . .' I asked her to go to Soho Square and tell Richard I couldn't see him.

'You'll know him, I am sure, when you see him.'

'I have seen him,' said Hannah, reminding me of how heads had craned, tongues had clacked.

'He's dishy,' said Hannah. 'If I were that way inclined I'd fancy him.'

'Ask him if tomorrow's all right?'

'Will do.'

In Dorothy Wordsworth Ward Annie was sitting straight up in bed, looking sullen and very ill.

As she saw me, she began: what was she doing here, she had been brought here against her will, she wanted to go home, she wanted her clothes, there was nothing the matter with her. On and on and on . . . The three other people in the ward, all of them ill, tried to shut it all out in various ways, but when the nurse came in, complaints. The nurse looked harassed: I knew that she knew nothing would shut up Annie. 'She is one of those, I suppose,' she said, whisking out of the ward and leaving her to me.

I sat by Annie, thinking of Richard, and fought to get a word in. At last I said that she had hurt her leg, she must know that—and, and, and, on. But what she needed was to complain. Annie has to complain: at home, in hospital, whatever her situation, grumbling is what she has chosen. I stayed three hours, lashed by that sour old tongue, until, hearing that I was leaving, she subsided, eyes bright and a little crazy with frustration, and said that at least she would have company in here, which was more than could be said for her at home.

At the duty desk I asked what was likely to happen to Annie next; but the night nurses had come on, and, not knowing Annie, smoothed me down with: The doctor . . . we'll have to . . . perhaps in a day or two . . .

As I left I heard Annie shriek, 'Nurse, nurse,' and the nurse said in the hushed voice of one trying to mollify a child, 'There's a bell, dear, a *bell* . . .'

'I don't want a bell, I want to go home.'

Just after writing that, when I was getting into bed, the

telephone. Richard. His voice had a breathy squeezed sound: anger. I could hear that he had been furious for hours.

'Your hit woman conveyed your message,' said he.

I was silent, adjusting myself from thoughts of Annie, what could be done for her, if anything, to this necessity: Richard wanted to know why I had not been able to see him for so long, day after day, then weeks: *I'm sorry, I can't.* He had decided he wasn't going to ask, didn't want to know: but his anger spoke differently.

I was in a panic. I could not, cannot, tell Richard about Matthew.

I said, 'What is this about Hannah? You're ridiculous! There was no one else to ask, only Hannah was left in the office.'

'That woman!'

'But Richard, why? What did she say? What did she do?'

'She certainly enjoyed her role.'

'I don't believe it! She's not . . .' I stopped. I could imagine Hannah's large, comfortable assurance: 'Janna's not coming,' and how easy it would be to hear an unspoken: She's got more important things to do. But Hannah would not have been thinking that at all. It is her style to impose a: This is how things are and that is how they have to be! on everything, while she surveys one with philosophically calm eyes, fingering a yellow bead necklace that lolls about on the smooth brown slopes of her breasts. I said, 'Hannah's sympathetic to us, and she's shown it in a hundred ways. You must have misunderstood.'

'I didn't misunderstand. She enjoyed telling me you were off somewhere.'

'I was with Annie, you know, I told you, the old woman I am involved with. I had to go. She hasn't got anyone but me, not really.'

'I suppose you were spending all your free time with her instead of with me recently, so that you couldn't even meet me for half an hour?'

I was thinking, Supposing I did say, 'I fell in love with your nasty son Matthew. But think nothing of it. I felt as if I'd been programmed to do it, you know, some sort of indoctrination.

He had only to say, I love you, and that was that. But you'll understand, I know.'

Amazed at the impossibility of explaining what seemed to me so pettifogging and unimportant to a man whom I knew to be the essence of sense and fairness, I said, 'You were for *weeks* visiting relatives you say mean nothing to you.'

'You weren't getting your own back?' I heard: incredulous, appalled, hurt. And I knew that he was incredulous as I would have been to think that he was capable of it; hurt because I could put that, a petty revenge, against our dwindling treasure of days and nights.

I said, 'No. How can you think . . .'

'I don't know what to think. You were in London. I was in London. Our time is running out. But you couldn't meet me. Not at all. Not once.'

I said, sounding awkward, almost stammering, certainly apologetic, 'If I told you . . .' And could not go on.

Silence. I could hear him sigh, shift the receiver about: he was calming himself, using his formidable self-discipline, bringing fairness to bear.

He said, 'Tell me, what actually did Matthew say to you? Was it Matthew? It was, wasn't it?'

And here was the moment when I could, if I would, speak out. Sitting there, holding that receiver with one hand, with the other holding close my white silk dressing gown at the throat as if he could see me, and as if our quarrel imposed a punishing modesty, I felt myself all at once invaded with the atmosphere, the 'taste' of being 'in love' with Matthew: I was breathing a sweet poisonous air, compounded of reluctant lust and yearning for something that was encompassing and far off, something distrusted and disliked. I could taste a sweet falseness on my tongue, and I felt sick.

'What on earth could he have said to you, to upset you so much you wouldn't even eat a sandwich in the square with me, for nearly three weeks?'

I said, 'Richard, he's not the point. Matthew's absolutely not the point.' And heard myself add, in a furious coldly contemptuous voice, 'I dislike him very much. I am sorry, but I simply cannot stand him.'

And so 'the truth', God help us, slid away for ever; though for a moment I was in a panic, knowing that there was something real and naked there in my voice, and that Richard, if he wanted, or could, might interpret it.

After a pause he said cautiously, 'Well, I suppose I'm not going to be told. And so it was pretty bad. I have had a feeling it was pretty bad. When Matthew is out to get his own way, then I know to my cost—the whole family does—that no holds are barred. He gets his way. And he has got it over you.' I was holding my breath, but he went on, 'He wanted to stop us meeting, and he succeeded. Temporarily, but for long enough. And now we are leaving soon he won't bother to try anything else. I don't know what he has been saying, whether it was about me, or Sylvia—or anything. I simply can't imagine what it could be, but I would have liked to have been able to believe that you would see through it. But then, why should you, Janna?'

I said, 'We can still meet tomorrow?'

'Yes, yes, I suppose so. Yes, why not!'

Outside the pub where I was going to meet Richard, our pub, Kathleen stood, a drooping silent figure, her back to the entrance, looking up into an evening sky that this time next week will be black: the clocks are going to be set back.

I went straight up to her, touched her on the shoulder, said, 'Kathleen, do please come inside with me.'

Her humble, pleased smile, that nevertheless had triumph in it, satisfaction. I thought, This has been talked over with Matthew, he has told her she must come into the pub with us.

Richard watched us both come towards him, pulled out two chairs, and said to the barman, 'Manhattan.'

Her tipple.

Her being there cancelled everything. We could not get the conversation going. The ordinariness of it, this momentous thing, seemed to shock her. Her dark full bold eyes—bold when not cringing with the memory of the awfulness of her thoughts about us—moved from his face to mine, from mine to his, as if somewhere there was a fact she needed which she could not lay her hands on.

Between me and Richard the current had been cut. When our eyes met, as we laboured over the talk, nothing was said. Soon, Richard said that he had to leave, and got up. Kathleen rose with him, with reluctance. She still was hoping for that final revelation about life or love or something.

We went to the door. The dark had come down, a lively companionable dark, full of people and busyness.

Richard's eyes did manage to communicate to me: This is *awful*—before he went striding off with Kathleen in tow.

Conference day. Once my favourite day of the week, when everything that was *Lilith* was concentrated in one place, the long formal room which came alive for the occasion; and at one time, Monday mornings, when you could sense how, after the dispersion of the weekends, everything was pulled together, you could feel the pulse of *Lilith*. The representatives of the departments, twelve or fourteen; and around the edges of the room on the chairs set back against the walls for that purpose crowded everyone who could spare an hour or two. Anyone was welcome, from the smallest typist. Anyone could contribute, come in with ideas. Conference day was ideas day. There was the formal agenda, the framework. But what really happened was that for three hours ideas and energy came bubbling forth, and all that was written down and kept so that nothing got lost. By Phyllis, once . . .

And now nothing of this happens. Why not? Easy to say, *Charlie*, and I know that in the lower reaches of *Lilith* they blame Charlie for everything. But I wonder! I think it is more the *spirit of the times*, that affliction that no one seems able to identify.

I do know this: that when this spirit, whatever it is, has entered an institution, you can pass resolutions, and send around reminders, till your brain aches, and nothing happens.

Monday after Monday I have reminded everyone that *Lilith* has always encouraged everyone to have ideas, to put them forward, and if possible to be responsible for them;

asked people to think of *Lilith* as a joint venture; asked that anyone who can shall come up and listen in to the proceedings, and join in too. But these days the chairs all around the edge of the room remain empty. And when the item on the agenda is reached: New Ideas, usually people look at each other in case someone else has an inspiration, doodle, wait for the next item.

Today there were only ten people: the lowest number ever. Outside the three tall beautiful windows September blazed, the trees stood about full of birds and bustle, the sky was a sprightly blue.

On the long table the Christmas issue lay spread around, still in its parts. Party time: glamour. The cover: two enormous dark eyes, a pink pout and a swirl of black velvet against falling snow. The January and February issues are merely adumbrated on the sheets of paper we have lying in front of us, though articles and photographs for those months are already on our desks. The men all have their jackets off. Jill's shoulders are smooth brown against the white straps of something not far off a sun-dress. Charlie is wearing a Russian peasant smock in cream linen, and he beams at us all as his secretary, who is as maternal as he, offers us tea. The aromas of Orange Pekoe and shortbread biscuits. It is a joke in the office—on the whole a friendly one—that Charlie cannot drink a cup of tea without evoking an atmosphere of occasion. Help yourself to everything I have, his affable smile seems to say, as he hands you a plate of cake.

Everything goes along efficiently and amiably, items on the agenda slide past on the oil of indifference: the decisions have already been made, things are already under way, what we do here is not to originate, but to record. And that is why everything is so smooth. And, basically, indifferent. I look at the faces of those who have been with *Lilith* long enough to remember how our conferences were; they were polite, but seem to be merely sitting the time out until they can get back to work. Jill knows that things were different, and so very recently. Hannah does not, nor Mark, for they weren't here. Charlie probably has never noticed anything very much.

Then we come to the item: New Secretaries. Charlie's and mine are both leaving. Among the applications are several from young men. A question of principle—and suddenly the room comes alive.

Henry from Production takes command. He is revolutionary. Stern and unsmiling. At least, with us, though I dare say with his comrades he allows himself a measured smile. His clothes evoke the military: his cropped hair, a black brush, is not high style as when Jill or the others suddenly decide to sprout a brief inch or two, but is meant to make one think of prison and guerrillas; probably terrorists, I wouldn't be surprised.

'I would like to remind you,' said he, 'of the Sex Discrimination Act.'

'Oh Lord,' said Charlie, dismayed, 'but why?'

'What is our policy on this?' demanded Henry, looking from one to the next around the table, so that his eyes enmesh with ours, a ploy which I am sure he has learned from some pamphlet: *How to Control Meetings.*

'I want a policy formulated, and voted on,' said Henry.

'I don't see why we should have a policy,' said Charlie, 'we can deal with each case on its merits.'

'I think we should have a policy,' said Hannah, and she and Henry were looking at each other: they have worked together in Production, and not, we hear, always amicably.

'I know what your policy is likely to be,' said Henry.

'Yes, positive discrimination, in favour of women,' said Hannah. 'This is one of the few industries women can work in.'

'That's my position,' I said; and saw Henry about to lay down some law or other.

But here Jill remarked, in the soothing voice she sometimes uses with Mark when his revolutionary principles threaten and she instinctively, her mother's daughter, tones them down, 'Oh yes, we ought to have a guideline, so that we know where we are.' She looked towards Mark. But he was sitting back in his chair, absorbed in making small perfect circles, red, blue and green, with his felt pens, all over a pale red cardboard folder. Such was his concentration, so accurate the circles, so compelling his deft and clever movements, that we all watched.

'As far as I am concerned, principles and policies cause nothing but trouble,' said Charlie, sounding really put out for once. 'I know that the lower echelons of *Lilith* seethe with both, but I do not want to know anything about it.'

'I entirely agree,' I said, watching Mark's hands but talking to Henry. 'You ought to know. You attend all those meetings downstairs.'

'*Downstairs* is good,' said Henry, with that small laugh which means, There they go again.

'Oh well, it's the spirit of the house, if you like.'

'We confer in the drawing room,' said Henry, and he laughed, genuinely. Everyone laughed.

'As I was saying, all I know is that a political meeting is a recipe for ill-feeling. People who are getting on perfectly well before a meeting are likely to be enemies after it,' I said.

'Or vice versa,' said Mark, his patterns proliferating.

'Then if they are all cemented into harmony, everyone else not at the meeting is an enemy,' I said.

Jill said, 'I really don't *know*, Jane. You can't even be called reactionary. You are so reactionary you are in some special category of your own.' I knew that these were not her own words really, but Mark's.

'Count me in on that,' said Charlie.

'So I believe I am described,' I said. 'But when I think about it, I wonder why. *Lilith* pays higher wages and salaries than anyone else in the field. The conditions are—so the union agrees—good. And under me—under us—'

'Oh, keep the credit, Jane,' said Charlie affably, 'it was you, we all know that.'

'—our policy is to employ young people. The average age in *Lilith* must be under thirty.'

Here Henry nodded, in a way that signalled, But that isn't the point.

'So,' I concluded, 'reactionary is not what reactionary does, or even *says*, but has something to do with some abstract standard that I, for one, do not believe that even Henry could define easily.'

Henry allowed himself a wry smile, which was meant to say, She's so off the point that . . . but she's harmless.

I said, 'You ask me, will I have a male secretary? If it is an issue, I will. Provided he is as efficient as a girl. I don't give a damn.'

'I give a damn,' said Charlie. 'I will not have a male secretary. I want a soothing charming girl like Mary, who so unluckily for me is leaving to attend to her lucky husband. She must flatter my ego and surround me with emotional security. I keep reading critical descriptions of male employers like me, but that is how I am, I am afraid.'

His beaming smiles, meant to deflect criticism, failed: the young men present were all careful not to let their eyes stray towards this elderly charmer. But their faces said it all.

Charlie, pressing on: 'The point is, I like women. I think they are a thousand times nicer than men, better in every way.'

'Good God what a put-down,' said Hannah, astounded at the sheer impossibility of Charlie.

'It seems to me very easy,' I said. 'I will have a male secretary and Charlie a female one.'

Hannah said, 'Janna, did you know this whole question has been discussed in the Association for weeks now?'

'Well, it has just been solved,' I said.

Henry said, 'As delegate from the Association downstairs, what shall I tell them?'

'Practically, it is solved. As a principle, shelved.'

'Then it must go on to the agenda for next Monday,' said Henry.

'Put it on the agenda,' I said. 'But I should like to make a point. This item is the only one that has been discussed with any interest at all. And yet whether we have male or female secretaries is not going to make any difference to *Lilith*. I mean, to making the magazine any better or worse.'

Here Henry looked briefly at me: acknowledged my point. He even nodded. But his eyes had turned sideways again, towards Mark's labours.

We were all looking at the design Mark was holding up for us to see.

'That would make the most marvellous dress material,' said Charlie, suddenly all real interest and animation.

'I take it this conference is over,' I remarked, and everyone was getting up as I spoke.

I went into the outer office with Jill and Hannah, leaving the others.

'What would you say if I took a week's leave?' I asked.

I was surprised at the vehemence with which Jill whirled around at me: 'Oh, Jane, no!'

'Why not?'

I looked at Hannah, arbiter and judge, and she asked, 'Are you thinking of leaving Kate alone?'

'Oh, *Jane!*' Jill's emotion made me see, and I should have seen it before, just how much she is possessed with worry over Kate, eaten up with it, whether she hates her or not.

'I can't leave London,' I said, 'if that is what you are worrying about, Jill. For one thing, there's Annie.'

'Oh, *her!*'

'Yes, I know what you think. But a week off from work?'

'But we are so busy,' moaned Jill; and I could see from Hannah that she agreed.

'Very well,' I said.

'Anyway,' said Hannah, 'it's much better for you to have something to keep your mind off it.'

I waited all afternoon for Richard to ring, but he did not. At six I went up to Annie in hospital. She was in a chair. As she saw me, she said, 'I want to go home, why are they keeping me here . . .' and on she went, and did not stop.

The three other women in the room were trying to shut it out; one of them told me that Annie was shouting for the nurse in the night, for she wouldn't use the bell, until they drugged her and shut her up.

Yesterday they talked as if she were staying in hospital for weeks: today they said they were sending her home. It is because she makes life impossible for everyone around her. But she cannot cope at home, she can hardly walk. She keeps saying, 'But you will all come in and see me, just as usual,' for now her loneliness and boredom is all forgotten, and home in her mind is all visitors and loving care. And when she is at home, she will say, 'It was nice in hospital, I didn't want to leave.' For she has done all this before. Wherever she is, Annie will grumble, and complain, and fill the world with gloom.

I sat there tonight, while she went on and on, suppressing a really violent and shameful impulse to hit her or shake her into silence. I was thinking that her mother, the poor old Irish woman who lived alone on a pittance in a meagre room off Holborn, hardly able to walk, keeping to her bed when it was cold to save coal, the mother that Annie thinks of now remorsefully, saying, *She* didn't have all this, people running in to her with food and doing her shopping—for that old woman, this hospital, the care Annie gets, would have seemed a miracle, so far beyond her she could not even think of it. She didn't have a doctor, Annie says. She didn't have money for that sort of thing.

Trying it out, I say to Annie, 'Do you know that if you paid for your bed here, it would cost a hundred pounds a week?' I say a hundred because it is a figure she can cope with, understand.

Her eyes glaze and she says, 'What do you mean?' Then: 'Yes, but I haven't got a hundred pounds a week.'

'If you had, that's what you'd have to pay.'

'If I had I wouldn't be here, I'd be somewhere nice, or I'd be with my sister. No, I'm just fed up and sick with it all. When is the doctor coming? I want to go home.'

As I came up the stairs I heard the telephone ring. It had stopped by the time I got in. Kate was asleep in the sofa, drunk. All over the flat I find rusty looking glasses, and there are empty bottles in the bin.

One of my little yellow chairs has wine stains on it.

My bed has a creased hollow: Kate has been lying on it. I don't like this, I feel invaded, soiled. For the hundredth time I think, What can I do? There must be something I should do, what is it?

* * *

The clocks went back today.

Richard picked me up outside my door, and we went off to Kent. It was cloudy, chilly, we wore thick sweaters. We found a pub, and ate sandwiches and drank Guinness, and then walked for a long time along lanes and little back roads. It was muddy and my shoes clogged up, and we tried to laugh at my silly heels as we did at the beginning, but I seemed to myself as tiresome and vain as I was afraid I did to Richard.

We were tired and low-spirited. We did not mention our families or problems, but held hands and went on walking.

When we came out of the pub to come home, a wind had got up. From a great ash outside the pub twigs and bits of leaf came pelting all over us as the wind stretched and pulled the branches about. It sounded as if rain were pattering down, but it was debris from the tree. As we drove on up a lane, through a little wood, rubbish from the trees pattered on the car's roof, and when we reached the big road cars seemed to be fleeing up it away from the wind. We joined the streams of cars, but stayed in the slow lane, to look at the yellow stubbly fields and the woods beyond. Then it was dusk, and the lights came on one by one as we drove towards them. The extremely tall, elegant slender pylons that held the single eye of light over the road were like stick insects; and then the dusk deepened and the pylons, absorbed by the dark, were merely sketched thin dark lines against dark, and the lights were delicate shapes like little oblongs of melon, or pink grapefruit, and they flicked past over us, as the wind seemed to grapple with the car, wanting to tip it over. Then the rain started.

We drove through a black plastic world, the lights, red and green and blue, swimming and glittering on the black shining streets. All the way into London, a low wet drive, in lines of traffic: the black gleam of plastic seemed to enclose us, and when the lights picked out a tree or a shrub, it was luridly green, unnatural.

When we turned into Waterloo Road, Richard stopped suddenly at the pedestrian crossing. The slanting lines of rain in the headlights had half obscured the shape of a man standing there who had stepped out on to the crossing and then back. When he saw we had stopped, he turned to our car and raised his arm in a jaunty wave: an old man, small, with nothing on his head, and only a short black plastic jacket. He went stepping across the road like a cat afraid to get its paws wet, making a play of it, but that was not it. He was acting being a pedestrian, hastily but carefully crossing the road while a great big powerful imperious motorcar waited for him, and as he stepped up on to the pavement he made it an enormous step, which he achieved only with difficulty, and he waved that insouciant, cheerfully cheeky arm again, hand upward, pronging fingers sketching the ghost of an insult, and vanished into the rainy dark towards Blackfriars, having in the space of twenty seconds mocked us and the powerful of this earth, himself and his compliance, and while he was about it had commented on and demolished the entire age of technology.

We exchanged quick glances in the dark of the car, and laughed. But then Richard drew the car up on the side of the road, and he said, as if it had been shaken or driven out of him, like a grief one cannot acknowledge, 'Oh, God, I do love this country, I do love this bloody marvellous country.' His rough breathing meant that he was going to cry if he wasn't careful, and in fact he did turn his face to me, and I could see the wet shining on his cheeks. 'Why do you all knock it so?' he demanded angry, amazed. 'Why do you? Why do you run it down? Why do you let it all go down the drain?'

I said, 'Then why do you leave it?' for I was angry, being helpless, because for a moment I had shared his feelings of being helpless.

'I?' he demanded. 'I've never left it.' And then he laughed, at himself. Started the car, and we drove on towards the Aldwych.

'I swear,' he said, in a sober voice, no longer the voice of a thwarted lover, 'that there's something here you find nowhere else. It's the people,' he said. 'Salty, and original. It's that little streak of—well, of what, then? You tell me. All I can say is, you keep coming on it. I have been coming on it during this trip, I'd forgotten . . . Do you think I'm raving?'

I said, 'I live here, don't I?'

He said, 'Anyone who lives anywhere else is mad.'

As we parted, we agreed to do the same next Wednesday: he picking me up after work here.

I said, 'Richard, can't I have your number? After all, Matthew and Kathleen know about me, and I suppose they will have made sure Sylvia knows.'

He hesitated, and was curt because he was embarrassed. 'I can't, it's not inside the terms of our contract. The unwritten contract.'

'Ah yes, these unwritten contracts. They are the worst.'

'Particularly when they are made with oneself.'

They brought Annie home. The Welfare people furious: she is not fit to be home, the Home Help says she will go in as usual and not do one thing more than she ought. The Good Neighbour, Lucie, a kindly soul, says she is doing as much as she can, as it is—which everyone knows is so far beyond what she is paid to do that the thing cannot be discussed in those terms at all—and Annie fights every night to make her stay, staging all kinds of ills, ailments, and crises, and she, Lucie, doesn't know how long she will stand it.

I went in and found her sitting in her shit.

Just as I am going into action, in hurries Lucie, for she has posted one of her children to keep an eye out for when I come in. She is a charming, pretty woman, with far too much to do, and she is fond of Annie. But now she is quite frantic with anxiety. She knows and I know that Maureen, because Lucie Fox can be relied upon to do her work for her, so often does not come in. We both know that 'they' will keep Annie at home as long as somebody, friend, kind-hearted Home Help, a Good Neighbour, will look after her; we know that it is a monstrous imposition because Annie, probably for good, will be incontinent; we know that Annie will not go into a Home. Fussed and fussing, we busy around, cleaning up, changing knickers and there aren't any clean ones left, we tidy up everything, and then Lucie goes, saying to Annie that she will come in later, at nine as usual, to give her a cup of tea.

Annie sits at her table, worn out. Soiling herself, not so

long ago, would have been a horror, to be concealed in any way she could—by cutting out the crotch of her knickers, for instance, and saying, I don't know what has happened to my knickers, I am sure. But now blessed vagueness has overcome her, and she says, 'I am all right, I have the commode, haven't I?' I then sit down and start on the impossible: a sensible conversation with Annie.

The situation: if she would go into a Home, then she would get used to it, and—grumbling, of course, every inch of the way—would make friends, and settle down. And live probably for a few years yet. If she won't, then she has entered that awful, shameful process, that might go on for a year, two years, that is the end of so many. Staggering or crawling around her room, getting or not getting to the commode in time, piles of dirty underclothes accumulating, for the Laundry Service cannot cope with the extremes of this condition, waking wet, or dirty, and unable to cope with it, waiting for a nurse to come—but it's not the nurse's job to change sheets and wash bottoms—when the nasty nurse has gone, waiting for the Home Help, who will clean her saying it is not her job, she is not supposed to do this kind of work, or who won't come that day, so that Annie must wait and wait for somebody to come and help her; and so it will go on all day, while Annie rages and boils and—falls down again, which will get her into hospital for a few days but from where she will be expelled the moment they can get rid of her. Meanwhile her blood pressure is soaring, with anger and frustration, and her old face is sometimes scarlet and sometimes a dull grey.

The room already smells horrible.

I say to Annie that she should go into a Home, and Annie says, 'You can't make me!'

'No, we can't. But you could go and try it out...'

But if she did agree to this, she would complain every second, demand to come home, where she would say, Oh I don't know, it was quite nice there, you have company at least. But taken back there, she would complain and demand to go home...

Now she says that she likes it in hospital, and she wouldn't mind having a spell in there.

I say that she grumbled all the time until she was brought home.

She says, 'I didn't! Why do you say that?'

She grumbles now, and I sit, trying to ward off that state of mind where the human condition is reduced to this: we are sewers, no more, machines for the production of urine and shit, and the whole of human life is a conspiracy to conceal this fact. Annie is 'viable' so long as she can manage to deposit her wastes in the right places; when she can't, that's the end. I look at Annie's gaping mouth, making words, words, and I see it as the opening into a conduit that runs, convoluted and disgusting, to the opening that is her anus and which looks, probably, the same.

The longer I sit there, the more amazed I get that we can conceal from ourselves what we all are: containers of dirt-filled intestines. And when this state of mind threatens to take over, I leave, Annie shouting after me:

'And now I am going to be alone all night.'

I shout: 'Lucie will be in.'

She shouts: 'And then I will be alone all night.'

I shout: 'Then why don't you go into a Home.'

She shouts: 'Because I am going to stay with my sister.'

Here I found Kate sitting at the kitchen table, in a foul mood. This encouraged me: anything better than the listlessness. She was eating pickled onions from a vast jar, one after another, with her fingers. I don't know why but it seemed to me a good sign, vinegar an improvement on sugar, and I said, 'Would you like to come to the pictures with me?'

'You don't want me to go with you to the pictures.'

I made myself a sandwich, and sat down opposite her.

'I want a sandwich too.'

'Then why don't you make one?' It struck me that without her belligerence, and the pickled onions, I would have offered her one. This made me laugh and at once she imploded, and sat, a sullen trembling child.

'It's not kind to laugh at people.'

'I wasn't. Do come to the pictures, Kate.'

It took me an hour of cajoling. Just as we were leaving, the telephone.

'Richard, I'd love to, but I can't. I'm going to the pictures with Kate.'

I am so amazed. And yet, not. When Richard said it, I was stunned. Now I think, Of course! Everything has led to it.

Sylvia and Richard were discussing the problems of their offspring. As, obviously, they often do. She said she thought it would be a good thing to 'defuse the situation' by us having dinner together—Richard and she and I, with Kathleen and Matthew. She could think of no other way to get rid of all these unhealthy emotions, she said. Richard put this to me, embarrassed, but not very, because he thinks it is a good idea too. If I knew, said he, the awfulness of what was going on, how Kathleen tormented them, he and Sylvia, I would be kind and say yes.

'What about Matthew?' I asked, and he gave me a quick look: so he did think there might have been something?

'Matthew, as far as I am concerned, can stew in his own juices . . . he does anyway. I never have the faintest idea of what he is thinking. But Sylvia thinks it would be good for him.'

When I got back to the office after lunch, Hannah was in their room alone. I told her what Richard had said. 'What do you feel about it?' she asked, like a psychotherapist.

'I don't know whether to laugh or cry.'

'Nothing strikes you as peculiar?'

'No more peculiar than anything else.'

'That it should be just you—you and them? Why not take Jill along, or even Kate?'

Our eyes meeting, we laughed. First, a small, even decorous amusement: then laughter overwhelmed us, and we bellowed and roared, and collapsed into chairs and could not stop.

'I don't know why I am laughing,' I said.

'I do,' she claimed.

* * *

The party will consist of Sylvia, Richard, Matthew, Kathleen. Their team. Me, Jill, Mark, Kate. And since I feel that in some way this is Hannah's occasion as much as ours, Hannah. Richard, hearing about this adjustment to Sylvia's plan, first gave a short surprised snort of laughter; then he fell about, so that the Irish barman raised his glass to both of us, spilled charm willingly over us all, said, 'Well, now then, and you must share the joke with the rest of us.'

'I don't know why it is funny,' said Richard.

I have booked the private room at the Gay Hussar. And ordered a dinner. Sylvia said, through Richard, that she would pay for it, since it was all her doing. But of course we are going halves.

And so this is what happened.

First, Kate. When I said there would be a dinner, and she was asked, she was pleased. Said she had nothing to wear. I felt this was a great step forward, and I went out with her to buy a dress. But although she put the dress on, made green circles around her eyes, and painted her nails green, at the last moment she said she wouldn't go. Nothing would make her.

I left her in her usual place in the sofa. She was not plugged in, but stared sullenly in front of her. I knew there was wine in the kitchen: she had brought in a two-litre bottle.

In the taxi down I was possessed by Kate, poor drab, nineteen years old, her precious years draining away; by Jill, with joy kept shut away from her, since joy, delight, are threats; by Kathleen, who has nothing better to do than trail around at a distance after her father's pleasures. Matthew I will not think about, and I was preparing myself not to think about him throughout the dinner ahead, but I know that there is not a cell in his body that could understand joy: he is all intention for the future. Hannah: supremely competent, rooted in her body, but it is only bodies like her own she will open her arms to.

I was thinking of them all as possessors of some treasure,

but they disregarded it; a marvellous inheritance, but they did not know it; though warnings enough reach them of the vast deserts, and nothing that I or anybody else can say will make the slightest difference.

A handful of years, and they will wake up one morning, and know that there is an absolute barrier between them and what they could have had, but did not, because they would not.

As I reached Greek Street I saw Richard on the pavement. He looked up and saw me. I stepped from the taxi into his arms, and he turned me towards him and said, 'I've been planning a speech!'

'So have I!'

'Gather ye rosebuds?'

'Exactly.'

'But it is no use?'

'None at all,' I said.

And, our faces three inches from each other, we laughed, brushed our lips together, valedictory, laid our cheeks together, feeling our separate lives pulsing, separated by a film of skin, and went up into the restaurant.

The pleasant room, soft lights, a table laid for nine, and Kathleen alone. She was soft and awkward with pleasure, and when her father went and sat down by her, leaving me to find my way, she flushed and was grateful.

Then Sylvia. She is a tall, slight woman, not an ounce of anything unnecessary about her. She wore a white suit. Her hair is tawny, with white in it, and is tied back with a black ribbon. She is good-looking, with regular features, brown and oiled with the summer. If I had passed her in the street I would have remarked a woman well put together and pleasant, but none of the adjectives that celebrate excess would have occurred to me: she is not handsome like Richard, nor beautiful, nor charming. And yet his heart has been aching over this woman for a third of a century.

She said, in a voice American, not English, 'I am sorry about Matthew, he wouldn't come.'

We said hello, and how are you, and she did not seem to need particularly to examine me, but sat on the other side of

Kathleen so the girl had the look of being held upright by her parents.

Hannah came in with Jill and Mark.

'Where's Kate?' Jill asked at once, sharp; I said she would not come, and I saw Hannah alert herself and look quickly at me for information.

Two places were removed, and seven of us sat around the table, like a family. Sylvia seemed abstracted, but smiled at once if she felt that someone looked at her: in a way that made it seem as if she were defending herself. Like Richard, her shoulders easily bow forward slightly. They are similar: married: their faces echo each other's, as married people's do who have been drawn to each other because they have seen their own features on this unknown. But Richard sat there large, careless, glowing, brown—splendid, oh splendid he is, full of life that comes out of him, his eyes, his smile; but she is all held in and controlled. Her manner is never anything but abstracted, as if listening for some call on a bleeper, or thinking about her next operation. Her hands are too large for her, or so they are made to seem, for while like everything else about her they are fined down and appropriate, they are long, very strong, and sensitive, everything the hands of a prominent if not world-famous surgeon ought to be. And she is careful with them; you'd think she was a musician, you see her flexing and unflexing them, as I have seen violinists and pianists do, with a quick examining look, *Are they all right? Ready for work?*

Mark and Jill sat side by side, and she was all held into herself and suffering, thinking of course of Kate. And he was exuding waves of warm support and love for her, and when he passed her the butter, it was his heart.

Hannah, rather isolated, or making herself look like that, sat back and watched. She watches. Magnificent in a short scarlet woollen dress over full purple silk trousers, she sat playing with a turquoise pendant the size of a saucer, her strong brown fingers stroking the stone as if it were flesh.

This occasion was for Kathleen; we all knew it, we all played up to it. Kathleen, this poor, handsome, blushing, ashamed girl, who has this sorrowful dark little spirit—the phrase has made me see her, and I suppose I always now will see her—as a small dark passionately sorrowful little girl, always trying to come to grips with something that evades her, joy emblemed in an idiot boy.

We addressed our remarks to Kathleen, we asked her questions, we watched the food on her plate and how she ate it, in case it was not to her taste.

And Sylvia sat abstracted, smiling, and I swear that not once the whole time did she look at me and think, This is my rival, or, He loves her, or even, My husband fancies her, or, I quite like her.

No, nothing of the kind: this scene had come to pass because it should, and here we all were, and we all—of course—were behaving beautifully, because we are the kind of people who do, and Kathleen will be the better for it. So she was thinking.

The Gay Hussar had made us a gorgeous pudding which was about to be shared out to our several plates, when I was called to the telephone, and I knew at once what I was to hear, and so did Hannah, for she had half risen by the time the man had finished saying, 'Mrs Somers, will you come to the telephone, it is urgent.'

The Jefferies in the next flat had found a note under their door half an hour after returning from somewhere:

Please telephone my aunt Jane at the Gay Hussar,
I have taken fifteen sleepers and drunk some wine.

I arrived back to find Hannah and Jill and Mark all standing, and looking. I was in a blaze of anger: as I suppose I had been expected to feel, but Jill's face slapped me down into proper concern.

I told them. Richard at once got up. Sylvia said, 'Oh, how tiresome,' and went on eating her pudding, putting out her hand to keep Kathleen in her place.

'You'd better go with them, Richard,' she directed, 'don't you think?'

'I'm sorry, Kathleen,' I said, thinking that it might very well have been Kathleen we all had to rise from a dinner to go and rescue.

We rushed downstairs, leaving Sylvia after all to pay the bill, and into a taxi.

I was sitting next to Richard and he had his arm around me. Mark had his arm around Jill, who was sitting immobile, her face like a knife, mouth pinched tight.

'They will have called the ambulance,' comforted Mark.

But they had not. The Jefferies had decided that they could deal with it. Wrestling Kate off my bed, where she had chosen to wait for rescue, they had made her sick, though she had been sick already, given her black coffee, and were walking her around and about the living room. Richard looked her over, said she must just have taken the stuff when she wrote the note—obviously had waited for the couple to come in before taking it. She seemed all right. Mark and Jill took over from the Jefferies and, one on each side, went on walking Kate. Who seemed annoyed, on the whole, but gratified that her sister was there.

And so there we all were. I made coffee. Richard, having remarked that he would never have known my room, it looked as if a war had been fought in it, kissed me like an old friend, or like a brother, and departed, saying we should have Kate checked in the morning by a doctor.

After about an hour, we put Kate into bed. Her bed, though she demanded to be allowed to sleep in mine.

Mark, Jill, Hannah, me.

Hannah said, 'I think you ought to let me take Kate to our house.'

I have never felt such a sense of defeat. At once Hannah enfolded me: I was happy to be cradled in those formidable arms. 'Poor Janna,' she said. 'But you must see that there is nothing you can do.'

I am writing this from a sleeping bag on my floor, since my bed is disgusting with vomit and pee. I keep seeing Kate, sacrificially extended on the white altar of my bed. I shall get the mattress taken out in the morning.

I woke Kate at about ten: I had not gone into the office. She came into the kitchen as if nothing whatsoever had happened. She sat down with a small girl's sniff, and rubbed the back of her hand against her nose, and said in a little voice, 'I am so thirsty.'

When she was set with coffee and toast, I said that she must see that I couldn't have that kind of thing happening, and that she—

'What kind of thing?' she broke in, 'what do you mean? I don't know what you are talking about.'

So, nothing has happened, just as nothing happened last time she staged a 'cry for help' at home; but while I agreed, by default, that I would be party to it, I went on to say that either she would have to agree to go home—and her head was already vehemently shaking itself back and forth, saying no—or go and stay for a while with Hannah.

She did not say anything, but lowered her face and watched her hands crumbling bits of toast.

'Why Hannah?' she asked in a tiny voice.

I said, 'She's kind and sensible. And there are lots of people in her commune.' I didn't say, Because no one else will have you.

Hannah came to fetch Kate today.

Kate did not look at me when she left. But she rang me up in her obedient little voice this afternoon to say that she liked the commune and she liked Hannah, and she had decided to stay there until she can find herself a flat of her own, when she will start training to be a model.

I went into a frenzy of energy in my flat, all the covers ripped off for cleaning, the carpets properly done, the walls washed down.

My bed is back to normal, a new mattress, the thick white of the bedcover, a square, cool, white place where I can lie and watch London's gauzy night skies, purple and orange, pink and pearl, in the frame of the window.

*   *   *

Today I had lunch with Richard. He said that Sylvia had suggested I might like to befriend Kathleen, who is going to stay in London to study. Economics and Politics.

'What a silly thing to study,' I said.

'Yes, when you look at the results . . .'

'Did Sylvia say what she had in mind? Take her out to dinner? Have her for the weekend?'

'You don't have to, you know, Janna,' he said, concerned for me, but of course he knew that I would. His eyes were full of restless energy, he seemed abstracted too, rather like Sylvia.

I said, 'What has happened? Apart from the decision that I should be a sister to Kathleen?'

He did laugh, but not much. 'We are going to live in Canada, Montreal. Sylvia has been offered a job—the best. She could not possibly refuse it.'

'But Richard, what about this clinic of yours you've set up?'

'True. Well, that has to go by the board. But you see, Janna, my hands are full of aces, you don't realize, but I'm that phoenix the old-fashioned family doctor. I'm pure gold, a prize. The poor bloody plebs have to put up with modern medicine and vast hospitals and specialists, but the rich can afford to pay for the best and they are paying for the old-fashioned doctor. Me and my kind. So I have already arranged, I and some like-minded associates, to start again in Montreal. Luckily I didn't take American nationality when Sylvia did.'

'That was surely a very drastic thing she did?'

'Single-minded, that's Sylvia.'

Listening in my mind to what he had said, playback, I heard *to start again,* and I felt I had heard everything.

'Janna,' he said quickly, 'I don't mind, I really don't.'

'It seems very hard.'

'It's no more than women have had to do, always.'

I knew that I looked dubious; and he said, 'Well, what would your Hannah say to that?'

'I don't know,' I said. 'I don't think she's in a condition to say anything. She's finding Kate hard going.'

'Janna . . . ?'

I knew what he had been going to say; but before he said it, it was censored. But I said, 'I can't see myself in Montreal.'

'Why not?'

'I can't imagine myself out of London.'

'I don't blame you.'

'But you do.'

'There must be fashion magazines in Montreal.'

What he was saying was, You have nothing to keep you here.

I said, 'I have worked for *Lilith* for . . . long before it was *Lilith*. Since after the last war.'

'Ah.'

'Well . . .'

'I thought you said you were going to retire.'

'Well, perhaps I will.'

'Well, Janna, the offer will be open.'

'How do you know? You may fall for somebody else?'

'Ah no, ours has been the marriage of true minds.'

'If not bodies.'

'Do you suppose if we had met earlier—no, of course not, that's silly.'

'Yes.'

'You would have been like Sylvia.'

'Yes.'

'You would have allotted me my share, what was left over from *Lilith*?'

'Yes.'

'Bloody stupid it all is, why do we go on with it all Janna?'—sounding amazed.

Richard is leaving in two days. We had planned to spend yesterday evening together, the last evening we will have, but just as I was starting off to meet him the hospital rang to say Annie was dying, and they were informing me since they supposed her sister could not be contacted? It seems she had a heart attack. I sat with her and held her hand. She was quiet, lying propped up a little, looking at the ceiling and at the curtains that were pulled around the bed. This peaceable sensible old woman has become a stranger to me; we have rarely enough caught a glimpse of this Annie whom one could like, even love. I would not have thought she was dying. Outside the bright orangy-yellow curtains there was silence in our ward: the three other women are all rather ill. There was a lot of noise, laughter and talk from the nurses' station down the corridor. Annie asked in a drowsy voice, 'What's all that noise?' and I could see she was trying to work it all out: where she was, and why, and what the laughter and voices meant. A little later she said, 'Why are we here?' and put out a hand, the one I was not holding, to try and twitch back the curtains.

'This is a very small room,' she remarked.

I said, 'This is the hospital, Annie.'

'Is it?'

A little later, her eyes closed. Her breathing seemed shallow and fitful. I sat on, thinking of Richard, who would have arrived at the pub, have waited, have realized something had happened and then gone home.

Annie died some time after midnight. All that happened was that she stopped breathing. I thought, No, this is just not possible! She has been breathing away for all those decades, day in, day out, and suddenly, for no reason, the breathing stops.

When I got back, into the empty flat, and looked at its cleanliness, its order, I thought how odd, that Kate should go off, that Annie should die, and suddenly, freedom! I could do as I liked now. But Richard won't be here, so it doesn't matter. Of course, there is Kathleen.

Well, Jane, so that's it!

I have spent all today with Richard. It was awful. We walked and walked; we walked, up and around and back and through London, hour after hour; and we stopped in pubs, but could not stay, for we were driven up and out again, and walked; and walked; and sometimes stood together under trees with the leaves beginning to fall, yellow leaves floating down, just one or two, pretty omens and harbingers. Richard put out his hand to catch one, and he put it in his wallet with the little photograph of me. I picked a brilliant yellow leaf off the pavement, as clear and sharp as a slice of lemon, and put it in my handbag.

A shiveringly bright blue sky, duck's-egg blue, and not a cloud anywhere.

In Theobald's Road he said to me, 'What are you going to do about Kathleen? What do you feel about it?'

'*Feel*,' I said. 'I wonder what I will be feeling, let's say in a year? Will I be fond of her? Affectionate? A sort of dismal hopelessness, like for Kate? Will I admire her? Perhaps I'll love her, because she's your daughter. I might even love her for herself, why not, when you think of all the jolly little surprises life has in store? Yes, I can imagine it. I'll say, Richard? Oh yes, Richard. Well, he's her father, isn't he?'

Just off the classier part of the Fulham Road, I stopped outside a house and said, 'Joyce lived here. This was her house. You know—Joyce? My friend, I told you about her. Years and years of being friends. And now I don't know her, so all that might have never happened!'

Finding ourselves for the second time on the borders of Regent's Park, we went in and sat on a bench that seemed to rock and lurch about because we had stopped the momentum of our fast walking. The ground under our feet was unstable and we looked at drying roses that burned and shimmered in the late afternoon sunlight.

Richard's face, his eyes, showed the chilly bright anguish I watched in Joyce when she was so unhappy, and I knew that he was seeing the same in me, for I could feel myself being consumed by a cold flame, that was making me shiver inwardly.

'You are a very strong woman,' he announced. 'You will certainly live to be ninety.'

'With all my faculties intact?'

'Ah, I didn't promise that.'

'And you?' I asked, curious to hear his verdict, examining this strong and handsome, this leonine man, whose shoulders were hunched under his invisible burden, and who today had an ashy look about him, as if attrition ate from within.

'Doctors have a poor life expectancy.'

'Perhaps we all have.'

'Ah yes, but we've forbidden that subject,' and we put out our hands towards each other, and got up at the same moment, in the same movement, and strode on and out towards Albany Street, and on and up to Camden Town and around again, with our time running out fast, for at eight he had to go to Sylvia to pack because of leaving tonight. Night fell at King's Cross station, and we walked slowly along Euston Road with a soft wind in our faces that will bring tomorrow in with rain. The great buildings dazzled with lights, and around their bases the wind was funnelled into cataracts of air, and we were held upright by walls and tunnels of wind, and staggered along with our arms around each other. We stood on the pavement at the bottom of Hampstead Road, and looked at the new building, all of mirrors, that reflects everything all day, skies and clouds and winds; lights and stars and people. Tonight it reflected part of the towering building behind our backs: black that had regular stars of light up and down it, outlined against the grey of the sky where light white clouds were driving, so that the mirror building dissolved into sky and reminders of building, but was blobbed and blurred with yellow light, and at one side of it a transparent glass lift outlined in smaller starry yellow lights, where people could dimly be seen, whizzing up and down, up and down, sprightly and frivolous, like a mobile birdcage.

We embraced. We wept. We clung because the wind was trying to batter us off our feet.

Then, a taxi, and I crawled into it crying fit to bust, and cried all the way home, the taxi driver remarking as I stepped out that he hoped it wasn't too bad, what I was crying about.

'No,' I said, 'not really.'

'That's the spirit,' said he, driving off to somewhere, 'you don't want to let things get you down.'

I am up here in my bedroom. I've caught myself listening for Kate.

It seems to me, tonight, that my life is nothing, nothing at all, and never has been, like my perfect rooms, my bedroom in which—so says Richard—he can find nothing of me, cannot see me. I am looking up into the theatrical London sky through which, an hour ago, Richard flew off towards his real life, accompanied by the woman he has lived with for over a third of a century. And I look around at this quiet, white, cool, orderly room where soon, I know, into the emptiness will steal one by one, at first lacklustre and inconsiderable, but then familiar and loved, all the little innumerable pleasures and consolations of my solitude.

I can see through the open door of my bedroom into my big living room. There is the grey linen sofa, immaculate now, and the two yellow chairs. Beyond are the windows where in black panes blur and blend the lights from the street.

A stage set! House lights down . . . the sudden hush . . . the curtain goes up . . .